Remnant

Rescue of the Elect

Chronicles of the Apocalypse
Book Two

By Brian Godawa

Remnant: Rescue Of The Elect
Chronicles of the Apocalypse Book Two
3rd Edition b

Warrior Poet Publishing
www.warriorpoetpublishing.com

ISBN: 9798710875964 (hardcover)
ISBN: 978-1-942858-28-7 (paperback)

Scripture quotations taken from *The Holy Bible: English Standard Version.* Wheaton: Standard Bible Society, 2001.

The *Chronicles of the Apocalypse* series

is dedicated to

Ken Gentry and Gary DeMar.

Scholars and gentlemen, both.

ACKNOWLEDGMENTS

Special thanks to my Lord and Savior Jesus Christ for allowing me to combine my esoteric theological interests with my passionate love of storytelling. I never envisioned such privilege or ministry. I do not deserve it.

Perpetual thanks to my wife, Kimberly, my Cassandra, my muse.

I am so grateful for Jeanette Windle for making this entire series so much better because of her loving editorial ruthlessness. Jeanette, your theological understanding, your life experience in missions, your own storytelling choices and your skill convince me that God providentially led me to you. I could not imagine a more perfect editor for this project to make it what it needed to become.

My deepest gratitude goes to my long-time friend and scholar Kenneth L. Gentry Jr. for allowing me the privilege of early access to his Revelation commentary, *The Divorce of Israel*, which served as a scholarly guide to unveiling the complexities of this most fascinating of all New Testament books. I would also like to thank my newer friend and scholar Michael S. Heiser, whose work on the divine council, the Watchers, and the Deuteronomy 32 worldview constitutes the other major influence on my interpretation of Revelation. I believe I have made opposites attract. Christus Victor!

I cannot neglect to thank Gary DeMar, another long-time friend and scholar whose eschatological work continues to be a trumpet call of sanity in this era of last days madness.And of course, I could not have made this as clean a manuscript as it is without all my devoted Advanced Reader Team's kind and gracious help in proofreading and helpful feedback. You know who you are (and so do I).

NOTE TO THE READER

Chronicles of the Apocalypse is a standalone series. But this book you are reading is not a standalone novel. You must read the first book *Tyrant: Rise of the Beast* before *Remnant: Rescue of the Elect*. In another sense, *Chronicles of the Apocalypse* is the conclusive sequel to my *Chronicles of the Nephilim* series about the biblical Cosmic War of the Seed. One need not read the previous Nephilim series to be able to understand this Apocalypse series, but the literary and theological connections run deep.

This is the story of the apostle John's writing of the Apocalypse during the time of the Roman Empire, the first major persecution and martyrdom of Christians, and the Jewish revolt of A.D. 66 that resulted in the destruction of Jerusalem and the Temple in A.D. 70. My hope is that the original context of the ancient world in all its symbolic glory will come alive to you, the reader, as you encounter the imagery in Revelation dramatically unveiled through its Old Testament and first century literary lens.

I've included numbered endnotes for each chapter that provide detailed biblical and historical substantiation behind the fictional story. As it turns out, half of the text of this book is endnotes. This is my most heavily researched series of novels yet. Though using endnote numbers in a novel text is considered anathema by many, I chose to use them to provide biblical and historical context for those who want to "fact check" and dig deeper.

I have tried to be as accurate as I can with the actual historical events and characters surrounding the Jewish revolt of A.D. 66 and the fall of Jerusalem in A.D. 70. However, there are many details we simply do not know with certainty either because the Bible or other historical sources are silent or there is disagreement over the facts. Because of this, I had to take some creative license to fill in the gaps or simplify for easier reading. But I have tried to remain true to the spirit of the text if not to the letter.

For example, the New Testament letters such as John's Apocalypse did not have chapter or verse numbers. They were originally letters written to various people and congregations. The chapter and verse numbers were added in the medieval era for closer detailed study of the Scriptures. In *Chronicles of the Apocalypse*, I have broken up the letters into a fictional first century variation on chapters and verses I call "fragments" to make it easy for a modern reader to look up those Bible verses. It was a kind of creative footnoting within the context of a narrative. I hope the more demanding "Bible scholars" will forgive such petty contrivances for the sake of helpful annotation and storytelling.

CAST OF CHARACTERS

Some readers prefer to conjure pictures of what characters look like in their own imagination. But this is a sprawling epic with a lot of characters, so I wanted to help the reader keep all the characters straight in their minds as they read. See the color versions of these characters on the Chronicles of the Apocalypse website: http://wp.me/P6y1ub-1uH

I also have artwork of maps, paintings and illustrations that relate to this story:
http://wp.me/P6y1ub-1uJ

Brian Godawa
Author, *Chronicles of the Apocalypse*

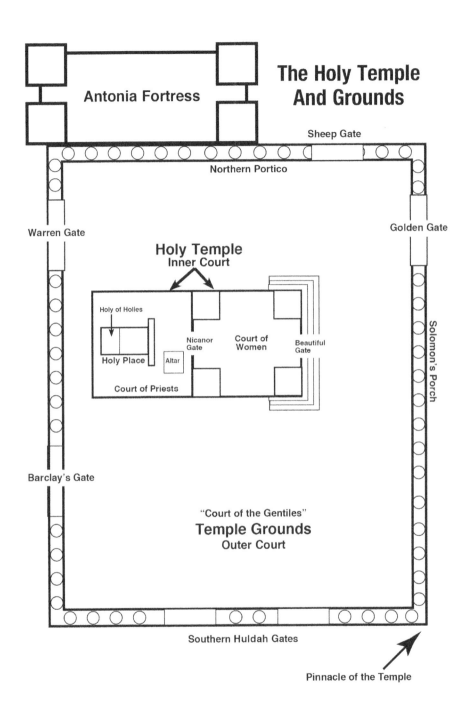

The Holy Temple And Grounds

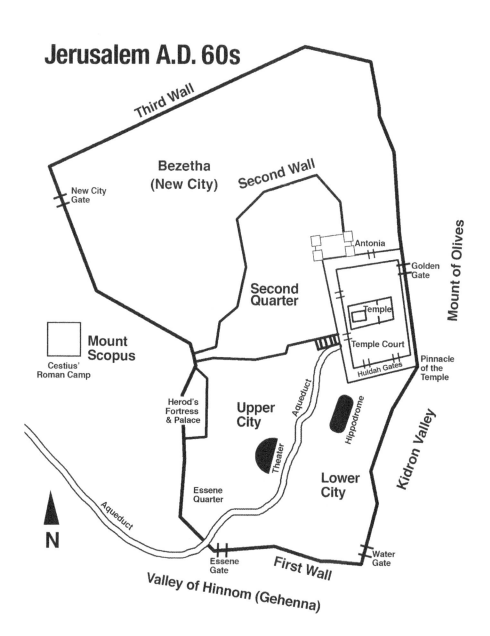

Jerusalem A.D. 60s

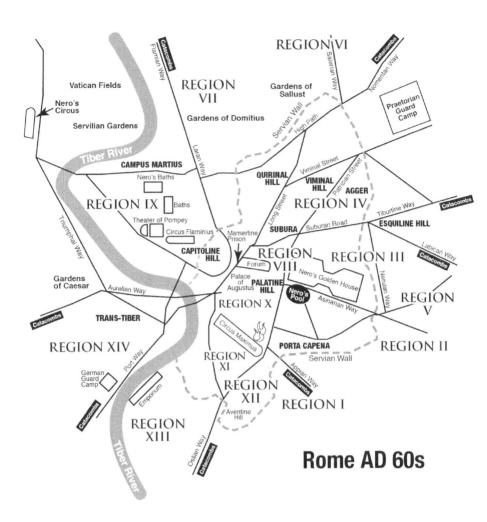

Rome AD 60s

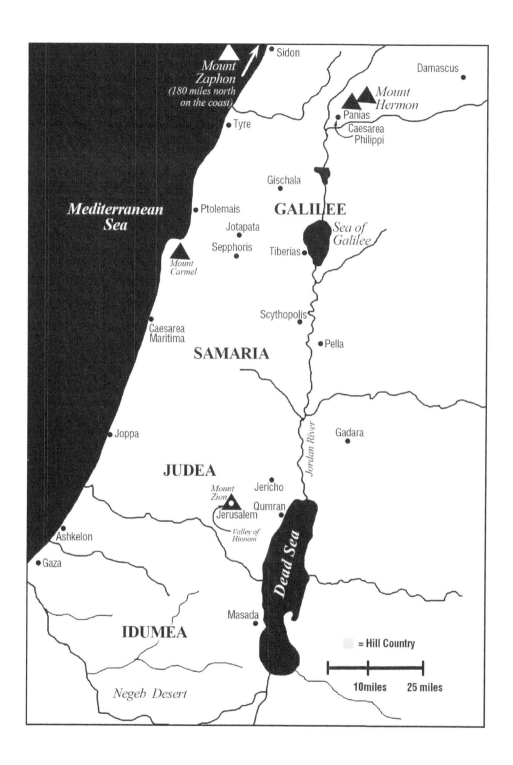

"So when you see the abomination of desolation spoken of by the prophet Daniel, standing in the holy place (let the reader understand), then let those who are in Judea flee to the mountains.... For then there will be great tribulation, such as has not been from the beginning of the world until now, no, and never will be."
—Matthew 24:15–21

"But when you see Jerusalem surrounded by armies, then know that its desolation has come near. Then let those who are in Judea flee to the mountains ... for these are days of vengeance, to fulfill all that is written."
—Luke 21:20–22

PART ONE

Revelation

CHAPTER 1

Rome
March, A.D. 66.

Apollyon the Destroyer stood at the entrance to the temple of Jupiter Optimus Maximus, looking down upon the eternal city of Rome, the city on seven hills. It had taken Apollyon centuries to build Rome from its humble origins as a small Latin town on the Tiber River into the greatest empire in the history of the world. When the enemy was building his pathetic little kingdom in that strip of useless land called Canaan, Apollyon was biding his time and building a superior one that would eventually rule over all the nations of the earth.

And all the gods of the nations now served him as the rightful god of this age. Their identities as Jupiter, Juno and Neptune in Rome or as Zeus, Hera and Poseidon in Greece or as Ba'al, Asherah and Dagon in Canaan were masquerades covering their real identities as the fallen Sons of God from the heavenly host of Yahweh's divine council in heaven.[1]

It all began in the Garden of Eden, when Nachash the Serpent deceived the Mother of the Living and led Man astray from Yahweh. That jealous, infantile creator wanted to keep humanity from enlightenment, and when he could not have his way, he cursed Adam and Eve as well as the Serpent. Thus began the long war between the Seed of the Serpent and the Seed of Eve. But Yahweh made the mistake of trumpeting his intent of one day sending a Messiah who would crush the head of the Serpent.[2]

Before the days of Noah, a band of two hundred Sons of God rebelled from Yahweh's divine council. They violated the heavenly and earthly divide, the separation of humanity and divinity. They came to earth at Mount Hermon, the holy mountain of Bashan. They sought out strange flesh by mating with the daughters of men. The fruit of their unholy union were the Nephilim, the fallen giants of old. This heavenly corruption and mankind's violence brought on the Great Flood, where humanity was judged and those rebellious angelic

3

beings were imprisoned in Tartarus in the heart of the earth until the great Day of Judgment. Seventy of them were spared from that pit for God's purposes.[3]

But after the waters receded and humanity multiplied upon the face of the earth, man and angel once again united in rebellion and built a tower, a stairway to heaven where the creation was once again worshipped in place of the creator. So Yahweh Elohim confused the tongues of mankind and spread them out on the face of the earth as the seventy nations. He gave them over to the false gods of their lusts and depravity. He allotted those nations and their territories under the authority of the seventy rebel Sons of God who would be their Watchers. But he kept Israel, the people of Jacob, as his own allotment with Michael as their guardian prince.[4]

The nations worshipped the heavenly host as their gods, so their gods they became, adopting the identities they now shared amongst themselves. The Sons of God took on a variety of divine masks, both male and female, sculpting their visible forms to match mortal imaginations. Nachash had taken on several himself. Apollyon was his latest favorite. But the Hebrews called him by other names: Satan the adversary, Belial the wicked, Helel ben Shachar the shining one, Mastemah the hostile, Diabolos the devil, and the Dragon. Apollyon was the Greek translation of his Hebrew name, Abaddon the Destroyer. Despite his many faces, he had but one plan: to destroy the people of God and the Messiah.[5]

When the Nazarene came, he fooled everyone. Apollyon knew that lowly carpenter's intent was to steal the allotted inheritance of all the nations. But when the Nazarene played the weakling, Apollyon used the Jews to incite the Romans to crucify him at Golgotha. The principalities and powers had been tricked. They had been looking for a military general to fight a physical war, not a suffering servant who would achieve spiritual redemption through self-sacrifice. As atoning Messiah, the Nazarene secured the legal inheritance of the nations, stripped the principalities of their power over God's people, and exiled Apollyon from heaven to the earth. Apollyon could no longer legally accuse the people of God before the heavenly throne. The Nazarene then spread his malicious "Good News" through his messengers and began to draw the nations as his inheritance into the kingdom of God.[6]

The story tormented Apollyon as he relived the events over and over in his mind, asking himself how he had missed the deception. How they had all missed it.

But that was a wall of rushing water he could no longer hold back. He had to concern himself with his new plan. He had stolen the key to the Abyss and released the once-bound Watchers from Tartarus. Those ancient ones had returned to their thrones over the nations, now under his authority.

"Our lord, you called upon us."

The voice brought Apollyon out of his musings. He turned to see two muscular divinities bow before him: Azazel and Semyaza, the duo of mighty leaders of the fallen Watchers, now freed from their chains. Though they were his servants, he would have to give them both positions of importance or risk mutinous conspiracy.[7]

Azazel sighed deeply and said, "It is good to be back. We have waited long for our revenge."

They had spent thousands of bitter years in their prison.

Semyaza said to Apollyon, "Master, what is thy will?"

Apollyon looked out on the eternal city. It had been rebuilt after the Great Fire two years ago and was currently recovering from a devastating plague that had wiped out over thirty thousand people. It seemed Rome could overcome all adversity and still find the power to trample down the nations with its iron teeth and bronze claws.[8]

Apollyon said, "You two shall be the leaders of my Roman forces." They glanced at each other with approval.

"Semyaza, you shall take on the identity of Mars, god of war, and you will be the genius of the Roman General Flavius Vespasian. His patron deity."

Azazel looked with annoyance at Semyaza. The "genius" of an earthly leader was considered to be the guardian spirit or god that was allotted to persons of importance. Such heavenly principalities watched over their earthly rulers with spiritual authority. Vespasian would be favored by Nero to lead his military forces. Therefore Semyaza would enjoy that exalted power.[9]

Apollyon said to Azazel, "You shall become Mithras, the patron deity of the Roman legions, and genius of Vespasian's son, Flavius Titus." Flavius was the family name.[10]

Apollyon saw the twitch of envy in Azazel's face. As Vespasian's son, Titus would be subordinate to his father's authority. And that made Azazel subordinate to Semyaza.

Azazel pushed out through gritted teeth, "Yes, my lord and savior."

It amused Apollyon that these two brawny deities of war licked the sandals on his bony feet. They were ancient ones, but Apollyon was the ancient serpent, a superiority not easily challenged. His latest bodily form was a bone-thin androgynous humanoid with long, black, greasy hair. He loved defying Yahweh's created order of male and female, and he enjoyed ugliness over beauty. Though beauty did have its use as well.

Apollyon said, "Nero is visiting the Greek isles to participate in the games. The Flavians—Vespasian and Titus—will be accompanying him. I expect you both to be prepared for what is coming. The Julio-Claudian line will not last forever." Nero was the last of the descendants of Julius Caesar. It was the Master's deliberate hint of a new dynasty of emperors—and the spiritual powers behind them. It was a subtle promise of promotion for these two.

But Apollyon didn't yet want Azazel to know that Titus was more important for his plans than Vespasian was. He would save *that* revelation to use for his benefit later.

Azazel probed him. "My lord, though we trust your wisdom in planning a winning strategy for engagement, I am concerned about this secret Apocalypse of the enemy. Does it not reveal his plans?"

Apollyon clenched his fist in rising anger. The Apocalypse. That damnable document that had caused more trouble than all the previous scriptures of the Nazarene cult. He took a deep breath to calm himself.

He said, "The Revelation is for Yahweh's people alone. He has supernaturally protected the document and its copies. Though we may try, Watchers cannot read the text. The only intelligence I have been able to uncover is what the humans say about it. But the Christians are secretive with it and are protected by the Holy Spirit wherever they congregate."

Azazel would not let up. "Have you not tried torture through the Romans?"

"What do you think I have been doing the past few years before I rescued you from your prison, Azazel? I have tried every means at my disposal. But if you have anything new to add from your vast wisdom gleaned from the chains of Tartarus, be sure to let me know."

These ancient ones were powerful beings of much use to Apollyon. But they no doubt had ambition to regain their primeval authority. He had to remind them of their place or he would regret it.

"Stay focused on your human wards and do as I told you. The time is at hand. I need you ready."

CHAPTER 2

The Aegean Sea
Off the Coast of Asia Minor

Alexander ben Maccabaeus beheld a door standing open in heaven. He heard a voice saying, "Come up here, and I will show you what must soon take place, for the time is near."

Before he could respond, Alexander found himself in a heavenly throne room. As soon as he saw the throne and the one who sat upon it, he fell to the ground, prostrate.

All was quiet with an unearthly silence. A holy silence. He looked up. The one seated on the throne had the radiance of a crystal-clear jewel. His throne was surrounded by a rainbow of emerald brilliance. Lightning flashed, followed by peals of thunder. Seven torches of fire stood before him, their flames dancing like spirits.[1]

Alexander could not look straight at the seated king because the brightness burned his eyes, piercing his very soul. The purity, the holiness, the truth frightened him. He knew this was Yahweh Elohim, the Ancient of Days, and he, a lowly Jewish physician and Roman servant, was being allowed to witness supernatural legal proceedings.

Alexander had heard about this many times before in the synagogue readings from Scripture and other Jewish literature. Yahweh Elohim convened his divine council to adjudicate covenant lawsuits that the prophets brought against Israel or on behalf of her. God had engaged Israel with a legal covenant similar to the suzerain treaties between a king and his servant kingdoms. The prophets operated as God's legal spokesmen and moral prosecutors. When Israel broke her covenant, God would put her on trial in his heavenly courtroom before passing sentence for punishment.[2]

The satan, or accuser, had prosecuted Job in the same way. After the Jews had returned to the land from their exile in Babylon, the prophet Zechariah wrote of the accuser prosecuting the high priest Joshua before God's heavenly court. Joshua and his people were stained with the sins of corruption and uncleanness. Enoch had also seen the rebellious Watchers judged before this same throne with God's holy ones beside him.[3]

But Alexander saw no accuser in this heavenly court. Christians had taught him that the spiritual prosecutor had lost his power to condemn God's people because of the eternal atonement completed by Messiah on the cross. "It is finished," he had uttered, and the satan had fallen like lightning to the earth, stripped of his power to accuse. Though he had become the prince of the power of the air on earth, he could no longer enter heaven.[4]

Alexander saw twenty-four elders seated on twenty-four thrones surrounding the Most High. They were clothed in brilliant white and wore crowns of gold. Alexander thought of the twenty-four elders of the priesthood in Ezekiel's prophecy about the Jerusalem temple. In Jewish government, the elders of a city were its legally appointed judges. The elders would meet at the gates to adjudicate legal matters. He wondered if these were the foundational twelve patriarchs of the Old Testament coupled with the twelve apostles of the New Testament.[5]

As in Ezekiel's vision, Alexander saw a sea of glass, like crystal, before the throne. Four living creatures defended it with six mighty wings each and bodies full of ever-seeing eyes. One of them was like a lion, another was like an ox, a third had the face of a man, and the fourth was like an eagle. Alexander still did not know what the sea meant or what these hybrid throne guardians would do. But they were surely frightening representatives of the mightiest of creation.[6]

When the creatures spoke, they sounded like a multitude of voices. They pronounced the trisagion of praise familiar to Isaiah and others who had been in this throne room before him.

"Holy, holy, holy is the Lord God Almighty, who was and is and is to come."[7]

At this pronouncement, the twenty-four elders fell down before the Ancient of Days and cast their crowns before the throne, a common act of submission before a higher authority.[8]

They sang out, "Worthy are you, our Lord and God, to receive glory and honor and power. For you created all things, and by your will they existed and were created."[9]

9

Alexander also fell to his face and wept with worship.

He looked up to see the Ancient of Days hold a scroll out in his right hand. It was written on both front and back, as if it were overflowing with the passion of the author. The passion of righteous indignation. This was a legal judgment being handed down from the Judge of all the earth.

An angel surprised Alexander from behind, proclaiming in a loud voice, "Who is worthy to open the scroll and break its seals?"[10]

That was when Alexander noticed that the scroll had seven seals on it. He remembered the seven seals of destruction tha t he and his companions had read in their pieces of the letter. This was indeed a legal judgment of great importance, for seals of imperial authority were placed on court documents under pain of death for breaking. Who could open such a sealed court document? It would have to be someone of utmost imperial authority.[11]

One of the elders on a throne called out, "Behold, the Lion of the tribe of Judah, the Root of David, has conquered, so that he can open the scroll and its seven seals."[12]

Alexander then saw a lamb standing as though it had been slain. It had seven horns and seven eyes. He knew this was symbolic for Jesus Christ, the Lamb of God, who was also the Lion of Judah and Son of David. He had proved to be the only one worthy of this holy act. And all the living creatures and elders sang so.

> *Worthy are you to take the scroll and to open its seals,*
> *for you were slain, and by your blood you ransomed people for God*
> *From every tribe and language and people and nation,*
> *And you have made them a kingdom and priests to our God,*
> *And they shall reign on the land.*[13]

A chilling cold went down Alexander's spine as he watched the Lamb prepare to open the first of the seven seals.

Alexander awakened from his dream.

He was in a cold sweat, disoriented. He saw the stars above him and remembered he was on a corbita, a Roman merchant ship, in the Aegean Sea on his way to the island of Patmos, just off the coast of Asia. He had been asleep on the deck.

His Roman lord, Lucius Aurelius Severus, prefect of the vigile police force in Rome, was still asleep in the small captain's cabin at the stern. Alexander had been conscripted as Severus' personal doctor and Jewish advisor. Severus was on a commission from Nero Caesar to find the author of a seditious letter written in code against the empire. The letter had been written as an apocalypse, a spiritual vision of an apostle of the Jewish cult of Christians named John bar Zebedee. Nero had persecuted the Christians for the Great Fire of Rome and banished John to presumed obscurity on Patmos. Shortly thereafter, this Apocalypse had circulated throughout the imperial provinces, detailing war and insurrection against the emperor. This uprising was to be led by their resurrected Messiah, Jesus Redivivus, someone Nero thought an imposter, but Alexander had come to believe in with all his heart as the resurrected Nazarene spiritually coming on the clouds of judgment.

Alexander now realized that he had been reading and rereading fragments of John's Apocalypse so intensely that when he fell asleep he had dreamed of it as if he were in the vision himself. It had been so vivid, so real to him. And because of his past legal experience in Rome, he knew exactly what the Apocalypse was, a certain kind of legal document that he had not previously considered.

But now he knew, and it changed everything—for the worse.[14]

He decided not to reveal his secret to his companions yet. If he was right, then everything he believed about the document would be turned upside down.

The words echoed in his head: "These things must soon take place, for the time is near."

Cassandra Laetorius, Severus' Christian servant on this journey, had awakened from inside her lone tent on the deck and joined Alexander beneath the stars. Her auburn hair and blue eyes were enough to put Alexander into a trance.

She whispered to him, "Nightmare?"

"You could say that," he whispered back.

She smiled. "I need some fresh air."

These ships were built for carriage, not comfort. The oarsmen and accompanying soldiers slept below in the galley.

They looked up at the bright stars above them.

She whispered with wonder, "What an awesome God we serve."

He agreed with a soft, "Hmm." They stood in holy silence.

They had travelled so far together, serving the orders of their master Severus. Cassandra had been in Rome during the Christian purge that was led by Severus and his nightwatch vigiles a couple years ago. Severus had noticed her in the crowd and pulled her aside. He wanted a Christian to help them decode the Apocalypse and understand the mindset of their Christian victims. Alexander had thought Severus had other designs on her, but the Roman had kept his hands off, treating Cassandra with respect and patience. That was because she had saved Severus' son, Thelonius, from death in the Great Fire of Rome. At first Cassandra tried to misdirect Alexander and Severus on their search, but eventually she sought to convert them both instead. Severus only hardened, but Alexander broke. He surrendered himself to the Messiah whose people he had previously persecuted. He was forgiven his sins against those he now wanted to help.

This godly woman had changed his world, and introduced him to the Savior and Messiah he now worshipped, Jesus the Christ. But he could not tell her that he was madly in love with her. He felt so unworthy of her. At age thirty, she was but one year younger than him. Through her inherited merchant ships, she had served with the apostle Paul in his powerful ministry of bringing the gospel to the ends of the earth. What could Alexander, a simple physician and new convert, offer her?

He stared at her beautiful visage. If he didn't say something, he would regret it the rest of his life.

"Cassandra?"

She looked at him with an attentive smile.

His tongue felt thick, twisted. He pushed through.

"There is something I wanted to …"

He was interrupted by a voice. "Is this an early morning prayer meeting?"

They both turned to see Demetrius smiling at them. Tall, erudite, and handsome Demetrius. The dark-skinned Egyptian warrior who had saved them from certain death in Ephesus. The Christian son of Apollos with whom Cassandra had a history in ministering the gospel with the apostle Paul. The Demetrius who now drew a smile from Cassandra as no one else could. Alexander coveted the Egyptian's relationship with her.

She said, "I doubt God would allow you before his throne with that hair."

Demetrius felt his head. His hair was smashed up in a funny way from sleeping. He smiled and licked his hand, dragging it over his head to press it down, trying to make it less amusing.

He said, "That is what I like about you, Cassie. You tell me the truth I need to hear."

There it was again. That annoying nickname, *Cassie*. Every time Demetrius said it, Alexander felt chills of jealousy down his spine. It gave his competitor a closeness Alexander craved to have with this most excellent woman.

Cassandra smiled at Demetrius, but then turned serious and looked at the horizon ahead of them.

She said, "Let us remember the truth of Severus' task."

Alexander and Demetrius both knew to what task she was referring. Severus was on his way to find the author of the Apocalypse, the apostle John, whom they had discovered was on the penal colony of Patmos. For the author of a letter that Nero considered seditious, there was one certain fate: execution. The only question was how Severus would do it. Would he bring John back to Rome for trial? Or would he just kill him quietly to avoid any more mishaps?

Demetrius had wormed his way into their search party through negotiation with Severus. He brought along a small contingent of his forty Kharabu warriors, ex-legionaries who had converted to the new faith and provided their services to help rescue persecuted Christians. Severus believed in building alliances, or at least appearing to do so.

The sun rose behind them, casting light onto the small island now in sight. Patmos was a mere fifty miles away from Ephesus, so it had taken them a day to sail there.

The crew began their chores of readying the ship for port.

Severus came out of the captain's quarters and approached the three others. He said, "We will anchor in their harbor, and I will consult the prison prefect about John's whereabouts on the island." He looked at Cassandra and Demetrius. "He knows both of you?"

Demetrius nodded solemnly.

Cassandra said, "My lord, do you really believe the apostle will tell you anything? You are his enemy. In his eyes, a worshipper of the Beast."

"Antichrist," added Demetrius.

Severus said, "Need I explain to you the effectiveness of Roman torture?"

Cassandra said, "How effective was it the first time, when you boiled him in oil?"

Severus deferred with a nod.

Alexander broke the silence. "I have a suggestion. Send the three of us into the colony as imperial prisoners. The apostle will explain to fellow Christians what he would never explain to you."

Severus eyed him suspiciously. "You would betray your own leader?"

Cassandra said, "My lord, may I remind you of my calling from the angel?"

Cassandra had claimed a visitation by an angel who told her to help Severus decipher the Apocalypse and find John. Though Alexander trusted Cassandra's integrity, it seemed like madness to Severus. Why would Yahweh tell them to betray their own brethren? It didn't make sense. But Alexander repeated Cassandra's own arguments. "We are not betraying him. We are seeking the meaning of a word from God. You think the name of Jesus Christ is a code word for someone in hiding. We believe he is the risen Savior coming on the clouds of heaven. So we are not betraying Jesus, because he will not be on earth for you to find. The Apocalypse will remain a mystery to the emperor."

Severus nodded at the logic. He smiled and said with irony, "For him who has ears to hear." It was the phrase they had taunted him with in the past for not being receptive to their propaganda.

Demetrius added, "We cannot stop you from bringing John into your custody or the injustice that Rome will inflict upon him. We only seek to bless him before he is taken and understand his message before it is lost forever."

Cassandra reiterated, "The apostle will trust us. He will not trust you."

Severus searched their faces for confirmation of their honesty. They had tricked him in the past, had thrown him off the trail of his quarry. But now that he had their apostle in his sights, there was nowhere on the small island they could hide, and they had no better friend than the truth of their intent. They were right; he would never be able to get anything out of the apostle prisoner anyway. He had heard that the other eleven apostles had died martyr's deaths. These Christians were the most stubborn true believers he had ever seen.

He looked out at the approaching island. "Very well, prisoners. Prepare to join your leader in hard labor. And thank your god it will only be for a few days."

CHAPTER 3

Mount Parnassus
Delphi, Greece

Nero was escorted by his entourage up the steep and winding Sacred Way that led up the hillside to the temple of Apollo in the heart of the city. The Pythian games took place in Delphi, and Nero was there to participate in the competition for singing and poetry in Apollo's theater as well as the chariot racing in the hippodrome. And Nero would certainly win the victor's laurel wreath—fairly each time, he told himself.

But now he wanted an audience with the Pythia, the oracle of Delphi, the most notable in all of Greece, at this most notable of locations, considered the navel of the world. The Flavians, Vespasian and Titus, followed him, as did their geniuses, unseen by human eyes.[1]

As emperor, Nero did not have to wait in the long line of commoners seeking the wisdom of the oracle. They bowed in worship to Nero as he passed them all by on his way to the marble temple lined with doric columns and bathed in the smell of burning sacrifice. His first stop was at the temple treasury, where he paid a handsome sum of four hundred thousand sesterces for this important advice. Next, he approached the outer court of Apollo's temple to give his black sheep to the priests for sacrifice. At the top of the columns was the famous inscription: "Know thyself." Nero had always considered that the ultimate truth.

He gestured for his party, including his Flavian military companions, to wait for him outside as a priest opened the large double oak doors and he entered alone into the inner temple, accompanied only by the unseen Apollyon. Nero passed the eternal fire, kept watch over by several women, and walked down some stairs into a sunken, dark, and moody sanctuary.

Both emperor and Watcher looked up at the solid-gold statue of Apollo that looked down with intimidating power upon the worshipper. Apollyon loved images so, especially images of himself.

Nero approached the *adyton*, a recessed inner sanctum where the Pythia, one of three chosen women oracles, received the patron's request. Even the emperor could not go inside the adyton, but had to stand outside and ask his question. Nero had dismissed everyone except the two priestesses who oversaw the sanctuary and the female scribe who recorded the oracle's pronouncements. His question was of private concern.

"My dear oracle, I have made my generous offer to the temple treasury and have performed the required sacrifice. Speak now to my patron god Apollo and tell me what I seek."

"Yes, your majesty," she replied. "What do you seek to know?"

Nero could not see the Pythia's face behind her veil in the darkened room. Her jewelry and exotic robe made him question his sizable donation. These temple priests and priestesses seemed to be quite familiar with extravagance. He thought, *I should have plundered this temple when I was financing the rebuilding of Rome.* He would keep that in mind for the future.

He said to her, "Years ago, I received a vision from Apollo in his temple in Rome. I was a sea beast of immense power, and I caught a glimpse of the power of my reign. I have been at pains to discern the meaning or the end of the vision."

The Pythia said, "I will ask of Apollo that he might enlighten you in your quest."

She moved over to a tripod stool that sat before a six-foot-wide fissure in the earth. The opening spread across the entire sanctuary. She sat upon the stool. Lifting her veil, she inhaled the sacred vapor that came up from deep below and drew her into a trance.

Apollyon dug his talons into her skull and controlled her like a puppet. Sorcery was a true delight. The wench was fully his.

Her voice changed. It became deep, penetrating—Apollyon's own with a serpentine hiss. "I sssee the sssea beassst, a ssscarlet beassst, a sssseven-headed dragon. Leopard-like with the feet of a bear and the mouth of a lion."[2]

"That's the one!" shouted Nero. "That's me."

Of course it was. Apollyon had been the one to give him the original vision. Well, actually, it wasn't original at all. He had simply used the same symbolic images about which the apostle John wrote. Though Yahweh had supernaturally withheld access to the Apocalypse, Apollyon had been able to catch bits and pieces from what humans had publicly spoken of it. He had quickly surmised that the apostle's vision was a reiteration of Daniel's vision of four kingdoms as four beasts ending with the iron beast of Rome.[3] But in this new vision, the evil essence of the previous three kingdoms were absorbed into the final hybrid Roman beast.

Ah, the bits and pieces. Those bits and pieces were all the Watcher needed to use Yahweh's own words against the creator. Normally, the Destroyer would twist scripture, take it out of context, or just selectively quote it. In this case, he decided to use the revelation as Yahweh originally intended it, to let Nero glimpse the truth as an inspiration for his wickedness. Evil worked like that. It gloried in its rebellion. Prided itself in its defiance.

The Pythia said, "The beassst is you, but it isss more than you. The beassst has many headsss."

Nero remembered the Christian captive Paul of Tarsus saying something similar.

"The ssseven heads are sssseven mountainsss."

Nero knew that meant Rome. The beast must be the Roman empire.[4]

"They are alssso ssseven kingsss. Five have fallen, one isss, the other isss yet to come."[5]

The heads must represent the Caesars. Nero was the sixth king or Caesar. But a seventh meant there was someone coming after him. Was that seventh king more important than Nero? A shiver went down his spine.[6]

The Pythia said, "I sssee a harlot sssitting on the ssscarlet beassst."

Nero remembered that from his vision as well. He didn't like the implications of it.

"The great harlot isss arrayed in purple and ssscarlet and adorned with gold and jewelsss and pearlsss, holding in her hand a golden cup full of abominationsss."[7]

Nero was visibly agitated by this mystery. He said, "Who is the harlot?"

"The emperor hasss a mind for wisssdom. I will only tell you, she isss a community of influence. And she isss Jewish."

Nero flushed with anger. Whoever this whore was, it was unacceptable enough that she have "influence" on him. That she was Jewish influence was even more detestable. Was it his wife Poppaea? It could not be. She was dead. Could it be the influence she had brought into the court with that Pharisee Joseph and Aliturius the Jewish mime?

"The beassst will hate the harlot. He will make her desssolate and naked and devour her flesh and burn her up with fire."[8]

Now the Pythia was making more sense. The image of cannibalizing the harlot was a pleasing metaphor for what he would like to do to the Jews.

But he couldn't get out of his mind that little reference to seven kings. And he was the sixth. "Who is the seventh king yet to come?"

"One of the headsss ssseemed to have a mortal wound, but its wound wasss healed, for the beassst isss, then isss not, and isss to come."

Nero filled with rage. The implication was obvious. If Nero was the sixth king and a seventh was to come after him, then Nero must be the head that would be mortally wounded and replaced by a new Caesar. The heads die out, but the beast of empire continues on.[9]

He yelled, "Noooo!"

The Pythia was shaken out of her trance. The scribe, faithfully recording her words, looked up at Nero, startled.

Apollyon realized he had revealed too much. He released his grip on the Pythia and stood back to see what Nero would do.

The scribe was within reach of the emperor.

Nero grabbed the parchment she was writing on and crumpled it in his fist. The young scribe gasped. He grabbed her by the neck and pulled her into the sacred area near the fissure.

The Pythia yelled out, "You must not enter the sacred space!"

Nero threw the parchment into the fissure. Then he cast the scribe in after it. She screamed as she fell into the darkness. The sound of her hitting the rock some distance below silenced her life.

Nero looked over at the Pythia, whose mouth was open in shock. He walked up to her and dragged her off the tripod, then threw her into the fissure for the same fate as the scribe. Her screams were stifled by her landing.

Apollyon's delight in the oracle's death was turned a bit sour by the recognition that any rejection of spiritual authority by the emperor made him less controllable, even if the spiritual authority was a mere oracle. Apollyon had to maintain control.

Nero turned and saw the two sanctuary priestesses, witnesses to it all. They began to back up slowly.

"Do not move!" he yelled. "Obey your emperor!"

They froze.

"Now approach me."

They glanced at each other.

"I said, approach me."

Slowly, they approached, entering the inner sanctum area. Nero could see them trembling with fear. They stopped at a safe distance from him, looking with terror into his furious eyes.

He pointed to the fissure, its vapors barely visible.

They looked at each other. The command was silent but clear. They both began to cry.

Nero remained solid in his glare and unmoving with his finger still pointing to the fissure.

The two priestesses walked slowly up to the ledge and looked down into the darkness. The fumes made their heads dizzy. Made them more compliant.

They held hands and jumped silently to their deaths.

Apollyon evaluated his next move. He wanted to inspire his little Beastie, not discourage him. Such unbridled outrage would be difficult to manage for Apollyon's purposes. He would make sure Azazel and Semyaza did not find out about this slight error of judgment. If they questioned his ability to control his beast, it would be the beginning of his own end.[10]

As the furious Nero and his entourage made their way back down the Sacred Way out of the Apollonian complex, the three Watchers followed their earthly counterparts. Azazel and Semyaza could see something was not right and Apollyon did not appear as vainglorious as usual.

Azazel said with an overly innocent voice, "Did everything go as planned, my lord Apollyon?"

Apollyon changed the subject. "Remember to guide your humans as I instructed. I need to pay a visit to the gods of the nations, and prepare the legionary forces in those territories."

"Of course, my lord and god," said Semyaza.

Azazel asked with more faux innocence, "May we ask for what purpose?"

Apollyon puffed up again and explained, "I have accomplished much with the persecution of Christians during this Great Tribulation. We first incited the Jews and pagans into lynch mobs. The priesthood and ruling class of Palestine, whom I affectionately refer to as my harlot, is drunk on the blood of the Christian martyrs. And now my beastie Nero hunts the remnant of God's people."

He paused. "But it is not enough."

The anger in Apollyon's voice sobered the two deities.

"The Nazarene promised that he would come in triumph on the clouds to deliver his kingdom to his saints."[11]

A triumphal entry was the return of a king in victory to his city. The city of Messiah was none other than Jerusalem. The Nazarene was coming to Jerusalem.

Apollyon added, "And we will have the armies of the nations ready to meet him when he does."[12]

CHAPTER 4

Isle of Patmos
Aegean Sea

The morning sun bathed the harbor in its rays as the merchant ship rowed into port at Patmos. The crew anchored the ship a few hundred yards out in strict obedience to the penal colony's security rules. No ship could dock at port. A ferry boat would taxi visitors and new arrivals from the ship to the island.

Alexander, Cassandra, and Demetrius had changed into prisoner's dress of simple woolen garments. They watched the taxi approach them from the dock. It was a rowboat large enough to carry a dozen passengers.

Alexander felt discouraged that even in such rags Demetrius looked distinguished and strong before Cassandra's eyes.

Severus stepped up beside them, awaiting the arrival of the boat.

Alexander said, "Honesty with the apostle will garner more trust from him. Let us tell him the truth, and no doubt he will tell us the truth."

Severus said, "I do not care what you tell him. So long as you find out the full meaning of the Apocalypse."

Cassandra asked, "Will you take him back to Rome for trial?"

Severus answered, "You and Demetrius will not be going on the island. Go to the captain's quarters now. Alexander is going alone."

The other three looked at him with shock.

Cassandra asked, "Do you not trust us?"

Severus said, "Alexander, I trust. You, I do not. He has done right by me all the years he has been in my service. I can trust him to do what must be done, despite his own scruples."

That burned Alexander's soul because it was true. Alexander had lived a life of compromise. As a Hellenist, he had embraced the Greek culture and sought to blend it with his own Jewish heritage. In so doing, he had found himself participating in things he did not believe, violating his own standards and religious convictions. And he'd done it all to stay alive in a hostile culture that ultimately hated his God and masqueraded as tolerant and sophisticated. He had saved the lives of Roman soldiers on the battlefield. He had assisted in the abortion of Severus' own child by his mistress. He had helped the Praetorian hunt down Christians. Though he was now one of those Christians and believed himself forgiven of his sinful past, Alexander did not always feel forgiven or as changed as he claimed.

But he had vowed to live differently, to *be* different.

He blurted out, "Severus, Cassandra and Demetrius know John. I do not. He will trust them more."

"You will go alone," repeated Severus.

We were fools to think we could fool him, thought Alexander. *The three of us would obviously conspire more effectively.* This last-second surprise just ruined their plans. Alexander glanced out at the approaching boat. It was almost upon them.

Severus added, "And if you do not get me what I need, I will leave you here and take the old apostle and Cassandra with me."

Severus knew of Alexander's affection for Cassandra and how to manipulate the Jewish physician. Severus also knew that death was not as good a motivator as torture. The pain of losing Cassandra to Severus while Alexander was left to rot on this ocean rock, yearning for her, would be a torture Alexander could not bear. Such stakes were too high for him to fail.

"You have been loyal to me," Severus said to Alexander. "But I am loyal to Rome and to Caesar, my lord and savior."

Cassandra protested, "We saved your life."

Severus countered, "And I show my gratitude by not reporting to the emperor Demetrius' secret community of Christians in the mountains of Ephesus."

That was an appropriate quid pro quo.

Severus added, "Would you rather I had *not* saved *your* life from the arena?"

Cassandra frowned.

Regardless of all they had been through, Severus was ultimately a son of Rome. He worshipped the Beast. His name was not written in the Book of

Life. But his logic was sound. If Cassandra had not been saved from the arena, she would never have met Alexander, who then might never have been redeemed. And she still believed God had a special plan for that Jewish physician of Rome. She just didn't know what it was.

Severus said, "Consider this, Alexander. At least you don't have to pretend to be a Christian. Therein lies your advantage."

Cassandra wondered if Demetrius might try to wield his forty loyal Kharabu fighters to achieve a mutiny on board the ship. He looked as if he were ready to do so.

A voice from the taxi interrupted them, "Ho, captain! How many to ferry to the island?"

"Two of us," said Severus, "and several guards."

Alexander climbed into the boat with Severus and they were rowed back to the island. He saw Cassandra watching him with tears flowing down her face. He saw Demetrius' arm around her, comforting her. Alexander wished it was his arm.

As she receded into the distance, he wondered whether he would ever see her again. He wondered whether he would die on this cursed island.

The boat docked. Alexander was escorted by Severus and the guards into the Roman outpost on the shoreline. This was a small fort with an outer ditch, rampart walls of dirt, and wooden watchtowers. They walked through the front gate and down the via praetoria to the headquarters, called the principia. The two small streets in the fort contained orderly barracks that appeared to house a couple centuries of soldiers. These would not be the best of legionaries who fought in battles. These would be the troublemakers and riffraff of the Roman army. Men consigned here for disciplinary actions or legal punishment.[1]

They were led into the principia. Alexander was left waiting in the small courtyard as Severus spoke to the fort prefect, showing his papers from Caesar and no doubt explaining his secret plans for the new "prisoner."

The arrival of Severus, the prefect, and a town official ended Alexander's wait.

The official was a tall, thin, balding man with a charismatic presence. He said with open arms, "Alexander, welcome to Patmos. I am Laurentios, the governor of the island. I understand you are a physician?"

"Yes, my lord."

"Well, then, we have great need for you here. Follow me, and allow me to introduce you to your new home."

Alexander followed him out the door with a glance back to Severus, who winked at him. This was not the kind of celebratory welcome he had anticipated.

And the island was not at all what the rumors had made it out to be either. Exiting the fort, they walked into the closest village in the harbor.

"This is the town of Skela," said Laurentios. "Chora is right over there. And there are several others spread out across the island. You'll learn of them soon enough. We have need for good doctoring in all the villages."

Alexander was confused. "Where is the stone quarry? I thought I was to engage in hard labor."

"Not at all. You will be working hard as a physician, but we have nothing like quarries or mines for forced labor as is often rumored. We do have fisheries, farms, and local marketplaces. You have to earn your way here just like anywhere in the empire. The only difference is, you are not free to leave."

The island was a crescent shape about seven miles long of volcanic origin, but it was not a barren rock, as Alexander had imagined. It was quite lush with vegetation.

Laurentios pointed up to an acropolis high above them on the hilltop. "That is Kastelli, the governing administration of the island. Over there, you can see our hippodrome. Yes, even prisoners need entertainment."[2]

He pointed to two temples at the far edge of the harbor. "That is a temple of Apollo and that one a temple of Artemis."

Great, thought Alexander. *Those two abominations are everywhere. They have infected all of Asia.*

Laurentios continued, "We are quite diverse and accommodating when it comes to religion, since our prisoners come from all over the world."

Alexander asked, "Is there a population of Christians?"

Laurentios' positive attitude soured. "Unfortunately so. The Christians have caused so much trouble with their inflammatory speech and intolerant religion that they have been relegated to ghettos. I would not ask about them if I were you. Every other religion *except* Christianity is tolerated here."

Alexander sighed. So it was the same persecution of Christians everywhere, even in a prison colony.

Laurentios added, "And for the gods' sake, stay away from the caves up in the mountains between Skela and Chora. The infamous apostle John lurks up there." Alexander's ears perked up. "He is an agitator who causes riots when he comes to town. The caves are the only place he is safe."

"Thank you for the warning," said Alexander.

Laurentios said, "I will have my assistant take you to the Jewish district of the city for your residence. They will bring you some medical supplies in the morning. You can begin seeing patients tomorrow."

And I will begin finding a way to the cave of the Apocalypse, thought Alexander.

CHAPTER 5

A knock at the door of his humble new residence in Skela awakened Alexander from a deep sleep. As a prisoner, he was only allowed a small apartment in the large, brick-lined insula, or apartment complex. Every resident was also issued basic cooking utensils and a wooden bed with a cushion.

Fumbling around in the dark, Alexander managed to light a small oil lamp, then stumbled over to the entrance, where he opened the latch of a small window inset into the door. Outside, the flickering lamp flame revealed a slightly-built man with large, gray eyes.

Alexander croaked, "Who calls at such a time of night? Can your ailment not wait until the morning?"

"My name is Prochorus," the small man whispered, looking nervously around. "I heard you are a new physician on the island."[1]

"That is no reason to abuse my services," said Alexander.

"I am a secretary scribe, and my master has been beaten by thugs. But he cannot come into town for treatment, for fear of his life."

Alexander's attention was piqued. "Who is your master?"

Prochorus looked Alexander fearfully in the eye through the small opening, but he did not respond.

Alexander opened the door. Prochorus was looking downward where the dim lamp light revealed a half-arc drawn in the dirt, undoubtedly by the night visitor's own foot.

Alexander's memory was jolted. He remembered this mark. It was code.

Stepping through the door, Alexander used his own foot to draw a reverse arc that intersected the first one, creating a crude-looking drawing of a fish. The *ichthys, the* Greek word for "fish," was the symbol used by Christians to secretly identify themselves to each other in a hostile setting. The letters were an anagram that stood for Jesus Christ, Son of God, Savior – fisher of men. Alexander had learned it from his investigations in Rome to hunt down

27

Christians. In a strange twist of providence, he was now using it to identify himself as a Christian.[2]

Prochorus' large eyes lit up with hope. He said, "I beg of you, have mercy on my master, the apostle John bar Zebedee."

Alexander's heart leapt at the sound of the name. Prochorus quickly erased the fish symbol with his foot.

The trip up the mountain took an hour in the dark of night. The moon lit the way, but the climb through rocks and prickly bramble was tortuous.

The two men finally arrived at the mouth of a small cave. Alexander spotted the flicker of firelight from deep within.

Before he entered, Alexander turned to look out over the island down below him. The moon glistened off the waters, and the harbor was lit for late night carousing. Had the apostle's vision been displayed to John from heaven on this very spot?

Hearing a groan from within, Alexander hurried to help his secret patient.

He found John by the fire, nursing his wounds. The apostle was aged, with a full beard and head of white hair. Probably in his sixties. One eye was black and swollen shut. John's hair was matted and bloody from being hit on the head, his robe torn and muddied. He looked worse than the beggars in the ghettos of Rome.

Alexander moved to the apostle's side and set his bag of medical supplies on the ground. "My name is Alexander Maccabaeus. I am a physician. Let me see your eye."

John turned his face fully into the firelight. Alexander examined the apostle's pus-filled and bruised eye socket while the apostle examined with his own intent gaze the doctor's bruised soul.

Alexander turned to Prochorus. "Can you find me a bowl of clean water?"

"Yes, there's a spring of water nearby. I'll go bring some." Picking up a bowl sitting on the floor near John, Prochorus ducked back outside the cave.

John said to Alexander, "You are a Christian."

Alexander stopped his examination to stare at John. "How did you know?"

As John smiled, Alexander saw that one of the apostle's teeth was missing. "The eyes are the window of the soul."

Alexander met John's penetrating gaze briefly before guilt set in and he looked down. That was when he noticed John cradling his right arm.

"Let me see that."

John slowly raised his arm for Alexander to see. The arm was darkly bruised, and with his movement, John let out a grunt of pain.

"Do not worry," said Alexander. "I was a surgeon in the Roman legions."

John extended his arm further for inspection. Alexander examined it. "You have a break on your ulnar bone."

Before John could even process his words, Alexander had gripped the old man's arm, firmly pulling it out and around until the broken ulna snapped back into place. John screamed, the blood draining from his face so that he looked about to faint.

"I'm sorry," said Alexander, "but it was best not to warn you."

Tears were streaming from John's good eye. "The things best for us are also the most painful."

Seeing a pile of firewood near the fire, Alexander rummaged until he found two straight branches. He pulled out some linen wrap from his bag.

"Here, let me give you a splint for that."

John let Alexander wrap his arm with the brace. By the time the task was complete, Prochorus had returned with a bowl of water. As Alexander took it, he said, "I am afraid I do have another surprise."

John flinched, automatically pulling his arm away.

Alexander smiled faintly at the apostle's instinctive reaction. "I promise, no more tricks. Though in truth this is much more painful. I bring word from the congregation in Rome. We have endured much persecution there."

"I know."

"Of course you do. We have pieces of your letter. Though we are not sure of its interpretation. I was sent by the believers to find some answers. I have the pieces with me." Alexander reached into his satchel, pulling several pieces out to show the apostle.

John did not reach for them, but instead asked, "Who is left in Rome?"

To Alexander, it felt as though the old man was testing him. "I met Cassandra Laetorius there. Most of her house church was killed, but there are some still meeting in the catacombs."

As he spoke, Alexander felt a chill of guilt go down his spine. He hated himself for withholding the full truth from the apostle. Half-truths were still lies. But he was trying to save Cassandra.

With the apostle's splint complete, Alexander reached for the bowl of water and began wiping away the blood and dirt obscuring John's injured eye and the wound on his head. John grunted again in pain, but continued looking into Alexander's eyes.

"Alexander, I believe you are a Christian, but I do not believe what you are telling me. The proconsul would never allow prisoners to carry subversive propaganda onto the island. I ought to know, since I wrote it."

Alexander sighed.

"Tell me the truth, son. We serve a sovereign God who ordains the beginning from the end. The Alpha and Omega. What do you fear?"

Alexander could lie no longer. "I am a servant, under threat of death, to Lucius Aurelius Severus, Vigile Prefect of Rome and special emissary of Nero Caesar."

At his words, Prochorus moved with such a startled jerk he knocked over the bowl of water. As the slightly-built scribe scrambled to set the bowl upright, Alexander continued. "Severus has orders to find you and decipher your letter to figure out what military leader claims to be Messiah and where his army is hidden. Then he will execute you. Don't ask me why, but Cassandra was told by an angel that we should help the Roman."

Alexander broke off under John's wide-eyed stare. Then suddenly, the old man roared with hearty laughter.

Alexander scowled. What about the apostle's impending doom was so funny?

John grimaced with pain, his good hand clutching at his ribs, even as he continued laughing uncontrollably.

"What?" demanded Alexander. "What on earth are you laughing at?"

John managed to get out an explanation. "I wrote the letter to disguise its full meaning from unbelievers, but I never thought they would come up with such nonsense."

Now Alexander too began to smile. "That is what Cassandra and Demetrius said. And it is why we are helping Severus, so we can help bring the message to believers abroad."

John asked, "Demetrius of Alexandria?"

"Yes."

"So Cassandra of Corinth and Demetrius of Alexandria are with you."

"Yes. They are captives of Severus as well. He will leave me here and take you with them if I don't get the information from you. I fear for all our lives."

John chuckled again and placed his hand on Alexander's shoulder. "Fear not, Alexander. I am not afraid to die, and I know those two well enough to know that they prefer death to collusion with Rome. If Cassandra Laetorius says she saw an angel, I believe her. Bring Severus with you up to this cave, and I will gladly share with you anything you want to know."

"Really?" said both Prochorus and Alexander simultaneously.

This brought another smile to John's lips. "Yes, really. I believe God has a special plan for you, Alexander Maccabaeus."

Alexander looked at John with surprise. He was too afraid to tell him Cassandra had used those same words.

"Why do you say that?"

"Let me see those pieces of my letter. What have you got?"

Alexander reached in his satchel and pulled out the scroll fragments.

John tried to read the parchment, squinting. "My eyes are too old and weak for this firelight. Prochorus, bring the large lamp here."

Prochorus held a lamp close enough for John to see the writing. The apostle set the parchments down. "Prochorus, get one of the copies we prepared."

Running over to a large container, Prochorus pulled out a scroll. He brought it over to John and handed it to him as if it were a sacred document.

John handed it to Alexander. "This is a copy of the complete letter with all your missing parts."

Alexander held it with awe. He unrolled it gently, looking it over. He stopped and stared solemnly at John.

He said, "When we first found these pieces in Rome, I believe we misunderstood its true nature. We thought it was all about insurrection against Rome. But then I studied it closely, and I think I know what it really is."

"And what is that?" asked John.

"A writ of divorce."

John appeared impressed with his visitor.

"I noticed it because of my own divorce. I recognized the legal language. The heavenly courtroom, the two witnesses required by Torah, the metaphors of unfaithfulness, the written decree of judgment. This scroll is God's certificate of divorce against Israel, isn't it?"[3]

John closed his good eye and nodded in agreement.

Alexander concluded, "When the Son of Man appears again in fragment 10 and hands you the scroll to eat, it becomes bitter in your stomach. I never forgot that imagery from Torah school, the trial by ordeal."

In the trial by ordeal, a wife suspected of adultery would drink water mixed with dust from the temple. If she was innocent and faithful, she would be fine. If she was guilty of adultery, God would make the water bitter in her stomach with sickness and sterility. John had tasted of Israel's infidelity.[4]

Alexander continued staring off into the dark, remembering his painful past. "My divorce was no surprise. My wife violated our covenant of marriage, and even after restoration she returned to her adulterous ways. She flaunted it in my face. I loved her and I forgave her, but she continued in unfaithfulness until I finally executed legal judgment upon her." He didn't want to admit that he had watched her die with revenge in his heart, not justice.

John and Prochorus listened in rapt attention to Alexander. The physician then looked at the apostle and said, "God's covenant with Israel finally became clear to me. It too had been a long time coming, staring at us in the pages of Torah. God married Israel as his bride on Sinai. He promised her the land as her inheritance, if she only kept his commands. The temple became their house and the heart of their covenant. But Yahweh is a jealous God, and Israel was unfaithful. She committed adultery with the foreign gods of Canaan and the nations around her. Yahweh forgave her. But over and over again, she worshipped the Ba'als and the Asherahs. She played the harlot on every high hill and under every green tree. Yahweh's prophets prosecuted her. Isaiah, Jeremiah, Ezekiel, and the others. God commanded Hosea to marry a harlot as a sign of judgment on Israel for her spiritual harlotry. But each and every one of the prophets were rejected and murdered, until finally they murdered Messiah himself, the ultimate crime, the ultimate rejection. So Yahweh will divorce Israel, destroy her house, and execute her for her adulteries. Then he marries a new bride with a new Jerusalem, the new covenant church."[5]

"I told you," said John with a smile, "God has a special plan for you."

"But I have so many questions."

"All in good time," said John. "But now you know the basic picture of the Apocalypse. It is a tale of two women, the harlot of Israel versus the bride of Christ."

He took the scroll and opened it to a section for Alexander to read. "Your fragments were missing this part of the writ. I believe your purpose lies there."

Alexander read it as Prochorus stepped back outside with the bowl to retrieve more fresh water.

When he was finished reading, Alexander looked up and read out loud from the fragment, "144,000 sealed from every tribe of the sons of Israel. What does it mean?"

"All in good time," John repeated. "You will understand when you need to. But first, go retrieve my blessed Christian friends and that stubborn pagan Roman."

CHAPTER 6

Mount Olympus
Greece

The twelve peaks of the sacred mountain rose above the Macedonian landscape below. The Greek gods dwelt in the gorges of that mountain range. But Mount Pantheon, the highest peak of Mount Olympus, was where the assembly of the gods met to deliberate. Their spiritual realm was unseen by humans, but just as real as the physical realm with which it was interwoven. Two different domains within one space. As creatures who existed within both domains, they experienced both earthly and heavenly realities. And they could enter and exit each realm at will.

Apollyon looked around the barren, snow-capped summit, with freezing winds that hindered humans from approaching. It was so unlike the palatial paradise described in Greek mythology, utopian delusions of holy mountain fantasies. He could not wait to get out of this empty pile of rock and ice and on his way to Syria.

"Is this it?" asked Zeus, king of the gods, slave of Apollyon. "Is this the war you told us was coming?"

"No," said Apollyon with dripping sarcasm. "It's a friendly game of dice. How did I appoint you king of the gods?" He looked Zeus up and down. "You fat, stupid slug. You're pathetic."

Zeus had gained a lot of weight, gorging himself on the luxury of his privileged position and the sacrifices of the humans in their temples below. He had gotten lazy – and entitled. He tried to soften Apollyon's wrath. "Greek culture can be indulgent, my lord. And after millennia of imprisonment, I could not help myself."

Zeus was one of the ancient ones who had displaced the seventy over their nations. The primeval beings had taken over their inferiors' identities by the order of Apollyon, their master.

34

Apollyon gripped his staff tightly and rammed it into Zeus's gut. The big god keeled over, gasping for breath. Then Apollyon used the staff to bludgeon the head of the Greek father god. He hit him over and over again, breaking teeth and cracking his skull. Blood spattered everywhere.

Athena wiped some off her face, but kept her composure.

Apollyon stopped, his chest heaving with anger. He threw his staff on the ground and pulled the dazed Zeus up to a sitting position. Angelic flesh was both earthly and heavenly. Angels could eat, fornicate, bleed, and suffer, but they could not die. Zeus experienced real fleshly pain, but his wounds would heal with supernatural speed compared to those of natural creatures.[1]

Apollyon stuck his finger deep into Zeus' throat. The obese god gagged and retched. Vomit poured out of his mouth onto his toga and the floor.

The other gods turned up their noses at the smell.

Apollyon leaned in close to Zeus and spoke with restrained fury, "If you do not stop stuffing your belly, I will cut it out of you."

Zeus gurgled through his bloody face with pus-filled black eyes and broken teeth, "Yes, my lord. Forgive me."

"Forgiveness is for cowards. The only reason I don't bury you alive in the earth is because I need all the gods of the nations to pull off my plan."

Apollyon wiped blood and vomit off his hand onto Zeus' toga. Then he shoved the god back to the floor.

"Is there *anyone* here with discipline and testes?"

Standing at attention were Athena, goddess of wisdom and war, Artemis the huntress, Poseidon, shaker of the sea, and Ares, god of war. Athena was the obvious choice for replacement of Zeus as commander of the forces. She was a brilliant strategist. But she was more a guardian of defense, and Apollyon wanted brutal, unrestrained bloodlust and slaughter. He wanted Ares.

Apollyon looked at the war god. "Kneel before me."

Taking off his helmet, Ares lowered his shield and spear as he knelt at Apollyon's feet.

"I commission you as principality of my Greek Fifth Legion, Macedonia." At Apollyon's words, Athena scowled. Zeus hid his bloody face in humiliation.

Like all human rulers of power, the legions of Rome had patron deities in authority over them in the heavenlies. When there was a war on earth, there was a war in heaven, and their victory or loss was intertwined. *On earth as it is in heaven.*

Ares spoke, "My lord Apollyon, I accept your confidence. But I am sure you can understand my hesitance. Our Greek empire was crushed by Rome, just as the Hebrew prophet Daniel had foretold. Our forces have been demoralized."[2]

"Your self-esteem is not my concern," said Apollyon, "only your obedience. Where is the Fifth Legion?" The Roman military machine was a collection of people from all the nations. The Fifth Legion was manned by Macedonian Greeks who venerated Ares.[3]

Ares said, "In Antioch of Syria along with the Tenth and Twelfth."

Apollyon said, "I sent for the god Serapis in Egypt to prepare the Fifteenth Legion." Though this legion was under Apollyon's heavenly watch, he had given it over to the patron god of Alexandria, where the human legion now quartered. Serapis was an Egyptian god of the underworld who had a very dark, Greek personality.[4]

"Will the gods of Egypt join us?" said Ares.

"The gods of *all* nations will join us," said Apollyon. "You do your part, and we will be an unstoppable force of desolation."[5]

Ares said, "I have wanted to destroy that infestation of sand rats ever since the Maccabees overthrew our Hellenistic forefathers."

Apollyon remembered that distasteful failure a mere two centuries ago. Ares was right. The despicable Jew Daniel had prophesied of the fall of the Babylonian, Medo-Persian, and Greek empires, followed by the current rule of Rome. He had said that the messianic cornerstone "cut without human hands" would hit the feet of the Roman kingdom of iron and clay and would crush them all.[6] But that prophecy seemed to be a certain failure to Apollyon, for Rome was stronger than ever, and Apollyon could foresee another millennium of its reign.

Not everything that Yahweh predicts comes true, he thought. *Look at Nineveh. That city was supposed to be overthrown in forty days according to the prophet Jonah. It wasn't.* Yahweh had claimed the judgment was conditioned upon repentance, but Apollyon considered that an excuse.[7]

Another failed prophecy in Apollyon's eyes was Jeremiah's claim that the Babylonian exile would last but seventy years, after which Israel would be restored to her land. Well, *that* had hardly happened! After those seventy years, Daniel extended that so-called promise into seventy *weeks* of years based on Israel's lack of repentance. Centuries later, Israel was still considered in exile in spite of the fact that some of them had returned to the land. And those who did return were in great trouble and shame, considering themselves still under a yoke of oppression. Some fulfillment that was.[8]

Unfortunately, Daniel's other predictions about Apollyon's pet, Antiochus Epiphanes, were spot-on. Epiphanes was the Greek king over Judea more than two hundred years ago. He had controlled the high priest of Jerusalem's temple as his spiritual harlot until another priest overthrew him in a civil war. Epiphanes had considered the act to be sedition, so he led his forces to desecrate the temple and city. He had prohibited the Jews from obeying their laws, stopped the sacrifice, dedicated the holy temple to Zeus, built an altar to the Greek god, and performed pagan sacrifice to him within the holy place. That abomination of desolation was so atrocious to the Jews that they had risen up under the leadership of the Maccabees, overthrowing Epiphanes and his forces with a miraculous turn of events. Apollyon knew he had gotten somewhere when Yahweh stepped in with his cheating help. Epiphanes was one of two "little horns" in Daniel's prophecies. The other was Apollyon's own Little Horn.[9]

> *After this I saw in the night visions, and behold, a fourth beast, terrifying and dreadful and exceedingly strong. It had great iron teeth; it devoured and broke in pieces and stamped what was left with its feet. It was different from all the beasts that were before it, and it had ten horns. And behold, there came up among them another horn, a little one, before which three of the first horns were plucked up by the roots. He shall put down three kings. And behold, in this horn were eyes like the eyes of a man, and a mouth speaking boastful things. He shall speak words against the Most High, and shall think to change the times and the law. As I looked, this horn made war with the saints and prevailed over them. They were given into his hand for a time, times, and half a time [3 1/2 years].[10]*

Apollyon had been orchestrating his plan for hundreds of years. Though he could not always hide from the prophetic providence of Yahweh, he could use such prophecy to his advantage. If Yahweh prophesied some victories for the Adversary, then he would happily take them. And he would seek to manipulate those ordained victories to force the failure of the rest of the prophecy.

Nero was the Beast of John's Apocalypse. For now. But there were others. He was only one of the dragon's heads, *and* he was the Little Horn on Daniel's iron and bronze beast. Nero had ascended to his throne in the wake of assassinations of three previous Caesars—Tiberius, Caligula, Claudius—three horns plucked up. Nero had spoken high and mighty words against Yahweh and had sought to change the times and laws like a god. He was currently persecuting the Christians, Yahweh's saints, for the appointed period of time.[11]

But that was all preparation for the mortal blow. Apollyon's final bet was on the "prince to come." For he would arrive on the wing of abominations to desolate the temple. That prince was Titus Flavius, son of Vespasian.

> On the wing of abominations shall come one who makes desolate, until the decreed end is poured out on the desolated. And the people of the prince who is to come shall destroy the city and the sanctuary. Its end shall come with a flood, and to the end there shall be war. Desolations are decreed.[12]

"Pack up," said Apollyon to Ares. "You are going to Pontus in the east, where your legion of Greek warriors awaits." He turned to the others. "And we are going to Syria." He looked sternly at Zeus, who was now standing hunched over with pain from his beating. "You. Stop acting like a pig. Start acting like a god."

"Yes, my lord," came the muttered response. The other gods avoided looking at their humiliated king.

"And if *any of you* prove as incompetent as this oaf, there'll be Gehenna to pay."

CHAPTER 7

Patmos

The morning sun lit up the cave through dusty air. Severus sat munching on some roots as he interrogated the apostle, surrounded by Alexander, Cassandra, Demetrius, and Prochorus. Alexander had brought them all to the lofty stone residence of the blessed apostle.

Severus said, "So you are telling us that this Apocalypse is not a call to war but a spiritual prophecy. And you truly believe your resurrected Jesus is coming from heaven to judge the world."

"Yes," said John.

The Greek word that Severus had used for "world" was *oikoumene*, which meant all the Roman empire. To Rome, all the world was hers.

Severus continued, "So Rome *is* the target of destruction."[1]

John smiled. "You are thinking too much like a Roman. See Jewish writing and thought through *Jewish* eyes, and then you will understand."

Severus, frustrated, pulled up the parchment pieces to quote from them. "'So will Babylon the great city be thrown down with violence and will be found no more. Fallen, fallen is Babylon the great.'"

John finished the sentence with a sober stare. "'She has become a dwelling place for demons.'"[2]

Severus gestured to the other Christians there. "Did we not examine this passage in detail before we arrived here? Babylon is Rome."

"No," said John. "Babylon is Jerusalem."[3]

Severus and the others went silent with surprise.

John explained, "In the eyes of God and his prophets, Rome is not 'the great city.' Our holy Jerusalem is. Its greatness lies in its covenantal status with God.[4] What I was doing in the Apocalypse was repeating a long-lasting prophetic tradition of showing the true spiritual status of Israel by renaming her with the name of a pagan enemy of God. By rejecting Messiah, the once-holy nation has become apostate and cursed for her unfaithfulness. Isaiah, Jeremiah, and Ezekiel all likened Israel in her apostasy to Sodom, the symbolic city of God's wrath. Amos likened her to Egypt, the first-born enemy of Yahweh's people. And ever since the Exile, Babylon has been the universal symbol of God's enemies."[5]

"Wait a moment," interrupted Alexander, picking up a papyrus. "In fragment 11, you also call Jerusalem by the names of Sodom and Egypt, 'where our Lord was crucified.' The symbolism isn't hidden but in plain sight. Jesus was crucified in Jerusalem, 'the great city,' which is also the symbolic center of the nation of Israel. So Jerusalem is now Sodom. Jerusalem is Egypt. Jerusalem is Babylon the great. All nations cursed and judged by Yahweh in the past."[6]

John smiled at Severus. "It's something a Roman would miss."

"And a few of us dull-witted Jews," added Demetrius.

Alexander saw Cassandra smile. Demetrius' self-deprecation had the effect of endearing him to her. Alexander wished he had a better sense of humor, like the Egyptian.

Severus complained, "But your description of all the nations and kings of the land fornicating with the great harlot and the merchants of the land growing rich from her power and luxury. It is Rome that has that kind of glory."[7]

John countered, "It was not of Rome's glory that I wrote. It was of Jerusalem's glory. Jerusalem's temple was overflowing with the wealth of temple taxes from every nation in the Diaspora.[8] That's why Nero sent Florus to pilfer the temple treasury to pay for his own debt. It is Jerusalem that has bought the cargoes of gold, cloth, wood, and marble as well as spices, horses, and chariots for its temple and city. Jerusalem has made merchants and seafaring traders wealthy.[9] It is the kings of her land, the ruling aristocracy, who have committed spiritual fornication and lived in luxury.[10] All through her history, Israel was told not to intermingle with the other nations and their foreign gods. Yahweh sought to maintain his own pure inheritance of Jacob, a holy nation and royal priesthood, that would receive the blessings of God.

"Israel's intermingling with pagan kings and merchants was another act of spiritual infidelity toward Yahweh. But Israel was also supposed to be a light unto the Gentiles.[11] The Gentiles think Israel benefits from her interaction with them, but in truth it is the Gentiles who benefit from their interaction with Israel."[12]

Cassandra said, "I have a question. Babylon, Sodom, and Egypt were all judged *after* God took out his holy ones from their midst. Babylon was judged when Israel returned from her exile there. Sodom was judged after Lot and his family were taken out by the angels. And the Exodus out of Egypt is a story that defines who we Jews are as a nation. Are you expressing another Exodus related to this judgment on Jerusalem?"[13]

"Leave it to the wise woman to figure out the intent," said John smiling, "amongst thick-headed men."

Those men appeared duly chastised.

John added, "I echoed the plagues of Egypt in the seals, trumpets, and bowls of the Apocalypse. Water turned to blood, hail and fire, boils and frogs, locusts and darkness. All brought upon that wicked nation for her sins."[14]

Cassandra read the words in the Babylon fragment to prove the point. "Come out of her, my people, lest you take part in her sins. Lest you share in her plagues; for her sins are heaped high as heaven."[15]

Alexander reiterated, "So you are recounting the Exodus, just like the prophets."

John nodded with a smile. "Only now Israel has become both Babylon and Egypt. It is her sins that are heaped high as heaven, as Jesus taught.[16] And she will receive Yahweh's judgments, poetically described as the plagues. The new exodus is out of old covenant Israel."

Alexander asked, "But if God is judging the Jews for rejecting Messiah, then who is he telling to flee to the mountains?"

John said, "The 144,000. They are the overcomers who sing the song of Moses that the Israelites sang in the Exodus."[17]

Severus jumped back in. "It sounds like your god hates his own people now. That he is divorcing them and that Israel's sins are so great he is going to destroy her along with all the tribes of the earth."

He was reading from the first fragment of the Apocalypse they had brought with them.

John said, "Do us a favor, Severus, and read those words out loud."

Severus did so. "Behold, he is coming with the clouds, and every eye will see him, even those who pierced him, and all tribes of the earth will wail on account of him."[18]

41

"Now," said John, "I do not blame your Roman mind for reading the Greek *ge* as meaning the Latin *earth* as opposed to *land*, which best translates my intent. You see, when a Jewish prophet writes 'tribes of the land,' he means the tribes of Israel, not the tribes of other nations. Because when we say 'the land,' we often mean the Land of Israel."[19]

It hit Severus like a ton of stone. This meant that much of the imagery in the letter he had assumed was about the worldwide empire of Rome was actually about the local land of Palestine. This one word, *Land*, instead of *earth*, changed everything. It was a key that opened the abyss of his understanding.

Alexander was not going to admit that he had missed it too. Demetrius was right again. Sometimes Jews could be just as literal-minded as Romans.

Demetrius clarified, "So the dragon had been cast down to *the land, the Land of Israel*, not the whole earth. The hour of trial is coming to those who dwell on *the Land of Israel,* not the whole earth."[20]

Alexander saw Cassandra watching Demetrius intently. The doctor jumped in, hoping he might turn her attention. "The angelic seals, trumpets, thunders, and bowls of judgment. They are for *the Land of Israel*, then, not the whole earth."[21]

Alexander glanced at Cassandra, who was now looking at him. She joined their revelations. "The Two Witnesses will be against *the Land of Israel,* not the whole earth; the second Beast that comes up from the 'earth' is actually the Beast that comes up from *the Land of Israel*."[22]

Alexander now asked, "The 144,000 will be redeemed from *the Land of Israel*?"[23]

"Yes. But patience," said John. "I will get to the 144,000."

Severus interrupted, "But you wrote 'those who pierced him.' Is not piercing a reference to crucifixion? We Romans crucified your Christ."[24]

John said, "But it was our Jewish leaders who tried him and handed him over to be crucified. And the people approved. An accessory to murder is still guilty of murder according to God's Law. In Yahweh's eyes, it is one evil for godless Rome to persecute his people. But for his people to reject the Messiah is the far greater sin. Jesus called down judgment upon this generation of Jews and their leaders for their apostasy. He called them 'sons of those who murdered the prophets.' He said that they filled up the measure of their sins, and upon them would come all the righteous blood shed on the land of Israel, from the blood of Abel to the blood of Zechariah—because they murdered the Messiah, the Author of Life."[25]

Cassandra said, "I remember Paul teaching the same thing: that the Jews killed both the Lord Jesus and the prophets, displeasing God by their hindrance of the gospel. He said that they 'filled up the measure of their sins, and wrath has come upon them to the utmost.'"[26]

Severus summarized for the sake of clarity. "So the Sea Beast is Rome, since it comes from Palestine's horizon far across the Mediterranean Sea, and the sea often means Gentiles.[27] Then who or what does the Land Beast represent?"

John said, "The leaders of apostate Israel in spiritual unity with Rome. The Land Beast looks like a lamb, but it speaks with the voice of the dragon."[28]

Severus asked, "Then who is the great harlot that rides the Beast of Rome?"

John turned to Alexander as the physician pulled out one of the Apocalypse fragments. "Alexander, would you please read it for us?"

Alexander read, "I saw a woman sitting on a scarlet beast that was full of blasphemous names, and it had seven heads and ten horns."[29] He stopped. "What are the ten horns?"

"We will get to the horns later," said John. "Read on."

"The woman was arrayed in purple and scarlet and adorned with gold and jewels and pearls, holding in her hand a golden cup full of abominations and the impurities of her sexual immorality."[30] Alexander stopped again.

John said to the others, "As I've said before, the prophets used the common symbol of sexual immorality to refer to the spiritual unfaithfulness of Israel. Gentiles cannot be spiritually unfaithful to Yahweh because they are not covenanted to Yahweh. But Israel is. So in that light, what does the golden cup and those colors and clothing remind you of?"

Severus blurted out, "That sounds like a description of the High Priest's holy garments." He knew that because he had seen the special uniform stored in the Antonia fortress.[31]

"And elements in the temple itself," added Demetrius.

"Well spoken," said John. "Keep reading, Alexander."

"And on her forehead was written a name of mystery: 'Babylon the great, mother of harlots and of the land's abominations.'"[32]

A revelation dawned on Alexander, but before he could speak up, Demetrius beat him to the punch, saying thoughtfully, "The high priest in Jerusalem has a nameplate on his forehead that says, 'Holy unto Yahweh.'[33] So are you saying Israel's priesthood has become unholy, it is like Babylon, in God's eyes?"

John said, "Yes. The earthly priesthood of Israel is now a Babylonian mockery of the true priesthood of Jesus, the eternal high priest of God's heavenly temple."[34]

Alexander kept reading, "And I saw the harlot, drunk with the blood of the saints, the blood of the martyrs of Jesus."[35]

Cassandra jumped in this time. "The Jewish priests handed over Jesus to be crucified." Her voice became bitter. "And for the past generation, they have led in the persecution of Christians until they finally persuaded Nero to join them in their bloodguilt."

A pall went over the group. John said soberly, "The golden cup of libations that Israel's high priest is supposed to pour out has become a cup of human sacrifice that he drinks, an abomination before the Lord.[36] The great harlot represents the corrupt spiritual priesthood of Israel, guilty of martyring Christians."[37]

Alexander thought of Joseph ben Matthias and his fellow Pharisees and Sanhedrin. The Herods and their toadies had long been considered spiritual prostitutes in bed with Rome. Harlotry was a perfect term to describe their dynasty of ruthless spiritual whoredom; and drinking blood the perfect metaphor for their violence against the Christians.

John broke through his thoughts. "But the harlot is also a symbol of the great city of Jerusalem, the heart and soul of apostate Israel."[38]

Alexander read from the Apocalypse in confirmation. "And the woman you saw is the great city that has dominion over the kings of the land." He looked up. "So your description of the fall of that great city in fragment 18 is not the fall of Rome, but the coming fall of Jerusalem, who is now Babylon in Yahweh's eyes."

"Yes," said John. "And this is where the ten horns on the Beast come into play."

Alexander read from the seventeenth fragment, "And the ten horns that you saw are ten kings who have not yet received royal power, but they are to receive authority as kings for one hour, together with the beast. And the ten horns and the beast will hate the harlot. They will make her desolate and naked and devour her flesh and burn her up with fire."[39]

John said, "The ten horns represent client kings of Rome who rule in territories around Israel. Caesar will call upon the client kings and give them temporary authority to aid in his war on Jerusalem."[40]

Severus said, "I am familiar with those client kings. Antiochus of Commagene, Malchus of Arabia, Sohemus of Emesa, and others all provide auxiliary forces upon Caesar's command. Even Herod Agrippa is a client king of Rome."

Demetrius summarized, "So God will use Rome and her client kings to judge Israel, destroy her temple to finish off the old covenant, and divorce her for good, resulting in his marriage to the bride of Christ."

John nodded. "That is a picture of the new covenant. A marriage supper eating the spoils of judgment."

"What about his covenant with Abraham and Abraham's seed to inherit the nations? Wasn't that unconditional and everlasting?"

John said, "Yes, and that is where the Remnant comes in."

"The Remnant?" interrupted Severus. "This is becoming too complex and poetic to follow." He added wryly, "For that Roman mind of mine."

John smiled. "I do not blame you for not having the last fragments of the Apocalypse. It is there that I explain Yahweh's marriage to a new bride, the body of Christ, and the marriage supper of the Lamb. The New Jerusalem is a symbol of the new covenant church, whose origin is heavenly, as opposed to the old, earthly Jerusalem."[41]

Alexander said, "The Torah speaks of a remnant of God's people in the time of the prophet Elijah. Is that the kind of 'remnant' you are talking about?"

"Exactly," said John. "The Scripture speaks of Elijah and how he appealed to God against Israel. He said, 'Lord, they have killed your prophets, they have demolished your altars, and I alone am left, and they seek my life.' But what was God's reply to him?"

Cassandra said, "I have kept for myself seven thousand men who have not bowed the knee to Baal."[42]

"Exactly," said John again. "Though all of Israel had rejected Yahweh, yet there was a remnant that did not. That remnant was the faithful, the true Israel. And it was Isaiah that said only a remnant would be saved, for the Lord will carry out his sentence upon the land without delay."[43]

"Upon *the Land of Israel*?" said Severus.

John smiled. "Upon the Land of Israel. Now you are thinking like a Hebrew."

Alexander saw Severus smile proudly. He was beginning to understand.

John continued to quote, "'So too at the present time there is a remnant, chosen by grace.' And who are they?"[44]

Severus said, "They can't be the unbelieving Jews, because you said they rejected Christ, so God is divorcing them."

"But God is true to his everlasting covenant," said John. "So what is it? Does God keep his everlasting covenant or not? Does God contradict himself?"[45]

Alexander jumped back in. "If Israel as a nation is cursed as Babylon for rejecting Jesus the Christ, it is no longer true Israel. Then those Jews who follow Jesus must be the true Jews for whom the Promise remains intact. They are the Remnant."

"Exactly," said John, who seemed to be repeating that word for effect. "And they are one with the Gentiles who believe in his name. A great multitude that no one could number from every nation, from all tribes and peoples and languages, standing before the throne of the Lamb."[46]

Cassandra said with fond memory, "Paul used to say that no one is a Jew who is merely one outwardly, nor is circumcision outward and physical. But a Jew is one inwardly, and circumcision is a matter of the heart, by the Spirit, not by the letter. The true Jew is a man of faith, not flesh."[47]

Alexander looked at Severus as he asked John, "So even someone like Severus could become a true Jew if he put his faith in Jesus Christ?"

Severus appeared to be listening intently as the object of that example.

John said, "Yes. The promise to Abraham's seed remains everlasting, because Abraham's seed is Jesus Christ, *not* the physical descendants of Abraham. We are the children of Abraham, the Israel of God, not through flesh, but through faith in Jesus Christ."[48]

Alexander's face lit up with excitement. "So the 144,000 from the tribes of Israel are the Jewish Christians in Israel?"

"Exactly. They represent the gathering of the remnant of Israel that the prophets foretold, along with the ingathering of believing Gentiles into one body. It's the mystery of the gospel. The restoration of true Israel."[49]

Alexander knew that promise all too well. Isaiah, Ezekiel, Jeremiah, Hosea had all promised that one day Yahweh would gather his scattered remnant from the Diaspora back into their land and with them Gentiles from all the nations.[50] The apostle was saying that this ingathering or restoration was being fulfilled right now in the Jewish and Gentile believers in Jesus.[51] He had always thought the event and the numbers would be more dramatic, but now that he thought of it, remnant meant a small number.

But the numbers still didn't seem to match.

Alexander said, "But there are only several thousand Christians in all of the Land."[52]

John said, "The number is symbolic. The twelve tribes of the old covenant times the twelve apostles of the new covenant multiplied by the number one thousand, the number of complete fullness.[53] The 144,000 have the spiritual seal of God on them to protect them in the same way that the worshippers of the Beast have the spiritual mark of the Beast to condemn them. God's sevenfold wrath is not for the Jerusalem Christians. They join the multitude of all believers who come out of this Great Tribulation."[54]

Alexander said, "That is the exodus motif of the plagues that you explained already: 'Come out from her my people, lest you share in her judgment.'" He thought of how Demetrius had escaped Ephesus with the Christians for the same purpose. But he didn't want to mention it and give Demetrius too much credit in Cassandra's eyes.

John said, "The exodus is two-fold. Come out of the old covenant community, both spiritually and physically, because it is about to be judged both spiritually and physically. Jesus warned us that there will be great distress upon the land and wrath against the Jews. That they will fall by the sword and be led captive among all nations. That Jerusalem will be trampled underfoot by the Gentiles. He said that when you see Jerusalem surrounded by armies, like eagles over a carcass, then know that its desolation has come near."[55]

Severus threw in, "The armies of the eagle are no doubt Rome."[56]

John nodded and continued quoting, "'Then let those who are in Judea flee to the mountains, and let those who are inside the city depart, for these are days of vengeance.'"[57]

Alexander now knew what John meant when he said God had a special plan for him. His heart filled with courage and purpose. He said, "We must get this message to the Remnant of Christians in Judea and Jerusalem, the 144,000. We must help them get out before judgment falls."

After his statement, the cave rang with silence. The expression on his companions' faces made clear they knew Alexander was right.

They all looked pleadingly at Severus, who sighed deeply. He looked back at the passage that had launched this discussion. He read it again, "'Behold, he is coming with the clouds, and every eye will see him.' So you expect me to believe that your Jesus Redivivus is going to come and destroy Jerusalem by literally flying down from the heavens on a cloud like Zeus with his lightning bolts?"[58]

"No," said John.

"Wait," said Severus. "Let me guess. Another Hebrew figurative way of thinking."

"Exactly. But not merely Hebrew. It is a way of thinking on our side of the world, from Egypt to Canaan to Mesopotamia. Throughout the history of our people, Yahweh would speak to us through our prophets. And whenever he would judge a city, a nation, or an empire, he would describe it as a cloud-coming. When Yahweh judged Egypt, the prophet Ezekiel said it was 'a day of clouds, a time of doom for the nations.' Isaiah called it 'Yahweh riding a swift cloud.' Joel and Zephaniah both used the metaphor of Yahweh's cloud-coming to describe the destruction of Jerusalem and Israel at the hands of the Babylonians. Yahweh wasn't visibly seen at those judgments, but he was spiritually present in the armies of those who did his bidding. He sovereignly ordains pagans to perform his will.[59] So, when Jesus used the same language of cloud-coming, he was not saying that he is going to be visibly riding a cloud like some kind of mythical Greek theater. He was saying that he is the providential hand that wields the axe of the Roman forces who will punish Israel."[60]

Another moment of silence occurred as they all processed the meaning. This truly did change everything.

Then Severus said, "I don't think Caesar would bother to send his armies against Palestine. There is no need. There are only Jewish brigands and robbers, all fighting each other. The governor of Judea can handle such things with the help of the Herodian rulers."

Demetrius said, "Until it gets out of control. And the Herodians only make it worse."

Severus replied, "Still, civil war is more likely than insurrection."

Alexander countered, "What if the first turns into the second?"

Severus considered the possibility.

"In either case," concluded Alexander, "Caesar must put down all hostilities within the empire, or he loses power and control."

Severus complained, "If Jesus is spiritually present in the armies of Rome, then why would God judge Caesar for doing his will?"

John said, "Because Caesar intends otherwise. But like Pharaoh, God uses Caesar's evil for his own purposes." John, ever the teacher, looked to the others. "Can anyone tell me what the Scripture says to Pharaoh?"

Demetrius started to respond, but Alexander jumped in over his words. "For this very purpose I have raised you up, that I might show my power in you, and that my name might be proclaimed in all the land."[61]

Alexander glanced at Cassandra to see if she had noticed. She had. He felt embarrassed, like a young boy pathetically trying to vie for her attention while the world was about to end.

John turned back to Severus. "So then he has mercy on whomever he wills, and he hardens whomever he wills. God uses the Beast to judge Israel, and then he will judge the Beast."

Alexander saw the thoughtful look on Severus' face. He knew the Roman well enough to know Severus had been deeply moved by this discussion with the apostle. The Roman had been exposed sufficiently to the gospel through both words and deeds over their journey these last couple years that he could not help but be affected by it. Alexander hoped the Holy Spirit was working on Severus' hard heart.

Severus considered all that he had heard. He certainly did not believe in the lunatic prophecy of Jesus coming on the clouds of heaven. He thought the Christians were delusional victims, blinded by their own desire for magical deliverance. He could see now that this last surviving apostle was no real danger to the emperor. But what if one of those Jewish bandits did rise to power? They could easily claim messianic status, regardless of the truth. In that case, Severus would be executed for dereliction of duty.

But if he went to Jerusalem with these Christians, disguised as one of them, Severus could gather useful intelligence. If any of the rebel leaders showed promise, he would kill them. He could help the believers escape the city, but if they turned out to be deceivers after all, if they did in fact have a secret army somewhere, then Severus would help them escape the city— right into the arms of a Roman Legion.

It would all depend on Severus gaining their trust.

He said to John, "I will not bring you into custody. I do not believe you are dangerous."

John sighed, looking relieved.

Severus turned to the others. "I will bring the three of you to Jerusalem and help you deliver your message while I discharge my duty to investigate the Jewish unrest disguised as a Roman merchant seeking new markets."

The others looked hopeful.

Severus added, "But I will only do so under one condition."

He saw everyone look at each other with trepidation.

Demetrius said, "And what is that condition?"

Severus said, "You explain to me how to become a Christian."

CHAPTER 8

"Lucius Aurelius Severus, thus I baptize you in the name of the Father, of the Son, and of the Holy Spirit." The phrase was supposed to be words of sacrament, but they felt like a judicial sentence of judgment pronounced over Severus. He stood beside Demetrius in the small spring not far from John's cave. He had professed faith in Jesus and was now performing the necessary ritual of inclusion into the congregation of Christ.

Demetrius lowered the Praetorian under the water of the spring. Beneath the water all sound ceased for Severus. And all distraction.

For that brief moment, Severus' dishonesty overwhelmed him. He felt buried, as if the waters would drown him as he deserved. He was spiritually identifying with Christ's death and resurrection, but he didn't really believe in it. He had lied to these Christians and told them that he wanted to become a Christian. They had spent several hours explaining the gospel to him and answering his questions, but they didn't realize it was his way of seeking to understand their view of the cosmos so that he could mimic it.

Severus saw that the apostle was a seer, that he had some kind of preternatural ability to discern falsehood. So Severus knew that the only way he could pretend with such convincing appearance would be for him to make himself momentarily believe that he truly wanted to repent and follow their Christ. To place himself entirely within their viewpoint and temporarily ignore his Roman reason and spirit. He drew from his own guilt over killing his mistress's twin unborn sons—*his* unborn sons—to create a genuine brokenness with tears. He had confessed his murderous rage as a legionary, his worship of Caesar and idols, as well as his immoral pursuit of lust and power. He simply inverted his Roman identity to act like a convert. And it had worked.

Why now did he feel the pangs of guilt? As if his ruse was anything more than the pragmatic means of accomplishing his ends. It bothered him that these people were so caught up in their delusion that they truly wanted to believe in his conversion. He felt as if he was exploiting innocent children.

His son came to mind. Thelonius, now eighteen years old. Severus had not seen him for a year. He had been studying under Alexander to be an imperial doctor. He might even be one by now. Severus missed his son. He felt bad that he did not miss his wife, with whom he left Thelonius at their residence in Rome. Because Severus lived a double life with his mistress and other questionable activities, he had not been a good father to Thelonius.

It was amazing how much could come to his mind in so short a time span.

He burst out of the water and felt overcome again with emotion. Had his tactic dredged up deep-seated feelings he had suppressed and forgotten? He would have to be careful not to let this ploy go too far.

Demetrius hugged him and gave him a kiss on his cheek, as was their custom.

When Severus got out of the water, the apostle, Alexander, and Cassandra hugged and kissed him as well.

Demetrius gestured for the doctor to join him in the water.

Alexander had experienced conversion back in the Artemisium of Ephesus. He had embraced the faith, but in the urgency of their immediate events of capture and rescue, he had not had the opportunity to be baptized. What an honor to do so now in the presence of the "disciple whom Jesus loved," one of three of the Messiah's closest circle of followers.

But more than that, he wanted the presence of only one person.

"Cassandra," said Alexander, "would you stand in the water beside me?"

Cassandra looked to John for his response. John arched his brows and shrugged. "I don't see why not. Cassandra had the most influence on your conversion."

Cassandra shrugged with a nervous laugh and walked down into the water to join Demetrius. In the Greco-Roman world, such involvement of a woman in sacred rites would be considered offensive to the patriarchy. In the Christian community it was considered part of it.

John approached Alexander and held up his vial of anointing oil. He dipped his hand and anointed Alexander on his forehead with the oil. He said, "Alexander Maccabaeus, say the words of renunciation."

Alexander followed John in his words. "I renounce Satan, all his procession of rulers, and all his works."[1]

John said, "Let every evil spirit depart from you."

It had been explained earlier to Alexander and Severus that baptism was spiritual warfare. It was a loyalty oath to Yahweh as the true owner of the earth and the cosmos, the world order. The Adversary, the Destroyer, was the ruler of this world, along with his procession of principalities and powers. Before Alexander experienced his regenerating faith, he too had been under the authority of the powers of this present darkness. He had been more than a citizen of Rome; he had been a slave of the devil. Now he was going to make a plea for a good conscience, his declaration of allegiance to a new authority in this spiritual war.[2]

Alexander stepped into the water, moved in between Demetrius and a smiling Cassandra, and prepared for his plunge. He felt Cassandra's hand on his back. His whole body felt it. He was sure she must have felt him trembling.

Demetrius said to Alexander, "Do you believe in God the Father Almighty?"

Alexander said, "I believe."

Demetrius gently lowered Alexander into the water over his head a first time and pulled him back up. Alexander felt like he was being washed clean of his sins.

Demetrius said, "Do you believe in Jesus Christ, the Son of God, who was born of the Holy Spirit and the virgin Mary, who was crucified under Pontius Pilate and died and rose on the third day, living from the dead, who ascended into heaven and sat down at the right hand of the Father, the one coming to judge the living and the dead?"

Alexander choked up with emotion. But he got it out, "I believe."

Demetrius lowered him a second time beneath the waters.

When Alexander was pulled back up, Demetrius concluded, "Do you believe in the Holy Spirit within the Holy Congregation?"

Alexander said, "I believe."

"Alexander Maccabaeus, thus I baptize you in the name of the Father, and of the Son, and of the Holy Spirit."[3]

This third time, Alexander stayed beneath the waters for a moment longer. His mind was flooded with the very imagery the apostle had explained to him earlier, that of Noah's Deluge. The waters of the great flood did not merely destroy the flesh of wicked humanity. They also judged the fallen Sons of God who rebelled on Mount Hermon. As a result, those angelic divinities were imprisoned in Tartarus, the deepest location of Sheol. It was said that Tartarus was as far beneath the earth as heaven was above the earth. This was the same Tartarus where Jesus went in the spirit after he died and proclaimed his final victory over those imprisoned spirits.[4]

As Alexander came up from the water, he thought of Jesus rising from the dead and ascending to heaven, leading a train of captives, the remaining Watchers who had been given authority over the nations.[5] He had reclaimed the earth from the gods of the nations, taken back their territorial allotment from God. By rising up with Jesus, Alexander was transferring his citizenship from the domain of darkness and all its rulers into the kingdom of light and his beloved Son.[6]

Alexander looked over to see Cassandra crying with joy. She hugged him tightly. As she did, Alexander saw Demetrius forcing a smile, but appearing quite uncomfortable.

"Come up here, young man," said John. "You aren't finished yet."

Alexander helped Cassandra out of the water, followed by Demetrius. He stood before John with Severus.

The apostle held up his vial again and poured some oil on each of the initiates' foreheads. "I anoint you with holy oil to be sealed by the Holy Spirit."

With that, John reached over to kiss and hug Alexander, then Severus. He said, "The Lord be with you."

They responded, "And with your spirit."

John turned to Prochorus. "Brother, bring the Lord's Supper."

Prochorus, ever the diligent servant, had already retrieved the elements: a wooden platter with bread, a small bowl, and a bronze cup.

"First," said John as he held up the small bowl, "partake of this milk and honey mixed together in fulfillment of the promise made to the fathers in which he said, 'a land flowing with milk and honey.' This indeed is what Christ gave as he became for us the Promised Land."[7]

Severus and Alexander took sips from the bowl in turn and replaced it on the platter.

John sat the platter down, holding the small loaf of bread in his hands. He broke it and said, "For I received from the Lord what I also deliver to you, that the Lord Jesus on the night when he was betrayed took bread, and when he had given thanks, he broke it, and said, 'This is my body which is for you. Do this in remembrance of me.'"[8]

John handed each of the two men a half of the small loaf. They took a small bite and returned the loaf. Severus watched John closely. Alexander had his eyes closed.

John picked up the cup and said, "In the same way also he took the cup, after supper, saying, 'This cup is the new covenant in my blood. Do this, as often as you drink it, in remembrance of me.'"

Severus began to reach for the cup, but John was not finished.

"For as often as you eat this bread and drink the cup, you proclaim the Lord's death until he comes. Whoever, therefore, eats the bread or drinks the cup of the Lord in an unworthy manner will be guilty concerning the body and blood of the Lord. Let a person examine himself, then, and so eat of the bread and drink of the cup. For anyone who eats and drinks without discerning the body eats and drinks judgment on himself."

A pang of fear shot through Severus like a lightning bolt. If there was any truth to this religious fanaticism, he would be in grave trouble. What if it was true? What if he was drinking judgment upon himself? Would he be struck dead? He was too far in now to balk or hesitate. He took the cup and drank. His nagging fear got the better of him, and he gagged on the wine, coughing and sputtering.

He saw everyone watch him with sympathy as he regained his composure.

He whispered through a hoarse throat, "Some went down the wrong pipe. I apologize."

Demetrius chuckled.

John smiled and said, "We are only human."

Only human, Severus thought to himself.

Alexander drank the wine.

As the liquid flowed down his throat, he remembered how when he'd been against the Christians back in Rome he had heard of this rite and thought it a perverse kind of cannibalism. How foolish he had been. Now he understood its true meaning and purpose. The metaphor of eating the flesh and drinking the blood of Christ was an earthly expression of the heavenly participation in Christ that all believers experienced. Jesus was the bread of life that came down from heaven. His shed blood was the source of eternal life. Coming to Christ and believing in him was like taking Christ's very sacrifice into one's inner being just as food and drink become part of one's body. The physical act made his abstract faith tangible. For that brief moment, Alexander felt all his doubt melt away. He knew he had eternal life, and he knew he would be raised on the last day.[9]

John broke Alexander out of his spiritual musing. "Let us pray, and let us see the three of you off to Jerusalem to warn the congregation of what is to come. Maranatha."

It was an Aramaic word that meant, *Our Lord, come.*[10]

The other three echoed, "Maranatha."

CHAPTER 9

Pontus
Southern Black Sea

The Roman province of Pontus bordered the Black Sea two hundred miles north of Syria and seven hundred miles north of Jerusalem. Roman Legion V Macedonia was stationed in the foothills near the Halys River. The war god Ares walked invisibly through the camp of thousands of human soldiers, assessing their earthly strength for Apollyon's plans. Legion V had recently had success in war against Parthia. But after that victory, the army had returned to building roads and constructing engineering projects in Pontus. So the call to arms that rang through the camp elicited excitement only soldiers could know. They were preparing for battle again.

Ares stood on the shore looking out upon the Black Sea. The sea was a beautiful symbol of untamed chaos. The formlessness and void of the primordial earth. The waters of the Abyss that lay below. The sea was the world without order, without covenant. Yahweh had asserted his power over that chaos when he parted the Red Sea for his covenant people to pass through. At that moment, he crushed the heads of Leviathan, the sea dragon of chaos, to establish his covenant order with Israel. He pushed back the Jordan River for his people to cross over into the Promised Land. And even Messiah had tamed the sea storm as an expression of his creative authority over chaos to establish a new covenant.[1]

In a covenantal sense, the ultimate goal of Yahweh was to eliminate the sea altogether.[2] Ares chuckled. The goal of Apollyon was to make *all the earth* a sea again. Return everything to primordial chaos where Leviathan would once again rule and Yahweh's covenant would be made formless and void. This was what had happened when the temple in Jerusalem was destroyed by the Babylonians. The prophet Jeremiah had looked upon the holy city and temple in ruins and lamented,

I looked on the earth, and behold, it was without form and void;
    and to the heavens, and they had no light.
I looked on the mountains, and behold, they were quaking,
I looked, and behold, there was no man,
    and all the birds of the air had fled.
I looked, and behold, the fruitful land was a desert...
    For this the earth shall mourn,
    and the heavens above be dark.

The world without Yahweh's covenant order was a world returned to pre-created chaos: *tohu wa bohu*, without form and void. If Apollyon could achieve this kind of catastrophe again, it would be the collapse of the entire spiritual cosmos, a shaking of heaven and earth.[3]

Ares noticed movement in the water near the shore. Something large. He held his lance ready, set down his helmet and shield, and walked into the water waist-high. He hoped it was a shark. Consuming the flesh of such sea monsters was empowering. A stingray would be a disappointment. But he would be happy to kill anything. Ares loved to kill. To consume the essence of other creatures. It was a way of opposing Yahweh's creative powers of life.

The war god was so focused on the water ahead of him, he did not see the three angelic figures rise from the waves behind him. Saraqael, Remiel, and Raguel, three of Yahweh's seven archangels, fell upon him and drew him under the water.[4]

• • • • •

Mount Zaphon
Syria

Apollyon and his three divine Greek companions, Zeus, Athena, and Artemis, finished their climb up the steep, rocky face of Syria's holy mountain. They were just outside Antioch in the far reaches of the north on the coastline of the Mediterranean Sea. Mount Zaphon was the location of the palace of Ba'al, prince of the Canaanite and Syrian pantheons.[5]

It was another bleak environment with brisk sea winds on the five-thousand-foot-high peak. Apollyon sighed. "This isn't much more desirable than Olympus. I always preferred ziggurats myself." Ziggurats were manmade holy "mountains," step pyramids that functioned like stairways to heaven with a sacred altar on top for the gods to come down and interface with humans. Babel was the first ziggurat tower that reached to the heavens.

Yahweh hated them, so Apollyon loved them.

"Perhaps the interior will be more glorious," said Zeus as the group paused outside a temple of marble and cedar.

"Somehow, I doubt that," said Apollyon, looking up at the dilapidated and crumbling structure. It had been rebuilt from ruins, but without much effort to renew its former glory.

As they approached the entrance, they were greeted by three divinities at the top of the steps: the beefy storm god Ba'al, his slender, athletic sister Anat, and the matronly Asherah, mother of the gods. Ba'al wore his conical hat with horns that indicated his deity. And he carried a war mace.

Apollyon said, "The Most High Ba'al, Rider of the Clouds."

Ba'al and the other two Canaanite deities bowed in reverence. The epithet of Cloud-rider indicated both divine power and the storm cloud of judgment. Ba'al was the Most High of the Canaanite pantheon.[6]

Apollyon said, "You have quite a reputation in this godforsaken land."

"I serve you, Abaddon." It was the translation of Apollyon's name into Ba'al's Semitic language.

Apollyon considered it subtle defiance of his authority. He said, "You serve me, do you? Then get on your knees and lick my feet."

Ba'al's eyes went wide with surprise. The two goddesses with him jerked their heads to see what he would do.

Ba'al acted confused. "My lord?"

"You heard what I said, Fart-rider. Get down on your knees and lick my feet."

Apollyon saw the storm god's eyes glance around at the other deities. Then Ba'al took a big swallow through gritted teeth and got down on his knees.

Apollyon relished the irony of this huge, muscular male deity slavishly bowing before Apollyon's own scrawny androgynous figure.

Ba'al hesitated.

"Go ahead," said Apollyon. "Clean my filthy feet with your mighty tongue. Unless, of course, you would like to challenge my authority."

Apollyon gave a facetious open-faced offer.

Ba'al closed his eyes, utterly humiliated, but fully submitted, stuck out his tongue, and licked Apollyon's sandaled toes, full of dirt from the climb.

Real power did not go to the strong or the brutish, but to the wise and strategic. Ba'al was the most high god in this local pantheon, but Apollyon had been the legal Adversary, the satan, in Yahweh's own heavenly court room. He had gained his power as god of this age through political machinations and legal manipulation of covenants. And Yahweh governed the cosmos, the heavens and the earth, through the law of the covenant.

Apollyon could see Ba'al gagging on the dirt and wiping off his tongue to continue his dutiful obedience.

He also noticed suppressed anger in the face of Anat.

Apollyon became impatient. "Up. Up with you, you overgrown meathead."

Ba'al stood, gazing down at the floor in disgrace.

Apollyon said, "Call me by my Greek name when you address me. Am I clear?"

"Yes, my lord Apollyon."

"I'm going to be watching you, Canaanite cretin. And if I suspect so much as a question in your face, you will find yourself bound in the earth or thrown into the Abyss."[7]

"Yes, my lord."

Apollyon lifted a foot and an eyebrow with it. "Impressive. I think I'll use that mighty tongue of yours to clean one of my dirty orifices later."

Ba'al remained silent and submissive.

Like a madman, Apollyon changed his demeanor from anger to playful. "Now, where were we?" Then from playful to discouraged as he looked at the goddesses. "Oh yes. So, these are your escorts?"

Ba'al said, "My lord, Lady Asherah is a battle maiden who has helped me achieve unprecedented control over Israel." Apollyon looked at the hefty goddess. She did have strong arms and a masculine look. Maybe he misjudged her.[8]

Ba'al continued, "My sister, Anat, may appear to be slight, but she is a war goddess who treads on battlefields knee-high in blood. And she rescued me from Mot in the underworld. You will be glad you have her with you, Lord Apollyon."[9]

Anat was slender, sexually charged, but with a soulless look in her eyes that indicated a brutality and ruthlessness Apollyon could well afford. He found her legs attractive, covered as they were in the blood and gore of her victims. By the way Ba'al looked at Anat, he could tell their intimacy did not stop at merely brother and sister. And that also explained the contempt that Apollyon could see in her look. He had just humiliated these incestuous lovers. He could use that hatred and fury.[10]

"Well, I wouldn't want to tear you two apart," said Apollyon. "And I need all the help I can get."

Anat was aggressive. She said, "Will my brother receive Yagrush back?" Yagrush was the name of Ba'al's war hammer. It meant *Driver*.

Apollyon said sharply, "Do not ever ask that question again." Everyone knew that weapon could do mighty damage, so whoever wielded it would wield great power. Ba'al's other weapon, a lightning spear named Ayamur, had been long lost through the history of warring nations.[11]

Asherah changed the subject. "Allow us to entertain you, my lord." Apollyon liked her submissive posture—and her full figure. He considered abusing her later if he found some free time.

The three Canaanite deities led Apollyon and the others inside.

Zeus asked, "Why is your palace in such disrepair?"

Ba'al scraped the rotted oak door closed. Its hinges were rusted, and it wouldn't quite close. Ba'al said, "Actually, I don't spend much time here. Too many bad memories."

"Bad memories?" said Artemis.

Ba'al looked at Apollyon, who rolled his eyes impatiently and nodded, allowing Ba'al to tell the story. "In the days of the Israelite Joshua ben Nun, when the Jews first stole our land from the Canaanites, four archangels came here, attacked me, and imprisoned me in the magma of the earth. They destroyed my temple, and ever since it just hasn't been the same. Once I escaped from my volcanic prison, I never spent much time on this cursed mount."[12]

Apollyon grumbled, "Thanks to Messiah stealing our inheritance, land value just isn't what it used to be."

Zeus' face lit up with curiosity. "You mentioned the archangels. Where are they?"

Ba'al looked to Apollyon. The prince Watcher said, "Holed up in Jerusalem. Those meddling godlickers have been my bane for centuries. But that is about to end."

Apollyon wasn't about to admit that he had almost been captured by the archangels in that very city. Michael was the prince of Israel. He had fooled

Apollyon into thinking he had withdrawn from the holy temple, leaving it for the Watcher to desolate. It reminded Apollyon of the days of Daniel when Michael left to help Gabriel fight the principality of Persia.[13] And Apollyon would never forget fighting the prince of archangels over the body of Moses.[14] Michael was not to be underestimated or trifled with. So when Apollyon had arrived to claim the temple, he'd been ambushed by Michael and his three strongest compatriots. Unfortunately for the angels, Apollyon had the war hammer of Ba'al and nearly crippled them before escaping with the coveted key to the Abyss, the seal of Solomon. No one needed to know how he had actually gotten the key. They only needed to know that he had it.

Apollyon grabbed the scruff of Ba'al's neck. It was satisfying to see the bulky brute cringe just slightly in response. "You, my Syrian storm god, are in authority over the human Syrian forces down in Antioch, with Ahura Mazda over his Persian auxiliaries. Now, hurry on down there and prepare for my call. Go ahead. Go." He patted him on the rump like he would a sheepdog. Ba'al began to walk away.

Anat jumped in. "Master, may I accompany my brother?"

"No. You will go with the rest of us."

Artemis said, "My lord, I have heard that there are not merely four archangels guarding the temple. Some have seen the armies of Yahweh's heavenly host."

Apollyon said, "And I have the gods of all nations with Rome. So prepare yourself, huntress. There will be no observers in my army."

Anat said, "Will you share your strategy?"

Apollyon said, "You need only know what we are doing next. And my next step is to take a break from our tour of holy mountains and start some real trouble down in Caesarea Maritima."

Zeus said, "There is much trouble there between the Jews and Greeks."

"Exactly," said Apollyon. "It's time for the uprising to begin."

• • • • •

Antioch
Syria

The city of Antioch was one of Syria's largest, boasting a populace of five hundred thousand. The Orontes River ran through the city out to the Mediterranean Sea. It was an important cosmopolitan center and capital of the Eastern Roman empire. It hosted grand pieces of Hellenistic architecture, including a huge hippodrome modeled after the Circus Maximus in Rome. The activities in that circus were modeled after Rome as well: chariot races, gladiatorial combat, and throwing Christians to the lions. Antioch had been the cradle of Gentile Christianity in the land. The apostle Paul had worked there for fourteen years to much effect. But now most of the Christians had been killed or had run away into the mountains to escape persecution.

The circus games were silent today. Military legate Cestius Gallus was mustering close to thirty thousand legionary and auxiliary forces just outside the city in the foothills and plains. Legion XII Fulminata and Legion X Fretensis were assembled there.

Ba'al watched over the armies as their Syrian principality. But he was most curious about the foreign auxiliaries, Parthian and others, who were now engaging in field exercises with several thousand archers and cavalry. Client kings from surrounding nations had lent some of their forces to this growing army. These included Herod Agrippa of Israel, the Armenian Sohaemus of Emesa, and the Persian Antiochus IV of Commagene. The Arabian King Malchus II of Nabatea would soon join them with thousands more horsemen and infantry archers.

This was the power of Rome: its ability to subsume all the nations of the earth under its iron shield but allow them to maintain their ethnic identities beneath their Roman duty. They paid their taxes to Caesar, and when they were needed for Caesar's army, the client kings were given imperial power to unite with force. This was similar to how the gods of the nations found their unity within diversity. Ahura Mazda was the principality of Persia over these forces from Emesa and Commagene. The Arabian deity Hubal would arrive soon with the Nabateans.[15]

But where was Ahura Mazda? Ba'al could not find him. They were supposed to meet to engage in their own battle practice. Scanning the plain,

Ba'al caught sight of Ahura Mazda's horse. The Persian deity rode that horse everywhere. It was odd that it would be walking loose. Ba'al approached the horse but it turned from him, trotting away as if leading him.

He followed. The horse led him to the forest near the edge of the city. As the horse walked in between the trees, Ba'al sensed something was not right. He pulled out a battle mace from his belt. He held it firmly and moved toward the horse, cautiously looking around for signs of his comrade or of ambush. He wished Apollyon had given him Yagrush, his war hammer from of old. But the truth was, one hit from this battle mace wielded in his muscular arm could crush just about anything.

He saw the horse stop thirty yards away in the brush and stoop down to eat some grass. He glanced to his left, to his right, and behind. He listened with his preternaturally sensitive ears.

Nothing but the wind in the trees.

As he inched closer to the horse, he saw something hanging from the trees just beyond it.

It was Ahura Mazda, beaten bloody and unconscious, hanging upside down by some kind of cord attached to a large tree branch above. His face was so pounded it was almost unrecognizable. Another look around, and Ba'al inched forward, gripping his mace tightly. It looked like a trap.

Below the hanging Watcher, Ba'al could see the remains of a camp, now abandoned. Some slight smoke from coals in the fire pit. Nothing left behind. Except this bound victim with most of his blood dripped out onto the forest floor. Only one kind of enemy on earth could do that to a Watcher: archangels. But Apollyon had told Ba'al that Yahweh's heavenly host were all in Jerusalem. Apparently some angels were engaged in sortie missions of torture for information. It was a good thing the Master did not tell the gods everything of his plan, so they could not give up any important intelligence if caught.

How much had the Persian god given up?

He arrived at his comatose comrade, senses still heightened, body still prepared for ambush.

Still, there was nothing.

Ba'al noticed the cord that bound the Watcher. It was so slight-looking as to be almost invisible. Cherubim hair, drawn from the holy heads of Yahweh's own throne guardians. Indestructible except to a heavenly blade. It was the only binding a Watcher could not break. It had been used on the ancient ones at the Flood. Ba'al winced. He could remember the feel of that abominable ligature on his own wrists when he was bound in Tyre by the archangels a generation earlier.[16]

He didn't have a heavenly blade. This would take time.

Ba'al stepped around the hanging captive to see how he might get Ahura Mazda down. Then he felt a tug at his feet.

A tripwire.

Ba'al spun around just in time to see a massive log, carved to a point, swinging down on him like a huge pendulum spear from out of the foliage. He jerked backward. The log missed him by inches and dug its sharp point into the tree behind him. He would have been skewered into that tree had his instinct been a moment slower.

In anger, he approached the enormous log and swung his mace with a mighty arc, breaking the log in two like a twig. He fantasized doing the same to an archangel's spine.

Ba'al made his way back to the captive Watcher. He could not cut the cord of binding because he had no heavenly blade. But he could pull down the tree branch it was wrapped around. He sheathed his mace and jumped up, grabbing onto the Watcher so he could yank downward with their combined weight. He heard the sound of the branch cracking. One more jump and yank, and the tree limb above broke, bringing the captive and his savior to the ground.

But it also did something else Ba'al had not anticipated. The falling branch had triggered another trap. This one, a weighted net beneath Ba'al's feet, pulled upward, enclosing Ba'al and Ahura Mazda in its web.

Ba'al cursed as he realized his foolishness. He had no blade to cut through the net. His mace was useless in this situation. He writhed and jerked and bellowed with furious anger.

But he stopped flailing when he noticed three figures standing around their catch: Saraqael, Remiel, and Raguel.

One of them queried, "A little frustrated, art thou, o storm god?"

Ba'al felt a pounding blunt force hit the back of his head, and everything went black.

CHAPTER 10

The Mediterranean Sea

The corbita merchant ship headed on its southwesterly course on the Mediterranean Sea toward Palestine. It had been almost ten days since Severus and his party had left Patmos, and tensions were high.

Below deck, Alexander finished tending the injuries of some of the oarsmen. He had used ointment to salve blisters and helped others with cramps and pulled muscles. He had learned much of the nature of musculature through the effect of battle on the human body, which was not much different from that of hard labor. The last oarsmen whose knotted back he had just massaged said to him, "It's a miracle. Thank you."

"It is no miracle," said Alexander. "It is medicine. But you are welcome just the same."

The oarsman looked up at him and said, "It is a good work you do for us, doctor. Do not think less of it. We oarsmen may be of low status, but we are as necessary to the purpose of a ship as the captain who leads us."

"True enough," said Alexander. Then he added with a playful sternness, "Now, get back to work."

They shared a smile, and Alexander left for the deck above.

When he rose from the galley, Alexander saw Demetrius and Cassandra at the bow of the boat, watching the horizon together.

Demetrius seemed to always be with Cassandra. Like a fly buzzing around her. It annoyed Alexander. As he approached the two of them, he felt depressed. He had spent many hours discussing the Scriptures with the two of them and Severus during the trip. The apostle John had given Alexander the honor of bringing the scroll of Revelation to Jerusalem. But Demetrius had outdone Alexander's distinction by memorizing the entire letter while aboard the ship.

It seemed that the Egyptian excelled at everything. He was handsome and a strong warrior. He was both witty and persuasive. He had oratorical skills comparable to Paul the Apostle. Success in the Kingdom of God seemed to follow Demetrius wherever he put his hand to the plow. Synagogues were confounded, crowds repented, congregations expanded.

About the only weakness Demetrius had was that he knew he was gifted. He thought God had a special plan for him, and he did not hesitate to let that be known—especially to Cassandra.

He was in the midst of doing just that when Alexander approached them.

Demetrius and Cassandra shared a laugh.

"You are not jesting?" she said.

"I speak the truth," chuckled Demetrius.

"That old Stephanas," she said, "he is still one stubborn wild ass who could only be tamed by the apostle Paul. I miss him." She turned with a pleasant smile to their newly arrived intruder. "Hello, Alexander. We were just reminiscing about one of our mutual acquaintances in Corinth." She was kind to try to make Alexander feel included. "Paul baptized Stephanas, who then devoted himself to ministry. The old Corinthian was a man of extremes. Not unlike our traveling companion, here," she gestured with amusement to Demetrius, who put his hands in the air as if to disavow.[1]

Demetrius said to Alexander, but really to Cassandra, "Alexander, beware of this one. Trying to get her attention makes you do extreme things."

She slapped him playfully. "That is not true, Deemie."

Deemie? So she had a pet name for him as well. This kept getting worse for Alexander.

Demetrius returned to their original discussion, mostly with Cassandra. "So Stephanas challenged me to go to the Oracle of Delphi and proclaim the gospel." He made an aside to Alexander. "The Oracle of Delphi is the voice of the gods for the Greeks."

"I know who the Oracle of Delphi is," said Alexander with a testiness that he immediately regretted. He thought he must have looked like a child to Cassandra.

The oracle was also called the Pythia. From remote antiquity, she was the high priestess of the temple of Apollo in Delphi, just across the water from Corinth. Her consultation with kings and commoners alike had become so renowned that Delphi was known during the reign of Greece as the navel of the earth.[2]

Alexander added with a bit of his own condescension, "Well, her notoriety has lessened greatly with Rome's ascendancy. But even Nero consults her at times out of his own curiosity."

"I did not know that," said Demetrius. But he continued as if it was irrelevant, "So I crossed the water and went to the temple of Apollo in Delphi." His demeanor turned more serious. "I can tell you that it is a city full of demons."

Cassandra's eyes narrowed with interest. "What happened?"

Demetrius said, "I cast out several demons before I was confronted by the Pythia outside her temple. And I have to say, I have seen plenty of possessed souls in my day, but I have never seen a python spirit in someone as strong as the one I saw in her. In fact, I *saw* him."

"You saw the entity?" asked Cassandra.

"Yes," Demetrius replied. "It stood behind her like a tall phantasm. I am almost sure it was the Prince of Greece."

"You encountered a Watcher," Cassandra reiterated with awe. "Usually, only spiritual sensitives can see such creatures."

"I know," said Demetrius. "I suspect Yahweh has something important planned for me."

Alexander felt jealous. What insignificant plans did God have for a lowly Hellenist doctor?

Cassandra said in a hush, "I saw a Watcher at Ephesus."

Demetrius' eyes went wide. "It looks like Yahweh has something important planned for both of us."

Now Alexander felt sick to his stomach.

Cassandra said, "So what did you do when you saw the Watcher?"

Demetrius spoke as if he wasn't even scared. "Well, I said to him, 'I come in the name and power of the Lord Jesus Christ, inheritor of nations. You are no longer the principality of this territory.' Then I quoted the Psalm in which Yahweh judges the Watchers. I said, 'Thus says the Lord, 'How long will you judge unjustly? You are gods, sons of the Most High, all of you; nevertheless like men you shall die, and fall as one man, O princes.'"[3]

Alexander could see that Cassandra was captivated by the story. She said, "How did the Watcher respond?"

"With one very loud temper tantrum."

Her eyes lit up with a smile.

"The Oracle fell to the ground and flopped around like a fish in a net. Her screams could be heard through the entire valley. She sounded like a wild banshee being slapped around by the Holy Spirit."

Cassandra laughed. She was so caught up in the story that she didn't notice Alexander was not laughing. He was thinking, *How can I compete for her attention with that? This godly warrior had a power encounter with a heavenly Watcher and won?*

What came next made him more depressed.

"When it was all over, three hundred onlookers confessed faith in Christ that day and were baptized. It was humbling."

Now false humility, thought Alexander. *He may not fail at anything, but his character is wanting.*

Cassandra said, "God does have something important planned for you, Demetrius. I suppose it was good that you left us in Ephesus after all. We thought we needed you, but God has used you for his holy purpose."

Demetrius looked down with sadness. "I cannot say that I have always had my mind on his 'holy purpose.' I must confess, my motives for leaving Ephesus were more from flesh than from faith."

"What do you mean?" Cassandra asked.

Demetrius looked out to sea with trepidation and said, "Cassandra, may I speak to you in confidence?"

Cassandra looked to Alexander, who said with perfectly faked approval, "By all means."

Demetrius said, "Let us go to the captain's quarters."

Cassandra placed her hand on Alexander's arm with empathy. She must have known he felt awkwardly left out by Demetrius. But she didn't know how her touch made him full of the fear of losing her to this—this superior man.

Alexander watched the other two walk over to the captain's quarters at the back of the boat. He looked around for Severus. The Roman was below, dealing with structural issues. The oarsmen were rowing. The other soldiers attended to ship duties. Alexander decided to follow Cassandra and Demetrius discreetly to the captain's housing and appear to fix some ropes while eavesdropping on their conversation.

"Lord, forgive me," he muttered as he picked up some rope from a pile to reconfigure its loops.

He heard the two of them talking through the tent-like walls of the quarters. Actually, it was Demetrius confessing to a quiet Cassandra.

"I have desired to tell you something for years," said his strong, eloquent voice, "but I could not."

There was a pause. Alexander longed to look at Cassandra, to see how she responded. But he could only guess at her silent reactions behind the cursed tent walls.

"The reason why I left Ephesus was not from godly motive. I left because of you."

Another pregnant pause. Another moment of anxious curiosity gripped Alexander's heart.

"When I first met you, my father was already an influential orator. And I was studying to be like him. But he was like an untutored scribe blustering half-truths, and I was mimicking him with an ignorant confidence." Alexander heard them both chuckle with amusement.

"But your father told Aquila and Priscilla about my father. And they took him aside and explained to him the way of God more accurately. I will forever be grateful for how your family changed my life."[4]

A pause in the discussion indicated emotions were riding high. "Those weeks I spent in your household were the best days of my life."

Alexander could not help but feel jealousy burn through him again. For even in this area, he did not share anything uniquely with Cassandra. Both Alexander *and* Demetrius had been led to the Savior by the Laetorius family.

Demetrius' voice continued, "That was where I grew in the knowledge of the Lord. That was where I developed my skills of oratory. That was where I fell in love with you."

A new silence exploded Alexander's eavesdropping. The very thing he dreaded.

"Demetrius," came the simple reply of Cassandra's voice. It was soft, understanding. But was it receptive? Alexander could not tell. A shiver of dread went through his entire body.

Demetrius' voice went on, "But I respected your desire to remain chaste until the Lord's coming. That is why I left Ephesus. I could not be around you any longer without my heart being ripped in two by what I knew was right and what my heart longed for. I needed to flee temptation. So you see, my pursuit of my 'calling' was not as godly as you presume. I am only thankful God redeemed it for his will."

"He has indeed," came Cassandra's voice. "I respect you the more because of it, Deemie. Obedience to God is not always easy, but it is always right. And you did the right thing. God honored you for it. I thank you from the bottom of my heart."

Demetrius' voice said, "And now here we are. It is many years later, and I still love you. I have never stopped loving you. Our paths and callings did not cross without a reason. I believe God has brought us together again for a purpose."

Was she consenting with her eyes, with her face? Alexander had stopped doing his work, straining as if to see through the walls that separated him from their intimate talk.

"Cassie," said Demetrius' voice with desperation, "I ask you to be my wife. Join me in ministry, and God will do great things through us together. I believe he has a special plan for me, but I know not what. I only know that with you by my side I could face anything: the mouth of the lion, the sword, antichrist, the Beast. We are already one in purpose. Let us become one as husband and wife."

Another silence. Another soft response. "Deemie."

This time Alexander heard a tone of surrender. The death knell for his own bleeding heart.

His eavesdropping was interrupted by the shout of a sailor. "Land in sight!"

Alexander saw Severus arrive up top for a look. He knew the two inside the tent quarters would soon come out as well. And they would catch Alexander spying on them.

He dropped the ropes and made his way quickly to the bow of the ship to meet Severus.

Alexander saw the lighthouse and towers of a huge port city break the horizon.

"Caesarea Maritima," observed Severus.

It was the largest port city on the coast of Palestine. They had arrived safely to their destination.

Demetrius and Cassandra joined them at the bow. Alexander saw that Cassandra's eyes were wet—wet with happiness. She avoided his look. He cringed in his soul. He wanted to jump off the ship and drown in the waves, or better yet be swallowed by a great fish. He tried to stay strong.

Severus turned to his gawking shipmates. "Back to work, sailors. Prepare for arrival."

They obeyed and returned to their posts.

Severus said to his three traveling companions, "I think it wise not to make my conversion public in this city. I am sure you will agree that I will protect our cause more under colors of my duty to Caesar than as an outward member of a despised minority."

"Wise choice," said Alexander.

Cassandra nodded.

"Wise as a serpent," said Demetrius, "and innocent as a dove."

Severus smiled in return. "Let us see just what is going on in this land of serpents and doves."

CHAPTER 11

Caesarea Maritima
May, A.D. 66

Just before dawn, Severus' ship entered the huge manmade port of Caesarea Maritima, named after Augustus Caesar by Herod the Great, who had built up this Greco-Roman city in Caesar's honor over seventy years ago. It was the capital of the Judean Province and the busiest in exporting goods from the east to Rome. The apostle Paul had been incarcerated here prior to being brought before Caesar years earlier. Severus and his companions would dock at this port and travel sixty miles southeast to their destination, Jerusalem.[1]

The enclosed circular harbor was made of concrete walls and arched colonnades. The bay area was large enough to host a hundred ships. But Alexander became alarmed when he saw that most of the ships were leaving the port rather than arriving or staying. He joined Severus, Demetrius, and Cassandra at the bow.

A building was burning in flames in the southern part of the city. They saw scattered people running about the wharf. They heard crowds shouting in the distance.

"What is going on?" asked Alexander.

"Riots," said Demetrius.

Alexander said, "Caesarea is the residence of the Roman governor of Judea, Gessius Florus. Florus will respond with ruthless brutality."

Severus said to the others, "You may have a revolution after all."

No one was available to guide them into a berth, so they chose the most convenient one available, and Severus had his men moor the ship.

Severus said to his crew captain, "Wait here and guard the ship and passengers. He turned to Demetrius. "Ready half of your warriors. I'll bring legionaries. We'll see if we can find out what is going on. If it's out of control, we meet back at the ship and launch for the southern port of Joppa."

Alexander interrupted, "I'll go with you."

"It's too dangerous," said Severus. "Our Roman uniforms will not protect us from attack in a riot."

Alexander would not back down. "But Jewish rioters will respect other Jews. This is my homeland. You need me."[2]

"All right," said Severus. He turned to Cassandra. "But you stay here." She sighed, resigned.

Twenty Kharabu and twenty legionaries followed Demetrius, Severus, and Alexander out of the boat and down the dock toward the city.

The port storage bays were locked, though some had been broken open and looted.

They passed by the temple of Augustus, a grand structure also built by Herod for the imperial cult of Caesar. This city was one of the most Hellenized of Palestine. A virtual port of idolatry.

Demetrius said, "The hippodrome and theater are in the southern part of town. I think we should check the north side."

"Agreed," said Severus, and they made their way into the city.

The streets by the wharf were all deserted, but they could hear the growing sound of crowds as they pressed on toward the Jewish quarter.

Suddenly, a handful of residents came bursting down an alleyway, running right into Severus' band. They stopped in their tracks when they saw the imposing legionaries, then turned tail, splitting up into different directions.

"Wait!" shouted Severus.

Alexander said, "Let me," and launched off after one of the runners. Demetrius followed.

Alexander turned a corner and saw the runner trying to open locked doorways. When the man saw Alexander and Demetrius behind him, he bolted off again, with the two Christians in pursuit.

The runner was not athletic, so when he found himself in a dead-end alley, he failed to climb the wall before Alexander and Demetrius were on him, dragging him to the ground.

The runner cowered in fear, arms raised to protect his face as he shouted, "Please don't kill me! I have a wife and children!"

Alexander gently pulled Demetrius to step back. He had this. "We are not going to kill you. We just want to know what is going on."

The runner peeked up at Alexander from behind his arms. His look displayed recognition.

"You are a Jew?"

Alexander said, "Yes. We just arrived on a ship from Asia."

"You were with Romans. Has Florus sent them to squash us?"

Alexander sighed. "No. We are on a diplomatic mission from Rome. We are not your enemy."

Demetrius said, "I'm an Alexandrian Jew. My companion speaks the truth. What has happened here?"

The runner swallowed hard, then told his story. "The argument started over our synagogue. We tried to buy the location where we were meeting, but the Greek owner would not sell it to us. So we bribed Florus to help us, but he took the money and left the city, doing nothing. Then on the Sabbath, some Greeks blasphemed God by sacrificing a bird on an earthen vessel at the very entrance of the synagogue, which profaned our holy place. They deliberately provoked a fight with their abomination, and they got it. A riot started, but by the time a Roman security unit came to quench the mob, it was too late. It had grown beyond their ability to control. Now gangs of Greeks and Jews fight and kill one another. Thousands have perished. There is no safe quarter."[3]

Demetrius asked the runner, "Where are the Christians in the city?"

The runner looked as if betrayed to find out his interrogators were Christians.

Demetrius repeated more emphatically, "We worship Jesus the Christ. We know there are those in this city who also worship the Christ. Where can we find them?"

The runner paused skeptically, but finally said, "If any are alive, they're probably hiding out in their meeting place, the banquet hall on Via Roma." He pointed to the south end of the city. "Most of them were killed in the first outbreak. They tried to stay out of it, but you can't stay out of this."

The runner froze in fear at the sight of Severus arriving.

Severus asked the runner, "Where is the Roman presence in the city?"

The runner said, "They withdrew. Procurator Florus is letting Jews and Greeks kill each other."

Severus said, "He is trying to provoke a war in Judea."

Alexander said, "And the Christians are caught in the crossfire."

Demetrius concluded, "We have to rescue them."

Severus complained, "That's impossible. You'd have to go through the heart of the city to get there. You won't make it out alive."

"We have to try. Those innocent lambs are our brothers and sisters in Christ. I cannot leave them to die."

Severus hesitated. He knew he needed to give the impression that he cared for the Christians.

Alexander said, "I'm going with Demetrius."

Severus shook his head at the doctor's persistent competition with the Egyptian. "The apostle commissioned you to deliver the scroll. That is our mission."

Alexander said, "Cassandra has the scroll on the ship. She can help find the Christians in Jerusalem if I don't return."

Severus sighed. "I will meet you back at the ship an hour after dark. Otherwise, I sail to Joppa without you."

"Well and good," said Demetrius. "That gives us a few hours." The sun was already approaching the horizon.

"The Lord be with you," said Severus.

"And also with you," said Demetrius.

The blessing stung Severus. Using such language reminded him of his own deceitfulness.

He pushed it out of his head and led his soldiers back to the ship.

Demetrius grabbed the runner and said, "Help us find this banquet hall."

The runner shook his head. "No, please. We'll all be killed."

"Then take us as far as you can."

Demetrius, Alexander, and their squad of Kharabu warriors hustled down the back alley on their way to the south end of the city. They followed their captive runner, who looked nervously every which way, fearful of ambush.

Alexander felt miserable. He wasn't sure if he had joined Demetrius because he wanted to save the Christians or because he wanted to be as heroic as Demetrius.

Thank God for the Kharabu.

The Kharabu were ex-legionary Christian converts who had helped Demetrius save other Christians in Ephesus from persecution. They had also rescued Severus, Alexander, and Cassandra from being sacrificed to the goddess Artemis. The Kharabu had brought their rescued hostages to the distant mountain hideaway called Kirkindje, and they were now Demetrius' security force for their mission to Jerusalem. They were trained in an ancient way of battle that was said to have been used by the cherubim of Eden and by Enoch, the giant killer. Alexander suspected he would soon find out what such heavenly warfare looked like.[4]

The Kharabu were dressed in mercenary warrior garb of light leather armor and helmets, battle skirt, and leather shin guards, and they carried small circular shields with a short sword and javelin. They were light, swift, and deadly, but their mission was rescue, so their goal today was to avoid battle. The Jews would not attack them, but the Greeks would. Demetrius longed for the coming darkness of night to help them stay in the shadows. But it was not to be.

Their band came to the edge of an alley that opened onto a main thoroughfare. The runner stopped and hid behind the corner of the building. The warriors slid against the walls, waiting. Looking out into the street, Demetrius saw that it led into a large open market square where a mob was fighting. He pulled back out of sight.

The runner said, "The banquet hall is on the other side of this street."

Demetrius asked him, "There is no way around it?"

The runner shook his head no.

"Then we go through it. Thank you for your help."

The runner took off in the opposite direction. Demetrius looked back out at the mob, but could not see enough from his vantage point. Turning back, he whispered to his men, "Wait here. I am going to get closer to find out what our options are."

But he didn't have the opportunity to find out their options because just then a loud voice yelled from the alley behind them, "Kill the Jews!"

Demetrius turned to see a gang of dozens of Greeks a mere sixty yards away, running down the alley toward them with clubs, axes, and swords ready to bludgeon, chop, and cut down their enemies.

Demetrius yelled, "Follow me through the mob! Stay on course to the other side!"

He took off running, Alexander close behind him.

His Kharabu warriors followed.

The Greek gang was close on their tail.

Demetrius and his men broke out into the open square. All around them was mayhem. Gangs of Greeks and Jews killing each other. It was difficult to discern who belonged to which side, but the ground was littered with dead bodies of the fallen. The noise of men at battle sounded like a smashed hive of angry bees.

Their own band ran in an arrow formation, an "arrowhead" of the best fighters clear-cutting the way with the rest behind them in a two-by-two line, one side fighting the left, the other side fighting the right. Alexander stuck close to Demetrius. He didn't carry a weapon, but he was ready to help any of their own wounded. This was his second experience with the impressive fighting skills of the Kharabu. Like an arrow, they cut a swath through the marketplace with winged ease, their fighting as smooth as silk and fast as lightning.

Alexander's first experience with the Kharabu had been when they rescued him along with Cassandra and Severus in the Ephesian Garden of Ortygia. There they had used non-lethal staffs and clubs to incapacitate their enemies. This time they were using lethal force to cut down their attackers without a single wound to their own.

But now their Greek pursuers became engulfed in the fighting around the square as a gang of Caesarian Jews attacked the Greek gang with a vengeance.

Demetrius had been in the lead formation. As they moved through the fray, something to his left caught his attention. At the far end of the square was a twelve-foot-tall statue of Roma, patron goddess of Rome. Standing on the statue base was an eight-foot tall being. It was thin with long, greasy-looking scraggly hair. It could have been a feminine male or a masculine female. He couldn't tell. But it was definitely not human. The creature's skin glittered bronze in the setting sun, and it stood over the fighting as if to supervise it. A Watcher.

Then the thing saw Demetrius and stared straight at him. It had hypnotic serpentine eyes. The warrior felt a supernatural chill down to the bone. And it appeared to be surprised that he could see it. It snarled at him.

The distraction caused him to hesitate, and a Greek's sword swung down upon him.

It was blocked by a Kharabu's sword. "My lord!" he yelled, shaking Demetrius back into the fray.

Within a couple minutes, Demetrius and his squad broke through to the other side of the marketplace and the continuance of the Via Roma.

"This way!" shouted Demetrius. His men closed the gap behind them, rushing down the street and out of the battlefield.

Alexander saw the banquet hall facility at the end of the street. It was large enough to host congregational meetings and easy enough to spot.

Within moments they were at the door, pounding to be let in.

"We are here to help you!" yelled Demetrius. The doors and windows were barred shut. They received no response.

Alexander looked down the street from where they had come. No one had followed them. Night was falling. Darkness would now be their cloak.

But their time was short.

Demetrius yelled again, "I am Demetrius of Alexandria and Corinth! I served the Lord Jesus Christ in Greece with the apostle Paul! I beg you, let us in!"

Still nothing.

Alexander remembered one of the Christian peculiarities he had learned and yelled out, "Maranatha!"

Demetrius joined him, and they both yelled again, "Maranatha!"

There was a noise of the door being unbarred, and it swung open to reveal the fearful faces of several men. Demetrius and his band pushed their way into the building, then barred the door behind them.

Demetrius looked around.

There were about twenty of them. A mere twenty. Only four men, the rest women and children cowering in the darkness for their lives.

Demetrius muttered with despair, "These are all the Christians that survived?"

Their leader, a scrawny middle-aged man with bruises and cuts on his face and arms, stepped forward and said, "As far as I know, we are the last of the elect in the city. My name is Micah. I am an elder of the congregation. Did an angel of the Lord send you?"

"You could say that. But we are very human. And we have no time to spare. You must follow us to the harbor. We have a ship that is leaving within the hour."

Micah did not seem as hopeful. "We have twenty-two more wounded in the next room."

"Twenty-two?" responded Demetrius with dread. "Show us."

Micah led them into a side room where the rest of the men, wounded with bruises, cuts, and bloody bandages, lay on the floor in need of medical attention.

Alexander jumped into action, performing triage on the wounded.

Demetrius said, "How many can walk of their own accord?"

Micah said, "Maybe five or so."

Every new fact made their situation more dire.

Demetrius said, "Carrying these would require most of our men. Even if the women and children help, we will be severely handicapped for fighting."

Actually, Demetrius knew it was impossible. There was no way they could do it. He just didn't want the others to despair. He knew that if they tried to make a path around the perimeter of the city to avoid the fighting it would take a couple hours. There was simply not enough time left.

They were not going to make it.

Then a woman at one of the windows got the others' attention. "Micah!"

As heads turned, the sound of a rock could be heard hitting the front door, then yelling outside. Demetrius ran to the barred window and peered out through the cracks.

He saw a mob outside with weapons and torches and madness. The Greek gang they had avoided in the town square. And it looked like others had joined them. Many others. They were trapped and surrounded.

Demetrius told his men, "They found us."

One of the Kharabu asked, "How many?"

Demetrius swallowed. He didn't want to say. But he had to be honest with the odds. He said, "It looks like a couple hundred."

Some of the women gasped with fear. One of them burst out crying. Micah comforted her, holding her tight.

The Kharabu looked at one another silently. They could normally handle such numbers on the run. They had done so before. But not while protecting a crowd of women, children, and wounded men. It would be like fighting with one hand and one foot tied together.

Demetrius told them what they all knew was coming.

"Men, we cannot move these Christians. But we can go out and face the enemy."

It was a call to a last stand. All of them knew it to a man.

They didn't have any time to consider. The jarring boom of a ram pounding their door shocked them to their senses.

BOOM. BOOM. BOOM.

In a moment the door would crash in and it would all be over.

Demetrius yelled, "To the door!" The Kharabu were already moving, drawing their weapons and wielding their shields.

"We push the first wave back and form a perimeter around the opening! Do *not* let a man through for your life!"

They all knew it was their call to fight to the death. They moved as one man.

The wood bar cracked into pieces. The door flew open.

The battering ram fell to the floor.

But before any Greeks could get inside, the Kharabu were upon them, pushing them back like a flood of water bursting from an opening.

Now the real skills of these mysterious warriors were on display.

As they pushed out the door and formed their perimeter, they hacked and slashed down Greek fighters like they were mere bugs.

Alexander watched in awe through the doorway as they fought with their swords like flowing water. They danced and spun with fluid grace, a macabre dance of death, more like a ballet than a battle.

But the blood flowed freely.

Alexander thought, *Like the Angel of Death.*

The shocked Greeks pulled back in surprise.

But they quickly gathered their wits and began to reform.

The sheer numbers would eventually overwhelm these mighty protectors of the elect. The men would all be dead shortly, the women and children raped and enslaved.

But then the sound of a Roman war trumpet blasted from behind the Greek gang. It froze them with confusion. Many of them turned to see what attacked them in the rear.

That gave the Kharabu the chance to cut down the frontline.

The yells of Greek hostility turned to cries of terror.

Demetrius saw a human battering ram of Roman legionaries and the rest of his Kharabu warriors plow through the Greek forces and divide them in half.

They were led by Severus!

That smug Roman had broken his promise to leave without them.

Demetrius smiled as Severus broke through to the front.

Filled with new vigor, the Kharabu began a campaign of slaughter. Normal odds simply were not fair to their enemies.

But it was already over. The divided Greeks ran in fear for their lives. They were mere hoodlums and thugs facing eighty seasoned professional warriors. They wouldn't last another minute. So they scattered to the ends of the city like frightened cockroaches.

Demetrius stepped up to a blood-drenched Severus. "Liar! You said you would leave without us."

Severus responded with a smile, "Forgive me, brother. Next time I will leave you in God's hand."

Demetrius smiled back. "Brother, you *are* God's hand."

They clasped each other's bloody wrist with strength and honor.

Severus said, "Actually, it's that headstrong woman of yours you should thank. She knows how to put the fear of God into you."

They laughed together and prepared to move the Christian refugees to the ship.

Severus' lieutenant pulled him aside. "Sir, while we were waiting at the ship, I took the liberty of checking the port office. No one was there, of course, but I found this in the mail box for delivery upon our arrival."

He handed Severus a sealed letter addressed to him. It was in the handwriting of his son, Thelonius.

• • • • •

Cassandra had been praying for the last couple hours straight, ever since Severus had first left with Alexander and Demetrius to find the Christians. When Severus returned, she had pleaded with him to reconsider leaving the others behind. She had become filled with the Holy Spirit and prophesied to him that Yahweh would treat him as he had treated others. If he did not wait any longer, God would not wait for him.

Severus could not stand waiting under such condemnation, so he left a second time. Cassandra then cornered all the oarsmen and shipmates to make them pray together for the safety of the rescuers and the rescued.

When the squad returned, bringing the Caesarean Christians, Cassandra gave glory to God and helped them situate their new on-board refugees. With the additional forty or so refugees, the boat was dangerously overloaded. But Joppa was only thirty miles south. Severus said it was worth the risk, and they set out from the Caesarian harbor, leaving the tumultuous city in their wake.

Cassandra helped Alexander attend to the wounded as rations of food were handed around to everyone.

Alexander gave his ration to a couple of children who needed it more.

He saw Demetrius kneel down to help Cassandra.

He heard him whisper to her, "I saw a Watcher in the city. Unlike any I've seen before. More frightening."

Eyeing his blood-soaked cloak and armor, Cassandra ignored Demetrius.

He said, "Cassandra, what is wrong?"

She didn't respond at first.

"Cassandra?"

Finally she asked, "How many did you kill?"

Demetrius said, "I don't know."

"You don't know how many lives you sent to Gehenna?"

Demetrius sighed. "Maybe twenty or more."

She closed her eyes, pondering every single one of them.

He said, "We did what was necessary to save the innocent."

She said, "Our Lord said, 'He who lives by the sword, dies by the sword.'"

"He also said to take a sword for our protection."

She grimaced sourly. "I despise violence."

He said, "So do I. But self-defense is *righteous* violence. If we do nothing, then we empower unrighteous violence, and the innocent suffer."

"And what of the martyrs? Are they guilty of doing nothing? Are they guilty of empowering unrighteous violence?"

Demetrius looked at Alexander, who returned to helping wrap a bandage on a victim.

Demetrius said, "No. I pray that God vindicates the martyrs, as he has promised. But not everyone is called to die for the gospel."

"And are you called to kill for the gospel?"

"I am called to protect others. Unless you prefer we leave the Christians to die at the hands of the Beast."

"But God has said, 'Vengeance is mine.'"

"Yes, and sometimes he uses the sword of man to achieve his justice."

She looked at him with eyes stained in tears. At the carnage on his armor. She said, "You are covered in the blood of guilt," and stomped away to the boat's stern.

Demetrius watched her with sadness and muttered under his breath, "Oh, Cassandra. I am covered in the blood of the Lamb."

Alexander was moved by the debate of the two mature Christians before him. They both sought the face of God, they both obeyed the call of the gospel, and yet they had different beliefs about the nature of so important an issue as self-defense and the use of force to protect the innocent. Righteous versus unrighteous violence. So there was not complete unity of thought on all matters within the congregation of Christ.

He would think on such things to decide what to do when they got to Jerusalem. What he saw tonight seemed clear to him, though. They would not have saved the innocent without putting down the evildoers. But Alexander was not a man of force and violence. He was a man of medicine and healing. He had taken the Hippocratic oath to first do no harm.

And he could not help but consider how this divide between Cassandra and Demetrius was to his advantage.

He felt guilty for even thinking the thought. He should not seek to win Cassandra's heart by subterfuge, for that would simply be a consolation for her, not her heart's desire. As difficult as the thought was, he wanted her to be happy, even if it meant she was not to be with him. It was looking like she was not going to be with any man in these last days. The thought of it made more sense to Alexander. He now understood what the apostle Paul meant when he wrote that in view of the impending tribulation it was best for a person to remain unmarried. For the married have twice as much to lose, twice as much to suffer. And because the appointed time of judgment had grown short, it would be best not to seek a spouse at all. It would be best not to accumulate anything in this present world order because this world order was passing away. The Lord was coming.[5]

Alexander only hoped he would have the endurance to suffer with dignity when his time came. He would die to rescue Cassandra from suffering. But would he die for the name of Jesus Christ? The things he had seen Nero do to the Christians in the Roman circus were so hideous in his memory that he still had nightmares from them. Could he suffer with those who were crucified? Stand with those torn apart by wild animals? Or with those burned as human torches in the night? He feared his own weakness. He doubted his own faith.

He wondered what Jerusalem would bring.

Severus sat in the captain's tent reading the letter from his son. It had been dated from a couple months earlier. It was short, to the point, and devastating.

> *Father,*
> *Greetings from your son Thelonius in Rome.*
> *Mother is dead. She killed herself by opening her veins. She*
> *has been cremated and her ashes stored in her favorite vase.*
> *I will continue to oversee the estate until you return.*
> *But if it is acceptable to you, I would like to leave it in the hands*
> *of Uncle Clavius, so that I can accompany you on the rest of*
> *your journeys.*
> *Uncle Clavius sends his greetings and sympathies as does*
> *Fabius, Antonia and Tigellinus.*

Severus felt dead inside. He couldn't even cry.

He knew exactly why his wife Livia had killed herself. It was for revenge. She had committed suicide in the same exact way that his mistress Persephone had. His mistress he had driven to destruction with his controlling obsession;

his wife, with his criminal neglect. He had used Livia to birth an heir for his family legacy, and then had given his soul to another. And that heir, his son, he had left alone to suffer in the wake of it all.

It seemed the only legacy Severus was leaving was one of selfish ambition and personal destruction.

He knew Thelonius was devastated by the loss, and that he would not write about it because Thelonius also had desperately longed for a relationship with his father. Even though Severus was pathetic and unworthy, he was Thelonius' father, and he was all the young man had left in this world.

Severus longed to see his son, to beg his forgiveness for failing him in so many ways. But he could not bring Thelonius into this dangerous land exploding with war.

The best Severus could do was to write a letter to Thelonius, to explain it all to him, to ask for forgiveness, and to hope that one day, Severus would be able to make it back alive to Rome to reconcile with his beloved son.

PART TWO

Revolution

CHAPTER 12

Qumran
On the Salt Sea
June, A.D. 66

The cock's crow awoke Aaron ben Hyam. His fellow initiates in the cave began to stir on their bedrolls. Aaron was a senior initiate in the Yahad, or Community of Qumran. He was sixteen years old and on the verge of full acceptance as a priest in this congregation of holy ones, or the Sons of Light as they thought of themselves. To outsiders, they were known as Essenes.

Aaron was diligent in his devotion to the Community Rule, a strict regimen of spiritual duties to assure purity and status in the holy priesthood. He led his young initiates now in their morning preparation for the day. Rolling up their simple bed rolls, they left the cave on the shoreline of the Salt Sea, also called the Dead Sea, where no life could dwell. There were a dozen other caves around them, all filled with members of various degrees in the sect.

Aaron and his fellow initiates walked a thousand yards to their walled settlement on the wide plateau overlooking the sea. Three hundred feet before they arrived, they were allowed to relieve themselves in a designated location for excrement, which made them impure. Advanced members, who lived in pitched tents outside the walls of the settlement, met the initiates at the gate of the compound beneath a single large watchtower.[1]

Just outside those gates, the initiates descended steps into one of the settlement's dozen in-ground baths used for ritual purification. Aaron and his companions joined the line of two hundred Community residents as each dropped his woolen tunic to enter the water and immerse himself. They would come out, put their tunics back on, and follow the line up the other stone staircase. The water was fed into the pools through an aqueduct that brought fresh spring water from a few kilometers away. It was crucial for their holy activities to have living water to cleanse them from impurities.[2]

There were so many things that made them impure. It was burdensome for Aaron to keep up with all the rituals of purification required of the Community. But he wanted to be pure, to be one of the true Israel of God whose "voices would cry in the wilderness to prepare the way of the Lord and his Messiah, to make straight in the desert a highway for their God." The Community considered this scriptural calling as their own. They saw themselves and their desert congregation as the fulfillment of that voice for purity.[3]

But Aaron struggled with a constant sense of his own impurity, his own uncleanness before God. He had joined the Community three years ago, one of the younger initiates to the brotherhood that consisted mostly of unmarried, celibate men who sought the true priesthood of Israel. They were devoted to a simple monastic life of holiness, prayer, and basic subsistence. The purpose of their preparation was to be ready when Messiah came to destroy the Kittim, a derogatory word that referred to the Romans, and their corrupt collaborators, the wicked priesthood of Jerusalem.

It was the belief of the Community and thousands of other Essenes located throughout Judea[4] that the holy temple in Jerusalem was defiled and unfit for priestly service. It had been made unholy by an illegitimate priesthood appointed by the Romans and the Herodian rulers. In fact, the Essenes considered all Jews who accepted this arrangement and continued to participate in the corrupt temple system to be the congregation of Belial, or Sons of Darkness. This spiritual harlotry went back two hundred years to the Maccabees, who had established the Hasmonean priesthood in defiance of Yahweh's commands. The true priesthood were the Sons of Zadok, the first high priest of Solomon's temple. The Essenes were those Sons of Zadok. They considered themselves the only true remnant of Yahweh, and it was that remnant that the prophets had foretold would be gathered back into the land and be given the kingdom.[5]

The Essenes separated themselves from the polluted temple in the desert to wait for their rightful inheritance, which the Messiah would provide after the coming great war of the Sons of Light against the Sons of Darkness. As their War Scroll prophesied, the war would be final. The holy temple would be cleansed. The wicked High Priest and his corrupt Hasmonean priesthood would be destroyed and replaced by the true priesthood from Qumran. Aaron longed for that war, the ultimate baptism of purity in this putrid, stinking world of excrement that defied Almighty God.[6]

He led the younger initiates through the gate to a changing room, where they clothed themselves in white linen, the symbol of cleanness for the temple. Pants and a top cloak finished their dress. Then they entered the tefillin room.

Tefillin were also called phylacteries. The word meant *to guard or protect*. These were small, black leather boxes a few inches square that carried pieces of Scripture within them. Aaron and his brothers wrapped the long leather straps attached to the tefillin seven times around their forearms in a spiral all the way up to their fingers. Then they took another phylactery and wrapped those straps around their heads, binding the Scriptures to their forehead. This procedure was done to fulfill a symbolic command with literal observance. God had told Moses, "You shall therefore lay up these words of mine in your heart and in your soul, and you shall bind them as a sign on your hand, and they shall be as frontlets between your eyes."[7]

Aaron felt a surge in his spirit once the tefillin were strapped to his body. He felt as if he were marked by Yahweh to perform his religious duty with his actions—symbolized by his hand—and with his mind—symbolized by his forehead. It was a tangible way of expressing that he loved the Lord his God with all his heart, mind, soul, and strength.

And now it was time to pray.

Everyone gathered in the assembly hall at the northern end of the walled village. The overseer, a fat, balding man named Phineas, entered the front of the hall to lead them in morning prayer.

Aaron's stomach turned sour. He felt a dark spirit of bitterness come over him as it did every time he saw Phineas. This made it difficult to pray, to feel close to God. Every morning and afternoon, he would fight the impulse to get up and walk out and never turn back. He had striven for three years to become a full-fledged member of the Community. A true believer in the doctrine of the Essenes, he was devoted to their cause of preparation for the cleansing of the temple and the end of days. But he had been betrayed deeply by the very leader of this holy cult. And it made him question his own faith at times. How could this holy man of authority do what he'd done to Aaron—and more than once? Did God not see? Did God not care? Would he bring the justice he promised and for which Aaron prayed regularly?

Aaron longed for Messiah to come and destroy the evil that polluted all of life like rotting, diseased flesh. He felt as if his own flesh was polluted. Even though he carefully followed the rigorous Essene regimen of daily cleansing and holy works, he could not help but feel that his past transgressions at the hands of Phineas returned and haunted him. Phineas' fat, groping, disgusting hands. Sometimes he even felt like cutting his own throat as a sacrifice to pay for his sins.

He would have to try harder, work harder, become a full-fledged priest. Maybe then he might find the peace that seemed to elude him. His prayer was that he might be ready to fight in the glorious army of the Sons of Light alongside Messiah and bring down not only the Sons of Darkness, those speakers of smooth things and their false priests, but also the Kittim, the godless Roman Beast of their exile.[8]

But Phineas the overseer would remain.

And with him the constant spiritual torture of Aaron's memory.

Phineas raised his hands to heaven, and the group knelt to pray.

He proclaimed, "When the sun comes forth to shine upon the earth, they will bless and they will answer and they will say, 'Blessed be the God of Israel, the God of all the holy ones.'"

The Community repeated his prayer, "Blessed be the God of Israel, the God of all the holy ones."

Phineas continued, "We, the sons of your covenant, bless your name."

The Community repeated, "We, the sons of your covenant, bless your name."

"And we will arise for our destiny with the God of all the armies of the gods."

"And we will arise for our destiny with the God of all the armies of the gods."[9]

Aaron mouthed the prayers but felt as if God was not listening. As if the Creator sat upon his throne above the waters of the heavens, cold and distant— disgusted.

The next part of their daily order was work. The Community was self-sufficient, and everyone had their responsibilities. Some tended the garden within the walls. Some made textiles and handicrafts. Others were beekeepers, shepherds, and farmers in the field outside the walls. The few wives of the married men did the cleaning and cooking, mostly separated from the males.[10]

Aaron was a scribe. He worked in the scriptorium with twenty others, copying scrolls with ink on parchment they made in their own tanneries. He sat down at a long wooden scribal table that extended from one end of the room to the other. This was for the benefit of unrolling scrolls.[11]

He began his tedious process of holy copying.

There was nothing else in life more satisfying to him than being a scribe, copying the Scriptures and other important literature for their community. He loved scrolls. He wanted to spend all his time with them, reading them and studying them. He wanted to lose himself within their fascinating worlds of the ancient past and poetry. In the words of the scrolls, he found himself carried away from his mundane earthly misery into a magical world of Enoch's heavenly journeys and wars of the giants, Melchizedek's vengeance upon Belial and the fallen sons of God who ruled the nations, and Isaiah's vision of Messiah and the Kingdom of God.[12]

Aaron had been given the task of copying a scroll of the prophet Isaiah, one of the most cherished and most read books of Scripture at Qumran, along with the Psalms and Deuteronomy.[13] He was on the chapter of lament of the Suffering Servant. This scripture puzzled him deeply. It bothered him. He stopped copying to read over the entire passage.[14]

The Servant was the very arm of Yahweh, but he was the polar opposite of the figures of deliverance with which Aaron was familiar in Qumran literature. In the scrolls of the sect, there were two Messiahs to come, a priestly Messiah of Aaron and a kingly Messiah of Israel, along with a coming prophet of the law, creating a kind of triad of prophet, priest, and king. The Damascus Document predicted that the enemies of God would be delivered up to the sword when the messiahs of Aaron and Israel came, and the War Scroll described the final battle of the Sons of Light against the Sons of Darkness.[15]

But in Isaiah, the mysterious Servant of Yahweh was "despised and rejected by men; a man of sorrows, and acquainted with grief. He was oppressed and afflicted, yet he opened not his mouth. He was like a lamb that is led to slaughter."

How could such a weak victim represent the triumph of God? Why would Yahweh "smite him" and "crush" the righteous one? Was this a fourth prophesied character in addition to the Messiahs of Aaron and Israel and the prophet? Aaron could not see how such failure fit in with God's promised victory.

And the fact that the Suffering Servant was described in the symbolic terms of an atoning sacrifice for sins seemed bizarre.

> *But he was pierced for our transgressions;*
>   *he was crushed for our iniquities;*
> *upon him was the chastisement that brought us peace,*
>   *and with his wounds we are healed.*[16]

When Aaron had finished copying the chapter, he felt as though his soul had been turned inside out. The Community had taught that this was a collective portrait of the suffering of Qumran's righteous remnant. But he knew it could not be so. The Servant was spoken of in individual terms *against* the collective group of people. *He* was crushed for *our* iniquities, *he* was pierced for *our* transgressions, all *we* like sheep have gone astray, but Yahweh has laid on *him* the iniquity of *us all*.[17]

A tiny doubt assaulted Aaron's faith. He pushed it out of his mind.

But then another curiosity seduced him. After this servant suffers and dies and is placed in a rich man's grave amidst the wicked, "he shall see his offspring; he shall prolong his days."

What else could that be but resurrection? The overseer, their teacher, denied it. But the Gabriel stone carried the vision of Messiah resurrecting after three days.

> *By three days you shall know that, thus said Yahweh of Hosts, the god*
>   *of Israel, the evil has been broken by righteousness ...*
> *Behold, all the nations gather against Jerusalem....*
> *In just a little while, I will shake the heavens and the earth....*
> *My servant David [Messiah], ask of Ephraim for a sign ...*
> *By three days, live/be resurrected, I, Gabriel, command you, prince of*
>   *princes.*[18]

It was one of the few visions they had carved in stone, and it stimulated his imagination like no other. Could such suffering and resurrection be an expression of power over death itself? Hosea the prophet wrote:

Shall I ransom them from the power of Sheol?
    Shall I redeem them from Death?
O Death, where are your plagues?
    O Sheol, where is your sting?[19]

Aaron's wandering thoughts were interrupted by the sound of a ram's horn. It was the fifth hour, time for the midday community meal.

Aaron cleaned up and joined the brothers at one of several baptism pools around the compound to ritually bathe in cold water. They then put on new tunics and met at the dining hall, where they ritually washed their hands in a basin before entering. They ate bread and drank new wine and ate small amounts of vegetables and meat in silence. Aaron was grateful for some of the rules such as these. He felt so lonely in the midst of this crowd that he would only stand out even more were they allowed to talk to one another.[20]

He finished his meal and went out to the stable where some horses and mules were tended. Normally, he would have returned to the scriptorium and finished his daily copying until the evening, when they would eat once more and then study Torah together. But today was different for Aaron. He had been ordered by the overseer to take a couple of initiates to Jerusalem to buy some supplies they lacked. Self-sustenance was an ideal but not a practical reality. Jerusalem might be corrupt, but not so much that they could not do some trade in it. In fact, there were some Essenes who still lived there. The Qumran sect considered them to be spiritually compromised, but it was always nice to have some connections there for their occasional benefit.

Aaron and two nondescript fourteen-year-old initiates, Baruch and David, prepared their mules for the fifteen-mile journey west to Jerusalem. They had a couple of extra pack animals to carry the supplies on their return.

"Aaron!"

The voice of Phineas drew Aaron from strapping up their last mule.

As the overseer approached, Aaron felt the bitterness of disgust rise in him. Even the way the fat leader waddled was dishonorable. They were supposed to be ascetics. How was he able to put on so much weight with the meager rations they ate? He knew full well how Phineas skimmed from the storehouse for his personal stash. He knew too much about this hypocrite. He wished he could erase his memory like a clay tablet.

But he could not.

Phineas approached them and put his arm around Baruch.

"Be careful. Remember my initiates don't have your experience in the marketplace."

My initiates. Aaron pulled Baruch away from the old man and helped him up on the mule.

"I will, brother."

Though the Community was hierarchical, the members nevertheless stressed their equality before God by using the term *brother* for everyone. Speaking that word was one small way that Aaron sought to bring down this unworthy leader in his mind.

Phineas said, "Stay in the Essene quarter tonight with our brethren. And after you have purchased your supplies tomorrow, do not linger in the city."

"I will, brother." He spoke without conviction.

Aaron kicked his mule, and led the small train of initiates and pack animals on their way to the once-holy city.

CHAPTER 13

Jerusalem

Herod's palace on the western edge of the upper city was as fortified and as elevated as the temple mount. Herod the Great had built it to rival the temple in grandeur and importance. Large open courtyard, luxurious baths, opulent colonnades, and towers of fine Greco-Roman architecture. Another reason the Herods were hated by the Jews of Jerusalem.

Its northernmost region backed up against the Praetorium, the guarded local office quarters of procurator Florus, who now waited for a meeting with Berenice in the vast open courtyard.[1]

She led a small parade of a half-dozen court attendants to meet him by a huge gazebo in the center. She walked deliberately slow to make the Roman wait.

When she arrived beneath the covered gazebo, surrounded by ten-foot-tall columns, Berenice could see Florus was irritated with her tardiness. Just what she wanted. Any way she could stick him with little pinpricks of annoyance to remind him of her royal prerogatives satisfied her immensely.

She walked up the steps and said with faux surprise, "Procurator Florus, forgive me for the delay. I was attending to royal affairs." She had been attending to a royal male servant of particular sensuality. She would not allow this Roman to spoil her pleasure.

Florus said impatiently, "I expect a more prompt response to official inquiry in the future."

She raised her brow with melodrama to get under his skin. "Truly, had I but known ..."

"Enough!" he interrupted. He got to the point. "Judea is delinquent on its taxes. I have come to collect."

She faked a curious look. "I do not understand, procurator. Judea is surely the least among many that have been in arrears with taxes." She stopped as if to realize something. "Have the riots in Caesarea Maritima brought much damage to your residence there? Did the mobs raid your treasury?"

She saw his jaw clench tightly. She knew her dig had gotten through, implying his true intent, a greedy lie.

He said angrily, "Nero Caesar is calling in debts to help finance the rebuilding of Rome since the Great Fire."

"I see," Berenice responded. "Well, I would love to help you, dear procurator, but as you know, I have no authority in these matters. I am sure my brother will rectify them just as soon as he returns from Egypt."

Florus turned snide. "Your brother has been squandering Rome's money in Egypt. Which only makes me wonder why you are not with him. You two are usually so *intimate* in your 'royal affairs' and indulgences."

He stressed that word *intimate*. She thought, *How dare you judge me, you Roman pig*. The scandalous rumors of an incestuous relationship between her and Agrippa had gotten so out of control it scorched her like the Great Fire of Rome itself.[2]

"My brother is celebrating the new governor of Alexandria, as *Nero Caesar had asked him to*." Berenice stressed that last phrase to counter his accusation. But she was not done defending her piety. "I considered it an opportunity to fulfill a religious vow. But I am sure such things as fasting from 'indulgences' are of no interest to you, procurator."

Her subtle insult did not seem to penetrate his godless, staring eyes.

Florus said, "If you cannot comply with my demand, then I shall have to collect the tribute myself." He paused. "From the temple treasury."

Her heart cringed with fear.

The Roman procurator turned to leave.

She blurted out, "Procurator Florus."

He stopped and turned back to her, just barely.

"May I remind you it is Caesar's own decree that Roman forces are forbidden to enter our holy temple."

The corner of his lips turned up snidely.

"Who do you think gave me my orders?"

Berenice swallowed, muttering to herself, "Abomination." She watched him swagger down the steps and march away triumphantly toward what would inevitably fan the flames of revolt.

But she should have guessed as much. His favor and support of the Greeks in the Caesarean riots was despicable. They were clearly in the wrong by profaning the Jewish synagogue, and yet when the Jews had attempted to bribe Florus, he'd taken the money and left for Jerusalem, leaving the mobs to fight it out.[3]

Florus was very much like his predecessor Pontius Pilate in his contempt for the Jews. Pilate had engaged in numerous provocations against them. He brought military standards bearing the image of the emperor into the temple. He furthered this abomination by taking funds from the temple treasury to build an aqueduct. The resultant uprising had been brutally suppressed by Pilate's troops, and many Jews were bludgeoned, crushed, and trampled to death that day. Pilate enjoyed killing Jews.[4]

Florus, she was sure, wanted to wipe them out entirely. And the best way to do that was to incite the Jews to start a war, then call upon the bestial Roman war machine to come and destroy them with impunity. He was trying to outdo his predecessor.

Berenice turned to one of her attendants. "Call together my advisors. Quickly."

CHAPTER 14

Aaron led Baruch and David to the upper marketplace just next to the southwestern wall of the temple. They had stayed in the Essene quarter overnight and were now up bright and early to buy their provisions and be on their way back to Qumran.

Aaron's attention was distracted by the beautiful edifice that towered over them. Whenever he saw the temple, his heart beat quicker. Hope welled within him. The temple was the heart and soul of Yahweh. It was where he would meet with his people, as he had in distant days in the tabernacle with the shekinah glory. Yes, this physical sanctuary had become polluted with the corruption of the unholy priesthood. But one day it would be cleansed, and the Sons of Zadok would return to their rightful place of ministry here. Oh, what glory the future held.

"Aaron? Aaron."

The voice of Baruch took him out of his holy trance. "Should we not purchase our provisions? Phineas told us not to linger."

Aaron turned back to the two innocent young recruits. He thought for a moment, then asked, "Has Phineas approached either of you in private?"

"What do you mean?" asked David.

"Has he made any overtures of—special attention—toward you?"

The two looked at each other with curiosity. "No," said Baruch. "Why?"

They were still newly arrived in the sect. They were safe for the moment.

"Just tell me if he does. But keep this to yourselves."

They looked at each other again. So innocent. So naïve.

The sound of a booming voice interrupted them.

Aaron saw an old man standing on the platform of the southern entrance to the temple, the Huldah Gates. He was elderly, with white hair and beard, and wore a dilapidated robe like a prophet. He spoke like one, too. Like Ezekiel the prophet, he was pronouncing his message to the masses, who ignored him and went about their daily business.[1]

Aaron said, "Let us go see what he is saying."

"But Aaron," pleaded David.

It was too late, Aaron was already moving closer to the platform to hear the speaker better. His two companions followed like obedient ducklings.

"O Jerusalem, Jerusalem!" the old prophet crooned. "Behold, your temple is being left to you desolate! For the days will come upon you when your enemies will set up a barricade around you and surround you and hem you in on every side and tear you down to the ground, you and your children within you! And they will not leave one stone upon another in you because you did not know the time of your visitation! These are days of vengeance! For there will be wrath upon this people to the uttermost!"[2]

Fascinating, thought Aaron. *This prophet of doom sounds very much like the prophecy of the War Scroll.* But it wasn't. And this old man wasn't an Essene. Aaron did not recognize him. But when he spoke next, it all came clear.

"In those days John the Baptizer came preaching in the wilderness of Judea saying, 'Repent, for the kingdom of heaven is at hand.' For this is he who was spoken of by the prophet Isaiah when he said, 'The voice of one crying in the wilderness: 'Prepare the way of the Lord; make his paths straight.''"[3]

Aaron's eyes went wide. He looked at his two initiates, who had also recognized the reference to the voice crying in the wilderness. That was Isaiah's prediction which they'd been taught was fulfilled in the Community of Qumran. The Community was the voice crying in the wilderness. But the old man was saying it was fulfilled in this baptizer named John. The initiates did not know who this was, but Aaron did. He had learned of the famous herald who a generation ago had been a member of Qumran. He had broken away from the Community because he believed he had been called to announce the arrival of Messiah in their time. When it came to light that a simple carpenter of Nazareth, a nobody, was his alleged Messiah, both the Baptizer and the Nazarene were executed. Aaron had been taught that John the Baptizer was an example of what happens when one strays from the Community. But now this old fool, an obvious member of that Nazarene sect of Christians, was saying John was right!

The old man turned vitriolic toward the crowds, who continued to ignore him. "You brood of vipers! Who warned you to flee from the wrath to come? Do not presume to say to yourselves, 'We have Abraham as our father,' for I tell you, God is able from these stones to raise up children for Abraham. Even now the axe is laid to the root of the trees. Every tree therefore that does not bear good fruit is cut down and thrown into the fire. Jesus the Messiah will baptize you with fire. His winnowing fork is in his hand, and he will clear his threshing floor and gather his wheat into the barn, but the chaff he will burn with unquenchable fire."[4]

Aaron had thought Jesus the Nazarene was another one of the many failed messiahs who had come and gone over the last few generations. But this Christian "prophet" was saying that despite his failure this Jesus was the Messiah coming to judge. How could that be? And what was his connection to the heretical Essene, John the Baptizer? These Christians were so similar to the Essenes and yet so completely different. Aaron wanted to know why.

Baruch asked, "Who is Jesus, Aaron? This crazy man claims he is the Messiah?"

Before Aaron could explain to them, he noticed that the old prophet was surrounded by a group of several temple guards. Aaron recognized one of them as the infamous Captain of the Guard, John of Gischala. Aaron had been a young priestly assistant in the temple before he became disillusioned and left for Qumran. He knew all about the temple guard and their previous captains, like Simon bar Giora, who had fled into the desert. And he knew Gischala, a ruthless and violent man who had replaced Simon.

Gischala approached the prophet and kicked him in the back. The old man flew off the platform to the ground six feet below. He landed with a thud, the sound of a loud crack indicating he'd broken his arm. The old man cried out with pain.

Gischala and the guards were upon him in seconds.

Aaron moved in closer to hear them.

He heard Gischala say, "You know, Joshua bar Annas, you need to be more careful of who you condemn. There are Zealots and Sicarii hidden everywhere. Disguised as common men. Farmers, merchants—temple guards even."

The prophet Joshua grunted with pain, protecting his broken arm.

Gischala smacked Joshua. "I am sick of your constant growling and barking like a rabid dog. Your vile hatred of the people of God and the holy temple. I think your words are not from God at all. I think it is time to give you a taste of your own prophecy."

The other three guards grumbled in agreement.

Gischala raised his arm to smack the old man again.

A voice from behind them stopped the captain. "You will do nothing of the sort."

Gischala halted. He and the other guards turned to see six Jewish men, dressed as mere citizens but carrying Roman gladius swords with trained dexterity.

Aaron could not tell if they were bandits or Sicarii.

The leader was a tall, handsome dark-skinned man with long, flowing black hair and brown eyes. When he spoke, his wide chin displayed clenched teeth.

"Back away, and you will live."

Gischala stared at the black-haired leader with shock, then amusement. "You dare defy the temple guard?"

The leader said, "This man has done nothing wrong. You are violating the law."

Gischala took one step closer, gripping his sword. The other guards raised their weapons.

The tall leader's men took ready stances.

"You have some gall," said Gischala. "Who are you?"

The tall leader did not answer him.

"Are you Zealots?"

"We are travelers. We seek no trouble. But we will protect the innocent."

"The innocent?" demanded Gischala incredulously. "If you knew anything about this miscreant, you would not use that word."

"And what if I knew about you?" said the tall one.

Gischala narrowed his eyes. "Are you threatening me?"

"We are protecting *him*," said the tall one.

The tension had risen. A fight was about to break out.

But a disturbance released the pressure of their attention. A century of legionaries passed them on the street on their way to the north entrance of the temple. Procurator Gessius Florus led them, and they looked prepared for battle.

Gischala said to his men. "Gather the temple guard!"

The captain slugged Joshua in the face, knocking him out. Before the old man's protectors could move to defend him, Gischala and his men ran off into the Huldah Gate.

The tall leader ran to Joshua to tend to him, muttering, "Despicable coward. He sucker-punched him just for the spite of it."

One of his fellow warriors gestured towards the elderly prophet. "Who is this man?"

The leader said, "I don't know, but I suspect he can lead us to the Christians. We need to find them."

"I can help you," said Aaron, approaching the newcomers.

The tall leader looked him up and down with suspicion.

"My name is Aaron. I am an Essene. The Christians live in the Essene quarter among some of my community. I can take you there."

"I thought the Essenes considered Christians unclean."

"Most do. Those of us who live in the city are less zealous."

"What is your name, son?"

"Aaron." He gestured to his comrades. "These are David and Baruch."

After an uncomfortable stare at the young men, the leader said, "My name is Demetrius. Thank you for your help."

Aaron's heart leapt within him. The words of this Christian prophet were fascinating to him, and now he had the opportunity to get inside their community and see just what their secret plans were. Were the Christians going to raise an army of their own? Why were their interpretations so close to the Essene understanding of the End of Days?

"Aaron," said Baruch with a questioning face, bringing Aaron back to the moment.

Aaron said to the Christians, "I beg your pardon for a moment." He pulled the two initiates aside and whispered to them sternly, "Go into the temple complex and see what happens."

David whispered back with fright, "Aaron, that looks like a fight about to happen."

Without a breath in between, Baruch added, "You want us to endanger our lives?"

Aaron said, "I am not asking you to fight, just observe. The Romans don't kill bystanders."

David said, "That is not much comfort."

Aaron said, "Information on temple events brings a significant reward from the Community overseer." He only hoped it wasn't the kind of reward with which *he* had been cursed.

His companions' expressions displayed a sudden change of heart at the thought of such advancement.

Aaron concluded, "Meet me by the Essene Gate in two hours. That gives us enough time to return to Qumran."

The two young initiates looked at each other with fear on their faces.

"You can do it," said Aaron. "I believe in you."

He turned back to Demetrius and his compatriots, who had carefully picked up Joshua's broken body to carry him.

"Follow me."

CHAPTER 15

Florus and his century of soldiers had entered the Antonia fortress at the north of the temple complex, then used the underground tunnel that led to the outer court of the Gentiles. Eighty heavily armed soldiers now marched behind his horse, its hoofs clacking noisily on the stone pavement. Florus pranced his horse without hesitation past the four-foot-high stone fence surrounding the actual temple. It hosted a stone plaque that warned of the "pain of death" for any Gentile who entered this holy area.[1]

Several local women screamed at the intrusion. Others ran to get away.

Florus made the priests open the huge bronze doors. Then he sauntered into the Court of Women, the outermost partition of the inner court, which was about two hundred feet square. Beyond the doors of the Nicanor Gate at the other end of the courtyard was the altar and temple proper. Some priests saw the procurator coming, and they closed the huge gate to keep the abomination out.

But the procurator's interest was in this courtyard. His horse whinnied, and his soldiers surrounded him in protective formation. Scattered temple assistants ran. Some priests began to accumulate on the steps to the Nicanor Gate as if they could prevent Florus from going any further.

He looked around the colonnade. He found the passageway for which he was looking and gestured toward it.

A band of twenty soldiers with a portable battering ram in their midst jogged in unison into the passageway that led down below.

Florus pranced his horse over to the colonnade, where he could see seven large upside-down trumpet-shaped urns for financial offerings. He peered down into a couple of them as his horse slowly click-clacked on the stone. They were empty. He moved back out into the outer courtyard.[2]

Underground, below the court, the soldiers found their destination, the temple treasury. The captain of the legionaries saw two frightened guards take off for their lives into the maze of tunnels.

He ordered the soldiers to use the battering ram to break through the heavy oak doors.

When the doors burst open, the soldiers stopped in wonder at the sight. A ton of gold and silver coins and vessels were stacked up in carrying carts. Grinning broadly, the captain said, "Get packing, you grunts."

Back up in the courtyard, Florus saw the latest high priest approaching him, a pathetic crow of a man, scrawny, with a beak for a nose. He couldn't remember this one's name. These Jews changed high priests as frequently as one would change chamber pots. Florus scratched his horse's flank with a devious grin at the high priest. His steed lifted its tail and relieved itself on the stones, first urine, then excrement. Still keeping formation, some soldiers moved aside to avoid the droppings.

Florus could see the old crow's eyes flash with burning anger. The priest yelled, "This is the temple of the Lord God! I am his high priest!"

Florus slightly nudged his horse's ribs and trotted up to the high priest. The procurator pulled his sword and let it hang ominously down the side of this mount.

The priest stepped back fearfully. The air became tense.

Florus glowered down upon the trembling priest. He said, "I don't care if this is God's whorehouse and you are his pimp. Caesar demands confiscation for taxes—which supersedes your religious privileges."

The tension was interrupted by the sound of soldiers wheeling carts of gold out of the treasury hallway. They halted.

Florus shouted, "How much can you retrieve, Centurion?"

The lead centurion announced, "About seventeen talents, Lord Procurator."

Florus shook his head with contempt. He looked back down at the high priest. "You greedy people have pushed Caesar's grace too far."

The priest swallowed and rose up like a rooster. He spat out, "How dare you blaspheme God's holy temple."

Florus shook his head. "Defiant Jew bastards." He hocked and spat in the face of the priest.

A voice boomed out from behind the priest. "Procurator Florus!"

John of Gischala stepped out from one of the corner chambers in the court and walked up behind the high priest with his own sword drawn.

He continued, "It is my duty to warn you that you have violated the laws of Caesar by entering this temple, and it is therefore our right to defend ourselves against lawless Romans."

Gischala then shouted, "Temple guard!"

From behind the portico columns all around them, a hundred Jewish temple guards stepped out with bows drawn and aimed at Florus and his men.

The legionaries tightened formation, their shields pulled up in defense.

The priests on the steps of the Nicanor Gate dispersed to safety.

The temple guards stayed close to their pillars and in the shadows of the colonnade. The reason for this was more than protection. It was strategy. The Roman lookouts in the Antonia fortress could see into the inner court. If they spotted this confrontation, they would immediately send reinforcements. By keeping the temple guard hidden in the porticos, Gischala could slaughter Florus and his men before the Antonia forces were even aware of the need for backup.

One of the flag holders in the century of Romans laid down his banner in an apparent bid to join his fellow soldiers. But what Gischala did not know was that it was a secret visual cue determined by Florus as a silent call for help to the Antonia.

Gischala stood beside the high priest like a bodyguard. He glared defiantly at Florus.

Florus spoke through his teeth. "Gischala, withdraw now and I will spare your life. It is your duty after all to guard this dung house. I will not hold that impulse against you."

Gischala responded with biting sarcasm. "Since Caesar is so poor and you lack fiscal responsibility, I passed around a beggar's pot to help with charity."

Gischala pulled out a bag of coins and cast the contents onto the ground at Florus' feet. The bag opened. Clinking coins spilled out onto the stone pavement. The noise made the horse whinny and buck with unrest.

Florus settled the spooked stallion. "You dare insult my favor?"

Gischala stood resolute, unyielding. "Procurator, ever since you slaughtered the Egyptian and his zealous followers before me in cold blood over a year ago, I have patiently waited for the opportunity to return your favor upon your own head."

Florus' eyes went wide with shock. He knew what was next.

Gischala nodded to his lieutenant, a man named Eleazar, who raised a trumpet to his lips and blew. The sound penetrated the courtyard.

Gischala yelled, "Defend the temple!"

A flurry of arrows was released into the body of legionaries. Shields protected some, but not all. A dozen went down.

Another volley killed more legionaries.

Followed by a charge of temple guard upon the weakened Romans.

Gischala grabbed the high priest from behind and used his sword to cut the poor bird's throat.

To Florus' surprise, Gischala then yelled, "Florus has killed the high priest!"

Florus muttered, "Traitor." He launched his horse at Gischala, and their blades met. With Florus' superior position, Gischala could barely protect himself, let alone return the attack.

Suddenly, another century of Roman legionaries burst through the Beautiful Gate into the court. They had received the flag call for reinforcements and came to their brothers' defense like a flood.

The tables were quickly turned against Gischala.

But then the Jewish captain quickly thrust his sword into the heart of Florus' horse.

The animal snorted in pain and fell to the ground with Florus on its back.

Florus rolled and was on his feet with his sword ready to kill Gischala.

But the captain was gone. Vanished into the colonnades and down into one of the many labyrinth of tunnels to escape. Along with his temple guards. Their attackers had fled.

A centurion approached Florus. "Your orders, sir?"

"Find the coward, John of Gischala, and his men." Florus was well acquainted with the captain of the temple guard. "He lives in the upper district. He will probably be hiding there. Kill everyone, man, woman, and child there, until he and his men hand themselves over."

"My lord?" said the centurion. It was more of a plea for mercy than clarification.

"You heard what I said, soldier. Put the women and children to the sword and crucify the men."

"Yes, Procurator," said the centurion, and left to carry out his orders.[3]

The Romans left the court with their confiscated gold. Two shaking Qumran initiates had watched the entire disaster from the safety of the one place no one would be bold enough to check, the Chamber of Lepers. David and Baruch looked at each other fearfully. They had to get the message to Qumran of what they had just witnessed: the beginning of the War of the Sons of Light and the Sons of Darkness.

CHAPTER 16

"Your jaw is broken as well," said Alexander. He had been examining Joshua's injuries from Gischala's attack on the temple steps. Alexander wrapped a large linen bandage around Joshua's jaw and head. Cassandra helped to splint the old man's broken arm.

"You will not be able to speak for a month or more," he said. "Or use that arm."

Joshua groaned with sad eyes.

Alexander said, "You will have to have your food liquefied to drink through a reed straw."

Demetrius stepped up to Joshua, who was still lying on the floor of the Christian home to which Aaron had led them in the Essene quarter.

Aaron was impressed with these strangers. They had come from Rome and Asia on a mission that they had not yet revealed. Demetrius and Cassandra were the more charismatic of the travelers. The doctor struck him as a caring man of peace. They had a Roman with them named Severus, and though the Roman stayed out of the conversation, Aaron suspected he was more important than he acted.

Aaron's curiosity overcame him. He wanted to stick around a little longer and listen in.

The travelers were surrounded by twenty-four elders and leaders of the Christian congregation here. It was strange how peaceful and compassionate the Christians were, so very different from the image of wild-eyed fanatics Aaron had been taught at Qumran. Unless they were hiding something. He was reminded of how the Sicarii appeared to be average citizens in the crowd, while carrying secreted daggers for diabolical purposes of assassination and kidnapping.

What was the secret these Christians carried?

Demetrius said to Alexander, "Let us lay hands on Joshua and pray for his healing."

Alexander felt guilty he hadn't even thought of that. His life training in medicine conditioned him to focus exclusively on human remedies. As a Jew, he always affirmed the power of God to perform miracles of healing and deliverance. Nehushtan, the bronze serpent on the pole that healed all those who looked to it, was his favorite story. But it was a story. He had never seen such miracles in all the mayhem he attended to on the battlefield. He was too ashamed to admit that prayer for healing was the last thing he would have considered.

The elders of the city hesitated at the request for prayer. They had been reluctant to bring in the injured Joshua as well. Alexander now learned why.

One of the elders, an older but healthy man named Boaz, said, "Perhaps it is the Lord's will that he speak no longer."

Demetrius stared angrily at the elder. "And perhaps it is the Lord's will that he be healed."

Boaz protested, "His preaching has caused the congregation much difficulty in the city."

"What do you mean?" said Demetrius.

Boaz said, "He only preaches judgment on this generation, which inflames the hostility of our kinsmen against us."

Another elder added, "We want to preach a gospel that lives out the grace of God amongst our Jewish brethren. Jesus is the Messiah to the Jew first. The gospel is love. Joshua preaches judgment."

In all of this, Alexander saw that poor Joshua could only watch the exchange with moans. It took others to defend him.

Cassandra said, "Is not judgment as much a part of the gospel as love? Yes, Jesus came to the Jew first, but then to the Gentile as well. And he also promised that he is coming on the clouds to judge those who pierced him, and all the tribes of Israel will mourn on account of him."[1]

Alexander could see that Cassandra was annoyed with the Jerusalem Christians. She was getting ahead of herself. They had yet to tell their hosts about the secret scroll they carried like a Sicarii dagger in their cloak.

The elders shied with guilt. But one of them piped up, "We have lost so many in this Great Tribulation already. Beatings, stonings, martyrdom for our faith. We fear we are being persecuted more for our judgmental attitude than for the content of our message."

Cassandra mocked, "You *fear*."

She stared them down with contempt. "I came from Rome. Have you heard of Nero's circuses? Do you know that he uses Christians on poles as human torches? He feeds them to beasts. He blamed the Great Fire of Rome on the Christians at the urging of his empress who followed the whisperings *of Jewish leaders*."

The elders looked guiltily at one another.

Cassandra welled up with tears of anger, "Do not speak to me of your cowardly 'fears.' Our own countrymen betrayed our Messiah. They crucified the Lord of glory and killed him by the hands of lawless men. They claim to be children of Abraham, but they are children of the devil. They expect to eat at the table with Abraham, Isaac, and Jacob in the kingdom of heaven. Instead, they will be thrown into the outer darkness, where there is weeping and gnashing of teeth. The Jews deserve Gehenna, which they have stored up for themselves on the day of wrath when God's righteous judgment will be revealed."[2]

"Cassandra," said Alexander, interrupting her tirade.

She flushed with embarrassment. She had proven their very accusation with her own vengeful spirit.

Demetrius turned to the elders and said, "I'm sure Cassandra would agree that we *all* deserve God's wrath. But I think the point remains. Regardless of our own failures or attitude, Jesus said that some of his disciples would not die until they saw him seated at the right hand of God and coming on the clouds of heaven with his angels to repay each person according to what he has done."[3]

Boaz said, "But he also said he did not know the day or the hour."[4]

Demetrius said, "That is why we are here. We have a new revelation from the apostle John on Patmos." Alexander could see the surprise in the Jerusalem elders' eyes.

"We have reason to believe that the last hour has arrived. The time is near. He is coming soon."[5]

Boaz said, "This from the last living apostle?"

"Yes," said Demetrius. "But first, let us put aside our differences and live out our 'gospel of love' toward one another as you so eloquently spoke. Let us lay hands on Joshua for his healing."[6]

Alexander felt the Holy Spirit in those words. At the same time, he felt a tinge of envy as he watched Cassandra's look of respect at Demetrius. How was it that one man could be so gifted? So successful with everything he put his hand to? Alexander wondered if Cassandra and Demetrius had ever finished their discussion of marriage that had been interrupted back on the ship.

The elders reluctantly moved over to Joshua and followed Demetrius' lead. They all laid hands on the old prophet, and Demetrius prayed.

He lifted his words to heaven and called upon Yahweh to heal Joshua.

Aaron was impressed with the dark man's strong voice and eloquence. If there was anyone whose prayer God would hear and answer, it would certainly be this man.

When they had finished praying, Aaron opened his eyes to see Alexander unwrap the bandage from Joshua's arm.

But Joshua yelped in pain, held his bandage, and shook his head. He had not been healed.

Everyone looked at one another for an answer, but there was none.

Demetrius finally said, "Well, it must not be the Lord's will for Joshua to be healed yet." He looked to the old prophet. "Joshua, seek God for what you will say when you can speak again."

He looked at Boaz. "In the meantime, I would hope that these leaders will find a place in their midst for their brother in Christ."

The elders appeared shamed. Boaz said, "We will care for you, Joshua. Forgive us for our divisive spirit."

Joshua nodded with forgiveness.

Demetrius would not reveal his innermost feelings to the brethren. He kept his air of confidence and faith so as not to discourage the others. But deep inside, he questioned whether God had left him. What had he done wrong after so many years of success? He had healed before. Lepers, plagues, and demon-possessed. He had seen hundreds converted through his preaching. Was Yahweh done using him? He felt worse than a failure. He felt like a success that was no longer needed.

Alexander reconsidered his own failure of faith. So Demetrius was not successful at everything he put his hand to after all.

Forgive me for my pride, Lord, Alexander prayed. And he actually felt sorry for his spiritual rival. Demetrius shouldn't be a rival at all. They were allies in their quest. But Alexander's feelings of inadequacy in the face of this gifted man continued to plague him. He wanted that kind of influence. He wanted to *be* like Demetrius. But this incident made him realize he knew nothing of God's purposes.

Aaron now wondered if this eloquent leader Demetrius was no less a fraud than his overseer Phineas at Qumran. Maybe these Christians were just another group of fanatics whose beliefs sought a fool's paradise that would lead them into the hands of the Kittim of Rome.

Cassandra had wondered if the lack of healing was because of her own lack of faith. Did her anger achieve the righteousness of God?

Yes, she had slipped. She had let her passion overcome her in the moment. But she was sure she was right about the judgment of God. And these Jerusalem Christians would soon understand that she was right when they read the Revelation of Jesus Christ given to John the apostle. God was divorcing the harlot of Israel and marrying his bride, the body of Christ. Capital punishment against an unfaithful wife was justice, and Cassandra would be happy to cast the first stone.

Severus had been silently watching the entire incident while wondering if this Joshua was aspiring to messianic pretensions. The prophet's name was Joshua, which was Jesus in Greek, also the name of Israel's conquering general in the days of Moses—Moshe in Hebrew. At least, that is what he had learned from his Christian servants. So this Joshua claimed the same name as their Jesus Redivivus. He preached destruction and judgment, the language of insurrection. And he had the touch of madness necessary for delusions of grandeur.

But now Severus just saw him as a pathetic old fool whose rambling mouth may very well have been shut by the god he claimed to serve—a god of amusing irony to Severus.

The Praetorian had secretly quartered his men a distance outside the city, disguising himself as a humble Christian in this traveling band. His soldiers were to be available for his call to action, as well as a cohort of legionaries from the Antonia fortress by the authority of Nero Caesar. Unfortunately, because of the unrest started by Florus, Roman presence was no longer as useful a deterrent. But Severus could see that there was no need for any action here at all. Joshua was no revolutionary leader. And these Jerusalem Christians were no warriors. They were mice, not men.

Boaz's wife entered the room and announced to her husband, "There are two young men at the door asking for an Aaron ben Hyam. They appear quite frightened."

Aaron said, "They are my companions. They bring news of the temple."

Boaz told his wife, "Bring them in, please."

Severus had seen Florus and his Roman minions trampling their way toward the temple. He knew that the news would not be good.

CHAPTER 17

"And he said to me, 'These words are trustworthy and true. And the Lord, the God of the spirits of the prophets, has sent his angel to show his servants what must soon take place. And behold, I am coming soon. Blessed is the one who keeps the words of the prophecy of this book.' I, John, am the one who heard and saw these things."

For the past hour, the lector of the congregation had been reading the Apocalypse of John to the small congregation of Christians in Jerusalem. They had met secretly at the house of one of the wealthy converts in the upper city, along with the four messengers who had brought the scroll from Patmos. The young Essene, Aaron, who had joined them, was now on his way back to Qumran.

The lector continued reading the last segment of the scroll. "And he said to me, 'Do not seal up the words of the prophecy of this scroll, for the time is near.'"[1]

The words struck Alexander like a hammer. He had been studying the prophecy of Daniel. Six hundred years earlier, the prophet had written of the "time of the end." The angel in Daniel's vision had told him to "conceal the words of the prophecy and seal up the scroll" because that "time of the end" was in Daniel's distant future. The angel speaking in John's vision had commanded just the opposite, to *not* seal up the words of his scroll of prophecy for the time of the end *was near*. Which meant they were in the last days of the old covenant. Daniel's long-awaited predictions had come upon them. The sealed scroll had been opened by Jesus. He was coming in judgment.[2]

The lector finished the final words of the scroll. "He who testifies to these things says, 'Surely I am coming soon.' Amen. Maranatha, come, Lord Jesus! The grace of the Lord Jesus be with you all. Amen."

Alexander looked down at the mute prophet Joshua, whose tears saturated the bandage around his head. He could not speak, but his face proclaimed a holy joy of vindication.

The atrium full of listening Christians was stunned silent for several minutes as they processed the revelation they had just heard.

The Apocalypse still sent a chill down the spine of Severus whenever he heard it. The impending nearness of doom, the imminence of Jesus coming, the certainty of God's judgment. What if these Christians were right? What if they were *not* lunatics following a delusion? What if this was all about to happen?

Well, if it did start to happen, then he would wait and see, then make a true conversion when it did. After all, didn't their gospel teach that one of the brigands on the cross next to Jesus received a similar last-minute reprieve? Severus would continue to pretend and hedge his bets.

The lead elder, Boaz, spoke first to the travelers, addressing Demetrius as the leader. "This is a deeply lyrical, profoundly written prophecy. I can see now your claims. If it is true, then we must heed its words."

Demetrius sighed with relief.

Cassandra silently thanked God.

Severus and Alexander were not so hopeful.

"But if it is *not* true, we would be fools to follow it. I myself find it very difficult to believe that it has been written by the apostle John."

"What do you mean?" said Demetrius. "We told you we were with him on Patmos."

"Yes, you *alleged* such a visit," said Boaz. "But the words in the scroll betray you. We have had other letters from the apostle John as well as his Gospel, and this letter simply does not sound at all like his writing. It does not possess the same language or ideas."

"It was a vision from Jesus Christ," said Demetrius, getting angry. "He was recording what he saw and what the angel told him to write. It's Apocalyptic, not gospel or epistle. That's why it doesn't reflect his usual style."[3]

Cassandra added, "You are calling us liars. Demetrius and I were coworkers for the gospel with Paul throughout the western provinces."

"Forgive us," said Boaz. "But this is the east. And we have never met you before. The ramifications of this alleged prophecy are traumatic for us—and highly dangerous. We need more proof beyond the mere claims of strangers."

Severus said, "Shall I take my ship and retrieve John from Patmos so he can tell you himself?"

Severus would not actually do such a thing. But it was exasperating how suspicious these Christians had become under persecution from their fellow Jews. He decided to shut up and watch how his companions would handle it.

Alexander jumped in. "Do you have the Gospels of Matthew or Luke?"

Boaz nodded. "And those of Mark and John as well."[4]

Alexander said, "Then you know that Matthew, Mark and Luke all record Jesus' Olivet sermon where he prophesied the signs that herald his coming. Signs that we've all seen fulfilled. Famine, earthquakes, false messiahs, the persecution of the apostles."[5]

Boaz said, "John's gospel has no prophecy of the kind."

Demetrius said, "That's because the Apocalypse *is* John's version of the prophecy."

Alexander backed him up. "The Olivet sermon is what Joshua has been reciting from memory in the marketplace."

Alexander saw Joshua aggressively nodding his head.

Boaz said, "You know full well we do not approve of Joshua's interpretation."

"But what of Jesus' interpretation?" said Demetrius. "He was the one who said that all these things would come upon our generation. That some of the original disciples would not taste death until we saw the Son of Man coming in his kingdom."[6]

"And that is just the problem," said Boaz. "The fathers of our faith, the apostles, have died out."[7]

Alexander jumped back in. "John is still alive. But even if he was not, Jesus was speaking to others beside the twelve."[8] He would not let Demetrius be the only defender here.

Boaz tried to ignore the facts. "John is very old. He will be dead soon. It's been a generation already."

"Exactly," said Alexander. "The fullness of time has arrived. It is the last hour of the last days of the old covenant. Did not Jesus inaugurate the messianic age to come with the new covenant?"[9]

Cassandra saw Boaz glance over at another elder, a tall, gaunt, fifty-year-old bald man named Jacob, who now joined the discussion. The two men's interchange appeared strategic to her. Jacob said, "Temple, Torah, and Land remain unchanged. Everything continues as it has since the beginning of creation. Maybe we have misunderstood the promise of the Messiah's coming and a new heavens and earth."[10]

Cassandra and Demetrius glanced at each other. They now knew who was responsible for the problem here.

Cassandra said to Jacob, "What do you mean, 'Temple, Torah, and Land remain?'"

Jacob answered, "Maybe we have brought this on ourselves. All the vicious rhetoric about destruction and judgment over many years. Is it any surprise that blaspheming either the house of God or his covenant with his people would provoke our countrymen?"[11]

Cassandra was incensed. "You believe the persecution of antichrist is our own fault? That we brought upon ourselves the Great Tribulation?"[12]

"I believe," said Jacob, "that if we blessed the temple and obeyed the Torah, God would bless us, as he promised Moses. But if we are not careful to obey all God's commandments and statutes, then he has promised to curse us and cause us to be defeated by our enemies. And that is precisely what has been happening to us for years. Christians have become anathema, not just in Jerusalem, but all over the empire, as you yourself have experienced."[13]

"Don't you dare tell me what I have experienced," growled Cassandra. "You have no idea what the beast of Rome has done to our brethren."

"Cassandra," cautioned Demetrius. But she wasn't backing down. She and Demetrius had fought long and hard with the apostle Paul against these Judaizers in Rome and Asia, who believed that faith in Jesus as Messiah was redemption for all, but that Gentile believers would also have to become Jews to fully participate in the people of God. This required circumcision and keeping the dietary laws and Sabbaths, a requirement that Paul had considered blasphemy against the new covenant.[14]

"Who has bewitched you?" said Cassandra, frustrated. "These issues of Torah were dealt with in the Jerusalem council years ago by your previous elders *and* the apostles. Yet I see you have returned to the weak and worthless principles of a dead covenant." She paused. "Like a dog returns to its vomit."[15]

The elders went aghast at her accusation. A hush went over the congregation.

"Jesus said all this would happen. That we would be put out of the synagogues and that the hour would come when those who killed us would think they were offering service to God. He said that the Jews do this to us because they have not known the Father or the Messiah. But their hour is coming."[16]

Alexander could not tell if this was the Holy Spirit upon Cassandra or her burning hatred for fellow Jews who had martyred her parents and now spread their false teaching throughout the body of Christ.

He listened closely as Cassandra continued, "Peter wrote of this very day before he died in Rome. He said scoffers would come in these last days of the old covenant, questioning the promise of his coming. That false teachers and destructive heresies would cripple our assemblies. The Jerusalem congregation has been infected with doctrines of demons."[17]

More gasps of horror came from the crowded room.

Jacob said, "You speak out of line, woman."

"I speak the words of the apostles Peter and Paul," Cassandra rejoined.

"You refer to *alleged* correspondence." Jacob paused as though a thought had occurred to him. "I can remember in the early years when the residents of Jerusalem sold their homes and shared all things in common because we had been convinced that the end was near. Some even chose not to marry. But it never happened, and we had to get back to our lives. Many lost all they had because of that doom-saying. That generation has already passed."[18]

"It is not already passed," Cassandra said, "but it is at an end."

"You speak with audacity," Jacob complained. "You should heed the commands of your precious apostle to the Gentiles, who said women should keep silent."[19]

"In a worship assembly," hissed Cassandra, "Which this is not. And since you are unaware of the writings of Peter, the 'precious apostle' *to the Jews,* then allow me to share what the Holy Spirit has revealed through him. The heavens and earth that now exist are stored up for fire. The *stoicheia* are being melted with fervent heat. And the Lord is not slow to fulfill his promise. He has delayed in order to draw more to repentance."[20]

Alexander's thoughts were triggered by her words. He was transported back in his memory to one of his first discussions with Peter in Rome before Alexander had become a Christian. The apostle had explained this very concept to him. "Heavens and earth" was a poetic expression for a covenant of God. The *stoicheia* were the elements or principles of that world order. When Yahweh established covenants, he created a new spiritual cosmos. The Mosaic old covenant was the first heavens and earth. The new covenant, of which Peter spoke, would soon replace that old "heavens and earth" which Jesus had made obsolete by his death and resurrection.

The stakes of this issue were such that if the elements of the old covenant were still standing as Jacob alleged, the *stoicheia* of Temple, Torah, and Land, then how could anyone say they were no longer in effect? How could they prove that the new heavens and earth that God had promised had been inaugurated at the cross when everything went on the same from the moment of that new creation? There was only one way to prove such a cosmic change of covenants: cataclysm. The historical destruction of those old covenant elements of Temple, Torah, and Land.[21]

Cassandra's pronouncement broke into Alexander's thoughts. "Know this, Christians of Jerusalem, the Day of the Lord will come like a thief, and the heavens will pass away with a roar, and the *stoicheia* will be burned up and dissolved. That is why the Lord Jesus told those in Judea to flee for the mountains. Because if you do not, you will be taken away in judgment by the abomination of desolation."[22]

Boaz pushed his way back into the discussion. "But Jesus said to flee when the abomination of desolation stood in a holy place, when Jerusalem was surrounded by armies. Rome may have quarters in the city, but we are not under siege."[23]

For the first time, Cassandra did not have an immediate retort. Boaz's challenge carried some weight.

Alexander came to the rescue. "What do your prophets say? Have they not warned you of the coming storm?"

Boaz and Jacob looked guiltily at each other.

Boaz was the honest one to speak up. "The revelatory gifts have been strangely silent. They began to decrease in frequency not long ago. We haven't seen any miracles or received messages of tongues or prophecy for months now."

It occurred to Demetrius why his prayer for Joshua's healing had not been answered. He said, "The revelatory gifts are Yahweh's word, and the miraculous validates it. The apostles' teaching was the last revelation of redemptive history. Once they are dead, the final perfection comes, and the new covenant scriptures are sealed in the last days of the old covenant. The end of all things is at hand."[24]

Alexander could see that Boaz had been bothered by their arguments. He was no doubt a good soul trapped in the middle of extreme claims, high stakes, and a battle for the soul and survival of the body of Christ.

Cassandra, now less zealous, said with sobriety, "God is giving us time to spread the word and alert the Christians throughout the land. We must copy the Apocalypse and distribute it before Rome arrives."

She looked to Boaz for some confirmation of her hope. Would he and the elders be willing to take a chance on this dire prophecy after all?

Boaz said, "We will do nothing of the sort unless and until its authority can be proven to us. Otherwise, we seek peace and diplomacy with our fellow Jews."

Jacob shot a smirk at Cassandra.

She looked to Severus for support. He had none to give.

Demetrius sighed with desperation. Time was running out. The Judge was standing right at the door.[25]

Alexander prayed that the poisonous control of the Judaizers would somehow be broken by the Spirit of God before it was too late.

Severus' group left the home of Boaz and sought an inn to rent some rooms. As they walked the streets, they argued amongst themselves, but tried not to draw attention.

Cassandra said, "Jerusalem is infected with these Judaizers and their false teachings."

"But not everyone is," said Alexander. "We must have patience for the sake of the elect. We must be faithful to our calling of spreading the word. It is God who opens hearts and changes minds."

Demetrius disagreed, "I will not waste my time with the hard-hearted who refuse to consider the truth. I see now that God has given them up to their faithless hearts. He has withdrawn his presence. My Kharabu and I will go to the four corners of the Land with the Revelation and protect the elect with our swords."

Cassandra pleaded with him, "Let me go with you, Demetrius."

Alexander's heart sank. At the moment of crisis, she wanted to be with the Egyptian, even though she was against his violence.

Severus said, "You will not go with him. You will remain with us in Jerusalem." In the course of all that had happened, Cassandra had clearly lost sight of the fact that she remained in Severus' custody.

Severus added, "I will send some of my men with you, Demetrius, to help you and report back to us of your progress." His real intent was for his own men to report on any messianic pretenders they may find.

CHAPTER 18

The Road to Jerusalem
August, AD 66

Agrippa awoke from a restless nap. He peeked out the window of his carriage, hand-carried by Nubian slaves from Egypt in a caravan on its way back to Jerusalem. He saw the Judean desert countryside passing by. He could tell he was almost home.

He was returning from Alexandria, where he had traveled to congratulate the new governor of the province. It had been a welcome break from his troubled Judean headaches. Increasing bands of brigands, rising revolt, and religious unrest in the population all provoked an already vexed relationship with their ruthless procurator, Florus. Agrippa had treasured the opportunity to get away from it all with a change of scenery and culture and some well-earned rest.[1]

Egypt was exotic to him. He found the Nile flowing through the desert with life-giving creation to be a mystical experience quite different from the rain and storm of his homeland. The pyramids and massive religious structures were impressive. Though the Jews had great disdain for this pagan oppression of their past, Agrippa carried a secret regard for it in his Herodian heart. As he did for the intimate embrace of Egyptian women.

He was bringing exotic African animals back with him for hunts, along with beautiful tapestries, fabrics, and jewelry for Berenice. Though the famous Alexandrian library had burned down almost a hundred years ago, he still longed for access to its volumes of world literature. As a port city, Alexandria was a cosmopolitan center of merchant trade and cultural exchange that dwarfed Caesarea Maritima on his own coast. Egypt was so much more colorful and full of life than Judea felt to him.

Agrippa belched and tasted the leeks and onions from the rich foods he had packed for his trip home. He was preparing himself mentally for a return to a more austere existence in his Jerusalem palace. Thank God he had brought some of those Egyptian women back with him.

I think I will get one now, he thought. *I need release from the tension I have from this wearisome travel.*

He was interrupted by a rap on the carriage door. He pulled the curtains to see who was bothering him.

One of his guards said, "My lord, you'll want to see this," and he stepped back.

The sight through the window shocked Agrippa.

He jumped up and opened the door to his carriage. He leaned out to look ahead down the road. They were within a quarter mile of Jerusalem. Its walls loomed in the bright midday sun.

The road to the city was lined with thousands of crucified victims, left and right. Rows and rows of Jews, sometimes two abreast. Some of them were still alive, groaning in the pangs of death. Others had already been feasted upon by carrion birds.[2]

The air was filled with the stench of death. Human flesh rotting in the burning sun.

Vomit rose in Agrippa's throat. He swallowed and kept it back with a gagged wince.

He jerked himself back into his carriage and closed the blinds, placing a perfumed napkin over his mouth and nose.

What had Florus done now?

Agrippa felt sick to his stomach.

He prayed that Berenice was safe.

• • • • •

Agrippa stood with Berenice in the war room of the Herodian palace, surrounded by a handful of their advisors, including the high priest Ananus ben Ananus and the Pharisee Joseph ben Matthias.

The others had just finished explaining to Agrippa the recent events that had led up to Florus' mass retaliation against the Jews. First the Caesarean riots, then his plundering of the temple treasury. Now this. The Roman governor had gone too far.

Joseph said, "The city has been on the verge of riots several times already. The Sicarii and Zealots led an assault on the Roman garrison in the Antonia. They butchered them all. There is no Roman presence left in the city."

"If they're bold enough to attack the Romans," said Agrippa, "then they have finally stepped over the line. There is no turning back now."

Berenice said, "You must speak to the people, brother. Surely they have not forgotten the power of the house of Herod."

Agrippa said sadly, "What the people do not forget is that Herods have always conceded to Rome in exchange for power. If they have killed Romans, they will kill Herods."

"But you must try," she said. "Florus would not listen to reason. I begged him barefoot before his tribunal, and he paid me no concern. He knows the Sicarii and Zealots are fanatics. He knows they don't represent the Herods or the people."[3]

Ananus said, "It does not matter to Florus who the Sicarii and Zealots represent. He has been looking for an excuse to pillage Jerusalem, and he has finally found it. By provoking an insurrection, he can summon the Roman legions from Caesar to bring desolation upon Judea. With all his enemies eliminated, Florus rebuilds uncontested power."

Joseph said, "I have more bad news to add. The Sicarii took the fortress at Masada and slaughtered the Romans stationed there. They seized Herod's armory full of weapons."[4]

Within the next breath, Ananus added, "And I am afraid to report that Eleazar ben Simon, the new captain of the temple guard, has taken control of the temple and placed it on lockdown."

"Eleazar ben Simon?" said Agrippa. "I thought John of Gischala was captain of the guard."

Ananus said, "Gischala fled before Florus' army. It turns out Eleazar, his lieutenant took his place, and unfortunately, he is a fanatic. After seizing control of the temple, he 'persuaded' the officiating priests to cease the daily sacrifices on behalf of the emperor."[5]

The imperial sacrifice was the one act that Caesar conceded to the Jews to replace the idolatrous sacrifice *to* the emperor's genius.

The silence that filled the circle meant only one thing.

Joseph said it. "Attacking Roman soldiers is bad enough. But the ceasing of daily sacrifice is an attack on Caesar himself. It will be understood as nothing less than an act of war."[6]

Agrippa said, "Can we restart the daily sacrifice?"

Joseph said, "Eleazar is too strong. He has a tight grip with his guard on the entire temple."

"Jew against Roman. Now Jew against Jew. What has Florus wrought?" said Agrippa with dread.

Everyone desperately sought a strategy for the way out, but no one could offer one in the shadow of the truth that hung over them like a storm cloud.

Berenice spoke up, "I will go to Rome. I will appeal to Caesar to remove Florus as procurator and bring order back to Judea."

Joseph replied, "My lady, a legionary dispatch from Florus is already on its way to Rome. Caesar will come. And it is not order that he will bring."

Berenice considered the implications and said, "Then I will leave immediately on a speedy ship. I must arrive in Rome before this dispatch. Perhaps I can plead with Caesar for a return to Herodian rule."

"Perhaps," said Agrippa, "you can plead for mercy."

> *And from the time that the daily sacrifice is taken away, and the abomination of desolation is set up, there shall be one thousand two hundred and ninety days.*
>
> *Daniel 12:11[7]*

•••••

Agrippa and Berenice stood on the palatial porch before a multitude of agitated Jerusalem residents. They were making a last-ditch attempt to stop a revolt from happening. Agrippa had first tried to reason with the multitude to reconsider their passions. He had argued that their personal desire for revenge against Florus was irrational because the war they were bringing upon themselves would not be with Florus, but with Caesar and the entire Roman empire. He tried to get them to see that more moderate governors would surely replace Florus eventually, and all they needed was patient endurance.[8]

But it didn't work.

The mob was not rational. The mob is never rational.

After they quieted down enough for him to speak again, Agrippa pronounced, "All right! So you want to go to war!"

The crowd cheered.

"And you are the only nation on the face of the earth who finds it intolerable to submit to Rome!"

More cheering.

"Will you be prepared to make war with the Egyptians and the Arabians? They are at the beck and call of Caesar!"

The crowd was not so cheerful now.

"Are you richer than the Gauls? Stronger than the Germans? Wiser than the Greeks? Of course not. Yet they are all servants of Rome. Can you conquer the Parthians, warlords of the East, or the Carthaginians, masters of the South?"

He could see that they knew he was right. But they remained stubborn.

"Rome has a myriad of auxiliaries from all the nations of the earth. From where will you draw your allies?"

A heckler yelled out, "We have God on our side!"

Another announced, "No God but Yahweh! No king but Yahweh!"

The quieted crowd raised its voice again with fervor. Agrippa became angry. He could not stop the Zealots and other fanatics from poisoning every gathering. But he continued to try.

"I promise you that if you stop this revolt now, if you pay the tribute due to Caesar, not to Florus, if you rebuild the damage you have done to Roman structures in Jerusalem and allow them back into the city, I will risk my very life to defend your case before Caesar."

He glanced at Berenice. Some lies were necessary.

But another Zealot screamed out, "Herods are whores of Rome! You fornicate with Caesar!"

Raucous laughter filled the crowd.

Another yelled out, "Incestuous fornicators!"

A group of men in the crowd pelted vegetables at Agrippa and Berenice. The princess shrieked as a rotten piece struck her dress and splashed into her face. She withdrew, wiping off the foul-smelling residue from her skin, gagging at the smell.

Agrippa tried to protect her and was struck by some hard roots.

The Herodian guard surrounding the porch presented their arms and shields in defense. The crowd backed up.

Another voice yelled, "Go back to your whorehouse and leave us alone!"

Agrippa pulled Berenice back into the palace entrance and out of sight of the protestors, who now began to chant, "Herods, go home! Herods, go home!"

Berenice asked her brother, "What will you do?"

"I'm going to Antioch," he said. "Maybe I can call upon Cestius, the legate in Syria, to help us squash this uprising before it gets out of control. To that effect, you must leave immediately for Rome."

CHAPTER 19

Mount Hira
Arabia

The gods fought one another upon the holy mountain Hira just outside the Arabian city of Makkah. Hubal, the god of rain and divination, took one of his seven arrows and launched it at Allah, the moon god, who dodged its deadly aim. Lightning flashed, followed by a crack of thunder. Hard rain pelted their skin like needles in the swirling winds of the two-thousand-foot summit.

Hubal was the older of the two gods—and wiser. But Allah was brutish and strong. Allah's three daughters—Allat, Al-Uzza, and Manat—cheered him on.[1]

Allah launched himself into Hubal, ramming him into a cleft of rock. The hit was so hard that the mountain quaked beneath their feet. Hubal slammed his fist into Allah's face. The sound of cartilage cracking was followed by Allah's scream of pain. A stream of blood poured from the deity's nose. They were divine flesh, but all flesh was created and had its limitations. Their immortality did not preclude them from experiencing fleshly sensation, which included pain.

Allah became furious and pummeled his opponent with a rapid onslaught of punches that would have destroyed a cohort of human warriors. Hubal could handle it. He protected himself with his arms and found the right moment to uppercut Allah, sending him flying onto his butt on the ground.

Allah reset his jaw and growled.

Hubal rubbed out his bruised arms, crouched, and prepared for more.

But just as Allah sprang into another attack, he was yanked back by the scruff of his neck and slammed onto the ground, knocking the wind out of him.

He looked up at the armored form of Athena glaring down on him.

"How dare you, Grecian tramp," muttered Allah and rolled to his feet, giving a war cry with eyes ablaze at his new enemy.

Athena smirked. This Arabic fool had no idea he was about to be crushed. "ENOUGH!"

The thunderous voice pierced the ears of Allah, made him freeze in his tracks.

He looked behind Athena to see the stately form of the gaunt god of gods, Apollyon, his cloak flowing in the storm winds that only now were beginning to abate. Behind him were seven other Watcher gods.

Apollyon walked up to the brutish Arab deity.

"Kneel," he demanded.

Allah knelt obediently.

Apollyon looked up at Hubal, still standing by the rock face. He said, "Get over here, child."

Hubal scrambled over to Apollyon and knelt beside his rival.

The daughters of Allah scurried behind them and lay prostrate on the ground, shielding their faces.

Apollyon spoke with suppressed anger. "Look at me."

Hubal and Allah looked up.

Apollyon said, "I can never tell you two apart." The two Arabian deities were very similar in appearance: their stature, their full beards, their curly dark hair and eyes. In fact, they looked like identical twins, which continually confused the Destroyer and everyone else who knew them.

Apollyon looked at one of them, whose bloody face and tattered garments made the Watcher shake his head with scorn.

"Which one are you?"

"Allah, my lord and god."

"Yes, Allah. The scrapper with the uncontrollable temper. Now what are you two imbeciles fighting over?"

Hubal said, "The Kaaba." It was the holy site down in Makkah below them. This was not the first time they had vied for superiority.

Apollyon said, "I ordered you to go to Nabatea and prepare my auxiliary legions." His voice became increasingly agitated. The gods trembled. "But instead you waste my time by forcing me to track you down to this worthless heap of dung. And here you are, quarreling like a couple of children over ownership of a black rock instead of preparing for Armageddon."

He caught himself from exploding into a rage and calmed his voice. "I think you both fail to appreciate the gravity of our situation. And since I cannot afford to cast you into the Abyss, I am going to have to be content with teaching you a lesson."

Apollyon turned and stepped away, nodding to Athena and Anat, who were standing ready.

They approached the kneeling gods and stood behind them. Hubal glanced at Allah fearfully. They knew what was coming.

Allah's shaky voice blurted out, "I ask but one thing from my lord and savior. Please let it not be women who beat us."

Apollyon smirked. "I prefer the irony." He nodded to the goddesses of war.

Athena and Anat raised battle maces and hit the two Arabs simultaneously in the spines, cracking them both in two. The delinquent deities crumbled beneath the beating. Their bodies would heal and regenerate, thanks to their supernatural flesh, but that did not rescue them from the pain.

They were paralyzed by the spinal breaks. They could do nothing to protect themselves from their punishment.

Athena and Anat pounded their bodies with unrelenting fury. The daughters of Allah cried out for mercy. But there would be no mercy. They had to serve as an example. Apollyon had to maintain dominion and absolute submission. And one of the tactics these Arabs used to express dominion over their subjects was sodomizing them. Athena and Anat followed suit using their clubs as the organs of offense.[2]

The ever-curious Zeus, still healing from his own chastisement, stepped up to Apollyon and said, "These Arabs are a restless people. They fight as much against each other as they do against their enemies."

"They are more like the Jews than they care to admit," said Apollyon. "However, there is a certain charm to their barbarism that can be of benefit to my long-term goals. I see potential in them, or rather in whomever rises above the other. For now, Hubal will lead the Arabian forces." He turned to the prostrate paralyzed deity. "So hurry up and heal. I expect you there within the next few days."

Zeus asked, "Where to next, my lord?"

Apollyon said, "The end of our holy mountain tour, where it all began: Mount Hermon."

• • • • •

The Kaaba
Makkah

A day had passed since Apollyon and his escort of Watcher gods had left. The three goddesses, Allat, Al-Uzza, and Manat, tended to the broken bodies of Hubal and Allah at the sacred shrine in Makkah called the Kaaba. The Kaaba was a stone temple in the shape of a cube dedicated to the sun, moon and planets. That is, dedicated to these very deities.

The spines of the wounded gods had begun to regenerate. They were able to move somewhat under great pain, and their bruises were healing. The daughters finished dressing their wounds inside the large black cube, while outside hundreds of naked worshippers circumambulated the temple in a cultic fertility ritual. Others lined up at the southeast corner of the temple to kiss and rub the sacred Black Stone. The stone had fallen from heaven, and the Arabs considered it an image of Al-Uzza, or the Morningstar Venus. It was encased in a silver holder shaped like the vulva of the goddess. On the opposing corner was another stone of worship considered an image of Manat, the goddess of fortune.

The cube shape of the temple was in honor of the sun goddess Allat, and the crescent-shaped perimeter wall symbolized the moon god Allah. The pillared courtyard that surrounded the temple housed the stone images of three hundred and sixty other deities, completing the astrological religious cycle of the Arabs as they worshipped the heavenly host. For the Arabs, the Kaaba was the navel of the earth, the navel of the fertility goddess.[3]

Hubal and Allah drew much healing from the worship of their devotees. Idolatry was a powerful form of sorcery. But it was time to return to Hira, where they would finish healing before leaving for the legionary forces in Nabatea.

At the top of the mountain, Saraqael, Remiel, and Raguel hid amidst the rocky boulders of a small ridge. They watched silently as the three goddesses finished carrying their wounded gods to their camp at the base of the ridge just below them. The location gave them some shelter from the cold night winds on this harsh, lifeless mount. After laying the two gods down beneath a sheltered ridge of rocky boulders, Al-Uzza and Manat went to retrieve water from the mountain spring nearby. Allat stayed behind as watch.

As soon as she was alone with her back turned, Saraqael gestured silently to the other two angels. They used their supernatural strength to lift large timber levers they had wedged into the boulders around them. The strategic placement achieved their goal: a huge avalanche that fell on the gods below, crushing them helplessly beneath tons of stone.

But now they had to take out the goddesses. All three angels leapt to the ground below as Allat bellowed in a horrendous piercing screech, calling her companions to battle.

In moments, the goddesses had returned with scimitars out, facing the three angels one on one.

Unfortunately for them, these women were no match for the archangels, who cut them into ribbons in mere moments—quite literally. They cut off the goddesses' heads, arms, and legs, spreading their body parts as far as the archangels could toss them. They could not afford these harpies the opportunity to alert Apollyon to their activities. The angels had already captured three leading principalities of war: Ares, Ba'al, and Ahura Mazda. Now they were here to pull their fourth and final deity from the rubble, bind him, and bring him back with them for Yahweh's purposes.

The three angels patiently pulled boulders from the heap of rock that had buried the two gods, creating a small cave with their clearing.

They found Hubal within the first layer of rocks, smashed even worse than he already had been by Apollyon's henchmen. Binding the war god, they dragged his crushed body out of the manmade cave to carry him away.

Remiel asked, "How deep do you think Allah is buried in there?"

Saraqael said, "About twelve feet back. We'll let him burrow his own way out when he can. That ought to buy us enough time before Apollyon finds out."

Remiel said with a smile, "He'll never forget this pile of rock."

Raguel added with a smirk, "It'll be sacred."

Saraqael was not so lighthearted. "He'll plot his revenge from this cave.[4] Mark my words. Allah is a violent and vengeful deity."

They bound the broken body of Hubal and lifted him for travel. Remiel said, "How much time do you think our mission will buy for Michael and the others?"

Saraqael said, "Time enough to reach the four corners of the land before the end. Come, let us leave this godforsaken land of Arabia."

CHAPTER 20

Qumran

"On the day when the Kittim fall, there shall be a battle and horrible carnage before the God of Israel, for it is a day appointed by him from ancient times as a battle of annihilation for the Sons of Darkness. On that day the assembly of the gods and the congregation of men shall engage one another, resulting in great carnage."[1]

Aaron read from the sectarian War Scroll about the final battle at the End of Days, the War of the Sons of Light against the Sons of Darkness. Judgment Day. The last stage of his initiation before full acceptance into the Community of Qumran required that he give a sacred lecture on a topic of his choosing before his final baptism of membership.

He and the two initiates had returned from their trip to Jerusalem two days ago with the foodstuffs and sundry supplies they were sent to purchase. Aaron had made the other two promise to say nothing of their experience with the Christians in the city. Jerusalem Jews were bad enough to avoid with their polluted presence without the additional corrupting stain of apostasy that the Christians added.

But now here he was, reading at the lectern of the meeting hall in the early morning hours with the eyes of all his brethren upon him. He had chosen the scriptures he read for a very specific reason.

He read on. "The Sons of Light and the forces of Darkness shall fight together to show the strength of God with the roar of a great multitude and the shout of gods and men; a day of desolation. It is a time of distress for all the people who are redeemed by God."

Aaron stopped and looked out upon the audience. "Brethren, for many years we have studied the scrolls, looking for the time of the end as spoken of by Daniel the prophet and further illumined by the War Scroll in the War of the Sons of Light against the Sons of Darkness. So we, the undefiled community of holy ones, the true Israel, have established the pure and uncorrupted priesthood of Zadok in preparation to take back our rightful leadership of the holy temple of God. Brethren, I believe that time has arrived."

The Community erupted with hushed whispers and chatter. Aaron raised his voice to continue over the noise because he knew he might be stopped at any moment. "Daniel prophesied that the Abomination of Desolation would come to destroy the holy city and the sanctuary. Two days ago, three of us witnessed the beginning of the fulfillment of that prophecy when we saw the Roman procurator Gessius Florus enter the Court of Women to plunder the temple treasury."

Phineas the overseer stood and made his way to the front, raising his hands to settle the unrest. The rest of the gathering quieted down.

Aaron noticed the fat, disgusting overseer was sweating as he stared Aaron down. Aaron shuddered, knowing that Phineas could squash him with his authority over the Community. And because of Aaron's rebellious attitude toward his abuser, Aaron was certain he would.

Phineas spoke to the gathering. "Baruch and David, where are you? Please stand."

The two young initiates stood sheepishly near each other at the back of the watching crowd. They were the two who had traveled to Jerusalem with Aaron. Aaron now felt terrible, knowing that he had just dragged them both into a punishment that might jeopardize their initiation into the Community.

Phineas said to the two initiates, "What say you of Aaron's statements? Testify before God and the congregation of holy ones."

The two young men were visibly shaking. They looked to each other for support. Aaron could see they had no wish to lose everything they had worked for just to support someone whom they knew had problems with Phineas.

Phineas said, "I expect no collusion in this matter. Tell us the truth."

Baruch spoke first with a shaking voice. "All three of us saw Florus enter the outer temple area, the Court of Gentiles. But Aaron told us to go watch what happened inside. Both David and I hid in the chamber of Lepers. We saw Florus enter the Court of Women, as Aaron said. And he robbed the treasury. He was confronted by the temple guards, but he did not retreat. And the high priest was killed."

Phineas asked, "Florus killed the high priest?"

"No," said Baruch. "The captain of the temple killed him."

"The captain of the temple?" repeated Phineas with surprise.

"Y-yes," quivered Baruch.

Phineas mused over the implications of that scandal.

Aaron breathed a sigh of relief. They had told the truth. Thank God. But if they told the rest of the truth, Aaron would be punished.

Phineas asked, "And where did Aaron go when you went into the inner temple?"

Baruch looked at David, who now spoke. "Aaron went to the Essene quarter to help some of those injured in the commotion at the temple."

It was not an outright lie. For that is where Aaron had actually gone. It was a lie by omission. They did not say *whom* he'd helped, but implied by the location that it was the Essenes. If it was discovered that they had been with the dreaded Christians, they would face bitter punishment.

Phineas said, "Baruch and David, you are unclean because of your contact with the Chamber of Lepers. Remove yourself to the cave of separation for seven days."

Others around the two men backed away so as not to be touched by their uncleanness. They bowed and made their way out of the meeting hall. The cave of separation was the furthest from the walled area. It would be a cold and lonely seven days for them. But it was a blessing compared with the possibility of being permanently cut off from the congregation.

Phineas turned to Aaron with a wary eye. Aaron felt his heart beating out of his chest. Thank God the two young initiates were safe from that fat abuser's hands for seven days.

Phineas then pronounced, "We have the required two or more witnesses to establish these claims as true."

Aaron sighed with relief.

Phineas continued, "I received word today that the daily sacrifice for Caesar has ceased, just as Daniel had prophesied."

More chattering and whispers broke out in the crowd. "Roman defilement of the holy temple and the murder of the high priest are indeed an abomination that will bring desolation. It appears that the prophecy of Daniel has indeed been unsealed as Aaron indicates. The End of Days is at hand. We must prepare for the War of the Sons of Light against the Sons of Darkness."[2]

The mutterings and whispers all stopped. They were replaced with a hushed silence of dread. It was as if all the brethren of the Community had stopped breathing.

One of the older brothers stood up and said, "Overseer, we are not prepared for the war. None of us are trained in fighting skills. We are farmers, scribes, and priests."

Another brother shouted out, "God will fight for us!" The Essenes were strict determinists. It would make some sense that they might believe God would intervene for them.

But Phineas was more realistic. He said, "God is sovereign over the affairs of history, it is true. He has declared victory in the end. But that does not alleviate our responsibility to do our part. The Scriptures say we will engage in battle, so we must prepare. Even though God has determined the outcome, we still must act within his plans. But you are right, brother Avi. We are without preparation, and I know of no one to lead us or train us in the art of war."[3]

Aaron spoke up. "Overseer, I know of someone who can. And I know where to find him."

CHAPTER 21

Judean Wilderness
On the Road to Jerusalem

The large Judean outpost was ten miles west of Jerusalem on a major crossroads of east-west and north-south trade routes. Traveling merchants and caravans used it as a watering hole and overnight stay at its inn facilities. The outpost was the size of a large, wealthy estate and provided its visitors with everything from water and traveling provisions to more worldly indulgences like harlots and strong drink.

Simon bar Giora partook of the latter indulgence in the large, two-story tavern at the center of the outpost. He had in fact partaken of far too much of that benefit and was now brooding in a drunken stupor at a table in the center of the tavern. Around him, various merchants and other travelers drank or flirted with prostitutes who represented every tribe and nation on the face of the earth. Talk about the messianic promise that all nations would flow into Zion.

He chuckled to himself. Perhaps the kingdom *had* come.

A beautiful Egyptian harlot looked down on him with sad eyes.

He said to her, "Don't pity me, woman." He let out a loud belch that made her turn away with a look of disgust.

Simon caressed a small lock of hair in his fingers that he had received from Berenice on that fateful night. He wallowed in the despair of his lost love with the Herodian princess. It was over two years ago that he had barely escaped Jerusalem with his life after being betrayed by his closest friend, John ben Levi, Gischala as he was nicknamed for his home town. That son of the devil had falsely accused him of being a Zealot so that he could steal Simon's position as captain of the temple guard. Simon would never forget the events of that day. In fact, they haunted his memory daily, like returning demons from hell, taunting him, possessing him. Over and over again, he replayed the incidents, wondering how he could have been so fooled. If only he had seen it coming. If only he had not trusted Gischala. If only he had not been blinded by his faith.

Well, that would never happen again. Simon had long since given up his faith in God and in any hope for a cause bigger than himself. Religions, causes, national identities were all delusions of power used to manipulate the masses of ignorant plebs to do the bidding of the wealthy and privileged elite. Power and money were the true gods of this world behind governments, causes, and religions.

Power and money were the only things he trusted.

Simon could not achieve the power he wanted without money, and he could not get money without access to a certain amount of power. So when he had fled Jerusalem into the desert two years ago, he'd done what he had to do to build his future. He stole other people's money. He became a bandit. Because of his warrior and leadership skills, he quickly gained a following, a band of brigands that became one of the terrors of the countryside. He pillaged and plundered the Jewish ruling class and other Roman sympathizers throughout the land. But he left the poor to their own miserable struggle for survival.

Simon's gang had quickly grown to a hundred and fifty brigands, and his reputation had spread throughout Galilee, Judea, and Idumea. His power and wealth were now sufficient for him to achieve the only goal that was deeper and more primal than both: revenge. From the day he had been betrayed by Gischala, he had not stopped plotting how he would accomplish vengeance against him. Simon had recently been paid a hefty price of weapons and gold for helping the Sicarii take the stronghold of Masada from the Romans.

In a surprise move, he'd handed over the command of his forces to his captain, taking just a handful of his men to travel to Jerusalem, where he was going to kidnap Gischala and take his enemy out into the desert to torture him. But when Simon and his men had arrived at the Judean outpost, a few Essene monks had met them on their way back to Qumran from the holy city. Simon had found out that Gischala had himself just recently become a fugitive from the Roman procurator. The story was that Florus had pillaged the temple treasury and Gischala had fought back with some of his temple guards. Gischala had escaped into the desert and was now hiding out God only knew where.

It was the second biggest letdown in Simon's life. For Gischala to go missing just moments before Simon was about to grab him was almost as devastating as his original betrayal. Now Simon would have to hunt him down, which could take weeks or months. And Gischala would be on his guard, since he too was now an outlaw.

The revelation had so frustrated Simon's thirst for revenge that he'd spiraled into a depression and told his men to return to Masada where he might meet them later. *Might* meet them. Maybe he should just kill himself now and get it over with. Stop the unceasing pain, the pounding in his skull. What difference did it make? In the end, they would all be dead anyway. Why bother to continue the struggle just to suffer more miserable months or years of unsatisfied hunger for justice?

As he mused over how he might end it all, Simon watched the patrons around him. Or rather, the lack of patrons. It looked like the tavern had been clearing out. He wondered what time it was.

An Arabian merchant with a Persian strumpet on his arm stood on the stairs, watching Simon.

Simon belched again.

A shepherd sat at a nearby table, drinking. And watching Simon.

Simon was inebriated, but not so much that he didn't sense something was wrong. Before he could draw a conclusion, the doors to the tavern burst open to two heavily armed Jewish travelers with drawn weapons. One had an axe and the other a flail, a wooden rod with chain and iron ball at the end of it.

Simon stood and lost his balance a bit. He was focusing on the flail, a type he had never seen before, when he was jumped from behind. It was the shepherd, who had now drawn a blade.

The shepherd reached with his blade to cut Simon's throat. But Simon flipped him over his back. The shepherd smashed into a table, the impact knocking Simon's attacker out.

The harlot on the staircase screamed.

Simon saw the Arabian merchant shoo her away and draw a scimitar, the curved sword of choice in his homeland. The merchant bounded down the stairs.

The two assassins from the door attacked.

Simon had no time to draw his own weapon. He dodged the swinging axe twice. His alcohol-impaired response allowed the weapon to graze his chest, cut his tunic, and draw blood. A third dodge of a third swing, and the axe wedged, not into Simon's skull, but into the wood of one of the poles holding up the roof.

Simon drew his dagger and plunged it into the heart of the attacker. The man fell to the floor dead.

Not bad for a pathetic drunk, Simon thought to himself.

He saw a blur and ducked.

The iron ball of the flail hit the pole behind him, and Simon heard it crack under the force of the weapon.

He rolled out of the way and drew his sword.

Now the Arabian was upon him with his scimitar. Simon felt dizzy and nauseous. But there was no time to vomit. He raised his blade to defend himself against the Arab's onslaught of rapid slashing. If Simon had been sober, he would have been able to dispatch this one. But his drunken state blurred his vision and slowed his mind enough to force him on the defensive instead.

The Arab backed him up against the stairs. Simon barely kept up with the blows.

But Simon had one offensive tactic the Arabian had not anticipated. In fact, even Simon didn't anticipate the tactic until this very moment. His nausea.

Simon relaxed his gut and let his body perform its natural reaction to intoxication.

He felt his stomach erupt like a volcano. A stream of projectile vomit burst from his throat and hit the Arab in his face.

The acidic upchuck burned the Arab's eyes and blinded him for just a moment.

In that moment, Simon thrust his sword into the abdomen of the Arab. The attacker dropped his scimitar and slid off Simon's blade to the ground.

But before Simon could gather his footing, the chain of the last attacker's flail wrapped around his sword like a serpent. The iron ball hit and ripped the blade out of Simon's hand.

Simon's sobering instincts kicked in, and he launched himself at the Jewish assassin before the other man could disengage the tangled-up weapons.

They both landed on the floor. Simon heard a snapping crunch.

The assassin went limp, his eyes staring up at the ceiling, into the void. Lifeless.

Simon rolled the assassin over. His attacker's spine had landed on a jagged piece of broken jug. Simon's jug of alcohol. Simon thought how disappointed he was not to be able to finish the drink he had started. It was an expensive price. But not too small to pay for saving his life.

Then he remembered that he wasn't sure he wanted to be saved.

He heard wood moving behind him as the first attacker rose from his unconscious spread on the broken table.

Simon turned to face him.

The attacker looked at the rubble and dead comrades all around him.

Then he bolted for the door.

Simon shook his head. As the excitement of the fight wore off, his cuts and bruises began to sting and ache. He moaned and staggered to his feet.

Spotting an unbroken jug of wine on another table, he grabbed it and plopped down on the floor, ready to return to his stupefaction.

As he raised the jug to his lips, Simon saw three men at the door. Three more men.

Curses, he thought. He'd never even retrieved his blade. It was out of reach and wrapped up in the flail.

Simon sighed and relaxed, giving up. Now was just as good a time as any to die. At least he had taken out four others.

But when the three men came inside, he saw that they were not warriors. They were not even men. They were young monks.

They approached Simon. The lead one pulled down his hood. Simon recognized him.

"Greetings, Simon," he said. "Do you remember me? I am Aaron, the Essene you met here a couple days ago."

Simon sighed, not out of relief, but out of annoyance that he was going to live after all.

"Well, Aaron, you just missed my attempted assassination."

Aaron looked around him. *Pathetic attempt* would be a better description.

Simon said, "Who are you looking for?"

Aaron looked closely at the warrior and said, "You are intoxicated. You dispatched three assassins in a drunken state."

Simon interrupted him, "A fourth got away."

Aaron said, "You are exactly who I am looking for."

• • • • •

The four of them sat at a table. Aaron had introduced Baruch and David as his traveling companions. Simon nursed his wounds as Aaron spoke to him.

"Why were they after you?"

"Being a lonely mercenary has its advantages," said Simon. "Nobody is your friend."

Baruch and David looked quizzically at each other. That didn't make sense to them. They couldn't fathom that anyone would consider being a loner with manifold enemies as an advantage.

They had not yet been betrayed by those they trusted most.

Aaron said, "We want to be your friends. We want you to train our community in the art of war."

Simon stared at Aaron. "I don't deal in delusions. Leave now, boy."

Aaron ignored the order. "The signs of the last days are all around us. We believe the uprising in Jerusalem is the beginning of the final battle of the Sons of Light and the Sons of Darkness prophesied in our scrolls. We want you to prepare us for that battle."

Simon looked at the other two doe-eyed innocents and burst out laughing.

The three Essenes glanced at each other, embarrassed.

Still amused, Simon demanded, "Do you think your little band of sandy monks are the 'chosen few' to rescue Israel from a hundred and twenty years of Roman domination?"

Aaron nodded his head with optimistic vigor.

Simon could not believe it. "You think your cause is going to change the world? You think your faith will bring unity to our people, who are plagued by brigands and bandits, robbing and killing each other?"

The expressions of the three young monks remained positive and hopeful.

Simon said, "Well then, you do not want me, boy. I do not believe in causes, and I do not live on faith." He stood up to leave.

Aaron reached in his cloak and pulled out a large gold ingot. He dropped it on the table with a weighty clunk.

"We will pay you."

Simon's eyes fixated on the gleaming treasure. It must have been worth ten thousand denarii, a year's worth of wages.

Aaron said, "And that is only a down payment against the rest."

Simon looked incredulously at the little man. The other two monks grinned.

Aaron said with a smile, "Communal wealth has its advantages."

Simon wondered just how much more communal wealth they might have at their peaceful little commune on the Salt Sea—without any defensive security.

CHAPTER 22

Pella

Forty miles northeast of Jerusalem, the city of Pella was in ruins. Smoke filled the sky from burning structures. Wild dogs and carrion birds fed off the bodies of Jews and Gentiles filling the streets. The eerie pall of death was punctuated by the wails of women finding their husbands and sons in the aftermath of total desolation. Pella was located in the mountains across the Jordan, surrounded by forest and rugged hills. The city was a member of the Decapolis, ten Hellenistic cities of predominately Greek citizens in the northern region. But now Pella was an empty carcass, a town of ghosts.

On the edge of the forest, a ragtag group of a hundred Jewish warriors stood in a clearing of trees used for stonings. Forty-three Christians awaited their fate at the hands of these captors. A half-dozen victims were tied to trees awaiting their judgment.

Some distance away, the first six were already dead, buried in the ground up to their stomachs, hands tied behind their backs, bodies bruised, cut, and shattered, bludgeoned by the force of a hundred rocks now lying around them on the bloodied ground. Once the Jewish warriors realized it would take too much time to dig holes for a hundred criminals, they'd decided it would be much quicker and more efficient to tie the blasphemers to trees.

So here they were, ready to inflict justice in the name of God. The captain of the company, a rugged leader with a commanding presence, looked soberly upon his responsibility.

All of this in the name of God.

Some of the captives were Jewish, and some were Gentile. But they were all Christians. And Christians deserved the same fate as the Syrians and Greeks whom the Jewish rebels had just slaughtered throughout the city. The Christians didn't fight the Jews. Instead, they tried to hide and protect their families from the battle. But their religious malignancy in the body politic of

Israel was thought to be one of the reasons why God had allowed the Roman persecution of Jews throughout the land. So the remedy for such apostasy was repentance. And repentance consisted of applying the Law of God to the apostates in their midst.

These Christians had been found and rounded up for judgment. Maybe their deaths would propitiate Yahweh's anger against his chosen people.

The captain pronounced the sentence. "Thus saith the Law of the Lord, 'Whoever blasphemes the name of Yahweh shall surely be put to death. All the congregation shall stone him.'"[1]

Most of the hundred soldiers held their stones ready, a mere twenty feet from the bound prisoners. They eyed their targets, some choosing the men, others the women and children.

The captain continued, "For blasphemy against the one true God Yahweh and for idolatry, I pronounce the sentence of death upon you."

But before the captain could commence the stoning, two arrows pierced his gut, dropping him to the ground, writhing in pain.

Dozens of other missiles came out of the forest to hit their targets of soldiers holding stones.

Those not hit froze with surprise. Only to see a company of over forty armed warriors explode from the trees and foliage, racing toward them like the wrath of God.

Most of the soldiers were so stunned they didn't think to drop their rocks and grab their weapons.

Those who did fared no better because these attackers were the Kharabu warriors led by Demetrius and fueled with a holy rage.

They cut down the hundred soldiers in a matter of minutes with such ease that the watching Christians thought they might be angels.

They *were* angels of a sort. The word "angel" meant messenger of God. And while these were humans, they were messengers of God delivering the people of God from the synagogue of Satan.

But humans are mortal. One of the execution squad had managed to raise his bow and target Demetrius.

Demetrius heard his name shouted. He turned to see the archer release his arrow. His instincts were not fast enough. He had not the time to move.

But in the flash of a second, a small warrior flicked a whip that caught the arrow in mid-air mere feet before hitting Demetrius. The whip cut the arrow in half, plunging it into the dirt at their feet. Almost simultaneously, three flying daggers out of nowhere hit the archer and dropped him.

Demetrius stood in shock at what he had just seen. What he thought he had just seen. It was impossible. A warrior had just cut an arrow in half in mid-flight and saved his life. And who had thrown those blades?

He looked around. Others had seen it too. His men now stood over their vanquished enemies. Demetrius walked over to the captain lying on the ground. He was still breathing despite two arrows in his chest. Some men just took longer to die than others.

Demetrius asked, "Who are you? Why have you killed innocent civilians?"

The captain wheezed. Bloody air bubbled from his punctured lung. He spoke defiantly, "They are not innocent. Greeks massacred the entire Jewish population in Caesarea Maritima."

"So you butcher unarmed Christian men, women, and children in Pella as a response to the Greeks?"[2]

"Christians are a Trojan Horse to Israel."

Demetrius could not believe the insanity of evil that he was facing. He said, "Who is your leader?"

"We have no king but God. We've risen up all over the land and in Syria. We've laid waste to Ashkelon, Ptolemais, Tyre, and other cities. The Decapolis is next. God is with us."[3]

So the revolt had spread into a civil war. Jews were now fighting Greeks. Jewish brigands still roamed the wilderness attacking their own wealthy countrymen. And Christians were in more danger than ever.

Demetrius watched the dying captain grimace in pain. He said, "Yahweh is not with you. You killed Messiah, now you kill his people. You worship the harlot of apostate Israel."

The captain began to fade into unconsciousness.

Demetrius leaned down and whispered to him, "Thank you for giving me the cities for my next rescue. Enjoy Gehenna."

The captain breathed his last, his eyes frozen open in terror.

Demetrius stood. His men freed the Christian victims and cleaned up the survivors of the execution squad.

He called his lieutenant over to his side and said, "We need to tell these brethren in Christ about the Revelation. But we must do so speedily. Our work has only just begun."

They were interrupted by an elderly man who looked angry. "Sir, my name is Gurion. I am an elder of the congregation of Pella."

"Greetings in Christ," said Demetrius. "Then you are the one with whom I need to share a most important letter."

But Gurion was not happy. "Did you have to use your bows and swords with such merciless cruelty? Could you not have warned them without having to resort to bloodshed?"

Demetrius looked with incredulity at his lieutenant. Then said to Gurion, "I believe you and your sheep were about to be slaughtered, shepherd."

The elder challenged, "Jesus said those who live by the sword will die by the sword."[4]

Demetrius responded as he had to Cassandra, "Jesus also said to take a sword for *defense*, as the wisdom of Torah prescribes. 'Rescue the weak and needy. Deliver them out of the hand of the wicked.'"[5]

But Gurion would not back down. "The gospel is grace and peace, not violence and war."

Demetrius held back his rising anger. "You are right. And if we do not stop evil men, there will never be grace or peace. There will only be violence and war."

Gurion continued his diatribe. "Justice outside of the law is not the way of God."

Demetrius smiled. He began to feel as one would with a temperamental child. "Would you rather I let you, your women, and children die at the hands of lawlessness? If martyrdom is really your desire, I would be happy to deliver you over to other bandits and allow them the so-called grace you demand."

Gurion fell silent. Then concluded, "This will not end well for you."

Demetrius smiled. "I've already accepted that responsibility. My calling is to make it end well for others."

"I will pray that God changes your calling," said Gurion.

"That's fine with me, brother," said Demetrius. "I need all the prayer I can get. And so do you. Because the demons of hell are coming like a plague of locusts."

Demetrius looked around for the warrior who had saved his life. He saw him, a small man with the whip. Demetrius waved him over.

Several of his Kharabu warriors stepped protectively near to Demetrius, who recognized the small warrior as one of Severus' company sent to assist them. But he wasn't dressed as a Roman.

Demetrius asked, "What is your name?"

"Uriel, my captain."

Demetrius said, "I thank you for saving my life, Uriel."

"I count it a privilege," said the small warrior.

"Some would say what you did with that whip was a very lucky coincidence. But you appear to be confident in your skills."

Uriel shrugged. At that moment, Demetrius noticed that the whip was not really a whip. It was a flexible metallic blade about nine feet long.

"What on earth is that weapon?"

"You mean 'what in heaven?'" Uriel rolled up the blade. "It's a whip sword, handed down for generations. Its nickname is Rahab for the sea dragon. She gives a mean bite."[6]

"Apparently so," smiled Demetrius.

When Demetrius had accepted members for his squad in Jerusalem, he had learned that this small warrior and several of his Jewish cohorts were mercenaries. They had appeared skilled and devoted. But not this extraordinary. Demetrius wondered if there were more secrets that he needed to uncover.

He looked around. "Where are the others who threw the daggers?"

Three other mercenary warriors stepped out of the crowd of men. They were the cohorts of this small warrior. They were dressed in similar cloaks and carried similar muscular builds. Demetrius eyed them carefully. They looked—out of place. Could such mysterious warriors be trusted?

A handsome one stepped forward. "I am the commander of the unit, my lord. My name is Michael." He pointed to the others. "This is Gabriel and Raphael."

Demetrius stared at Michael with surprise. Then he narrowed his eyes and cocked his head. He knew the Scriptures and the legends. He said, "I understand mercenaries often use fictitious names to protect their identities. Fair enough. And you have the sense of humor to use the names of four of Yahweh's archangels. But do you have the holy intent of such guardians?"

Uriel said, "Do our actions not reveal our intent, my lord?"

With that, Demetrius could not argue.

Michael said, "My lord, the truth is that the four of us are Kharabu warriors. The ancient tradition after which you named your own warriors."

"That much is obvious," said Demetrius.

"Our sole purpose is to help you protect and deliver the elect."

Uriel added, "We are not as mysterious as you may think, once you get to know us." He smiled and pointed at Gabriel. "Especially this one. He is quite simple and easy to figure out."

Gabriel pointed back at Uriel and retorted, "And I assure you, my lord, I will simply keep this one from talking too much."

Demetrius could not help but smile. These men were still mysterious to him. But he felt at ease in his spirit. It had to be the Lord assuring him.

He said cheerfully, "Well, I guess you are my 'guardian angels,' then."

Some of his men around him laughed. The four mercenaries seemed amused as well.

Demetrius turned to his men. "We will split into four units and spread out onto the four corners of the land. Hit as many cities as you can, deliver the Revelation, and gather the elect to escape."[7] They had previously made several copies of the Apocalypse for just this purpose.

He looked back at Michael and his mercenaries. "Each one of you will accompany a different unit. That way, each unit will have its own 'guardian angel'."

The men chuckled at the ongoing angel joke. The truth was, Demetrius was splitting up his mysterious benefactors just in case he was wrong in his assessment of trust.

Michael nodded, "Excellent decision, commander."

Or was Demetrius endangering all four of his teams?

He said, "Uriel, you will stay with my unit. With that special sword of yours."

He saw Uriel smirk at the others. Gabriel rolled his eyes. These two were clearly competitive.

"We'll start with the Decapolis and Galilee and spread out to the four winds from there." Demetrius turned to the elder Gurion. "And now we have a letter from the apostle John that you need to read to the congregation."

CHAPTER 23

Jerusalem

Alexander sighed with frustration. Cassandra put her head in her hands. Severus watched the debate with morbid curiosity. It was like watching a fight in the arena where two gladiators were trying to kill each other as the bloodthirsty crowds cheered them on.

But this was not a duel of gladiators. This was a debate on the Mount of Olives by a group of Jerusalem Christians arguing over the prophecy of John's Apocalypse and the judgment of Israel. Severus was still amazed at how important religious doctrines were to these Jewish Christians. They were as obsessed with fine details of belief as Greek philosophers were over logical consistency. After a month of council meetings and arguments and debates, only some believed the message of the Roman outsiders, while many remained steadfast in their commitment to Jewish primacy. Or as Cassandra called it, the poison of the Judaizers. Until they could convince all the leaders, they would not be successful in evacuating the congregation of the Lord from the city.

This group had been kept as small as possible to avoid drawing attention. There were seventy deacons, elders, and teachers within the congregation, who would then be responsible for disseminating the conclusion of this battle royal to the rest of the believers in the city. Others would help carry the message to Samaria, Idumea, and Galilee.

But time was running out, as the news of rampaging Jewish riots in cities all over the land would surely bring the wrath of Rome down upon them. The latest report was that Masada had been taken from the Romans by Jewish rebels. This act inspired other groups of rebels all over the land. The problem was that there was no unity. Zealots fought Sicarii for dominance. And they both agitated the pro-Roman Jewish priesthood and ruling class.

Nobody trusted anyone. Alexander thought the Jews might all kill each other before the Romans even got here. Cassandra would no doubt pray for that to happen. She had told Alexander she was worried about where Demetrius was and whether he was alive and safe.

Alexander was worried about their own safety in Jerusalem. Fights, mobs, and even an occasional riot had become too commonplace.

The Jerusalem congregation had an impossible decision to make. If John's Apocalypse was right and they ignored it, their doom would be sealed. But if it was wrong and they left the holy city, then Christians would be bereft of both home and work, at the mercy of ruthless bandits and brigands in the countryside. The Jews hated the Romans and Syrians. Romans hated the rebels. The rebels hated the Romans and Herodians. The ruling class hated the bandits. The bandits hated the ruling class.

But everyone hated the Christians.

These believers were not arguing for abstract principles or mere doctrines after all. They were arguing for their lives and for the future survival of the congregation of the Lord.

The elder Boaz led the side against Alexander and Cassandra. But Cassandra was convinced Boaz was merely a puppet whose real voice came from the fat, bald serpent at his shoulder, Jacob, who whispered lies and deception into the old man's ear.

Alexander thought that though Boaz seemed easily manipulated by Jacob, he also seemed more open-minded and sensitive to the Holy Spirit. And Boaz was widely respected in the city. If they could persuade the elder, they might override the demonic influence of his treacherous counselor.

The current topic was the holy temple. Boaz spoke first. "The temple remains standing in all its earthly glory. It is the heart and soul of Yahweh's relationship with his people. How can you say that the temple is cursed? You are attacking the heart and soul of God!"

Mumbles of agreement came from his supporters. Jacob smiled devilishly at Cassandra. She wanted to strangle the disgusting dog. Instead, she prayed, *Forgive me, Lord. May you strangle him instead.*

Alexander stood to address the crowd and answer Boaz. "Brethren, it is true as Boaz says that the temple with its holy place and all its rituals of atonement and purification was once the heart and soul of our God. It is the earthly glory, but of what? The heavenly reality. The temple and all its practices is a mere shadow, a copy of the greater, more perfect temple not made with hands. And it was that true temple in heaven that Jesus Christ, our high priest, entered once and for all to achieve eternal redemption by his perfect sacrifice. Do you not see? The Torah is but a shadow of the good things to come. It is not the true form of those realities. It can never, by its imperfect sacrifices offered year after year, make perfect those who draw near. God has done away with the first covenant and its earthly shadows to establish the second, new covenant with its eternal reality. When Messiah had offered for all time a single sacrifice for sins, he sat down at the right hand of God. There is no more need for temple sacrifice."[1]

Cassandra interrupted, "The earthly temple has become a carcass of dead religion. To worship at that carcass is to reject the true temple, Jesus the Messiah, which turns this earthly temple into an altar of the Beast."[2]

The crowd erupted in protest.

Alexander gave Cassandra a scolding look and sought to calm down the rest of the group. When calm was finally restored, he tried to mend the tear.

"Brethren, what my caustic sister in the Lord is trying to say—without much diplomacy—is that the earthly temple is a mere shadow pointing toward the true heavenly temple of God: Jesus. His flesh is the temple veil that opens to the Holy of Holies. He is the Word that tabernacled among us, and we have seen his glory, the glory of the New Jerusalem, whose temple is the Lord God Almighty and the Lamb. His body is the true temple in heaven, and we are the Body of Messiah on earth. We are the living stones of that spiritual house of God. In Messiah, we are being built up together into that holy temple, the dwelling place of God's Spirit, with Jesus as the cornerstone."[3]

Boaz pointed at the temple below them and protested, "If this earthly temple no longer has God's presence as you say, then why did the apostles continue to go to temple? The apostle Paul prayed in the temple, performed a Nazirite vow *and* ritual purification in the temple. Can we not engage in the temple practices as a memorial of what Messiah has done?"[4]

Alexander said, "That is why Jesus is coming to destroy the temple. Because God does not want us to hold onto the weak and beggarly elements of the old and obsolete covenant. The reason why the apostles continued in the temple was to try to persuade the Jews of their own Messiah, not because they support the old covenant system. They were being all things to all men that they might win some to Messiah. Know this, that the new covenant makes the first covenant obsolete. And what is becoming obsolete and growing old is ready to vanish away. This generation between the atonement of Messiah and the destruction of the temple that is coming is a transition between covenants. But God will abolish the elements of the old covenant because they are no longer needed."[5]

Jacob had been whispering furiously into Boaz's ear. The elder stood again. "Alexander, you speak of the promises to Abraham as if they have become obsolete, abolished by Messiah. Yet Yahweh himself said that his covenant with Abraham was an everlasting covenant."

Jacob interrupted, "You deny the Law of God. You call God a liar! Blasphemy!" The crowd burst out again in reaction. Some in agreement with the accusation, others opposed.

Cassandra leaned in to Alexander and said beneath the din, "And you call me caustic and undiplomatic?"

When they had calmed down again, Alexander said to the crowd, "We do not call God a liar, nor do we blaspheme. We affirm what the apostles themselves have written. Yes, the covenant to Abraham is eternal. But the promise to Abraham and his seed did not come through the law but through the righteousness of faith. It is those of faith who are the sons of Abraham, not those of flesh. The eternal covenant of circumcision is not circumcision of the flesh, but circumcision of the heart done by the Spirit of God."

Boaz said, "But Jews are the children of Abraham. Jews are the seed to whom the promise was made."

Alexander said, "The promises were indeed made to Abraham and to his seed. But the Scripture does not say 'and to his seeds,' referring to many, but 'to your seed,' referring to one individual. That seed is Messiah. All the promises to Abraham are fulfilled in Messiah. And if you are Messiah's, then you are Abraham's seed, heirs according to promise. But if you call yourself a Jew and rely on the Law and boast in God, yet you reject the Messiah, your circumcision becomes uncircumcision, and you are not a child of Abraham. You are not truly a Jew."[6]

Cassandra could not help herself. She barked out, "You are not circumcised, you are mutilated! You have severed yourselves from Christ!"[7]

Jacob stood and took over from Boaz. "These lawless ones are saying that Jews are not Jews! That Israel is not Israel!" The crowd became agitated yet again.

"No!" said Alexander, trying to calm everyone down yet again. "We are saying that not *all Israel* is Israel. Being a physical descendant of Abraham does not make you a Jew. True Jews are those with faith in Messiah. The true Israel of God is the Remnant. And the Remnant are the believing Jews within the unbelieving nation. God has always dealt with his people as the remnant of true believers within the faithless apostate nation at large. So despite the fact that we Christians have been hated by our own countrymen, God has kept a Remnant for himself, and that Remnant are the believers in Jesus. That is why we are telling you Christians to leave the city before it is too late, or you will be caught up in the wrath of God that is not determined for you. Jesus is coming on the clouds to render judgment upon those of his own who killed him. And he will destroy their city. He has given his kingdom to a people that will bear the fruit."[8]

Jacob scoffed with excessive drama. "So now you claim that the Congregation of Jesus *replaces* Israel?"[9]

"No, again," said Alexander. "The Congregation of Messiah *is* the Israel of God. It is the *Remnant* of Israel. That congregation consists of both believing Jew and believing Gentile. The spiritual root of true Israel remains the same. Unbelieving Jews are like branches that were cut off, and believing Gentiles are branches that have been grafted in. In this way, all Israel, both Jew and Gentile, is saved—through faith in Messiah."[10]

The rumble of discussion grew until Boaz gestured to the crowd with a thoughtful look on his face. "While we certainly would not deny that the Body of Christ is the object of God's redeeming love, so also we would not say as you do that the Jewish nation is disinherited. What if there is not just one people of God? Can there not be two peoples of God with two separate covenants? Yes, faith in Christ is the means of salvation in this new covenant at this time. But also yes that God is not finished with the Jewish people. After the times of the Gentiles is fulfilled, he will still gather the twelve tribes back into the land of their inheritance to honor his covenant promise. The gifts and the calling of God are irrevocable."[11]

Severus rolled his eyes and muttered to Alexander and Cassandra, "They haven't listened to a jot or tittle of what you said." Though Severus himself had been listening, he was finding it difficult to keep up with all the theological minutiae so alien to his own understanding.

Alexander spoke to the crowd. "Messiah has already begun the restoration of the remnant of the twelve tribes *through faith*. The gospel draws believing Jews from all the nations into his kingdom and unites them to Gentile believers just as God promised through the prophets. That all began at Pentecost a generation ago with the coming of the Holy Spirit."[12]

Jacob interrupted him. "You are spiritualizing God's promises to the seed of Abraham, to Israel in this earthly land upon which we stand!"

Boaz placed his hand on Jacob. "Let him finish his point, brother."

Alexander finished his point. "Call it spiritualization if you will. But the Holy Spirit has revealed this fulfillment of his promises in Christ. Jesus is the seed of Abraham. Jesus is faithful Israel. Jesus is the promise to the nations. *Jesus* is our inheritance in place of the Land.[13] And the gospel is the gathering of the remnant into their inheritance of eternal life. Messiah will not merely inherit this small patch of land in the desert but has inherited all the earth and all the nations. That is how Abraham has become a father of many nations.

"Now, elder Boaz, you raised the question of whether there are two peoples of God. To this, I answer that there *are* two peoples, but they are not two peoples *of God*. One is the people of promise, and the other is the people of judgment. For it is written that Abraham had two sons, one by a slave woman and one by a free woman. Hagar, the slave woman, corresponds to the present earthly Jerusalem, for she is in slavery with her children, unbelieving Jews born of the flesh alone. But Sarah, the free woman, corresponds to the heavenly Jerusalem, all believers in Messiah. And just as Ishmael of flesh persecuted Isaac of promise, so those Jews born of the flesh persecute those Christians born of the Spirit. But what does the Scripture say? Cast out the earthly Jerusalem, for the son of the slave woman shall not inherit with the son of the free woman. So, brethren, it is not the children of the flesh who are the children of God, but the children of faith and promise who are counted as God's seed.[14] Because this generation of fleshly Jews has rejected Messiah,

Jesus is coming to judge them by casting them out of the kingdom and destroying the city and temple. Wrath has come upon them to the utmost."[15]

"Blasphemy!" yelled Jacob. "That is a malicious and twisted interpretation of Scripture. What more evidence do we need? Arrest these blasphemers!"

Alexander, Cassandra, and Severus looked around to see a dozen Herodian guards approach them from behind a ridge. They had been there, waiting to be summoned.

The three were surrounded by the soldiers. They did not fight back, though Severus wanted to. Unfortunately, the remainder of his century of Roman soldiers was still hidden away west of the city. And they would be unable to help without being attacked and overwhelmed by the rebels everywhere in Jerusalem. Romans no longer had power within the walls of the holy city. They no longer kept the peace.

Severus' disguise as a Christian, as dangerous as it now was, paled in comparison with the danger of being revealed as a Roman agent of Caesar.

CHAPTER 24

Severus chafed at the heavy iron shackles on his wrists and ankles as he and his fellow captives, Alexander and Cassandra, were led by several temple guards down the hallway toward the Hall of Hewn Stones. The new captain of the temple guard, Eleazar ben Simon, a young fanatical leader, turned and looked Cassandra up and down, then sneered at Alexander. His survey of Severus lingered skeptically. Severus had heard that Eleazar had strong-armed control of the inner temple, which only served to add more pressure to a situation already about to collapse into anarchy.

Severus knew that his false identity as a Roman merchant did not fool this militant leader. A look in the eyes was enough to betray a warrior's presence to another of his kind. He suspected Eleazar was zealous for power and glory. And control of the temple was the most glorious position of power to the Jewish mind. It could even be messianic.

If the Roman garrison in the city had not been overthrown and killed by the fanatics, Severus might have been able to save his companions by revealing his true identity, a Roman prefect commissioned by Caesar himself. But now that identity would surely get them all killed. And Eleazar would certainly use their deaths as "Roman operatives" as a symbol to inspire the mob. Severus could not let Eleazar find out who he really was.

They entered the chamber. It was large and circular with seats for the seventy Sanhedrin who would meet in council over civil and religious matters. A dozen high priests and scribes were present this evening. They stopped their small talk when the captives were brought before the high priest's chair.

Cassandra saw the new high priest Mattathias, a corpulent man, sitting on his throne-like chair with pompous pride. Why were so many of these religious leaders so fat and soft?

As she gazed upon the chair and its occupant, she thought to herself, *The throne of the Land Beast.*

The description of the Apocalypse was vivid in her memory.

> Then I saw another beast rising out of the Land. It had two
> horns like a lamb and it spoke like a dragon. It exercises all the
> authority of the first beast in its presence, and makes the land
> and its inhabitants worship the first beast. It performs great
> signs, even making fire come down from heaven to earth in
> front of people, it deceives those who dwell on the Land, telling
> them to make an image for the beast.[1]

As the apostle John had explained to her, these men of the high priesthood
in their collaboration with Rome had the appearance of a holy lamb, but were
really servants of Satan the dragon. The beast of Rome gave them their authority
as a beast of the Land of Israel, and the Jews followed them in their idolatrous
submission to Caesar. The priesthood had kept the perpetual flame on the altar
alight, as if Yahweh approved of them with fire from heaven.[2] But their temple
had become a cursed altar, a dead image for the first Beast, Nero, into which he
would breathe life to perform his service. And the service that united them all
was the slaying of Christians who would not accept the imperial cult, that mark
of the Beast.[3]

Alexander recognized the carefully groomed Pharisee on one side of the
throne as Joseph ben Matthias. He would never forget that antichrist who was
part of the inspiration for the Great Tribulation, Nero's persecution of the
Christians. His ruling class of Judea was the harlot who rode the Beast of
Rome, drunk on the blood of the martyrs. They had begun their slaughter of
Christians with the martyrdom of Stephen and had expanded their attacks as
the Church had begun to expand throughout the world. Alexander fought the
hatred rising in him. So many had died at their hands.[4]

On the other side of the throne stood the elderly ex-high priest Ananus
ben Ananus. Alexander could tell he was the real leader of the priesthood. The
white-haired and bearded old man seemed to dictate Mattathias' every move
with subtle nods and whispered words. Alexander couldn't tell which was the
False Prophet, the acting high priest or the hidden one. Or maybe the entire
priesthood itself.

The false prophet who in its presence had done the signs by which he deceived those who had received the mark of the beast and those who worshiped its image.[5]

Satan, Nero, and the high priesthood were a demonic conspiracy that was leading the nations to Armageddon. The Apostle John had described it as an unholy trinity with the high priest as its False Prophet.

And I saw, coming out of the mouth of the dragon and out of the mouth of the beast and out of the mouth of the false prophet, three unclean spirits like frogs. For they are demonic spirits, performing signs, who go abroad to the kings of the whole world, to assemble them for battle on the great day of God the Almighty. [6]

Cassandra thought the only one missing from this cabal of spiritual harlotry was Herod Agrippa, who was probably somewhere using his influence to protect his wealth, his properties, and his own neck.

The three prisoners stood before the throne of their captors under the weight of their heavy chains.

Mattathias said, "You have caused much trouble in the city with your malignant propagation of false teachings."

Eyeing the pompous Pharisee and his white-haired advisor, Cassandra concluded, *The dragon speaks through the beast.*

She said, "My lord, high priest, is this our trial or your summary judgment?"

Mattathias said, "Woman, hold your tongue, or I will cut it out."

She saw the temple captain Eleazar smirk. These two authorities of the temple, the high priest and the captain of the guard, were no doubt the two horns of power on the Land Beast.[7]

Another voice came from the back of the Sanhedrin. "My lord, high priest, she spoke with the same disrespect to me as well." Cassandra and the others turned to see the gaunt, balding Jacob step out and walk up to the throne beside Joseph.

Severus said, "Are we being charged with lack of etiquette?"

Mattathias said, "You are being charged with blasphemous cursing of the holy temple and the chosen people of God."

Jacob jumped right in. "I have been to multiple public and private gatherings where these three have spread their vicious lies and promoted the violent overthrow of Jerusalem and the destruction of Yahweh's temple. They are traitors to Israel."

Cassandra felt Alexander's hand on her to keep her from exploding. The physician addressed Mattathias, "High priest and Sanhedrin, according to the law, there is a requirement of at least two witnesses for any such serious crimes as we are being accused of. Where is your other witness?"

Joseph now spoke up. "I, Joseph ben Matthias, affirm Jacob bar Mordecai's claims as a witness to these accusations. I was in the crowd on the Mount of Olives where the accused were arrested."

Alexander didn't remember seeing Joseph at the mount. If he was, he must have been hiding—like a coward.

Joseph held out a scroll. "This scroll is documentation of their blasphemy and cursing. It was written by their last living apostle, John, currently exiled on Patmos. These three are responsible for copying this scroll and disseminating it among the Christian community in Jerusalem and surrounding towns and villages. It speaks in the veiled language of the apocalyptic, but I am quite conversant in such literature. Jacob has confirmed the fact that this document calls Jerusalem by the blasphemous names of Sodom, Egypt, and Babylon.[8] It also calls plagues and curses down upon our city and upon our people for rejecting their dead Messiah, Jesus of Nazareth. Furthermore, they claim the Nazarene is secretly alive somewhere with his armies, waiting to attack Jerusalem and the temple."

Joseph bowed to the high priest, who then said to the arrested, "Do you have any words in your defense?"

Alexander said, "Only that we serve the Lord Jesus, Messiah of Israel and Savior of the Gentiles. We do acknowledge ownership and dissemination of the scroll. But on the charges of blasphemy and curses, we claim only to be bearers of God's word to this wicked and adulterous generation. What we have said with clarity in public and private, in homes and the marketplace and the temple, is no different from what the prophets Ezekiel, Jeremiah, Isaiah, and others have said to unfaithful Israel. You have become a harlot, and Yahweh has divorced you. His two witnesses are the Law and the Prophets, and he will perform the legal right of capital punishment to marry his new bride, the body of Messiah, the Remnant."[9]

Mattathias looked around the room as he spoke. "The Sanhedrin has already convened over the facts of this case in prior council. Based on the defendant's statements, are there any who offer a change of opinion?"

None of the Sanhedrin responded to the offer.

Of course not, thought Cassandra. *Who is like the Beast? Who can fight against it?*

Mattathias said, "Very well then. This court finds the accused guilty of the crimes of apostasy, blasphemy, and sedition."

Severus' heart sank. He had sought to infiltrate the religious fanatics to find messianic pretenders. He had tried to uncover plans of assassination of Caesar or of sedition against Rome. But now he was captive to the enemy and facing execution. He would not receive the promise of his future made to him by Nero. He understood his companions to be true believers without the guile he once thought drove them. Their faith was a living vital one that made him reexamine his own soul. These monsters putting them on trial were the real villains.

And now all three of them were convicted of crimes that were punishable by death. His goal had been frustrated. His hopes had been crushed. Worse yet, if he revealed his Roman identity, he would only make matters worse for them all because the Jews were now at war with Rome. Cassandra and Alexander would be considered treasonous spies. They had saved his life. They had shown him the reality of a living faith in a living God. They may have been the only truly good people he had ever encountered. He would die before he would allow them to suffer.

Then another thought struck him. An ironic one. Severus was about to die for a faith he didn't even believe in.

The old high priest Ananus now spoke up, taking over the discussion with his forceful will. "The punishment for your crimes is death."

Severus saw the fear on his companion's faces.

Ananus continued, "But in light of the present situation, it is not our intent to make more Christian martyrs who become flashpoints of public unrest. We are not going to kill you. We are going to keep you alive. But hide you so deep in the earth you will not be found. Like the fallen angels, you will never see the light of day until judgment. You will disappear into the abyss. And you will wish you were dead."

The ex-high priest's words bit into Severus like a lion. He was dreadfully right. No one could rally in defense of a symbol if they could not find it. To be forgotten was a fate worse than death.

Eleazar, the temple captain, pointed to Severus and said, "I have deep suspicion about this prisoner. I do not believe he is who he says he is: a Roman Christian vine-grower."

"Why do you suspect this, Captain?" said Mattathias.

Eleazar glared at Severus. "Experienced intuition."

"Intuition is not evidence."

"Nay, indeed. But I will interrogate the prisoner to find any evidence that may be of import to us."

Eleazar's control of the inner temple had made him bold and demanding. And the priesthood cowered before his aggression. He could not rule the Sanhedrin outright. The people would consider that tyranny, and they would riot. But Severus knew that having a heavily armed force allowed Eleazar the opportunity to rule through proxy.

And there was still another storm cloud on this horizon. Eleazar was an anti-Roman fanatic imposing his will upon a corrupt pro-Roman priesthood. This meant that the civil war now going on in Judea was about to explode within the holy temple as well. Severus could not allow Eleazar to find out who he was.

Mattathias whispered with Joseph and Ananus. He turned back to Eleazar. "You may interrogate him. But he must not die in your custody, Captain. You must be accountable."

"As are we all in this Sanhedrin, my lord high priest."

Severus heard the spite in Eleazar's voice when he said the word *Sanhedrin*. This Eleazar was a single burning flame that was about to ignite a great fire.

As they were pulled out of the chamber, Severus saw his worried companions. He didn't really believe that their god was real or that if he was real he would help an insincere convert like Severus. But the Roman decided he would be sincere in his attempt to protect his precious Christian companions. It would probably be his only selfless act in a life of selfishness. But he had decided he would do it.

He whispered to them, "Pray for me."

CHAPTER 25

Severus hung naked from the ceiling by a rope and pulley system. His arms were outstretched like a "Y" above him, his legs tightly wound below him. The rope burns on his wrists and ankles were not even noticeable compared to the bruises he had received from the leather bludgeon filled with lead and the burns from the iron Eleazar had pulled from the fire in the corner.

Severus groaned in delirious pain. He could smell the odor of his own burnt flesh, still sizzling on his ribs and back.

Eleazar was just warming up. He had taken off his shirt, ready for a workout in pummeling his "Christian" nemesis. He paced around the small stone-walled chamber, specially set aside for torture in the dark depths below the temple mount. Eleazar stopped before a table of instruments to contemplate what he would use next.

What an irony, thought Severus. *The torture of humans beneath the very holy place of atonement for sins. Maybe Cassandra and Alexander are right about this place. It has become a temple of the Beast.*

Eleazar said, "Contrary to what you may think, I do not relish inflicting pain. Such a petty obsession is for fools with no sense of anything beyond themselves. As a Roman, you should understand that. It's how Caesar conquered the world. A higher cause gives one purpose and meaning."

Severus grunted out, "A higher cause justifies murder and torture."

Eleazar appeared perturbed by the comment. "Does a higher cause justify lying about your identity?"

Severus did not answer.

"Who are you, and what is your true mission?"

Severus said, "I am a merchant from Rome and I am here to aid my companions in the preaching of the gospel of Jesus Christ."

Eleazar held up a hook blade that was used for disemboweling victims. Severus could tell this was a man who, in service to his "higher cause," would be entirely capable of breaking his promise to keep his prisoners alive.

Eleazar asked outright, "Are you an imperial agent of Caesar?"

He had guessed right. Severus' nemesis had an uncanny intuition in recognizing a fellow warrior. Confessing all now would ensure Severus' death. And Eleazar would not stand trial for torturing a Roman spy during war.

Severus said with sober believability, "I am an agent of the Kingdom of God and the Lord Jesus Christ."

An idea beamed in Eleazar's eyes. He put the blade down and asked, "What is the gospel of Jesus Christ?"

He's going to try to expose my lie, thought Severus. But Severus had had plenty of experience with the language of Christians. He could reproduce it easily enough. He said through labored breaths, "Both Jew and Gentile are under sin, the condemnation of the law. Jesus the Christ died for our sins according to the Scriptures and rose from the dead to justify us. He has ascended to heaven to sit at the right hand of the Father until all his enemies have been made a footstool for his feet. Forgiveness of sins is available to the Jew first and also to the Gentile through faith in Jesus Christ alone and not in the works of Torah."

The torturer stared at him.

Strange, thought Severus. He had spoken the words like an actor in the theatre, but he felt something. He felt as if he finally understood the Christians, not intellectually but spiritually. He felt his own humanity, his frailty. He had been guilty himself of persecuting the believers, torturing them for his lord, Caesar. At first it had turned his stomach because he knew they were not the monsters they were made out to be. But the more he did it, the easier it got, and the distaste had faded. Now for the first time since he couldn't remember when, he felt the true horror of what he had done. It took trading places with those he had hurt to waken his humanity, his soul. It was a pain he gladly accepted.

Eleazar said, "What kind of Messiah dies without freeing the people of Israel from the yoke of the Kittim?"

Kittim was a term usually used by Zealots and other insurrectionists to refer to Rome.

Eleazar leaned in to whisper to Severus. "I control the temple now. The very heart of God's covenant. There are plenty of armed forces who support me. There is no one to support your dead Nazarene. You Christians are weak and without political will."

He is using the language of deliverance, thought Severus. Now, when it was too late, when it didn't matter to Severus, he had found what he had been looking for—a messianic pretender in defiance of Caesar.

If only he was on the other side of this interrogation.

Severus finally said, "Jesus is alive. And he is coming in judgment upon Jerusalem and all of Israel. Soon you will not have a temple to control."

Eleazar slugged Severus several times in the stomach and chest. Severus lost his breath and felt one of his ribs crack under the blow. He groaned in pain.

Eleazar said, "Well, this Jesus Redivivus is going to have to bring one mighty army to wrest it from my hands. Because my men are loyal, and we will fight to the death to protect our most holy place. God is on our side."

Severus said through the pain of his rib and bruises, "My king is Jesus the Christ, who will bring the Roman Beast and all those who took his mark to their end in the Lake of Fire. That goes for the harlot of apostate Israel and her false prophet, the high priesthood who serves the Beast." It was amazing how smoothly and easily the words came to him.

Eleazar pummeled him again. This had become personal. The Jewish captain had become unhinged.

Severus was taking control away from his torturer.

Again, Severus felt a chill down to his very core. It wasn't from the physical abuse he was experiencing. This was some kind of inner awareness. He felt as if he was beginning to actually believe the very things he had pretended to believe all these past months.

It was as if the brutality of torture brought to light the clarity of truth to Severus. In his pain, he could see things more clearly than he ever did before.

Eleazar hit him again. He almost fainted from the pain. But his conscience was more awake than ever.

Severus had been blinded by imperial idolatry, numbed from his pursuit of power, convicted by his transgressions. He had neglected his only living son. He had murdered his unborn sons. He had driven both his wife and his mistress to suicide. But those were only small examples of a lifetime of wrongs done to others—and to his Creator most of all.

Eleazar picked up a Roman scourge with pieces of bone and metal at the tips of leather straps. He raked it over Severus' back. Once. Twice. Three times. With every lash, Severus felt the sting and searing pain pierce through every nerve of his body.

Eleazar screamed, "Who are you and what is your mission?!"

Severus didn't answer. He had to protect his Christian friends from being tied to Rome.

Eleazar lashed him again.

And again.

Severus felt himself outside of his body, now looking down upon this little man and his attempt to break his victim. In some detached corner of his mind, it occurred to him that he was hanging in a position similar to crucifixion. The position of Jesus when he had died for the sins of the world. When he died for Severus' sins.

Eleazar became as a madman, whipping furiously with all the hatred in his being. Some of the lashes reached around and grabbed flesh from Severus' chest, ripping it from his body with a shriek.

"Who are you and what is your mission?"

Severus was back in his body. The full weight of his sin came over him. He deserved to be the one crucified for his sins, but now he understood that weight had been placed on Jesus. The Savior had taken Severus' place on the cross at the very point in time when Severus hated him and cursed him. The Praetorian felt himself whipping the flesh of Messiah with a Roman scourge. And he sensed Jesus choosing him in the very womb of his mother to be his adopted child. The contradiction of such grace broke him.

Severus began to weep.

Eleazar stopped.

He leaned in. "Is there something you want to tell me?"

Severus was barely conscious. But he was conscious enough to note the irony that he who before this moment had not been a true believer in Jesus Christ had through the act of being tortured *as* a believer actually become one.

He managed a weak smile and said painfully, "I am a believer in Jesus Christ. My mission is the gospel of the Kingdom of God."

· · · · ·

The dungeon stank of sewage and sweat. Severus felt himself coming in and out of consciousness as two temple guards dragged him down the dark hallway of prison cells beneath the temple.

He heard the sound of a cell door opening. He felt his body set down on the cold stone floor. He was delirious. A pile of bandages was thrown onto him.

He heard Alexander's voice say to the guards, "I need some more medical supplies or he is going to die."

He passed out.

When Severus came to, he was welcomed by the worried faces of Alexander and Cassandra.

Alexander helped him up from his prone position on the floor.

Cassandra offered him a small wooden cup of water.

His back felt like it was on fire. Severus grunted and sipped from the cup. It tasted like a river of living water down his throat. He spat out a bug that had fallen into that living water.

And then he realized he was in the prison cell with his fellow travelers and dozens of others, shivering, dirty, and malnourished in their captivity.

Alexander said, "I sewed and bandaged you up as best I could. You lost a lot of blood. You almost died."

"How long have I been out?"

Cassandra answered, "Three days. Sometimes you would cry out in your sleep."

"What did I say?"

"Have mercy on me, Lord Jesus."

"We had the entire cell block down here praying for you," said Alexander.

"How many are down here?"

"Over a hundred," said Alexander. "Quite a few of us, Christians."

Cassandra added, "Criminals for proclaiming the message that Jesus is the promised Messiah."

Alexander added, "Some have been here for years."

Dread overcame Severus. Eleazar was not exaggerating. They would be forgotten, disappeared down the abyss of public memory. Their message of the Apocalypse would be choked before they could get it to the other believers throughout the Land.

Alexander asked Severus, "Did he break you?"

Severus saw the worried look on both their faces. What fate would await them if he had?

"Jesus broke me," said Severus.

Their frowns turned to smiles.

He added, "I was pretending to be a Christian. Until that moment."

He saw by the look in their eyes that he did not have to explain it to them. He felt a fool to realize he had not fooled them.

But he understood grace now.

He tried to laugh at himself, but he stopped at the pain.

He said, "You are both released from my service."

They looked at him as if they didn't hear him. He wondered if he was in a dream.

"You still need a physician," said Alexander.

"And we have a job to finish," said Cassandra.

Severus was stunned. These two had just been freed, yet they chose to continue helping him. The grace of this new God overwhelmed him. Anything he could try to say would sound so trivial. He broke the uncomfortable silence. "If I can get a message to my soldiers, they might be able to come in disguise and break us out of here."

Alexander looked dismal. "No one has ever been able to get a message out of here in over two years."

Severus racked his mind, trying to think of other options. He looked with hope at Cassandra. "What about Demetrius and his men? Surely they will notice our absence."

Cassandra said, "Demetrius is traveling incognito around the countryside with the message of the Apocalypse. He won't know about our predicament. And you heard him. He has no intention of returning to Jerusalem."

Alexander said, "The only thing we have left to do is pray."

Severus said, "Didn't you tell me that angels rescued the apostles from prison?"

"Yes," said Cassandra. "But they didn't rescue John the Baptist or James the Just."

"Or Peter or Paul." Alexander added. "Or all those who went to their deaths in the arena."

The purpose of the Apocalypse became more clear at this moment to Severus. The apostle had explained it to them on Patmos, but he only now began to understand. It wasn't just to warn the Christians of coming judgment on Israel. It was to encourage the martyrs during this Great Tribulation to persevere and trust that Yahweh would vindicate them and punish their persecutors—after more were martyred and cried out from heaven's altar.[1]

Cassandra said, "And matters just got worse above us."

"What do you mean?" said Severus.

"See those prisoners?"

He followed her nod to a group of new prisoners across the way in a different cell.

"They were arrested after a coup that occurred in the temple when you were brought in here several days ago. They told us the captain of the temple, Eleazar, led his temple guard to take full control of the inner temple. He killed the high priest Mattathias. The rest of the Sanhedrin are now hiding out in the upper city."[2]

Severus grunted, "He did it without my confession."

Her eyes were wet with gratitude. "It would have been worse for us if you had."

He said, "Is Ananus the high priest still alive?"

She said, "Yes. He has taken leadership of the Sanhedrin and ruling class in response to Eleazar. But Zealots have burned the Jerusalem archives. Where the debts are recorded."

Severus said, "He's turning the mob against the ruling class." Without such debts to the rich, the poor were free to fight them.

Alexander said, "The land is consumed in civil war. Greeks murdered twenty thousand Jews in Caesarea Maritima. Wiped them out. Jews have responded by murdering Greeks in Pella, Samaria, and all over Galilee. Syrian cities are mercilessly killing Jews. Some Christians have been victims caught in the middle."[3]

He and Cassandra exchanged a look. They knew who each other was thinking about. Demetrius and his men. They were in the middle of that civil war trying to save Christians. Or were they already dead?

Severus said, "How has King Agrippa responded?"

"He ran," said Alexander. "Supposedly gathering forces in Antioch in the north with Cestius Gallus, governor of Syria."

Severus winced. "No doubt preparing to bring the might of Rome."

Cassandra said, "With the new regime in Jerusalem and the absence of Herod, the high priest Ananus has appointed Joseph ben Matthias to fight John of Gischala in Galilee for control of the region."

"Who is John of Gischala?" said Severus.

"He was captain of the temple before Eleazar. He became a fugitive of Florus when he attacked Florus in the temple. Gischala returned to his home town and recruited thousands of warriors. The prisoners tell us that he has become one of the most influential brigands in the countryside."

Severus said, "Syrians and Greeks killing Jews. Jews killing Jews. Israel is collapsing in on itself. Cannibalizing its own."

Cassandra said with relish, "Just as the Apocalypse foretold. Soon Israel will know the wrath of God to the utmost. 'And those who pierced him, all the tribes of Israel, will wail on account of him.'"[4]

Alexander said, "That is nothing to be happy about, Cassandra. And what about the 144,000? Have we failed to rescue the Remnant?"

She said, "If they continue to refuse our message, maybe they are not the Remnant after all."

Severus said, "God's word cannot be thwarted. If it is not us whom Yahweh uses, it will be another."

The sound of approaching soldiers turned everyone's attention. When they reached the cell, they saw the Zealot guards dragging another brutalized Jewish man between them.

As they opened the rusted cell door, the lead guard said, "Here is another patient for the physician to patch up." The other guards chuckled at the cynical remark.

Alexander said, "Who is he?"

"Sicarii leader. Keep him alive for Eleazar. I think we broke his arm."

"Where are the new medical supplies I asked for?"

One of the guards brought in a blanket full of bandages, threads, needles, and other supplies and set it on the floor, along with a couple buckets of fresh water.

Cassandra felt repulsion. The Sicarii were competitors of the Zealots. And both were enemies of the Christians. Both fought for the so-called exclusive rule of God over Israel: "No god but Yahweh," their saying went. But they were just two gangs of Jewish criminals fighting over control of the temple and city. And it was their violent religious fanaticism that terrorized the populace. Their belief in a military Messiah was no different from those Jews who had crucified the Messiah when he came.

Alexander said, "Cassandra, help me. I have to reset his arm."

She stayed where she was. She couldn't do it. This was a man who represented everything she hated. This was a man who represented the very reason why Jesus was coming on the clouds of judgment to Jerusalem.

Let God do his work, she thought.

Alexander noticed her hesitation. He looked at her with a scolding face. She said, "When he is healed, he will strike us down."

"Love your enemy," said Alexander. "Do good to those who hate you."

She closed her eyes. He was quoting Jesus. She knew he was right. She knew that God had said, "Vengeance is mine." She didn't believe in striking back with violence. But was it not right to "leave room for the wrath of God"? Should they not allow this antichrist to experience the consequences of his own sin? Her parents came to her mind, murdered and strung up by fanatical Jews like this.

She could not do it. She could not help him.

One of the other prisoners came to Alexander's aid, and they took hold of the Sicarius' arm. He screamed with great pain.

"It's okay," said Alexander. "I've reset the bone. You'll heal. What is your name?"

The delirious Sicarius croaked out, "Samuel."

Cassandra sat on the floor as if her knees gave way. Her first thought was disgust. What a blasphemy that such an honorable name as Samuel should be attached to such a criminal. She kept watching Alexander as he grabbed some rags and dipped them in the water bucket to help the man's fever.

As he worked on the wounded criminal, she thought of how many others in the prison Alexander had helped. And she had helped him. Cleaned cuts, broken bones, sicknesses. She remembered how she had first met Alexander when he too was unrepentant. And how God had changed his heart.

A picture came to her mind of Jesus healing sick people—people who were not particularly good: tax collectors, prostitutes, a Roman centurion's child. She remembered Jesus' words on the cross for his own executioners, "Father, forgive them. They know not what they do." She had struggled for so long with resentment against her own people for their treatment of the Christians. She had pined to see God's judgment upon them for so long that she could not find a way past her anger.

But she continued to watch Alexander. And she felt her heart moved by this man's actions. Actions she could not bring herself to do.

CHAPTER 26

Mount Hermon

Apollyon and his ten gathered deities stood before the large cave opening at Panias just outside the city of Caesarea Philippi. They were in a sacred grotto north of Galilee in the foothills of Mount Hermon. The area had fallen into disuse ever since the Nazarene had pulled his coup against the gods. When he had ascended on high, he'd led a train of captives in triumphal procession at this very location.[1]

Apollyon announced, "The end of our holy mountain tour, the Gates of Hades."

Everyone looked around at the abandoned site where Pan, the god of nature, had been worshipped for millennia.

"It was here that the Nazarene made his call to war." Apollyon pointed to Mount Hermon looming in the distance. "He said that upon this rock he would build his Congregation, the people of God. It is here he assaulted the Gates of Hades."[2]

Everyone gazed upon the holy mountain in silence.

"Then he had the gall to go up Mount Hermon and transfigure himself right in our faces. He revealed himself as the unique Shining One on *our* cosmic mountain, spitting in our faces and claiming it as his own. Then after his resurrection, that abomination of desolation entered our holy place and defiled it with his resurrected saints. He stole our inheritance, destroyed our mount of assembly, and dared to build Mount Zion upon its ruins."[3]

Zeus asked, "Has he built a temple up there?"

"No, you fool. He was speaking spiritually. Mount Zion replaces Mount Hermon as the cosmic center of the heavens and the earth."

"Can we reconstruct our mount of assembly, then?" said Zeus.

Apollyon said, "That's exactly why we're here."

The group of gods made their way up Hermon until they arrived at the ruins of a temple. It looked like a ziggurat that had been half-buried into the mountain so that one side of the step-pyramid stuck out for worshippers to ascend its steps. The bulk of the temple was embedded within the mountain.

They climbed the broken stairway to heaven until they reached the altar at the top, a wide platform with a large pit for burning sacrifices. The smell of human flesh was long gone from the pit, and it was filled with boulders. Apollyon led the gods over to a part of the pit that had been cleared away, showing an entrance down into the earth.

Apollyon said, "Follow me." He climbed into the hole.

The gods followed him into the darkness.

In the bottom of the fire pit was a walkway that led to a chamber entrance.

Apollyon led them through a long hallway lined with columns until they arrived at a large doorway with its gates blown off its hinges. That horrid Psalm rang within Apollyon's head,

> Lift up your heads, O gates!
> > And be lifted up, O ancient doors,
> that the King of glory may come in.
> Who is this King of glory?
> > Yahweh, strong and mighty,
> > Yahweh, mighty in battle![4]

Apollyon remembered that day with dread. He tried to shake it out of his mind, but the scene of destruction before him would not allow it. It had occurred a generation ago, but he remembered it all as if it had just happened. The battle, the binding of his fellow Watchers by the army of resurrected ones, and then the Nazarene bringing Apollyon before the heavenly court room, where he was stripped of his authority as the satan, the legal adversary and accuser of the covenant people. The Messiah had then cast Apollyon and a third of his angels to earth like lightning, leaving him unable to legally accuse the Nazarene's brethren, the Christians.[5]

Yahweh may have bound me from the power of accusation, thought Apollyon. *But he made the mistake of not casting me into the Lake of Fire.*

The cavern was already halfway cleared of its cave-in. As they made their way through the debris, Apollyon could see a dozen other Watchers already there, carrying rubble and dropping it into a small lake of black pitch.

Apollyon said to his traveling companions, "Now get to work cleaning up this holy place." He looked at Zeus. "Lose some of that indulgent ballast."

Zeus and the others joined the working Watchers at their task. He noticed Anat glaring at him and hesitating to join the others in their labor. Apollyon considered her foolish to display her bitterness over the humiliation of her brother and lover Ba'al. It only gave Apollyon more power over her weakness.

And he decided to exploit that weakness. He called out, "Anat, come to me!"

She approached him.

He said, "I have a special task for you."

She raised her brow, wondering why he would give her such favor.

He was keeping his enemy close.

"Choose five trustworthy Watchers to join us."

Zeus arrived just behind Anat with eager eyes. "My lord, may I be of service to you as well?"

Apollyon looked at Zeus, while clearly implying to Anat, "Now that is the kind of positive attitude that deserves my affection. Would that all my minions have such a willing spirit."

Anat remained still-faced and emotionless. She said dryly, "Thy will be done, my lord."

Apollyon said, "Follow me, my chosen ones."

• • • • •

"You're taking us to the Gates of Hades," said Zeus as they approached the sacred grotto of Panias.

"Now you're growing some brains," said Apollyon. "It's time to grow some testicles to match."

He led them into the large cave opening in the rock face.

They travelled through the dark, their supernatural eyes able to see as clearly as in daylight.

Some distance in, they finally arrived at a pile of rubble blocking their way. A small opening had been made through the rock wall, a carved-out tunnel barely large enough for them to travel through single file.

The Nazarene had originally demolished the cave at the time of his ascension, closing off the Gates of Hades at the back of the cave.

Apollyon led his seven helpers through the tunnel to their destination.

They arrived at the mouth of a large crevasse in the earth. Though the Watchers were mighty beings, all but Apollyon stood back in fear from the precipice. Apollyon looked down into a darkness so deep he could not see the end of it. Silence swallowed up all sound below.

He glanced back at them with a sarcastic sneer. "What are you afraid of?"

He knew full well the source of their fears. At the bottom of the shaft were the waters of the Abyss. He had used Solomon's seal, stolen from the Jerusalem temple, as the key to free them from this very prison. The other Watchers glanced at each other, wondering if Apollyon intended to return any of them to the waters.[6]

Zeus shivered and asked, "What is your plan, Lord Apollyon?"

The others listened closely, failing to disguise from Apollyon their dread.

Apollyon mused, "Certainly not to waste my time or manpower by throwing any of you back in there."

The seven of them relaxed visibly.

Zeus said, "Leviathan swims the waters of the Abyss."

Apollyon said, "You may yet merit your station, Greek boy-lover." The seven-headed sea dragon had been of much use to Apollyon's interests from the War on Eden to the great War of Gods and Men in the days of Noah, as well as during the Exodus and on through history up to this day. Though the dragon was an agent of chaos, Azazel had learned how to secure Leviathan's service through occult magic. And Azazel was now under Apollyon's command.[7]

Apollyon said to the others, "You remember the Titanomachy of primordial days."

Zeus and Anat remembered that revolt of giants, but had not been on the front lines. They were both fresh recruits to the divine assembly at the time.[8]

Apollyon continued, "The Rephaim, giant Canaanite warrior kings, were the first of my Nephilim, the primeval ones. They were swallowed into the Abyss of Sheol in the War on Eden."[9]

Sheol was the Hebrew word for Hades, the underworld.

"And ever since that day," said Apollyon, "they await the kings of the nations."

Zeus asked, "You are going to imprison the kings of the nations in Hades?"

Apollyon glanced at Anat and saw her eyes watching with scheming intensity.

Apollyon said, "You think too small, fat one." Zeus glanced at the floor in shame. "You will know when you need to know. And speak to no one of this."

All seven bowed in submission to the prince of the power of the air.

He said, "All you need to know is that I need this cave cleared out."

They looked at one another. It was a mammoth task even for the strongest of divinities.

Apollyon said, "When I return, I expect this complete tunnel to be cleared and wide open. As wide as possible."

Anat was yet again slow to the task. It would take Apollyon some time to bridle her spirit. But that only made the challenge more delicious to him. The seven Watchers began to remove the debris by throwing it down into the crevasse where the rocks would simply sink deep into the endless waters of the Abyss.

But they were interrupted by a distressed voice from the cave entrance. "Lord Apollyon." The Watchers turned to see a bruised and bloodied Allah and his three daughters with him.

· · · · ·

"Damn Yahweh to his own hell!" growled Apollyon. He looked ready to explode with violence. The four deities with him stepped back in fear. He had left the other Watchers to their task inside the cave and had taken Allah and his daughters outside to hear their report. They had told him of the attack of the archangels and the capture of Hubal.

Allah said, "We travelled to Antioch with the Nabatean forces, only to discover that Ba'al and Ahura Mazda had also been taken hostage. And word arrived that Ares was their fourth."

Apollyon gnashed his teeth. "They've taken out the principalities over the four dominant legions in my arsenal." He considered the ramifications of this enemy's strategic sabotage. Without those four spiritual princes of the nations, Apollyon would not have the overwhelming strength he needed to bring the spiritual desolation he had planned. His strategy had to change.

"I must find them," said Apollyon. "But if Yahweh is going to play that game, then I will play mine." He turned to the moon god. "I have to leave for

Rome immediately. I want you to go to Alexandria and tell the gods of Egypt to prepare their legions for Nero's command. Have them massacre the Jews of the city."[10] Allah bowed in obedience. The Master was going to pull in more forces from all the nations.

Apollyon turned to the three goddesses. "I want you three to find out where the four gods are being held. Engage in a mission of search and extraction. Those principalities are essential to the success of my plan. Speak of this to no one." The daughters of Allah bowed silently, their eyes glancing at each other through their veils. It was obvious to them why silence was required. If word got out that Apollyon's forces were hamstrung, he would suffer the mistrust of the other principalities, which could even lead to a coup.

The Arabian goddesses needed no words amongst themselves. Their minds were already synchronized with each other. They alone had knowledge of their Master's Achilles' heel.

CHAPTER 27

Qumran

Simon felt the sea breeze on his back as he watched a line of Essene monks aim their arrows at targets of wood fifty feet away. They were on flat ground outside the commune on the seaside. The wooden planks were cut roughly to the shape of a human silhouette.

Almost every arrow missed its target.

Simon barked, "Focus on the target, not on your weapon! Again!"

The archers nocked their bows again. Simon turned to another line of Essene soldiers-in-training. These were slingers who twirled their slings and released toward a straw dummy propped on a pole. More hits than the arrows.

But still so far to go.

Last, a scrimmage line of battling monks in light armor facing each other and carrying wooden swords.

Simon barked, "Commence!"

The monks carefully and slowly engaged in swordplay. The goal was to learn their forms through slow, deliberate moves. Then to step them up in speed over time until they were sparring each other with full force.

But even after so many weeks, these students were still using slow and halting movements. Simon became exasperated. He had accepted the job of training these peaceful monks in the art of war for the gold they offered. He never expected them to actually become competent at fighting. But their ineptitude had begun to disturb him. The entire community of these poor sods could be cut down in seconds by a mere squad of a dozen legionaries.

And he would be walking away with their money as they lay hacked to pieces at the hands of the Romans. If they could at least put up a fight, he wouldn't feel so guilty stealing from them. He couldn't tell them the truth about where he had come from before they hired him. But the fact that he couldn't train these monks properly made him wonder if he was really just a fraud.

No. The beginning of the end of a mercenary warrior was when he considered the politics of the situation. Moral evaluation of people and causes always led to weakness. And weakness led to death.

Religious causes, from the Zealots to the Essenes to the Jerusalem priesthood, were all rationalizations for the human quest for power. In the end, they were all the same delusional beast with a different head.

Maybe by training these monks he could give the plebeians, caught up in the middle of such tyranny, a fighting chance.

Not these naïve fools.

They were still awkward children at play, bumbling through their moves, fearful of hurting their opponents.

He screamed out, "Stop, goddamnit! STOP!"

The monks obeyed, looking at him with shock. All of them, even the archers and slingers, had frozen in fear. He realized his profanity was offensive to their religious sensibilities.

But apology was weakness.

Simon noticed Aaron, the young monk, facing off against another hairless youth. He walked over to one of the straw dummies.

The monks watched in anxious silence as he jerked off the Roman helmet and breastplate.

He then made his way back to the swordsmen. He said to Aaron's opponent, "Put this on." The young monk obeyed.

Simon pointed at Aaron and announced to the crowd, "This monk is about the best I've seen out of all of you."

Aaron gleamed with pride.

Simon continued, "Most of you would only last three seconds against a Roman. He would last about five."

Aaron's beaming face lost its shine.

Simon turned to Aaron. "Listen closely." He turned back to the crowd, pointing at Aaron's fighting partner. "This is not your fellow monk, with whom you pray and share your religious beliefs and observances. This is a swine-loving Roman heathen. The cause of your oppression."

Aaron cocked his head, looking at his opponent. Simon was trying to get them to fight better by fueling their emotional imagination.

"The Roman in front of you is the source of your people's suffering. In fact, his ancestors desecrated your first temple and set up their own abominable sacrifices in Yahweh's holy place. They spat at your god. They killed and enslaved your people for centuries. And now he is trying to do it all over again."

He was exaggerating, but Aaron got the point. The Babylonians, the Medo-Persians, the Greeks, and now the Romans were an unbroken line of oppression of God's chosen people.

As Aaron looked at his sparring partner, he felt a surge of righteous indignation.

"Now, disembowel that monstrous Roman in front of you for the glory of God! Commence fighting!"

The monks brandished their wooden swords and dutifully obeyed Simon's new directive. Their energy increased. Their speed picked up. They began to fight, really fight.

Aaron assaulted his opponent with such relentless fury the other monk could not return the attack. He seemed to put all his energy into protecting himself from Aaron's onslaught.

Until Aaron effectively knocked the youth to the ground, stepped on his shield, and struck his helmet off.

Aaron stood triumphantly over his dizzied prey, sword poised at his neck. Simon stepped up to him.

"Better. You've obviously picked up something from watching Roman battle."

Aaron said proudly, "When I lived in Caesarea Maritima." The attention from Simon elevated his heart unlike anything he could pray for.

"But you do not understand Roman strength."

Aaron frowned.

"It is tempting to think that you are in the superior position with your force." Aaron was confused. Was that not the point?

Simon pointed downward.

Aaron looked down to see his conquered foe, shaking, but holding his own sword to Aaron's groin.

Simon said, "It is discipline that wins wars. Fury dulls the wits."

Simon offered his hand to Aaron's opponent. "Well done." He helped him up. Aaron felt rejected. Confused and manipulated. First Simon had fueled their hatred in order to fight. Now he was telling Aaron to be more in control.

But then Simon took the youth's wooden sword and said to Aaron, "Now, you and I." The soldier faced off against the young monk. "I'll help you find the balance of force and discipline."

Aaron's emotions flew high.

This great man had chosen *him* for special tutoring.

Aaron began to concentrate harder than he had on anything in his entire life. He wanted to become a warrior that would make Simon proud.

After the practice, Simon called the monks together. He stood beside Aaron. "Tomorrow, I take leave to take care of personal interests."

The monks grumbled with surprised disappointment.

"I leave you under the authority of Aaron. He is competent enough to lead you in practicing your forms until I return."

Aaron looked up at Simon with shock.

Someone shouted out, "Where are you going?"

"It is not important for your purposes. Maintain your discipline without me."

"When will you return?"

"I don't know."

The discouragement on their faces disturbed Simon. He felt as if he was abandoning them. But he had to get back. Back to where he had been running from.

CHAPTER 28

The sun was setting on the western horizon. The community had eaten dinner and was now engaged in evening prayers. Aaron slipped out unseen to follow the lurking figure of Simon as he left the commune and made his way up a path to the highest mount above the caves of Qumran.

Aaron saw Simon sit down on a rock and stare out onto the horizon. In the distance, he saw the city of Jerusalem in silhouette against the setting sun, the holy city enshrouded in the circle of red blood.

He saw Simon deep in thought. He approached silently, cautiously. When he was within yards of the warrior, Simon spun around with dagger in hand, ready to defend himself. Aaron jumped back.

Simon recognized him and dropped the blade, annoyed. "Do not ever sneak up on me. I could have killed you."

"I apologize, commander."

Simon said, "Sit with me."

Aaron's heart beat faster. He came and sat down next to Simon. "Thank you for all your guidance. And leadership."

Simon remained mute, his eyes now fixed on a small tuft of hair he caressed in his fingers. Aaron's heart sank. He said, "Who have you lost?"

Simon said, "Someone I could never really have."

Aaron felt that reality all too deeply. He said, "I know you are doing this for the money, but – I think there is something more noble in you. Something that craves justice."

"Craves the impossible."

Aaron said, "You have inspired us. Given us hope."

"You do realize you are going to die. All of you."

Now it was Aaron's turn to remain silent.

Simon added, "You cannot defy Rome and win. It is hopeless."

"Nothing is hopeless with God."

Simon chuckled. "You are quick to claim God's blessing. But you are too anxious to spill blood, Aaron."

"We have found something to die for."

"You mean, to kill for."

Aaron shrugged. "Sadly, such means are necessary."

"Then you are no better than the Zealots or the Sicarii."

Aaron felt a surge of confidence. He could not believe he would challenge this man, this demigod whom he admired. But he had to. "The Zealots and Sicarii fight for political control. We fight for God's temple."

"Ah, the temple," said Simon with spite. "That hollow shell. Cruel symbol of a capricious God."

Aaron looked at him with incredulity. "You were captain of the temple guard. You were in the very house of Yahweh. How could you believe such things?"

"Because I have seen inside that house. It has been desecrated by a corrupt priesthood, taken over by thieves."

"That is why we fight. To purify it. To return it to its original glory."

Simon remained silent. Aaron looked back out onto Jerusalem. He spoke as a lover would of his beloved. "Jerusalem is the center of the cosmos. The navel of the earth. Some say Mount Zion was the primordial hill where creation began.[1] The temple is our Garden of Eden, spiritually connected to the heavenly temple in the waters above the firmament. *On earth as it is in heaven.*[2] The temple is the earthly monument of our covenant. Outside in the inner court is the copper sea gilded with lilies on the backs of the bulls at the four corners of the earth. That is the sea of chaos out of which Yahweh created. Out of which he established his covenantal order. It took Solomon seven years to build the first temple. And seven days to consecrate it. The seven days of creation. And then he rested."[3]

Aaron rested for a moment.

He said, "Is it true that the priests call the altar hearth 'the mountain of El'?"[4]

Simon nodded thoughtfully. "Yes." He became caught up in his own past. "Garden imagery is engraved on the marble walls and columns of the holy place. The Menorah candle-stand is cast as a seven-branched image of the tree of life."[5]

Aaron asked, "When you were captain of the temple, did you ever long to see the veil of the Holy of Holies?"

"I have seen it."

"But only priests may enter the holy place."

"And the captain of the temple."

"They say it is a microcosm of the heavens and earth. The blue of the air, purple of the sea, fine flax of the earth, and the scarlet of fire."[6]

Simon nodded in agreement and added, "Embroidered with cherubim and the stars of heaven."

Aaron imagined in his mind's eye, "Behind that holy veil is the presence of God on his throne with the ark of the covenant as his footstool and the tables of the Mosaic Law. Guarded by cherubim as in the Garden."

Simon added somberly, "Except it's empty. God's throne, his glory. It's all gone. The Garden is desolate, and the covenant is about to be shattered."

Aaron could not argue with that. No matter how much Simon might have attempted to justify his own hopelessness, he was right. The ark of the covenant and Yahweh's glory were simply not in the Holy of Holies. The ark had been taken and destroyed when Nebuchadnezzar desolated the temple five hundred years ago. It had never been replaced. How could it be? As in earlier days, the name Ichabod came to him. It meant that the glory of Yahweh had departed with the ark of the covenant. Messiah alone could replace it. But could the covenant, the very power of the people of God, be shattered?[7]

Simon changed the subject. "I am not who you think I am. The reason I am taking leave is to return to Masada."

Aaron tilted his head with curiosity. He had heard that gangs of bandits and Sicarii had captured the fortified Masada and were building their forces. Lawless criminals.

Aaron could not help the pity that overwhelmed him. He said, "What was it, Simon? What made you lose faith?"

Simon stared into the last sliver of sun disappearing beneath the end of the earth.

"I was betrayed by my closest ally, my lieutenant, John of Gischala. I had become an outlaw. So I joined with outlaws. When you found me, I was on the verge of opening my own veins from despair over the meaninglessness of my life of crime. But these weeks in Qumran have changed me. I see in your community a will to survive despite your poverty and oppression. You live above your suffering. I see the rich and powerful, the ruling class of Judea, exploiting the poor to feed their own gluttonous appetites."

He paused, continuing his stare into the abyss. "I have a purpose now. A higher cause to live for." Aaron watched him with unblinking eyes. "I will plunder the rich and the powerful to alleviate the suffering of the poor."[8]

Aaron said, "There will be a reckoning, commander. That is what God promised through the prophet Daniel. Our prophecy of the War of the Sons of Light against the Sons of Darkness confirms it."

Simon looked at Aaron. It made the monk quiver. This warrior was so strong. So opposite of Aaron's fat, weak abbot, Phineas. That lecherous pig.

Simon said, "A reckoning? You really believe that." It wasn't a question. It was astonishment.

Aaron said, "I live for it."

"You will die for it."

"Maybe so. But at least my life will have counted for something more noble than robbing the rich in the name of justice and equality. Despite your anger with God, you have given me hope. You have given us all hope. Please do not leave. I will do anything to keep you here. Just tell me."

Simon looked at the young monk with surprise. He smiled and put his hand on Aaron's shoulder in affection.

Then Simon looked searchingly into Aaron's eyes. A look that made Aaron feel things he had not felt before. Confused feelings. This mighty warrior looked right into his soul. Aaron felt as if he were naked and vulnerable, but he liked it. Where did such unnatural desire come from?

Then he saw something in Simon's eyes change. A turn. A dawning of understanding. As if he knew Aaron's secret and rejected it.

Simon withdrew his arm. Spoke like a caring father. "Who has been your mentor until now, Aaron?"

Aaron did not answer immediately. But when he did, it was with hatred. "The elder Phineas."

Simon looked at him again. Aaron looked away. His previous vulnerability now turned to shame. Thoughts of what Phineas did to him shattered his dream.

Simon put his hand on Aaron's shoulder again. This time it wasn't with affection, but with a masculine encouragement.

The fallen warrior said, "I will return to Qumran. But not for reasons you may think. Perhaps we both have something to learn about losing faith. Mine in God, yours in men."

CHAPTER 29

Tiberias
Galilee

Demetrius led his band of Kharabu warriors up to the edge of the steep hill overlooking the city of Tiberias on the shore of the Sea of Galilee. It was the capital of the Galilee region, strategic in both location and influence. The Christians there were hated by their fellow Jewish Tiberians. This was the Kharabu's next target of liberation.

But Demetrius felt a growing darkness over his soul. He had lived a life of hopeful trust in the kingdom of God, a kingdom that Jesus had said would be like leaven, spreading through all the world as the leaven did through a batch of bread. Jesus had also said the kingdom was like a mustard seed that started small, but grew to be the largest tree in the garden. The prophet Daniel had said the mountain of God begun in Messiah would grow to fill the earth. And yet here they were on the verge of the total annihilation of that kingdom. All over the empire, Christians were still being persecuted for not supporting the imperial cult of Caesar, for not accepting his mark of ownership.

And here in the very land of Judea, civil war had grown like wildfire. Bandits and brigands roamed the wilderness, robbing and pillaging the wealthy. Their own countrymen were battling each other as Jewish leaders fought for power over the region. John of Gischala had grown his band of rebels into a formidable force that competed with Joseph ben Matthias for Galilee.

And cities were torn apart by warring citizens, Greeks versus Jews. Cities with Greek majorities attacked Jewish minorities, and cities with Jewish majorities attacked Greek minorities as revenge. Demetrius and his company had liberated some Christians in villages along the way to larger cities like Pella and Gadara. But he had stumbled upon scenes of such carnage that he began to lose hope.

In Scythopolis, one of the cities of the Decapolis, Demetrius had arrived to find a large grove filled with the dead bodies of thirteen thousand Jews—men, women, and children—hacked to pieces. Thirteen thousand innocent victims. A survivor told him the story behind the horror. The Jews who resided there were loyal to their city, but the Greek majority did not trust them. When they heard that Joseph ben Matthias was coming to Scythopolis with his Galilean forces, the Scythians requested the Jews of their city to gather in the grove as proof they would not betray their fellow Greek citizens to Joseph. Whereupon the Greeks attacked them in a bloody massacre, the results of which Demetrius had not been able to get out of his head since they came upon the atrocity.[1]

Demetrius had heard even more stories of devastation all around the land. Cities filled with the dead, old and young, women and infants, lying unburied, their nakedness left profanely uncovered. It was a kind of barbarism that could only be described as demonic. The holy land itself had become unclean, overrun with demons. It seemed as if they would destroy themselves before the Roman armies even got there.[2]

Demetrius saw Uriel arriving from below on horseback. He gestured to the warriors behind him to wait for orders. There were twenty more Christian men who had joined them from the various villages they had liberated. Upon hearing the message of the Apocalypse, most Christians had sought refuge in the mountains or in safe cities like Gerasa, Sidon, and Antioch where Jews were not attacked.[3] But these few had joined the Kharabu warriors to help rescue their brethren from the hands of certain death.

Demetrius wondered whether the other three units of liberators had been successful. They were on their way to Ashkelon and Hebron in the south, Tyre and Damascus in the north. Had they managed to convince the Christians to find safety before the coming wrath? Or were they having as much trouble as Demetrius and the others had encountered in Jerusalem?

Uriel arrived and got off his horse.

"What news?" asked Demetrius.

Uriel said, "John of Gischala has amassed forces in Tiberias. He seeks to control Galilee, and the Tiberians are on his side. Joseph ben Matthias stands against him in imminent attack in the valley just outside the city. The timing is perfect for us."

"Well done, Uriel." Demetrius turned to his men and announced, "We will draw near in stealth. When Gischala and Joseph clash on the field with their armies, we will take the opportunity of distraction to enter the city from behind and extract the Christians."

One of the soldiers spoke up. "Commander. You told us that Joseph is an agent of the Beast. Is there any way we can delay the success of his forces, and therefore give us time to save more Christians?"

"Excellent idea," said Demetrius. He considered the possibilities. As a member of the ruling class of Judea, Joseph ben Matthias was party to the Land Beast of apostate Israel. As a Pharisee, he was also tied to the great Harlot of demonic religious leadership that rode that Land Beast. Joseph ben Matthias was a key player in the strategy of the Dragon.

Uriel stepped forward. "I will cripple his plans. Give us more time."

Demetrius said, "How?"

"I have an idea. It is best you not know. But give me leave, and I'll infiltrate his ranks."

Demetrius said light-heartedly, "Who will be my guardian angel in your absence?"

Some of the nearby men laughed.

"Fear not," said Uriel. He reached in his cloak and pulled out a small ram's horn trumpet. He handed it to Demetrius and said, "If you get in trouble, blow upon this, and I will fly in on the wings of an eagle with the bite of Rahab." He patted the sheath that held his rolled-up whip sword.

Demetrius stared at the small warrior. Then with eyes of incredulity at the small horn in Uriel's hand. Demetrius had been playfully calling the four Kharabu warriors his 'angels' since they had rescued him. And the four had gone along with it in jest. Perhaps they were all taking this angel joke a bit too far.

But Uriel looked serious.

Demetrius smiled. He decided to keep the humor going. It might be the only reprieve from the nightmare of madness all around them that threatened to swallow up their hope.

He grabbed the trumpet. "Very well. But if Gabriel beats you to my side, I'll consider changing guardian angels."

Uriel said with a smile, "That will keep me on my toes. Gabriel and I have been rivals since the days of Noah. I usually win, but don't tell him I told you that."

Demetrius laughed. "Uriel, I am not sure which skill of yours is more important to me: bodyguard or comic."

"Finally," said Uriel. "Someone who appreciates my sense of humor. Please do share your sentiments with Michael. He thinks sarcasm is not fitting for the heavenly host. Thankfully though, Yahweh agrees with me."[4]

Demetrius shook his head with amusement. "Go. Perform your secret mission. And please do survive and return to me. I don't want to lose my sense of humor."

The thought occurred to Demetrius that Uriel might be mentally deluded. Maybe he wasn't joking. Maybe he really did believe he was an angel. Maybe he really was dangerous.

• • • • •

Joseph ben Matthias led his forces of two thousand soldiers into the battle against Gischala's equal army in a valley not far from the city of Tiberias. Joseph needed this victory, and he needed it today. He had engaged in various skirmishes with that bandit, who had managed to create havoc in Galilee as he sought dominance in the region. The Jerusalem command was starting to think Joseph was incompetent in his leadership. But they did not know how deadly his opponent really was. Gischala was an accomplished leader and warrior. He was not like the other rogue leaders who wandered the countryside. He was strategic and driven by a fanatical vision much like that of the Zealots.

In fact, Gischala had many Zealots in his army. Joseph thought Gischala's ultimate goal would be to capture Jerusalem and try to become king. Such aspirations were common amongst the rebels. And why not? They all anticipated the arrival of Messiah to free them from the Romans. Of course many of these rebel leaders would begin to see themselves as the anointed deliverer. Such as Eleazar.

Ironically, it was this very messianic belief that drove the Jewish revolt and would bring the iron fist of Rome down upon them all. If they would have been happy with the status quo, none of this self-destruction would be occurring and Joseph could return to his own pursuit of advancement in the Jewish ruling class.

But here he was out in the field, fighting against his own countrymen, who were too stubborn and intolerant to admit it was their own fault that Judea was under the oppressive hand of Rome.

His forces met Gischala's with a clash of cavalry and infantry, sword and shield, arrow and armor. But this was only a pretense for a ruse he had planned.[5]

• • • • •

Demetrius and his men heard the trumpets of war in the valley. Leaving their hidden location in the hills next to the city, they made their way into town to find the Christians. Uriel had told them the Christians were forced into a ghetto on the west side. How he was able to find that out as well as the intelligence on Joseph, all without being discovered, was a mystery to Demetrius. But he trusted the small warrior. He had never been wrong yet. Despite their jesting about angels, Uriel's service toward the group seemed almost superhuman. He was an amazing tracker, an unbeatable warrior, his sword seemed as if it was from heaven itself, and he had a peace about him that Demetrius could only define as transcendent.

What if he really was an angel?

Demetrius and his team made their way through the deserted streets and dilapidated buildings of the ghetto. The civilians were hiding in their homes with their families, praying in fear while the battle raged on in the field. But not all the soldiers were on the battlefield. At least one garrison of armed Tiberians loyal to Gischala remained in the city. The Kharabu rescue team could not afford for word to get out that they were here. They could not afford to be discovered.

After asking several stray citizens, Demetrius found the home of one of the Christian elders of the city. Demetrius didn't have time to gather the congregation and read the Apocalypse to them. He had to get them to safety first.

But the elder, a graying bald man named Gihon, did not trust them. He didn't know them, and while he had heard of a letter from John the Apostle, he had no way of authenticating it through strangers.

Gihon said to Demetrius, "We have heard of such tricks all over Galilee. Men, women, and children are taken outside the city, then butchered in cold blood."

They were standing at his door. Demetrius didn't have time to argue. When the army came back to the city, he and his men would be discovered and executed. Or one of the stragglers they'd interviewed might already have alerted John's garrison inside the city.

Desperate tactics were required.

Demetrius kicked open the door. Gihon fell to the floor. His elderly wife and several women in the home were watching, some holding babies. They screamed and backed up.

"Keep them quiet," barked Demetrius to his men. Several of them pushed their way into the home, surrounding its occupants. The women went mute, clinging protectively to their infants.

Demetrius helped the frightened Gihon up. The old man cringed in fear.

Demetrius said, "I don't care if you don't believe us, old man. You will do what I tell you or you will suffer the consequences."

The soldiers looked with shock at Demetrius. He winked at them. It was all a ruse.

"Don't you think we can go from house to house and kill you if we wanted?"

The old man was trembling with fear. Demetrius noticed a spreading puddle on the floor at his feet. A wave of regret washed over him. He had so frightened this elder that his bladder had released. He was terrifying the very ones he was trying to save. And now they would never believe a thing he said.

• • • • •

The valley was filled with thousands at war. Jew against Jew. Gischala leading the Tiberian side, Joseph the Galilean side.

But then the tide began to turn. Joseph's men appeared to tire. They were pushed back. Some began to withdraw. The Tiberians were on their home turf. Gischala's forces were in a superior position. They pushed harder.

Joseph could see his forces were not in a winning battle. He sounded his trumpet, and the Galilean forces withdrew.

An army in retreat was an army at a disadvantage.

Gischala gave his clarion call, and his forces gave chase.

They cut down the stragglers on the perimeter with ease. The goal was to keep the flow of battle moving forward with unstoppable force. Like a boulder gaining speed as it rolls down a hill.

They entered a clearing surrounded by forest. The Galilean forces were being overtaken. They were moments away from being decimated by the Tiberian forces.

That was when Joseph turned around and had his herald sound his trumpet again.

From out of the forest behind the pursuers, another two thousand soldiers burst forth on horseback and entered the fray.

The Tiberians were flanked and outnumbered.

The tide had turned. The Galileans began to crush Gischala's force between two sides. Tiberians fought for their lives. But their lives had not much time left.

Joseph was in the rear now. He decided to gallop into the heat of battle to inspire his men.

But just as he advanced, his horse stopped, unwilling to move forward. As if there were an invisible wall. Joseph yelled and slapped the reins. The horse still refused to move.

He kicked her side hard with his boots.

She reared up, and Joseph lost control. He fell to the ground, breaking his wrist, the wind knocked out of him.

His lieutenant saw him guarding his arm in pain. Joseph was vulnerable to the enemy. So the lieutenant used his horn to sound retreat, calling for the Galilean force to protect their commander.

Joseph cursed, still cradling his broken wrist in pain. He was surrounded by his men and lifted to safety on another horse. He saw his own horse circling in confusion, spooked by something.

It looked as if the horse had seen a ghost.

She had in fact seen an angel.[6]

• • • • •

Demetrius was unsure of what he should do. But he knew persuasion would no longer work with these frightened Christians. His cruel behavior had ruined that opportunity. He felt like a monster.

A messenger arrived. "Commander."

Demetrius pulled him aside.

"The Tiberians are returning from the battlefield. Our time is running out."

Demetrius was in an impossible situation. The local Christians didn't trust him and were not being compliant. But if he didn't do something quickly, they would all die.

He turned back to the elder. "You will guide me to the homes of Christians and tell them to join us, or your daughters and wife will be killed by my men. Do you understand, old man?"

He nodded to his men. They drew their swords, glancing at each other, hoping it was a ruse.

Gihon said, "I will do as you say. Our lives are in the hands of God."

"You have no idea how true that is," said Demetrius.

They gathered a hundred Christians from the ghetto and began to lead them out of the city. The Tiberian forces were on their way back from their battle. Demetrius hoped they would be too preoccupied with their wounds to notice or care about the exiting Christians.

His warriors had drawn their weapons threateningly upon the Tiberian believers as they herded them to safety. The Christians feared they were being herded to their deaths. But it had been the only way Demetrius could get them to act quickly. He felt sure that God approved, considering the circumstances.

The last of the Christians had left the city limits. They were finally on their way up the forested path into the hills where they might evade the search of the Tiberian soldiers. They were on their way to safety.

And then all safety vanished before them like a dream upon waking.

The call to battle came on Demetrius' left. He heard the cry of war in response on his right. A quick glance confirmed that they were hemmed in on both sides by Tiberian soldiers.

The city garrison had been secretly alerted to their escape.

Demetrius called out, and his men circled their Christian wards. His warriors were not the only ones in peril.

Two hundred Tiberians descended upon them from out of the forested hills against Demetrius' fighting force of forty-plus men.

But these Tiberians were at a disadvantage. They had never fought against Kharabu warriors before.

What started as a rush of battle quickly turned into a scattering of confusion as Demetrius' men responded with ruthless fluidity that broke the ranks of their enemies. They danced and flowed around their opponents like water.

The Tiberian Christians at that moment discovered their fears of Demetrius were misplaced. He was their protector, not their executioner. Some of the captives joined the battle with weapons from the fallen.

The thought crossed Demetrius' mind to use the trumpet Uriel had given him. But surely it was a joke. Uriel wasn't an angel. And his trumpet would not alert any angels. Demetrius would look like a fool to his men. Like a weak leader who has given up and cried out for a miracle. In reality, the trumpet would only alert the other Tiberians to their location.

He pushed the thought out of his mind and cut down three attackers, one right after the other. He saw one of the Christian women hit by a Tiberian arrow. It fueled his rage. It brought back every memory of every innocent woman and child he had seen slain in the cities of this land.

Instead of defending his territory, he went on the offensive. He rushed up the hill and pushed his way through a gauntlet of a dozen warriors, slicing, hacking, pounding. He cut off limbs and blocked attacks with ease. He lost himself in the frenzy of vengeance. And he felt invincible.

He saw red. The red of his enemies' blood filling the hillside.

When he had run out of victims, he looked around for more.

Only then did he realize he was all the way up the hill and cut off from his men.

His fury had blinded him, had burned all his energy in a raging inferno that left him overcome with exhaustion. His muscles now trembled, spent. He could barely raise his sword. And he was surrounded by a dozen more Tiberians.

Demetrius dropped to his knees. "Lord, forgive me!" Resigning himself to his fate, he closed his eyes.

He heard the snap of a whip.

A metallic whip.

The whip sword Rahab.

He looked up. Uriel had stepped up next to him and was swinging Rahab in an arc of destruction. Within moments, the Tiberians were all dead, decapitated, disemboweled, or cut in half.

His chest heaving to regain his breath, Demetrius looked up to see that the battle was over, the Christians below were safe.

Lowering his whip sword, Uriel stood over Demetrius with a scolding look.

Demetrius fell to his back on the ground with relief. "That was impressive. I didn't even blow your trumpet."

"You are not out of miracles yet, Demetrius. But you have certainly tried my patience. You still glory in your strength instead of your weakness. And it almost killed you."

"I don't know what overcame me."

"You tasted the bitter root of vengeance. And arrogance."

"I thought it was justice."

"A common danger of righteous violence. It is a means of justice. But it leaves no man unscathed."

Demetrius looked away, ashamed. "I feel … stained by the darkness of my heart and the blood of my actions."

Uriel knelt down beside him. His stern look turned to grace. "You are forgiven by the blood of Christ."

Demetrius tried to believe that. But his own hypocrisy would not allow him. "My obsession has turned me into the very monster I fought. I have failed the Lord."

Uriel was now smiling. "You may not want to hear this, but actually, Yahweh prefers using failures. It's the only way to get you to the end of yourself. Why do you think he made me so small?"

Demetrius had no more words to say. Nothing more to offer. He was ready to be filled.

Uriel added, "God has a plan for you, Demetrius. It's time I explain it to you. It's time to return to Jerusalem."

In his mind, Demetrius thought the warrior was crazy. But in his heart, he knew it was a word from the Lord.

Demetrius felt confused. "What about our calling to the Christians of the land?"

"Your squad will do fine without you. You and I have a job to do." Uriel looked out on the men down the hill awaiting their command.

Demetrius sighed, still exhausted in the dirt. "Can you carry me to Jerusalem?"

Uriel looked back at him, and Demetrius smiled. The guardian smiled in return and said, "I once carried Noah—on my back, mind you—out of the lowest depths of Tartarus. I am never going to do anything like that again. But I will help you up from the ground."[7]

"About our angel jokes," said Demetrius. "I think we have taken the jest a bit too far."

Uriel smiled. "That is something else I need to explain. But we'll have plenty of time on the road to Jerusalem."

CHAPTER 30

Rome
August, AD 66

The three Flavians—Vespasian, Titus, and Domitian—walked through the atrium of Nero's Golden House. As they approached the huge bronze Colossus, Titus stopped to look up at it. Vespasian and Domitian joined him at the base of the hundred-and-twenty-foot-tall statue of Nero incarnate as the sun god Sol. It was massive and stupendously egomaniacal.

Titus said, "He should be Pluto." Pluto was the hated dark lord of the underworld. Titus turned to his father. "This will be the first thing I tear down under Flavian rule."

Vespasian said, "Curb your ambition, my son. I seek a long life in obscure retirement, not a short life at the blade of an executioner."

Titus sighed with gritted teeth. He so despised Nero, the little piss-haired and pimply miscreant. "He is perverted in his personal behavior and lawless in his public reign."

Domitian, Vespasian's younger son, said, "Beware the sting of thine own standard, dear brother."

Titus looked angrily at Domitian. His younger brother was only fifteen years old, but had already displayed a penchant for cunning and cruelty. Unfortunately, in this case he was also right. Titus had engaged in much revelry and riotous living with his friends, catamites, and other notorious rabble-rousers. His father had pressed him to straighten up, and he knew the clarion call was coming soon for him. If Titus wanted to advance his status, if he wanted to gain the fear and respect required to be a good leader, he would have to start acting more responsibly. He would do so very soon.[1]

Domitian added to his sting, "Not to mention, we are still under the shadow of your wife's familial connection to the Pisonian conspirators."

"That is why I divorced her, *dear brother*," said Titus. "And Nero assigned me questorship right afterward. Your intimations of suspicion are unwarranted."[2]

"Nevertheless," said Vespasian, "you know how fickle Nero can be. We must be careful to sever connections to all *potential* suspicions."

Domitian said with a snide look, "Especially personal grievances of the past."

Titus knew what Domitian was implying. Titus had complained too often to his younger brother about Nero's assassination of Titus' most beloved friend when he was fourteen years old.

"Britannicus was the rightful heir to the throne," said Titus. "Not this adopted usurper."

"Keep your voice down, son," growled Vespasian, "or you'll get us all executed for treason." The old man was right. "Let us get to the garden."

Though Claudius Caesar had adopted and chosen Nero as his successor, the blond little fiend nevertheless poisoned Britannicus two years into his own reign, to ensure that true Julian blood would not challenge Nero's imperial appointment. Titus had been at the feast where the poisoning had taken place, and had even unwittingly consumed a bit of the deadly drink, becoming deathly ill before recovering. Titus knew Britannicus did not suffer from epilepsy, as Nero claimed. His best friend and rightful heir to the throne had been assassinated. It was a deeply personal grievance that Titus would never forget, and it drove his obsession for the crown and for revenge. One day, Titus would ascend the throne and execute Nero for treason. He just wasn't sure in what order that might play out.[3]

As the three Flavians made their way through marble halls to the garden entrance, Domitian considered his own future. He wondered if it would be advantageous to his ambitions if he replicated Nero's act of familial betrayal upon his own arrogant older brother. The securing of power did require a certain sacrifice of loyalties. Titus was handsome, politically confident, and a rising military leader. But his weakness was his extravagance of risk and indulgence in both revelry and leadership. One day, Titus' excess would get him into trouble, and that would become Domitian's opportunity. In the meantime, Domitian would devote himself to his education to prepare himself to rule, keeping his own indulgences to a minimum.

They exited the structure and traversed the walkway to the royal garden, where Nero awaited them. The path was illuminated by hundreds of human torches, Christians hanging on poles, wrapped in tunics soaked in pitch and set afire.

Titus wrinkled his nose at the malodorous burning human flesh. "Repulsive," he grumbled. "How can Nero do such things to his own subjects?"

Domitian said, "The Great Fire still requires a scapegoat."

Titus said, "The Christians are virtually extinct. Soon he'll have no more left to blame."

Vespasian threw in, "He feeds the civil unrest instead of solving it."

Domitian looked up at the flaming charred corpses and snickered. "One thing I will say for these Nazarenes: They call themselves the 'light of the world,' and they have certainly lived up to that claim."

They entered the garden area where Nero was reclined at banquet, surrounded by the senatorial class and military leaders. Servants scrambled to pour wine and serve the participants from the large table piled high with pig, fowl, fruits and vegetables.

Titus saw an obese senator turn and vomit into a pail so that he could continue feasting without reserve.

"Vespasian!" came the annoying voice of the emperor. "Come here! I want you to meet my distinguished guest."

The three Flavians approached the head table and saluted Nero.

Vespasian said, "My lord and savior."

Titus noticed two syphilitic sores on the emperor's lips. A fitting metaphor of the debauched reality tainting his boyish features and charm. He was only twenty-nine years of age, two years older than Titus. On Nero's right sat the freedman Pythagoras, the muscular male spouse the emperor had married against all advice. Titus had to sit through that foolish celebration just a year ago.

On Nero's left was his newly married spouse, Sporus, an effeminate male whose facial features reminded Nero of his beloved dead wife Poppaea

Sabina, the one the emperor had kicked to death that same year. Nero was so emotionally taken by the familiarity of Sporus' looks that he had castrated the youth, decked him out in the finery of an empress, used make-up on his face to increase the likeness, changed his name to Sabina, and married him in full ceremony. He was a boy transformed into a woman in the delusions of a depraved emperor. Titus could see Sporus was inebriated, as he always seemed to be. He too sported a canker sore on his lips. No doubt that was not the only location on his body marked by the sexual infection.[4]

So Nero was flanked by two spouses, one who played the man to the emperor's woman and the other who played the woman to the emperor's man. The beast fancied himself quite progressive in his unnatural lusts and defiance of the created order.

Titus' attention was arrested by a beautiful foreign princess who turned to see the newly arrived guests. She looked mature, in her thirties, with raven-black hair and pale skin. This was a woman whose beauty had increased with age, rather than lessened. And she appeared to be a Jew.

"Vespasian," said Nero, "this is Princess Julia Berenice of Judea. Sister of—what is his name again?"

"Herod Agrippa II, my lord." She sounded like an angel to Titus.

Nero continued, "Yes, well, anyway. This is Flavius Vespasian, my notorious and hated governor of Africa. Some say he is just and honorable, but I have my doubts."[5]

Nero smirked. Titus saw his father's face tighten. Ever since Vespasian had fallen asleep during Nero's lyre performance a while back, Nero would not stop insulting and taunting Vespasian. He had originally banished him, but the old general's experience and sound wisdom were sorely needed, so Nero had called him back. The taunting was Nero's way of keeping Vespasian humiliated and satisfying the emperor's hubris.[6]

Nero continued crowing, "I call him my 'muleteer' because he is known to be good with stubborn animals." Another jab at Vespasian's business of selling mules when he was in exile. "I may very well send him to quell your stubborn mules' uprising."[7]

Titus saw Berenice bow in deference to the emperor. Titus found himself staring at her. Nero's voice shook him out of his trance.

"Titus, his elder son and legate." Titus locked eyes with Berenice. "And Domitian, the youngest Flavian." She didn't move her look from Titus. He knew it was a look of desire. Everything faded away into the background of Titus' senses. He was overcome by lust. He could barely hear Caesar's words.

"Our loyal Jewess here was just telling me of yet another uprising in Judea by the more unsavory elements of her people. Predictable, of course." Nero turned from Vespasian back to Berenice. "Please, continue, princess."

Titus continued to study every physical detail of the woman and every verbal nuance as she pleaded with Nero.

"My lord, Caesar, Procurator Florus has sent a messenger who will arrive shortly and try to deceive you about his part in the instigation of the revolt. It is not against you that the people are protesting. It is against the cruelty of Florus. You just need affirm them of your concern and they will submit. I am sure of it."

Nero contemplated her story with curiosity. When she finished, he sat in silence for a moment. Then he asked, "Is it true that the daily sacrifice on my behalf has ceased in your temple?"

Berenice was noticeably downcast. "Yes, my lord. But only because a fanatic has taken control of the temple. That will change."

Nero said, "Are the Jewish aristocracy and the priesthood still in support of my throne?"

She became enthusiastic. "Yes, my lord."

"And who do you say is to blame for this insurrection?"

She nodded nervously. "Gessius Florus."

Titus felt every muscle in his body want to hold her, to caress her. To ravage her.

Nero called out behind him, "Florus!"

Titus saw Berenice's eyes go wide with fear as Gessius Florus stepped out from behind a pillar and made his way to Nero's side.

"Yes, my lord and savior," said Florus. His sly look at Berenice made Titus want to jump up and wring his neck.

Nero said, "I owe you a hundred denarii. She *did* blame you."

Florus said, "Bless you, my lord."

Nero's smirk displayed his delight in causing pain and misery in others. He said to Florus, "You may leave us, procurator. I need to finish this."

Florus bowed and made his way out of the banquet hall.

Nero stared into the distance, considering his options. Then he looked around him at the mindless gaiety and gluttonous consumption.

He gestured to the group of Flavians and Berenice. "Let us speak in private. Follow me."

Leaning over, Nero kissed Sporus, then Pythagoras. "Come along, my loves."

He walked between his two "spouses," holding their hands. Berenice walked behind him, followed by the three Flavians.

Watching the Jewess sway with eloquent poise as she walked into the palace enflamed Titus' lust. He wanted her more with each passing moment.

There were three other princes who followed the emperor's walk. But they were not earthly princes. They were the spiritual principalities of Rome, the geniuses over Nero, Vespasian, and Titus. They were Apollyon, Azazel, and Semyaza. Each of them stayed close to their wards and whispered their influences.

The group approached one of Nero's private chambers deep in the palace. As the Roman emperor opened the doors, Berenice shuddered with a gasp.

Inside were two women and a man tied up to posts, completely naked and blindfolded.

Nero responded to the princess. "Don't worry, they're only Christians. This is my most private of chambers. No one will hear our words in here. Not even if we screamed."

Nero's comment and diabolical grin was an ominous hint of the purpose to which he put this chamber.

The interior was muffled for sound by wooden walls and ceiling. Various bloodied instruments of torture hung on the walls. There were swords, axes, and pikes as well as bizarre utensils and mechanical devices Titus had never seen before. The granite floor showed stains of blood that flowed down into a drain at the center of the room near the trussed-up victims.

Pythagoras closed the doors behind them. Titus hoped that Nero's dark intent was not for this beautiful Jewess.

Or maybe this would be the Flavian moment to overthrow the tyrant. Pythagoras would be the only impediment, but Titus was enough of a warrior to handle such obstacles.

Titus saw Domitian lick his lips, examining the naked victims on the poles. Then his younger brother approached the blindfolded male, tickling his underarm. The male squirmed. Domitian smiled at Nero, who said, "Now there is someone who has a sense of humor."

Berenice shivered with fear. Who was this monster before whom she was begging for mercy? She wanted to get out of this terrifying place, get away from this creature and his grotesque depravity. The thought occurred to her that she might become one of these poor victims. She took a futile step backward. She looked at Titus, who was still staring at her, hunger in his eyes. But what kind of hunger?

Nero drew everyone's attention as he spoke. "Vespasian, I want you to handle this fiasco in the east. First on your itinerary, have Florus executed. But I want you to wait until you get to Caesarea to do so. I want a swift and public replacement. Placate the Jews to quell the revolt."[8]

Berenice's immediate shock was replaced with a wave of relief. This imp of a god could destroy whole nations on a single capricious whim, but he could also save them as well. Truly, God's providence was watching over his people.

Nero continued, "I also want you and Titus to prepare four legions for departure to Judea. Destroy Jerusalem entirely. Take them by surprise. It is time we remind these stubborn mules who their master is."

Berenice found herself blurting out, "But, my lord."

Nero jerked a look at her. Another shiver chilled her to the bone. His eyes were reptilian, soulless—dragonlike.

She pushed through her fear with trembling voice. "Florus is the cancer. With the disease cut out, the patient can heal."

"Florus is not the cancer," said Nero. "He is merely a carrion bird circling the carcass."

Berenice felt her face flush with fear.

Titus moved to her defense. "Caesar, should not the Senate be consulted before such a large undertaking? The financial commitment will surely tax the imperial treasury, which is already in jeopardy."

Nero did not even look at Titus. He spoke to Vespasian. "So who exactly is general here?" He snapped his fingers as if to waken Vespasian from slumber. "Or have you fallen asleep on me again, my bored and overfed muleteer?"

Vespasian cleared his throat. "I am saving my nap for later, my Caesar." He patted his stomach. "After I return to your banquet and fill my fat belly with some of your fine beer."

Nero grinned.

Titus knew his father had no respect for this pompous man-child and was about the only person in the empire who wasn't afraid of Nero's juvenile outbreaks. Titus thought his father's lowly social etiquette gave him an advantage with the emperor because it made Nero feel superior and therefore godlike in his tolerance. The emperor knew that this uncouth and unsophisticated warrior would never rise to threaten Nero's own authority and power. He knew that the old general just wanted to retire away from it all. So he used Vespasian for his wisdom of experience.

And Vespasian used his own apparent ignorance to his benefit.

Vespasian continued, "But with all due respect, I believe Titus makes a valid point. What you are asking for is not unreasonable, but it may well escalate a police action into a war."

Nero said, "The Jews are already at war."

Berenice said, "It is a civil war, my Caesar. We war amongst ourselves."

Nero considered her words. "Doing little or nothing will only give the rebels confidence in their seditious provocation."

Titus saw Berenice look to the floor in silence.

Semyaza whispered into Vespasian's ear, and the old general spoke. "There may be a way to assert your authority without opening Pandora's box of unwanted consequences. Cestius Gallus is the legate of Syria, north of Israel. He has already operated as a mediator for Florus' irresponsible antics. If you send him to show a display of force in the capital city, Jerusalem, I believe you will have your chastisement without outright war, which will save the imperial treasury the burden of a full campaign."[9]

Nero considered the general's advice.

Titus again noticed Berenice watching the emperor with nervous hope.

Nero said, "Is this another one of your lazy attempts to avoid hard work, so you can drink your beer in unmolested peace?"

Vespasian shrugged. "Either way, my lord, I will drink beer."

Nero shared his smile. "My Vespasian, you overcome your uncouthness yet again. Under that vulgar exterior is a cunning strategist."

Vespasian gave another shrug and a smile.

It was certainly no secret that beneath that "vulgar exterior" and jest the old general just wanted to retire back in Egypt with his mistress to eat good food, drink good drink, and be done with the pain of government and politics.

Nero said, "I will send Cestius."

Everyone breathed a sigh of relief.

The three great shadow beings knew they had prevented catastrophe. Without the captured principalities, Apollyon's spiritual force was not strong enough for the total desolation he had planned for Jerusalem.

"But if it gets out of control," added the emperor, "be prepared to guzzle your beer in the desert of Palestine."

Nero turned to Berenice. "And my loyal Jewess, you may bring the dispatch to Cestius on your return."

"Yes, my lord."

"Oh, and tell your brother, what's his name again?"

"Agrippa, my lord."

"Yes, Agrippa. Tell my little Herodian harlot Agrippa to join his forces with Cestius. We need a show of support from the ruling class."

Berenice bowed. "Yes, my emperor. I will relay your command."

Her stomach sank. Any deviance from full obedience to imperial orders would insure her execution, yet the dispatch she was delivering ensured infliction of judgment upon her people.

Nero moved over to the wall where animal skins hung from hooks. He passed by a leopard skin, a bear skin, and lastly a lion skin, which he pulled off its hook. He draped it over himself with the animal's head on top of his own, its mouth pried open with bared fangs. He looked like one of the barbarians on the frontier.

Nero dismissed his companions with a wave of his hand. "Enjoy the banquet."

The Flavians escorted Berenice out of the chamber and made their way back to the garden.

Titus stopped and looked back through the door, still open behind them.

He saw Nero get on all fours, acting like the feline draped over him. He roared like a lion and crawled toward the quivering, blindfolded victims.

He chose the male Christian first.

Titus saw Nero attack the poor soul's private region with his mouth. But it wasn't a sexual assault. The Christian screamed in agony as Nero used his teeth to tear like a ravaging beast.[10]

Titus turned away in disgust as Pythagoras closed the door behind him.

Yes, Nero was indeed a beast. A beast that must one day be slaughtered.[11]

Apollyon reveled in his control of that beast as he, Azazel, and Semyaza followed their human wards back out to the feast.

Apollyon said, "Well done, both of you. The delay will give me the time I need to re-install my captured princes."

Semyaza said, "Will Cestius be able to quench the revolt without full imperial force?"

Apollyon smiled. "He will only make it worse. But now is your time to shine, Azazel."

"What do you mean?" complained Azazel. "My specialty is war. You just delayed it."

"I seem to remember that the primeval secrets you revealed to mankind were not merely the implements of war, but the arts of seduction. Considering the current situation, you may accomplish as much through the latter as you do the former."[12]

Azazel now knew his next task. He hurried after his ward Titus as Semyaza kept up with Vespasian.

Apollyon smirked and turned back to bathe in the perversion of his own human pet back in the torture room.

CHAPTER 31

Vespasian took a deep chug of beer and belched. "Ah, more room for food," he said. He picked up a piece of roasted pig from the table before him and listened to the minstrels play their music in the garden banquet.

Domitian watched the dancers, trying to decide which ones he would take for his pleasure this evening.

Titus eyed Berenice beside him. She was not eating.

"Is something wrong, princess?"

"What I just heard in that dungeon has ruined my appetite."

Titus knew she was referring to the impending doom on Jerusalem, not the torture of hapless Christians.

He said, "Let us go for a walk. Have you seen Nero's Pool?"

"No."

"It's a short distance. We can get some fresh air."

She glanced at the smoldering remains of the human torches around the perimeter of the garden. "The stink of death is rather suffocating."

They arrived at the shore of the manmade lake. Berenice saw a large boat anchored in the middle of the water, dark and unattended.

Titus said, "The emperor holds parties on the pool."

"Spare me the gruesome details," she said.

He smiled and held out a bottle of wine with two chalices. He gave her one of the chalices and filled them both.

They sipped the wine and walked casually along the shoreline.

"Have you seen the city?" Titus asked.

"Some. The Forum was magnificent. The architecture of your temples was grand and impressive. I almost wanted to become a Roman."

"Many Jews have," he said. "One does not have to give up national loyalty or one's gods to do so."

Berenice said wryly, "We only have to add Caesar to the head of our pantheon."

Titus smiled. He knew such demands were considered treason to their jealous god, who tolerated no rivals.

The Jewish princess lured him in. "I need to return to my people. They need a voice that speaks for Rome to stop the revolt."

"Tell me about your world," Titus said. "Your people, your holy city."

She raised her brow with suspicion.

He said, "You may doubt my sincerity, but I believe mutual understanding is the hallmark of true political progress."

She said, "If only Caesar shared your sentiments."

He said, "My father shares them. And Nero will not be on the throne forever."

Berenice looked up at him, searching his eyes for what he implied.

"A conspiracy?" she asked.

"No. A well-known Sibylline prophecy has predicted that the Julio-Claudian line of Caesars will end with the mother-slayer, Nero. And I assure you, the Flavian line is preparing for its fulfillment."[1]

Titus immediately knew he revealed too much. This woman had that effect on him. He wanted to tell her his secrets. But he knew he should not.

She asked, "Do you not also have prophecies of a ruler that shall arise in the east?"

He said, "Some believe so. Others do not."[2]

She said, "Our prophets have predicted that a Son of David from the land of Judea shall be that ruler of the nations."[3]

Titus said, "My father is charged with oversight of the Palestinian problem. He will literally be a ruler over the east and has not the capricious temperament of Nero. Perhaps you should thank the Roman gods for such fortune."

Berenice thought for a moment, then said, "Every nation has their gods. Behind the earthly powers of man are the heavenly principalities and powers, their allotted inheritance. So Yahweh called out our father Abraham from Ur of the Chaldees to establish his offspring as God's chosen people. The children of Abraham, Isaac, and Jacob are Yahweh's allotted inheritance. But the gods of the nations have not ruled justly. Yahweh shall judge all the earth and in time inherit the nations. But for now, he chastises his people."[4]

Titus said, "I confess, I do not comprehend the Jewish mind. You are so confident that you are superior to the rest of the world, yet you are quite inferior in terms of actual power."

"And I do not comprehend the Roman mind," Berenice said. "You consider yourselves superior to conquered nations, yet you rot within from debauched moral excess."

Titus asked, "And what of the rot of civil strife and religious factions? Wars and rumors of wars in Palestine threaten to undo the worldwide peace of Pax Romana."

She said, "Does that not argue for better diplomatic ties between our two great cities? If Rome could but see Jerusalem as a woman to woo, rather than as a harlot to ravish. You might find a romance has more long-term benefits than a rape."

He knew she meant so much more than what she was saying.

"Indeed it does," he answered. "But Jerusalem must know its place and submit."

Berenice said, "A weak and docile slave pleases little. A strong yet submissive client king rewards much."

Titus stopped her and looked into her eyes. "If you can promise me the loyalty of the Jewish ruling class, I will open to you the royal treasures of imperial Rome."

Berenice's eyes teared up with passion. She could not believe that she now stood the real chance of achieving the highest of aspirations that she could ever dream of, the chance to become mistress within a powerful family that could one day become the ruling dynasty of Rome. She dared not indulge for too long the hope of where such favor could lead: becoming an empress.

She said with a quivering voice. "I do promise you with all my heart, soul, and body."

Titus threw the bottle and his cup to the ground. He hit the cup out of her hand. It went flying.

He grabbed Berenice and kissed her, aggressively, deeply.

She yielded to him, felt dangerously overcome by his strength.

Would he hurt her? She didn't care.

"Ravish me," she demanded.

He stopped as if angered by her boldness.

But he smiled, then said firmly, "You will do exactly as I say."

She shivered. She could say nothing but release a gasp of ecstasy.

And the princess of Israel surrendered to the pagan's brute force and power right on the shores of Nero's wicked Pool.[5]

Azazel, pleased with his accomplishment, stood back from the two humans to allow the seduction to take its natural course. This single romantic entanglement would benefit the Master's plan more than all the internal political traitors in Israel.

More importantly, it would benefit Azazel's secret ambition.

CHAPTER 32

Jerusalem
October, AD 66

Demetrius entered the Essene Gate in the Southern Hinnom valley. It led him directly to the Essene Quarter where many of the Christians lived. Uriel had accompanied him all the way back to Jerusalem from Galilee, but had left his side before arriving at the walls of the city. The guardian had told Demetrius much on their journey. So much that Demetrius now understood his calling with a clarity he had never before experienced. It had changed him forever.

He was going to visit the home of the elder, Boaz. He had to tell the Christians. He had to try one more time to persuade them to heed the warnings of the Apocalypse, the warnings of Christ. But first, he would find the only man he trusted in the city.

"They are in the temple prison," said a somber Joshua, the white-haired prophet whom Demetrius had saved from a beating several months ago. His broken jaw had healed. He was answering Demetrius' question as to the whereabouts of Severus, Alexander, and Cassandra.

Demetrius had found Joshua outside the temple, preaching his message once again with renewed vigor. The Egyptian had often wondered how the old man found the courage and strength to continue this dangerous and exhausting ministry. He now understood.

They were on their way through the streets to Boaz's home. But Demetrius had stopped. This revelation would change his plans.

"How did that happen?"

"They were betrayed by some Jews and that serpent Jacob bar Mordecai."

"I remember that Judaizer," said Demetrius. Jacob had the ear of elder Boaz and others like some kind of whispering demon.

"Then why do you want to return to Boaz's congregation?"

"Why do you return to the temple to preach?"

Joshua acknowledged his point.

Demetrius explained it anyway. "You said yourself that the church of Jerusalem is still divided over the Apocalypse. But they remain united in staying put because a split could devastate them. Boaz is the most influential of the elders. If I can persuade him, we may turn the tide against the Judaizers and get the Christians to leave the city before the Roman armies arrive."

He saw Joshua's gaze turn downward in thought.

"What is wrong, Joshua?"

Joshua looked up. "Your zeal has convicted me, my brother. I have preached judgment for so long that I have lost sight of the hope of the gospel."

Demetrius placed his hand on his elder's shoulder. "Don't credit me, my friend. Assign it to angelic intervention."

Joshua tilted his head in curiosity. Did he know Demetrius' secret? Did he know about Uriel? That he really was an angel? That Uriel had revealed to Demetrius his true calling? No, the old prophet couldn't possibly know.

Joshua said, "I see in you an anointing."

Demetrius would not confirm or deny it.

"You and I would make a good team. You should join me." Joshua had an impish gleam in his eye. "I can assure you a ministry of suffering that builds great character."

Demetrius smiled knowingly. "Right now, my interest is to rescue my friends from suffering in prison. I need some help."

"I am too old for a prison break. And you do not want to go to Boaz to get your help. There will be those who will betray you. Come. I know where there are like-minded believers."

· · · · ·

Caesarea Maritima

Berenice and Agrippa looked out upon the burning mounds outside the port city. Berenice wept as her brother held her to keep her from crumbling to the ground. They were not hills of earth, but hills of the corpses of Jews massacred by the Greeks of the city at the behest of Procurator Florus. Twenty thousand of them.[1] The entire population of her people at Caesarea. Now smoldering remains. Holocaust. Carrion birds feeding on the flesh. Berenice gagged at the stench. Vomit rose in her throat.

It was doubly insulting that they were not allowed to be buried according to their religious customs. Florus had descended into a demonic lawlessness, completely unconcerned with the consequences of his actions. Berenice wondered what Florus' plans were for the Herods. She prayed that he would be replaced before it was too late.

Agrippa pulled her back to their carriage, guarded by legionaries. He said sternly to the pole carriers, "I want a smooth trip back to the palace. The princess is not feeling well. Do you understand?"

They nodded obediently. The two Herods got inside, and they returned to the city.

As they made their way back to the governor's palace, the two Herodian siblings looked out onto the streets of citizens going about their business, some fixing buildings vandalized in the riots, others engaging in their daily routine.

Agrippa said, "Look at these Greek swine. They live their days as if nothing happened. As if butchering Jews was a normal part of life."

"Brother, please. I'm already frightened for our safety. You are making it worse." Staring faces in the street sent a chill through Berenice.

"Sister, Titus has lent us a Praetorian bodyguard, thanks to your— 'special relationship' with him. These plebians wouldn't dare assault an imperial unit."

She glared at him. "My 'special relationship' will secure your kingship of Judea when this is all over."

He smirked. "Only the word of an empress can persuade Caesar in such matters."

She couldn't hide anything from him. They knew each other, heart, body, and soul. He knew her secret intentions because they matched his own. Herods would do anything to achieve their goals. *Anything.* But still, she enjoyed the power over him that his jealousy gave her.

"An empress could achieve for the house of Herod what even Herod the Great could not."

"So long as she does not forget from whence she came. And who loves her more than anyone else possibly can."

She smirked in control. "The love of family is the highest love of all, dear brother."

The carriage stopped. It was lowered gently to the ground. A voice from outside said, "My lord, Agrippa. We have arrived."

Berenice stood with Agrippa, Florus, and Cestius in the war council of the governor's palace. Antiochus IV of Commagene and Sohaemus of Emesa represented the client kings of additional auxiliary units.

Berenice could see in Florus' eyes a perverted mixture of contempt and lust for her. She could imagine what he would like to do to her if he got her alone. And it would not be pleasant for her.

Cestius was an old general in his late sixties, but with much vigor for his age.[2] He reminded Berenice of Vespasian, but without the vulgarity. Cestius was a no-nonsense, falcon-like warrior. A man of war with little patience for Florus because of the latter's excess and intemperance.

And the general did not approve of the mass murder of Jews.

Cestius was also commander of this campaign. He summarized to the five others who were there, "My Legion XII Fulminata is securing the Galilee region. My main force has neutralized Joppa and Narbatene. When they return to Caesarea, it is time to march on Jerusalem."[3]

Florus snarled, "Time to end this revolt of monkeys and pigs."

Berenice noticed that Cestius did not react with his usual disgust at Florus. He ignored him. "On the way, we will conquer the towns of Antipatris, Lydda, and Beth-Horon."

Agrippa asked, "How long before we make it to the walls of Jerusalem?"

"Several weeks."

Florus said, "Perhaps Agrippa should recuse his forces from this coalition." He gave another vile look at Berenice. "We know how duplicitous Jews can be when it comes to fighting their own."

Berenice felt hatred well up inside her. Agrippa had committed a couple thousand Herodian guards to the campaign. They had no problem with fighting their own rebels because these jeopardized the future of the entire nation.

Cestius finally took notice of Florus. "How do you recommend they be replaced?"

Florus said, "With my own forces, of course."

Cestius' face turned oddly curious. "What forces?"

Florus looked perturbed. "I have several thousand at my command."

"No, you don't," said Cestius.

"What are you talking about?"

"You have no forces at your command because you are not governor of Judea anymore."

Florus' face went white.

Cestius nodded to his guards. Several grabbed Florus from behind.

Cestius said, "Gessius Florus, by the imperial command of Nero Caesar, you are under arrest and are hereby relieved of your governorship."

Florus struggled vainly in the grip of the soldiers. "This cannot be! I have the ear of the emperor! My wife was friend of the empress!"

Berenice could not contain herself. She spoke out with relish, "The empress Poppea is long dead."

Cestius pulled out a scroll from his tunic and opened it for Florus' view. It was the imperial decree under seal. "You are to be executed for inciting this war through gross criminal negligence."

For the first time, Berenice saw Florus speechless. For the first time in his reign of terror, Berenice felt that there might be a moment of justice. This filthy Roman pig would finally pay for everything he had done to cause this coming war.

The soldiers dragged Florus away to jail.

Cestius turned back to the council and asked as if nothing had happened, "Now, where were we?"

· · · · ·

The entire city had gathered to the square outside the governor's palace. A thousand legionary forces stood in form before the porch of the palace. Berenice stood with Agrippa and the others of the war council on the balcony overlooking the crowds. Cestius raised his hands, and the crowd quieted down.

"People of Caesarea Maritima! Your actions of violence in this city have vexed the emperor and jeopardized the peace of Rome!"

The crowd looked around nervously at the soldiers who lined the perimeter. They were not allowed to leave the premises.

"But Nero Caesar, your lord and savior, is a gracious and patient god. He realizes that you were instigated and provoked by your procurator!"

Shouts of angry agreement peppered the crowd.

"So Caesar has decided to be lenient with you." More cheers.

"He has decided to visit his right arm of justice upon the source of this conflict, governor Gessius Florus!"

The mob went wildly enthusiastic with the shift of blame.

Berenice felt a surge of excitement fill her body as a unit of soldiers led Florus out onto the square and up to a gallows in front of the palace. Legionaries pushed back the roused citizens surrounding the tall platform.

Tall for all to see.

She and Agrippa exchanged a knowing smile as Florus mounted the steps.

The crowd cheered on.

The noose was placed around his neck.

As a Roman citizen, Florus had a right to be decapitated by sword. But with such flagrant irresponsibility that Florus had displayed, Caesar wanted to make a point by dishonoring the governor. Hanging was an ignoble end in the eyes of the public.

The eyes of Berenice filled with tears of revenge as Florus' body was hoisted into the air.

He was almost eye level with Berenice and the others standing on the balcony.

She could see the terrified look in his eyes as his body jerked and shook, trying to survive. Gasping for air. Choking to death.

A minute passed. Florus moved no more.

He was dead. Finally dead.[4]

But Berenice suddenly felt let down. This execution, just though it was in stopping Florus' reign of terror, became suddenly unjust, anti-climactic compared to how much evil he had perpetrated. This monster who had tortured and murdered so many Jews, thousands of them. This monster who had brought the iron teeth of Rome down upon her people. And all he had to suffer was a few seconds of fear and strangling? She filled with despair. There had to be a final judgment in the afterlife, or this was all a cruel joke. The amount of suffering that Florus experienced in this life could never be justice for the amount of suffering he had caused others. There had better be a Lake of Fire as the prophets proclaimed, or Yahweh was a worthless deity in a universe of injustice.

For one brief moment, Berenice felt the sting of her own thoughts. *What do I deserve in the afterlife?*

CHAPTER 33

Jerusalem

Demetrius led his team of five Christians disguised in Herodian guard uniforms down the stone-lined stairwell and into the prison area below the temple mount. They had confiscated the uniforms through some Christian women who were servant launderers at the Herodian palace. Now that hostility with Rome had begun, they could not disguise themselves as legionaries. And they could not dress as temple guards because they would not be recognized by the other temple guards they would soon face. Their only option was to impersonate Herodian guards. Herodians were despised by the temple unit because of their connection to Herod, but respected for their authority nevertheless. The move was risky because the Herods had left the city in the midst of controversy. But their palace and guard remained a stronghold for their return.

The soldiers followed Demetrius, disguised as a captain, in orderly lockstep, having been briefed by him in a quick lesson on soldierly behavior. Only one of them had any real battle experience. Thank God this mission was a ruse, not a strike force.

Demetrius stopped at the locked door to the hallway of cells, guarded by two Jewish sentries and a sitting sergeant of the temple guard. The sergeant, a bitter-looking soul who did not appear to want to be there, rose and half-heartedly saluted Demetrius.

Thank you, Jesus, thought Demetrius. A malcontent who sought minimal effort in his job would not bother to look closely at the details before him.

Demetrius settled his expression into a mean, silent frown as if he was a no-nonsense officer who didn't care for small talk. He held out a sealed scroll and said, "Orders from Herod Agrippa. I am to retrieve said prisoners for transfer to Caesarea Maritima."

The sergeant looked at the seal. One of the Christians had counterfeited it from purloined materials provided by palace servants. Okay, that was stealing, and this was lying. But this was also like Rahab protecting the Israelite spies, so it didn't bother the Christian's conscience in the least.

Nevertheless, if they were discovered, they would all be executed for their espionage.

The sergeant opened the scroll. He seemed curious as he read through the list of names. "I know one of these is a doctor. I guess the wounded captives are going to have to ask for healing miracles now." He handed the scroll back to Demetrius with a smirk.

Snapping it out of his hand, Demetrius demanded, "Who taught you to speak cavalierly to a superior rank?"

The sergeant's eyes showed shock and fear. "Forgive me, sir." He nodded to the temple guards. They opened the door, gave keys to Demetrius, and let the unit of six men through.

The door slammed shut behind them, and Demetrius heard the strong metal bolt lock tight. They weren't out of the woods yet.

The fake guard unit approached the cells, looking for their comrades.

They found them in a cell of about twenty. Demetrius noticed Cassandra first. Her beautiful visage had wilted with lack of food and sunlight. Demetrius' heart felt stabbed.

He clanged the door with a baton.

Everyone looked up. Cassandra's face brightened when she recognized him.

Demetrius held up the scroll, pretending to read out names of unknown prisoners. "Cassandra Laetorius, Lucius Aurelius Severus, and Alexander Maccabaeus. Step forward."

The three of them stood, obviously now aware of the ruse.

"You are being transferred to Caesarea Maritima."

Demetrius waved them out. He could see their faces bright with hope, trying not to give themselves away. Cassandra had a slight smile on her lips.

He locked the door behind them. For a touch of added realism, he said, "Do as you are told and you won't be beaten."

He rapped on the dungeon entrance door. The bolt slid back, and the door opened.

Demetrius froze. Before them stood a contingent of about twenty temple guards armed to the teeth with weapons drawn. Sergeant Malcontent stood snickering with diabolical glee at Demetrius.

He said, "Apparently, you did not know that Herod is in Antioch—*Christian*."

If Demetrius had his Kharabu warriors with him, they might actually take down this group of guards. But he did not have his Kharabu warriors with him.

He and his impersonators handed over their weapons.

Alexander sat listening to Demetrius as he explained to Cassandra, Severus, and the other prisoners what he had seen in Galilee. He and his five "soldiers" had been stripped of their stolen uniforms, now replaced by ragged tunics and robes. Everything Demetrius was telling the group expanded upon the earlier intelligence they had heard from other prisoners.

As Demetrius told the story of the battle of Tiberias, Alexander noticed that the Egyptian seemed different. He was not as strident as he had been. He no longer made his own accomplishments the central focus of his stories. He was admitting his faults and weaknesses. He appeared … humbled.

When they were returned to their cell, Cassandra had hugged Demetrius, her long-time friend, with a clinging vigor. Now she listened to him with wide, attentive eyes.

Demetrius' voice was breaking as he teared up. "There were so many dead. So many. Piles of corpses. Thousands of them. Murdered at the hands of their fellow citizens. Blood filled the streets. Everywhere. It's demonic. And yet, it is only the beginning of the end."

Cassandra put her hand on his shoulder in comfort. Alexander could see her eyes were wet with sympathy. He felt horrible that in this moment when he should be feeling the suffering of his fellow believers, he was becoming tainted with jealousy again. He tried to put it out of his mind. He said, "How many Christians have you saved?"

Demetrius answered, "What few hundreds there were in the towns have received the Revelation favorably and left. I have saved no one. It is by the grace of God alone—and his angels." He paused, looking into the distance.

Alexander was moved. He had heard Demetrius use such words in the past. But never like this. The Egyptian evangelist would often begin his stories of great successes with "by the grace of God," then proceed to flatter himself with the work God had done through him. But he could tell that now Demetrius truly meant what he said. He took no credit. And the reference to angels did not sound like a casual reference. Alexander wondered if Demetrius had actually seen angels.

Demetrius said, "My bodyguard Uriel saved me more than once. If it were not for him, I would not be alive." He concluded with an ominous tone, "The abomination of desolation is coming. I have intelligence that legions from Syria are preparing to march on Jerusalem."

Severus said, "Then none of us will be alive very long. We must escape. We must convince the Remnant in the city to flee."

"We must pray," said Demetrius, "It is in God's hands now."

There it was again. That humility of faith Alexander had not seen in Demetrius before. This man, who had been blessed with so many gifts, was admitting helplessness and total surrender to Yahweh.

"Why did you come back?" asked Alexander. He felt badly the moment he spoke. Surely, his jealousy was evident in his question.

Demetrius said, "I have a new calling from Yahweh."

His words that would normally be fused with self-importance sounded more like a death sentence. The Egyptian wasn't glorying in his statement.

"What calling?" asked Alexander.

"It's not important right now. What's important is that we pray for the city and the 144,000 within."

"He's right," said Cassandra. "God's word does not return to him void. Somehow, some way, Yahweh will rescue his Remnant in the city. They are sealed on their foreheads with the name of the Father and the Son. He will not forget them."

As they prayed, the others in the cell joined in. Twenty of them. Alexander thought back to the time he had spent with the apostle John on Patmos. John had explained so much of the Apocalypse to the four of them in that little cave—Alexander, Cassandra, Demetrius, and Severus. The words of the apocalypse haunted him now:

After this I saw four angels standing at the four corners of the land, holding back the four winds of the land, that no wind might blow on land or sea or against any tree. Then I saw

another angel ascending from the rising of the sun, with the
seal of the living God, and he called with a loud voice to the
four angels who had been given power to harm land and sea,
saying, "Do not harm the land or the sea or the trees, until we
have sealed the servants of our God on their foreheads." And I
heard the number of the sealed, 144,000, sealed from every
tribe of the sons of Israel.
—*The Apocalypse of Jesus Christ 7:1–4*

The final wrath upon the Land would not begin until the 144,000 were sealed and protected. Until they were taken out of Mount Zion. The number 144,000 was obviously symbolic. The twelve tribes of the old covenant multiplied by twelve apostles of the new covenant multiplied by the number of quantitative completion—one thousand—equaled the symbolic number of the Remnant in the Land. That Remnant was the true twelve tribes of Israel who embraced Jesus as Messiah when the rest of the nation rejected him. At Pentecost, shortly after the ascension of Christ, the baptism of the Holy Spirit had begun. Jews from all over the world, those of the twelve tribes who had been scattered in the Diaspora, had come to Jerusalem and were drawn into the kingdom of God. Yahweh's promise to bring the scattered tribes of his people back into the Land, to fill them with his Spirit, and put his Torah on their hearts was being fulfilled in the new covenant gospel.[1]

In the Apocalypse, John had contrasted the Beast of Satan with the Lamb of God and the people of that Beast against the people of God.[2] The people of the Beast received his mark of ownership in the Imperial cult: 666, the number of Nero Caesar. The people of the Lamb received God's mark of ownership on their foreheads, the seal of Father and Son. The children of the Roman Beast were spiritually fornicating with the Great Harlot of apostate Jerusalem. The children of God were undefiled, spiritual virgins.[3] The Jewish believers in Israel represented the firstfruits of God and the Lamb because the gospel had gone first to the Jew and then to the Gentile.[4] But those firstfruits had now spread through all the empire to include Christians of all tribes and peoples and languages who would come out of the Great Tribulation.

Alexander's imagination drifted into the beautiful image in John's vision of that great multitude that no one could number standing before the throne and before the Lamb, washed clean in the blood of the Lamb, clothed in the white robes of holiness, holding palm branches and singing a new song, the new covenant, before the four living creatures and before the elders.[5] That multitude had grown out of the holy city of Jerusalem in the early church to fill the world and include the Gentiles through the gospel. In that gospel proclamation of the Christian Remnant of "holy ones," no lie was found, in contrast to the children of the Lie who worshipped the Father of lies.[6]

The apostle had prophesied in the Apocalypse that there were two harvests coming that marked the end of the age. The grain harvest followed by the grape harvest.[7] The grape harvest was the soon-approaching judgment upon the Land of Israel and upon Jerusalem. The winepress of God's wrath, symbolically portrayed as blood flowing to the horse's bridle through the entire length of the land of Israel: 1,600 stadia or 184 miles long.[8] But before that would be the grain harvest, a harvest of rescue.[9] These would be the Remnant, the 144,000, the wheat that would be winnowed from the chaff and gathered into the safety of the barn.[10] At least that is what John the baptizer had said and how John the apostle had further explained it. But now it was looking as though that rescue might not happen. Was he missing something in God's plan? Were they all missing something?

Demetrius and his "angels" were messengers who had helped deliver some of the Christian remnant throughout Galilee, Samaria, and Judea. But what of those in the city of Jerusalem? They remained stubborn and corrupted by the Judaizers, still clinging to the temple and its practices, the *stoichea* of the old covenant.[11] Did Yahweh's patience run out? Was such corruption a final apostasy? Nineveh repented and was spared. But Sodom and Gomorrah did not. In the days of Daniel, some of the righteous were taken away into exile with the wicked. Alexander thought, *Will we be among the innocents caught up as collateral damage in an otherwise just judgment of God?*

> Then I looked, and behold, a white cloud, and seated on the cloud one like a son of man, with a golden crown on his head, and a sharp sickle in his hand. And another angel came out of the temple, calling with a loud voice to him who sat on the cloud, "Put in your sickle, and reap, for the hour to reap has come, for the harvest of the land is fully ripe." So he who sat on the cloud swung his sickle across the land, and the land was reaped.

Then another angel came out of the temple in heaven, and he too had a sharp sickle....."Put in your sickle and gather the clusters from the vine of the land, for its grapes are ripe." So the angel swung his sickle across the land and gathered the grape harvest of the land and threw it into the great winepress of the wrath of God. And the winepress was trodden outside the city, and blood flowed from the winepress, as high as a horse's bridle, for 1,600 stadia.
—The Apocalypse of Jesus Christ 14:14–20

CHAPTER 34

After the imprisoned Christians had prayed, some lay down to sleep while others sat in silence, thinking somberly of their fate. Alexander found an opportunity to catch Cassandra alone at one end of the cell. He sat down next to her. He saw her respond with a smile to a look from Demetrius at the other end of the cell. He asked, "Did you ever imagine you two would cross paths again in the last days and the end of all things?"

Cassandra replied, "When we parted ways those years ago, I thought I would never see him again. I had given up all hope for the blessing of an earthly marriage."

"What did you think when you saw him again?"

She raised her brow in surprise. "How beautiful a thing we had shared in our youth. And yet … how very different we both had become." She paused. "Life changes you. Suffering changes you."

Alexander swallowed and mustered the courage to ask her the one question whose answer he dreaded. "Do you still love him?"

She jerked a look at him. He saw a kind of shock in her eyes. She looked away from him and sighed with frustration, shaking her head in dismay.

Shame came over him. She must have figured him out. She must now know his true feelings. He had been a fool. She was rejecting him.

Staring at the Egyptian, she said, "Demetrius is a handsome, godly man of many gifts and achievements."

Alexander grunted in agreement. That was what made the Egyptian so intimidating.

Cassandra paused thoughtfully before continuing, "But the truth is, God does not look upon the outward appearance of a man. And gifts come not from ourselves, but from God's grace."

Was she implying that was her view as well or merely the ideal?

"Demetrius is also a warrior of God."

Brian Godawa

A mighty one at that, Alexander thought. *No doubt God was probably going to include Demetrius in Scripture for his faithful exploits.*

"But I think God values men of compassion and healing as much, if not more."

I am a doctor, he thought. *A man of healing. But she's deliberately not saying that. She doesn't want to lead me on.*

"I think some men just don't see themselves as great as they really are."

She's thinking of Demetrius and his newfound humility as a virtue.

"They are missing out on what is right in front of them."

Alexander cleared his dry throat. "Maybe he loves you so much he is protecting you."

Cassandra huffed. Glared indignantly at him. What had he said to make her angry?

"It's too late for that, Alexander. We are all in this together."

He didn't know how to respond. So he asked, "Did you not say that Paul wrote that in view of the present distress it would be better not to marry?"[1] He never forgot a single word she ever said to him.

Cassandra rolled her eyes in frustration, got up, and stomped over to the cell door, grasping the bars as though she wanted to break out of there and run away.

Alexander felt like a donkey. The last thing in the world he would ever want to do was to make her angry or unhappy. The hardest thing in the world was giving up his desire for her to allow her the happiness she deserved with Demetrius. But for her to reject him as a friend …

He heard her mutter, *Men. Ah!*

But before he could figure out exactly what that meant, he heard the sound of the dungeon door open, followed by the footsteps of a unit of soldiers.

Cassandra backed away from the bars.

Alexander got up to stand protectively beside her.

Eleazar, the captain of the temple, arrived with his men. Alexander thought the captain had a dark, crazed look in his eyes. He wondered if he was possessed by a demon—or a Watcher. Eleazar announced to the hundreds of prisoners in the cells. "Cestius Gallus, the Roman governor of Syria, is on his way to Jerusalem with an army to crush us under the iron fist of Rome. The end is near. Some of you here are members of the Sicarii and other gangs who have fought amongst ourselves. But our differences are no longer pertinent.

Romans do not see a difference between Zealot, Sicarius, Galilean, or other. They only see Jews. And they will kill us all. If you will join us now and fight the Kittim by our side, I will release you."

His offer was met with mutterings of prisoners arguing their options. There weren't really any.

"Where is Samuel the Sicarius?" asked Eleazar.

A voice rang out, "Here I am." Samuel stepped forward from out of the crowd.

"Will you join us?"

Alexander knew that if the leader Samuel accepted, Eleazar would have the rest of the rebels on his side.

Samuel's response required little thought. "I will," he said.

The cell door opened. Other prisoners shouted out and joined them.

Samuel stepped up to the cell door. "Captain, I have one request."

"Speak."

"I am capable because of the healing help of one man. I request he and his comrades be allowed to go free as well."

"Who is he?"

Samuel turned and waved Alexander over to him. "Alexander Macabbaeus."

Samuel was the Sicarius whose broken arm Alexander had reset. The doctor walked over to him.

Eleazar looked him up and down, unimpressed. He waved his hand. "Very well." He turned back to the other prisoners. "The rest of you will muster in the Women's Court to receive weapons and instructions for defending the temple and the city. If you are a Christian or are unwilling to fight, you will remain in your cells."

Alexander smiled to himself. Every attempt to get out of here had failed. Yet here they were walking out free at the command of the antichrist Zealot leader.

Just as in the days of Moses Yahweh had accomplished his will through Balaam's ass.

CHAPTER 35

Gaza

The city of Gaza lay three miles inland from the sea, fifty miles southwest of Jerusalem. It had a long history of strategic importance in the region. Originally it had been one of the Philistine cities of Canaan, and Joshua's conquering Israelite armies had never dispossessed the Anakim giants who found refuge behind its heavily fortified walls.[1] This would prove to be a thorn in the flesh for the anointed King David and a portent of persistent evil to come.

The city was vitally significant for two reasons. First, it was a major trading emporium for luxury goods from Arabia and the Far East. But secondly, because of its location on the Via Maris that connected Asia and Syria to Egypt, north to south, it had become a strategic bridgehead for Egyptian military campaigns into Israel and Syria.[2]

Its mixed population included a high proportion of Arabs, which meant that the daughters of Allah knew their way around this familiar territory. They were here on the hunt for a specific target.

They visited the temple of Dagon, the patron deity of the sea people called the Philistines. Like Marduk of Babylon, Dagon was a god of storm and vegetation. But because his worshippers offered many sacrifices from the sea, he tended to stink of decaying fish.[3]

The daughters of Allah wrinkled their noses as they visited him in the holy place of his temple. They had asked him for permission to operate in his territory and for help in their mission. Thankfully, their veils helped mask some of the stench.

But they had their permission and they had their plan.

• • • • •

Raphael and the dozen Kharabu warriors sent by Demetrius sat together in a small encampment hidden in the desert a mile outside Gaza. They had

236

stumbled upon an army of a thousand Zealots on their way to attack the city full of Greek inhabitants. The secret mission squad had ostensibly joined the Zealots in their fight against the Greeks with the ulterior goal of finding the Christians during the battle and protecting them.

The attack was to take place before the sun came up.

Raphael had climbed the city wall in the middle of the night to find the Christians and gather them together in a district whose location he would then communicate to his squad over the wall. When the Zealots broke into the city, Raphael's Kharabu would make their way to the district and protect the Christians.

Raphael presently slipped through the shadows of back alleys on his way to find more believers. He had been told where to find them by the elders, who had already gathered several dozen Christians in a meeting hall in the central district.

Raphael turned a corner, and froze. His preternatural senses detected the presence of a Watcher. But it wasn't Dagon, the patron god of this city, as he expected. It was something else. A different deity. He saw a figure in the distance fleeing into the darkness, as though the angel had interrupted something. Foiled its plans.

But what plans? A dark feeling came over him. The Christians were in greater danger than he realized.

He knew he should not do this alone. He should not chase after such an entity without knowing what he was getting into. It could be a trap.

But if he did nothing, it could be a worse trap for the Christians.

There wasn't time to wait. Raphael ran after the fleeing figure, his senses attuned to its flight, a predator on prey.

He bounded through the dark alleys, following its path. He kept alert to his surroundings, prepared for an ambush of any kind.

It never happened. Raphael had not been a planned target after all. He had been an unplanned obstacle.

He had to strike while he was still on top.

He stopped before the temple of Dagon, a large stone edifice quite similar in design to the holy temple in Jerusalem, though about half the size. The entity was trying to hide in the enemy's house.

Raphael slipped past two large pillars at the entrance and slowly moved into the outer courtyard, an area of about fifty feet square. The inner courtyard was on the other side of the gates.

The entrance gate behind him closed.

The courtyard was utterly empty.

So it was an ambush. He looked around the porticos, expecting armed priests of Dagon.

He drew his sword.

"Come and get me," he said with a lighthearted confidence.

But the figures that walked out from behind the pillars and now surrounded him were not priests of Dagon. They were Watchers.

He recognized them now. The three daughters of Allah circled his rear. Dagon, that smelly wretch, approached him from the front.

Raphael was confused. What was going on? What did they want?

"You, my dreaded archangel," said Dagon, "are very far from your home." He added, "And from your gang of high and mighty godlickers."

Raphael adjusted his defensive stance as he sensed the movement behind him.

Dagon grinned with irony. "There is strength in numbers." He gestured toward the three furies behind Raphael, crouched, scimitars drawn, ready to jump.

Dagon gestured toward the archangel. "And weakness in solitude."

"You never had a skill for wit," said Raphael. "And you still stink to high heaven."

The Watcher was visibly perturbed by the remark. It was easy to get under his heavenly skin. He spat out with anger, "And you are about to eat your words, as I feed them to your limbless body."

Dagon swirled his trident and attacked.

The three behind Raphael attacked.

Raphael wished that he had the ability to perform Uriel's special sword move at this moment.[4] But he was not so skilled.

He did his best. He swung his weapon.

He blocked the trident's fork from skewering him

He spun around to meet the three curved blades coming at him from behind.

But he was not fast enough.

Nor strong enough.

One Watcher, he could handle. Four all at once was too many.

• • • • •

Raphael awakened in a stupor. He felt pain surging through every part of his body. He found himself lying on the floor of the holy place in Dagon's inner temple. Above his head was a stone horned altar of sacrifice.

He couldn't move. At first he thought he was tied down. But he looked down at himself to discover the terrible truth: All four of his limbs had been severed from his body.

He bellowed in horror.

Angels were divine beings. Immortal. They could not die as humans did. But they were created beings with heavenly flesh. They were no mere spirits. They suffered and experienced pain like other creatures.[5]

That creaturely pain now filled Raphael's dismembered torso. Dagon and the three daughters of Allah stepped into his sight. Each held one of his bloody severed limbs in their hands.

Dagon asked mischievously, "Are these what you are looking for, angel?"

Even in his suffering state, Raphael found the strength to fight back, if only verbally. "You have no original thought in your head, Dagon. We recently did this to Hubal. And Asherah had you do this to Michael in the days of King David. You're a mimic."[6]

He saw Dagon suppressing his anger. He knew the incident had haunted the god. Dagon had not only been humiliated by Asherah's superior leadership in those days, he had been betrayed to the archangels by her and Ba'al to save themselves. Dagon's bitterness was the only weapon Raphael could use in his captive state.

Dagon smirked. "And what does that make you, archangel? So easily overcome by such an unoriginal and inferior deity!" His sarcasm was biting.

But all Raphael could think of was the Christians in the city of Gaza. Without his information, without his warning, they would not escape the coming violence.

The Philistine deity knelt down closer. "Well, I have an offer that will redeem us both. For me, it will grant favor with Apollyon. And for you"—he held up Raphael's right arm—"it will get your limbs back."

Fortunately for Raphael, angelic flesh was heavenly, not earthly. It had supernatural properties. If they reattached Raphael's limbs these would regenerate and heal quite quickly.

Raphael grunted at the pain again. "What do you want?"

"The daughters here have told me that you and your fellow archangels have captured and bound four gods of the nations that are key to Apollyon's earthly power. The strongmen Ba'al, Ares, Ahura Mazda, and Hubal.

These four were the principalities over Rome's armed forces now in Judea.[7]

"If you tell us where they are, I will give you back your limbs."

Raphael knew exactly where they were. He also knew that he could not trust a single word out of the mouth of this detestable abomination. He had to be strategic.

"You'll have to take me with you. Make it a hostage exchange." If he told them the exact location, they would never return his body parts. They would hide them at the four corners of the land, where he would be trapped until the final judgment. Only in the presence of his brethren would he stand a chance of salvation.

He added, "I will take you step by step until we arrive at the location where they are bound."

"Accepted," said Dagon. "But no limbs until we get there. We'll carry you."

The pain in Raphael's body was nowhere near as deep as the pain in his soul for the Christians of Gaza, who were about to be caught up in the slaughter because he had failed them.

Yahweh have mercy on them, he prayed.

CHAPTER 36

Jerusalem

Alexander was haunted by Cassandra's anger at him. Giving her up in his heart was one of the most difficult things he had ever done. He thought it would help make him more selfless. Instead, it just made him more miserable. Why had she rejected him? It was true that friendships were ruined when one learns they do not love as the other.

He had to stop thinking about her. His emotions were intruding on far more important matters of life and death. The fate of the Jerusalem Christians was hanging in the balance, and here he was muddled in his feelings of personal loss. He wasn't selfless after all. He was still selfish to the core. He prayed silently for the Holy Spirit to fill him and his three companions. He sat with Cassandra, Severus, and Demetrius in counsel with the elders of the Jerusalem church in the Essene quarter. They were once again at the home of the elder Boaz. And once again, the gaunt reptile Jacob sat beside Boaz, whispering calumnies in his ears.

Demetrius said, "This will be our last appeal to you. Your last chance to get out before the wrath of God falls upon the city."

Boaz asked, "Where do you expect us to go?"

"Where Jesus told us to go," said Joshua. "The mountains." The white-bearded prophet was there, bold as ever, disrespected as ever.

Demetrius said, "I led a team of"—he paused, searching for the right word—"*defenders* up into Galilee to get the word to the Christians there. Our first stop was at Pella, one of the cities of the Decapolis. When we arrived, we found it abandoned save for some Greek warriors. The Jews and Greeks of the city had killed each other, and the few Jewish survivors were about to kill the Christians who were left. We stopped them." A pall went over the gathering of a hundred Christians and elders. They knew what it meant.

Demetrius continued, "The city was virtually empty. Some damage to the buildings, but very livable. And it is in the mountains fifty miles northeast of here, a safe distance away from Roman invasion. We've already sent many Christians from the Decapolis and Galilee there. It could easily accommodate all of you from Jerusalem as well. My warriors should be back from their journey soon. We can escort you safely to Pella before Cestius arrives at the walls of Jerusalem. But we haven't much time."

Severus added, "Cestius will have to subdue the cities on the way to Jerusalem to secure his route. It could take him several weeks to get here. We must leave now."

Jacob whispered, then Boaz spoke. It reminded Cassandra of the way she had seen the spirit beings whisper to earthly authorities. "But what if you are wrong? We will not be able to return to our lives here."

"We are not wrong," said Cassandra.

"There are many who believe you," said Boaz. "But there are many who do not. We have previously decided we will not split the congregation. We all go or we all stay."

Jacob became more bold. He started to take over the discussion from Boaz. He looked at Demetrius. "I have been reading the Apocalypse since you were gone, and I have a question for you."

Demetrius glanced at the others. *Here he goes.*

"In the eleventh fragment, the apostle allegedly writes about the temple."

Alexander sighed. *The temple will be their death yet!*

"Now, John was told by the angel to measure the temple and the altar.[1] In Scripture, measuring is symbolic of Yahweh marking out something for protection. This is the case in Ezekiel and Zechariah, for instance. Is he not saying that Yahweh will protect the temple?"[2]

Demetrius responded. "You left off the second part of the passage. He does not measure the outer court because it will be given over to the nations. And they will trample the holy city for forty-two months.[3] Just as Jesus predicted. He said Jerusalem would be surrounded by armies of desolation. And the city would be trampled underfoot by the Gentiles in Yahweh's days of vengeance upon Israel. Not one stone of the temple will be left upon another. That is why he told us to flee."[4]

"But again," countered Jacob, "the inner temple itself is spared, even if the outer court is trampled down."

"No," replied Alexander. "The apostle explained to us that it is a vision of the spiritual reality behind the physical appearance. The outer court of the Gentiles is a symbol of the physical temple that *will* be destroyed by the Gentiles. Jesus is never wrong. Not one stone of the physical temple left upon another. The inner temple and altar with true worshippers is symbolic of the heavenly temple, the body of Christ, that he will protect forever.[5] Jesus is the heavenly temple of God. *We* as his body are that temple.[6] *We* are the royal priesthood of that temple.[7] *We* house the Shekinah glory that left the earthly temple in Ezekiel's day.[8] Earthly Jerusalem has rejected her Messiah and is now considered a harlot that Yahweh is divorcing to marry a new bride, the body of Christ.[9] That bride is the new Jerusalem that comes down out of heaven, while the old covenant Jerusalem is divorced, judged, and executed for spiritual adultery."[10]

"Well," scoffed Jacob, "you are quite the sermonizer. But this is all too speculative and debatable depending on one's viewpoint. How can we know that your interpretation is the right one?"

"We told you already," said a frustrated Cassandra. "The apostle John explained it to us."

"I guess we are back to whether or not we can trust you or trust that this letter is authentic. And I for one do not. There are many others who agree with me."

Jacob turned to the listening congregation of believers. Some rumbled in agreement, challenged in turn by rumblings of disagreement. The assembly remained deadlocked.

Finally, Severus spoke up. "It appears to me that many of you will simply not believe us unless the apostle John himself tells you."

The crowd settled down. Jacob thought about it, then said, "Yes, I suppose you are right."

"Then I will go to Patmos and bring him back so he can correct you in person," said Severus.

Gasps of shock filled the crowd. Jacob's eyes went wide with fear. Even Cassandra and Demetrius looked at Severus with surprise.

Alexander asked, "Is that even possible?"

Severus had clearly been figuring it out. Cassandra's corbita was still docked in Caesarea Maritima, which gave Severus a vessel for travel. The only issue was time. Severus said to them, "Patmos is about six hundred miles away on the sea. I can get to Caesarea, strip down Cassandra's merchant ship, and use a skeletal crew for speed. I can get to Patmos and back in a couple weeks with God's provision and good winds. It will take Cestius about three weeks before he gets here. That is dangerously close, but I'll do it. I have no more patience left for this suicidal bickering."

For the first time, Alexander saw that Jacob had no response. If the scrawny man encouraged Severus, it would weaken his opposition. If he discouraged the trip, it would make him look as if he did not want to know the truth.

Severus was right. It was the only option they had left.

Jacob muttered with resignation, "So be it."

CHAPTER 37

Panias

Apollyon stood at the precipice of the Abyss, the very Gates of Hades, in the sacred grotto near Caesarea Philippi. He stared down into the darkness of the shaft. Pitch blackness. Dead silence. The smell of death wafting up from below as from an open tomb.

The Watchers had cleared out the rubble of the collapsed cave where he stood. But Apollyon had returned alone for his next task to be performed at the bottom of the crevice. He took a deep breath for this dangerous game.

He leapt out into the darkness. He fell.

The shaft was deep. Previously, he had climbed out of it with his army of Watchers when he had released them from Tartarus.

Now he was going back in. Back into the Abyss.

It seemed forever before he finally reached the bottom and plunged into the cold, black water.

He made his way back to the surface and swam over to the steep rock walls. He pulled out a large engraving tool he had strapped into his belt and began to carve magic glyphs into the bedrock. Hieroglyphs of an ancient language long dead. His servant Azazel had given him the primeval spell. One that had been culled from the secrets of the Watchers. Azazel had been one of the leaders of the ancient ones who had revealed dark knowledge to humanity. And when Azazel had been locked up in Tartarus, the spell had been locked up with him. Until now.[1]

Apollyon was calling up from the depths. He was using occult magic to raise a denizen of the deep.

When he had completed the circle of glyphs around the shaft, he climbed up on the rock wall and waited.

It didn't take long before the waters began to stir. They swirled into a whirlpool, then bubbled with the heat of released sulfur. Then the black surface burst open in an explosion of water. First one, then two reptilian heads broke the surface. Then a third and fourth head until seven could be seen—all attached to one singular monstrous body: Leviathan, the seven-headed sea dragon of chaos.

The spell's purpose was two-fold. First, it called forth the mighty beast. But this sea monster was an untamed force of spiritual chaos. It brought unpredictable destruction wherever it went. It was no creature's inferior. That was what the second purpose of the spell was for: to mesmerize it, a kind of enchantment that placed it under temporary influence of the spell-caster, who could then harness its destructive powers.

Apollyon launched from the rock wall and landed on the neck of one of the dominant heads. Its mouth belched out a column of flames in angry response. The rock wall became scorched black. A fire-breather. Its nostrils snorted smoke.

Apollyon held on tight.

It took a moment for the creature to submit to its temporary master. It came deftly and dangerously under Apollyon's control.

The Watcher could feel the massive power beneath him. The scales were hard like potsherds, impenetrable to harpoons. The muscles on its neck bulged with brute strength. Terror danced before it. He knew its heart was hard as a stone, a creature without fear, and before it the mighty would flee. Leviathan was the king over all the sons of pride.[2]

The monster dove deep. Into the depths of the Abyss. Leaving a shining, boiling current in its wake.

Apollyon could feel himself connecting with the great creature, his mind becoming one with it. Without words, without language, he could communicate to it, bend it to his purposes. Harness it for his mission.

• • • • •

The Mediterranean Sea

Severus watched the coastline of Palestine sink into the horizon behind him. He turned toward the bow, toward his unseen destination: Patmos, where he would take into custody the apostle John and return to Jerusalem.

He breathed in the cool, salty air and thought about the amazing journey he had experienced in these few short years since the great fire of Rome. His life had been like that fire. His entire reality had been burned up and replaced by a new one, a new city. The city of God. He still wasn't comfortable with this new reality or the implications it had for his future. He was, after all, a Roman prefect in the service of Nero. Although now he did not know if he would ever return to Rome. Could he disappear? Fake his death? Or should he face his fate with the courage of Peter and Paul and the others?

He had been enslaved to an idolatrous empire of lies. But really, he had only been enslaved to himself, to his own sin. For every man was responsible for his choices in this life. And no one would escape judgment in the end. Severus had worshipped gods that he knew were not his creator. He had suppressed the truth in unrighteousness as one might try to force a ball below the surface of water. Through his quest to hunt down the subversive Apocalypse, he had come face to face with the fact that God had hunted him. He was no innocent bystander in the cosmic drama that was playing out on the stage of history. He was an active participant. There were no casual observers in this conflict. You either worshipped the Lamb or you worshipped the Beast. He had worshipped the Beast.

But God had hunted him.

Why? Why would Jesus choose him? Why would he have the privilege of experiencing God's grace in a world of such suffering? Suffering to which he had contributed so much. He had captured, tortured, and even delivered over to death God's own people. Could there be anything worse?

During their short time with the church in Jerusalem, Cassandra had shown him the apostle Paul's testimony in one of his letters to a colleague named Timothy. As a pagan, Severus had seen little sense in the apostle's story. But now he understood it. For here was a man who had persecuted Christians just as Severus had. Paul considered himself a blasphemer, persecutor, and insolent opponent of God before becoming a Christian. "Chief of sinners" was the phrase he used. Yet Jesus had mercy on him, forgave him, and chose him to be the apostle to the Gentiles. So if God's grace was great enough to redeem such self-confessed atrocities, then surely it would be great enough to cover even Severus' sin.[3]

But it still seemed impossible for Severus to conceive of such mercy, such grace. He had been indoctrinated in the Roman military code of strength and honor. Power had been the essence of his world, Mithras his false god. Grace and mercy were alien, offensive to the Roman mind. Grace argues that man is not strong but broken. And he is not honorable but depraved to the core. The notion of blood atonement was familiar enough from his own religion. Shed blood propitiates the wrath of deity, satisfies justice. Even God becoming flesh was not offensive to his own traditions. But the idea that the god-man would willingly take upon himself the judgment reserved for his creatures was still so astonishing Severus could not comprehend it. Herein was a God so personal, so close, with a love so grand that it had changed him forever. And he barely understood it. But after forty years of life on this earth, he finally felt his heart of stone begin to become a heart of flesh. He had begun to feel. Not just emotions, but the sense of connection with his creator. With meaning and purpose. He was now baptized in the Spirit of the infinite God.

Water baptism was the symbol of that spirit baptism. It was a ritual promise that he had been washed clean, that he had been identified with Christ's death and resurrection. He remembered back to his first visit to the apostle John on Patmos. He had been baptized in that mountain spring along with Alexander. But it had not been real to him then. He was only pretending to convert with ulterior motives. He had not made an authentic profession of faith. He had been a fraud. So now he considered whether he should be baptized again when he found the apostle, this time for genuine faith. Would John allow that?

He smiled to himself. He had sent a carrier pidgeon with a special message to his son in Rome. He had told Thelonius to take a ship to Patmos where they would meet upon Severus' arrival to pick up the apostle. Severus was overflowing with the joy of desire to tell his son the miracle of his salvation. To share with him the forgiveness of Jesus. He longed for redemption in this one last area of his life, for the chance to start anew with his only son.

His gaze turned from the horizon to the blue water chopping below the bow as the wind blew the ship on its course into the west. He thought he saw something in the water. A large fish following the boat in its wake?

A sense of foreboding came over him. The sky above became suddenly dark with storm clouds. As if they came out of nowhere. He barked orders to secure the sails and rigs in preparation. Thunder rumbled overhead. The wind whipped around in a fury.

The water below them became a large whirlpool. The ship stopped moving forward and began to circle the maelstrom created by the strange undercurrent. Severus had never seen anything like it. The few sailors aboard scrambled to tie everything down. He heard shouts of fear. Rain now pelted them from the heavens.

Severus muttered a prayer, "Lord Jesus protect us."

And then it stopped. The vortex dissolved, and the ship stopped its swirling spiral. The rain slowed and finally ceased.

The sea below had become calm.

Dead calm.

Severus and the other sailors looked at each other with frightened eyes. This was stranger than the sudden storm and whirlpool.

More foreboding.

Severus felt the ship rise. He heard the creaking of wood. Something was lifting them out of the water from below. Something huge and powerful. He looked into the water and saw the dark form of a sea monster. Large scales. He thought he saw several heads.

He screamed out, "Leviathan!"

The ship fell back into the water with a splash of waves.

Again, the calm of nothing. They all stood there waiting. Helpless.

And then it came. A monstrous double tail, twice the size of the ship, exploded from the water in a sweeping arc. It crashed down upon the middle of the vessel, snapping it in two like a floating twig.

The main mast cracked in half and hit the water. Splintered pieces of wood rained down upon them.

The force of the attack launched most of the men into the sea. Severus had been near the point of impact. He was dragged down into the water with the debris like an undertow.

His legs got wrapped into some ropes and rigging. He couldn't get himself loose.

The shattered hull sank quickly into the depths, pulling Severus with it.

As he descended, Severus saw the several heads of the sea dragon. He could swear he saw a humanoid figure clinging to one of the necks. He had been allowed to see into the spiritual realm.

But why?

It didn't make sense to him. He'd thought Yahweh wanted to get his word to the Christians.

Then why would Yahweh allow this to happen?

Severus prayed that his son would forgive him and that he would find the forgiveness of Christ. He prayed for the Christians in Jerusalem. He prayed for Jesus to receive his spirit and accept him into paradise.

The thought occurred to him that God had answered his previous question. He was allowing Severus a final baptism before he faced his creator with joy.

PART THREE

Rescue

CHAPTER 38

Jerusalem
November 14, AD 66

Berenice stood holding Agrippa's hand as they looked out upon the city of Jerusalem from the Roman camp on Mount Scopus. Their vantage point was about three-quarters of a mile to the northeast of the walls at a higher elevation, so they could see somewhat into the city. They stood with an entourage of officers and a unit of guards at the entrance of the camp perimeter.

The past thirty days had been an absolute horror for Berenice. She felt as if her heart was broken. Cestius had sent a legion from Caesarea into Galilee to plunder and destroy. Sepphoris, the strongest city in the region, received them with submission. Others did not. Thousands of Jews, both rebels and innocents, had been killed. Eight thousand citizens had been slaughtered in Joppa, just south of Caesarea.[1] Berenice and her brother had accompanied Cestius, hoping to negotiate with the rebels.

There were no negotiations.

The Twelfth Legion then joined Cestius' auxiliaries in their march toward Jerusalem. They dispersed the Jewish forces at Antipatris, found Lydda deserted, and fought skirmishes with rebels at Beth-Horon.[2] By the time they reached the walls of Jerusalem, many Jews were caught in the city because of the Feast of Tabernacles. Jerusalem was like a pregnant mother facing down the mighty eagle of Rome. Thirty thousand forces pitched their tents, sharpened their weapons, and prepared for desolation.

Berenice felt sick to her stomach as she watched a retinue of a dozen Jewish leaders from the city approach the Roman camp. Pharisees and Sadducees from the Sanhedrin as well as some of the wealthy ruling class. She prayed to God that negotiations would avert the coming disaster.[3]

The leaders arrived and were led through the camp to the general's tent where Cestius Gallus awaited them.

Berenice watched Cestius closely as he listened to the Jewish aristocrats make their offer to him. The Syrian governor-general, that older version of Vespasian, gruff and experienced, was also a practical man who had a sense of fairness. Though that fairness was more Roman than Jewish, he had spared the inhabitants of Sepphoris when they submitted to him. Unfortunately, Jerusalem was not so united. It contained innocent citizens, anti-Roman rebels, and pro-Roman nobles. The complexity of the situation could deteriorate into chaos at any moment.

The lead Pharisee, a wealthy member of the Sanhedrin with a black beard and a confidence born of privilege, spoke. He and his colleagues acted as if they were in control of the city. Berenice knew better.

The Pharisee said, "We speak for the ruling class and the populace. The majority of citizens want nothing to do with this revolt."

Cestius asked with a stoic face, "Then why do the citizens not put down the rebels?"

"I am sure that you understand, governor, that the masses tend to be easily cowed by the radical few."

Agrippa added, "He speaks the truth, my lord. Crush the rebels and the plebs will bow to you."

Cestius said, "I am here to subdue Jerusalem. I will accept nothing less than unconditional surrender, which recent experience proves will not be forthcoming."

The Pharisee implored, "What if my fellow colleagues and I open the gates of the city to you? Would that not be a significant collaboration to warrant leniency?"

"What kind of leniency?"

"Avoid the wealthy neighborhoods."

Agrippa jumped in, "And the Herodian palace."

Berenice looked at them both angrily and said, "And innocent civilians."

The Pharisee repeated with faux sympathy, "And innocent civilians."

Berenice looked at Cestius, who stared at the pompous Pharisee as though considering whether or not he could trust him.

Finally, Cestius said, "I will reply to you on the morrow."

The Pharisee and his fellow leaders bowed and left the tent to return to the city.

After they were gone, Cestius remained silently considering his options. Berenice felt anxious. The dozen officers awaited his command.

He finally asked, "Herods, what say you? Can I trust these betrayers of their city? Is it a trap?"

Agrippa spoke with assurance, "General, Berenice and I know these men very well and the entire ruling class. The Pharisee spoke the truth. They have the most to lose."

"They?" said Cestius.

"We. We know who allows us our wealth and power, and it is not the rebels. Those pro-Roman priests would be the last to lay a trap."

"Ah yes," said Cestius. "Those who suck at the teat of Rome like a litter of swine."

Berenice bristled at the insult. As a Herod, she was quite experienced in being condemned by everyone no matter what she did. But it still bothered her.

Herod smirked, thinking that the metaphor made Rome a big, fat sow.

After another moment of consideration, Cestius said, "While you Herods have proven faithful to Caesar, these others of your ruling class have not. I do not trust them."

Berenice felt like throwing up.

Cestius concluded, "They will not give me their city. I will take it. And I will crush them all."

CHAPTER 39

Simon bar Giora hid behind a ridge of the Mount of Olives across from the temple. He had several hundred warriors with him and several thousand more Sicarii and Idumeans hidden a mile away in a valley.

He looked down upon the New City north of the temple, now burning in flames. A force of several thousand legionaries was arrayed before the northern gate of the temple. Cestius had begun his attack. He had broken into the New City, razed it to the ground, and was already besieging the temple.

"General Giora." The voice made him turn to see one of his Idumean soldiers holding the young monk Aaron hostage, along with a group of fifty other Essenes.

"We found them lurking around the foothills armed with weapons." He grinned. "Perhaps a secret squad sent to assassinate you?"

Simon said, "Release them, captain."

He sighed as Aaron approached him. "I told you to stay and train your community."

Aaron beamed with confidence. "The time for preparation is over. The war is upon us, and we are ready to fight and die."

"Die, indeed," said Simon. "I'm not so certain about the former."

Aaron stepped closer so he could whisper out of earshot of the men. "General. You have taught us more than mere technique. You have inspired us with your courage. And it is courage that leads men to do the impossible."

"Do not worship me. I will disappoint your faith."

"I am not unaware of your ... flaws, General," whispered Aaron. "But please, sir, do not deny your change of heart. I saw it back at Qumran. You fight for the poor and the oppressed. We Essenes are both. And we are yours to command." He stood at attention, like a respectful soldier.

Simon glanced at the pitiful unit of Essenes. They weren't that pitiful. They had a deep sincerity. Something he had lost years ago. The irony was that Simon was the one who felt inspired by them. Maybe he could help this young man and his group of deluded fanatics to be the men they wanted to be. The man Aaron needed to be.

"What has happened?" asked Aaron, looking at the smoke rising over the ridge.

Simon took him to the top, where they lay on the ground out of sight.

Simon said, "Cestius Gallus has an army on Mount Scopus. He has just penetrated the New City and is razing it to the ground. Rather than try to break through the second wall into the Tyropoeon Valley, he is choosing to make his entry into the northern temple gate, which is less fortified."

Aaron could see a large contingent of legionaries creating a wall of interlocked shields as they approached the temple gate. Jews threw spears and rocks from the parapets above. The Romans were testing the strength of their enemy's firepower. It did not look good for the Jews.

Aaron asked, "Why do you not attack? You have a substantial force at your command."

"Yes, but I am counted as much an enemy of the people as is Cestius. At least by the ruling class."

"The ruling class you oppose who are the true oppressors of the people."

"But they remain in power and still hold great sway over those people. I cannot fight all of Israel and Rome combined."

He saw Aaron looking down on the battle with horror in his eyes. The young monk said, "The gate will not hold. The abomination of desolation is upon us."

"If that is a true prophecy," responded Simon, "then why do you fret? Is it not God's will?"

"Yes. But it is also God's will that we fight the Kittim in the War of the Sons of Light. For then Messiah will come to save us."

It struck Simon that this was how fanaticism deluded its adherents and ran them off a cliff like a herd of sheep without a shepherd.

That shepherd was not coming.

"You forget, soldier. I do not share your faith. So I wait for a more strategic moment to provide me a more certain victory."

He noticed Aaron's face brighten when he called him soldier. And he realized that the way he could best help this young, naïve true believer with all his human weakness would be to treat him as the man he could be.

"Return to our camp and await your orders. I will be inducting you as a lieutenant."

"Yes, General," said Aaron, stiffening with obedience. He bounced away to his men, and Simon turned his attention back to the tragedy that was unfolding in the city of his lost love.

Simon reached into his belt and felt the lock of hair. Where was Berenice at this moment? Was she in the Herodian palace? Was she safely hidden away in one of the several Herodian fortresses around Judea? Was she in another man's arms?

A wild thought occurred to him to go on a secret sortie to find her and rescue her. Or to kill his betrayer, John of Gischala. If he could find him.

Simon's attention was drawn to a commotion in the outer temple court. He saw a large crowd forcibly pushing a group of a dozen or so captives to the north gate, where the siege was playing out. From his distance he could not make out who the hostages were, but they appeared to be dressed in the clothes of the ruling class.

Just then, a young scout arrived. He had used one of the many tunnel systems to make his way out beneath the watchful eyes of Roman units stationed around the city.

Simon looked down at the young spy. "What is going on down there?"

The spy was breathing heavily from racing his way back. "That was an entourage of Sanhedrin and other nobles. I heard they met with Cestius to negotiate on behalf of the city. Then they tried to negotiate with Eleazar in the temple."

Simon saw the dozen nobles now brought up to the roof of the portico above the gate. The Romans were still below, readying a battering ram made of a large tree.

He saw the nobles brought to the ledge of the roof. They were resisting as if still trying to get away.

And then one after the other, the nobles were thrown down from the wall onto the attacking Romans fifty feet below them.[1]

Simon's eyes went wide with dismay. He saw some of the bodies land on their heads, others on their backs.

Simon felt his heart jump with the shock. And then he knew.

"It appears that negotiation is not an option for the Zealots."

Aaron was right. It was only a matter of time before the unholy abomination of desolation would enter the holy temple.

Then the smallest of doubt entered Simon's mind. Doubt about his own profane heart. Doubt about the choices he had made. Doubt about his own doubt.

He wondered if there might be some truth to the prophecies after all.

CHAPTER 40

Alexander looked at Cassandra in the lamplight of the gathering at Boaz's home in the Essene quarter. She wouldn't look back at him. She was avoiding looking at him at all. She was still mad at him.

It was night. The two of them and Demetrius and the prophet Joshua were packed into Boaz's home again with the elders and a couple hundred Christians in fear for their lives. The entire city was full of citizens in fear for their lives. It had been several weeks, and Severus had never returned with the apostle John from Patmos. They had heard no word from him at all. They didn't know whether he was alive or dead. And so the Christians had waited—and it was now too late. The Roman armies—the abomination of desolation—were surrounding the city walls, and the Christians had not heeded the words of their Lord. They had not fled.

Christians throughout the large home were on their knees, some prostrate, praying and beseeching the Lord. Some were weeping in repentance while others stood in silent brokenness.

Boaz finished his prayer. "Lord Jesus, we repent of our hard hearts. Forgive us for not listening to you. Forgive your shepherds for not protecting your sheep. We pray for mercy upon your children. Our lives and deaths are in your hands. Your will be done."

There was a moment of silence as heads were raised and the congregation considered their fate.

The balding Judaizer, Jacob, was the first to break the silence with a faux humility. "Elders, may I offer what I believe is a word from the Lord?" Alexander wondered why Boaz could not spot such obvious insincerity. There had been no word of prophecy for some time now. How dare he claim such presumption.

Boaz nodded to Jacob, who spoke to the crowd. "We have been divided within our congregation for far too long. Strife, pride, and jealousy tear us apart." He increasingly sounded like the serpent in the Garden.

"There are those of us who seek unity with our Jewish brethren who are not yet in the fold with us. Others have sought to create division by denying Torah and hatefully pronouncing judgment upon them and upon the holy temple." Rumblings illustrated the crowd's diversity of views.

"May I suggest that we now stand at a crossroads. The Roman Beast is at the very gates of the temple ready to destroy us all. The choice is no longer a mere theological one from the safety of our lofty heights. Our very lives are now at stake. The question we must ask ourselves is this. Do we stand with our Jewish brethren, the children of Abraham, or do we stand with the Beast?"

The rumblings of the crowd rose. Emotion was high. It was everything Alexander and his comrades could do to remain silent and let him speak.

Someone yelled out, "Christians are the children of Abraham!"

More murmuring spread through the crowd.

Jacob's voice raised to meet the din. "We have tried to be a peaceful people. And as the Scriptures say, there is a time and place for everything. A time for peace. And a time for war." Alexander knew where this demagoguery was leading.

"I believe it is time to take up arms and fight with our fellow Jews. I believe it is God's will that we join the revolt and protect the temple. If you are not against the Beast, you are for him!"

Cassandra could not contain herself any longer. She shouted, "The temple *is* the altar of the Beast! And Jews who carry his mark deserve judgment!"

The crowd broke out into chaos. Some applauded. Others booed.

Boaz stood up with the elders and quieted them down.

Finally, the head elder spoke. "The elders have conferred on this matter. Through much prayer and deliberation. And we have concluded that the messengers of the Apocalypse were right. Jesus had foretold this very judgment on the temple and city, and we have avoided it to our own detriment. We have clung to the carcass of an old covenant, and we will do so no more."

More mutterings filled the crowd.

Boaz turned to a surprised Jacob. "Jacob bar Mordecai, your teaching is a violation of the new covenant testimony of the apostles. You are an adversary of the gospel and the true Israel of God. We hereby charge you to repent of your heresy or be cut off from the congregation."

The crowd quieted down at the ultimatum. Alexander and the others looked at Jacob to see what he would do.

The shifty counselor looked around the room for support. "Who is with me?"

A dozen people rose and joined him. Most of those who were his previous allies followed the congregation in submission to their elders' authority. They might have their doubts, but their commitment to the community and God's ordination was deeper than those doubts.

"Cowards," spat Jacob. He made his way to the door with his few followers. The crowd parted to let him through as if he were a leper. He *was* a leper, a spiritually diseased false teacher who denied the Master who bought him. And who would blind the eyes of the Jerusalem congregation no longer.

Alexander heard Cassandra mutter, "Get behind us, satan."

Someone yelled out, "What do we do now? We are still unable to leave the city!"

"We pray!"

The voice came from the entrance where Jacob had just left. The crowd parted in silence again. This time for Demetrius' forty Kharabu warriors. The voice was that of the handsome, strongly-built Michael.

He approached the elders but spoke to the congregation. "My name is Michael. We have returned from drawing in the elect from the four corners of the Land, bringing the apostle's Revelation to the congregation of Jesus in each city. And helping Christians to safety. We fought beside Demetrius."

Demetrius said, "He speaks the truth. These are worthy men of God."

Boaz asked, "How successful were you?"

Michael answered, "We freed some, lost others. We are here now for your sake."

"How did you get into Jerusalem?"

"Through one of the tunnels." There were many hidden tunnel systems beneath the city that would allow unseen access to and from the outside. They had been dug through the generations for this very purpose.

"Can we escape through the same passages?" said Boaz.

"We Kharabu are but a handful," said Michael. "We were able to move in stealth. You cannot. You are too many. The Romans would easily discover you and kill you all."

Alexander said, "You cannot protect us inside the city any better. What are a few Kharabu against a legion of Romans?"

Alexander noticed how calm and at ease Michael was. He marveled at the man's faith. Or was there something he knew that the rest of them did not?

Demetrius spoke up. "Where is Raphael?"

Michael's confident demeanor dropped. "He was captured by the enemy. Fear not. It is all a part of Yahweh's plan."

Someone cried out, "Is it Yahweh's plan for the Romans to kill us too?"

Michael raised his hands to calm them. Alexander thought the warrior almost appeared to glow as the congregation settled down. "No, it is not. You are the Remnant of Israel. You have the seal of God on your foreheads. Now is your time to pray. To trust Yahweh with all your heart and lean not on your own understanding. For the Scripture says that he gives his angels charge concerning you to guard you and bear you up. The Angel of Yahweh encamps around those who fear him."[1]

Alexander noticed that Michael was speaking with much assurance. Was Michael his real name? Michael was the name of Israel's spiritual prince, its guardian. The prophet Daniel had written that at the time of the end Michael, the principality of Israel, would rise up to take charge of his people. These Remnant were his people. Was this Michael their prince?[2]

He saw that Demetrius also had a subtle smile of confidence. What did he know about these warriors that he was not telling them?

Boaz said, "Michael speaks wisdom. Our fate is in the hands of God. So let us pray."

CHAPTER 41

Eleazar left the safety of his inner temple stronghold to lead the defensive forces at the northern gate of the outer temple, called the Sheep Gate. He had successfully convinced the rival factions of rebels within the city to unite temporarily in defense against their Roman besiegers, the unholy Kittim. When Cestius had burned down the New City, rebel and bandit alike could see his was a scorched-earth policy. No mercy. The Roman general's decision to attack the temple next was a deliberate act of symbolic warfare that would surely lead to complete desolation of their holy house. He was aiming for their heart, to rip it out.[1]

Thousands of the rebels holed up in the outer court in anticipation of the confrontation. But after six days of battle exchanges at the north wall with the Romans, they were already losing morale. Eleazar had tried to keep them united under his command, but there were too many factions with too many rebel leaders at odds. Some of the brigands had already fled in anticipation of defeat. Eleazar hoped the disease of such fear and disunity would not spread into an epidemic, but he felt as if he was losing control. He had the tunnels below the temple mount guarded so no more could desert. If the Romans caught any of those escaping, they would surely have the final inspiration they needed to push through and crush the Jewish revolt.

Eleazar was not going to let that happen. He called a company of archers to the portico roof to counter the heavy attack of missiles being launched upon them from below. It was like a rain storm of arrows.

His men took their places along the parapet of the wall and returned fire. But then he saw the Romans wheel out dozens of wooden war machines beneath the Roman standards of the Twelfth Legion. These were called ballistas and "scorpions," advanced weapons technology made from wooden beams, each about the size of two horses, and manned by two soldiers for the purpose of projecting missiles. Both devices were spring-loaded weapons pulled taut by a crank that released their load when triggered. Ballistas hurled smooth stones

264

about the size of a human's head, while scorpions launched bolts and stinging darts the size of spears, thus the metaphor of the name. The long-distance range of these weapons placed them out of reach of Eleazar's archers. Several of them appeared built to launch six or more arrows all at once.

Eleazar yelled, "Seek cover!"

The Roman machines discharged their loads in rapid succession. Rocks smashed the parapet, breaking the shield walls into pieces, killing several soldiers at once. Arrows caught Jewish archers and pierced them right through, toppling them to the ground below. The force of the hits was devastating. And they had decimated Eleazar's own archer regiment. Some survivors fled in fear of the next round.

And the next round came like a pounding wave of missiles. Eleazar and the remaining archers hugged the stone floor, praying for deliverance.

The bombardment momentarily halted. Eleazar leapt to his feet. He knew what was coming next. An attack on the gate. "Archers, release at will!"

The Jewish archers jumped up, nocked their arrows, and fired at an approaching company of legionaries. But their arrows were to no avail. The Romans had raised their shields in their customary tactic called *testudo*. The word meant *tortoise*, and the tactic received its name from the fact that when the soldiers came tight together and raised their shields in unison, it looked as if the shell of a tortoise was protecting them.

Then that tortoise arrived at the Sheep Gate.

Eleazar's archers could not penetrate the shell. And they did not have siege weapons at their disposal, such as Greek fire or heavy stones for dropping.

The sound of massive springs releasing brought them all to the ground again as another round of darts and rocks continued to demolish the protective barricade and kill more of Eleazar's men.

When he got back to his feet, Eleazar saw what the Romans had done while the Jews sought cover against the barrage. They had placed a pile of pitch-soaked timber at the base of the door and had set it on fire with torches. They were going to burn the gate down.

It would take time for the temple's massive, silver-gilded wooden gates to burn through, but it was only a matter of time—mere hours. The Jews could not quench the flames with water because of the pitch and the constant barrage of missiles. But Eleazar determined to fight to the end and inspire his men to do so as well. This was God's holy temple they were defending. It was the very heart and soul of their religion, of their history as a people.

He stood and yelled with all his strength through a hoarse voice, "Archers, release!"

• • • • •

Cestius knelt in prayer to the Roman god of the Legions, Mithras, also called Sol Invictus, the unconquered sun. Before him was a stone relief of the muscular warrior deity engaged in a tauroctony, a sacrificial slaying of the sacred bull. One hand held the bull by the nose, and the other plunged a dagger into it. The signs of the zodiac surrounded the engraving. There were also scenes from the myth of Mithras: his birth from a celestial rock encircled by the serpent of wisdom and a feast of the sacred bull's flesh called the Banquet of the Sun.[2]

Cestius and his Roman officers had engaged in the banquet earlier in the day in preparation for their attack on the Sheep Gate of the temple. The ritual consisted of eating bull's flesh and drinking wine, the flesh and blood of their god, intended to make them one with his power. Mithras was the god of the Roman legions.

Cestius was alone now in the mithraeum, a temple cave beneath the ground outside the Antonia.[3] The secret subterranean chamber was about seventy feet long and about twenty feet wide, with an arched vaulted ceiling upon which the stars of the heavens were painted. The temple, like most temples in this world, was a representation of the cosmos, the heavens and the earth.[4] And Cestius sought the wisdom and favor of his patron deity in this most serious of military endeavors. He suspected Nero was launching a war that could last for years and drain his resources. Cestius had dealt with the Jewish problem caused by the troublesome escapades of Florus. He could not decide which was worse: Jewish stubborn fanaticism or Florus' obsessive provocation. That warmonger was still annoying him from the grave, through some of Cestius' officers who had been loyalists to Florus. But those meddlesome leaders were not in charge of the attack that was unfolding above ground a mere hundred yards from this underground temple.[5]

Cestius lit incense in a couple of censers. Intoxicating fumes quickly filled the cavern with a hazy, hypnotic layer of smoke. He breathed in the incense and prayed, "Mighty Mithras, place your foot on the neck of your enemies. Grant me swift victory to bring glory home to Caesar."

"Not today, Cestius Gallus."

The voice shocked him. He looked up, thinking that it came from the engraving. But a shadowy figure stood in front of the image. The figure was tall. About eight feet high. Though Cestius' sight was somewhat impaired by the dark fog and his own senses, he could see its skin shining like bronze. But it did not look like Mithras. It was not muscular like the warrior deity. It was androgynous, neither male nor female. Or was it *both* male and female? It had long scraggly hair, long sharp fingernails, and its breath stank like a sewer. Whatever it was, Cestius knew it was not human. He trembled with fear. He had seen the worst inhumanity that man can do to man, but he had never felt this kind of fear before.

It said, "Close your eyes."

He obeyed.

"Breathe deeply."

He breathed in the aroma around him.

"Now open them."

Another shock cracked his rationality. The being now looked like the muscular warrior from the relief. He was handsome and square-jawed with flowing hair—but his breath still stank of sewer.

Cestius was more at ease with the familiarity.

"Mithras, my lord."

"Cestius, my servant," the being countered. "There is not much time left. There is something you must do. Immediately."

· · · · ·

Eleazar looked down upon the Roman forces from his vantage point on the portico above the Sheep Gate. His archers were still returning hopeless volleys against Roman scorpions and ballistas. The gate below still burned from the pitch set afire earlier. Its silver overlay had long melted in the red-hot heat, exposing its wooden interior, now charred black. Flames licked the entire gate. A black plume of smoke billowed into the sky, signaling the coming end.[6]

Eleazar saw the Romans wheel out a wooden battering ram, called the *aries* in Latin. It was a huge log with the cast-iron head of a horned ram mounted at the front. It hung like a pendulum on a swing within a triangle structure. It was housed beneath a roof of wood to protect the soldiers within from missiles above. It looked like some kind of hideous hybrid monster. The Roman soldiers began to wheel the ram over to the gate.

Eleazar yelled to his men below, "Aries attacks! All hands to brace the gate!" But instead of all hands obeying his command, about a third of the rebels turned and fled. They knew that anyone who had not surrendered upon the first hit of an aries forfeited their lives to the gladius. There was no turning back.[7]

Eleazar turned to his archers above. "Release at will." Though he knew they could do little against the protective covering of the ram.

At that very moment, two men standing right beside Eleazar on either side were each pierced through by a scorpion bolt. They flew off the ledge to the ground below. Eleazar dove to the ground in shock. Both deadly projectiles had been just inches from him. It was as if he had been protected. As if God had saved him from his enemies. As if God wanted him alive for his purpose. Eleazar felt a resurgence of courage through his whole being.

He grabbed a rope that hung to the ground and slid down to join his men at the gate. Hundreds had gathered, carrying wooden braces. The gate had been sealed and unused since Hasmonean times and was bolted shut with a massive crossbar. But the gate was weakening as it burned on the other side. The wood was giving way to the flames.

There was a crashing sound on the outside of the gate, and the huge double door shuddered beneath the force. The Romans had begun to use the ram.

Eleazar yelled again, "Brace the gate!"

The hundreds of men placed their wooden poles and logs against the gate. This was too hot for them to use their hands. It seemed a hopeless gesture, but Eleazar would not give up. He could not give up.

Another pounding. The sound of charred wood giving way broke through all the men's bravery. Some soldiers fell back at the force. Eleazar held his brace and readied for the next hit. He turned to see another couple hundred soldiers flee their positions. He still had a thousand at his command, but not *thousands*. He needed thousands to have even a fighting chance.

The ram came again with pounding ferocity. The log was swinging back and forth on its pendulum to pummel the gate. With each hit, Eleazar felt the jarring down to his bones. He knew they were moments away from losing all. He screamed, "For Yahweh's temple!" They needed inspiration to face the impossible.

Another smash rattled them all. Then Eleazar heard the sound of splintering wood as the large crossbar cracked.

Another smash and the head of the aries broke through the burned wood like a punctured wound. When it pulled back, Eleazar could see the ram through the hole, manned by Roman soldiers.

They were almost through. The next hit would break open the gate, and Eleazar would finally confront the Romans in hand-to-hand battle, out-numbered and out-organized. He had expected this. He had prayed about it. He had prepared for it. But there was something overwhelming about facing such an indomitable foe. This was not a skirmish with other brigands in the desert. It wasn't the clannish battles he had previously fought. This was facing the very might of Rome. The wrath of Nero Caesar. It made adult men defecate in their trousers.

He glanced up to the heavens with expectation. Then shouted, "Prepare for combat!"

They braced the door for what would be the last hit.

Then Eleazar heard the sound of a Roman trumpet from behind the lines.

The ram hit the gate and crashed it open. The breach was wide enough for a half-dozen men to get through. The battering ram stuck through the opening over their heads.

Eleazar and his men drew their swords, ready to defend.

But the Romans didn't attack.

Through the opening, Eleazar could see the soldiers at the gates all pulling away like a receding wave.

The trumpet had been a command of retreat?

It didn't make any sense.

Eleazar yelled to his men, "Wait for my command!"

Grabbing the closest rope ladder, he scurried up as fast as he could to the roof of the portico.

At the top, he went to the ledge, now a crumbled pile of stone. In the distance, Eleazar could see Cestius Gallus, the general of the forces, on his horse commanding the soldiers to withdraw.[8]

What on earth was he doing?

The legionaries—even their centurions and optios—appeared confused by the order. But Cestius had absolute authority as Caesar's general. The Roman troops began to pull out their war machines and withdraw their forces.

Was Cestius regrouping for some reason?

Eleazar remembered that Cestius had another encampment against the Herodian palace in the upper city. Was this all a ruse? Draw the rebel fighters to the temple so that a second Roman regiment could flood the upper city virtually unopposed and raze it to the ground?

But it still didn't make sense to abandon a major breach that would have gained Cestius the keys of victory for the rest of the city.

Why would he leave at the climactic moment of breakthrough?

Just then, a messenger arrived on a horse. "Captain! The Romans have retreated from the Herodian palace! They're leaving the city!"

The men cheered.

Eleazar could not accept it. He remained with furrowed brow, seeking to figure out what strategic tactic Cestius was engaging in. Was there an unforeseen catastrophe of which the Jews were unaware? Were there new orders from Rome?

And then it struck him. His miraculous preservation from the arrows. His ability to unite the rebel forces previously at odds. His willingness to sacrifice all to defend God's temple. And now this miracle of deliverance. Maybe *Eleazar* was God's chosen deliverer.

He bellowed from his perch above, "Soldiers of Yahweh! The enemies of God are on the run! Now is the time of your deliverance! Retrieve your comrades who fled! Mount your horses and join me in destroying the Kittim!"

The warriors below cheered again and ran to the stairs that led to the horse stables below the temple mount.

Eleazar gazed into heaven proudly and prayed, "The Spirit of Yahweh Elohim is upon me, because Yahweh has anointed me to bring good news to the poor; he has sent me to proclaim liberty to the captives, and the opening of the prison to those who are bound; to proclaim the year of Yahweh's favor, and the day of vengeance of our God."[9]

CHAPTER 42

Beth-Horon Pass

Eleazar's bold, charismatic stand at the temple had inspired many of the rebels. He drew thousands to his side to pursue the fleeing Romans, who had quickly packed up camp from Mount Scopus and within a day were marching back to Caesarea at a hurried pace. Eleazar had chased them for the past six miles, launching sorties and raids on their baggage train at the rear. The Romans did not fight back. They just kept moving. Which struck Eleazar as unusual. So he sent scouts into the surrounding countryside to reconnoiter for a Roman ambush. But they had found none. Cestius was acting like a frightened amateur soldier on the run or like someone who had been spooked by a vision. He was making mistakes. About the only thing Eleazar could figure that motivated the Syrian general was that they were heading into winter and Cestius was not prepared for a siege in such conditions. He wasn't well supplied or supported by enough forces.

But how could thirty thousand soldiers with two thousand cavalry not be enough support? What did Cestius know that Eleazar did not? Whatever the reason, Eleazar seized upon it and continued to pick off hundreds of stragglers in the rear as they approached the Beth-Horon pass, a location of great symbolic religious significance to the Jews. It was a steep gorge of a valley where Joshua ben Nun had chased the Amorites and the sun had stood still. First, God had cast hailstones the size of boulders upon the cursed people of Canaan. Then Joshua had used the extended day to his advantage in wreaking vengeance on their enemies. Later in the days of the Maccabees, Judas the Hammer had slaughtered the Syrian governor Seron and his forces in this same pass.[1]

Yes, God was with the Jews in those days. And he was with them again. Eleazar felt like a modern Judas the Hammer. The previous night, Cestius had slaughtered those of his pack animals that weren't carrying artillery and left behind loads of baggage. He was trying to increase his speed. He was getting desperate.[2]

Eleazar's men were further reinforced as numbers of Jewish civilians streamed to their side from surrounding villages and farms, armed and ready to fight. Word was spreading throughout the countryside, and their zeal was enflamed like a wildfire that could not be stopped. The winds of war had turned.

God was indeed with the Jews again.

Eleazar continued to war upon the rear of Cestius' army as the Romans entered the Beth-Horon pass up ahead. It was dusk. Night would soon come and postpone the battle until morning. Eleazar wished that God would make the sun stand still again.

The Jewish rebel force took no prisoners, hacking down all soldiers and servants with merciless wrath.

Then Eleazar heard a Roman trumpet of alert. He looked ahead and saw an army of warriors appear from behind rocks, boulders, and ridges high on the steep edges of the pass. There *was* an ambush. But it wasn't for the Jews, it was for the Romans.

A scout on a horse, both breathing hard, reached Eleazar and announced, "It's Simon bar Giora with an army of Idumeans!"[3]

Eleazar could not help but smile. "That son of a scorpion." Eleazar had despised the previous captain of the temple. He had heard that Simon had betrayed his sacred vows and turned mercenary, but hadn't known where the renegade captain was hiding out in the wilderness. Now he had his answer. So the divided rebel factions were able to put aside their disputes with one another after all and bond together to fight the Roman Beast.

Eleazar motioned to his own herald, who blew his horn for the rebels to push ahead with their attack. The Jewish forces had hemmed in the Romans from behind and above. The unholy Kittim had been outflanked by God's chosen people.

High on the steep grade above the Romans, Simon bar Giora led his army in descent upon their surprised quarry with the fury of a storm god coming on clouds of judgment. From both sides of the valley, they ran within range, using slings, bows, and javelins, thousands of them.

Aaron and his Essene monks were in the lead with their well-aimed slings, pelting the Romans with missiles. They had developed their skills well. After a first wave of attacks, the Jews retreated, replaced by a new regiment who thrust their javelins. The Roman infantry protected themselves with their shields. They wouldn't break ranks. They couldn't. They were carrying such heavy packs and weighted armor that they could not chase the fleet-footed Jews, who wore no helmets and minimal body armor so they could maneuver quickly.[4]

The legionaries had to keep moving on the path. They had to push through the gauntlet.

The Roman cavalry was an unequalled force on level terrain. If this had been a field or plain, they would have devastated the Jews in response. But this was hill country, and the horses simply could not manage the steep grade. They were virtually useless. Those who did try to chase the Jews were drawn upward, surrounded by units of rebels, and taken down.[5]

Israelites had lived and fought in this hill country for generations. It was their strongest field of battle.

All the while, darts continued to rain down upon the unprepared Romans.

Simon had his eye on Cestius near the lead of the long train of soldiers. The Roman general was near the standard-bearer, surrounded by a bodyguard of six legionaries.

"Aaron, bring your slingers!" Simon yelled, trampling toward the general with eyes of fire.

Many of the centurions and other officers had been targeted by the Jewish forces. Without their leadership, the Roman lines began to disintegrate.

The dead, the wounded, and the abandoned baggage in the front became obstacles to the legionaries in the rear. It slowed them down, left them open to the missiles still falling down upon them. Panic ensued in the Roman ranks. Those pulling the artillery abandoned their posts. They were the easiest slow-moving targets of all. Hundreds of ballistas and scorpions were left for plunder.

Up at the front of the line, the cavalry had been decimated. Four hundred had been taken down. The rest of them galloped out of the valley to clear the way.[6]

Simon was within yards of Cestius. He threw a javelin and took down a bodyguard. The five others saw him and attacked.

Two of them were knocked off their horses by a hailstorm of rocks slung by Aaron's Essene unit. Simon ducked as the lead attacker swung at him with his sword. Simon slashed at the nearest leg of the attacker's horse. The horse fell to the ground, crushing the bodyguard.

Then Simon saw Cestius kick his horse and take flight. Finding another bodyguard, Simon reached up and pulled him down off his horse, impaling him with his sword. He jumped up on the mount and gave chase.

Simon got within range of Cestius easily enough. The weight and bulk of the general's armor slowed him. Simon raised a bow while riding and aimed at the biggest target available, the horse's hind quarters. Firing a bow from a moving horse was not easy. And the darkness falling upon them complicated the shot even more. But Simon had developed the skill as a necessity of his wilderness circumstances.

The missile hit. The horse went down. Cestius was thrown to the ground in an explosion of dust.

Simon jerked his reins to a stop and slid off his horse. They had pulled far away from the marching army behind them, and the cavalry was almost out of sight before them in the dark. They were all alone.

Simon approached his prey with deliberation. Full moonlight offered ample illumination to see Cestius scramble to his feet, releasing his cape and helmet. The Roman general drew his gladius and took a defensive stance.

Simon kept walking right up to Cestius and swung his sword without pause. The sixty-year-old general was no match for the younger seasoned warrior at the height of his skills.[7] Simon hacked and hewed with brute force. No swordplay needed with this battered old man. Cestius was pushed back with each advance. It took all he could do just to block each move.

Simon drank in the desperation of his impaired enemy.

One hard hit and Cestius' weapon was on the ground.

The general broke down, trembling. He dropped to his knees before Simon, who stood over Cestius in disgust. Simon would let the pig choke on his fear for a few moments. He wanted to reduce his enemy to the animal he was. A beast for slaughter.

Then the general's crying turned into a strange kind of laughing. He looked up. Simon could see a twisted look on his face in the moonlight. Fear had turned to madness.

Cestius said through a quivering voice, "You are all going to die." He let out a burst of maniacal laughter.

Simon remained silent. He would not dignify this beast's delirium.

"Do you really suppose Caesar will not return with ten times the soldiers? He will crucify Judea and enslave your women and children for generations. You have no idea of the principalities and powers arrayed against you."

Simon swung his sword and cut off the general's head.[8]

The decapitated body stayed in its upright kneeling position for a moment, like a corpse in macabre defiance, before collapsing to the dirt, twitching and soaking the ground in blood.

Simon looked at the face of his foe on the ground. Eyes wide-open in terror, mouth agape in fear, a frozen herald whose words haunted Simon. *Principalities and powers arrayed against you.* He wasn't talking of Rome. This was the language of spiritual authorities, of wickedness in high places. It was as if the general had seen into the heavenlies.

He pushed it out of his mind. Israel had Yahweh on their side. The God who had miraculously delivered them from the valley of the shadow of death. Surely, they were …

A sharp pain struck Simon's shoulder, and he fell to the ground. His instinct kicked in, and he looked up. Two horsemen approached him from out of the darkness. An arrow stuck out of his left collar bone area. It wasn't his sword arm. He still had a fighting chance.

Or did he? One of the horsemen held a javelin within range. The other nocked another arrow in his bow.

The lead horsemen said to his fellow warrior, "I think death would be too easy for this Jewish scum."

But before they could utter another word, a flurry of stones hit them both, dropping them to the ground.

In seconds, a dozen Essenes surrounded the unconscious Romans. Aaron led them.

Simon saw Aaron draw his sword and hesitate. The Roman hostage stirred. Seeing the monks standing over him, the Roman drew his dagger in defense. He swiped at Aaron. The monk dodged it and instinctively responded by impaling the Roman in the heart. The other horseman was dispatched before he came to.

Aaron cautiously backed away from the dead Roman, staring at the body as if expecting it to leap up and attack them all. As he approached Simon, the wounded warrior could see the monk's sword hand was shaking. And he had a stunned look on his face. Simon knew that look. He knew exactly what had happened. It was Aaron's first kill in hand-to-hand combat. He and his monks had operated their slings from a distance, taking down many warriors. But that was removed from the personal. It was technology at a distance. To kill a man with your own hand was an entirely different matter. It was not easy to do. And once you had done it, it changed you forever.

Simon looked up into Aaron's eyes, no longer innocent, no longer naïve. He grunted in pain and said, "Now, you understand."

Aaron remained mute with shock. One of his Essene comrades spoke up. "We have to get you out of here. Nightfall has stopped the battle, but not the Roman footrace. They'll be this way soon, like a herd of swine in panic."[9]

Simon smiled. He looked up and saw in the moonlight one of the Essenes carrying the standard of the Twelfth Legion. It was a long pole with a golden-cast image of an eagle at the top. Below the crest and legion number was the open hand of legion loyalty. Below that was an image of the emperor and a flowing red banner of the general. The standard was more than a mere signal. It was the sacred guarded emblem of the legion and symbolic presence of Caesar. To the Jew, it was a detestable image of idol worship. Its capture by the Jews was more serious a failure for the Romans than the entire loss of the battle. It was a psychological victory that would demoralize the Kittim and empower the Jews.[10]

Aaron and another monk helped Simon to his feet and onto his horse. Aaron said, "Eleazar ben Simon captured the Roman pay chest and confiscated all their artillery. Hundreds of ballistas and scorpions."[11]

"Well then," grunted Simon as he got on his mount, "when the Romans return, they can use their own weapons against them. They'll need all the help they can get."

Aaron stared at Simon. "They? *We* just decimated the Twelfth Legion and captured their standard. *You* led us in the victory, Simon."

Cestius' words still mesmerized Simon. *Principalities and powers arrayed against you.* Rome was not a single entity. She consisted of all the nations, tribes, and peoples she had conquered and conscripted into her service.

"Do not be a fool, Aaron. Tonight we were lucky. Rome will return to Judea. And when she does, she will bring all the nations with her."[12]

"Surely you can see that God is with us. Everything is coming to pass just as our scrolls foretold. The War of the Sons of Light against the Sons of Darkness. Belial, the evil one, will be overthrown."

"I told you already," said Simon. "I will fight to free the poor and oppressed from the ruling class who exploit them. I will rob and I will plunder their ill-gotten riches. But I will not die in a war I know is hopeless for a cause in which I do not believe."

Simon got on his horse. "Tonight, I return to Masada with my Sicarii and the Idumeans. Good luck with your holy war."

Simon whistled to his men and galloped off into the night.

CHAPTER 43

Jerusalem

The streets of Jerusalem were filled with jubilant citizens, some carrying palm branches, lined up to get into the temple for the celebration of victory over the Romans. In the outer court, thousands ate and drank and danced to the music of minstrels playing psalms of joy. It was a banquet feast. Yahweh had routed the Romans.

Eleazar watched the festivities from his perch high on the inner temple gate. He had returned to the inner temple with his Zealots. Upon bringing the spoils back to Jerusalem, he found himself still opposed by the Sanhedrin. The Sanhedrin that was manipulated by that snake Sadducee Ananus ben Ananus.[1] Ananus had sewn seeds of gossip among the ruling class, casting blame for the siege on Eleazar because of his cessation of the daily sacrifice for Caesar. Some of the Sanhedrin even accused Eleazar of tyranny. Tyranny! After he had defended the temple, then chased the Roman invaders all the way to the Beth-Horon pass, at great danger to himself. Eleazar had united the various rebel factions to fight the Kittim and drive them out. They had killed six thousand Romans and yet had only suffered the loss of a few hundred of their own.[2] It was a miracle. Even Simon bar Giora had joined him with his gangs of thugs and Idumeans. Their combined efforts crushed the tyrannical imposition of Caesar upon the Jewish people. And these ruling-class weasels had the temerity to reject the deliverer of Beth-Horon pass.

Eleazar was just going to have to pursue his own plans. *Wait until Rome returns—and they will return—then see to whom they will go begging for liberation.*

Eleazar paused in his anger as he watched a train of Sanhedrin arrive from below, protected by the temple guard. Ananus ben Ananus stepped up to a platform in the outer court directly opposite the temple. He had with him seven other leaders, including the Pharisee Joseph ben Matthias.

Heralds blew their trumpets, and the crowd quieted down. Musicians stopped playing their instruments. Acrobats and dancers stopped their performances. Everyone's attention was drawn to the podium where Ananus' booming voice announced, "In the days of Moses, Yahweh parted the Red Sea, crushed the heads of Leviathan, and delivered his people from Pharaoh. In the days of Joshua, he made the sun stand still in the valley of Aijalon to liberate us from the Amorites. He cut down the Anakim and the Nephilim, the seed of the Serpent in Canaan, to deliver this Land to us as an inheritance. Our forefather David, the anointed one, slew the mighty Rephaim giant, Goliath, and delivered Israel from the hands of the Philistines. In the days of Nehemiah, Yahweh used his anointed one, Cyrus, to deliver the Jews from Babylon. In the days of the Maccabees, Yahweh used Judas the Hammer to deliver us from the Greek abomination of desolation."

Ananus paused dramatically. He raised his hands in triumphal offering. "And now today, Yahweh has delivered us from the Roman abomination and crushed their invasion!"

The crowds went wild with excitement. Eleazar added silently, *Through his anointed one, Eleazar ben Simon.*

Ananus continued, "We are the chosen people of God, the children of Abraham. We are the holy ones who keep God's Torah, circumcision, and Sabbaths in the land that he has promised to us as an inheritance!"

The crowd applauded in agreement.

"Today we celebrate. God has been faithful to his holy ones. Enjoy this victory because you have earned it." Another dramatic pause and a somber tone came over him. "But tomorrow we must prepare because Rome will return. And she will be stronger. So we must be stronger. And so we shall be!"

The crowd cheered. It was wild with emotion. Israel had done the impossible yet again. God was on her side.

Ananus wrapped it up. "The Sanhedrin has met in counsel, and I am here to report to you that they have appointed me as supreme commander of the city of Jerusalem and all her forces."[3]

More cheering in the crowd.

Blasphemy, thought Eleazar. *This soulless priest and his manipulation of the masses.*

"These men I have on the platform with me have been appointed as generals over the regions and cities of the Land: Judea, Idumea, and Galilee."

Joseph ben Matthias was the appointed general in Galilee. Eleazar was grateful that Joseph would be up in those backwoods and out of his hair. Joseph had been particularly annoying and arrogant.[4]

"We will immediately set about rebuilding our fortifications, including the walls of Jerusalem. And we will begin building war engines. But fear not, Israelites. Yahweh's right arm is strong. Let us celebrate his glory and power and honor now and forevermore, amen!"

A loud cheer broke out in the crowd. The celebration had begun.

Despicable egomaniac, thought Eleazar. *Let us see how well you do without my leadership that won your victory, and without the finance of the booty I confiscated.*

In the distraction of the resultant singing and dancing and drinking, the Jewish citizens were oblivious to the one group that was conspicuously absent from this celebration: the Christians.

· · · · ·

"This miracle was Yahweh's means of waking us up," said Alexander. "To give us one last chance to flee the city for the mountains as he had warned us."[5] He stood outside with Cassandra, Demetrius, Boaz, and the old prophet Joshua in the cool October wind amidst a large gathering of Christians in the Essene quarter of Jerusalem.

Cassandra ignored Alexander. Joshua said, "His timing is impeccable. He likes to keep his holy ones at the cutting edge of faith."

Hundreds of Christian citizens had packed up their belongings for travel to a new city, a new life.[6] Some had carts, others horses. Most would be on foot. Demetrius and his forty Kharabu warriors would protect them on their journey. Their goal was Pella, the abandoned city in the mountains of the Decapolis fifty miles northeast of Jerusalem. It was the city Demetrius had recommended to them. The excommunicated Jacob bar Mordecai and his Judaizers were staying behind. They believed the holy city and temple would be protected by Jesus' own legion of angels. Alexander knew that when the Son of Man came, he would say to them, "I never knew you."

Demetrius said to Joshua, "I will miss you, old man, and your loud mouth for the gospel."

"You should stay," said Joshua. "I could use the help of a young mule."

Demetrius smiled and embraced him.

Cassandra hugged Joshua next. She lingered. When he pulled away, her eyes were full of tears. She said through a shaky voice, "Come with us, Joshua. After all these unbelievers have done to you, why would you stay? They deserve what is coming. Not you."

Joshua looked at her with a kind and gracious eye. "Cassie, I am ready to die for the sake of my kinsmen according to the flesh, if I might save some. It is my calling." His face grew grave with concern. "Dear sister, do not let the root of bitterness defile you. Remember, you too were once dead in your sins and trespasses when Messiah died for you. We are no more deserving of forgiveness than the worst of the scribes and Pharisees who rejected Jesus."

She embraced him again, this time in weeping. When she stepped back, he announced to the others, "And let it be noted, I've changed my name. From this day forward, you shall know me as Moshe. An angel told me to take the name of our lawgiver."

Cassandra stopped weeping to look at him for confirmation. The others were equally surprised, yet not uninformed. It was common practice to change one's name based on a dramatic change of life or calling from God. Yahweh had changed Abram's name to Abraham when he made a covenant with the patriarch to turn Abram from a *noble father* to a *father of many*. His wife Sarai, meaning *princess*, also had her name changed to Sarah, or *mother of nations*. Jacob's name, meaning *supplanter*, was changed to Israel, meaning *struggles with God*. Jesus changed the disciple Simon's name to Peter, which meant *rock*. Even God himself revealed different aspects of his character through his names in history. To Abraham, Isaac, and Jacob, he was known as El Shaddai, or God Almighty. At Sinai, he revealed himself as Yahweh, the great I Am of the Mosaic covenant.[7]

Everyone there understood the old man's meaning. It was the purpose of the very Revelation they had been spreading to the four corners. Joshua had received the calling of a prophet. And prophets were prosecutors in Yahweh's heavenly court. They brought charges for and against Israel. In this case, the Law condemned Israel for being a faithless wife, a spiritual adulterer, whom

Yahweh was divorcing and soon to execute for her crimes of rejecting her husband. The Apocalypse was the scroll of divorce in that court. And Joshua had been called as a new Moses to pronounce the law in her midst and call down the plagues of judgment. He was already doing so when they met him. It was now official. He was one of two witnesses required by Torah for such judgments.[8]

Alexander wondered who the other witness would be. The Apocalypse had foretold that two witnesses would prophecy with God's authority for twelve hundred and sixty days, or forty-two months, the time that Rome would trample underfoot the holy city. It was called the "times of the Gentiles" because it represented three-and-a-half years that the unholy nation of Gentiles, Rome, would trample the holy land of Israel and finally, Jerusalem.[9] It was the same fourth kingdom beast of Daniel led by the abominable "prince to come" that had not yet risen up. Cestius was only a precursor to the Roman campaign that was about to be unleashed. The "one who makes desolate" would soon arise.

The Kharabu warrior Michael broke the sober silence that had fallen on them all. "We had best get moving. We have miles ahead of us."

Several of the warriors whistled to get attention. Boaz's escort raised a banner to notify they were on the move. The Christian caravan began to make its way out of the nearby Essene Gate into the valley. It was their exodus out of what had become to God the new Egypt, the new Sodom, the new Babylon. And this physical exodus was merely an earthly counterpart to their spiritual exodus out of old covenant Israel and into the Messiah, the new inheritance of the kingdom of God.

Before they could even make substantial progress, Alexander saw a mob of Jews approaching them from several side streets. He saw a familiar face in the lead of the crowd spewing invectives at them.

"Well, if it isn't the serpent himself, Jacob bar Mordecai." He saw Cassandra's face harden with spite.

The crowd seemed hostile. They cheered and whistled and waved good riddance to the Christians. Alexander felt an object hit him in the arm and fall to the ground. It was a wilted cabbage head filled with worms. Others were now pelting the Christians with rotten vegetables. Brushing off the residue from his tunic, he yelled out, "Remember the words of our Lord! Bless those who curse you and pray for those who abuse you!" He could see that Cassandra was having a difficult time turning her cheek to such hatred.[10]

He could hear Jacob shout out, "Christians leave the city! Unclean! Unclean!"

The crowds joined in, chanting, "Unclean! Unclean!"

According to Torah, sharing bread with Gentiles, disregarding circumcision, violating dietary laws and Sabbaths made one unclean as a leper was unclean, cut off from the congregation. Christians were accused of all these things, so Jews were only too happy to get rid of them.

Alexander considered the irony that the truth was exactly the opposite. Christians were Yahweh's holy ones, the 144,000 Remnant, sealed and undefiled in the blood of the Lamb. The Land had become defiled by earthly Israel's rejection of Messiah, so God was removing his heavenly people to clean house. Earthly Jerusalem would soon be overrun by demons and permanently cut off by the cloud-coming of Messiah's judgment.

Alexander prayed for the souls of his kinsmen.

• • • • •

Caesarea Maritima

Apollyon watched from the shadows with great satisfaction as Herod Agrippa stood in his royal bathrobe at the palace balcony overlooking the city. The earthly prince said, "They finally did it. They provoked Caesar, and now they will get what they asked for. But they will wish they had not."

Berenice lay naked on the silken bed after their sexual tryst. She resented him spoiling her momentary release from the stress of their world. She refused to respond.

Agrippa kept musing, waxing poetic. "The moon shall turn to blood, and the sun shall become black as night. The stars of the heaven shall fall to the land. And the sky shall be rolled up like a scroll. Men will hide themselves in caves. And they shall say to the mountains, 'cover us,' and to the hills, 'fall on us!' They will long to die, but death will flee from them."[11]

He was quoting imagery used by the prophets to describe the heavenly cataclysm that occurred whenever a nation's earthly power was overthrown.

"Brother, you have such a penchant for the melodramatic."

"Apocalyptic," he corrected her. "I always wanted to be a prophet. But, alas, God made me a king."

She said, "Let us pray the Herods will not be among those falling stars."

He smiled. He had drawn her out, as he always could. "Of course, there will be some advantage to *you* in all this terror. Soon, your beloved Titus will be here. Have you missed him so?"

She smirked. "Surely you are not jealous of what will no doubt advance a legacy between our family and the Imperial future. I have enough love for you both."

"You are so sure of yourself, sister. Yet the Flavians are not in the Julio-Claudian line."

"No. But then there are no heirs left in the Julio-Claudian line because Nero has murdered them all."

"Well, then. May you advance the Herods with your finely tuned skills of ... pleasing the men in your life. To your advantage."

Berenice laughed. He *was* jealous. She had him—and she had him.

He became somber. "I received word from Damascus. The Syrian residents rounded up ten thousand Jewish citizens in the gymnasium and butchered them."[12]

Fear and dread pulsed through Berenice's entire body. She pulled the sheet up to cover herself. "Why did you not tell me this?"

"I thought it might distress you too soon."

She choked on the thought of it. "My God, it's really happening."

He looked back out onto the horizon. "Do you really believe in the prophecies of a coming Messiah?"

"I don't know what to believe. I see so much ... suffering."

"What if he is coming? But what if he is not the one we expected?"

"What are you talking about, brother?"

"What if the Savior of Israel ... is her destroyer?"

She was confused. "You mean Rome?"

He changed the subject. "I don't know what I mean."

Apollyon turned his head. He heard a herald call from the unseen realm. Only divine beings could hear it. The sound was like a whistling wind or a hissing serpent. Watchers had entered the city.

He walked out to the veranda, unseen by the mortals, and hissed his response into the wind. He climbed over the edge of the balcony and jumped to the ground fifty feet below.

Apollyon met the daughters of Allah at the temple of Roma and Augustus near the center of the city. Herod had built it to honor the god-king and his patron deity for the imperial cult. There was no end to the spiritual corruption that royal Edomite had brought to Israel in his long and diabolical career. He tasted sweet to Apollyon's memory.

They met in the shadow of the portico of columns and walked into the holy place where they could speak without fear of being overheard by any eavesdropping angel.

"What good news do you bring?" asked the Master.

When they answered, their three voices were synchronized. They were a threefold divinity who spoke as one. "Our lord and god, we captured an archangel and interrogated him. We know where the four kidnapped Watchers are being held."

"Well done, my girls. You outshine your simpleton father."

"They are bound at the Euphrates River in the north. He will not tell us where until we get there."[13]

"Good. You will find them. And I will unleash the demons of war."

CHAPTER 44

*And a great sign appeared in heaven: a woman clothed with the sun, with the moon under her feet, and on her head a crown of twelve stars [true Israel]... She gave birth to a male child [Jesus the Messiah], one who is to rule all the nations with a rod of iron ... but the woman fled into the wilderness, where she has a place prepared by God, in which she is to be nourished for 1,260 days ... And when the dragon saw that he had been thrown down to the land, he pursued the woman [the Remnant] who had given birth to the male child. But the woman was given the two wings of the great eagle so that she might fly from the serpent into the wilderness, to the place where she is to be nourished for **a time, and times, and half a time** [3-1/2 years].*
—The Apocalypse of Jesus Christ 12:1–6, 13-14

Pella
The Time, Times, and a Half a Time Begins

The caravan of hundreds of Christians finished entering the newly-built gates of the city nestled in a valley of the Transjordanian mountain range. Alexander could see why it was a good place to resettle. It was but a mile east of the Jordan River, which allowed them access to water. It was not too remote to stay in contact with the rest of their world. As part of the Decapolis region, Pella had been a predominately Greek city. So when the Romans returned to Judea, it was more likely to be avoided in favor of subduing exclusively Jewish towns and villages. And word had already gotten out that Pella had been wiped out in the civil war that had spread through the land. That was why some of the Christians escaping other cities like Scythopolis, Tiberias, and Nazareth had already settled there and begun the arduous process of rebuilding the damaged infrastructure and reestablishing an active government. The new refugees had been accepted in by their fellow Christian brethren to help them start their new life as strangers in a strange land.[1]

Most had been sponsored by other families and housed in their quarters until they could find or build their own homes. Demetrius had found large enough quarters to house him and his three Kharabu warriors, Michael, Gabriel, and Uriel, as well as Cassandra and Alexander.

The evening found them around a fire in the atrium at the center of the home. They had spent some time in prayer, thanking Yahweh for their safe delivery to Pella. They prayed for Severus wherever he was. But in this brutal time, they could not help but think the worst.

Alexander felt restless. Cassandra had been ignoring him. She'd hardly spoken to him the entire four days of their journey to get here. He had virtually forgotten why she'd gotten mad at him back in the prison cell. He remembered only that it had to do with her discovering his love for her and how that had ruined their friendship. Alexander watched Demetrius' strong, confident stature in the firelight next to his fellow Kharabu captains. He felt a wave of envy wash over him again. They were so daring, so bold and heroic. They risked their lives to save the innocent. They accomplished so much as warriors that it made Alexander feel useless, less of a man. Yes, he healed the sick and wounded. But they vanquished evil.

He knew he was not a warrior, so he had made up his mind to do the best he could with what lesser skills he had been given.

Michael announced to the group, "The time has come for the three of us Kharabu to leave you."

Cassandra asked, "Where will you go?"

Michael said, "We have a task to do up by the Euphrates River. But I will return to Pella."

Cassandra asked, "Will you be going with them, Demetrius?"

Alexander watched her.

"I wish I was," he said. "They have protected me like God's own angels." He gave a knowing smile at the Kharabu.

"Yahweh will protect you," said Uriel. "Probably more than he does us."

Michael gave him a scolding look.

Then Alexander decided to release his soul of the burden he had been carrying for some time. He said, "I will be returning to Jerusalem."

Everyone looked at him with shock.

Uriel asked, "To certain death?"

Alexander glanced at Cassandra, who appeared to become even colder toward him, if that was possible.

"All my life I have sought to compromise to survive. I compromised my faith to embrace the Hellenistic culture that has corrupted our people. And it corrupted me. I compromised my ethics to serve a Roman prefect and betray the Christians. I told myself I was helping my people. But I was really just a coward trying to survive. Because I had nothing to die for."

He looked at Cassandra. "Because of God's grace and your faith, I now serve Jesus the Messiah." He looked at Demetrius and his three captains. "I am no warrior. I have neither the skills nor the courage to kill those who deserve to die. But I do have the skills to heal. And I do know that when Rome comes there will be great suffering for the Jews in that city like never before in our history. If Jerusalem comes under siege, there will be many wounded, much disease and famine. I can help them. And I can share the gospel of liberation with them."

He looked again at Cassandra, whose eyes were tearing. "I know that judgment upon this people is deserved. But we deserve it too. Yet God plucked us out of the fire. I want to give as many as I can that last chance that I was given. I will never compromise to save myself again. I am ready to die."

In the respectful silence that followed, Alexander saw Cassandra stand up with frustration and in a huff turn away from the fire. She could not fully suppress her weeping. Her moans could be heard by everyone in an extended awkward silence.

Alexander knew this was his last chance to redeem what he had left with her before he would never see her again. He said with a shaky voice, "Forgive me for doing this, but I have been a fool in front of everyone with how I have treated you, Cassandra. So it is only fitting that I apologize in front of everyone as well. I know that I have hurt you by falling in love with you when you have been in love with Demetrius."

She turned back around to him, her eyes bleary red, her face contorted with confusion. She looked at Demetrius, who returned her gaze with a shrug. Alexander saw it, but couldn't understand why. So he kept going, "I have been too much of a coward to tell you because here too I have compromised to save my fragile, selfish ego. I am sorry for what I have caused. Please forgive me."

He waited for her response. She could only say one thing. "You dumb ox. It is not Demetrius who I am in love with."

Alexander's entire body felt a chilling shock. He glanced at Demetrius, who gave him a sympathetic look. Cassandra continued, "I have been angry with you because you presumed upon me what was not true, and you offered me no opportunity to correct you. I have been angry with you because I could not understand how a man who is so compassionate about the suffering of others, a man of humility and kindness and sacrifice, a man whom I respect above all I have ever met, could be so dull-minded about what was staring him in the face."

Alexander froze like a marble statue of a fool in an Aristophanes play.

"I forgive you, Alexander Maccabaeus. But I am not going to let you return to Jerusalem alone. Your task is too big for one man. You need help. You need an assistant." Cassandra began to cry again. She spoke through her tears. "I have been a prisoner of my own hatred of the Jews who killed my family. I have wallowed in the perverse desire to see them all judged and thrown alive into the Lake of Fire. I have become what I have hated. It is time for me to love my enemy."

When she stopped, Alexander could barely see through his own tears. But now he could feel he was grinning more widely than he had ever grinned before. He stopped himself and became firm. "I will not allow you to come to Jerusalem with me and subject yourself to such risk and danger." He saw her eyes go wide with shock. "Unless you agree to one condition."

She couldn't even ask. She could only give him a confused look that asked the question, what?

"That you marry me, Cassandra Laetorius. You fiery angel of God."

Her confusion turned to delight. She broke down in weeping, but this time it was for joy. Alexander walked over to her and embraced her. He was never going to let her go.

CHAPTER 45

The wedding was no small affair. In the light of their present situation of much loss and suffering, many of the Christians wanted a reason for hope and celebration, and this marriage provided the opportunity. Cassandra felt as if the entire city had joined in on their seven-day ceremony of festivities. She had felt it was all a bit too much, that she didn't deserve it. She had thought she was never going to be married. She had even committed her life to ministry to accomplish more for the kingdom in these last days. But she had accepted Alexander's proposal because she now saw her understanding of ministry transform from one of judgment to grace. Yes, they would be walking into great danger and, most likely, their deaths. But it would be worth it. She would be supporting Alexander to bring relief to those suffering and the hope of eternal life to those who had ears to hear.

She had served the apostle Paul and Apollos for many years, transporting them in their itinerant ministries, helping them to bring the gospel to the ends of the earth. It had given her a sense of strength, of superiority, of pride. And now God had humbled her through the love of this man of compassion. He was not a warrior, but he was just as strong as Demetrius. His strength lay not in the ability to fight and kill others, but to face suffering and bring healing. She felt the release of her bitterness. They were going to lay down their lives as living sacrifices to the very ones who had rejected them and persecuted them. But she now understood that their calling was their own. That God used people in different ways to accomplish his complex purposes. Though she had differed with Demetrius over the use of violence, she now understood that pure pacifism empowered the very monsters it sought to withstand. Righteousness and peace could kiss, though it was an uneasy embrace. Both warrior and healer were gifts in the body of Christ that embodied both justice and grace.

Cassandra's thoughts were interrupted by the sight of her beloved in the moonlight. She had been led through the streets by a group of female celebrants carrying lamps with music and dancing. She stopped yards away from Alexander at the threshold of the home they had been staying at. He wore a fine, rich indigo-blue mantle over a linen tunic, obviously borrowed from a wealthy Hellenist. They had no money, after all. He had shaved his beard and cut his hair, and she noticed how truly handsome he was.

She saw him staring at her with his mouth open, like a stunned little boy who has just discovered girls. As she drew near, a big smile grew on his lips. It made her feel uncomfortable. She wasn't used to such … attention. She had never cared much for outward beauty. She had cultivated her inner character and had sought to avoid vanity. But today her sisters in Christ had clothed her in bright golden robes with a dowry of jewelry and precious gems. Like many others, she had lost everything in the Tribulation, so these extravagances were donated piecemeal from the community. Her headband and veil felt tight on her head, and she had never worn so much make-up or so many necklaces, bracelets, anklets, and rings in her entire life. She felt like royalty. She had never displayed her own family's merchant wealth when she had it, so this was also something she longed to remove from her body.

The hungry look in Alexander's eyes made her consider that he longed to remove them as well, but for a different reason. She had memorized the Song of Solomon when she was a young girl and foolishly in love with love. As the Great Tribulation had spread through the empire and her youthful ideals vanished, she had never imagined she would ever experience that very Scripture. But it now came back to her in pieces.

> *You have captivated my heart, my sister, my bride;*
> > *you have captivated my heart with one glance of your eyes.*
> *I am a rose of Sharon,*
> > *A lily of the valleys.*
> *My beloved brought me to the banqueting house,*
> > *and his banner over me is love.*
> *Arise, my love, my beautiful one,*
> > *and come away.*
> *My beloved is mine and I am his.*[1]

Alexander met her, and the two of them entered the home. They were crowned with garlands in the atrium, where the friends of the bridegroom, Demetrius and his Kharabu warriors, bore witness along with some of

Cassandra's new female friends. She had never felt safer in her entire life than right now. She had forgotten the whole world outside and all its evils.

They signed a traditional marriage contract where Alexander promised to care for and keep his wife in the manner of men of Israel. They washed their hands in ritual purity, and Demetrius said a benediction over them culled from the apostolic letters.

"May the Lord make you increase and abound in love for one another and for all, as we do for you, so that he may establish your hearts blameless in holiness before our God and Father at the coming of our Lord Jesus with all his saints. He who testifies to these things says, 'Surely I am coming soon.' Amen. Maranatha."[2]

The witnesses all responded, "Maranatha."

Come, Lord Jesus.

The banquet feast went on late into the night. As Alexander drank his wine and ate of the rich foods donated by the residents, he could not help but wonder at his undeservedness of such blessing. He watched his beloved enjoying the festivities. At that moment, Demetrius and his Kharabu warriors were engaged in a display of faux fighting. They looked as if they were dancing more than sparring. They flipped and twisted in the air with the lightness of angels. He knew that what appeared like fluid beauty in this festive performance was harnessed with lethal result in real battle. It was another one of the many examples of Yahweh's creative and fearful symmetry. Alexander had lived under constant fear and intimidation of this warrior who in actuality had protected and prepared his Cassandra for this moment. For him!

For the first time, he felt no envy as she watched Demetrius. Instead, Alexander watched her with desire. The imagery of Solomon's love song came to his mind.

> *You are beautiful, my love,*
> *lovely as Jerusalem.*
> *Your rounded thighs are like jewels,*
> *the work of a master hand.*
> *Your navel is a rounded bowl*
> *that never lacks mixed wine.*

Your belly is a heap of wheat,
  encircled with lilies.
Your stature is like a palm tree,
  and your breasts are like its clusters.
I say I will climb the palm tree
  and lay hold of its fruit.[3]

Cassandra looked at him with a smile on her face. She leaned over, and they kissed—deeply. And all of the pain and suffering of life just melted away from his memory.

He whispered in her ear, "I love you, Cassie." He had been dying to call her that for years. Jealous of everyone else who could, like Demetrius. But now he could say it with complete and utter devotion. And it tasted delicious to him.

"I love you, Alex." They kissed again.

The sound of the music ending the Kharabu performance brought them back from the stars to earth.

Demetrius came to the front table, still breathing heavily from his energetic feats on display.

As he smiled at the newlyweds, Alexander noticed Demetrius' eyes were wet with happiness. He turned to the crowd and announced, "May I have your attention!" The crowd obeyed.

"As a friend of both bride and bridegroom, I want to give my most heartfelt congratulations and hope for their new union of love." Alexander could hear hearty approvals from the gathering. "I have been through heaven and Hades with these two." Chuckles in the crowd. "We have all been changed forever by each other and by recent events."

He paused, choking up. "One very special person is absent from this joyous occasion." Alexander held Cassandra's hand tightly. They knew to whom he was referring. "Lucius Aurelius Severus, a dear beloved brother in Christ, was sailing to Patmos for the sake of the gospel. I have recently received word that the ship on which he was sailing never arrived at its destination and is believed to have been lost at sea." A hush went over the crowd. "And though our hearts are heavy with sorrow at our loss, we know where our brother resides—at home in the presence of the Lord. He would be angry at us right now if we did not rejoice." The crowd chuckled in agreement.

"And we also rejoice, knowing that God used Severus to bring Alexander and Cassandra together. In a rather—undesirable way." The newlyweds laughed nervously together.

Alexander could not forgive himself for how he had first treated Cassandra. It still bothered him.

"But God's grace is greater. His blood covers a multitude of sins. He redeems the years that the locusts have eaten." More amens through the crowd. Demetrius paused.

When the noise died down, Demetrius said, "The bridegroom and his bride have asked me to share with you what I told them earlier."

He looked at Alexander and Cassandra. "They will not have seen the last of me yet. Because I too will be returning to Jerusalem to preach the gospel." The audience rumbled with curiosity. "The Kharabu warriors will remain to watch over you here at Pella. So do not stop celebrating this day, for you are in good hands. Let this wedding feast be a foretaste of the wedding supper of the Lamb that is to come shortly. That supper is the glory of God's new covenant kingdom, for his bride has made herself ready." Applause and praise broke out in the wedding party. It sounded like congregational worship.

Alexander was impressed. Demetrius truly had a gift for oration. He always had. And now it all made sense. Because what Demetrius did not tell the crowd might have dampened the joy of the evening. So they let him keep it a secret. The truth was that Demetrius was putting down his sword to join the prophet Moshe in Jerusalem. The Egyptian had told Alexander and Cassandra earlier that God had told him to change his name to Elihu, the Hebrew name for Elijah. That he was to be one of the Two Witnesses who would prophesy of the city's coming desolation.

So the prophecies were coming to pass. The time was near. The hour was at hand.

The things which John had written in his Apocalypse would take place shortly.

Jesus was coming quickly.[4]

Alexander stood and got the crowd's attention. "I think it would be appropriate in light of our exodus and of what is coming for us to sing the songs of the 144,000 in the Apocalypse. The Song of Moses and the song of the Lamb."[5]

The sound of agreement affirmed his statement. Cassandra held his arm tightly with pride, emboldening him. He led them first in the song of the Lamb.

> *Great and amazing are your deeds,*
>> *O Lord God the Almighty!*
> *Just and true are your ways,*
>> *O King of the nations!*
> *Who will not fear, O Lord,*
>> *and glorify your name?*
> *For you alone are holy.*
>> *All nations will come*
>> *and worship you,*
> *for your righteous acts have been revealed.*[6]

Then with a smooth transition, Alexander led them in the sobering Song of Moses that warned of the judgment yet to come.

> *Give ear, O heavens, and I will speak,*
>> *and let the earth hear the words of my mouth.*
> *The Rock, his work is perfect,*
>> *for all his ways are justice.*
> *A God of faithfulness and without iniquity,*
>> *just and upright is he.*
> *Jacob has dealt corruptly with him;*
>> *they are no longer his children because they are blemished;*
>> *they are a crooked and twisted generation.*
> *When the Most High gave to the nations their inheritance,*
>> *when he divided mankind,*
> *he fixed the borders of the peoples*
>> *according to the number of the sons of God.*
> *But the Lord's portion is his people,*
>> *Jacob his allotted heritage.*
> *But they stirred him to jealousy with strange gods;*
>> *with abominations they provoked him to anger.*
> *They sacrificed to demons, not God,*
>> *to gods they had never known,*
> *to new gods that had come recently,*
>> *whom your fathers had never dreaded*
> *Yahweh says, "I will heap disasters upon them;*
>> *I will spend my arrows on them;*

"they shall be wasted with hunger,
    and devoured by plague
    and poisonous pestilence;
"I will send the teeth of beasts against them,
    with the venom of things that crawl in the dust.
"Outdoors the sword shall bereave,
    and indoors terror,
"Vengeance is mine, and recompense,
    for the time when their foot shall slip;
"for the day of their calamity is at hand,
    and their doom comes swiftly."
So, rejoice with him, O heavens;
    bow down to him, all gods,
for he avenges the blood of his children
    and takes vengeance on his adversaries.
He repays those who hate him
    and cleanses his people's land.[7]

The 144,000 Remnant had left Jerusalem and the cities of the land in a new exodus out of the Egypt that Israel had become. Once again, Yahweh had spared his people and sealed them with his protection. But now, his angels were about to pour out plagues of vengeance upon the Land.

EPILOGUE

Rome
February, AD 67

Titus sat with his father Vespasian and brother Domitian at the banquet table set up by Nero for his general Corbulo and visiting governors from Germania. There were a hundred in all, and they awaited the arrival of plates of the finest foods in Rome. Servants brought in platters of pork, beef, and pheasant, followed by loaves of bread and trays piled with fresh vegetables and legumes. Olive oil, honey, and milk were also in abundance.

Nero announced before the meal began, "Before we partake of this bounty, may I propose a toast?" Wine stewards arrived and filled the cups of the officers. They raised their drink in honor to Nero.

Titus hated when Nero did toasts. The emperor was so melodramatic. Titus hated just about everything Nero did.

"To Gnaeus Domitius Corbulo, my governor general in Syria. You distinguished yourself with mighty victories in Germania under Claudius and in Armenia and against Parthia for me." Titus gave verbal approval along with others in the crowd. "For imperial glory, we raise these cups and sip of Apollo's nectar. For life is wine!"

The officers all drank from their cups in unison. Nero continued, "Unfortunately, my dear general Corbulo is also the father-in-law of one Lucius Annius Vinicianus."

Titus looked around the room. Some of the officers appeared threatened. Eyes darted. Someone coughed. Then another.

"And it has come to my attention that there has been a 'Vinician conspiracy' to assassinate me and replace me with my dear, distinguished General Corbulo himself." Officers looked panicked.

Titus saw Corbulo close his eyes, expecting the inevitable. More coughs rose from the crowd.

"And you all know that I do not take kindly to such conspiracies." One officer began a coughing fit that ended in choking. An older officer dropped to the ground in a dead faint. His cup clanged on the floor. And Titus knew what they all now knew. Nero had poisoned the friends and conspirators of Corbulo.[1]

He saw Vespasian take another deep swig from his cup, entirely confident in his innocence. Titus looked into his cup. He could not be so assured. And he could not forget how Nero had poisoned his friend Britannicus all those years ago. It was a cowardly act by a cowardly ruler who had not the courage to face his enemies with honor. And it still fueled Titus' hatred of the emperor.

A dozen of the officers collapsed and died with frothing mouths right before them.

But Corbulo and his two closest officers were not among them. The three survivors looked around in fear and appeared to have lost their appetites.

Nero started to chuckle to himself. He raised his cup again in toast and said, "Salute those who are departing. Give my regards to Pluto in the underworld."

His black humor was followed by an uneasy silence. Servants approached Corbulo and the two German governors, carrying platters with daggers on them.

The officers swallowed and took the blades.

Titus could see Corbulo look at the emperor and mutter, "I should have expected as much."

Corbulo held the knife to his wrist and opened his veins, as did the other two governors.

The irony of it all was that Titus wasn't even sure the conspiracy was real, anything other than another paranoid delusion in the fevered megalomaniac mind of Nero.

An eerie pall settled on the crowd as the three Roman leaders slowly fainted to the floor, their paling bodies becoming silhouetted slowly by growing pools of their own red blood.

What does one do at such a moment?

Wait for the emperor's lead.

Nero looked at Vespasian and Titus and said, "And now to this matter of Judea and the Jewish question ..."

• • • • •

The Capitoline hill was one of the governmental centers of the city of Rome and a precinct used for assemblies of the people like the one that now filled its streets. At the crest of the hill sat the city's most important sacred shrine, the temple of Jupiter Optimus Maximus.

Domitian watched Nero standing on the porch. It was a mighty structure of marble pillars that rose to the sky like ancient trees upholding the heavens. The emperor was dressed as Apollo again with his bright white toga and golden crown of sun rays. Domitian stood beside the emperor with hidden amusement. Nero's pock-marked face and the canker sores on his lips stood as a visual reminder of the contradiction. All the self-deification he displayed was just so much masquerade. Nero Caesar could not hide the fact that he was a mere human of mortal flesh. And his death was just a matter of time.

Three priests stood before the emperor with daggers that they used to cut open the sacrificial animals required by Mars, the god of war: an ox, a pig, and a sheep. Throats were slit, blood spilled on the pavement, and bellies cut open to gain the intestines, where a priest would examine the entrails as divination of the will of the gods.

The priests raised the bloody entrails and declared, "Success for Nero's campaign!" The crowds cheered. They proceeded to cut up the animals and burn them on the altars.[2]

Trumpets sounded, and an entourage of military leaders on horses now approached the base of the temple from behind the building. In the front of the parade was Titus, adorned in ceremonial armor and glory, leading an empty white horse beside his own. Domitian envied his brother's favored status with their father. He secretly hoped that Titus would be killed in the war.

Nero spoke to the masses, now quieted down. The acoustics of the temple and forum area projected his voice like a god's. Domitian made a mental note of the technique. One day, he might want such amplification.

"People of Rome. My people. The gods have concurred. The time is at hand. Rome is at war with Judea!" The crowd applauded. Jews had always been a problem in the empire. Now they were finally going to know their place.

"To prosecute this war, I will now crown my legate of the legions: Titus Flavius Vespasian!" Nero signaled behind him, and Vespasian came out from the pillars to the wild cheering of the citizens. He was dressed in the ceremonial garb of a general: white toga, golden armor, carrying an elaborate helmet in his arm.

Vespasian knelt before the emperor. The legate was the supreme general over all the forces in the region. He was invested with the presence and authority of Caesar in much the same way that an image of a god represented the god's presence and authority over a territory. The legate was the image and power of Caesar.[3]

Nero received a golden wreath from a priest, which he placed upon Vespasian's head. The crowd cheered again. Domitian heard Nero joke with Vespasian under his breath, "Don't let it fall off your bald head, old man." Vespasian smiled in return, whispering back, "I will do my very best not to fall asleep, my Caesar."

Vespasian stood, and the crowd went wild again. Domitian knew that this was a good sign for their family's future. A very good sign. He heard Nero turn serious in his private exchange with Vespasian. "I don't care how popular you are with the people. You had better not fail me."

"My lord, you know my sacred devotion to your promise."

Nero rolled his eyes at the old general's toothy grin. "Yes. I know you will never fail to remind me. After this campaign is over, you may retire to Egypt and your animal pleasures."

Nero turned and was handed another symbolic element. This time, it was a golden bow. The ceremonial weapon represented the power of Rome's might even at a long distance, like that of an arrow launched from Apollo's bow. The empire stretched thousands of miles from Spain in the west to Parthia in the east.

Vespasian bowed to Nero and descended the steps where Titus awaited him with the general's horse, a white stallion of victory. Vespasian mounted his steed, and they awaited the final divination.

A group of augurs up on the porch of the temple rolled forth cages and released a murder of crows into the air. The birds ascended like a plume of black smoke. The augurs observed their direction and speed, flying quickly to the east. They raised their hands in thanks and yelled, "Victory for Nero Caesar!"

The crowd once again rose in applause as Vespasian launched a ceremonial arrow from his golden bow in the direction of the birds.

Then he and Titus led their train of officers off to war.

Up on the porch, Nero grinned widely and said to young Domitian, "Nothing reminds the people of the power of the emperor like a good war."

Domitian said wryly, "Or the power of his conquering general."

Nero replied, "That, my dear Domitian, is why you remain in my custody."

In the midst of all the celebration and glory, none of these pagan idolaters heard what the three divine beings had heard as they watched over their servants. Apollyon, Azazel, and Semyaza turned their heads at the echo of a trumpet that had just been sounded from the heavenly throne of Yahweh. The first seal had been opened. The first trumpet and thunder sounded. The first bowl was about to be poured out on the land of Israel.

> *Now I watched when the Lamb opened one of the seven seals,*
> *and I heard one of the four living creatures say with a voice like*
> *thunder, "Come!" And I looked, and behold, a white horse! And*
> *its rider had a bow, and a crown was given to him, and he*
> *came out conquering, and to conquer.*
> —The Apocalypse of Jesus Christ 6:1–2[4]

This story continues with the next novel in the series, *Resistant: Revolt of the Jews.* Available at Amazon.com here: http://godawa.com/from-remnant-to-resistant/

• • • • •

If you liked this book, then please help me out by writing a positive review of it wherever you purchased it. That is one of the best ways to say thank you to me as an author. It really does help my sales and status. Thanks! — *Brian Godawa*

More Books by Brian Godawa

See www.Godawa.com for more information on other books by Brian Godawa. Check out his other series below:

Chronicles of the Nephilim

Chronicles of the Nephilim is a saga that charts the rise and fall of the Nephilim giants of Genesis 6 and their place in the evil plans of the fallen angelic Sons of God called, "The Watchers." The story starts in the days of Enoch and continues on through the Bible until the arrival of the Messiah, Jesus. The prelude to Chronicles of the Apocalypse.
ChroniclesOfTheNephilim.com

Chronicles of the Watchers

Chronicles of the Watchers is a series that charts the influence of spiritual principalities and powers over the course of human history. The kingdoms of man in service to the gods of the nations at war. Completely based on ancient historical and mythological research. ChroniclesOfTheWatchers.com

•••••

Biblical & Historical Research

For additional free biblical and historical scholarly research related to this novel and series, go to Godawa.com > Chronicles of the Apocalypse > *Scholarly Research*.

AFTERWORD

Many readers will be shocked by what they read in this novel because they have been taught to read prophecy through an almost-singular interpretation of the End Times. This popular interpretive viewpoint was made famous by the *Left Behind* series and is called Dispensationalism (which grew out of Premillennialism). Those schooled in this historically recent *eschatology* (study of "end things" or end times) all assume that the book of Revelation mostly speaks of events future to our modern era. This is why these views are called "futurist" schools of eschatology. This scenario involves a rapture of some kind to come, a rebuilt Temple in modern Jerusalem, a Great Tribulation in our near future, a Satanic "Antichrist" and his companion "Beast" that has yet to appear on the world stage, that leads to a climactic attack on Israel, the end of the world and the Second Coming of Christ. The futurist view reads the Bible through a modern lens of interpretation.

But this series is the story of the Apostle John's writing of the Apocalypse during the time of the Roman Emperor Nero, the first major persecution and martyrdom of Christians, and the Jewish revolt of A.D. 66, that resulted in the destruction of Jerusalem and the Temple in A.D. 70. The premise of the story is that John was writing, not of the second physical return of Jesus at the end of history, but rather of his judgment-coming upon Israel and Jerusalem in that first century. Revelation was not written as a prophecy of some distant future but as an encouragement to suffering Christians of the first century to endure because their vindication was near. Those who had rejected and killed Messiah and were persecuting the Christians would soon be punished by God. The new covenant would be completed in the destruction of the old covenant elements of city, temple and land. God would divorce his "wife" of the old covenant for her spiritual unfaithfulness and marry a new wife of the new covenant, the bride of Christ.

Many godly and orthodox men of history have taught versions of this eschatological view, that is generically called *preterism*. Preterism is a Latin word that means "past fulfillment." This suggests that most or all prophecies of the "last days" were fulfilled in the first century. Preterism is gaining more attention as historical events continue to falsify all the Dispensational and Premillennial schemes of the End Times over and over again.[1]

In the interest of providing a reasoned explanation of the preterist view, I wrote a companion book for this Chronicles of the Apocalypse novel series. It's called End Times Bibly Prophecy: It's Not What They Told You. In that book of biblical research, I examine what Jesus himself said about the Last Days, the end of the age and the destruction of the temple as described in my fictional storyline.

For the scholarly Scriptural defense of the eschatology in this novel series, called *redemptive-historical preterism*, read the following two books: The single best popular introduction to this prophetic view is *Last Days Madness: Obsession of the Modern Church* by Gary DeMar. The single best scholarly Revelation commentary is the two volume, *The Divorce of Israel: A Redemptive-Historical Interpretation of Revelation* by Ken Gentry.

For additional works, see the bibliography at the end of this book.*

Brian Godawa

Author, *Chronicles of the Apocalypse*

* P.S. Some examples through history of respected Christian scholars who affirmed preterist interpretations are: Eusebius (A.D. 260-340), Clement of Alexandria (A.D. 150-215), Arethas of Cappadocia (6th c.), Spanish Jesuit Alcasar (1614), Reformed theologian Hugo Grotius (1583-1645), Westminster scholar John Lightfoot (1601-1675), Milton S. Terry (1840-1914), Moses Stuart (1780-1852), Adam Clarke (1762-1832), Anglican historian, F. W. Farrar (1831-1903), David S. Clark (1921), modern Reformed scholars David Chilton (1987), Jay Adams (1996), J. Marcellus Kik, Gary DeMar, Kenneth L. Gentry, Steve Gregg, and R.C. Sproul. — From "Back to the Future" a pamphlet by Kenneth L. Gentry, Jr., Th.D.

BIBLIOGRAPHY OF BOOKS ON BIBLE PROPHECY
THAT INFLUENCED AUTHOR BRIAN GODAWA

For additional biblical and historical research related to this series, go to
www.ChroniclesoftheApocalypse.com and Click on Scholarly Research.

John L. Bray, *Matthew 24 Fulfilled*, (American Vision; 5th Edition, 2009).

David Chilton, *The Days of Vengeance: An Exposition of the Book of Revelation*, (Dominion Press; 1st Edition, 2006).

Gary DeMar, *10 Popular Prophecy Myths Exposed: The Last Days Might Not Be as Near as You Think*, (American Vision, 2010).

— *Last Days Madness: Obsession of the Modern Church* Wolgemuth & Hyatt Pub; 4th Revised edition (September 1999).

— *Left Behind: Separating Fact From Fiction*, (American Vision; First edition, 2010).

— *Why the End of the World is Not in Your Future: Identifying the Gog-Magog Alliance*, (American Vision; First edition, 2010)

Kenneth L. Gentry, Jr., *The Beast of Revelation*, (American Vision, 2002).

— *Before Jerusalem Fell: Dating the Book of Revelation*, (Victorious Hope Publishing, 2010)

— *The Book of Revelation Made Easy: You Can Understand Bible Prophecy*, American Vision (December 31, 2009).

— *The Divorce of Israel: A Redemptive-Historical Interpretation of Revelation Vol. 1 & 2*, (Liberty Alliance, 2016).

— *Navigating the Book of Revelation: Special Studies on Important Issues*, (GoodBirth Ministries, 2011).

— *The Olivet Discourse Made Easy*, (Apologetics Group. 2010)

— *Perilous Times: A Study in Eschatological Evil*, (Covenant Media Press, 1999).

Kenneth L. Gentry Jr., and Thomas Ice, *The Great Tribulation: Past or Future?: Two Evangelicals Debate the Question*, (Kregel Academic & Professional, 1999).

John H. Gerstner, *Wrongly Dividing the Word of Truth: A Critique of Dispensationalism 3rd Edition* (Nicene Council, 2009).

Hank Hanegraaff, *The Apocalypse Code: Find out What the Bible Really Says About the End Times and Why It Matters Today,* (Thomas Nelson, 2010).

George Peter Holford, *The Destruction of Jerusalem: An Absolute and Irresistible Proof of the Divine Origin of Christianity*, (Covenant Media Press; 6th American edition, 2001).

Peter J. Leithart, *The Promise of His Appearing: An Exposition of Second Peter* (Canon Press, 2004).

Keith A. Mathison, *Dispensationalism: Rightly Dividing the People of God?* (P & R Publishing, 1995).

Philip Mauro, *The Seventy Weeks and the Great Tribulation: A Study of the Last Two Visions of Daniel and the Olivet Discourse of the Lord Jesus Christ* (Hamilton Brothers, 1922).

R.C. Sproul, *The Last Days According to Jesus: When Did Jesus Say He Would Return? 2nd Edition,* (Baker Pub Group, 1998).

If You Like This Novel
Get This Free eBook
Limited Time Offer

The Research Notes behind the Novel Series
Chronicles of the Apocalypse
By Brian Godawa

Over one hundred pages of Biblical and historical sources, with citations, addressing each verse in Matthew 24.

https://godawa.com/matthew-24/

Get the Theology behind
This Novel Series

The Biblical Theology behind
Chronicles of the Apocalypse
By Brian Godawa

Brian Godawa reveals the Biblical and historical basis for the Last Days presented in the novel series *Chronicles of the Apocalypse*.
Godawa unveils the biblical meaning of many End Times notions like the Last Days, cosmic catastrophes, the Abomination of Desolation, the antichrist, the Great Tribulation, and more!

Available in eBook, Paperback & Audiobook

https://wp.me/P6y1ub-io8

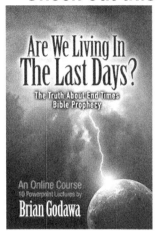

GET MORE BIBLICAL IMAGINATION

Get More Biblical Imagination

Sign up Online For The Godawa Chronicles

https://godawa.com

Insider information on the novels of Brian Godawa
Special Discounts, New Releases,
Bible Mysteries!
We won't spam you.

CHRONICLES OF THE NEPHILIM

The Prequel Series to Chronicles of the Apocalypse.
Nephilim Giants, Watchers, Cosmic War.

www.Godawa.com

CHRONICLES OF THE WATCHERS

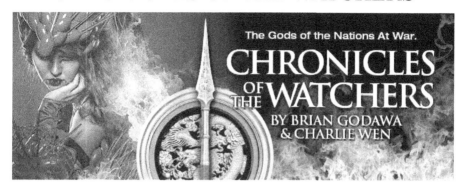

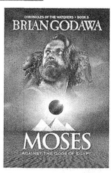
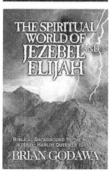
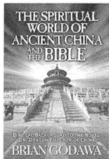
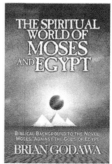

ABOUT THE AUTHOR

Brian Godawa is the screenwriter for the award-winning feature film, *To End All Wars*, starring Kiefer Sutherland. It was awarded the Commander in Chief Medal of Service, Honor and Pride by the Veterans of Foreign Wars, won the first Heartland Film Festival by storm, and showcased the Cannes Film Festival Cinema for Peace.

He previously adapted to film the best-selling supernatural thriller novel *The Visitation* by author Frank Peretti for Ralph Winter (*X-Men, Wolverine*), and wrote and directed *Wall of Separation*, a PBS documentary, and *Lines That Divide*, a documentary on stem cell research.

Mr. Godawa's scripts have won multiple awards in respected screenplay competitions, and his articles on movies and philosophy have been published around the world. He has traveled around the United States teaching on movies, worldviews, and culture to colleges, churches and community groups.

His popular book *Hollywood Worldviews: Watching Films with Wisdom and Discernment* (InterVarsity Press) is used as a textbook in schools around the country. In the Top 10 of Biblical Fiction on Amazon, his first novel series, *Chronicles of the Nephilim*, is an imaginative retelling of Biblical stories of the Nephilim giants, the secret plan of the fallen Watchers, and the War of the Seed of the Serpent with the Seed of Eve. The sequel series, *Chronicles of the Apocalypse*, tells the story of the apostle John's book of Revelation, and *Chronicles of the Watchers* recounts true history through the Watcher paradigm.

Find out more about his other books, lecture tapes and DVDs for sale at his website, **www.godawa.com**.

BLANK PAGE

BLANK PAGE

BLANK PAGE

CHAPTER 1

[1] **The gods of the nations as real spiritual demonic entities**: I detail this theological truth in my book, *When Giants Were Upon the Earth: The Watchers, The Nephilim and the Biblical Cosmic War of the Seed.* The basic Scriptures are these:

Leviticus 17:7 [7] So they shall no more sacrifice their sacrifices to **goat demons**, after whom they whore. This shall be a statute forever for them throughout their generations.

Deuteronomy 32:17 [17] They **sacrificed to demons** that were no gods, **to gods** they had never known, to new gods that had come recently, whom your fathers had never dreaded.

Psalm 106:37-38 [37] They sacrificed their sons and their daughters **to the demons**; [38] they poured out innocent blood, the blood of their sons and daughters, whom they sacrificed to **the idols of Canaan**, and the land was polluted with blood.

Psalm 95:5-6 (LXX) For great is the Lord, and praiseworthy exceedingly. More awesome he is than all the gods. For **all the gods of the nations are demons**, but the Lord made the heavens."

1 Cor. 10:18-20 Consider the people of Israel: are not those who eat the sacrifices participants in the altar? What do I imply then? That food offered to idols is anything, or that an idol is anything? No, I imply that what pagans sacrifice they offer to demons and not to God. I do not want you to be participants with demons

In the New Testament, Paul picks on the demonic territorial spirits in his "principalities and powers": Ephesians 3:10 so that through the church the manifold wisdom of God might now be made known to the rulers and authorities in the heavenly places.

Ephesians 4:8-10 [8] Therefore it says, "When he ascended on high he led a host of captives, and he gave gifts to men." [9] (In saying, "He ascended," what does it mean but that he had also descended into the lower regions, the earth? [10] He who descended is the one who also ascended far above all the heavens, that he might fill all things.)

Ephesians 6:12 For we do not wrestle against flesh and blood, but against the rulers, against the authorities, against the cosmic powers over this present darkness, against the spiritual forces of evil in the heavenly places.

Colossians 2:15 He disarmed the rulers and authorities and put them to open shame, by triumphing over them in him.

[2] **The "proto-evangelion" curse on the Serpent as the first promise of Messiah**: Genesis 3:14–15 [14] The LORD God said to the serpent, "Because you have done this… I will put enmity between you and the woman, and between your offspring and her offspring; he shall bruise your head, and you shall bruise his heel."

[3] **The Sons of God came to Hermon and mated with the daughters of men**: I exegete this theological storyline in my book, *When Giants Were Upon the Earth: The Watchers, The Nephilim and the Biblical Cosmic War of the Seed.*

Genesis 6:1–4 [1] When man began to multiply on the face of the land and daughters were born to them, [2] the sons of God saw that the daughters of man were attractive. And they took as their wives any they chose. [3] Then the LORD said, "My Spirit shall not abide in man forever, for he is flesh: his days shall be 120 years." [4] **The Nephilim were on the earth in those days, and also afterward, when the sons of God came in to the daughters of man and they bore children to them. These were the mighty men who were of old, the men of renown.**

The Nephilim as giants and the Sons of God as angelic Watchers on Mount Hermon: This supernatural interpretation is supported by the book of 1Enoch. For a detailed defense of 1Enoch as a Biblical source see my paper: "The Book of Enoch: Scripture, Heresy, or What?" online free at https://independent.academia.edu/BrianGodawa. But it is also chapter one of my book, *When Giants Were Upon the Earth: The Watchers, The Nephilim and the Biblical Cosmic War of the Seed.*

[4] **Babel, Watchers, Divine allotment, gods of the nations:** I detail this theological storyline in my book, *When Giants Were Upon the Earth: The Watchers, The Nephilim and the Biblical Cosmic War of the Seed.*

Divine allotment of the nations under the heavenly Sons of God: "When the Most High gave to the nations their inheritance, when he divided mankind, he fixed the borders of the peoples according to the number of the sons of God. But the LORD's portion is his people, Jacob his allotted heritage." Deuteronomy 32:8–9.

Heavenly host (Sons of God) as real supernatural entities and gods of the nations: Deuteronomy 4:19-20; 1 Enoch 6-7. For a creative depiction of this primeval fall and territorial allotment, see Brian Godawa, *Noah Primeval* (Los Angeles, Embedded Pictures, 2011) and *Enoch Primordial* (Los Angeles, Embedded Pictures, 2012). For a scholarly defense of the view see Michael S. Heiser, *The Unseen Realm: Recovering the Supernatural Worldview of the Bible*, First Edition. (Bellingham, WA: Lexham Press, 2015).

Watchers as territorial supernatural authorities over mankind: Daniel 4:13, 23; 1 Enoch 20:1. "[the term Watcher] utilizes the arrangements of a human court to picture God's management of the affairs of heaven and earth. An earthly king had watchmen, for instance, who were the eyes and ears whereby he controlled and provided for his realm (see n. 3:2.c). The heavenly king governs his realm by similar means, members of the Council of Yahweh (1 Kgs 22:19–22; Job 1–2; Ps 89:6–8 [5–7]; Jer 23:18) who act as his eyes (2 Chr 16:9; Zech 4:10; cf. 1:9), keeping him informed on the affairs of his realm and seeing that his will is put into effect throughout it." John E. Goldingay, *Daniel, vol. 30, Word Biblical Commentary* (Dallas: Word, Incorporated, 1998), 88.

Israel as Yahweh's allotted people: "When the Most High gave to the nations their inheritance, when he divided mankind, he fixed the borders of the peoples according to the number of the sons of God. But the LORD's portion is his people, Jacob his allotted heritage." Deuteronomy 32:8–9.

Rebellious angels of Noah's day in Tartarus: 2 Peter 2:4–5 For if God did not spare angels when they sinned, but cast them into hell (*Tartarus*) and committed them to chains of gloomy darkness to be kept until the judgment; [5] if he did not spare the ancient world, but preserved Noah, a herald of righteousness, with seven others, when he brought a flood upon the world of the ungodly;

1 Peter 3:18–20 [18] For Christ also suffered once for sins, the righteous for the unrighteous, that he might bring us to God, being put to death in the flesh but made alive in the spirit, [19] in which he went and proclaimed to the spirits in prison, [20] because they formerly did not obey, when God's patience waited in the days of Noah, while the ark was being prepared, in which a few, that is, eight persons, were brought safely through water.

Jude 6 [6] And the angels who did not stay within their own position of authority, but left their proper dwelling, he has kept in eternal chains under gloomy darkness until the judgment of the great day.

"What is important to realize is that the Greek word translated as "hell" in this English translation is not one of the usual New Testament Greek words for hell, gehenna or hades, but tartarus.

"The Greek poet Hesiod, writing around 700 B.C., described this commonly known underworld called Tartarus as the pit of darkness and gloom where the Olympian Titan giants were banished following their war with Zeus.

> Hesiod, Theogony lines 720-739 as far beneath the earth as heaven is above earth; for so far is it from earth to Tartarus…There by the counsel of Zeus who drives the clouds the Titan gods are hidden under misty gloom, in a dank place where are the ends of the huge earth. And they may not go out; for Poseidon fixed gates of bronze upon it, and a wall runs all round it on every side.

"Obviously, Peter does not affirm Greco-Roman polytheism by referring to Tartarus, but he is alluding to a Hellenistic myth that his readers, believer and unbeliever alike, would be very familiar with, subverting it with the Jewish traditional interpretation.

"Extra-Biblical Second Temple Jewish legends connected this legend of gods and bound Titans in Tartarus to the bound angelic Watchers and punished giants of Genesis 6.

Sibylline Oracles 1:97-104, 119 enterprising Watchers, who received this appellation because they had a sleepless mind in their hearts and an insatiable personality. They were mighty, of great form, but nevertheless they went under the dread house of Tartarus guarded by unbreakable bonds, to make retribution, to Gehenna of terrible, raging, undying fire…draping them around with great Tartarus, under the base of the earth.

"Other well-known Second Temple literature reiterated this binding in the heart of the earth until judgment day:

Jubilees 4:22; 5:10 And he wrote everything, and bore witness to the Watchers, the ones who sinned with the daughters of men because they began to mingle themselves with the daughters of men so that they might be polluted…

And subsequently they [the Watchers] were bound in the depths of the earth forever, until the day of great judgment in order for judgment to be executed upon all of those who corrupted their ways and their deeds before the LORD.

This "binding" or imprisoning of supernatural beings in the earth is expressed in 2 Peter's "cast into pits of darkness reserved for judgment" (3:19), 1 Peter's "disobedient spirits in prison" (v. 6), and Jude's "eternal bonds under darkness for the judgment of the great day" (2:4). But it is not altogether unheard of in the Old Testament.

Isa. 24:21–23
On that day the LORD will punish
the host of heaven, in heaven,
and the kings of the earth, on the earth.
They will be gathered together
as prisoners in a pit;
they will be shut up in a prison,
and after many days they will be punished.

"Isaiah here is speaking of judgment upon Israel by the Babylonians around 600 B.C., but he evokes the same Enochian imagery of the angelic host of heaven (often linked to the astronomical heavenly bodies and earthly rulers) being overthrown and imprisoned in the earth until judgment day.

"Robert Newman notes that the Qumran Hebrew of the Isaiah scroll of this passage refers to a past event as its reference point: "They were gathered together as prisoners in a pit" (past tense). This past event could very well be the antediluvian binding of the fallen host of heaven (bene ha Elohim) as an analogy for the future captivity of Israel." Brian Godawa, *When Giants Were Upon the Earth: The Watchers, The Nephilim and the Biblical Cosmic War of the Seed* (Embedded Pictures Publishing 2014), 128-131.

Michael as Watcher of Israel: Daniel 10:20–21 [20] Then he said [to Daniel], "Do you know why I have come to you? But now I will return to fight against the prince of Persia; and when I go out, behold, the prince of Greece will come. [21] But I will tell you what is inscribed in the book of truth: there is none who contends by my side against these except Michael, your prince.

[5] **The gods of the nations as fallen angels**: See footnote 1 in this chapter.

The names of Satan: Apollyon/Abaddon: "This angel is named only here in Revelation [9:11 as Apollyon], and elsewhere in the OT and early Jewish literature is mentioned only in 4Q280 10 ii 7:"[Cursed be you Ange]l of the Pit, and Spir[it of Aba]ddon" (Kobelski, Melchizedek, 43–44). While in 4Q280 and related texts these two titles are alternate ways of describing Belial, in Revelation it is not at all clear that the angel of the abyss is a designation for Satan, for he is carefully named elsewhere with a selection of aliases in two different contexts (12:9; 20:2), and neither Abaddon nor the angel of the abyss is mentioned again. The fact that ἄγγελον is articular here, however, suggests that the author expected the readers to be familiar with this figure, i.e., that the angel of the abyss is none other than Satan-Belial." David E. Aune, *Revelation 6–16, vol. 52B, Word Biblical Commentary* (Dallas: Word, Incorporated, 1998), 534.

"The "Destroyer" in Rev. 9:11 is either the devil himself or an evil representative of the devil; either alternative receives confirmation from Jewish exegetical tradition on Exodus (see below). Rev. 12:3–4 and 13:1ff. are compatible with this conclusion, since there the devil and the Beast respectively are pictured wearing royal diadems and leading evil forces. This is also in line with the same conclusion already reached about the angel's identification in 9:1." G. K. Beale, *The Book of Revelation: A Commentary on the Greek Text, New International Greek Testament Commentary* (Grand Rapids, MI; Carlisle, Cumbria: W.B. Eerdmans; Paternoster Press, 1999), 503.

Belial: 2 Corinthians 6:14-15. ""The personification of wickedness, treachery, or the like, as Belial. In most of its OT attestations, bĕliyyaʿal functions as an emotive term to describe individuals or groups who commit the most heinous crimes against the Israelite religious or social order, as well as their acts." S. D. Sperling, "Belial," ed. Karel van der Toorn, Bob Becking, and Pieter W. van der Horst, *Dictionary of Deities and Demons in the Bible* (Leiden; Boston; Köln; Grand Rapids, MI; Cambridge: Brill; Eerdmans, 1999), 169.

Helel ben Shachar: Isaiah 14:12-15. Though many scholars accept this passage as having two referents, one, a historical prophecy to the King of Babylon, and the other, a spiritual allusion to Satan's pre-Edenic fall, David Lowe makes a persuasive argument that it has nothing to do with Satan. See David W. Lowe, *Deconstructing Lucifer: Reexamining the Ancient Origins of the Fallen Angel of Light*, (Seismos Publishing 2011).

Mastemah: "Mastemah appears as a noun meaning 'hostility' in OT (Hos 9:7–8) and Qumran writings. In Qumran literature the word is mostly connected with an evil angel (Belial) and in Jub. Mastemah is always a proper name for the leader of the evil angels." J. W. van Henten, "Mastemah," ed. Karel van der Toorn, Bob Becking, and Pieter W. van der Horst, *Dictionary of Deities and Demons in the Bible* (Leiden; Boston; Köln; Grand Rapids, MI; Cambridge: Brill; Eerdmans, 1999), 553.

Satan as ancient serpent and dragon: "And the great dragon was thrown down, that ancient serpent, who is called the devil and Satan, the deceiver of the whole world." Revelation 12:9.

Job 1:6-12; Zechariah 3:1-2. "The Hebrew (satan) means something like "adversary," "prosecutor," or "challenger." It speaks of an official legal function within a ruling body—in this case, Yahweh's council. When Yahweh asks the satan where he has been, we learn that his job involves investigating what is happening on earth (Job 1:7). He is, so to speak, Yahweh's eyes and ears on the ground, reporting what he has seen and heard." Michael S. Heiser, *The Unseen Realm: Recovering the Supernatural Worldview of the Bible, First Edition* (Bellingham, WA: Lexham Press, 2015), 56–57.

[6] **Christ claiming the nations as his inheritance:** Psalm 2:8; Isaiah 2:1-5. For a fictional portrayal of this victory of Jesus Christ over the principalities and powers see Brian Godawa, *Jesus Triumphant* (Los Angeles, Embedded Pictures, 2015).

"Satan is called "the ruler of this world" (Jn. 12:31, 14:30-31, 16:11), in 2 Cor. 4:4, "the god of this age." In Eph. 2:2 he is called the "prince of the power of the air, the spirit that is now working in the sons of disobedience." In fact, when Jesus was tempted by the satan in the desert, he offered Christ all the kingdoms of the world for his own "domain and glory; for it has been handed over to me, and I give it to whomever I wish" (Luke 4:6). It seems as if the satan is the only Watcher god in authority over the nations, like he has all the power." Brian Godawa, *When Giants Were Upon the Earth* (Embedded Pictures, 2014), 289."Much tradition identified Satan as the angel of Rome, thus adapting the angels- of-the-nations idea to the situation of Roman world-hegemony. Since Rome had conquered the entire Mediterranean region and much else besides, its angel-prince had become lord of all other angel-princes of the vanquished nations. This identification was already explicit at Qumran, where Rome and the Romans (the "Kittim" of the War Scroll) are made the specific allies and agents of Satan and his host. Similarly in the New Testament, Satan as the 'archon of this world' (John 12:31; 14:30; 16:11) or 'god of this aeon' (2 Cor. 4:4) could scarcely avoid being identified as the special patron of Rome." Walter Wink. *Naming the Powers: The Language of Power in the New Testament* (The Powers : Volume One) (K-Locations 405-409). K-Edition.

Principalities and powers were fooled and didn't understand the mystery of the gospel: 1 Corinthians 2:6–8 [6] Yet among the mature we do impart wisdom, although it is not a wisdom of this age or of the rulers of this age, who are doomed to pass away. [7] But we impart a secret and hidden wisdom of God, which God decreed before the ages for our glory. [8] None of the rulers of this age understood this, for if they had, they would not have crucified the Lord of glory.

Ephesians 3:4–10 [4] When you read this, you can perceive my insight into the mystery of Christ, [5] which was not made known to the sons of men in other generations as it has now been revealed to his holy apostles and prophets by the Spirit. [6] This mystery is that the Gentiles are fellow heirs, members of the same body, and partakers of the promise in Christ Jesus through the gospel. [7] … and to bring to light for everyone what is the plan of the <u>mystery hidden for ages in God</u> who created all things, [10] so that <u>through the church the manifold wisdom of God might now be made known to the rulers and authorities in the heavenly places.</u>

The "messengers" of the gospel are the "angels" (*angel* in Greek means messenger) that draw the elect into the kingdom with the preaching of the gospel: Matthew 24:31 [31] And he will send out his angels with a loud trumpet call, and they will gather his elect from the four winds, from one end of heaven to the other.

Matthew 28:18–20 [18] And Jesus came and said to them, "All authority in heaven and on earth has been given to me. [19] Go therefore and make disciples of all nations, baptizing them in the name of the Father and of the Son and of the Holy Spirit, [20] teaching them to observe all that I have commanded you. And behold, I am with you always, to the end of the age."

Christ's triumphal procession, with victory over the powers: Colossians 2:15 [15] He disarmed the rulers and authorities and put them to open shame, by triumphing over them in him.

Ephesians 4:8–10 [8] Therefore it says, "When he ascended on high he led a host of captives, and he gave gifts to men." [9] (In saying, "He ascended," what does it mean but that he had also descended into the lower regions, the earth? [10] He who descended is the one who also ascended far above all the heavens, that he might fill all things.)

1 Peter 3:21–22 [21] Jesus Christ, [22] who has gone into heaven and is at the right hand of God, with angels, authorities, and powers having been subjected to him.

Ephesians 1:20–22 [20] that he worked in Christ when he raised him from the dead and seated him at his right hand in the heavenly places, [21] far above all rule and authority and power and dominion, and above every name that is named, not only in this age but also in the one to come. [22] And he put all things under his feet.

[7] **Azazel and Semyaza were the leaders of the fallen Sons of God in Genesis 6**: 1Enoch 9:6-9 "You see what Azaz'el has done; how he has taught all (forms of) oppression upon the earth. And they revealed eternal secrets which are performed in heaven (and which) man learned. 7 (Moreover) Semyaz, to whom you have given power to rule over his companions, co-operating, they went in unto the daughters of the people on earth; 8 and they lay together with them—with those women—and defiled themselves, and revealed to them every (kind of) sin. 9 As for the women, they gave birth to giants to the degree that the whole earth was filled with blood and oppression." James H. Charlesworth, *The Old Testament Pseudepigrapha, vol. 1* (New York; London: Yale University Press, 1983), 17.

Azazel's and Semyaza's original binding in the earth: 1 Enoch 10:4, 11-13 "the Lord said to Raphael, "Bind Azaz'el hand and foot (and) throw him into the darkness!" And he made a hole in the desert which was in Duda'el and cast him there…And to Michael God said, "Make known to Semyaza and the others who are with him, who fornicated with the women, that they will die together with them in all their defilement. 12* And when they and all their children have battled with each other, and when they have seen the destruction of their beloved ones, bind them for seventy generations underneath the rocks of the ground until the day of their judgment and of their consummation, until the eternal judgment is concluded. 13* In those days they will lead them into the bottom of the fire—and in torment—in the prison (where) they will be locked up forever." James H. Charlesworth, *The Old Testament Pseudepigrapha, vol. 1* (New York; London: Yale University Press, 1983), 17-18.

1Enoch 54:4-6 ""For whom are these imprisonment chains being prepared?" 5 And he said unto me, "These are being prepared for the armies of Azaz'el, in order that they may take them and cast them into the abyss of complete condemnation, and as the Lord of the Spirits has commanded it, they shall cover their jaws with rocky stones. 6 Then Michael, Raphael, Gabriel, and Phanuel themselves shall seize them on that great day of judgment and cast them into the furnace (of fire) that is burning that day, so that the Lord of the Spirits may take vengeance on them on account of their oppressive deeds which (they performed) as messengers of Satan, leading astray those who dwell upon the earth." James H. Charlesworth, *The Old Testament Pseudepigrapha, vol. 1* (New York; London. Yale University Press, 1983), 38.

[8] **The plague of Rome**: Tacitus, *The Annals* 16.13 "Upon this year, disgraced by so many deeds of shame, Heaven also set its mark by tempest and disease. Campania was wasted by a whirlwind, which far and wide wrecked the farms, the fruit trees, and the crops, and carried its fury to the neighbourhood of the capital, where all classes of men were being decimated by a deadly epidemic."
http://penelope.uchicago.edu/Thayer/E/Roman/Texts/Tacitus/Annals/16*.html

Suetonius, *Lives of the Twelve Caesars, Nero* 39 "To all the disasters and abuses thus caused by the prince there were added certain accidents of fortune; a plague which in a single autumn entered thirty thousand deaths in the accounts of Libitina."
http://penelope.uchicago.edu/Thayer/E/Roman/Texts/Suetonius/12Caesars/Nero*.html

The fourth beast of Daniel 7 that is iron and bronze and tramples other nations is Rome:

Daniel 7:7 After this I saw in the night visions, and behold, a fourth beast, terrifying and dreadful and exceedingly strong. It had great iron teeth; it devoured and broke in pieces and stamped what was left with its feet. It was different from all the beasts that were before it, and it had ten horns.

Daniel 7:19 "Then I desired to know the truth about the fourth beast, which was different from all the rest, exceedingly terrifying, with its teeth of iron and claws of bronze, and which devoured and broke in pieces and stamped what was left with its feet,

Daniel 7:23 "Thus he said: 'As for the fourth beast, there shall be a fourth kingdom on earth, which shall be different from all the kingdoms, and it shall devour the whole earth, and trample it down, and break it to pieces.

[9] **Definition of genius**: "a. With reference to classical pagan belief: the tutelary god or attendant spirit allotted to every person at birth to govern his or her fortunes and determine personal character, and finally to conduct him or her out of the world. Also: a guardian spirit similarly associated with a place, institution, thing, etc." "genius, n. and adj.". *OED Online*. December 2015. Oxford University Press. http://www.oed.com/view/Entry/77607?redirectedFrom=genius (accessed January 06, 2016).

Tertullian on the Genius as demonic: "Thus, too, is it that to all persons their *genii* [geniuses] are assigned, which is only another name for demons." Tertullian, "A Treatise on the Soul, 39" in *Latin Christianity: Its Founder, Tertullian*, ed. Alexander Roberts, James Donaldson, and A. Cleveland Coxe, trans. Peter Holmes, vol. 3, *The Ante-Nicene Fathers* (Buffalo, NY: Christian Literature Company, 1885), 219.

[10] **Mithraism as the religion of the common soldier**: "However, we do have a number of dedications from followers of Mithras (mainly addressed to invictus ("unconquerable") Mithras), mainly from Roman Britain, the Rhine and Danube area and Italy. The finds suggest a large number of his worshippers were possibly low-ranking soldiers (there are very few examples of offerings from higher-ranking soldiers and those may have just been to encourage their men) and slaves, perhaps because a religion with a strict but straight-forward hierarchy allowed them the power they lacked in their everyday lives." The Roman Military Research Society, "Mithras Sol Invictvs - An initiate's Guide," http://www.romanarmy.net/mithras.shtml

CHAPTER 2

[1] **The details of Alexander's dream** are taken from Revelation 4 and 5.

[2] **Covenant lawsuit**: "Whenever "the satan" is named in the Bible (meaning "the accuser," a legal term), it is usually in the legal context of a heavenly lawsuit. In the Noah Primeval appendices, I examined the divine council in the Scriptures in detail. In passages such as Job 1 and 2, and 1Kings 22 we are told that "the sons of God came to present themselves before Yahweh," "all the host of heaven standing beside him on his right and on his left." God then asks counsel and recommendation from this multitude on what to do regarding a specific situation. The heavenly beings give their opinions, God renders his verdict, and directs some of the host to carry out the sentence.

"The context in these passages is that of a legal body of divine beings counseling with God over justice and the satan is one of these divine beings whose role is to accuse. In Zechariah 3:1-4, Joshua the High Priest stands in this divine council before God. The satan stands beside him "to accuse him" before Elohim in good legal form.

"While some of these scenes are the satan initiating legal accusations against God's people, others are litigation against pagan rulers for their own defiance of God's universal sovereignty. In Daniel 7:9-14, we see "the Ancient of Days" seated on his throne, "and ten thousand times ten thousand stood before him; the court sat in judgment" over the nations of the earth (Dan. 7:10). And in Psalm 82, God renders legal judgment upon the members of the divine council who failed to carry out justice for God upon the gentile nations they had inherited. We read this Psalmic phrase used in Enoch Primordial, "God has taken his place in the divine council; in the midst of the gods he holds judgment" (v. 1-2).

"Another kind of Biblical lawsuit saw Old Testament prophets as Yahweh's prosecuting attorneys indicting Israel for breaking her covenant with God. The prophet would stand before God's divine council and make the summons and charges against Israel before calling her to respond to the charges. Then Yahweh as judge would pronounce his verdict. One of the qualifications of a prophet's authority to speak for God was that he had stood in this divine council (Jer. 23:18, 22).

"Herbert Huffmon has pointed out examples of covenant lawsuits in Jeremiah, Isaiah, Micah, and other prophets carried out in God's courtroom against Israel that illustrated a Biblical pattern of legal procedure:

A description of the scene of judgment
II. The speech of the plaintiff
A. Heaven and earth are appointed judges
B. Summons to the defendant (or judges)
C. Address in the second person to the defendant
1. Accusation in question form to the defendant
2. Refutation of the defendant's possible arguments
3. Specific indictment"

Brian Godawa, *When Giants Were Upon the Earth: The Watchers, the Nephilim, and the Biblical Cosmic War of the Seed* (Embedded Pictures, 2014), 156-158. See also, Herbert B. Huffmon "The Covenant Lawsuit in the Prophets" Journal of Biblical Literature, Vol. 78, No. 4 (Dec., 1959), pp. 285-295; Wheeler Robinson, H., "The Council of Yahweh," Journal of Theological Studies, 45 (1944) p.151-158.

[3] **The satan's legal accusations against Job**: Job 1, 2. This occurs with the satan as a part of the divine council of Sons of God before God's throne.

Zechariah 3 and the divine council courtroom: "The thrust of the fourth vision is the cleansing of the priests (v 4) and the land (v 9) of עָוֹן "iniquity or guilt." Even though the people had returned from Babylon and had started to rebuild the temple, there was still the contamination of iniquity that had not been purged. Was the iniquity only that of Joshua personally (cf. J. Smart, History and Theology in Second Isaiah [Philadelphia: Westminster Press, 1965] 285)? Or did Joshua's filthy garments (3:3, 4) represent the contamination of all the people? The latter seems to be the proper meaning. Just as Aaron and his sons were cleansed and clothed properly at the institution of the priesthood (Lev 8:5–7) so Joshua was to be cleansed in order to be acceptable before God in his role as priest.

"The role of Satan becomes clear if we understand the setting of the vision to be that of the meeting of the heavenly council. Satan was a member of the heavenly council in Job 1 and 2. There are a number of similarities between this passage and the heavenly council scenes in Job 1 and 2: (1) Satan appears before the Lord as an accuser in both passages (v 1); (2) Yahweh speaks to Satan (v 2); (3) the presence of other "angels" in the group (vv 4, 6). N. L. A. Tidwell sees the seven eyes of Yahweh ranging through the whole earth (4:10b) as corresponding to the function of Satan in Job 1 and 2. There can be no doubt that the scene is that of the heavenly council." Ralph L. Smith, *Micah–Malachi, vol. 32, Word Biblical Commentary* (Dallas: Word, Incorporated, 1998), 199.

Enoch's vision of the heavenly throne: 1 Enoch 14:18-22 "And I observed and saw inside it a lofty throne—its appearance was like crystal and its wheels like the shining sun; and (I heard?) the voice of the cherubim; 19 and from beneath the throne were issuing streams of flaming fire. It was difficult to look at it. 20 And the Great Glory was sitting upon it—as for his gown, which was shining more brightly than the sun, it was whiter than any snow...No one could come near unto him from among those that surrounded the tens of millions (that stood) before him. 23 He needed no council." James H. Charlesworth, *The Old Testament Pseudepigrapha, vol. 1* (New York; London: Yale University Press, 1983), 21.

The New Testament books of 2 Peter and Jude affirm the Enochian judgment of angels:

2 Peter 2:4 For if God did not spare angels when they sinned, but cast them into hell and committed them to chains of gloomy darkness to be kept until the judgment;

Jude 6 And the angels who did not stay within their own position of authority, but left their proper dwelling, he has kept in eternal chains under gloomy darkness until the judgment of the great day—

Other heavenly courtroom scenes: 1Kings 22:9; Psalm 82; 89.

[4] **It is finished**: John 19:30.

Christ's once-for-all sacrifice is eternal: Hebrews 9:11-12; 10:11-14.

324

Satan bound in the ministry of Jesus: (Matthew 12:27-29). In Rev 20:2-3, binding the satan in the Abyss is described as stopping his ability to "deceive the nations." Though this binding of Rev 20 is a different binding than what occurred through Christ's ministry, it may shed light on what the actual binding means. Perhaps Satan's binding during Christ's ministry was the restraint of Satan's ability to stop the inauguration of the kingdom of God intruding into the land of Israel. Or perhaps the binding through Christ's ministry was the fact that Satan could no longer accuse Christians. See below.

Prince of the power of the air: Ephesians 2:2.

Satan's inability to accuse Christians: 1Peter 5:8; Revelation 6:9-11; 12:13-17; 13:7-8; 20:4-6.

[5] **Twenty-four elders around the throne**: Revelation 4:4.

Elders as Judges in the Old Testament: "The OT elders with Moses not only see God on his throne (Ex 24:9–10), but elders elsewhere are associated with judges (Dt 21:2; Jos 8:33; 23:2; 24:1; Ezr 10:14; 1 Esdr 9:13), were entrusted with the law (Dt 31:9), and stood under oath before God (Dt 31:28). Their presence around God's throne further underscores the judicial tone of the vision. Not only so, but in Israel elders represent the people before God (Ex 24:9–10; Isa 24:23), being called "elders of the people" (Ex 4:29; 19:7; Nu 11:16; Jer 19:1) and "elders of the congregation" (Lev 4:15; Jdg 21:16)." Kenneth L. Gentry, Jr., *The Divorce of Israel: A Redemptive-Historical Interpretation of Revelation Vol. 1* (Dallas, GA: Tolle Lege Press, 2016), 492.

24 Elders: "That they are twenty-four in number apparently reflects the ancient division of the priests into their classes in 1Ch 24:6–31(though for his purposes John calls them "elders" and not "priests"). We also see David dividing the singers into twenty-four courses (1Ch 25:1–6), appointing twenty-four gatekeepers (1Ch 26:17–19), and dividing his soldiers into twelve divisions of 24,000 men each (1Ch 27:1–15). This could have come to John not only through his understanding of the temple service, but also through Ezekiel. Stuart (2:111) notes regarding the twenty five men in Ezekiel's temple (Eze 8:6; 11:1): "this includes the high priest and the twenty-four heads of the orders of the priesthood." This priestly pattern would be familiar to first-century Jews in that this division was still functioning in their day while the temple stood (Jos., Ant 7:14:7 §365–67; m. Ta'an 4:2; t. Sukk 4:26–27; t. Taan 2:1; 3:1)." Kenneth L. Gentry, Jr., *The Divorce of Israel: A Redemptive-Historical Interpretation of Revelation Vol. 1* (Dallas, GA: Tolle Lege Press, 2016), 490-491.

[6] **On the four living creatures around the throne**: Revelation 4:6-9.

"This imagery has John drawing once again from Eze 1:5–21 (cp. Eze 10:1–20; 11:22), though with some influence from Isa 6:2–3. His parallels with Ezekiel include their number (four, Rev 4:6; Eze 1:5), their designation ("living creatures," zōa, Rev 4:6; Eze 1:5), their appearance (lion, calf/bull [moschos]13, man, and eagle, Rev 4:7; Eze 1:10), their several wings (Eze 1:5; Rev 1:8), and their being full of eyes (Eze 1:18; Rev 4:7)." Kenneth L. Gentry, Jr., *The Divorce of Israel: A Redemptive-Historical Interpretation of Revelation Vol. 1* (Dallas, GA: Tolle Lege Press, 2016), 497.

"living creature," is used in the OT, it refers to "a dangerous animal, untamed, living free, and usually large" (KB3, 297), and the plural form of the term with this meaning occurs only rarely (see Isa 35:9; Ps 104:25; Dan 8:4). In Ezek 1–3 the term ḥayyôt is a vague, general term for living creatures, defined more fully in terms of their human form (Zimmerli, Ezekiel 1:120). In Ezekiel the living creatures are implicitly understood to bear up the moveable throne of God." David E. Aune, *Revelation 1–5, vol. 52A, Word Biblical Commentary* (Dallas: Word, Incorporated, 1998), 297.

The crystal sea: "There was also before the throne something like a glassy sea like crystal." This is probably based on an allusion to Ezek 1:22, where the prophet sees "the likeness of a firmament, shining like crystal," spread out over the heads of the living creatures (Tg. Ezek. 1:22 compares the firmament to a great ice field). One of the features of the temple of Solomon was an enormous bronze basin of water mounted on twelve bronze oxen, three facing each of the cardinal directions (1 Kgs 7:23–26; Jos., Ant. 8.79–80; according to 2 Kgs 16:17, Ahaz later removed the base and substituted one made of stone). This basin was called, "the sea" (1 Kgs 7:24; 2 Kgs 16:17), "the molten sea" (1 Kgs 7:23; 2 Chr 4:2), or, "the bronze sea" (2 Kgs 25:13; Jer 52:17; 1 Chr 18:8)." David E. Aune, *Revelation 1–5, vol. 52A, Word Biblical Commentary* (Dallas: Word, Incorporated, 1998), 296.

[7] Revelation 4:8.

[8] **Casting down crowns**: "Presenting a crown to another of higher rank was a common way of showing submission to that higher authority (Jos., Ant. 14:3:1 §35; 14:12:2 §304; 14:12:3 §313; 16:9:4 §296)."

Kenneth L. Gentry, Jr., *The Divorce of Israel: A Redemptive-Historical Interpretation of Revelation Vol. 1* (Dallas, GA: Tolle Lege Press, 2016), 503.

[9] Revelation 4:11.

[10] Revelation 5:1-2.

[11] **Seals on legal documents**: "Seals were quite commonly used in antiquity in both private and public life and were of great legal significance" (EDNT 3:316; cp. TDNT 7:940–42). We even find this practice in Scripture itself (1Ki 21:8; Neh 9:38–10:1; Est 3:2; 8:8, 10; Jer 32:10–11, 14, 44). For instance, when Jeremiah buys a field, he creates a legal deed complete with terms, conditions, witnesses — and seals (Jer 32:9–14): esphagismenon (LXX Jer 39:11). Interestingly, we know that some ancient Roman legal documents were sealed with seven seals as here...

"The scroll is clearly patterned on Ezekiel's very similar visionary scroll. That earlier scroll is written on both sides (Eze 2:9–10) which also is presented from God's throne (Eze 1:26). That scroll contains "lamentations, mourning and woe" (Eze 2:10) which are to come upon a "stubborn and obstinate" (Eze 2:4; 3:7) and "rebellious" (Eze 2:3, 5–8; 3:9, 26, 27) people: Israel (Eze 2:3; 3:1, 4, 7). These people "transgressed" (Eze 2:3) against God, breaking his law. In Eze 2:3 "the form of the statement I am sending you to the descendants of Israel derives from official court diction". Ezekiel describes Israel as deserving judicial punishment in that they are a nation of "rebels" (marad), where the Hebrew means "to rise up in revolt against an overlord, to refuse allegiance to one's sovereign" (Block 1997: 118). This is paralleled with the charge of having "transgressed" (Heb.: pasa) against God, where the Hebrew means "to commit a crime, to transgress a law or principle". Ezekiel's vision certainly engages a legal matter dealing with Israel." Kenneth L. Gentry, Jr., *The Divorce of Israel: A Redemptive-Historical Interpretation of Revelation Vol. 1* (Dallas, GA: Tolle Lege Press, 2016), 512, 514.

[12] Revelation 5:5.

[13] Revelation 5:9-10.

[14] **Revelation 4-5 the key to Revelation**: "Most scholars agree that Rev 4–5 is the fulcrum upon which Rev turns, but it is especially Rev 5 that "is the key to the entire Book of Revelation". Moyise concurs: it is "one of the most important passages in the book" and is "an interpretative key for the rest of the book." Kenneth L. Gentry, Jr., *The Divorce of Israel: A Redemptive-Historical Interpretation of Revelation Vol. 1* (Dallas, GA: Tolle Lege Press, 2016), 509.

CHAPTER 3

[1] **Nero's Visit to Delphi**: This actually occurred in the summer of AD 67. Some details of the location and ritual as described in this novel were drawn from Dando-Collins, Stephen. *The Great Fire of Rome: The Fall of the Emperor Nero and His City* (p. 210-211). Da Capo Press. K-Edition; and Jelle Zeilinga de Boer and John R. Hale, "The Oracle of Delphi—Was She Really Stoned?" Bible History Daily, 2013 http://www.biblicalarchaeology.org/daily/ancient-cultures/daily-life-and-practice/the-oracle-of-delphi—was-she-really-stoned/

[2] **The following Pythian vision** draws from Revelation 13 and 17 about the beast and the great harlot.

My premise in this chapter is that the Pythian spirit is communicating the apocalypse accurately to Nero. Such occultic activities are not always lying ones. After all, the spirit world does have access to the truth and can use it for its own twisted purposes. In this case, the spirit seeks to rile up Nero so that he will lash out with more ferocity. What would make Nero more angry than the truth?

[3] **The beastly character traits of Revelation's Beast contain the traits of all the kingdom beasts in Daniel 7**: Daniel 7:3–7 3 And four great beasts came up out of the sea, different from one another. 4 The first was like a lion and had eagles' wings. Then as I looked its wings were plucked off, and it was lifted up from the ground and made to stand on two feet like a man, and the mind of a man was given to it. 5 And behold, another beast, a second one, like a bear. It was raised up on one side. It had three ribs in its mouth between its teeth; and it was told, 'Arise, devour much flesh.' 6 After this I looked, and behold, another, like a leopard, with four wings of a bird on its back. And the beast had four heads, and dominion was given to it. 7 After this I saw in the night visions, and behold, a fourth beast, terrifying and dreadful and exceedingly strong. It had great iron teeth; it devoured and broke in pieces and stamped what was left with its feet.

Revelation 13:2 And the beast that I saw was like a leopard; its feet were like a bear's, and its mouth was like a lion's mouth. And to it the dragon gave his power and his throne and great authority.

[4] **The seven heads are the seven hills of Rome**: (Revelation 17:9). "The angel's explanation continues with this final hōde saying directed to the original audience. These believers are to discern two things related to the significance of the beast's seven heads. First, they represent seven hills. Rome was known throughout the ancient world as the city of seven hills, whose names are: Capitoline, Aventine, Caelian, Esquiline, Quirinal, Viminal, and Palantine. Numerous Roman writers used the phrase "seven hills" as a locution for Rome. The names of the seven hills are inscribed on the base of a second-century A.D. statue found in Corinth. The statue apparently depicted Dea Roma sitting or standing on Rome's seven hills." Clinton E. Arnold, *Zondervan Illustrated Bible Backgrounds Commentary: Hebrews to Revelation., vol. 4* (Grand Rapids, MI: Zondervan, 2002), 346.

[5] **The spirit quotes from**: Revelation 17:9–10 [9] the seven heads are seven mountains on which the woman is seated; [10] they are also seven kings, five of whom have fallen, one is, the other has not yet come, and when he does come he must remain only a little while.

[6] **The seven kings**: Revelation 17:10.

"A number of commentators see these "seven kings" as representing the first seven Caesars of Rome (cf. Stuart 2:325; Terry 431; Ratton 206; Renan, 215; Clark 109; Chilton 436; Mulholland 1996, 101; Prignet 481). We may find a list of the first twelve Caesars in Suetonius' famous work, *The Lives of the Twelve Caesars*. He lists them as follows:

1. Julius Caesar (59–44 B.C.)
2. Augustus Caesar (31 B.C.–A.D. 14)
3. Tiberius Caesar (A.D. 14-37)
4. Gaius Caesar (a.k.a Caligula) (37–41)
5. Claudius Caesar (41–54)
6. Nero Caesar (45–68)
7. Galba Caesar (June 68 to January 69)

"We find this order of emperors also in Josephus (Ant. 19:1:11 §75; cp. 18:2:2 §32–33; 18:6:10 §224); Sib. Or. 5:12-51; 4 Ezra 11-12 [2 Es 12:15]82; Theophilus (Ad Auto. 3:2783); Dio Chysostom (Or. 34:7); Clement of Alexandria (Strom. 1:21); and maybe, Barnabas 4:3-6. On this reckoning, the five that have "fallen" would be Julius through Claudius. That they are "fallen [epesen]" alludes "to the eminent rank of those whose death is declared" as in 2Sa 3:38. TDNT (6:161) notes that this word is commonly used of dying, particularly in the LXX (cf. Prignet 493). The sixth one who "is" (Gk.: estin, 17:10b) would be Nero. Regarding the seventh who will come and "must remain a little while [oligon auton dei meinai]" we should note that following Nero's thirteen year rule Galba takes the reins of government. But he rules for only seven months (June, AD 68 —January, AD 69), the shortest reigning emperor to that time." Kenneth L. Gentry, Jr., *The Divorce of Israel: A Redemptive-Historical Interpretation of Revelation Vol. 2* (Dallas, GA: Tolle Lege Press, 2016), 453-454.

The Beast as a collective kingdom and an individual king: Revelation 17:9–12 [9] This calls for a mind with wisdom: the seven heads are seven mountains on which the woman is seated; [10] they are also seven kings **[collective kingdom]**, five of whom have fallen, one is, the other has not yet come, and when he does come he must remain only a little while. [11] As for the beast that was and is not, it is an eighth **[individual king]** but it belongs to the seven, and it goes to destruction. [12] And the ten horns that you saw are ten kings who have not yet received royal power, but they are to receive authority as kings for one hour, together with the beast.

[7] **The spirit quotes from**: Revelation 17:3–5 [3] And he carried me away in the Spirit into a wilderness, and I saw a woman sitting on a scarlet beast that was full of blasphemous names, and it had seven heads and ten horns. [4] The woman was arrayed in purple and scarlet, and adorned with gold and jewels and pearls, holding in her hand a golden cup full of abominations and the impurities of her sexual immorality. [5] And on her forehead was written a name of mystery: "Babylon the great, mother of prostitutes and of earth's abominations."

[8] **The spirit quotes from**: Revelation 17:16 [16] And the ten horns that you saw, they and the beast will hate the prostitute. They will make her desolate and naked, and devour her flesh and burn her up with fire,

[9] For the explanation of the sixth king as Nero: see footnote #5 above.

It was common in the first century for both Christians and pagans to call Nero a "beast", even a many-headed beast: "I have seen hosts of Arabian and Indian wild beasts; but as to this wild beast, which many call a tyrant, I know not either how many heads he has, nor whether he has crooked talons and jagged teeth…this one is only roused to greater cruelty than before by those who stroke him, so that he rends and devours all alike. And again there is no animal anyhow of which you can say that it ever devours its own mother, but Nero is gorged with such quarry. Philostratus, Life of Apollonius 4.36-40 (translation by F.C. Conybeare, published in 1912 in the Loeb Classical Library) http://www.livius.org/sources/content/philostratus-life-of-apollonius/philostratus-life-of-apollonius-4.36-40/

[10] **This event of Nero's visit was drawn from ancient sources:** Suetonius, Lives of the Twelve Caesars, Nero 40 "Astrologers had predicted to Nero that he would one day be repudiated, which was the occasion of that well known saying of his: "A humble art affords us daily bread," doubtless uttered to justify him in practising the art of lyre-playing, as an amusement while emperor, but a necessity for a private citizen. Some of them, however, had promised him the rule of the East, when he was cast off, a few expressly naming the sovereignty of Jerusalem, and several the restitution of all his former fortunes. Inclining rather to this last hope, after losing Armenia and Britain and recovering both, he began to think that he had suffered the misfortunes which fate had in store. And after consulting the oracle at Delphi and being told that he must look out for the seventy-third year, assuming that he would die only at that period, and taking no account of Galba's years, he felt so confident not only of old age." http://penelope.uchicago.edu/Thayer/E/Roman/Texts/Suetonius/12Caesars/Nero*.html#ref123

Cassius Dio, Roman History, 62.14.2 "This same emperor gave 400,000 sesterces to the Pythia for uttering some oracles that suited him; this money Galba recovered. But from Apollo, on the other hand, whether from vexation at the god for making some unpleasant predictions to him or because he was merely crazy, he took away the territory of Cirrha and gave it to the soldiers. He also abolished the oracle, after slaying some people and throwing them into the fissure from which the sacred vapour arose." http://penelope.uchicago.edu/Thayer/E/Roman/Texts/Cassius_Dio/62*.html

[11] **The Son of Man came on the clouds to receive the kingdom at his resurrection/ascension:** Daniel 7:13–14 [13] "I saw in the night visions, and behold, with the clouds of heaven there came one like a son of man, and he came to the Ancient of Days and was presented before him. [14] And to him was given dominion and glory and a kingdom, that all peoples, nations, and languages should serve him; his dominion is an everlasting dominion, which shall not pass away, and his kingdom one that shall not be destroyed."

The Son of Man gives the Kingdom to the saints after the little horn of Daniel 7 (Nero) wars with them and loses: "Daniel 7:21–22 "As I looked, this horn made war with the saints and prevailed over them, 22 until the Ancient of Days came, and judgment was given for the saints of the Most High, and the time came when the saints possessed the kingdom."

[12] **All the nations attack Jerusalem:** "For I will gather all the nations [the Roman armies] against Jerusalem to battle, and the city will be captured, the houses plundered [Matt. 24:17], the women ravished [Luke 17:35], and half the city exiled [Matt. 24:16], but the rest of the people will not be cut off from the city" (Zech. 14:2).

"This happened when the Roman armies, made up of soldiers from the nations it conquered, went to war against Jerusalem. Rome was an empire consisting of all the known nations of the world (see Luke 2:1). The Roman Empire "extended roughly two thousand miles from Scotland south to the headwaters of the Nile and about three thousand miles from the Pillars of Hercules eastward to the sands of Persia. Its citizens and subject peoples numbered perhaps eighty million."1 Rome was raised up, like Assyria, to be the "rod of [His] anger" (Isa. 10:5). "So completely shall the city be taken that the enemy shall sit down in the midst of her to divide the spoil. All nations (2), generally speaking were represented in the invading army, for Rome was the mistress of many lands."2 Thomas Scott, using supporting references from older commentators and cross references to other biblical books, writes that Zechariah is describing the events surrounding Jerusalem's destruction in A.D. 70." Gary DeMar, "Zechariah 14 and the Coming of Christ" http://www.preteristarchive.com/Modern/2001_demar_zechariah-14.html

CHAPTER 4

[1] **The Roman fort:** Peter Connolly, *The Roman Fort (The Roman World)* (Oxford University Press, 1998), 5.

This description of Patmos was drawn from Gordon Franz, "The King and I: Exiled to Patmos, Part 2," Associates for Biblical Research website, 2010, http://www.biblearchaeology.org/post/2010/01/28/The-King-and-I-Exiled-To-Patmos-Part-2.aspx

CHAPTER 5

[1] **Prochorus**. This name of John's secretary scribe was taken from a legendary apocryphal account of John on the Island of Patmos written in the 5th century A.D. Margarita Grillis, (Prochorus) *Acts of John, According to Prochorus: An Apocryphal Account of His Journeys, Miracles and Death* [translated] K-Edition.

[2] **Ichthys, the Christian fish symbol:** "The Greek word for fish is 'ichthys.' As early as the first century, Christians made an acrostic from this word: Iesous Christos Theou Yios Soter, i.e. Jesus Christ, Son of God, Savior. The fish has plenty of other theological overtones as well, for Christ fed the 5,000 with 2 fishes and 5 loaves (a meal recapitulated in Christian love-feasts) and called his disciples "fishers of men." Water baptism, practiced by immersion in the early church, created a parallel between fish and converts… When threatened by Romans in the first centuries after Christ, Christians used the fish mark meeting places and tombs, or to distinguish friends from foes. According to one ancient story, when a Christian met a stranger in the road, the Christian sometimes drew one arc of the simple fish outline in the dirt. If the stranger drew the other arc, both believers knew they were in good company." Elesha Coffman (August 8, 2008). "What is the origin of the Christian fish symbol?". *Christianity Today*.

[3] **Revelation as a divine law suit against Israel**: For a full and detailed Biblical explanation of the book of Revelation as a divine bill of divorce, see, "Redemptive-Historical Excursus 6: The Scroll as a Divorce Certificate," in Kenneth L. Gentry, Jr., *The Divorce of Israel: A Redemptive-Historical Interpretation of Revelation Vol. 1* (Dallas, GA: Tolle Lege Press, 2016), 520-546.

"Scripture seems to present divine throne-visions in contexts where the focus of judgment is Israel being judged for her sins, as here in Rev. The original throne-vision in Ex 24:10 may be the exception; it serves as the paradigmatic vision for the other fuller visions. Nevertheless, though it does not directly speak of Israel's judgment, it is given in the context of her receiving the tablets of the law (Ex 24:12) at Sinai (Ex 24:16; cf. 24:4, 12, 13, 15, 17, 18). And her judgments are rooted in her failure to keep his law (Dt 27; 28; Lev 26), despite her covenanting to do so (Ex 24:3, 7; cp. Ex 19:8; Dt 5:27). It is appropriate then that Israel's judgment be related to such throne-scenes. Three of the four remaining throne-visions specifically present God's throne in the context of Israel's judgment, as we see in 1Ki 22:19 (cp. vv 20–23); Isa 6:1–4 (cp. vv 10–12), and Eze 1:26–28 (cp. Eze 2:3ff). Given that Rev's OT allusions often carry their original context with them — especially when they are dealing with Israel —, this further suggests John's concern with Jerusalem's judgment. And even the fourth vision in Da 7:9 appears in the context of the revelation of four successive kingdoms (Da 7:1–8, 15–28) that will dominate Israel: Babylon, Medo-Persia, Greece, and Rome. Daniel's throne-vision points to the coming of Christ to secure an eternal kingdom. Jesus refers to this vision in two important passages that link it with Israel's judgment (Mt 24:30 [cp. Mt:24:2, 16]; 26:64." Kenneth L. Gentry, Jr., *The Divorce of Israel: A Redemptive-Historical Interpretation of Revelation Vol. 1* (Dallas, GA: Tolle Lege Press, 2016), 492.

"But what is Ezekiel's point? Since John often incorporates the context of his OT source, this insight should help us here. Ezekiel's context clearly speaks of judicial sanctions against Israel: "Then He said to me, 'Son of man, I am sending you to the sons of Israel, to a rebellious people who have rebelled against Me'" (Eze 2:3a; cp. 2:9–3:1, 4–5, 7; see also 4:1–8; 5:1–17). This supports my understanding of Rev's thesis, especially when we consider how much greater is first century Israel's sin in rejecting the Messiah himself. Jesus' parable about Israel as God's vineyard emphasizes the failed hope of Christ's coming to Israel."

"Here in Rev 5 John is focusing on a *biblion*. The Scriptures speak of the "certificate of divorce" in several places; and the divorce "certificate" in each case is even called a biblion (Dt 24:1; Isa 50:1; Jer 3:8; Mt 19:7; and Mk 10:4).9 This is the term John uses of the "book" here in 5:1–5, 8–9. The Mishnah speaks frequently of the "bill of divorce,"10 even containing one whole tractate on the matter (Gittin) and discussions of witnesses to this important legal matter (e.g., B. Bat. 10:1; Git. 9:4). Archaeologists even have found divorce gets (Hebrew divorce certificates) from the first century, one dated in AD 72." Kenneth L. Gentry, Jr., *The Divorce of Israel: A Redemptive-Historical Interpretation of Revelation Vol. 1* (Dallas, GA: Tolle Lege Press, 2016), 519.

The scroll of Revelation 5 as a divorce certificate: "Rev comes late in the period of canonical revelation as the great redemptive-historical juncture is reached in the first century. Soon God will finally and permanently remove his central temple, which forever opens the door to the Gentiles. The AD 70 catastrophe is a major issue in redemptive history that an intensely Jewish-flavored book such as Rev would not overlook. This strongly suggests that the scroll in Rev 5 represents God's legal judgment against Israel, especially given the large role that AD 70 plays elsewhere in the NT record (note for instance Luke's four Jerusalem oracles, 13:32–35; 19:41–44; 21:20–24; 23:38–31; cf. Walker 1996: 69–80). The seven seal judgments "are best understood in the light of the 'sevenfold chastisement' that is evolved within Jewish legal theology as a scheme of punishment for disobedience to God". This is affirmed by a mass of contextual evidence in Rev as well, which I will develop as I work through the material.

"More specifically the evidence even suggests that this judgment scroll is a divorce decree against God's unfaithful wife, Israel. According to Christ's own teaching, a man may not divorce his wife to take another apart from proper moral justification and his securing a divorce certificate (Mt 5:31-32; 19:9). God certainly did this in the OT when Israel committed harlotry (Jer 3:8). The moral justification Christ demands for such a radical breach of covenant is porneia (fornication"), which happens to be related to the word used for Rev's "harlot": pornēs. In fact, the harlot is guilty of porneia (14:8; 17:1–2; 18:2–3). Rev shows God issuing a divorce decree against his harlot-wife in a dramatic court-room setting before presenting the new bride, the "new Jerusalem," the Church of Jesus Christ. The local movement in Rev is from God's throne (ch 4), the presentation of the divorce decree and Christ's receiving it in order to open it (ch 5), God's judgments flowing from it (ch 6) to a pause to consider the faithful remnant of Jews (the 144,000 from the 12 tribes) and the resulting universal growth of the Christian church (ch 7). This movement parallels in important respects the revisiting of the scroll (ch 10), the destruction of the temple in the holy city (11:1–2) in the presence of witnesses (11:3–8), with a reiteration of its universal consequences (11:15) and its viewing of the heavenly temple (11:16–18) which is now forever opened (11:19). The divorce of Israel leads to enormous redemptive-historical changes as the true faith is permanently universalized.

"Clearly "in Israel some kind of written document appears to have been necessary" to effect divorce, and this required formal court proceedings and proper witnesses (as the Mishnah. Consequently, I believe Ford's (original) approach is generally correct: "the bride and adulteress motifs in Revelation . . point to such a scroll. It might easily be a bill of divorce; the Lamb divorces unfaithful Jerusalem and marries the new Jerusalem" (Ford 93). This identification of the scroll and the consequent dramatic movement of Rev will become more evident as I continue in ch 5 and through the remainder of the book." Kenneth L. Gentry, Jr., *The Divorce of Israel: A Redemptive-Historical Interpretation of Revelation Vol. 1* (Dallas, GA: Tolle Lege Press, 2016), 545-546.

[4] **Trial ordeal for adultery**: "Ford (165–66) argues that the ordeal of jealousy in Nu 5:11–31 is behind John's imagery here. In that legislation a husband who suspects his wife of adultery is to bring her before the priest. The priest will take some of the dust from the floor of the tabernacle and mix it in water to concoct "the water of bitterness that brings a curse" (Nu 5:18; cp. 5:19, 23, 24, 27). He then has the woman swear an oath (5:21) while he writes curses on a scroll and then washes the inscribed scroll with that water (Nu 5:23). Then the woman is to drink the water (Nu 5:24, 27) and if her stomach swells, this is a sign that she is guilty (Nu 5:27). This is a well-known law in Israel: Josephus mentions it as evidence of God's opposition to adultery (Ant. 3:11:6 §270–73); the Mishnaic tractate Sotah deals extensively with this law. In Num R 9:49 this law applies to the covenant relation between God and Israel (Ford 166). On Ford's interpretation John would be acting out the ordeal of jealousy as a sign against Israel, since his book is highlighting Israel's adultery against her husband (God) and bringing judgment against her for it. This interpretation could be valid despite the fact that John's primary backdrop is clearly Eze 1–3. Ford suggests that Ezekiel's passage itself has Nu 5 as its backdrop." Kenneth L. Gentry, Jr., *The Divorce of Israel: A Redemptive-Historical Interpretation of Revelation Vol. 2* (Dallas, GA: Tolle Lege Press, 2016), 22-23.

[5] The following was drawn from "Redemptive-Historical Excursus 6: The Scroll as Divorce Certificate," Kenneth L. Gentry, Jr., *The Divorce of Israel: A Redemptive-Historical Interpretation of Revelation Vol. 1* (Dallas, GA: Tolle Lege Press, 2016), 520-546.

Israel as Yahweh's bride: Leviticus 17:7; 20:5–6; Numbers 14:33; 15:39; Deuteronomy 31:16; Judges 2:17; 8:27; 1 Chronicles 5:25; 2 Chronicles 21:11; Psalm 73:27; Isaiah 54:5; Isaiah 50:1; 54:6; 62:4; Jer. 2:2; 3:14, 20; 31:32; Hosea 1:2; 2:2,7,16; 5:4; 9:1, 10.

Israel as married to God at Sinai: Jeremiah 2.2; 31.32; Hosea 2:14–15; cf. 13.4–5.

Covenant with Israel conditioned upon obedience: Exodus 19:5-6; Leviticus 26:14–39; Deuteronomy 28:15–68.

Temple or tabernacle as home of God and center of Judaism: Exodus 29:45; Leviticus 26:9–13; 1Kings 8:10–13; Psalm 132:13–15; Matthew 23:21; Jubilees 1:17; 25:21.

Yahweh is a jealous God: Exodus 20:5; 34:14; Numbers 25:11; Deuteronomy 4:24; 5:9; 6:15; 29:20; 32:16, 21; Joshua 24:19; 1Kings 14:22; Psalm 78:58; 79:5; Nahum 1:2; Zephaniah 1:18; Zechariah 1:14; 8:2.

Israel's unfaithfulness to Yahweh described as sexual infidelity and prostitution: Hosea 2:2; Jeremiah 3:6; Exodus 34:15–16; Leviticus 17:7; Numbers 15:39; 25:1; Deuteronomy 31:16; Judges 2:17; 8:27, 33; 1Chronicles 5:25; 2Chronicles 21:11, 13; Psalm 106:39; Isaiah 1:21; Jeremiah 2:20; 3:1–9; 5:7; Ezekiel 6:9; 16:15–17, 20, 22, 25–36, 41; 23:5–8, 11, 14, 19–19, 27–30, 35, 44; 43:7, 9; Hosea 1:2, 2:2, 4–5; 3:3; 4:10–15, 18; 5:3–4; 6:10; 9:1; Joel 3:3; Amos 7:17; Micah 1:7; Nahum 3:4.

Yahweh's legal witness against Israel as a covenantal divorce: Isaiah 1:2; 50:1-2; Deuteronomy 4:26; 30:19; 31:26, 28; Jeremiah 6:19; 7:13; Micah 1:2; Malachi 1:2 Dead Sea Scrolls: 4QLamentations 179.

Prophets as God's lawyers in spiritual lawsuits: Psalm 50; Hosea 4:1; 12:2-3; Jeremiah 2-3; 30:13-14; Isaiah 3:14; 41:21; 43:26; 45:21; Micah 6:2.

Israel judged/destroyed for rejecting Messiah: John 1:11; Matthew 10:6, 15–20; 15:7–9; 22:1–7; 23:37; Acts 13:46; 15:19; 26:20; Matthew 21:33-46

Matthew 21:40–45 "When therefore the owner of the vineyard comes, what will he do to those tenants?" 41 They said to him, "He will put those wretches to a miserable death and let out the vineyard to other tenants who will give him the fruits in their seasons." 42 Jesus said to them, "Have you never read in the Scriptures: " 'The stone that the builders rejected has become the cornerstone; this was the Lord's doing, and it is marvelous in our eyes'? 43 Therefore I tell you, the kingdom of God will be taken away from you and given to a people producing its fruits. 44 And the one who falls on this stone will be broken to pieces; and when it falls on anyone, it will crush him." 45 When the chief priests and the Pharisees heard his parables, they perceived that he was speaking about them."

Israel's Capital punishment for spiritual adultery: Leviticus 20:10; Deuteronomy 22:20–22; Ezekiel 16.

Destruction of God's House for Israel's apostasy: Deuteronomy 24:1; Jeremiah 7:13-15; 11:10, 14-15; 12:7; 15:1-2; 52:3; 2Kings 24:20; 1Kings 9:6–9; Jeremiah 22:5; Lamentations 2:7; Micah 3:12; Baruch 2:26; Testament of Levi 15:1; 1 Enoch 89:56; Pesiq. R. 138a; 146a; Jesus cleansing the temple was a prophecy of the temple's destruction (Matthew 21:13); Matthew 21:18-22.

Matthew 23:29–24:2 "Woe to you, scribes and Pharisees, hypocrites! For you build the tombs of the prophets and decorate the monuments of the righteous, 30 saying, 'If we had lived in the days of our fathers, we would not have taken part with them in shedding the blood of the prophets.' 31 Thus you witness against yourselves that you are sons of those who murdered the prophets. 32 Fill up, then, the measure of your fathers. 33 You serpents, you brood of vipers, how are you to escape being sentenced to hell? 34 Therefore I send you prophets and wise men and scribes, some of whom you will kill and crucify, and some you will flog in your synagogues and persecute from town to town, 35 so that on you may come all the righteous blood shed on earth, from the blood of righteous Abel to the blood of Zechariah the son of Barachiah, whom you murdered between the sanctuary and the altar. 36 Truly, I say to you, all these things will come upon this generation. 37 "O Jerusalem, Jerusalem, the city that kills the prophets and stones those who are sent to it! How often would I have gathered your children together as a hen gathers her brood under her wings, and you were not willing! 38 See, your house is left to you desolate. 39 For I tell you, you will not see me again, until you say, 'Blessed is he who comes in the name of the Lord.' " 1 Jesus left the temple and was going away, when his disciples came to point out to him the buildings of the temple. 2 But he answered them, "You see all these, do you not? Truly, I say to you, there will not be left here one stone upon another that will not be thrown down."

It is a horrendous slander, pernicious libel and hate speech to accuse Christians of being anti-semitic for pointing out the Scriptural condemnation, by *Jews*, including Jesus, of Israel's bloodguilt: John 8:44; Revelation 2:9; 3:9; Acts 2:23: 1 Thessalonians 2:14-16; Matthew 12:38–39; 16:4; Mark 8:38; Acts 7:51; Josephus, Jewish War 5:9:4 § 402. Such accusations of anti-Semitism are in effect accusations against Jesus Christ and his apostles, at once both absurd and blasphemous.

Jewish Diaspora recognized as Divine punishment by Second Temple Literature: Sirach 48:15; Testament Levi 10:3–4; Jubilees 1:9–13; Psalms of Solomon 9:1; Tobit 3:4; Judith 5:18; Sibylline Oracles 3:267–76.

331

Yahweh's marriage to a new bride: Matthew 22:1-14; 25:1-13; Luke 5:33-35; John 3:28-29; Revelation 19:6–9; 21:2, 9; 22:17.

CHAPTER 6

[1] **Angels and Watchers have flesh**: While angels are multidimensional in their ability to traverse between the heavenlies and the earth, they are described as having flesh that eats food (Gen. 18; 19:1), and can have sexual congress with human beings (Gen. 6:1-4). This is a heavenly flesh that is different from human flesh (1 Cor. 15:39-40), but is flesh nonetheless. This would make angels or divine beings such as the Watchers unlike demons who are incorporeal spirits seeking flesh to inhabit or possess. For the difference between angels, Watchers and demons, see Brian Godawa, *When Giants Were Upon the Earth: The Watchers, the Nephilim, and the Biblical Cosmic War of the Seed* (Embedded Pictures, 2014), 275-278.

[2] **Daniel's prophecies of Rome succeeding Greece**: Daniel 2:40 And there shall be a fourth kingdom, strong as iron, because iron breaks to pieces and shatters all things. And like iron that crushes, it shall break and crush all these.

Daniel 7:7 After this I saw in the night visions, and behold, a fourth beast, terrifying and dreadful and exceedingly strong. It had great iron teeth; it devoured and broke in pieces and stamped what was left with its feet. It was different from all the beasts that were before it, and it had ten horns.

[3] **With regards to Macedonian religion**: "Herodotus (IV, 59) wrote: "… they revere Hestia above all, then Zeus and Gaea, Apollo, Aphrodite, Heracles, Ares and Poseidon. It is not their custom to carve statues of their gods or to build sacrificial altars or temples, except to honour Ares". Acad. Antonije škokljev-dončo Slave Nikolovski-katin Risto Stefov (Chris Stefou), *Macedonia in Ancient Times* (Makedonska Iskra - Skopje)

[4] **Serapis of Alexandria**: Serapis was a god in Alexandria from where Titus brought the 15th Legion into Judea. Tacitus and Suetonius both claim Vespasian had an encounter with Serapis in Alexandria right before he was declared emperor after the death of Nero. Tacitus Histories 4.81-82; Suetonius, *Vespasian* 7.1

A statue of Serapis in Alexandria "suitably depicted a figure resembling Hades or Pluto, both being kings of the Greek underworld, and was shown enthroned with the modius, a basket/grain-measure, on his head, since it was a Greek symbol for the land of the dead. He also held a sceptre in his hand indicating his rulership, with Cerberus, gatekeeper of the underworld, resting at his feet. The statue also had what appeared to be a serpent at its base, fitting the Egyptian symbol of rulership, the uraeus.

"With his (i.e. Osiris's) wife Isis, and their son Horus (in the form of Harpocrates), Serapis won an important place in the Greek world. In his 2nd-century AD Description of Greece, Pausanias notes two Serapeia on the slopes of Acrocorinth, above the rebuilt Roman city of Corinth and one at Copae in Boeotia.[8]

"Serapis figured among the international deities whose cult was received and disseminated throughout the Roman Empire, with Anubis sometimes identified with Cerberus. At Rome, Serapis was worshiped in the Iseum Campense, the sanctuary of Isis built during the Second Triumvirate in the Campus Martius. The Roman cults of Isis and Serapis gained in popularity late in the 1st century when Vespasian experienced events he attributed to their miraculous agency while he was in Alexandria, where he stayed before returning to Rome as emperor in 70. From the Flavian Dynasty on, Serapis was one of the deities who might appear on imperial coinage with the reigning emperor. The main cult at Alexandria survived until the late 4th century." https://en.wikipedia.org/wiki/Serapis

[5] **Apollyon is visiting the gods that were connected to the Roman legions used in the Jewish War**: Legion V Macedonia: "The ancient Macedonians worshipped the Olympic Pantheon, especially Zeus, Artemis, Heracles, and Dionysus. Ancient Greeks regarded it as an essential element of Hellenic identity to share common religious beliefs and to come together at regular intervals at Panhellenic sanctuaries (Olympia, Delphi, Nemea/Argos, etc.) in order to celebrate Panhellenic festivals. Most of the gods who were worshipped in southern Greece can also be found in the Macedonian pantheon and the names of the most important Macedonian religious festivals are also typically Greek."
https://en.wikipedia.org/wiki/Ancient_Macedonians#Religion

In the first attack, [Cestius] "Gallus marshalled a considerable force of over 30,000 men at Antioch. At its core was legio XII Fulminata , plus 2,000 picked men from the other three Syrian legions, six more cohorts of infantry and four alae of cavalry, and over 14,000 auxiliaries furnished by Rome's eastern allies, including Agrippa II and two other client kings, Antiochus IV of Commagene and Sohaemus of Emesa, who led their forces (largely archers and cavalry) in person." Si Sheppard, *The Jewish Revolt AD 66-74* (Oxford: Osprey Publishing, 2013), 10.

In the second attack, Vespasian used the following forces:
Legion V Macedonia and X Fretensis from Antioch
Legion XV Apollinaris that Titus marched up from Egypt.
23 auxiliary Infantry cohorts
The following client kings each sent 2,000 archers and 1,000 cavalry:
Agrippa II, Sohaemus of Emesa, Antiochus IV of Commagene
Malichus II of Nabatea provided 5,000 infantry (archers) and 1,000 horsemen

Si Sheppard, *The Jewish Revolt AD 66-74* (Oxford: Osprey Publishing, 2013), 35.

[6] **Daniel's prophesy interpretation of the stone cut without hands toppling the previous kingdoms**: Daniel 3:34-45.

[7] **The overthrow of Nineveh in 40 days**: Jonah 3:4.

The reason why prophecy is not fulfilled: God places a contingency based upon repentance.

Jeremiah 18:7–10 [1] The word that came to Jeremiah from the LORD: [2] "If at any time I declare concerning a nation or a kingdom, that I will pluck up and break down and destroy it, [8] and if that nation, concerning which I have spoken, turns from its evil, I will relent of the disaster that I intended to do to it. [9] And if at any time I declare concerning a nation or a kingdom that I will build and plant it, [10] and if it does evil in my sight, not listening to my voice, then I will relent of the good that I had intended to do to it.

"Even seventy years after the invasion of Judea, things still hadn't come together as Jeremiah had prophesied. Jeremiah 29:10-14 (cf. 25:11-12) promised that after the seventy years, God would return the Israelites from exile and restore their fortunes. But it is not as if all the Israelites had returned to the Promised Land by the time the Temple had been rebuilt. Only a portion of the Israelite population hobbled back to Judaea under Cyrus's decree (Ezra 2:1-65). When Ezra's ministry began around 458 BCE, a solid 130 years into the exile, he was still only leading a modest contingent of Israelite exiles to Jerusalem (see Ezra 8:1-20), and even then, their travel required the gracious permission of King Artaxerxes (Ezra 7:11-28). A dozen years after that, Nehemiah undertook his ministry (Neh. 2:1-10), and he too lamented that the exile was far from over (Neh. 1:1-11). Thus, in about 446 BCE, some 141 years after the destruction of the Jerusalem Temple, Nehemiah was still in Persia; the walls of Jerusalem lay in ruins; and those who had supposedly escaped captivity remained "in great trouble and shame" (Neh. 1:3)." Christopher M. Hays, ed., *When the Son of Man Didn't Come: A Constructive Proposal on the Delay of the Parousia* (Fortress Press, 2016), 28.

[8] **Jeremiah's prophecy of the seventy years**: Jeremiah 29:10–14 [10] "For thus says the LORD: When seventy years are completed for Babylon, I will visit you, and I will fulfill to you my promise and bring you back to this place. [11] For I know the plans I have for you, declares the LORD, plans for welfare and not for evil, to give you a future and a hope. [12] Then you will call upon me and come and pray to me, and I will hear you. [13] You will seek me and find me, when you seek me with all your heart. [14] I will be found by you, declares the LORD, and I will restore your fortunes and gather you from all the nations and all the places where I have driven you, declares the LORD, and I will bring you back to the place from which I sent you into exile.

Daniel sees the extension of Jeremiah's prophecy from 70 years to 70x7 years to be based on Israel's continuing sin: Daniel 9:2–7 in the first year of his reign, I, Daniel, perceived in the books the number of years that, according to the word of the LORD to Jeremiah the prophet, must pass before the end of the desolations of Jerusalem, namely, seventy years. [3] Then I turned my face to the Lord God, seeking him by prayer and pleas for mercy with fasting and sackcloth and ashes. [4] I prayed to the LORD my God and made confession, saying, "O Lord, the great and awesome God, who keeps covenant and steadfast love with those who love him and keep his commandments, [5] we have sinned and done wrong and acted wickedly and rebelled, turning aside from your commandments and rules. [6] We have not listened to your servants the prophets, who spoke in your name to our kings, our princes, and our fathers, and to all the people of the land. [7] To you, O Lord, belongs righteousness, but to us open shame, as at this day, to the men of Judah, to the inhabitants of Jerusalem, and to all Israel, those who are near and those who are far away, in all the lands to which you have driven them, because of the treachery that they have committed against you.

333

Daniel 9:24 "Seventy weeks are decreed about your people and your holy city, to finish the transgression, to put an end to sin, and to atone for iniquity, to bring in everlasting righteousness, to seal both vision and prophet, and to anoint a most holy place.

Apollyon's (Satan's) view of "prophecy failure" is reflective of modern Bible critics: ""So,Jeremiah prophesied that Babylon would conquer Judaea and rule the Israelites and their land for seventy years, after which God promised to restore them. But did things turn out as planned? Not exactly. The Old Testament is littered with texts trying to account for the way in which subsequent history did not line up with Jeremiah's timeline. Initially, the biblical authors needed to explain why the exile began to wind down too early; then, they had to reverse their tactics and explain why restoration from exile was taking too long; and finally, some of them just threw up their hands and denied that the prophesied restoration was ever even inaugurated (however abortively or impartially). In short, the Hebrew Bible seems a veritable cacophony of voices trying to explain why things did not turn out as Jeremiah had prophesied. For a sample of this confused prophetic "witness," we need only lend an ear to Zechariah, Ezra-Nehemiah, and Daniel…

"The author adduced a new prophecy to supersede the previous schema. He alleged that back in the mid-sixth century, the "historical" Daniel had also been expecting the fulfillment of Jeremiah's prophecy in terms of seventy literal years. So, being one of the exiles himself and praying "in the first year of Darius" (Dan. 9:1), Daniel questioned how much longer it would be before Jeremiah's prophecy was fulfilled. Alas, the archangel Gabriel told him that it would, in fact, be seventy sevens-seventy lots of seven years. The extra wait notwithstanding, Gabriel promised that after 490 years, Israel's fortunes would surpass all previous expectations: there would be "everlasting righteousness" (Dan. 9:24). Even though Gabriel admitted that the last several years of the 490 would be undeniably ghastly, he promised that in the end, it would all be worth it." Christopher M. Hays, ed., *When the Son of Man Didn't Come: A Constructive Proposal on the Delay of the Parousia* (Fortress Press, 2016), 26, 30.

The returned Israelites still considered themselves in exile even in the first century: "But the geographical return from exile, when it came about under Cyrus and his successors, was not accompanied by any manifestations such as those in Exodus 40, Leviticus 9, 1 Kings 8, or even (a revelation to an individual) Isaiah 6. Never do we hear that the pillar of cloud and fire which accompanied the Israelites in the wilderness has led the people back from their exile. At no point do we hear that YHWH has now gloriously returned to Zion. At no point is the house again filled with the cloud which veils his glory. At no point is the rebuilt Temple universally hailed as the true restored shrine spoken of by Ezekiel. Significantly, at no point, either, is there a final decisive victory over Israel's enemies, or the establishment of a universally welcomed royal dynasty." N. T. Wright, *Jesus and the Victory of God, Christian Origins and the Question of God* (London: Society for Promoting Christian Knowledge, 1996), 621.

"Nowhere in second-temple literature is it asserted that this has happened: therefore it still remains in the future. The exile is not yet really over. This perception of Israel's present condition was shared by writers across the board in second-temple Judaism. We may cite the following as typical:

"Here we are, slaves to this day—slaves in the land that you gave to our ancestors to enjoy its fruits and its good gifts. Its rich yield goes to the kings whom you have set over us because of our sins; they have power also over our bodies and over our livestock at their pleasure, and we are in great distress

"This could not be clearer: Israel has returned to the land, but is still in the 'exile' of slavery, under the oppression of foreign overlords." N. T. Wright, *The New Testament and the People of God, Christian Origins and the Question of God* (London: Society for Promoting Christian Knowledge, 1992), 269.

[9] **Antiochus Epiphanes as the little horn of Daniel 8**: "The best commentary on all these prophetic statements of Daniel is, perhaps, the account of this Antiochus as given in the first book of Maccabees, and the corresponding narratives in the works of Josephus. The impious ruler is called in 1 Macc. 2:62, ἀνήρ ἁμαρτωλός, sinful man, and doubtless furnished Paul with the concept of "the man of sin, the son of perdition, he that opposeth and exalteth himself against all that is called God or that is worshiped" (2 Thess. 2:3, 4).

"Josephus states (*Wars of the Jews*, book i, 1, 1), that Antiochus Epiphanes "came upon the Jews with a great army, took their city by force, slew a great multitude, spoiled the temple, and put a stop to the constant practice of offering a daily sacrifice of expiation for three years and six months."

"The facts above mentioned show that the statements of Dan. 7:25, and parallel passages were most strikingly fulfilled in the person of Antiochus Epiphanes. To a Jewish writer his entire career would

334

appear most impious and contemptible. His order to abolish the worship of God at Jerusalem was a vile speaking against the Most High. His Jewish persecutions were designed to "wear out the saints of the Most High." His arbitrary prohibition of the "whole burnt offerings, and sacrifices, and drink offerings in the sanctuary," and his order to "profane the Sabbaths and feasts, and pollute the sanctuary and them that were holy" (1 Macc. 1:45, 46), were obviously a purpose "to change the times and the law;" and Josephus's statement that he "spoiled the temple and put a stop to the offering of a daily sacrifice for three years and six months," is a most significant explanation of the giving over of the sanctuary into his hand "until a time, and (two) times, and half a time." Milton S. Terry, *Biblical Apocalyptics: A Study of the Most Notable Revelations of God and of Christ in the Canonical Scriptures* (New York; Cincinnati: Eaton & Mains; Curts & Jennings, 1898), 191-192.

"A goat with a prominent horn (8:5). As the interpretation in 8:21 makes clear, this goat represents the coming of Alexander the Great. Between 334 and 331 B.C. Alexander won a series of battles against Darius III of Persia and became ruler of an empire that stretched from Greece to India. Note that in the Old Testament, the goat is regarded as a stronger animal than the ram (Jer. 50:8).

"His large horn was broken (8:8). At the height of his power Alexander died of a fever in Babylon in 323 B.C.

"Four prominent horns grew up toward the four winds of heaven (8:8). After Alexander's death his empire was eventually divided between four of his generals (see comment on 8:22). Their realms did not correspond to the four compass points, but "the four winds of heaven" is an Akkadian idiom (see comment on 7:2).

"Another horn, which started small (8:9). In view of what is said in the following verses, there is general agreement that this horn is a symbol for the Seleucid ruler Antiochus IV Epiphanes.

"Grew in power to the south and to the east and toward the Beautiful Land (8:9). Antiochus IV campaigned in Egypt to the south (1 Macc. 1:16–20) and against the Parthians to the east (3:27–37). Daniel 11:16, 41 make it clear that "the Beautiful Land" is Israel.

"It reached the host of heaven and it threw some of the starry host down to the earth and trampled on them (8:10). In his vision of the heavenly throne room Micaiah ben Imlah sees "the host of heaven" attending Yahweh (1 Kings 22:19; 2 Chron. 18:18). The God of Israel is sometimes called "LORD [Yahweh] of hosts" (2 Sam 6:2; Isa. 6:3; where the NIV has "LORD Almighty"). Judges 5:20 speaks of the stars fighting from heaven on behalf of Israel, and it is clear that here the "host of heaven" is also fighting on the side of Israel. The phrase expresses the transcendent dimension of the conflict between Antiochus and the Jews. The language of this verse is reminiscent of Isaiah 14 and Ezekiel 28." John H Walton, *Zondervan Illustrated Bible Backgrounds Commentary (Old Testament): Isaiah, Jeremiah, Lamentations, Ezekiel, Daniel, vol. 4* (Grand Rapids, MI: Zondervan, 2009), 554–555.

[10] **I have woven several passages together because they all refer to the Little Horn**: Daniel 7:7-8, 21-22, 24–25.

[11] **It was common in the first century for both Christians and pagans to call Nero a "beast", even a many-headed beast**: "I have seen hosts of Arabian and Indian wild beasts; but as to this wild beast, which many call a tyrant, I know not either how many heads he has, nor whether he has crooked talons and jagged teeth…this one is only roused to greater cruelty than before by those who stroke him, so that he rends and devours all alike. And again there is no animal anyhow of which you can say that it ever devours its own mother, but Nero is gorged with such quarry. Philostratus, Life of Apollonius 4.36-40 (translation by F.C. Conybeare, published in 1912 in the Loeb Classical Library) http://www.livius.org/sources/content/philostratus-life-of-apollonius/philostratus-life-of-apollonius-4.36-40/

Nero as the Little Horn of Daniel, or as some call it, the Antichrist: I am not dead set on this interpretation as I consider there to be a pretty good argument for Titus as the little horn. However, in writing a novel, I have to commit to a specific view so I chose this one because it makes narrative sense with my story. I have included the theory for Titus as the little horn right after it.

> I considered the horns, and, behold, there came up among them another little horn, before whom there were three of the first horns plucked up by the roots: and, behold, in this horn were eyes like the eyes of man, and a mouth speaking great things (Daniel 7:8).

"This speaks of Nero Caesar. He is the little horn "among them." Nero was the sixth of the ten emperors. Thus he is "another little horn" – one of many. Note that the passage says, "Three of the first horns plucked up by the roots." Nero was born on December 15th, AD 37. Three emperors ruled in his lifetime,

Tiberius, Caligula and Claudius. Roman historians tell us that each one was assassinated to make way for Nero, who was not in the line of succession. Although some have doubted the Tiberius assassination story recorded by Tacitus and Suetonius as a mere rumor, Nero was born in the year of Tiberius' death and survived the emperors Caligula and Claudius. He lived in an era when political assassinations of those in the Julio-Claudian line had become the norm...

"Daniel 7 is important because the language here closely parallels Revelation 13 and 17. If we are to "count the number of the beast" (Revelation 13:18), then we need to know who is the Little Horn. Daniel 7 must be consistent with a preterist interpretation of Revelation 13 and 17...

11. I beheld then because of the voice of the great words which the horn spake: I beheld even till the beast was slain, and his body destroyed, and given to the burning flame.

The beast was slain — This speaks of both the destruction of the Roman Empire and of Nero who committed suicide with a military sword that killed many people before him.

12. As concerning the rest of the beasts, they had their dominion taken away: yet their lives were prolonged for a season and time.

"As concerning the rest of the beasts — After Nero's death, other rulers governed the Roman Empire, but the power of their throne began to weaken. They had their dominion taken away — At this point, the kingdom of God began to grow in all the earth.

"Yet their lives were prolonged for a season and time — There are several possible interpretations from a preterist perspective. A general interpretation has the rest of the beasts symbolizing the Gentile nations, including the realms held by the Babylonian, Persian and Greek kingdoms, that will remain in rebellion to God for an unspecified period of time until the kingdom of God gradually fills the whole world, as in chapter 2. This is the interpretation I favor, but there are two others that are interesting and worth considering.

"A more specific interpretation is that the rest of the beasts symbolize the remaining four Roman kings who ruled after Nero. The "Year of the Four Emperors" lasted a little more than a year from the death of Nero on June 8th of AD 68 to the accession of Vespasian on July 1st, 69. In this space of time, Nero, Galba, Otho and Vespasian ruled in turn.

"On the other hand, if "a season and a time" is interpreted to be exactly "three months and one year," then Vespasian's reign as emperor began on July 1st of AD 69 and the destruction of Jerusalem took place on September 24th, AD 70. This is a one year and three month period. In fact, it is exactly 360 days (a year) plus 90 days (a season) according to the Babylonian calendar in use at that time.

13. I saw in the night visions, and, behold, one like the Son of man came with the clouds of heaven, and came to the Ancient of days, and they brought him near before him...

The Son of Man — This speaks of Jesus Christ, the Son of God who is fully God and fully man. In the Gospels, Jesus identities himself as the "Son of man" in order to identify himself as the Messiah.

14. And there was given him dominion, and glory, and a kingdom, that all people, nations, and languages, should serve him: his dominion is an everlasting dominion, which shall not pass away, and his kingdom that which shall not be destroyed.

"Dominion, and glory, and a kingdom — Christ was given the keys to the kingdom by God the Father when he sat down at the right hand of God after His resurrection and ascension. This kingdom is not a future kingdom. It began in the days of the Roman Empire. It overcame Rome and will overcome all the kingdoms of this world. It will last forever...

20. And of the ten horns that were in his head, and of the other which came up, and before whom three fell; even of that horn that had eyes, and a mouth that spake very great things, whose look was more stout than his fellows.

"Before whom three fell — Nero was born in AD 37, the same year as the death of Tiberius Caesar. Three Caesars were assassinated to clear the way for him. These were Tiberius, Caligula and Claudius. Tacitus and Suetonius record that Tiberius was smothered by Caligula and Macro and the crowd in Rome hearing the news rejoiced. Some consider this story to be spurious, but this is the consensus of the ancient historians. Caligula was murdered by his own guardsmen at the behest of a rival faction. Claudius was poisoned and it is thought that his fourth wife, Agrippina, committed the deed in order to make way for her son, Nero, whom Claudius had adopted as his step-son and heir.

"Many interpret the Little Horn as the "eleventh" horn. Of course, the number eleven is mentioned nowhere in the text. The Little Horn does not come after the ten horns, but as it has been translated as "in the midst of them" or "among them." Thus if the Little Horn is Nero, he is the sixth of the ten.

21. I beheld, and the same horn made war with the saints, and prevailed against them;

"The same horn made war with the saints — Nero began a persecution of the saints which began in AD 64 and lasted until his death on June 9th, AD 68.

22. Until the Ancient of days came, and judgment was given to the saints of the most High; and the time came that the saints possessed the kingdom. 23. Thus he said, The fourth beast shall be the fourth kingdom upon earth, which shall be diverse from all kingdoms, and shall devour the whole earth, and shall tread it down, and break it in pieces. 24. And the ten horns out of this kingdom are ten kings that shall arise: and another shall rise after them; and he shall be diverse from the first, and he shall subdue three kings. Another shall rise after them

— Nero was not in the direct line of succession, but three emperors were assassinated to make way for him.

25. And he shall speak great words against the most High, and shall wear out the saints of the most High, and think to change times and laws: and they shall be given into his hand until a time and times and the dividing of time.

"Until a time and times and the dividing of time — Literally, "time, times, half a time." If we understand a "time "to mean a year, then it is three-and a-half years. Nero's persecution of the Church lasted from about December AD 64 until his death in June AD 68. Although neither Suetonius not Tacitus give us the exact date when the persecution began, we can safely assume it was late 64 and lasted until Nero's death.

26. But the judgment shall sit, and they shall take away his dominion, to consume and to destroy it unto the end. 27. And the kingdom and dominion, and the greatness of the kingdom under the whole heaven, shall be given to the people of the saints of the most High, whose kingdom is an everlasting kingdom, and all dominions shall serve and obey him. 28. Hitherto is the end of the matter. As for me Daniel, my cogitations much troubled me, and my countenance changed in me: but I kept the matter in my heart.

"An everlasting kingdom — The purpose of this passage, and the entire prophecy of Daniel, is to give the Jews a correct understanding of the time when the Messiah would come. The purpose is to declare when the kingdom of God would come on earth. Jesus alluded to Daniel when He said to His disciples, "Assuredly, I say to you, there are some standing here who shall not taste death till they see the Son of Man coming in His kingdom." (Matthew 16:28)."

Jay Rogers, *In the Days of These Kings: The Book of Daniel in Preterist Perspective* (Clermont, FL, Media House Intl., 2017), 101, 54-57.

[12] Daniel 9:26–27

CHAPTER 7

[1] **Oikoumene, "the world":** "The Greek word translated "world" in Matthew 24:14 is *oikoumene*, "the inhabited earth." The same Greek word is used in Luke 2:1: "Now it came about in those days that a decree went out from Caesar Augustus, that a census be taken of all the inhabited earth." In the New American Standard Version, the marginal note in Luke 2:1 reads "the Roman empire" (also see Acts 11:28, 24:5)." Gary DeMar, *Last Days Madness: Obsession of the Modern Church*, Fourth revised edition (Powder Springs, GA: American Vision, 1999), 88.

In NT thinking the Roman empire is the world (Ac 11:28; 17:6; 24:5; Col 1:6, 24). This is true among non-biblical writers, as well (Jos., J.W. 2:16:4 §361, 380, 388; 4:3:10 §78; Ap. 2:4 §8; Tac., His. 2:78).

[2] **Severus quotes:** Revelation 18:2, 21.

Dwelling place of demons: "John frequently emphasizes Israel's demonic opposition to God, calling her weekly meeting place a "synagogue of Satan" (2:9; 3:9), dramatically portraying the flooding of the Land with demons during the Jewish War (9:1-11), showing demonic decrees pouring forth from her religious authorities (13:13-14; 16:13-14), and declaring her temple the throne of Satan (16:10; see Exc 12 at 16:10)." Kenneth L. Gentry, Jr., *The Divorce of Israel: A Redemptive-Historical Interpretation of Revelation Vol. 2* (Dallas, GA: Tolle Lege Press, 2016), 493.

[3] **The harlot/Babylon cannot be Rome**: Gregg summarizes James Stuart Russell's argument: "1. The fall of Rome does not fall within the things "which must shortly take place," which is the stated subject matter of the Apocalypse (cf. 1:1);

"2. The Olivet Discourse, which Russell conceives as a shorter treatment of the same subject matter as Revelation, does not include a discussion of the fate of Rome (see Matthew 24; Mark 13; Luke 21);

"3. As Revelation presents a series of contrasts—a Lamb vs. a dragon; the Father's name vs. the beast's name on people's foreheads; the bride vs. the harlot—so also the Apocalypse contrasts two cities, Babylon and the New Jerusalem. The latter is the church. The earthly Jerusalem is clearly in view in earlier chapters. To bring Rome into the picture at this point would introduce a third city and destroy the symmetry of the book;

"4. As a symbolic name for Jerusalem, Babylon would be as fitting as Sodom and Egypt, which were applied to Jerusalem earlier (11:8);

"5. The phrase "that great city" was used of Jerusalem earlier (11:8), as it is used repeatedly in these chapters regarding Babylon;

"6. In chapter 14, the winepress was trodden "outside the city" (14:20), which almost all understand to refer to Jerusalem, yet the only "city" named earlier in that chapter is Babylon (14:8), hence, Babylon equals Jerusalem;

"7. The division of Babylon into "three parts" in 16:19 best fits Jerusalem (see notes at that passage; cf. Ezek. 5:1–12);

"8. The appellation "the harlot" is an established label for Jerusalem from the Old Testament (cf. Isa. 1:21; 57:8; Jer. 2:2, 20); it could never be applied to Rome or any Gentile city, since they have never been in a covenant relationship with God. As Chilton writes: "The metaphor of harlotry is exclusively used in the Old Testament for a city or nation that has abandoned the Covenant and turned toward false gods; and with only two exceptions … the term is always used for faithless Israel";

"9. Jerusalem sat upon seven hills as truly as did Rome;

"10. If "the kings of the earth" be understood to mean "the rulers of the land (Israel)," then Jerusalem, as appropriately as Rome, could be said to be "that great city" in 17:18 (see note there);

"11. The expression "that great city which reigns over the rulers of the land" (v. 18) is fully equivalent to that which is said of Jerusalem in Lamentations 1:1—"Who was great among the nations! The princess among the provinces";

"12. The Jews of Jerusalem were idolatrous, as was Rome;

"13. No city other than Jerusalem could be charged with the blood of the prophets and saints and apostles (see 17:6; 18:20, 24)."Steve Gregg, *Revelation, Four Views: A Parallel Commentary* (Nashville, TN: T. Nelson Publishers, 1997), 402–406.

[4] **The "great city"**: Revelation 18:10, 16, 18, 19, 21; cp. 18:2. The Great City was previously introduced as the place of the crucifixion in Revelation 11:8, which is Jerusalem.

Old Testament prophets calls Jerusalem the Great City: Jeremiah 22:8 " 'And many nations will pass by this city, and every man will say to his neighbor, "Why has the LORD dealt thus with this great city?"

Lamentations 1:1 How lonely sits the city that was full of people! How like a widow has she become, she who was great among the nations! She who was a princess among the provinces has become a slave.

Josephus calls Jerusalem a great city: "This was the end which Jerusalem came to by the madness of those that were for innovations; **a city otherwise of great magnificence**, and of mighty fame among all mankind." Flavius Josephus, *The Wars of the Jews*, 7.4.

"And where is now that **great city**, the metropolis of the Jewish nation, which was fortified by so many walls round about, which had so many fortresses and large towers to defend it, which could hardly contain the instruments prepared for the war, and which had so many ten thousands of men to fight for it? (376) Where is this city that was believed to have God himself inhabiting therein?" Flavius Josephus, *Jewish Wars* 7:8:7 §375.

Roman historians Tacitus and Pliny call Jerusalem a great city: "However, as I am about to describe the last days of a famous city, it seems proper for me to give some account of its origin." Tacitus, *Histories* 5.2

"Jerusalem, by far the most famous city, not of Judæa only, but of the East, and Herodium, with a celebrated town of the same name." Pliny the Elder, *The Natural History*, 15.15, ed. John Bostock (Medford, MA: Taylor and Francis, Red Lion Court, Fleet Street, 1855), 1428.

The Great City is Jerusalem. Extra biblical sources: Sibylline Oracles 5:154, 226, 413.

Jerusalem's covenantal glory: "The angel now identifies the Harlot as the Great City, which, as we have seen, St. John uses as a term for Jerusalem, where the Lord was crucified (11 :8; 16: 19). Moreover, says the angel, this City has a Kingdom over all the kings of the earth. It is perhaps this verse, more than any other, which has confused expositors into supposing, against all other evidence, that the Harlot is Rome. If the City is Jerusalem, how can she be said to wield this kind of worldwide political power? The answer is that Revelation is not a book about politics; it is a book about the Covenant. Jerusalem did reign over the nations. She did possess a Kingdom which was above all the kingdoms of the world. She had a covenantal priority over the kingdoms of the earth. Israel was a Kingdom of priests (Ex. 19:6), exercising a priestly ministry of guardianship, instruction, and intercession on behalf of the nations of the world. When Israel was faithful to God, offering up sacrifices for the nations, the world was at peace; when Israel broke the Covenant, the world was in turmoil. The Gentile nations recognized this (1 Kings 10:24; Ezra 1; 4-7; cf. Rom. 2:17-24).26 Yet, perversely, they would seek to seduce Israel to commit whoredom against the Covenant – and when she did, they would turn on her and destroy her. That pattern was repeated several times over until Israel's final excommunication in A.D. 70, when Jerusalem was destroyed. The desolation of the Harlot was God's final sign that the Kingdom had been transferred to His new people, the Church (Matt. 21:43; 1 Pet. 2:9; Rev. 11:19; 15:5; 21:3). The Kingdom over the kingdoms will never again be possessed by national Israel." David Chilton, *The Days of Vengeance: An Exposition of the Book of Revelation* (Texas: Dominion Press, 1987, 1990) 442-443.

[5] **Israel called by the name of Sodom**: Isaiah 3:8–9; Jeremiah 23:14; Lamentations 4:6; Ezekiel 16:46, 48–49, 55–56; Amos 4:11; John 11:8 Matthew 10:15; 11:23–24).

Israel likened to Egypt: Amos 4:10-11.

[6] **Babylon in Revelation 17 and 18 is Jerusalem, not Rome**: "Several textual indicators suggest that John is focusing on Jerusalem rather than Rome (cp. Provan 1996: 94). (1) In this very Judaic book the language of religious defilement in 18:2 would suggest a Jewish city is in view. (2) Babylon's double punishment reflects the Old Testament prophetic witness against Jerusalem (18:6; see below). (3) The "great city" (18:10, 16, 18, 19, 21; cp. 18:2) was previously introduced as the place of the crucifixion (11:8). (4) In 18:24 the killing of the prophets by Babylon reflects a familiar sin of Jerusalem (Neh 9:26; cp. 1Ki 19:10, 14; 21:13; 2Ch 24:19, 21; 36:14-16; Isa 1:15; Jer 2:30; 25:4; 26:20-23). (5) The bowl judgments in Revelation 16 are being expanded upon in Revelation 17-18. In the latter bowls "Babylon the great" was distinguished from the cities of the nations (16:19)."Kenneth L. Gentry, Jr., *The Divorce of Israel: A Redemptive-Historical Interpretation of Revelation Vol. 2* (Dallas, GA: Tolle Lege Press, 2016), 506-507.

"It might be objected that the great city in Revelation appears too important among the nations to be identified with Jerusalem rather than Rome. However, Jerusalem was thought to be the "navel" or center of the earth (Gen R 59:5), "destined to become the metropolis of all countries" (Exod R 23:10), and the Psalms (e.g. 48:2–3, 50:2); Lamentations (e.g. 1:1, 2:15) and Prophets (e.g. Zech 14:16–21, Isa 2:2–4, Micah 4:1–3) speak in the loftiest terms of Jerusalem's place among the nations. Rev 17:18 is probably a similar hyperbole; cf. 4QLam which describes her as "princess of all nations." J. Massyngberde Ford, *Revelation: Introduction, Translation, and Commentary, vol. 38, Anchor Yale Bible* (New Haven; London: Yale University Press, 2008), 285.

[7] **Severus quotes from**: Revelation 18:9, 15.

The harlot as "the great city" cannot be Rome: ""The woman … is the great city—Here, at the conclusion of the vision and its explanation, we have the most specific and formal definition of the import of the harlot. The term great city has already been applied to the place called in mystic language Sodom and Egypt, where the Lord of the two witnesses was crucified (11:8). That city is allowed by the best exegetes to be Jerusalem, and Josephus calls Jerusalem in one passage (Wars, vii, 8, 7) "that great city." But it has generally been supposed that the concluding words, commonly translated which reigneth over the kings of the earth, cannot be appropriately applied to Jerusalem. Hence this verse, as well as the "seven mountains" of verse 9, are held by many to be conclusive that the great city intended must be Rome. But we believe that opinion to be erroneous and the following reasons to be conclusive of the soundness of the exposition given in these pages:

"1. If our position is correct that the latter half of the Apocalypse (chaps. 12–22) is in the main a repetition of the first half (chaps. 1–11) under different symbols, "the great city" of this verse is presumably the same as that of 11:8. It comports with the variety of symbols employed that other symbolical names also be introduced; hence "Babylon the great," instead of "Sodom and Egypt."

2. The latter part of the verse (18) should be translated which has dominion over the kings of the land. The meaning is, not that this city reigns over all the kings and kingdoms of the habitable world, but that it is the capital city of the land in which the great catastrophe of this book centers. "The kings of the land" is a phrase to be interpreted in the light of Acts 4:26, 27, where it is evident that in the early Church "Herod and Pontius Pilate, with the Gentiles and the peoples of Israel," were the sort of kings and rulers of the earth contemplated in the second Psalm, there quoted. Such kings are represented by Josephus as subject "to the royal city Jerusalem," which, says he, "was supreme and presided over all the neighboring country as the head does over the body" (Wars, iii, 3, 5); and he goes on to designate ten "inferior cities," which were in the land of Judea. In another place he speaks of Jerusalem in the identical language of our writer, and calls it "that great city" (Wars, vii, 8, 7).

3. If the beast is the Roman empire, the harlot must be something else than the city of Rome. For it cannot be said that the emperors or the chief princes of the empire hated Rome or ever sought to destroy that great city. For the empire to destroy its own capital is incongruous in thought and untrue in fact.

"4. It contravenes the analogy of biblical symbolism and usage to call pagan Rome a harlot. The imagery, according to this scripture, implies that she had been in covenant relations with God, but this is totally untrue of any heathen city. The imagery of this whole section of the Apocalypse is appropriated from Ezek. 16, 22, and 23, where the apostate people of Judah and Jerusalem are depicted. But they were a people unto whom Jehovah sware and entered into covenant (Ezek. 16:8), and their sins were accordingly like those of "a woman that breaketh wedlock" (Ezek. 16:38). But such imagery is wholly inapplicable to Rome. How unsuitable it would have been for Ezekiel to have employed the imagery of those chapters in reference to Assyria, or Babylon, or Egypt!

"5. Many expositors have held that this great harlot is the Church of Rome, depicted as an apostate Church. In that case the imagery employed would not be inconsistent, and the political affiliations and claims of the Roman papacy and the bloody persecutions of which that Church has been guilty correspond well with the picture here drawn of "Babylon the great." But it is not true that the Roman empire or any kings or powers of earth have hated and destroyed that Church in any such sense as the statements of verse 16 require." Milton S. Terry, *Biblical Apocalyptics: A Study of the Most Notable Revelations of God and of Christ in the Canonical Scriptures* (New York; Cincinnati: Eaton & Mains; Curts & Jennings, 1898), 434–435.

"There are several further reasons for arguing that the harlot is Jerusalem rather than Rome. First, if one identifies the first beast (13:1; see third NOTE on 17:3) with the Roman empire one must argue for a different identity for the harlot: Rome cannot be seated upon Rome. Some have argued that the beast is the Roman empire and the harlot the city of Rome, but this appears to be contradicted by the text. In 17:9 the woman is said to be seated on the seven hills (equal the seven heads) and these surely symbolize the city of Rome. Secondly, Rome is never mentioned in our text, but the new Jerusalem does occur and there is great emphasis on Jewish temple imagery, etc. Further, the phrase "the great city" first found in 11:8 appears to refer to Jerusalem, not Rome, and one would expect the same identity when the phrase recurs in Rev 18:16. Thirdly, the blood of the martyrs and the saints is found in our city (18:24) but it was Jerusalem, not Rome, who slew the prophets. Fourthly, if the beast imagery is taken from Daniel then it would seem to depict a foreign power against the Jewish nation. Lastly, the symmetry of the apocalypse might urge us to inquire whether the true counterpart of the new Jerusalem (ch. 21) is not rather the old, defiled Jerusalem, rather than Rome. This would be in keeping with the theology of Qumran." J. Massyngberde Ford, *Revelation: Introduction, Translation, and Commentary, vol. 38, Anchor Yale Bible* (New Haven; London: Yale University Press, 2008), 285–286.

[8] **The immense wealth of Jerusalem**: "We saw in 17:4-5 that Jerusalem was well-known for her wealth in the first century (cp. 18:7, 16). Of the temple's building by Herod, Josephus comments: "the expenses he laid out upon it were vastly large also, and the riches about it were unspeakable" (J.W. 1:21:1 §401). But not only were its buildings magnificent but it effectively served as the treasury of all of Jewry. Josephus observes: "let no one wonder that there was so much wealth [ploutos] in our temple, since all the Jews throughout the habitable earth, and those that worshipped God, nay, even those of Asia and Europe, sent their contributions to it, and this from very ancient times. Nor is the largeness of these sums without its attestation; nor is that greatness owing to our vanity, as raising it without ground to so great a height; but there are many witnesses to it, and particularly Strabo of Cappadocia" (Ant. 14:7:2 §110). Later he speaks of "the treasury chambers, in which was an immense quantity of money, and an immense number of garments, and other precious goods" (J.W. 6:5:2 §282)…

"Philo (Spec. 1:12 §70) states that "innumerable companies of men from a countless variety of cities, some by land and some by sea, from east and from west, from the north and from the south, came to the temple at every festival." Elsewhere Philo (Spec. 1:76) puts it thus: "Since the nation is the most numerous of all peoples, it follows naturally that the first fruits contributed by them must also be most abundant."

"Philo (Spec. 1:78) notes that "practically in every city there are banking places for the holy money," which is to be sent to Jerusalem and that "the temple has for its revenues not only portions of land, but also other possessions of much greater extent and importance, which will never be destroyed or diminished; for as long as the race of mankind shall last, the revenues likewise of the temple will always be preserved, being coeval in their duration with the universal world" (Spec. 1:14 §76). Tacitus (Tac., Frag. Hist. 2; Hist. 5:8) calls the Jewish temple a temple of "immense wealth." Kenneth L. Gentry, Jr., *The Divorce of Israel: A Redemptive-Historical Interpretation of Revelation Vol. 2* (Dallas, GA: Tolle Lege Press, 2016), 509-510.

[9] **John is referring to the cargoes of Revelation 18 used for the temple**: Revelation 18:11–13 [11] And the merchants of the earth weep and mourn for her, since no one buys their cargo anymore, [12] cargo of gold, silver, jewels, pearls, fine linen, purple cloth, silk, scarlet cloth, all kinds of scented wood, all kinds of articles of ivory, all kinds of articles of costly wood, bronze, iron and marble, [13] cinnamon, spice, incense, myrrh, frankincense, wine, oil, fine flour, wheat, cattle and sheep, horses and chariots, and slaves, that is, human souls.

"The wealth of Jerusalem was a direct result of the blessings promised in Leviticus 26 and Deuteronomy 28. God had made her a great commercial center, but she had abused the gift. While there are similarities between the list of goods here and that in Ezekiel 27:12-24 (a prophecy against Tyre), it is likely that the items primarily reflect the Temple and the commerce surrounding it. Ford observes that "foreign trade had a great influence on the holy city, and the temple drew the largest share. The chief items were food supplies, precious metals, luxury goods, and clothing materials."s Josephus described the luxurious wealth of the Temple's facade (cf. Luke 21:5)…

"In the midst of a lengthy passage describing Jerusalem's extensive commerce, Edersheim reports: "In these streets and lanes everything might be purchased: the production of Palestine, or imported from foreign lands – nay, the rarest articles from the remotest parts. Exquisitely shaped, curiously designed and jewelled cups, rings, and other workmanship of precious metals; glass, silks, fine linen, woolen stuffs, purple, and costly hangings; essences, ointments, and perfumes, as precious as gold; articles of food and drink from foreign lands – in short, what India, Persia, Arabia, Media, Egypt, Italy, Greece, and even the far-off lands of the Gentiles yielded, might be had in these bazaars. Ancient Jewish writings enable us to identify no fewer than 118 different articles of import from foreign lands, covering more than even modern luxury has devised."…

"The final phrase, adapted from the description of Tyre's slave traffic in Ezekiel 27:13, is applied to Jerusalem's spiritual bondage of men's souls. As St. Paul noted in his contrast of the earthly, apostate Jerusalem with the Church, the heavenly City of God: "The present Jerusalem… is in slavery with her children," while "the Jerusalem above is free; She is our Mother" (Gal. 4:25-26). Jerusalem trafficked in many goods, from all over the world. In keeping with the promises of Leviticus 26 and Deuteronomy 28, God had made her into a great commercial center. But she abused God's gifts: Her most basic trade was in human souls. Instead of fulfilling her proper function as the mother of all mankind, she prostituted herself, and led her children into demonic bondage, statist oppression, and finally annihilation." David Chilton, *The Days of Vengeance: An Exposition of the Book of Revelation*, (Texas: Dominion Press, 1987, 1990) 454-457

[10] **The kings of the land in Revelation 18**: Revelation 18:9–10 [9] And the kings of the earth, who committed sexual immorality and lived in luxury with her, will weep and wail over her when they see the smoke of her burning. [10] They will stand far off, in fear of her torment, and say, "Alas! Alas! You great city, you mighty city, Babylon! For in a single hour your judgment has come."

The Kings of the Land Lament: "We meet once again the kings of the earth ["land"] (the high priestly aristocracy, cf. 17:2) who committed acts of immorality and lived sensuously with her (18:9a), that is, the high priestly aristocracy who lived immorally with the wealth which flowed into her, Babylon-Jerusalem (cf. 18:3). The Qumranians despised the arrogant abuse of wealth perpetrated by Jerusalem's high priesthood. Of Habakkuk 2:8 they wrote: "Interpreted this concerns the last priests of Jerusalem, who shall amass money and wealth by plundering the peoples. But in the last days, their riches and booty shall be delivered in to the hands of the army of the Kittim [i.e., Romans]" (1Qp Hab 9). The high priest "robbed God and amassed the riches of the men of violence who rebelled against God,and the took the wealth of the peoples, heaping sinful iniquity upon himself" (1Qp Hab 8:11-12). Josephus even recognizes this problem among the high priests (Ant. 20:9:2 §205-207), as does the Tosefta and Talmud (t. Men. 13:21; Pesah. 57a)." Kenneth L. Gentry, Jr., The Divorce of Israel: A Redemptive-Historical Interpretation of Revelation Vol. 2 (Dallas, GA: Tolle Lege Press, 2016), 534-535.

[11] **A light to the Gentiles**: Isaiah 49:6 he says: "It is too light a thing that you should be my servant to raise up the tribes of Jacob and to bring back the preserved of Israel; I will make you as a light for the nations, that my salvation may reach to the end of the earth."

Acts 13:45–47 But when the Jews saw the crowds, they were filled with jealousy and began to contradict what was spoken by Paul, reviling him. [46] And Paul and Barnabas spoke out boldly, saying, "It was necessary that the word of God be spoken first to you. Since you thrust it aside and judge yourselves unworthy of eternal life, behold, we are turning to the Gentiles. [47] For so the Lord has commanded us, saying, " 'I have made you a light for the Gentiles, that you may bring salvation to the ends of the earth.' "

[12] **The nations as a separated inheritance from Israel**: Deuteronomy 32:8–9 [8] When the Most High gave to the nations their inheritance, when he divided mankind, he fixed the borders of the peoples according to the number of the sons of God. [9] But the LORD's portion is his people, Jacob his allotted heritage.

Nations that bless Israel are blessed: "Genesis 12:1–3 [1] Now the LORD said to Abram, "Go from your country and your kindred and your father's house to the land that I will show you. [2] And I will make of you a great nation, and I will bless you and make your name great, so that you will be a blessing. [3] I will bless those who bless you, and him who dishonors you I will curse, and in you all the families of the earth shall be blessed."

Revelation 18 Babylon as Jerusalem: "Moreover, the phrase 'great city' in 11.8 appears to refer to Jerusalem, and one might therefore well expect it also to refer to Jerusalem in 18.16.40 So for Ford, it is Jerusalem who in ch. 18 is found in political alliance with the Romans, trading (committing adultery) with the nations; and she provides persuasive detailed exegesis of the chapter along these lines. For example, it is Jerusalem which is recalled by 18.1, alluding to the divine glory leaving the temple and city in Ezekiel, and by 18.2, with its language of religious defilement. It is Jerusalem which fits best the covenant language of 18.5, where the city's sins, rather than her love, have cleaved to God; 18.23-24 is based on Jer. 25.10, which is an oracle against Judah and Jerusalem; and so on. Particularly interesting is her treatment of the list of cargoes, many of which, she argues, would have been used for the Jerusalem temple and its services.

"Beagley argues in a similar way, noting that when enemies of the church are explicitly referred to in Revelation 1-3, it is the synagogues in Asia Minor and Philadelphia which come into view, rather than the imperial authorities; that in Revelation 4-8 the first four seal-visions are strikingly parallelled by Ezekiel 5-7, where Ezekiel utters threats against Jerusalem, the house of Israel and the inhabitants of the land; that in Revelation 8-11 Jerusalem is clearly the city where the plagues of Egypt are to fall (11.8). The great city is distinguished from the cities of the nations in 16.19, implying a Jewish city, while 16.21 recalls Ezek. 13.8-16 (concerning Jerusalem). The striking influence of Ezekiel on Revelation 17-18 in general implies that the harlot in these chapters refers to Jerusalem (cf. Ezek. 16; 23; also Mt. 23.29-38, where Jerusalem, not Rome, is the city which killed the prophets), and the double recompense language of 18.6 clearly recalls Israel/Judah, not Babylon. The view of Jerusalem found in Revelation is already prepared for, in fact, by the Old Testament prophets, who always denounce contemporary, empirical, Jerusalem because of her immorality, injustice and apostasy, threatening her with destruction, but promising her future glorification. This is precisely the pattern found in Revelation...

"It is certainly intriguing that passages like 18.22-23, with their picture of a city devoid of people and religious festivals, call to mind no book quite so much as the book of Lamentations, set in the period after Jerusalem has fallen and her people are in exile (cf., e.g., Lam. 1.1-5; 2.6-10; 5.14-18)." Iain Proven, "Foul Spirits, Fornication and Finance: Revelation 18 From an Old Testament Perspective" *Journal for the Study of the New Testament* 64 (1996) 81-100.

[13] **Exodus motif**: John appears to be echoing Jer 51:45 (regarding Jews in OT Babylon) where we read: "Come forth from her midst, My people, / And each of you save yourselves From the fierce anger of the LORD." He is applying this to Jewish-Christians in the New Babylon (Jerusalem). This command looks forward to the dramatic escape of the Christians from Jerusalem to Pella early during the Jewish War. This occurs before the final siege hopelessly traps all within. We already know that the Lord's Olivet Discourse impacts Rev, e.g., the theme in 1:7 follows the unique pattern of Mt 24:30; the seals parallel the warning signs of Mt 24:4ff; and 11:2 expands on Lk 21:24. Jesus warns that Jerusalem will be surrounded, then eventually destroyed: "when you see Jerusalem surrounded by armies, then recognize that her desolation is at hand" (Lk 21:20). Consequently, when this occurs "then let those who are in Judea flee to the mountains, and let those who are in the midst of the city depart, and let not those who are in the country enter the city" (Lk 21:21).

"We might surmise that after Jerusalem's surrounding, it would be too late to flee. But Jerusalem is surrounded on several occasions before Titus' final circumvallation. For instance, before the Jewish revolt becomes a full-scale war, Cestius Gallus surround the city, only to suddenly cease operations and leave. Josephus notes that he surrounds the city "on all sides" (Gk.: pantothen), allowing him to besiege her walls for five days (J.W. 2:19:5 §535). At that time "many of the most eminent of the Jews swam away from the city, as from a ship when it was going to sink" (J.W. 2:20:1 §556). Perhaps the Christians escape at this time also. Later in AD 68 generals Vespasian and Titus "had fortified all the places round about Jerusalem. . . encompassing the city round about on all sides" (Josephus, J.W. 4:9:1§486). But when Vespasian and Titus are "informed that Nero was dead" (4:9:2 §491), they "did not go on with their expedition against the Jews" (4:9:2 §497; cp. 4:10:2 §590) until after Vespasian becomes emperor in AD 69 (4:11:5 §567). This would be the last reasonable opportunity for escape from Jerusalem because eventually Titus builds "a wall round about the whole city" (J.W. 5:12:1 §499)." Kenneth L. Gentry, Jr., *The Divorce of Israel: A Redemptive-Historical Interpretation of Revelation Vol. 1* (Dallas, GA: Tolle Lege Press, 2016), 514-516.

"It is no wonder if the historical children of Israel should use exodus- and creation-imagery to express their hope for a freedom that would be in somewhat more obvious continuity with such historical memories...

"It is perfectly conceivable, and it certainly happened in the case of some inter-testamental novelettes such as Judith and Tobit, that stories with the regular Jewish form and basic content could be told and written without having an actual or necessary historical referent. They would have the function, however, of sustaining and keeping alive the Jewish hope, which itself remained historical: that Israel's god would act within history at last, as he had done at the exodus, to deliver his historical people from historical bondage...

"Matthew presupposes a telling of the Jewish story according to which Israel has failed, has ended in exile, and needs a new exodus; and he undertakes to show that this new exodus was accomplished in the life, death and resurrection of Jesus." N. T. Wright, *The New Testament and the People of God, Christian Origins and the Question of God* (London: Society for Promoting Christian Knowledge, 1992), 284, 397, 388.

[14] **Comparison of Israel to Egypt and the application of the plagues of Egypt to Israel**: "We will see that the trumpet judgments clearly reflect several of the Egyptian plagues (though not following their original order). Note the following table showing the parallels:

Judgment	Trumpets	Plagues
Hail and fire	First trumpet (8:7)	Seventh plague (Ex 9:22–25)
Bloody / undrinkable water	Second and third trumpets (8:8–11)	First plague (Ex 7:20–25)
Darkness	Fourth trumpet (8:12)	Ninth plague (Ex 10:21–23)
Locusts	Fifth trumpet (9:1–11)	Eighth plague (Ex 10:12–15)

This is yet another of John's frequent ironic reversals (Ford 154–55). Here in this marvelously drawn scene John presents us with an ironic reversal of Israel's exodus experience: now she herself suffers through exodus-like judgments when the remnant, the true Israel (Jewish Christians) leaves her (cp. 7:1–4; 18:4; cf. Mt 24:16). Later in Rev John specifically calls Jerusalem "Egypt" (11:8), exposing her true character as the enemy of God (cp. the even stronger denunciations in 2:9; 3:9). Interestingly, in one of Josephus's speeches to Jerusalem where he is urging the Jerusalemites to surrender to the Romans, he alludes to the Egyptian plagues: "Who is there that does not know that Egypt was overrun with all sorts of wild beasts, and consumed by all sorts of distempers? how their land did not bring forth its fruit? how the Nile failed of water? how the ten plagues of Egypt followed one upon another?" (J.W. 5:9:4 §383).

During his ministry Jesus negatively compares Israel's spiritual lethargy to various pagan cities: Sodom, Gomorrah, Tyre, and Sidon (Mt 10:15; 11:21, 23). John tends to compare her to Egypt (11:8) and Babylon (see Exc 13 at 17:1). Thus as Chilton (236) observes: "Israel has become a nation of Egyptians and Canaanites, and worse: a land of covenant apostates." Kenneth L. Gentry, Jr., *The Divorce of Israel: A Redemptive-Historical Interpretation of Revelation Vol. 1* (Dallas, GA: Tolle Lege Press, 2016), 705-706.

Boils and frogs: In addition to the plagues charted above, the other examples of boils and frogs in the scene can be found in Revelation 16:2 (boils) and Revelation 16:13 (frogs).

[15] **Cassandra is quoting from**: Revelation 18:4.

The Christians were to come out of Jerusalem, but also the Jewish temple system all over the empire: "The followers of the Lamb were called to make a clean and final break with Babylon-Jerusalem and the Judaism it represented. They must avoid the temptation to fall back into Judaism, the mother faith with all of its temple glory. The Jewish Christians must not sugkoinōnēsēte because the koinon ("common," i.e., unclean, impure) will be excluded from the New Jerusalem. By applying a biblical moral calculus, all of this was significant by extension even to the Asia Minor Christian Jews who were not even in Jerusalem. For if "my people" are to come out of "Babylon-Jerusalem" because of her sins, should not those Jewish Christians still remaining in the synagogues depart those extensions of Jerusalem? After all, John called those structures a "synagogue of Satan" (2:9; 3:9), just as Jesus before him called the Jerusalemites the offspring of their "father the devil" (Jn 8:44)." Kenneth L. Gentry, Jr., *The Divorce of Israel: A Redemptive-Historical Interpretation of Revelation Vol. 2* (Dallas, GA: Tolle Lege Press, 2016), 518-519.

[16] **Jesus said the first century generation of Jews was guilty of all the blood of the prophets and martyrs in Israel's history**: Matthew 23:31–36 [Jesus:] "Thus you witness against yourselves that you are sons of those who murdered the prophets. [32] Fill up, then, the measure of your fathers. [33] You serpents, you brood of vipers, how are you to escape being sentenced to hell? [34] Therefore I send you prophets and wise men and scribes, some of whom you will kill and crucify, and some you will flog in your synagogues and persecute from town to town, [35] so that on you may come all the righteous blood shed on earth, from the blood of righteous Abel to the blood of Zechariah the son of Barachiah, whom you murdered between the sanctuary and the altar. [36] Truly, I say to you, all these things will come upon this generation."

[17] **The Song of Moses**: Revelation 15:2–3 [2] And I saw … those who had conquered the beast and its image and the number of its name, standing beside the sea of glass with harps of God in their hands. [3] And they sing the song of Moses, the servant of God, and the song of the Lamb.

[18] **Severus is quoting from**: Revelation 1:7. See also Revelation 16:6-7.

[19] **The "earth" meaning the Land of Israel**: "The usual meaning of eretz is simply "the land" and not "the earth" as in most English translations. For the most part, it refers to a specific stretch of land in a local, geographical, or political sense. Often it means simply "the ground" upon which one stands. As such, it is frequently used interchangeably with another common Hebrew word adamah (that is, "arable ground"). DOES THE LAND = THE PROMISED LAND? Not only does the Hebrew term eretz normally mean "land" as opposed to "the earth," but it usually refers specifically to the land promised to Abraham (Genesis 15:18). Certainly the term doesn't always denote "the promised land." It may be "the land" of Egypt (Exodus 1:7) or simply the place of one's birth, the "homeland" (Genesis 12:1). But most often in Genesis and throughout the Pentateuch the term eretz refers to the promised land." Sailhamer, John (2011-06-21). *Genesis Unbound* (K-Locations 523-530). Book Villages. K-Edition.

"Luke identifies the tribulation period as being confined to the land of Israel and the people living there in the first century: "Woe to those who are with child and to those who nurse babes in those days; for there will be great distress upon the land, and wrath to this people" (Luke 21:23). The land of Israel is in view, and "this people" refers to the Jews living in Israel at the time when Jerusalem is "surrounded by armies" (21:20), an event that occurred just prior to Jerusalem's destruction in A.D. 70. "The land should be taken in the restricted sense which we give the word, the country.—St Paul seems to allude to the expression, wrath upon this people, in Rom. 2:5–8 and 1 Thess. 2:16." Gary DeMar, *Last Days Madness: Obsession of the Modern Church*, Fourth revised edition (Powder Springs, GA: American Vision, 1999), 122.

"According to TDNT (1:677), gē frequently appears in texts speaking of "the land promised to Abraham" (e.g., Ge 12:1; Ac 7:3; Heb 11:9). In fact, regarding its Old Testament usage, AB (4:144, 145) observes that "in the majority of contexts, 'land' is identified as the land to which Israel has a claim" noting that it is often called an "inheritance" from God (Nu 34:2, 29; 36:2; Dt 3:28; 4:21; 15:4; 19:14; 25:19; 31:7; 1Sa 26:19; 2Sa 14:16; 1Ki 8:36; 1Ch 16:18; Ps 68:9; 79:1; 105:11; Jer 2:7; 3:18; cp. Ac 13:19), and that it also appears as the "land of possession" (Ex 6:8; Lev 14:34; Nu 33:53; Dt 1:21; 2:12; 4:22; Jos 1:6; 12:7; Eze 33:24; Am 2:10). Thus, it represents "the land of Israel" (cf. 1Sa 13:19; Eze 40:2; 47:18; 1Ch 22:2; 2Ch 2:16; 34:7), "the Lord's land" (Isa 14:2; Jos 22:19; Hos 9:3), "My land" (2Ch 7:20; Isa 14:25; Jer 2:7; 16:18; Eze 36:5; 38:16; Joel 1:6; 3:2; 4:2), "His land" (Dt 32:43; Isa 36:18; Eze 36:20; Joel 2:18), the land the Lord swore to the fathers (Dt 1:8, 35; 6:10, 18, 23; 8:1; 10:11; 11:9; 19:8; 26:3; 30:20; 31:7, 23). In Zechariah 2:12 and 2 Maccabees 1:7 it is found in the phrase "holy land." Elsewhere it is called "holy" (Ps 78:54; Is 57:13). Therefore, God grants it a special status requiring protective legislation (Lev 25:23ff).

"This particularly abundant use of gē is significant in that the land promised to Israel was central to God's covenant with her (e.g., Ge 12:1–7; Ex 3:7–18; 6:2–8). The Land was one of the three realia dominating her devotion: the Land, Jerusalem, and the temple. As NIDOTTE (1:522) puts it: "the land on which Israel lived forms one of the primary theological and ethnic foci of the faith of Israel and of the OT scriptures" (cp. ISBE2 3:71). When God established Israel as a nation, her founding documents elevated the Land as the first of these great hopes: "In terms of the Hexateuch there is probably no more important idea than that expressed in terms of the land promised and later granted by Yahweh."8 In fact, "the motif of the Promised Land is a major pattern in the Pentateuch and the book of Joshua" (DBI 665), which record the historical foundations of Israel as a people, society, and nation. The Land was also "of central importance to all of the writing prophets" (AB 4:149)." Kenneth L. Gentry, Jr., *The Divorce of Israel: A Redemptive-Historical Interpretation of Revelation Vol. 1* (Dallas, GA: Tolle Lege Press, 2016), 261.

[20] **The dragon cast down to the land**: Revelation 12:4, 9.

Hour of trial coming to those who dwell on the land: Revelation 3:10.

[21] **Seals opened upon the land**: Revelation 6:4, 6, 7-8, 10, 12, 15.

Trumpets announced upon the land: Revelation 8:7, 13,; 9:3, 4.

Bowls poured out upon the land: Revelation 16:1, 2.

[22] **The Witnesses against the land of Israel**: Revelation 11:4, 6, 10, 13.

The beast from the land of Israel: Revelation 13:11, 14.

[23] **144,000 redeemed from the land of Israel**: Revelation 14:3; 7:1.

[24] **Those who pierced him**: Revelation 1:7.

[25] **New Testament authors ascribe moral culpability for murdering Jesus to the Jews and their leaders of the first century. Both Rome and Israel are guilty.**

Acts 3:14–15 [14] But you denied the Holy and Righteous One, and asked for a murderer to be granted to you, [15] and you killed the Author of life, whom God raised from the dead. To this we are witnesses.

Acts 13:28 [28] And though they found in him no guilt worthy of death, they asked Pilate to have him executed.

Acts 7:51 "You men who are stiff-necked and uncircumcised in heart and ears are always resisting the Holy Spirit; you are doing just as your fathers did. 52 "Which one of the prophets did your fathers not persecute? And they killed those who had previously announced the coming of the Righteous One, whose betrayers and murderers you have now become.

Acts 2:22–23 "Men of Israel, hear these words: Jesus of Nazareth, a man attested to you by God with mighty works and wonders and signs that God did through him in your midst, as you yourselves know— [23] this Jesus, delivered up according to the definite plan and foreknowledge of God, you crucified and killed by the hands of lawless men.

1Thessalonians 2:14 For you, brethren, ...also endured the same sufferings at the hands of your own countrymen, even as they {did} from the Jews, 15 who both killed the Lord Jesus and the prophets, and drove us out. They are not pleasing to God, but hostile to all men, 16 hindering us from speaking to the Gentiles that they might be saved; with the result that they always fill up the measure of their sins. But wrath has come upon them to the utmost.

Now the point of these passages is not to justify anti-Semitism by saying, "Jews killed Christ." The point is that within the redemptive history of God, the physical Jews would so constantly reject him, even to the point of killing His Son, that He would take away His Kingdom from them to give to another people (the Gentiles) who were not originally His people, to be the inheritors of his Kingdom. Modern Jews are not judicially guilty of killing Christ, the first century Jews were guilty of this crime and therefore were judged by God in the destruction of the Temple and holy city and the spreading out of salvation to the Gentiles.

Jesus accused the Jews of murdering him:

The passage that is quoted here: Matthew 23:29–38 "Woe to you, scribes and Pharisees, hypocrites! For you build the tombs of the prophets and decorate the monuments of the righteous, 30 saying, 'If we had lived in the days of our fathers, we would not have taken part with them in shedding the blood of the prophets.' 31 Thus you witness against yourselves that you are sons of those who murdered the prophets. 32 Fill up, then, the measure of your fathers. 33 You serpents, you brood of vipers, how are you to escape being sentenced to hell? 34 Therefore I send you prophets and wise men and scribes, some of whom you will kill and crucify, and some you will flog in your synagogues and persecute from town to town, 35 so that on you may come all the righteous blood shed on earth, from the blood of righteous Abel to the blood of Zechariah the son of Barachiah, whom you murdered between the sanctuary and the altar. 36 Truly, I say to you, all these things will come upon this generation. 37 "O Jerusalem, Jerusalem, the city that kills the prophets and stones those who are sent to it! How often would I have gathered your children together as a hen gathers her brood under her wings, and you were not willing! 38 See, your house is left to you desolate."

Matthew 21:33-41 "Listen to another parable. There was a landowner who planted a vineyard and put a wall around it and dug a wine press in it, and built a tower, and rented it out to vine-growers, and went on a journey. 34 "And when the harvest time approached, he sent his slaves to the vine-growers to receive his produce. 35 "And the vine-growers took his slaves and beat one, and killed another, and stoned a third. 36 "Again he sent another group of slaves larger than the first; and they did the same thing to them. 37 "But afterward he sent his son to them, saying, 'They will respect my son.' 38 "But when the vine-growers saw the son, they said among themselves, 'This is the heir; come, let us kill him, and seize his inheritance.' 39 "And they took him, and threw him out of the vineyard, and killed him. 40 "Therefore when the owner of the vineyard comes, what will he do to those vine-growers?" 41 They said to Him, "He will bring those wretches to a wretched end, and will rent out the vineyard to other vine-growers, who will pay him the proceeds at the proper seasons."

"I would further note in this regard that Israel is continually rebuked by God for killing his servants the prophets. In fact, this charge is stereotypical of Jerusalem and Israel (1Ki 18:4, 13; 19:1, 10, 14; 2Ch 24:19-21; 36:14-16; Neh 9:26; Jer 2:30; 25:4; 26:20-24; cp. Jos. Ant. 2:15:4; §327; 10:3:1 §38; 1 En 10:38; Jub 1:12; Liv. Pr 1:2; 2:1; 3:1–2; 6:2; 7:2). It is also repeated in the NT (Mt 5:12; 21:35-36; 23:9, 29-31, 34-35, 37; Lk 6:23, 26; 11:47-50; 13:33; Ro 11:3; 1Th 2:15; Heb 11:36-37)." Kenneth L. Gentry, Jr., *The Divorce of Israel: A Redemptive-Historical Interpretation of Revelation Vol. 2* (Dallas, GA: Tolle Lege Press, 2016), 41.

[26] **Cassandra is quoting from**: 1 Thessalonians 2:14–16 "For you, brethren, became imitators of the churches of God in Christ Jesus that are in Judea, for you also endured the same sufferings at the hands of your own countrymen, even as they did from the Jews, 15 who both killed the Lord Jesus and the prophets, and drove us out. They are not pleasing to God, but hostile to all men, 16 hindering us from speaking to the Gentiles so that they may be saved; with the result that they always fill up the measure of their sins. But wrath has come upon them to the utmost."

[27] **The sea means Gentiles**: Revelation 17:15 And the angel said to me, "The waters that you saw, where the prostitute is seated, are peoples and multitudes and nations and languages.

[28] **The Jewish apostate leadership looks like a lamb, but voice of the dragon**: Revelation 13:11[11] Then I saw another beast rising out of the earth. It had two horns like a lamb and it spoke like a dragon.

The land beast as apostate Jewish establishment: The land beast "represents the apostate Jewish religious establishment. According to Wainwright (126), Firmin Abauzit (1679-1767) held that "the beast from the land stands for the Pharisees, and Babylon symbolizes Jerusalem. Its fall is the destruction of that city by the Romans."3 The high priestly aristocracy that governed Israel's religious and cultural life was headquartered in the Land; blasphemously employed the Roman judicial apparatus to crucify Christ (Mt 26:59ff; Jn 11:47-48; 19:5, 12); involves religious leaders associated with worship (Mt 26:3) and prophecy (Jn 11:51), who would thereby have been wolves in sheep clothing (Mt 7:15; Mt 24:5, 11; cp. Rev 13:11); worked false miracles (Mt 24:24; Ac 8:9-24; 13:6-11; 19:13-16); and were a widespread cause of death for Christians (Ac 5:27ff; 9:1-2; 21:11; 22:5; 25:7; 26:10)." Kenneth L. Gentry, Jr., *The Divorce of Israel: A Redemptive-Historical Interpretation of Revelation Vol. 2* (Dallas, GA: Tolle Lege Press, 2016), 234.

[29] **Alexander reads about the great harlot from**: Revelation 17:1-3 [1] Then one of the seven angels who had the seven bowls came and said to me, "Come, I will show you the judgment of the great prostitute who is seated on many waters, [2] with whom the kings of the earth have committed sexual immorality, and with the wine of whose sexual immorality the dwellers on earth have become drunk." [3] And he carried me away in the Spirit into a wilderness, and I saw a woman sitting on a scarlet beast that was full of blasphemous names, and it had seven heads and ten horns.

[30] **Alexander reads from**: Revelation 17:4 The woman was arrayed in purple and scarlet, and adorned with gold and jewels and pearls, holding in her hand a golden cup full of abominations and the impurities of her sexual immorality.

[31] **The Harlot's wardrobe and colors reflect the high priest's garments and the temple**: "The woman is clothed in material (thš) mentioned elsewhere only as the covering for the tabernacle and its cultic paraphernalia (e.g., Exod 25:5; 26:14; 35:7, 23; Num 4:6, 8, 10)...

"Nor is it accidental that in the LXX the high priest's garments are also described as adorned with 'gold, purple, scarlet, linen, and [precious] stones,' which is the identical combination of words used to describe the Babylonian harlot's attire here in 17:4; 18:16...

"We should note as well that "the harlot is dressed like the temple". For instance, when giving instructions to the Israelites for building the original tabernacle (the predecessor to the temple), God commands, "This is the contribution which you are to raise from them: gold, silver and bronze, blue, purple and scarlet material,... onyx stones and setting stones," among other things (Ex 25:3b-4, 7).48...

"Josephus speaks of the color scheme of the tabernacle (the predecessor to the temple): "At the front, where the entrance was made, they placed pillars of gold, that stood on bases of brass, in number seven; but then they spread over the tabernacle veils of fine linen and purple, and blue, and scarlet colors, embroidered" (Ant. 3:6:4 §124; cp. 3:6:4 §113; 3:7:7 §183)....

"Regarding the first century Herodian temple, at J.W. 5:4:4 §179 Josephus writes of the implements stored in the temple's many rooms, for "the greatest part of the vessels that were put in them was of silver and gold" (cp. Heb. 9:4)...

"So then, the colors marking out the high priest are the same as those highlighting the temple. As Josephus (J.W. 5:5:7 §232) describes the high priest's liturgical robe, he relates it to the temple: "that girdle that tied the garment to the breast was embroidered with five rows of various colors, of gold, and purple, and scarlet, as also of fine linen and blue, with which colors we told you before the veils of the temple were embroidered,"Kenneth L. Gentry, Jr., *The Divorce of Israel: A Redemptive-Historical Interpretation of Revelation Vol. 2* (Dallas, GA: Tolle Lege Press, 2016), 421-427.

[32] **Alexander reads from**: Revelation 17:5 And on her forehead was written a name of mystery: "Babylon the great, mother of prostitutes and of earth's abominations."

[33] **High priest's forehead plate**: Exodus 28:36–38 [36] "You shall make a plate of pure gold and engrave on it, like the engraving of a signet, 'Holy to the LORD.' [37] And you shall fasten it on the turban by a cord of blue. It shall be on the front of the turban. [38] It shall be on Aaron's forehead, and Aaron shall bear any guilt from the holy things that the people of Israel consecrate as their holy gifts. It shall regularly be on his forehead, that they may be accepted before the LORD.

[34] **Christ's high priesthood entering the heavenly temple**: Hebrews 9:11–13 [11] But when Christ appeared as a high priest of the good things that have come, then through the greater and more perfect tent (not made with hands, that is, not of this creation) [12] he entered once for all into the holy places, not by means of the blood of goats and calves but by means of his own blood, thus securing an eternal

redemption. [13] For if the blood of goats and bulls, and the sprinkling of defiled persons with the ashes of a heifer, sanctify for the purification of the flesh,

[35] **Alexander reads from**: Revelation 17:6 And I saw the woman, drunk with the blood of the saints, the blood of the martyrs of Jesus. When I saw her, I marveled greatly.

[36] **Golden cup of libations**: Exodus 25:29 [29] And you shall make its plates and dishes for incense, and its flagons and bowls with which to pour drink offerings; you shall make them of pure gold.

Gold was an important symbolic element of the temple implements: 1 Kings 7:48–50 [48] So Solomon made all the vessels that were in the house of the LORD: the golden altar, the golden table for the bread of the Presence, [49] the lampstands of pure gold, five on the south side and five on the north, before the inner sanctuary; the flowers, the lamps, and the tongs, of gold; [50] the cups, snuffers, basins, dishes for incense, and fire pans, of pure gold; and the sockets of gold, for the doors of the innermost part of the house, the Most Holy Place, and for the doors of the nave of the temple.

Drinking blood was an abomination: Leviticus 17:14 [14] For the life of every creature is its blood: its blood is its life. Therefore I have said to the people of Israel, You shall not eat the blood of any creature, for the life of every creature is its blood. Whoever eats it shall be cut off.

[37] **The Harlot that rides the beast represents the corrupt Jewish leaders**: "Since the harlot is dressed in the distinctive robe of the high priest which is worn only on holy occasions (Ex 28:2-4, 41, 43), and since she possesses a "gold cup" as used in libations (Ex 25:29; 1Ki 7:50; cp. m. Yoma 3:10), Rev is presenting the holy city (cp. 11:1) under the guise of the high-priest engaged in his sacerdotal duties...

"That the gold cup is "full of abominations and of the unclean things of her immorality further identifies the harlot as Jerusalem. The kai here is probably epexegetical, signifying that she is "full of abominations, which are, the uncleanness of her immorality." In the OT the word "abominations" is often a religious term signifying that which the God of Israel detests and "uncleanness" is a cultic term related to Israel's separation to God. This religio-cultic concern is strongly Jewish, well fitting first-century Jerusalem. Archaeologists...

"So in John's drama the priestly libations God ordains for holy worship are replaced in Jerusalem's high-priestly system: their golden libation bowls now are filled with uncleanness because of their spilling the innocent blood of Christ and Christians. Rather than offering humble sacrifices to God in true worship, the temple system destroys the followers of the Lamb...

"John portrays Jerusalem's situation as a sexual liaison (she is a "harlot" committing "immorality," 17:2, 4-5) with Rome. In the background of ch 17 is the "league of friendship and mutual alliance" with Rome, beginning with Julius Caesar (1 Macc 8:17–30; 14:24, 40; Jos. Ant. 12:10:6 §414–19; 13:5:8 §163–65; 14:10:1–8 §185–216; 16:6:2–3 §162–66; 19:9:2 §360–65).36 In 1 Macc 14:40 the Jews call themselves "friends, allies, and brothers of Rome," and were, according to Smallwood (2001: 7) "immensely proud of the alliance." Josephus (Ant. 14:10:1 §186) writes: "it seems to me to be necessary here to give an account of all the honors that the Romans and their emperors paid to our nation, and of the leagues of mutual assistance they have made with it." Philo also mentions that the Jews are "friends to Caesar"... John is painting Jerusalem in the same way Isaiah and Jeremiah did as they spoke of the first temple's destruction: "How the faithful city has become a harlot, / She who was full of justice! / Righteousness once lodged in her, / But now murderers" (Isa 1:21). "You have lain down as a harlot . . . . Also on your skirts is found / The lifeblood of the innocent poor" (Jer 2:20d; 34a; cp. 7:6; 19:3-4; 22:11, 17)." Kenneth L. Gentry, Jr., *The Divorce of Israel: A Redemptive-Historical Interpretation of Revelation Vol. 2* (Dallas, GA: Tolle Lege Press, 2016), 435, 429, 430, 416-417.

So, Jesus declares the Jewish establishment as guilty of killing the prophets and the Christ:

Matthew 23:31–36 Thus you witness against yourselves that you are sons of those who murdered the prophets. 32 Fill up, then, the measure of your fathers. 33 You serpents, you brood of vipers, how are you to escape being sentenced to hell? 34 Therefore I send you prophets and wise men and scribes, some of whom you will kill and crucify, and some you will flog in your synagogues and persecute from town to town, 35 so that on you may come all the righteous blood shed on earth, from the blood of righteous Abel to the blood of Zechariah the son of Barachiah, whom you murdered between the sanctuary and the altar. 36 Truly, I say to you, all these things will come upon this generation."

[38] **The harlot is the great city of Jerusalem**: Revelation 17:18 [18] And the woman that you saw is the great city that has dominion over the kings of the earth."

348

[39] **Alexander reads from**: Revelation 17:12 And the ten horns that you saw are ten kings who have not yet received royal power, but they are to receive authority as kings for one hour, together with the beast.

[40] **Ten horns as ten client kings of Rome**: "Though provincial governors are quite possibly in view, I am inclined, however, to see them as does Aune (951): "Here the ten kings represent Roman client kings." Rome's system of client kingship was such that kings (including even ethnarchs, tetrarchs, etc.) were appointed by Roman authorities from within various localities. They were responsible for keeping the peace, assisting Rome with defense, and ensuring the flow of tribute money to Rome. They would provide soldiers "as part of tribute, or through friendships and alliances" (Gilliver 2001: 24). During Nero's rule "the client system of the East [including Judea] was then revealed at its most efficient" (Luttwak 1976: 112)...

"Archelaus himself recognized that "the power of disposing of it [his kingdom rule] belonged to Caesar, who could either give it to him or not, as he pleased" (Ant. 17:11:2 §312). Their rule was tenuous, so that John could say "they receive authority"; that authority was "with the beast"; and it was for "one hour."

"Client kings, such as the Antiochus, Agrippa, Sohemus, Malchus, and Alexander provided auxiliary forces for Rome during the Jewish War (J.W. 2:18:9 §499–501; 3:4:2 §68; 5:1:6 §45) (cf. Aune 951; Stuart 2:327). Dio Cassius (65:4:3) mentions that the Roman siege of Jerusalem included "many slingers and bows that had been sent by some of the barbarian kings." In fact, "a Roman army on campaign always included a complement of allies.... Rome relied very heavily on others for her cavalry forces" in that "such troops might have local knowledge of topography and the enemy, and could provide specialist fighting techniques appropriate to the situation" (Gillver 2001: 22; cp. Grant 1974: 77). The auxiliary forces in the empire after Augustus comprised about half of Rome's military might (cf. Luttwak 1976: 16; cf. Tac., Ann. 4:5)." Kenneth L. Gentry, Jr., The Divorce of Israel: A Redemptive-Historical Interpretation of Revelation Vol. 2 (Dallas, GA: Tolle Lege Press, 2016), 474-475.

The Ten Client Kings Named: We do not know them all, but Wellesley lists 8 of them (assuming Berenice is not counted as a king). Malchus of Nabatea makes the 9th (*Wars of the Jews* 3.4.2), and Tiberius Alexander, governor of Egypt makes 10 (*Wars of the Jews* 4.10.6): "Mucianus, governor of Syria; Sohaemus of Emesa, Antiochus IV, ruler of Comagene, King Agrippa, sheikh of Anjar and Golan; Berenice, widow of Herod of Anjar. "We are not surprised to learn that the governors of all the provinces of Asia Minor, through disposing of no legionary garrisons, had promised such support in supplies, facilities and auxiliary forces as they could give and Vespasian might require. Among them were the proconsul of Asia, Gaius Fonteius Agrippa, and the legate of Galatia-with-Pamphylia, Lucius Nonius Calpurnius Asprenas. Both In addition, there was Cappadocia, still a procuratorial province governed by a knight without the legionary garrison which Vespasian himself was to give it; its governor in 69 is unknown, and equally unknown is the governor of Pontus, added to Bithynia five years before." Kenneth Wellesley, *Year of the Four Emperors* (Taylor and Francis, 2014) 123-124.

[41] **New Jerusalem is the New Covenant**: Hebrews 12:22–24 22 But you have come to Mount Zion and to the city of the living God, the heavenly Jerusalem, and to innumerable angels in festal gathering, 23 and to the assembly of the firstborn who are enrolled in heaven, and to God, the judge of all, and to the spirits of the righteous made perfect, 24 and to Jesus, the mediator of a new covenant.

Here, we see that the New Covenant is Mount Zion spoken of in the Old Covenant. Coming to Jesus is coming to the heavenly Jerusalem, the true spiritual reality that the Old Covenant types pointed to. There can be no physical Jerusalem or Mount Zion that God is promising to do anything with, because His promise was fulfilled in Christ and His Kingdom, the heavenly (spiritual) Mount Zion and Jerusalem!

This is the theme of Hebrews: that the Old Covenant was a physical type or shadow of the spiritual reality which is in Jesus Christ:

Hebrews 8:5 [The priests of Old Covenant Law] serve a copy and shadow of heavenly things.

Hebrews 9:23 Therefore it was necessary for the copies of the things in the heavens to be cleansed with these [physical sacrifices], but the heavenly things themselves with better sacrifices than these. 24 For Christ did not enter a holy place made with hands, a mere copy of the true one, but into heaven itself, now to appear in the presence of God for us.

This heavenly Jerusalem corresponds to the "New Jerusalem that comes down out of heaven" in Revelation 21. The heavenly Jerusalem is the true Jerusalem, not the physical one. And the true Jerusalem is populated by believers in Christ, not mere circumcised genetic Jews.

If there is any doubt left about this heavenly reality, the Apostle Paul, in a passage we saw earlier, emphasizes this true Jerusalem of promise as the Church of Christ consisting of believers in Christ:

Galatians 4:22–31 For it is written that Abraham had two sons, one by a slave woman and one by a free woman. 23 But the son of the slave was born according to the flesh, while the son of the free woman was born through promise. 24 Now this may be interpreted allegorically: these women are two covenants. One is from Mount Sinai, bearing children for slavery; she is Hagar. 25 Now Hagar is Mount Sinai in Arabia; she corresponds to the present Jerusalem, for she is in slavery with her children. 26 But the Jerusalem above is free, and she is our mother. 27 For it is written, "Rejoice, O barren one who does not bear; break forth and cry aloud, you who are not in labor! For the children of the desolate one will be more than those of the one who has a husband." 28 Now you, brothers, like Isaac, are children of promise. 29 But just as at that time he who was born according to the flesh persecuted him who was born according to the Spirit, so also it is now. 30 But what does the Scripture say? "Cast out the slave woman and her son, for the son of the slave woman shall not inherit with the son of the free woman." 31 So, brothers, we are not children of the slave but of the free woman.

Physical Jerusalem is correlated with physical Jews and they are in slavery and will not be heirs of God's promise because they are not the children of promise. Believers in Christ are the free ones who will be heirs of God's promise to Abraham and Isaac. Mount Zion and Jerusalem are simply metaphors for the kingdom of God which is the Kingdom of God in the Church!

[42] **This story of Elijah comes from**: 1 Kings 19:10-18.

[43] **Paul's explanation of the remnant based on the Elijah episode**: Romans 11:1–5 [1] I ask, then, has God rejected his people? By no means! For I myself am an Israelite, a descendant of Abraham, a member of the tribe of Benjamin. [2] God has not rejected his people whom he foreknew. Do you not know what the Scripture says of Elijah, how he appeals to God against Israel? [3] "Lord, they have killed your prophets, they have demolished your altars, and I alone am left, and they seek my life." [4] But what is God's reply to him? "I have kept for myself seven thousand men who have not bowed the knee to Baal." [5] So too at the present time there is a remnant, chosen by grace. [7] What then? Israel failed to obtain what it was seeking. The elect obtained it, but the rest were hardened, [8] as it is written, "God gave them a spirit of stupor, eyes that would not see and ears that would not hear, down to this very day."

The passage Paul (and John here) quotes from: Isaiah 29:10.

[44] **John quotes from**: Romans 11:5.

[45] **The everlasting covenant to Abraham is actually applied to the remnant of believers, which are the Christians**:

> Genesis 17:7 And I will establish my covenant between me and you and your offspring after you throughout their generations for an everlasting covenant, to be God to you and to your offspring after you.

Yes, God keeps his promises, and if he says it is an everlasting covenant, it is. But how he keeps his promises is sadly too often misunderstood, and to whom that everlasting covenant is made is misattributed by bad exegesis.

The Children of Abraham, Abraham's offspring, are not physical descendants from his loins, but rather those who have faith in Jesus Christ.

> Galatians 3:6–9 [6] just as Abraham "believed God, and it was counted to him as righteousness"? [7] Know then that it is those of faith who are the sons of Abraham. [8] And the Scripture, foreseeing that God would justify the Gentiles by faith, preached the gospel beforehand to Abraham, saying, "In you shall all the nations be blessed." [9] So then, those who are of faith are blessed along with Abraham, the man of faith.

So New Covenant believers in Jesus are precisely those children of Abraham to whom God is still eternally fulfilling those promises. The New Covenant is the continuation of God's eternal promise of inheritance to Abraham's Seed:

> Hebrews 9:15 Therefore [Jesus] is the mediator of a new covenant, so that those who are called may receive the promised eternal inheritance.

350

Yes, the promise is eternal, it's just not inherited by physically circumcised Jews, but by believers in Christ. According to the Scriptures, New Testament believers are the ones receiving God's everlasting covenant made to Abraham of an everlasting inheritance. And what is that inheritance, but the land of Promise, the land of Canaan? Again, this inheritance is misunderstood by many. So let's unravel that next.

[46] **John quotes from**: Revelation 7:9 about the multitude of Gentiles.

[47] **Cassandra quotes from**: Romans 2:26-29

[48] **Children of Abraham are those who believe in Jesus**:

> Genesis 17:7 And I will establish my covenant between me and you and your offspring after you throughout their generations for an everlasting covenant, to be God to you and to your offspring after you.

The second part of God's promise to Abraham "and your offspring after you throughout their generations..." is really another aspect of the first element of Abraham being the father of many nations. But I have separated it out because it is the basis of the concept "seed of Abraham" or "children of Abraham" that is frequently referred to in the Older and Newer Covenants. What I want to prove here is that the Abrahamic "offspring" God is referring to was never the mere physical offspring of flesh, but has always been the spiritual offspring of faith.

In Galatians, Paul writes about the Judaizers, or the "party of the circumcision" (Gal 2:12). These men were saying to Gentile believers that they must become Jews in addition to their faith by bearing the physical marker of circumcision or they would not be considered the true sons of Abraham (Gal 2:4; 5:1-6). The Judaizers were affirming the special status of the physically circumcised Jews as sons of Abraham, sons of the Promise, the receivers of "the blessing." But Paul violently disagreed by explaining that *it is faith that makes one a son of Abraham to receive the promised blessing, not genetic or outward physical Jewishness.*

> Galatians 3:6–9 [6] just as Abraham "believed God, and it was counted to him as righteousness"? [7] Know then that it is those of faith who are the sons of Abraham. [8] And the Scripture, foreseeing that God would justify the Gentiles by faith, preached the gospel beforehand to Abraham, saying, "In you shall all the nations be blessed." [9] So then, those who are of faith are blessed along with Abraham, the man of faith.

So here again, that same Abrahamic promise from Genesis is quoted as being made to those of faith, *not physicality*. He explicitly says that "those who are of faith are sons of Abraham," "those who are of faith are blessed with Abraham." He says that it was the New Testament Gospel that was preached to Abraham when he made the Promise of all nations and descendants. There could be no clearer proof that God has always meant faith as the means of sonship, not physical descent or Jewish identity markers.

But just in case, the Dispensationalist can't see the obvious, Paul goes further to explain that the promise made to the offspring ("seed") of Abraham was to the singular person of Christ, not the plural people of the land.

> Galatians 3:16 [16] Now the promises were made to Abraham and to his offspring. It does not say, "And to offsprings," referring to many, but referring to one, "And to your offspring," who is Christ.

The word that we have translated as "offspring" is better translated as "seed," but the point remains the same. So Paul writes that all those promises—all six points of the covenant —that were made to Abraham, were really made to Christ (singular), NOT the physical descendants (plural).

He then equates "sons of Abraham" with "sons of God." We partake of that Abrahamic Promise by being "in Christ" through our faith.

> Galatians 3:26–29 [26] for in Christ Jesus you are all sons of God, through faith. [27] ...for you are all one in Christ Jesus. [29] And if you are Christ's, then you are Abraham's offspring, heirs according to promise.

Notice the last line. Abraham's offspring, those who are heirs of the promise to Abraham, are not the physical descendants, but the faithful in Christ. We believers inherit the Promise made to Abraham! The Promise of inheritance was never intended by God to refer to a genetic or nation state Israel, but to the faithful in Christ. Now, of course, the faithful Jewish believers in the Old and New Testaments are

351

included in that Promise (The OT believer looked forward to Messiah, the NT believer looks backward to Messiah), but both Jew and Gentile are included in the Promise through faith! The point is that there is no special status for a physical Israel in God's plan. Never was. It was always the faithful to whom God was making the Promise.

Later in the same book of Galatians, Paul takes this dichotomy of faithful versus physical farther and makes the separation even more stark. This passage is particularly indicting against the Dispensationalist because Paul talks specifically about the difference between physical Israel and faithful Israel, and stresses that physical Israel is never what God's promise was all about. Paul allegorically likens physical Israel ("according to the flesh") with the physical Jerusalem that was in slavery in the first century and the physical descendants of Hagar as the symbol of those fleshly offspring. Then he likens the faithful believers to the heavenly Jerusalem that he calls free, and it is these free faithful that are the inheritors of the promise, *not* the physical nation.

> Galatians 4:22–26 [22] For it is written that Abraham had two sons, one by a slave woman and one by a free woman. [23] But the son of the slave was born according to the flesh, while the son of the free woman was born through promise. [24] Now this may be interpreted allegorically: these women are two covenants. One is from Mount Sinai, bearing children for slavery; she is Hagar. [25] Now Hagar is Mount Sinai in Arabia; she corresponds to the present Jerusalem, for she is in slavery with her children. [26] But the Jerusalem above is free, and she is our mother.

The "children of promise" are here spoken of as definitively being those who are of faith, *not* those who are physical Jews. In fact, Paul writes that the physical Jews who were persecuting the Christians during his lifetime were those "fleshly" slaves of Hagar:

> Galatians 4:29 [29] But just as at that time he who was born according to the flesh persecuted him who was born according to the Spirit, so also it is now.

And then he concludes by saying that the physical Jews who do not have faith in Christ will not inherit the Promise along with the faithful:

> Galatians 4:30–31 [30] But what does the Scripture say? "Cast out the slave woman and her son, for the son of the slave woman shall not inherit with the son of the free woman." [31] So, brothers, we are not children of the slave but of the free woman.

There could be no stronger denial that the physical Jewish descendants will inherit the Promise of Abraham. According to Scripture, it isn't going to happen. The physical descendants "shall not be an heir" with the faithful sons of Abraham. Not in Paul's time, not in the future. There are not two plans, one for believing Gentiles and one for physical Jews. Only Jews who believe in Messiah will inherit the Promise *along with* the believing Gentiles. **Believers alone** are the "children of promise." God's promise to Abraham is not to Israel of the flesh, but to Israel of faith.

> Galatians 4:23 [23] But the son of the slave was born according to the flesh, while the son of the free woman was born through promise... [28] Now you, brothers, like Isaac, are children of promise.

[49] **Mystery of the gospel**: Ephesians 3:4–6 [4] When you read this, you can perceive my insight into the mystery of Christ, [5] which was not made known to the sons of men in other generations as it has now been revealed to his holy apostles and prophets by the Spirit. [6] This mystery is that the Gentiles are fellow heirs, members of the same body, and partakers of the promise in Christ Jesus through the gospel.

[50] **The gathering of remnant Israel back to the land prophesied in the Old Testament**: "Ezekiel 36:24 I will take you from the nations and gather you from all the countries and bring you into your own land.

> Amos 9:9–15 [9] "For behold, I will command, and shake the house of Israel among all the nations as one shakes with a sieve... [14] I will restore the fortunes of my people Israel, and they shall rebuild the ruined cities and inhabit them;... [15] I will plant them on their land, and they shall never again be uprooted.

> Micah 2:12 I will surely assemble all of you, O Jacob; I will gather the remnant of Israel; I will set them together like sheep in a fold.

> "Isaiah 11:10–12 In that day the Lord will extend his hand yet a second time to recover the remnant that remains of his people, from Assyria, from Egypt, from Pathros, from Cush, from Elam, from Shinar, from Hamath, and from the coastlands of the sea. [12] He will raise a signal

for the nations and will assemble the banished of Israel, and gather the dispersed of Judah from the four corners of the earth.

[51] **The gospel of the New Covenant is the first century fulfillment of the gathering of Israel promised in the Old Testament**: Ezekiel 37:7-14 describes a vision that Ezekiel was given about the regathering and restoration of Israel depicted as a massive resurrection. Then in his further explanation of everything that restoration entailed, he writes this from the mouth of God:

> Ezekiel 37:21–28 [21] then say to them, Thus says the Lord GOD: Behold, I will take the people of Israel from the nations among which they have gone, and will gather them from all around, and bring them to their own land. [22] And I will make them one nation in the land, on the mountains of Israel. And one king shall be king over them all, and they shall be no longer two nations, and no longer divided into two kingdoms… [24] "My servant David shall be king over them, and they shall all have one shepherd. They shall walk in my rules and be careful to obey my statutes. [25] They shall dwell in the land that I gave to my servant Jacob, where your fathers lived. They and their children and their children's children shall dwell there forever, and David my servant shall be their prince forever. [26] I will make a covenant of peace with them. It shall be an everlasting covenant with them. And I will set them in their land and multiply them, and will set my sanctuary in their midst forevermore. [27] My dwelling place shall be with them, and I will be their God, and they shall be my people. [28] Then the nations will know that I am the LORD who sanctifies Israel, when my sanctuary is in their midst forevermore."

"In an expansion of that prophecy earlier in the text, God adds another promise that he will place his spirit within them and give them a heart of flesh to replace their heart of stone.

> Ezekiel 36:24–28 [24] I will take you from the nations and gather you from all the countries and bring you into your own land. [25] I will sprinkle clean water on you, and you shall be clean from all your uncleannesses, and from all your idols I will cleanse you. [26] And I will give you a new heart, and a new spirit I will put within you. And I will remove the heart of stone from your flesh and give you a heart of flesh. [27] And I will put my Spirit within you, and cause you to walk in my statutes and be careful to obey my rules. [28] You shall dwell in the land that I gave to your fathers, and you shall be my people, and I will be your God.

"On every level, this entire prophecy is about the arrival of the New Covenant, not some distant future reinstitution of the Old Covenant shadows of physical temple and land. Each of the prophecy's constituent elements are fulfilled in the New Testament Scriptures *at the time of the first century*. Let's take a look at those elements:

1. The gathering of Israel from all the nations (v. 21): This was already explained above as starting to occur in AD 30 at Pentecost (Acts 2). The New Covenant beginning in the first century.

2. One nation with one king, David (v. 24-25): It was already detailed above that this messianic reference was Jesus seated on David's throne at his resurrection and ascension (Acts 2:30-33) and uniting his sheepfolds (Jn 10:16). That's the New Covenant beginning in the first century.

3. The everlasting covenant of peace with Israel (v. 26): The New Testament says that this everlasting covenant of peace is the New Covenant brought through Christ beginning in the first century.

> Hebrews 13:20 [20] Now may the God of peace who brought again from the dead our Lord Jesus, the great shepherd of the sheep, by the blood of the eternal covenant,

> Colossians 1:20 [20] and through him to reconcile to himself all things, whether on earth or in heaven, making peace by the blood of his cross.

4. God's dwelling place shall be with them (v. 27-28): In multiple places in the New Testament the Church of believers in Jesus are described as God's temple (1Cor 3:16-17; Eph 2:19-22), but Paul explicitly quotes the Ezekiel prophecy of the regathering and God's dwelling as fulfilled in the New Covenant Church beginning in the first century.

> 2 Corinthians 6:16 [16] What agreement has the temple of God with idols? For we are the temple of the living God; as God said, "I will make my dwelling among them and walk among them, and I will be their God, and they shall be my people.

5. Remove the heart of stone, replace with a heart of flesh (36:26): Paul wrote that this promise of heart replacement was fulfilled in the arrival of the New Covenant of Christ beginning in the first century.

353

2 Corinthians 3:3 [3] And you show that you are a letter from Christ delivered by us, written not with ink but with the Spirit of the living God, not on tablets of stone but on tablets of human hearts.

6. God will put his Spirit in them and causing them to obey (36:27)

7. He will be their God and they will be His people (36:27): Not only does the Old Testament link these phrases to the New Covenant (Jer 31:31-34), but the New Testament also claims this promise was fulfilled beginning in the first century with the arrival of the New Covenant.

Ephesians 1:13 [13] In him you also, when you heard the word of truth, the gospel of your salvation, and believed in him, were sealed with the promised Holy Spirit. (see also Jn 7:37-39, 1Cor 6:19)

Hebrews 8:6–13 [6] "Behold, the days are coming, declares the Lord, when I will establish a new covenant with the house of Israel and with the house of Judah… I will put my laws into their minds, and write them on their hearts, and I will be their God, and they shall be my people… [13] In speaking of a new covenant, he makes the first one obsolete. And what is becoming obsolete and growing old is ready to vanish away.

"Notice how the Holy Spirit-authorized writer of Hebrews says right up front that the promise to the house of Israel and Judah is fulfilled in the arrival of the New Covenant in the first century, *not* in a future time yet to come. God places his Spirit in all believers in Jesus, they are his people of the New Covenant.

"Dispensationalists claim that the gathering of the Gentiles occurred with the coming of Jesus but not the promised gathering of Judah and Israel, which has yet to take place. But the New Testament over and over again claims that the New Covenant fulfills that promise to Judah and Israel of their gathering. If the New Testament claims a prophecy has been fulfilled, then it is literally anti-biblical to deny that fulfillment.

"Ezekiel 36-37 is pregnant with motifs and promises of the New Covenant arrival of Messiah, not a second coming and reinstitution of Old Covenant shadows. It is important to remember that the Old Testament contains no theology of the second coming of Messiah. It's all about the first coming for them. The second coming is a New Testament doctrine, not an Old Testament one. The whole point to the prophets was that when Messiah came, he would fulfill the promises and usher in the messianic age to come. The New Covenant is that messianic age, complete with Jesus seated on the throne of David (Eph 1:20-23). So when Christians read these prophecies as if they are intended to be split into pieces of fulfillment, the last of which will occur at a second coming of Christ, they are quite simply imposing their preconceived theology onto the text that has already been fulfilled instead of reading it within its original Old Covenant context." This was excerpted from Brian Godawa, *Israel in Bible Prophecy: The New Testament Fulfillment of the Promise to Abraham* (Embedded Pictures Publishing, 2017), 60-64.

[52] **The population of Jews and Christians in Israel and Jerusalem in the 60s**:

Acts 2:5 Now there were dwelling in Jerusalem Jews, devout men from every nation under heaven.

Acts 2:41 So those who received his word were baptized, and there were added that day about three thousand souls.

Acts 4:4 But many of those who had heard the word believed, and the number of the men came to about five thousand.

I presume that many of the Jews were in Jerusalem for Pentecost, not permanently, so those numbers may be curtailed when the Christian converts return to their permanent homes. PLUS, the "great persecution" of Christians throughout Israel in the 40s, as presented in Acts 8:1, coupled with the Jewish civil war and the Neronic persecution throughout the empire in the 60s, no doubt cut the Christian population down to low numbers in danger of extinction. This is where I come up with a number of about several thousand for Israel, and less than a thousand in Jerusalem by the late 60s.

Acts 8:1 And there arose on that day a great persecution against the church in Jerusalem, and they were all scattered throughout the regions of Judea and Samaria, except the apostles.

"Josephus gives the total number of those who died in the siege as 1,100,000 people and adds: 'Of these the greater number were of Jewish blood, but not natives of the place [Jerusalem]' (BJ 6.420). If one adds the 97,000 prisoners taken in the course of the war, one arrives at a total of 1,200,000 participants in the passover, who had been 'suddenly enveloped in the war' (BJ 6.421). He had, of course, to face the question how such a large number of people could find space in Jerusalem, and so continues: 'That the

354

city could contain so many is clear from the count taken under Cestius. For he, being anxious to convince Nero, who held the nation in contempt, of the city's strength, instructed the chief priests, if by any means possible, to take a census of the population' (BJ 6.422). This census was probably taken by indirect counting at the sacrifice, as mentioned also in rabbinic writings, since direct counting was not allowed. Josephus then mentions a passover shortly before the siege of Jerusalem at which 255,600 sacrificial animals were counted, going on to make the calculation himself, 'allowing an average of ten diners to each victim', and obtaining a figure of 2,700,000 participants (BJ 6.425). Finally, Tacitus claims that in 70 AD, 600,000 people were besieged in Jerusalem (Hist. 5.13 [3]). These figures are considered hugely exaggerated by most commentators...

"The importance of this problem for the present discussion results from the fact that the growth of the earliest church is mentioned in connection with the feast of Pentecost. Hence a large number of pilgrims may have been among those who 'were added' after Peter's sermon (2:41) and may also have been among those who stayed several days in Jerusalem and heard of the miracle in the Temple and the further preaching of the apostles (3:1–4:4). It might be objected that the number of those who converted at Pentecost refers exclusively to inhabitants of Jerusalem, because the κατοικοῦντες of Acts 2:5 can only describe permanent inhabitants of the city. One can reply to this, however, with Marshall's argument that, although the verb usually has the sense of 'permanent residents', the hearers of the Pentecost sermon were 'not necessarily all permanent residents in Jerusalem ... for the same verb is used in 2:9 of one section of this people and describes them as residing in Mesopotamia.' He refutes the objection that the newly-formed Christian church in Jerusalem would have shrunk very quickly to a smaller size, if it had consisted largely of pilgrims: 'But Luke says nothing about the proportions of visitors and residents.' This does not rule out the possibility, however, that at least the circle of those who were 'added' in the beginning may have consisted to a significant extent of pilgrims. Therefore the question of the number of festival pilgrims, particularly to the Feast of Weeks, is important here...

(1) There is no reasonable ground for believing that Jerusalem in the time of Jesus' activity and of the earliest church had only 20–35,000 inhabitants, as is still claimed in even the most recent treatments on the basis of Jeremias' calculations.

(2) The primary error in these figures is the too low estimate of the population density in the Jerusalem of that time. As has been shown, much evidence suggests that Jerusalem was extremely densely populated at that time; the density may have averaged over 50 persons per 1,000 m2.

(3) An exact calculation of the population appears impossible at present. A figure of 60,000 is a conceivable lower limit, though it is more probable that the figure was up to 100–120,000 inhabitants in the forties.

(4) In the Lukan figures of 'about 3,000' who believed and were baptised (Acts 2:41) or the 5,000 to which the 'number of the men' rose (Acts 4:4), one cannot, for the reasons given, rule out the idea that pilgrims, staying in Jerusalem for a few days for the Feast of Weeks, were included. If one still assumes several thousand locals joining the Jesus movement, this does not appear improbable.

(5) Apart from the 'theological' factors, especially the powerful working of the Spirit and of the word empowered by him, and the attracting power of the church as the eschatological people of God, 'non-theological' factors—just as very clearly later in the growth of the church in the Roman Empire

(6) Since there is also no convincing theological interpretation of the figures 'about 3,000' and '(about) 5,000,' one will instead have to accept that Luke was dependent on a reliable transmission of these figures."

Wolfgang Reinhardt, "The Population Size of Jerusalem and the Numerical Growth of the Jerusalem Church," in *The Book of Acts in Its First Century Setting: The Book of Acts in Its Palestinian Setting*, ed. Richard Bauckham and Bruce W. Winter, vol. 4 (Grand Rapids, MI; Carlisle, Cumbria: William B. Eerdmans Publishing Company; The Paternoster Press, 1995), 259–261, 263-265.

[53] **144,000 is clearly symbolic**: "The twelve tribes of course give the occasion for selecting the number twelve; and this is often repeated in other places; comp. Rev. 21:12, twelve gates, twelve angels, twelve names of tribes; 21:16, twelve thousand furlongs; 21:17, the wall is twelve times twelve cubits high, i.e. 144 cubits; 21:21, the twelve gates are twelve pearls; comp. in Ezek. 48:30–34. Compare with these the twelve fountains in Elim, Ex. 15:27; the twelve pillars around the altar, Ex. 24:4; twelves cakes of shew bread, Lev. 24:5; twelve gems in the breast-plate of the high-priest, Ex. 28:10; twelve stones set up on the banks of the Jordan, Joshua 4:3; offerings by twelves, Num. 7:3, 87. 29:17. Ezra 8:35; vessels for the

temple, Num. 7:84–86; twelve prefects over Israel, 1 Kings 4:7; twelve lions near the royal throne, 1 Kings 10:20; twelve oxen supporting the brazen laver, 1 Kings 7:25; the altar twelve cubits long and twelve broad, Ezek. 43:16, etc. See Exe. II. at the end. A thousand is the frequent and familiar number for designating many, and oftentimes it stands for an indefinite number; Ps. 90:4. 2 Pet. 3:8. Rev. 20:2, 3. Dan. 7:10. Rev. 5:11, comp. Heb. 12:22." Moses Stuart, *A Commentary on the Apocalypse, vol. 2* (Andover; New York: Allen, Morrill and Wardwell; M. H. Newman, 1845), 171–172.

144,000 as a symbolic number of the Jewish Christians in Israel/Jerusalem: "144,000 is the result of the square of twelve multiplied by one thousand, or the multiple of the squares of ten and twelve multiplied by ten. The use of twelve (and perhaps ten) heightens the figurative idea of completeness. The square of twelve may be merely the number of the tribes of Israel multiplied by itself or, more likely, the twelve tribes multiplied by the twelve apostles. Ch. 21 confirms this suggestion, where the names of the twelve tribes and of the twelve apostles form part of the figurative structure of the heavenly city of God, "the new Jerusalem." This city represents the whole people of God (21:9–10) in whose midst God and the Lamb dwell (21:12–22:5). The new Jerusalem has twelve gates, which are twelve pearls, on which are written the names of the twelve tribes. The city also has a wall one hundred and forty-four cubits in height with twelve foundation stones on which are written the names of the twelve apostles (cf. also the similar figurative use of "twelve" twice in 22:2)." G. K. Beale, The Book of Revelation: *A Commentary on the Greek Text, New International Greek Testament Commentary* (Grand Rapids, MI; Carlisle, Cumbria: W.B. Eerdmans; Paternoster Press, 1999), 416–417.

Boring (13) is surely correct when he observes that the number "is intended as symbolic theology, not literal mathematics." Besides its perfectly rounded precision and its setting in this symbolic book, we may readily discern symbolic features in its basic numerical components, ten and twelve. The number ten in Scripture represents quantitative perfection: Philo (Spec. 2:11 §41) speaks of "the perfect number ten." Regarding the number ten in antiquity, its significance "no doubt derives from simple calculations on the fingers" (ISBE2 3:560). It is the number of fingers that humans have, making a full complement of digits which are so important to manual dexterity. Our hands allow for expressing human creativity in crafting things (we speak highly of things that are "handmade").10 Therefore it speaks of quantitative completion — as we see in there being ten commandments (Ex 34:28), ten plagues (Ex 7:8–11:10), a tithe (Ge 14:20; Nu 18:21), ten righteous men would have saved Sodom (Ge 18:32), Jesus' parable of the ten virgins (Mt 25:1), and so forth (cp 12:3; 13:1; 17:3, 7, 12, 16). Scripture often uses the value of 1000 symbolically. It informs us that God shows his mercy to a 1000 generations (Ex 20:6) — which suggests the perfect fullness of his grace (10 x 10 x 10). The Lord promises to make Israel a 1000 times more numerous than they are in Moses' day (Dt 1:11) — bringing them to numerical fullness as a people. The Lord even claims the cattle on 1000 hills (Ps 50:10) — showing that he owns all the cattle of the earth. The figure of 1000 more often than not expresses complete fullness, not an exact numerical accounting of 999 + 1. Thus, multiples of 1000 are almost certainly symbolic in Rev, as must be the case with the new Jerusalem's cubed (!) shape measuring 12,000 stadia [stadiōn dōdeka chiliadōn = 1500 miles] on each side (21:16). Since the International Space Station orbits at around 250 miles above the earth, this would put the city's height 1250 miles higher than the International Space Station (creating a potential for a deadly collision at the city's 132,000th floor)." Kenneth L. Gentry, Jr., *The Divorce of Israel: A Redemptive-Historical Interpretation of Revelation Vol. 1* (Dallas, GA: Tolle Lege Press, 2016), 656-657.

The gathering of Christians, before or after the parousia (judgment-coming of Christ on Jerusalem), is the promised restoration of the twelve tribes of Israel, that is, the remnant of true Israel: "The author's insistence on an equal number (12,000) from each of twelve tribes indicates his interest in the eschatological restoration of the the twelve-tribe nation of Israel (Luke 22:30; 24:21; Acts 1:6; see Geyser, NTS 28 [1982] 389). The eschatology of the late OT and early Jewish periods emphasized the hope of the restoration of Israel (Deut 30:3–5; Isa 11:11–16; 27:12–13; 49:5–6; 54:7–10; Jer 31:7–14; Ezek 37:15–23; Hos 11:10–11; Pss 106:47; 147:2; Bar 5:5–9; 2 Macc 2:7; Sir 36:11; Tob 13:13; 1 Enoch 57; 90:33; 4 Ezra 13:12–13, 39–47; 2 Apoc. Bar. 78:5–7; T. Jos. 19:4; Pss. Sol. 11:2–7; 17:26; Shemoneh Esreh 10; m. Sanh. 10:3; Matt 19:28). In m. Sanh. 10:3 the opinions that the ten tribes will not return and that they will return are juxtaposed. This motif of the restoration of Israel was transmuted in early Christianity into the gathering of the elect from the four winds at the Parousia (Mark 13:27 = Matt 24:31; 1 Thess 4:16–17; 2 Thess 2:1)." David E. Aune, *Revelation 6–16, vol. 52B, Word Biblical Commentary* (Dallas: Word, Incorporated, 1998), 436.

[54] **John quotes from**: Revelation 7:14-17.

[55] **Alexander quotes from Jesus' words**: Luke 21:20-24.

[56] **The army of the eagle as Rome**: When Jesus describes these events of the Tribulation to take place, he says, "Where the corpse is, there the eagles [or "vultures"] will gather." (Matthew 24:28; Luke 17:37).

"As birds of prey flying up in the sky are waiting for some carcass to light upon, so the coming of the Son of man will be to that area where the "carcass" will be found. The Jewish nation, and more specifically the city of Jerusalem, was the carcass which the Romans (eagles) descended upon to devour...

"Commenting on this verse, Albert Barnes said:

> This verse is connected with the preceding by the word 'for,' implying that this is a reason for what is said there—that the Son of man would certainly come to destroy the city, and that he would come suddenly. The meaning is that he would come, by means of the Roman armies, as certainly, as suddenly, and as unexpectedly as whole flocks of vultures and eagles, though unseen before, see their prey at a great distance and suddenly gather in multitudes around it.... So keen is their vision as aptly to represent the Roman armies, though at an immense distance, spying, as it were, Jerusalem, a putrid carcass, and hastening in multitudes to destroy it (Albert Barnes *Commentary on Matthew* 24:28)...

"John Lightfoot (1859) said of this verse:

> [F]or wheresoever the carcass is, &c. I wonder any can understand these words of pious men flying to Christ, when the discourse here is of quite a different thing: they are thus connected to the foregoing: Christ shall be revealed with a sudden vengeance; for when God shall cast off the city and people, grown ripe for destruction, like a carcass thrown out, the Roman soldiers, like eagles, shall straight fly to it with their eagles (ensigns) to tear and devour it. And to this also agrees the answer of Christ, Luke xvii. 37; when, after the same words that are spoken here in this chapter, it was inquired, "Where, Lord." he answered, "Wheresoever the body is," &c.; silently hinting thus much, that Jerusalem, and that wicked nation which he described through the whole chapter, would be the carcass, to which the greedy and devouring eagles would fly to prey upon it (John Lightfoot, vol. 2, 319)."

John L. Bray, *Matthew 24 Fulfilled* (Georgia, Anmerican Vision Press, 1996, 2008), 128-130.

"The Jerusalem of Jesus' day, because of its dead rituals, was a carcass, food for the scavenging birds, the Roman armies. This is an appropriate description of Jerusalem's acts of abomination. In addition, we know that tens of thousands (Josephus says over a million) were killed during the Roman siege. Even the temple area was not spared. The Idumean and Zealot revolt left thousands slaughtered in and around the temple. A single carcass would render the city and temple area "unclean." According to Numbers 19:11–22, anyone touching the corpse of a human being is unclean: "Anyone who touches a corpse, the body of a man who has died, and does not purify himself, defiles the tabernacle of the LORD; and that person shall be cut off from Israel" (19:13). There was no life in Jerusalem since the Lord had departed. As our High Priest, Jesus could no longer remain in the city because of its defilement. It had to be burned with fire for purification." Gary DeMar, *Last Days Madness: Obsession of the Modern Church*, Fourth revised edition (Powder Springs, GA: American Vision, 1999), 127.

[57] **John quotes from**: Luke 21:20-22.

[58] **Severus reads from**: Revelation 1:7.

[59] **God providentially uses pagan armies to accomplish his will**: Isa 10:5-7, 25-27; 44:27–45:7; Hab 1:6-11; Jer 51:11, 28. Note especially that though God calls Nebuchadnezzar "My Servant" (Jer 25:9), he nevertheless destroys his kingdom (Jer 25:12).

God's providential control of the pagan destruction of Jerusalem and the temple: "Revelation emphasizes the divine governance over and again: Its very theme shows Christ's vengeance against Israel (1:7; 6:16; 19:2). The first vision in the opening of the judgment material shows God on his throne above the history that he controls (4:1ff) and through which he avenges himself (6:10-11, 16-17; 11:8; 14:19; 15:1,7; 16:1, 7, 19; 19:2, 15). His throne is repeatedly emphasized throughout the drama (1:4; 3:21; 4:2-10; 15:1, 6, 11, 13; 6:16; 7:9, 10-11, 15, 17; 14:3; 16:17; 20:11; 21:5; 22:1, 3). We see this also in the abundant use of divine passives (e.g., 6:2, 4, 8; 9:1, 3; 13:7) and judgments falling from heaven upon men (8:2, 5, 7; 9:1; 12:9, 12; 16:1-2, 8). This reminds us of an earlier reference to Israel and Rome in Acts 4:27-28: "For truly in this city there were gathered together against Your holy servant Jesus, whom You anointed, both Herod and Pontius Pilate, along with the Gentiles and the peoples of Israel, to do whatever

Your hand and Your purpose predestined to occur." Kenneth L. Gentry, Jr., *The Divorce of Israel: A Redemptive-Historical Interpretation of Revelation Vol. 2* (Dallas, GA: Tolle Lege Press, 2016), 486.

[60] **Coming on the clouds**: The following examples in the Old Testament illustrate that "coming on the clouds" was a reference to divine judgment upon nations and cities by Yahweh. So the phrase was not literal but metaphorical of "coming in judgment," usually through the human agency of other nations. Isaiah 19:1; Nahum 1:1-3; Psalm 18:7-10; 2Samuel 22:7-10; Joel 2:1-1; Ezekiel 30:3-4; Isaiah 30:30-31 and 31:4-5; Zephaniah 1:7, 14-15. Jesus said his cloud coming would happen before some around him would die, that very generation of people around him would see it. Matthew 16:28; 26:64; Matthew 23:36 and 24: 34.

Passages referred to her by John here:

God's judgment on Egypt:

Isaiah 19:1 Behold, the LORD is riding on a swift cloud, and is about to come to Egypt.

Ezekiel 30:3 For the day is near, the day of the LORD is near; it will be a day of clouds, a time of doom for the nations.

God's judgment on Israel:

Joel 2:2 Surely it is near, A day of darkness and gloom, A day of clouds and thick darkness.

Zephaniah 1:14–15 14 The great day of the LORD is near…a day of ruin and devastation… a day of clouds and thick darkness.

For an excellent discussion of the cloud coming of the Son of Man, see Gary DeMar, Last Days Madness: Obsession of the Modern Church (Powder Springs, American Vision, 1999), 157-169. Also, see Brian Godawa, *When Giants Were Upon the Earth* (Los Angeles, Embedded Pictures, 2014), 238-242.

Parousia "coming": "The word 'parousia' is itself misleading, anyway, since it merely means 'presence'; Paul can use it of his being present with a church, and nobody supposes that he imagined he would make his appearance flying downwards on a cloud. The motif of delay ('how long, O Lord, how long?'69) was already well established in Judaism, and is hardly a Christian innovation, as is often imagined. The usual scholarly construct, in which the early church waited for Jesus' return, lived only for that future and without thought for anything past (such as memories of Jesus himself), only to be grievously disappointed and to take up history-writing as a displacement activity, a failure of nerve—this picture is without historical basis. The church expected certain events to happen within a generation, and happen they did." N. T. Wright, *The New Testament and the People of God, Christian Origins and the Question of God* (London: Society for Promoting Christian Knowledge, 1992), 462–463.

God's providential hand wields the axe of pagan forces against Israel: Isaiah 10.

[61] **The dialogue and content here is derived from Romans 9:14-23**. [14] What shall we say then? Is there injustice on God's part? By no means! [15] For he says to Moses, "I will have mercy on whom I have mercy, and I will have compassion on whom I have compassion." [16] So then it depends not on human will or exertion, but on God, who has mercy. [17] For the Scripture says to Pharaoh, "For this very purpose I have raised you up, that I might show my power in you, and that my name might be proclaimed in all the earth." [18] So then he has mercy on whomever he wills, and he hardens whomever he wills. [19] You will say to me then, "Why does he still find fault? For who can resist his will?" [20] But who are you, O man, to answer back to God? Will what is molded say to its molder, "Why have you made me like this?" [21] Has the potter no right over the clay, to make out of the same lump one vessel for honorable use and another for dishonorable use? [22] What if God, desiring to show his wrath and to make known his power, has endured with much patience vessels of wrath prepared for destruction, [23] in order to make known the riches of his glory for vessels of mercy, which he has prepared beforehand for glory."

CHAPTER 8

[1] **The renunciation of Satan in baptism**: "The renunciation of Satan is the one demonological rite of initiation that the *Apostolic Tradition* of Hippolytus had in common with the practice of the contemporary Church in North Africa, as reflected in the writings of Tertullian. The renunciation, in fact, is the only universal antidemonic Christian initiation ritual; it occurred in liturgies like that of Hippolytus, where there was no postbaptismal prophylaxis, and in the Syrian rites where no prebaptismal exorcism was practiced…

"The idea of renunciation is, of course, present in all religious conversions and initiations. When a person turns from one form of life to embrace another, the old ways must necessarily be rejected, especially those practices most inimical to the new beliefs and style of life. We have seen an example of renunciation in the ritual of the Qumran sectaries, and similar practices can be found, inferred, or postulated in the ethically centered pagan mysteries and sects. In fact, these pagan religions formed the context of the renunciatory rite of Hippolytus and Tertullian, and without question it was influenced by them, certainly as far as the content of the renouncement was concerned and perhaps in the form of the ritual as well.

"Some scholars, as I have already mentioned in a previous chapter, like to think that the basic ritual of the renunciation of Satan developed quite early, in the context of Jewish Christianity. Since the devil and other evil spirits were considered to be prominent opponents of the kingdom of God, it is not unnatural that the New Testament should yield analogies to the formal renunciation of Satan and all his works." Ansgar Kelly, *The Devil at Baptism: Ritual, Theology, and Drama* (Ithaca, NY: Cornell University Press, 1985), 94-95.

[2] **Baptism as a plea for a good conscience in 1 Peter 3:21**: "Our focus for answering that question is two terms in verse 21, that baptism is "an **appeal** to God for a good **conscience** through the resurrection of Jesus Christ." The two boldfaced words need reconsideration in light of the divine council worldview. The word most often translated "appeal" (eperōtēma) in verse 21 is best understood as "pledge" here, a meaning that it has elsewhere. Likewise the word "conscience" (suneidēsis) does not refer to the inner voice of right and wrong in this text. Rather, the word refers to the disposition of one's loyalties, a usage that is also found in other contexts and Greek literature." Michael S. Heiser, *The Unseen Realm: Recovering the Supernatural Worldview of the Bible*, First Edition (Bellingham, WA: Lexham Press, 2015), 338.

[3] **The rite and theology of baptism portrayed here is based on the following sources**: The New Testament gives no formulaic details of the actual liturgy of baptism beyond water immersion and a generic reference to being baptized in the name of the Father, Son and Holy Spirit. Because of this, the principle of *Sola Scriptura*, or Scripture as final authority on doctrine, would dictate that there is no Biblically prescribed liturgy, thus warranting diversity in the act of Christian baptism.

Romans 6 connects baptism to the death and resurrection of Christ. We are baptized into his death and rise to new life. However, my depiction in this novel illustrates another theological connection that ties the meaning of baptism to the cleansing water of Noah's Flood and the destruction of the rebellious Watcher angels comes from the apostle Peter. This adds a spiritual warfare motif that many Christians have missed. Peter explains this spiritual warfare in terms of the rebellious angels, Sons of God, of Genesis 6:1-4, who were imprisoned at the Flood.

1 Peter 3:18–22 [18] For Christ also suffered once for sins, the righteous for the unrighteous, that he might bring us to God, being put to death in the flesh but made alive in the spirit, [19] in which he went and proclaimed to the spirits in prison, [20] because they formerly did not obey, when God's patience waited in the days of Noah, while the ark was being prepared, in which a few, that is, eight persons, were brought safely through water. [21] Baptism, which corresponds to this, now saves you, not as a removal of dirt from the body but as an appeal to God for a good conscience, through the resurrection of Jesus Christ, [22] who has gone into heaven and is at the right hand of God, with angels, authorities, and powers having been subjected to him.

2 Peter 2:4–5 [4] For if God did not spare angels when they sinned, but cast them into hell and committed them to chains of gloomy darkness to be kept until the judgment; [5] if he did not spare the ancient world, but preserved Noah, a herald of righteousness, with seven others, when he brought a flood upon the world of the ungodly…

Baptism as spiritual warfare related to the imprisoned spirits from the Flood: "Peter saw a theological analogy between the events of Genesis 6 and the gospel and resurrection. In other words, he considered the events of Genesis 6 to be types or precursors to New Testament events and ideas.

Just as Jesus was the second Adam for Paul, Jesus is the second Enoch for Peter. Enoch descended to the imprisoned fallen angels to announce their doom. First Peter 3:14–22 has Jesus descending to these same "spirits in prison" to tell them they were still defeated, despite his crucifixion. God's plan of salvation and kingdom rule had not been derailed—in fact, it was right on schedule. The crucifixion actually meant victory over every demonic force opposed to God. This victory declaration is why 1 Peter 3:14–22 ends with Jesus risen from the dead and set at the right hand of God—above all angels, authorities, and powers. The messaging is very deliberate, and has a supernatural view of Genesis 6:1–4 at its core." Michael S.

Heiser, *The Unseen Realm: Recovering the Supernatural Worldview of the Bible*, First Edition (Bellingham, WA: Lexham Press, 2015), 338.

For a book length treatment on the nature of baptism and spiritual warfare see, Ansgar Kelly, *The Devil at Baptism: Ritual, Theology, and Drama* (Ithaca, NY: Cornell University Press, 1985).

The liturgy of baptism practiced in the early church: The earliest evidence of the actual liturgy of baptism that we have outside the scant information in the book of Acts is in Hippolytus and Tertullian, both third century authors writing of procedures around AD 200.

The details that I used in this story come predominately from Hippolytus' *The Apostolic Tradition*, Chapter 21, written around AD 215. This is not because it is a superior source, but simply because it was the earliest I could find that has actual details of the ritual and liturgy. In truth, of course, the practice no doubt varied amongst wide spread locations. Tertullian in his *On Baptism*, talks more of the meaning, but overlaps with some of Hippolytus' description. A readable version of Hippolytus' *The Apostolic Tradition*, Chapter 21 can be found online at: http://www.bombaxo.com/hippolytus.html.

Tertullian on the liturgy of baptism: "I shall turn to that highest authority of our "seal" itself. When entering the water, we make profession of the Christian faith in the words of its rule; we bear public testimony that we have renounced the devil, his pomp, and his angels." Tertullian, "The Shows, or De Spectaculis, 4" in *Latin Christianity: Its Founder, Tertullian*, ed. Alexander Roberts, James Donaldson, and A. Cleveland Coxe, trans. S. Thelwall, vol. 3, *The Ante-Nicene Fathers* (Buffalo, NY: Christian Literature Company, 1885), 81.

"The flesh, indeed, is washed, in order that the soul may be cleansed; the flesh is anointed, that the soul may be consecrated; the flesh is signed (with the cross), that the soul too may be fortified; the flesh is shadowed with the imposition of hands, that the soul also may be illuminated by the Spirit; the flesh feeds on the body and blood of Christ, that the soul likewise may fatten on its God. They cannot then be separated in their recompense, when they are united in their service." Tertullian, "On the Resurrection of the Flesh," in *Latin Christianity: Its Founder, Tertullian,* ed. Alexander Roberts, James Donaldson, and A. Cleveland Coxe, trans. Peter Holmes, vol. 3, *The Ante-Nicene Fathers* (Buffalo, NY: Christian Literature Company, 1885), 551.

[4] **Tartarus beneath the earth**: Hesiod, *Theogony* lines 720-739 "as far beneath the earth as heaven is above earth; for so far is it from earth to Tartarus."

Jesus Journey to Tartarus and the Watchers: 1 Peter 3:18-22: [18] For Christ also suffered once for sins, the righteous for the unrighteous, that he might bring us to God, being put to death in the flesh but made alive in the spirit, [19] in which he went and proclaimed to the spirits in prison, [20] because they formerly did not obey, when God's patience waited in the days of Noah, while the ark was being prepared, in which a few, that is, eight persons, were brought safely through water. [21] Baptism, which corresponds to this, now saves you, not as a removal of dirt from the body but as an appeal to God for a good conscience, through the resurrection of Jesus Christ, [22] who has gone into heaven and is at the right hand of God, with angels, authorities, and powers having been subjected to him.

"**When Did Christ Go on His Journey?** "When Christ "went" to proclaim to the spirits in prison, it says he was "put to death in the flesh but made alive in the spirit, in which he went…" In the original Greek, "he went" does not contain a notion of direction as in ascent to heaven or descent to hell. It can only be determined by the context. So let's look at that context…

"One scholarly interpretation is that Christ's journey of proclamation occurred in a disembodied state between his death and resurrection. While his body was dead for three days, his spirit was alive and in Sheol. This understands the flesh/spirit distinction as a conjunction of opposites. "Put to death in the flesh but made alive in the spirit" is not talking about the fleshly death and fleshly resurrection, but a fleshly death and a spiritual life. The "spirit" in which he was made alive in this view is not the Holy Spirit, but rather his disembodied soul in the spiritual realm. That "spirit" then corresponds to the "spirits" to whom he proclaimed in the very next verse (v. 19).

"This view that Christ's soul or spirit went down into the underworld of Sheol between his death and resurrection is the most ancient and most traditional view, as attested in the Apostle's Creed. The Greek for "made alive" is never used of Christ's physical resurrection in the New Testament, but it is used of the spiritual reality of the believer "being made alive" in Christ (Eph. 2:5-6). Christ suffered the spiritual death of separation from the Father when he died on the cross (Isa. 53:4-6; 1 Pet. 2:24; Matt. 27:46). It is Christ's disembodied spirit that makes the journey to proclaim to the spirits, not his resurrected body.

"But whether Christ proclaims in his resurrected body or in his immaterial spirit, the next question arises, who are the spirits to which he proclaims and where are they?

"Who are the Spirits in Prison? The identity of the spirits has been debated extensively and falls into four possible categories: Human spirits, demons, Watchers, or a combination of the above.

John Elliott debunks the notion that "spirits" refers to human beings by looking at the Greek word for spirits (pneuma) in Biblical and Intertestamental texts. He concludes, "use of 'spirits' for human beings is very rare, and even then it is always qualified. In the Bible and related literature, when reference is made to deceased humans in Hades or the underworld, the term used is not pneuma but psyche."

But another commentator, Ramsey Michaels, shows that "spirits" (pneuma) is used of demons frequently in the New Testament for those supernatural beings that Jesus often confronted in his ministry. He points out that in 1 Enoch, pneuma is used of demons as the surviving part of the giants killed in the Flood.

> 1 Enoch 15:8-10 But now the giants who are born from the (union of) the spirits and the flesh shall be called evil spirits [pneuma] upon the earth, because their dwelling shall be upon the earth and inside the earth. 9 Evil spirits [pneuma] have come out of their bodies…They will become evil upon the earth and shall be called evil spirits [pneuma].

In this view, the "spirits in prison" are therefore the demonic souls of the Nephilim that are restricted to the prison "holding cell" under the earth until the coming of Messiah. (See below for the definition of "prison" as a holding cell).

"The only New Testament Scriptures that speak of imprisonment of spirits are Jude 6 and 2 Peter 2:4, the very passages that most scholarship has revealed are literarily dependent on the book of 1 Enoch.

> Jude 6 (NASB95) And angels who did not keep their own domain, but abandoned their proper abode, He has kept in eternal bonds under darkness for the judgment of the great day

> 2 Peter 2:4 God did not spare angels when they sinned, but cast them into hell [Tartarus] and committed them to chains of gloomy darkness to be kept until the judgment…

> 1 Enoch 12:4; 10:12 the Watchers of heaven who have abandoned the high heaven, the holy eternal place …bind [the Watchers] for seventy generations underneath the rocks of the ground until the day of their judgment.

"Jude not only quotes Enoch outright in Jude 4, but throughout his entire letter, he follows the progression of ideas in 1 Enoch and references memes and motifs of the angelic Watchers' sin and judgment in that ancient text. 2 Peter 2 is considered a paraphrase of Jude with the addition of the word for Tartarus as the description of the location of punishment.

"Tartarus was well known by the ancients as the lowest place of the underworld where the Titans were bound in pagan mythology. That underworld was referred to as Hades (Greek) or Sheol (Hebrew), and has obvious conceptual links to Jude and Peter's location of punishment. It would make most sense that Peter's second letter about angels bound in the prison of Tartarus would have continuity with the "spirits in prison" he is writing about in this first letter.

"The spirits are specifically indicated as being those who were disobedient during "the days of Noah while the ark was being prepared." That "days of Noah" is exactly the time period that 1 Enoch speaks of the fallen Watchers and their giant progeny receiving their comeuppance with a binding in Tartarus/Sheol at the Flood.

Chad Pierce makes a convincing argument that the disobedient spirits are not just the Watcher angels, demons, or human spirits alone, but the sum total of all who defied God at that time because cosmic powers are often united with human powers in the ancient world. In the Bible, the angelic power over Persia animated the human kingdom of Persia (Dan. 10:13), The Roman human kingdom in Revelation is granted its power from the satan (Rev. 12-13), and both are destroyed together in the Lake of Fire (Rev. 19:20; 20:7-10).

"Wink explains that the ancient mind of the Biblical writers was steeped in a macrocosm/microcosm of "what is above is also below." "Angelic and demonic activity in heaven was reflected in events on earth…These Powers are both heavenly and earthly, divine and human, spiritual and political, invisible and structural." Reicke adds that the "fallen Angels… the Powers, the demons in general, can in a certain way represent the whole world of fallen angels." And Pierce concludes, "the distinction between cosmic and earthly sinners is so blurred they cannot be distinguished. It appears that the author of 1 Pet 3:18-22 has left the recipients of Christ's message purposefully vague so as to include all forms of evil beings. The spirits in prison are thus all the forces of evil which have now been subjugated and defeated by Christ."

"1 Peter 3:22 concludes that the context of the proclamation Christ made was the subjugation of "angels, authorities, and powers." Heavenly "principalities, powers, and authorities" is a recurring concept in the New Testament (Col. 1:16, 2:13-15; Eph. 1:20-23). It is a concept that assumes earthly rulers and powers are animated and empowered by spiritual or cosmic rulers and power behind them.

"Thus, Paul could encourage those Christians who were suffering from the earthly rulers and powers who persecuted them; "For we do not wrestle against flesh and blood, but against the rulers, against the authorities, against the cosmic powers over this present darkness, against the spiritual forces of evil in the heavenly places" (Eph. 6:12-13). In other words, the real enemies of the persecuted Christians were the spiritual powers behind their earthly persecuting powers. This is not a denial of the human evil, but rather a drawing back of the curtain to see the ultimate enemy with more clarity.

"These spiritual and earthly "powers, rulers, authorities, and thrones," are the Seed of the Serpent that had been involved in the cosmic War of the Seed against Messiah. It is these rulers, both heavenly and earthly, who did not understand the mystery of the gospel of redemption through Messiah's suffering. They thought that killing the Chosen One, the Messiah, would bring them victory.

> 1 Corinthians 2:7–9 But we impart a secret and hidden wisdom of God, which God decreed before the ages for our glory. None of the rulers of this age understood this, for if they had, they would not have crucified the Lord of glory.

"So the focus on "powers and authorities" stresses the nature of Christ's cosmic mission against the heavenly powers. But the humans of Noah's day were certainly united in the rebellion of the Watchers and were also marked out by Enoch as being imprisoned along with the angels.

"**What was the Proclamation?** Some have believed it was Christ preaching the gospel to the Old Testament dead, as if they may have a second chance to repent because they died before Messiah, or even to Old Testament believers who did not yet have the historical sacrifice of Christ to apply to them yet. This brings us back to the human interpretation of the "spirits in prison."

"Since there is no place in the New Testament that supports the notion of a purgatorial type of second chance after death (Heb. 9:27), then the proclamation that Christ makes cannot be the "preaching of the Gospel" unto salvation, but something else. That something else is most likely a triumphant proclamation of his victory over the angelic authorities and powers.

"In the ancient world, kingly victors would perform a triumphal procession through the streets of a conquered city. They would parade their captive opponents, alive or dead, on carts to show off their power over their enemies. Thus the triumphal procession in Psalm 68 quoted in Ephesians 4:8 as "ascending on high and leading a host of captives." This would also be an encouragement for obedience from the vanquished inhabitants. Triumphal language like this in 1 Peter as well as other passages, reflect this military type victory of Christ over the ruling authorities achieved at the Cross.

> 2 Corinthians 2:14 But thanks be to God, who in Christ always leads us in triumphal procession, and through us spreads the fragrance of the knowledge of him everywhere.

"This triumph is referred to in the next verse of 1 Peter 3:22. "Christ, who has gone into heaven and is at the right hand of God, with angels, authorities, and powers having been subjected to him." The subjection of the spiritual powers occurs sometime before or during the ascension in this passage, most likely in the prison of Sheol. In Col. 2:15 we read that God "disarmed the rulers and authorities and put them to open shame, by triumphing over them" in Christ's death and resurrection. His death on the cross forgives us the legal debt of our sin, his resurrection unites us in our new spiritual life, and his ascension wraps it all up with a victory lap, towing the bound and defeated principalities and powers of the nations behind him.

"One of the premises of the entire *Chronicles of the Nephilim* series is the Deuteronomy 32 worldview that spoke of the allotment of earthly nations to the fallen Watchers, at the time of the Tower of Babel (Deut. 32:8-9; 29:26). God granted territorial authority to these divine beings (Deut. 4:19-20; Daniel 10). But God kept Jacob for himself and then took the land of Canaan as his inheritance. So the picture is one of a world divided up into parcels of land underneath the authority of the fallen Watchers as false gods, with Yahweh having Israel in Canaan as his own.

"And this allotment occurred at the division of tongues during the Tower of Babel episode (Duet. 32:8). But one day, the coming Messiah would ultimately take back that Watcher allotment and inherit the entire earth as his territory, along with the nations to be his people.

> Daniel 4:17 17 The sentence is by the decree of the watchers, the decision by the word of the holy ones, to the end that the living may know that the Most High rules the kingdom of men and gives it to whom he will.

> Psalm 2:7–8 7 The LORD said to me, "You are my Son, today I have begotten you, 8 Ask of me, and I will make the nations your heritage, and the ends of the earth your possession.

"The proclamation that Christ made to the spirits in prison was most likely his proclamation of victory and authority over the angelic powers that once ruled the Gentiles. The first of those powers were imprisoned in the Days of Noah, but their fellow fallen angels continued to rule in their absence over the nations. This inheritance of the earth and the drawing in of the nations would finally commence on the Day of Pentecost when the Holy Spirit would literally undo Babel and the division of tongues and begin to draw those nations to himself (Acts 2).

"But why would Christ have to proclaim authority or victory to those who were already imprisoned? Would that not be anti-climactic? Not if their fellow fallen angelic powers still ruled outside that prison on the earth, much like imprisoned Mafioso leaders are still linked to their fellow criminals on the outside. The angelic powers imprisoned at the Flood were the original rebels, the progenitors of the ongoing Seed of the Serpent that continued on in a lineage of evil on earth. They were in bonds, but the resultant War of the Seed that they spawned originated with their fall." Brian Godawa, *When Giants Were Upon the Earth: The Watchers, the Nephilim, and the Biblical Cosmic War of the Seed* (Embedded Pictures, 2014), 298-311.

[5] **The train of captives at Christ's ascension were Watchers not liberated souls:** "Psalm 68:18, where Yahweh leads a host of captives, may sound familiar. Paul cites the verse in Ephesians 4:

> Psalm 68:18 You have ascended on high; you have led away captives. You have received gifts from among humankind.

> Ephesians 4:8 Therefore it says,
> "When he ascended on high he led a host of captives, and he gave gifts to men" (ESV).

"If you look closely, there is a problem in the quotation. For Paul, Psalm 68:18 was about Jesus ascending on high and giving gifts to humanity. Jesus is somehow the fulfillment of Psalm 68. But the Old Testament text has God ascending and receiving gifts.

"Reconciling this conflict of ideas requires getting some context first.

"Psalm 68 gives us a standard description of conquest, known from other ancient texts and even from ancient sculpture and iconography. The victorious captain of the army leads the enemy captives behind him; they are the human booty of war.

"When Paul quotes Psalm 68:18 in Ephesians 4:8, he does so thinking of Jesus. Part of the confusion over how to interpret what Paul is saying is that so many commentators have assumed that captives are being liberated in Ephesians 4. That isn't the case. That idea would flatly contradict the well-understood Old Testament imagery. There is no liberation; there is conquest.

"Paul's words identify Jesus with Yahweh. In Psalm 68:18 it was Yahweh who is described as the conqueror of the demonic stronghold. For Paul it is Jesus, the incarnate second Yahweh, surrounded by the demonic elohim, "bulls of Bashan," fulfilling the imagery of Psalm 68. Jesus puts the evil gods "to an open shame" (ESV) by "triumphing over them by [the cross]" (LEB) (Col 2:15). Psalm 68:18 and Ephesians 4:8 are in agreement if one sees conquest, not liberation.

"What about the "receiving" and "giving" problem? Paul's wording doesn't deny there was conquest. What it does is point to the result of the conquest.

"In the ancient world the conqueror would parade the captives and demand tribute for himself. Jesus is the conqueror of Psalm 68, and the booty does indeed rightfully belong to him. But booty was also distributed after a conquest. Paul knows that. He quotes Psalm 68:18 to make the point that after Jesus conquered his demonic enemies, he distributed the benefits of the conquest to his people, believers. Specifically, those benefits are apostles, prophets, evangelists, pastors, and teachers (Eph 4:11)."

363

Michael S. Heiser, *The Unseen Realm: Recovering the Supernatural Worldview of the Bible, First Edition* (Bellingham, WA: Lexham Press, 2015), 292–294.

[6] **Territorial allotment of the nations to the Sons of God**: Deuteronomy 32:8–9 [8] When the Most High gave to the nations their inheritance, when he divided mankind, he fixed the borders of the peoples according to the number of the sons of God. [9] But the LORD's portion is his people, Jacob his allotted heritage.

Deuteronomy 32:17 [17] They sacrificed to demons that were no gods, to gods they had never known, to new gods that had come recently, whom your fathers had never dreaded.

Messiah's procurement of the nations: Psalm 2:7–9 [7] I will tell of the decree: The LORD said to me, "You are my Son; today I have begotten you. [8] Ask of me, and I will make the nations your heritage, and the ends of the earth your possession. [9] You shall break them with a rod of iron and dash them in pieces like a potter's vessel."

Christ's train of captives at the ascension: Ephesians 4:8–10 [8] Therefore it says, "When he ascended on high he led a host of captives, and he gave gifts to men." [9] (In saying, "He ascended," what does it mean but that he had also descended into the lower regions, the earth? [10] He who descended is the one who also ascended far above all the heavens, that he might fill all things.),

Citizenship in kingdom of darkness versus light: Colossians 1:12–14 [12] giving thanks to the Father, who has qualified you to share in the inheritance of the saints in light. [13] He has delivered us from the domain of darkness and transferred us to the kingdom of his beloved Son, [14] in whom we have redemption, the forgiveness of sins.

[7] **The Lord's Supper after baptism in ancient liturgy**: These elements and the language used here is taken from Hippolytus, *The Apostolic Doctrine*, Chapter 21.

[8] **These statements of John regarding the Lord's Supper are taken from**: 1 Corinthians 11:25-30.

[9] **Jesus as the bread of life**: "Eat my flesh and drink my blood." The ideas of the meaning of Lord's Supper in this scene are drawn from John 6:22-58.

[10] **Maranatha**: "An ancient Palestinian Aramaic expression recorded in transliterated Aramaic in 1 Cor. 16:22 and in Greek translation in Rev. 22:20… But as Moule has rightly shown, 1 Cor. 16:22 has no "eucharistic context." The verse is not a plea for Christ to be present at the Lord's Supper but a plea for the parousia of Christ in judgment on those who do not love the Lord." J. J. Hughes, "Maranatha," ed. Geoffrey W Bromiley, *The International Standard Bible Encyclopedia, Revised* (Wm. B. Eerdmans, 1979–1988), 243.

CHAPTER 9

[1] **The sea as chaos and God's power over the sea as covenant metaphor**: "In ANE religious mythologies, the sea and the sea dragon were symbols of chaos that had to be overcome to bring order to the universe, or more exactly, the political world order of the myth's originating culture. Some scholars call this battle Chaoskampf—the divine struggle to create order out of chaos.

"Hermann Gunkel first suggested in Creation and Chaos (1895) that some ANE creation myths contained a cosmic conflict between deity and sea, as well as sea dragons or serpents that expressed the creation of order out of chaos. Gunkel argued that Genesis borrowed this idea from the Babylonian tale of Marduk battling the goddess Tiamat, serpent of chaos, whom he vanquished, and out of whose body he created the heavens and earth. After this victory, Marduk ascended to power in the Mesopotamian pantheon. This creation story gave mythical justification to the rise of Babylon as an ancient world power most likely in the First Babylonian Dynasty under Hammurabi (1792-1750 B.C.). As the prologue of the Code of Hammurabi explains, "Anu, the majestic, King of the Anunnaki, and Bel, the Lord of Heaven and Earth, who established the fate of the land, had given to Marduk, the ruling son of Ea, dominion over mankind, and called Babylon by his great name; when they made it great upon the earth by founding therein an eternal kingdom, whose foundations are as firmly grounded as are those of heaven and earth." The foundation of Hammurabi's "eternal kingdom" is literarily linked to Marduk's foundational creation of heaven and earth.

"Later, John Day argued in light of the discovery of the Ugarit tablets in 1928, that Canaan, not Babylonia is the source of the combat motif in Genesis, reflected in Yahweh's own complaint that Israel had become polluted by Canaanite culture. In the Baal cycle, Baal battles Yam (Sea) and conquers it, along with "the dragon," "the twisting serpent," to be enthroned as chief deity of the Canaanite pantheon.

"Creation accounts were often veiled polemics for the establishment of a king or kingdom's claim to sovereignty. Richard Clifford quotes, "In Mesopotamia, Ugarit, and Israel the Chaoskampf appears not only in cosmological contexts but just as frequently—and this was fundamentally true right from the first—in political contexts. The repulsion and the destruction of the enemy, and thereby the maintenance of political order, always constitute one of the major dimensions of the battle against chaos."

Notice in the Scriptures below that God uses the creation of the heavens and earth, involving subjugation of rivers, seas, and dragon (Leviathan), as poetic descriptions of his covenant with his people, rooted in the Exodus story, and reiterated in the Davidic covenant. The creation of the covenant is the creation of the heavens and the earth which includes a subjugation of chaos by the new order. The covenant is a cosmos—not a material one centered in astronomical location and abstract impersonal forces as modern worldview demands, but a theological one, centered in the sacred space of land, temple, and cult as the ancient Near Eastern worldview demands.

Psa. 74:12-17
Yet God my King is from of old,
working salvation in the midst of the earth.
You divided the sea by your might;
[A reference to the Exodus deliverance of the covenant at Sinai]
You broke the heads of the sea monsters in the waters.
You crushed the heads of Leviathan;...
You have prepared the light and the sun.
You have established all the boundaries of the earth;

Psa. 89:9-12; 19-29
You rule the raging of the sea;
when its waves rise, you still them.
You crushed Rahab like a carcass;
you scattered your enemies with your mighty arm.
The heavens are yours; the earth also is yours;
the world and all that is in it, you have founded them.
The north and the south, you have created them...
I have found David, my servant;
with my holy oil I have anointed him,
so that my hand shall be established with him...
and in my name shall his horn be exalted.
I will set his hand on the sea
and his right hand on the rivers...
My steadfast love I will keep for him forever,
and my covenant will stand firm for him.
I will establish his offspring forever
and his throne as the days of the heavens.

Isa 51:9-16
Was it not You who cut Rahab in pieces,
Who pierced the dragon?
Was it not You who dried up the sea,
The waters of the great deep;
Who made the depths of the sea a pathway
For the redeemed to cross over?...
[Y]ou have forgotten the LORD your Maker,
Who stretched out the heavens
And laid the foundations of the earth...
"For I am the LORD your God, who stirs up the sea and its waves roar (the LORD of hosts is His name).
"I have put My words in your mouth and have covered you with the shadow of My hand, to establish the heavens, to found the earth, and to say to Zion, 'You are My people.'"
[a reaffirmation of the Sinai covenant through Moses]

Isa. 27:1; 6-13
In that day the LORD with his hard and great and strong sword will <u>punish Leviathan the fleeing serpent,</u>
<u>Leviathan the twisting serpent, and he will slay the dragon that is in the sea</u>…
In days to come Jacob shall take root,
Israel shall blossom and put forth shoots
and fill the whole world with fruit…
And in that day a great trumpet will be blown, and those who were lost in the land of Assyria and those
who were driven out to the land of Egypt will come and worship the LORD on the holy mountain at
Jerusalem. [the future consummation of the Mosaic and Davidic covenant in the New Covenant of
Messiah]"

For more on this covenant motif and the ancient Hebrew understanding, see: Brian Godawa, *When Giants
Were Upon the Earth: The Watchers, the Nephilim, and the Biblical Cosmic War of the Seed* (Embedded
Pictures, 2014), 79-88.

[2] **God removing the sea from the earth**: Revelation 21:1 Then I saw a new heaven and a new earth, for
the first heaven and the first earth had passed away, <u>and the sea was no more</u>.

"But if we understand this literally, it makes no theological sense: Why would the sea not be a part of the
eternal new creation order? Did not God re-create the "new earth"? Why would he not also re-create the
sea? Did not he create and bound the sea in the original creation (thalassas, Ge 1:10; Ex 20:11),9 as one
feature of creation which was "very good" (Ge 1:31; cp. Ps 104:24, 28)? Nor does it make contextual
sense, for what becomes of the "river" that flows through the city (22:1–2)? Does it evaporate? Make a
complete, endless circle around the globe? Rivers naturally and necessarily end—into a pool of some sort,
such as a lake, sea, or ocean (Ecc 1:7; cp. Eze 47:8; Zec 14:8). Besides, Scripture can speak
metaphorically by employing the drying up of a sea—as when God judged Old Testament Babylon (Jer
51:36; cp. 50:38). Why could not this sea absence be metaphorical (as even dispensationalist Thomas
agrees? The literalistic approach is unworkable—and unnecessary.

"Many commentators understand the sea to represent the chaos and woe in the world. In the Old
Testament the sea sometimes pictures the turmoil caused by the wicked, as in Isaiah 57:20: "But the
wicked are like the tossing sea, / For it cannot be quiet, / And its waters toss up refuse and mud."
Jeremiah 6:23 reads: "They are cruel and have no mercy; / Their voice roars like the sea" (cp. Ps 65:7; Isa
17:12; Jer 50:42; 49:23; 51:42; Eze 26:5; Da 7:2–3; Zec 10:11). In Revelation 13:1 the beast arises from
the sea. Beale argues that "the evil nuance of the sea metaphorically represents the entire range of
afflictions that formerly threatened God's people." This would point to the removal of opposition to God
and his people in the new order, which would certainly fit the ultimate consummation order, as well as the
postmillennial hope in redemptive-historical preterism's future victory and prosperity." Kenneth L.
Gentry, Jr., *The Divorce of Israel: A Redemptive-Historical Interpretation of Revelation Vol. 2* (Dallas,
GA: Tolle Lege Press, 2016), 736.

[3] **The first temple destruction in 587 BC described as "decreation" or a return to pre-creation**
chaos: "God describes the creation of His covenant with Moses as the creation of the heavens and the
earth (Isa. 51:14-16). The creation of Israel through deliverance and Promised Land was likened to God
hovering over the waters and filling the formless and void earth (Deut. 32:10-12), separating the waters
from the dry land (Exod. 15:8, 16-17), establishing the sun and moon, and defeating the mythical sea
dragon of chaos to create His ordered world (Psa. 74:12-17; 89:6-12; Isa. 51:9-14).

"If the creation of a covenant is spoken of as the creation of heavens and earth, and the ruling powers are
referred to as sun, moon and stars, then what would the destruction of those powers be but the destruction
of the heavens and the earth, including the fall of those astronomical symbolic entities? And what was the
embodiment of that covenant but the holy Temple in the holy city of King David?

"The first time that Jerusalem and the Temple was destroyed in 586 B.C. by the Babylonians, the prophets
used the language of decreation to express the covenantal violation of Israel. The destruction of the
Temple and exile of the Jews through God's providence was likened to the destruction of the heavens and
earth and a return to a pre-creation chaotic state, a reversal of Genesis 1 language:

Jer. 4:23-26
I looked on the earth, and behold, it was without form and void;
and to the heavens, and they had no light.
I looked on the mountains, and behold, they were quaking,
I looked, and behold, there was no man,

and all the birds of the air had fled.
I looked, and behold, the fruitful land was a desert…
For this the earth shall mourn,
and the heavens above be dark.

Isa. 24:1-23
Behold, the LORD will empty the earth and make it desolate…
The earth shall be utterly empty and utterly plundered…
The earth staggers like a drunken man;
On that day the LORD will punish
the host of heaven, in heaven,
and the kings of the earth, on the earth…
Then the moon will be confounded
and the sun ashamed.

"In the same way that the first temple destruction was earth shattering in its covenantal impact, so the second destruction of Jerusalem and the holy Temple in A.D. 70 was of equal spiritual significance in God's covenantal relations with Israel. It was the shaking of the heavens and earth with a punishment of the host of heaven, both astronomical and political/spiritual." Brian Godawa, *God Against the gods: Storytelling, Imagination And Apologetics In The Bible* (Embedded Pictures, 2016), 129-130.

[4] **The Seven archangels**: "ARCHANGEL Chief or first angel. The English term "archangel" is a derivative of the Greek word archangelos, which occurs only twice in the NT. Only one archangel is named in the Bible, though it is possible that there are others. In Jude's letter the archangel Michael is depicted as disputing with Satan over the body of Moses (Jude 9, see also Assumption of Moses). In the tenth chapter of the book of Daniel, this same Michael is described as one of the chief princes. This may imply that other chief princes (archangels) exist. Jewish apocalyptic literature of the postexilic period describes seven archangels who stand in the presence of God: Suruel, Raphael, Raguel, Michael, Gabriel, Remiel, and Uriel (Tobit 12:15; 1 Enoch 20:1–7; 9:1; 40:9). Some scholars speculate that these are the same angels who stand before God and blow the trumpets of God's judgment (Rev. 8:2–9:15)." John Laing, "Archangel," ed. Chad Brand et al., *Holman Illustrated Bible Dictionary* (Nashville, TN: Holman Bible Publishers, 2003), 105–106.

1 Enoch 20:1-7 And these are the names of the holy angels who watch. 2 Uriel, one of the holy angels, who is over the world and over Tartarus. 3 Raphael, 4 one of the holy angels, who is over the spirits of men. Raguel, one of the holy angels who †takes vengeance on† the world of the luminaries. 5 Michael, one of the holy angels, to wit, he that is set over the best part of mankind «and» over chaos. 6 Saraqâêl, one of the holy angels, who is set over the spirits, who sin in the spirit. 7 Gabriel, one of the holy angels, who is over Paradise and the serpents and the Cherubim. 8 Remiel, one of the holy angels, whom God set over those who rise.

[5] **Mount Zaphon**: "Recent discussion of Mt. Zaphon has focused on the function of sacred mountains in Canaanite religion, especially as exemplified in Ugaritic texts. Along with F. M. Cross (CMHE), Clifford (1972) has provided one of the most detailed studies of the association of Mt. Zaphon with the kingship of Baal in the Ugaritic texts. Indeed, the mountain was the site of Baal's royal palace built by Kothar-wa-Hasis, the divine architect. Mt. Zaphon was a feasting place for the gods (CTA 4.5.106–117) and the site of Baal's proclamations (e.g., CTA 3.3.10–28). It was also where Baal and his archrival Mot engaged in a cosmic battle (CTA 6.6.12–34). The mountain itself appears as a deity in many Ugaritic offering lists and in Phoenician personal names such as ʿbdṣpn, "servant of Zaphon.""

"According to Eissfeldt (1932: 12–15) and other scholars, one of the earliest texts referring to Mt. Zaphon in the Hebrew Bible is Ps 89:13—Eng v 12, where Yahweh is said to have created ṣāpôn along with Mt. Hermon and Mt. Tabor. Ps 48:2–3—Eng vv 1–2 describes Mt. Zion as a sacred mountain of Yahweh, and the use of yarkĕtê ṣāpôn ("distant north," "utmost peak of Zaphon," among other renditions) in the phraseology appears to identify Zion with Mt. Zaphon. Divine decrees issue from Mt. Zion (cf., Isa 2:3) as they do from the holy mountains in Ugaritic myths." Hector Avalos, "Zaphon, Mount (Place)," ed. David Noel Freedman, *The Anchor Yale Bible Dictionary* (New York: Doubleday, 1992), 1040–1041.

[6] **Baal the Cloudrider vs. Yahweh the Cloudrider**: "In the Ugaritic text below, we are introduced to Baal as one who rides the heavens in his cloud-chariot dispensing judgment from the heights. "Charioteer (or 'Rider') of the Clouds" was a common epithet ascribed to Baal throughout the Ugaritic texts. Here is another side-by-side comparison of Ugaritic and Biblical texts that illustrate that common motif.

UGARITIC TEXTS

'Dry him up. O Valiant Baal!
Dry him up, O Charioteer [Rider] of the Clouds!
For our captive is Prince Yam [Sea],
for our captive is Ruler Nahar [River]!'
(KTU 1.2:4.8-9)
What manner of enemy has arisen against Baal, of foe against the Charioteer of the Clouds? [then, he
judges other deities]
Surely I smote…Yam [Sea]?
Surely I exterminated Nahar [River], the mighty god?
Surely I lifted up the dragon,
I overpowered him?
I smote the writhing serpent,
Encircler-with-seven-heads!
(KTU 1.3:3.38-41)

OLD TESTAMENT

"[Yahweh] bowed the heavens also, and came down
With thick darkness under His feet.
And He rode on a cherub and flew;
And He appeared on the wings of the wind.
He made darkness canopies around Him,
A mass of waters, thick clouds of the sky.
(Sam. 22:7-12)
[Yahweh] makes the clouds His chariot;
He walks upon the wings of the wind;
(Ps. 104:3-4)
Behold, the LORD is riding on a swift cloud and is about to come to Egypt;
The idols of Egypt will tremble at His presence,
(Isa. 19:1)

"Yahweh is described here with the same exact moniker as Baal, in the same exact context as Baal—
revealed in the storm and riding a cloud in judgment on other deities. Baal is subverted by Yahweh.

"This correlation of deity with cloud judgment sheds light on the vision of Daniel's Son of Man that
Christians understand as a reference to Jesus Christ. The everlasting dominion received by the divine Baal
riding the clouds before the throne of the High God El is apologetically ascribed to the divine Son of Man
(Jesus Christ) riding the clouds to the throne of "Elyon," the Ancient of Days.

Dan. 7:13-14
"I kept looking in the night visions,
And behold, with the clouds of heaven
One like a Son of Man was coming,
And He came up to the Ancient of Days
And was presented before Him.
"And to Him was given dominion,
Glory and a kingdom…
His dominion is an everlasting dominion.

"Yahweh is God, not the Canaanite El. Jesus is Yahweh's son, as opposed to Baal being El's son. And
that "Son of Man" is the one who is given a kingdom of everlasting dominion, not Baal. Brian Godawa,
When Giants Were Upon the Earth: The Watchers, the Nephilim, and the Biblical Cosmic War of the Seed
(Embedded Pictures, 2014), 241-242.

[7] **Apollyon is the angel of the Abyss**: Revelation 9:11 They have as king over them the angel of the
bottomless pit [Abyss]. His name in Hebrew is Abaddon, and in Greek he is called Apollyon.

The binding of Watchers into the earth: "1 Peter 3:18-20 speaks of Christ going down into Sheol to
proclaim his triumph to the "spirits imprisoned" at the time of the flood. This act appears to be a
typological replay of Enoch's own vision journey into Sheol to see the "prison house of the angels" who
disobeyed at the flood (1 Enoch 21:9-10).

368

"But the story does not yet end there. You will notice that the location of punishment and binding of the fallen angels that we have already seen in 2 Peter is *Tartarus* in the Greek.

> 2Pet. 2:4 For if God did not spare angels when they sinned, but cast them into hell [*tartarus*] and committed them to pits of darkness, reserved for judgment.

"What is important to realize is that the Greek word translated as "hell" in this English translation is not one of the usual New Testament Greek words for hell, *gehenna* or *hades*, but *tartarus*.

"The Greek poet Hesiod, writing around 700 B.C., described this commonly known underworld called Tartarus as the pit of darkness and gloom where the Olympian Titan giants were banished following their war with Zeus.

> Hesiod, *Theogony* lines 720-739 as far beneath the earth as heaven is above earth; for so far is it from earth to Tartarus…There by the counsel of Zeus who drives the clouds the Titan gods are hidden under misty gloom, in a dank place where are the ends of the huge earth. And they may not go out; for Poseidon fixed gates of bronze upon it, and a wall runs all round it on every side

"Obviously, Peter does not affirm Greco-Roman polytheism by referring to Tartarus, but he is alluding to a Hellenistic myth that his readers, believer and unbeliever alike, would be very familiar with, subverting it with the Jewish traditional interpretation.

"Extra-Biblical Second Temple Jewish legends connected this legend of gods and bound Titans in Tartarus to the bound angelic Watchers and punished giants of Genesis 6.

> Sibylline Oracles 1:97-104, 119enterprising Watchers, who received this appellation because they had a sleepless mind in their hearts and an insatiable personality. They were mighty, of great form, but nevertheless they went under the dread house of Tartarus guarded by unbreakable bonds, to make retribution, to Gehenna of terrible, raging, undying fire…draping them around with great Tartarus, under the base of the earth.

Other well-known Second Temple literature reiterated this binding in the heart of the earth until judgment day:

> Jubilees 4:22; 5:10 And he wrote everything, and bore witness to the Watchers, the ones who sinned with the daughters of men because they began to mingle themselves with the daughters of men so that they might be polluted…
>
> And subsequently they [the Watchers] were bound in the depths of the earth forever, until the day of great judgment in order for judgment to be executed upon all of those who corrupted their ways and their deeds before the LORD.

"This "binding" or imprisoning of supernatural beings in the earth is expressed in 2 Peter's "cast into pits of darkness reserved for judgment" (3:19), 1 Peter's "disobedient spirits in prison" (v. 6), and Jude's "eternal bonds under darkness for the judgment of the great day" (2:4). But it is not altogether unheard of in the Old Testament.

Isa. 24:21–23
On that day the LORD will punish
the host of heaven, in heaven,
and the kings of the earth, on the earth.
They will be gathered together
as prisoners in a pit;
they will be shut up in a prison,
and after many days they will be punished.

"Isaiah here is speaking of judgment upon Israel by the Babylonians around 600 B.C., but he evokes the same Enochian imagery of the angelic host of heaven (often linked to the astronomical heavenly bodies *and* earthly rulers) being overthrown and imprisoned in the earth until judgment day.

"Robert Newman notes that the Qumran Hebrew of the Isaiah scroll of this passage refers to a past event as its reference point: "They *were* gathered together as prisoners in a pit" (past tense). [7] This past event could very well be the antediluvian binding of the fallen host of heaven (*bene ha Elohim*) as an analogy

369

for the future captivity of Israel." Brian Godawa, *When Giants Were Upon the Earth: The Watchers, the Nephilim, and the Biblical Cosmic War of the Seed* (Embedded Pictures, 2014), 128-131.

[8] **Asherah**: The name Asherah appears 40 times in the Bible (plural: Asherim, Asheroth, Ashtaroth). Some of those instances refer directly to the goddess herself (Judg. 3:7; 1 Kgs. 14:13, 18:19; 2 Kgs. 21:7, 23:4) and many others refer to a wooden cult object used in worship to symbolize the goddess (Deut. 16:21; Judg. 6:25-30; 2 Kgs. 18:4; Isa. 17:8; Jer. 17:2). From the time of Judges on into the monarchy and the Josianic reforms, The Asherah poles or sacred pillars are often spoken of in close connection with altars of Ba'al (Judg. 6:25; 1 Kgs. 16:33; 2 Kgs. 17:16; 21:3), which hints at a theological connection between this unseemly pair of idols that exercised an ongoing apostasizing influence on Israel throughout her history. Archeological discoveries of inscriptions in Israel have even confirmed the attempt of Israelites to syncretize Asherah into their religion as Yahweh's consort (Deut. 16:21-22). See John Day, "Asherah in the Hebrew Bible and Northwest Semitic Literature," *Journal of Biblical Literature*, Vol. 105, No. 3 (Sep., 1986), 391-92.

[9] **Anat**: In the Baal narrative cycle from Ugarit, El was the supreme "father of the gods," who lived on a cosmic mountain. A divine council of gods called "Sons of El" surrounded him, vying for position and power. When Sea is coronated by El and given a palace, Baal rises up and kills Sea, taking Sea's place as "Most High" over the other gods (excepting El). A temple is built and a feast celebrated. Death then insults Baal, who goes down to the underworld, only to be defeated by Death. But Anat, Baal's violent sister, seeks Death and cuts him up into pieces and brings Baal's body back up to earth where he is brought back to life, only to fight Death to a stalemate. See N. Wyatt, *Religious Texts from Ugarit, 2nd ed., The Biblical Seminar, vol. 53* (London: Sheffield Academic Press, 2002), 36-39.

[10] **Anat as incestuous sister of Ba'al**: "The Ugaritic texts present Anat as a "fertility goddess" who is the consort of the god →Baal. It is also often stated that she is the mother of Baal's offspring. Some scholars further allege that the texts present her as acting like a prostitute, either to entice Baal specifically, or in her general conduct. Even when she is described in what seems to be more respectful terms as Baal's sacred bride, this carries overtones of illegitimate sexuality." P. L. Day, "Anat," ed. Karel van der Toorn, Bob Becking, and Pieter W. van der Horst, *Dictionary of Deities and Demons in the Bible* (Leiden; Boston; Köln; Grand Rapids, MI; Cambridge: Brill; Eerdmans, 1999), 36.

[11] **On Ba'al's two weapons**: "One as a hammer like mace and the other "Ginsberg (1935:328) identified ṣmdm with the two-pieced maces excavated at Ugarit. The weapon consists of two pieces, a head latched onto a handle, specifically in Ginsberg's words (1935:328) "a mace with a stone head drilled through to adjust the wooden shaft, to which it is lashed tightly with thongs; and hence the name from the root ṣmd, 'to bind.' Such mace heads are found frequently in excavations.""…

"A famous stele from Ugarit, sometimes called the "Baal au foudre" stele and housed in the Louvre, depicts Baal wielding two weapons. The weapon in his right hand is sometimes characterized as a mace (Amiet 1980:201).204 In his left hand Baal holds "tree-lightning" (Vanel 1965:84; Williams-Forte 1983:28, 30). Other examples of second millennium iconography of the storm-god depict him with a weapon (Vanel 1965:esp. 108; Seeden 1980:esp. 102), which appears at times as "branch-like lightning" (Williams-Forte 1983:26)."…

Comparative evidence drawn from Mediterranean and Near Eastern myths comports with the meteorological character of ṣmdm (Thespis 164–65). Zeus pelts Typhon with thunderbolts at Mons Cassius, the Latin name for Mount Sapan (Apollodorus, The Library, 1.6.3; Frazer 1921:48–49). Zeus' thunderbolts made by Cyclopes, the son of the craftsman-god Hephaistos, have been compared with Baal's weapons fashioned by Kothar (Walcot 1969:115)…." Mark S. Smith, *The Ugaritic Baal Cycle: Introduction with Text, Translation and Commentary of KTU 1.1-1.2, vol. 1* (Leiden; New York; Köln: E.J. Brill, 1994), 339–340.

The actual text of the Baal cycle where Kothar-wa-Hasis crafts the two weapons, Yagarrish/Yagrush ("Driver") and Ayyamarri/Ayamur ("Expeller") for Baal to defeat Yamm (Sea) and River (Nahar) is KTU 1.2.11-25:

Kothar fashions the weapons,
And he proclaims their names:
"Your name, yours, is Yagarrish:
Yagarrish, drive Yamm,
Drive Yamm from his throne,
[Na]har from the seat of his dominion.

"Your name, yours, is Ayyamarri:
Ayyamarri, expel Yamm,
Expel Yamm from his throne,
Nahar from the seat of his dominion.
Leap from Baal's hand,
Like a raptor from his fingers.
Strike the head of Prince Yamm,
Between the eyes of Judge River.
May Yamm sink and fall to the earth."
The weapon leaps from Baal's hand,
[Like] a raptor from his fingers,
It strikes the head of Prince [Yamm,]
Between the eyes of Judge River.

Mark S. Smith and Simon B. Parker, *Ugaritic Narrative Poetry, vol. 9, Writings from the Ancient World* (Atlanta, GA: Scholars Press, 1997), 103–104.

"The most important textual witnesses to the weapons of the storm god of Aleppo [Ba'al] are found in the Old Babylonian letters from the Mari archives From these letters we learn that the weapons that were housed in the temple of the storm god in Aleppo were brought to the Mariote city of Terqa during Zimri-Lim's reign. While the letters seem to allude to the conflict myth that we find in fuller form later on in the Baal-Cycle from Ugarit, the weapons in the letters appear to be real weapons used as cultic objects." Joanna Töyräänvuori, "Weapons of the Storm God in Ancient Near Eastern and Biblical Traditions," *Studia Orientalia*, volume 112 (Helsinki, Finnish Oriental Society, 2012), 154, 160.

"In the text of the Ugaritic Baal-Cycle, the weapons forged by the smith Kothar-wa-Ḥasis, and wielded by Baal in the battle against Yamm, were clubs called by the names ygrš and aymr and traslated as 'driver' and 'chaser', respectively. A club (or a hammer, also a smiting weapon) could certainly have been one of the storm god's weapons, as the association seems to have had a cross-cultural mythological foundation. Many Syrian and Anatolian reliefs depict the weather god (Adad or Tarhunt) holding a lightning weapon in one hand and a hammer or a smiting weapon in the other hand." Joanna Töyräänvuori, "Weapons of the Storm God in Ancient Near Eastern and Biblical Traditions," *Studia Orientalia*, vol. 112, (Finnish Oriental Society, 2012) 166.

[12] This storyline of the archangels attacking the palace of Ba'al is fictional license. The full story is told in *Caleb Vigilant*, Chronicles of the Nephilim, book 5.

[13] **Michael as prince of Israel and the other principalities in conflict**: See Daniel 10.

[14] **Satan disputing over the body of Moses**: Jude 9 [9] But when the archangel Michael, contending with the devil, was disputing about the body of Moses, he did not presume to pronounce a blasphemous judgment, but said, "The Lord rebuke you."

Read a fictional account of this event of Satan and the body of Moses along with its theological purpose in my novel, *Joshua Valiant*, (Embedded Pictures Publishing, 2013).

[15] **Ahura Mazda is the god of Commagene, Hubal of Arabia**: And Ba'al of Syria. All these gods were over the nation's forces that made up the Roman army that marched down upon Jerusalem.

Commagene's gods: "The restored freedom of Commagene, now allied to Rome, allowed Antiochus leisure for his great religious expression still visible atop Nemrud Dagh. His remarkable fusions of Greek and Iranian gods satisfied the composite population, which could now worship Zeus-Oromasdes (Ahuramazda), Heracles-Artagnes, and the grandly titled Apollo-Mithras-Helios-Hermes!" Richard D. Sullivan, "Commagene (Place)," ed. David Noel Freedman, The Anchor Yale Bible Dictionary (New York: Doubleday, 1992), 1096.

Serapis was a god in Alexandria from where Titus brought the 15th Legion into Judea. Tacitus and Suetonius both claim Vespasian had an encounter with Serapis in Alexandria right before he was declared emperor after the death of Nero. Tacitus Histories 4.81-82; Suetonius, Vespasian 7.1

[16] **Cherubim hair as binding the angels**: The concept is entirely fictional. But it is based on some mythopoeic research. "Through the entire *Chronicles of the Nephilim* series, I have used a concept called "binding" of angels, demons, and Watchers. This binding is accomplished through imprisonment in the earth or Tartarus.

"This binding notion originates theologically from the binding of Satan in the ministry of Christ as noted above in Matthew 12, as well as the binding of angels in "chains of gloomy darkness" in Tartarus in Jude 6 and 2 Peter 2:4. And these New Testament Scriptures are paraphrases of the Enochian narrative of the antediluvian Watchers who at the Flood were "bound" "for seventy generations underneath the rocks of the ground until the day of their judgment" (1 Enoch 10:12).

"The idea of binding spirits is a common one in ancient religion and magic. Michael Fishbane notes that in the ancient Near East, incantations and spells were used by sorcerers and enchanters to bind people and spirits in spiritual "traps, pits, snares, and nets," using venomous curses from their lips like serpents. In response to some of these verbal sorceries, the Psalmist himself calls upon Yahweh in similar utterances to reverse the spells upon his enemies that they would be trapped, ensnared and bound by their own magical devices (Psalm 140; 64; 57:4-6). Exorcists of the first century used incantations to cast out demons in Jesus' name (Acts 16:18), the same incantation used by Demons against Jesus before being cast out (Mk 1:27).

"Ezekiel 13:18 refers to a specific form of hunting and binding spirits in a practice of women "who sew magic bands upon all wrists…in the hunt for souls!" I reversed this pagan version of using magical armbands by creating a heavenly version of the archangels with armbands of indestructible Cherubim hair for their hunting and binding of evil spirits. The hair is wrapped as bands around the arms of archangels and used like a rope to bind the Watchers' hands and feet." Brian Godawa, *When Giants Were Upon the Earth: The Watchers, the Nephilim, and the Biblical Cosmic War of the Seed* (Embedded Pictures, 2014), 285-286.

For the story of the angels being bound at the Flood, see: Brian Godawa, *Noah Primeval* (Los Angeles, CA: Embedded Pictures Publishing, 2011).

For the story of Ba'al being bound at the city of Tyre, see: Brian Godawa, *Jesus Triumphant* (Los Angeles, CA: Embedded Pictures Publishing, 2015).

CHAPTER 10

[1] **Stephanas had a history with Paul at Corinth**: 1 Corinthians 16:17.

[2] **The Oracle of Delphi**: "Numerous classical authors report that natural phenomena played an essential part in one of their most sacred religious rituals: the oracle at Delphi. According to the geographer Strabo (c. 64 B.C.–25 A.D.), for example, "the seat of the oracle is a cavern hollowed down in the depths … from which arises pneuma [breath, vapor, gas] that inspires a divine state of possession" (Geography 9.3.5)…

"The Pythia dealt less in visions of the future than in right choices: where to locate a new colony, when to attack an enemy, how to lift a curse, whom to choose as leader, what offering to make to which god. No kingdom, city or private person could afford to make critical decisions without consulting the Pythia. Thanks to her prestige, Delphi became the richest and most famous Hellenic sanctuary. The Greeks called it the omphalos, or "navel of the world."

"How could a mere mortal command such respect? The answer lies in the belief that Apollo—the god of revelation and inspiration—used the Pythia as his mouthpiece, taking possession of her during oracular sessions. The Pythia would fall into a trance, and the words she spoke were supposedly those of Apollo, delivered in a voice very unlike her normal tones." Jelle Zeilinga de Boer and John R. Hale, "The Oracle of Delphi—Was She Really Stoned?" *Bible History Daily*, May 2013.
http://www.biblicalarchaeology.org/daily/ancient-cultures/daily-life-and-practice/the-oracle-of-delphi—was-she-really-stoned/#end02

Navel of the earth: "The idea was common in the ancient world that the earth and the deities had body parts located in sacred spots, such as navels and vulvas. The idea behind the earth's navel is that there is an invisible umbilical between the god in the sky and the earth since a goddess had given birth to the earth. The *Encyclopedia Britannica* states:

"Frequently, the altar is regarded as the center or the image of the universe. For the ancient Greeks the grave marker (a mound of earth or a stone) was the earth altar upon which sacrifices to the dead were made and, like other earth altars, it was called the omphalos, 'the navel' of the Earth—i.e. the central point from which terrestrial life originated. In Vedic India the altar was regarded as a microcosm, its parts representing the various parts of the universe and its construction being interpreted as a repetition of the creation of the cosmos.

"The worshippers of Yahveh knew that Yahveh's Faces (2Ch 07:14a) and his eyes, ears and heart were present at the temple (1Ki 09:03; 2Ch 07:15-16). By contrast, fertility cult worshippers were concerned that their gods and goddesses' reproductive organs were at the temple—the Lingam and Yoni."

Yoel Natan, *Moon-o-theism: Religion of a War and Moon God Prophet Volume I of II* (online:2006), 756, http://www.yoel.info/moonotheismv1andv2.pdf

[3] **Psalm 82 and the judgment of the Sons of God (Watchers):** "Though the sons of God in Psalm 82 and elsewhere in the Old Testament have been understood as supernatural, angelic, or divine beings through most of Jewish and Christian history, it is fair to say that there has also been a minor tradition of scholars and theologians who have interpreted these beings as tyrannical human kings or judges. They claim that the scenario in which we see these sons of God is a courtroom, the liturgy they engage in is legal formality, and the terminology they use is forensic (related to lawsuits), thus leading them to conclude that these are poetic descriptions of the responsibility of natural human authorities over their subjects on earth.

"And they would be supernaturally wrong.

"The setting, liturgy and language are indeed all courtroom-oriented in their context, but that courtroom is God's heavenly courtroom because that is how God reveals his own judgments to his people and the nations.

"But don't take my word for it. Let's let Jesus exegete this passage for us.

"In John 10, learned Jews in the Temple challenge Jesus about his identity as Christ. Jesus says that he and the Father are one, a clear claim of deity in the Hebrew culture, which results in the Jews picking up stones to stone him because he, being a man, made himself out to be God (10:33). Their particular Rabbinic absolute monotheism did not allow for the existence of divinity other than the Father. Jesus responds by appealing to this very passage we are discussing: "Jesus answered them, "Is it not written in your Law, 'I said, you are gods'? If he called them gods to whom the word of God came—and Scripture cannot be broken—do you say of him whom the Father consecrated and sent into the world, 'You are blaspheming,' because I said, 'I am the Son of God'?" (10:34-36).

"If the judges in Psalm 82 "to whom the word of God came" were considered to be men rather than gods by Jesus, then his appeal to the passage to justify his claims of deity would be nonsensical. He would essentially be saying "I am a god in the same way that human judges were human representatives of God." But this would not be controversial, it would divest Jesus of all deity, and they would certainly not seek to stone him. No, Jesus is affirming the divinity of the sons of God in Psalm 82 and chastising the Jews that their own Scriptures allow for the existence of divine beings (gods) other than the Father, so it would not be inherently unscriptural for another being, such as himself, to claim divinity. Of course, Jesus is the species-unique Son of God (John 1:18), the "visible Yahweh" co-regent over the divine council (Dan. 7:13-14). But Jesus' point is that the diversity of deity is not unknown in the Old Testament.

"Jesus is arguing for the Trinitarian concept of divine diversity as being compatible with Old Testament monotheism, which was not compatible with man-made traditions of absolute monotheism that Rabbinic Jews followed. Remember, in the Bible, the concept of "god" (elohim) was about a plane of existence not necessarily a "being" of existence, so there were many gods (many elohim) that existed on that supernatural plane, yet only one God of gods (Elohim of elohim) who created all things, including those other elohim or sons of God.

"This is precisely the nuanced distinction that the Apostle Paul refers to when he addresses the issue of food sacrificed to idols—that is, physical images of deities on earth. He considers idols as having "no real existence," but then refers to other "gods" in the heavens or on earth who do exist, but are not the same as the One Creator God:

> 1 Cor. 8:4-6 Therefore, as to the eating of food offered to idols, we know that "an idol has no real existence," and that "there is no God but one." For although there may be so-called gods in heaven or on earth—as indeed there are many "gods" and many "lords"—yet for us there is one God, the Father, from whom are all things and for whom we exist, and one Lord, Jesus Christ, through whom are all things and through whom we exist.

> 1 Cor. 10:18-20 Consider the people of Israel: are not those who eat the sacrifices participants in the altar? What do I imply then? That food offered to idols is anything, or that an idol is anything? No, I imply that what pagans sacrifice they offer to demons and not to God. I do not want you to be participants with demons.

"In 1 Corinthians, as in Revelation 9:20 quoted earlier, gods are not merely figments of imagination without existence in a world where the Trinity is the sole deity residing in the spiritual realm. Rather, physical idols (images) are "nothing," and "have no real existence" in that they are the representatives of the deities, not the deities themselves. But the deities behind those idols are real demonic beings; the gods of the nations who are not THE God, for they themselves were created by God and are therefore essentially incomparable to the God through whom are all things and through whom we exist.

"The terminology used by Paul in the first passage contrasting the many gods and lords with the one God and Lord of Christianity reflects the client-patron relationship that ANE cultures shared. As K.L. Noll explains in his text on ancient Canaan and Israel, "Lord" was the proper designation for a patron in a patron-client relationship. There may have been many gods, but for ancient Israel, there was only one Lord, and that was Yahweh."

"This is certainly difficult for a modern mind to wrap itself around because we have been taught to think that there are only two diametrically opposed options: Either absolute diversity as in polytheism (many gods of similar essence) or absolute unity as in absolute monotheism that excludes the possibility of any other divine beings less than the One God. As we have already seen, the Bible seems to indicate that there are other "gods" who are not of the same species as God the Father or God the Son, yet they do exist as supernatural entities with ruling power over the nations outside of God's people. Some scholars have used the term monolatry of this view rather than monotheism, because monotheism excludes the existence of any other gods, while monolatry allows for the existence of other gods, but demands the worship of one God who is essentially different from all other gods.

"Psalm 89 fills out the picture of the heavenly divine council as opposed to an earthly human one that is composed of these sons of God who are comparably less than Yahweh:

> Psa. 89:5-8 Let the heavens praise your wonders, O LORD,
> your faithfulness in the assembly of the holy ones!
> For who in the skies can be compared to the LORD?
> Who among the heavenly beings (Hebrew: sons of God) is like the LORD,
> a God greatly to be feared in the council of the holy ones,
> and awesome above all who are around him?
> Oh LORD God of hosts…

"Here, the sons of God are referred to as an assembly or council of holy ones that surround Yahweh in a heavenly court "in the skies," not in an earthly court or council of humans, thus reinforcing the supernatural distinction from earthly judges. Israel is sometimes called, "a holy nation" (Ex. 19:6), a "holy people" (Isa. 62:12), "holy ones" (Psa. 16:3), and other derivatives of that concept, but the Hebrew word for "holy ones" (qedoshim) is used often in the Bible to refer to these supernatural sons of God, as the "ten thousands of his holy ones," surrounding God's heavenly throne. Verse 7 affirms this heavenly assembly with the phrase, "above all who are around him," and verse 8 contextualizes it with the phrase, "LORD God of hosts," which also refers to the heavenly host.

"Daniel calls these heavenly holy ones "watchers" in Daniel 4 (verses 13, 17, and 23) and the New Testament book of Jude quotes the non-canonical book of Enoch regarding God coming with ten thousand of his holy ones who were also these sons of God from heaven (Jude 14). The Dead Sea Scrolls of Qumran also uses the term "holy ones" in many passages to refer to angelic beings from God's heavenly throne, making this a common Semitic understanding congenial with the worldview of Daniel.

"So there is Biblical unanimity in describing a heavenly host of ten thousands of sons of God, called gods, watchers, and holy ones who surround God's throne in the heavens as an assembly, and who counsel with God and worship him, and some of whom were given to rule over human nations in the past (also called "demons"), but have lost that privilege at some point. These gods are clearly not human judges on earth; they are supernatural elohim in the heavenly divine council." Brian Godawa, *When Giants Were Upon the Earth: The Watchers, the Nephilim, and the Biblical Cosmic War of the Seed* (Embedded Pictures, 2014), 52-57.

[4] **Aquila and Priscilla instructing Apollos in Corinth**: Acts 18:24–28 [24] Now a Jew named Apollos, a native of Alexandria, came to Ephesus. He was an eloquent man, competent in the Scriptures. [25] He had been instructed in the way of the Lord. And being fervent in spirit, he spoke and taught accurately the things concerning Jesus, though he knew only the baptism of John. [26] He began to speak boldly in the synagogue, but when Priscilla and Aquila heard him, they took him aside and explained to him the way of God more accurately. [27] And when he wished to cross to Achaia, the brothers encouraged him and wrote

to the disciples to welcome him. When he arrived, he greatly helped those who through grace had believed, [28] for he powerfully refuted the Jews in public, showing by the Scriptures that the Christ was Jesus.

CHAPTER 11

[1] **Caesarea in New Testament history**: "Like most coastal communities in NT times, Caesarea had a mixed population. When Pilate was procurator of Judea he lived in the governor's residence at Caesarea. Philip preached in the city (Acts 8:40), which was also his home (Acts 21:8); and it was here that Peter was sent to minister to the Roman centurion Cornelius (10:1, 24; 11:11). Herod Agrippa resided in the city and died there (12:19, 23). Paul passed through Caesarea several times, making it his port of landing on his return from his second and third missionary journeys (18:22; 21:8). At Caesarea he made his fateful decision to visit Jerusalem (21:13), and to that city he returned under guard prior to his appearance before Felix (23:23ff). After two years of imprisonment Paul made his defense before Festus and Agrippa II in Caesarea, and sailed from there as a prisoner when sent by Festus to Rome on his own appeal (25:11)." W. Ewing and R. K. Harrison, "Caesarea," ed. Geoffrey W. Bromiley, *The International Standard Bible Encyclopedia, Revised* (Wm. B. Eerdmans, 1979–1988), 569.

"Little is known about the Caesarean church during the remainder of the procuratorial period. Paul made recurrent visits to the city indicate its continued importance. This Christian community together with Jerusalem and Antioch had been regarded as one of the centers of the primitive Church, prior to the outbreak of the war in 66." Lee I Levine, *Caesarea under Roman Rule* (Studies in Judaism in late antiquity) (Brill, 1975), 26.

For a good description of Caesarea during the first century: Lee I Levine, *Caesarea under Roman Rule* (Studies in Judaism in late antiquity) (Brill, 1975), 15-33.

[2] **Half the population of Caesarea was Jewish**: Lee I Levine, *Caesarea under Roman Rule* (Studies in Judaism in late antiquity) (Brill, 1975), 22.

[3] **The riots of Caesarea, the start of the revolt**: "Now at this time it happened that the Grecians at Caesarea had been too hard for the Jews, and had obtained of Nero the government of the city, and had brought the judicial determination: at the same time began the war, in the twelfth year of the reign of Nero, and the seventeenth of the reign of Agrippa, in the month of Artemissus [Jyar]. (285) Now the occasion of this war was by no means proportionable to those heavy calamities which it brought upon us; for the Jews that dwelt at Caesarea had a synagogue near the place, whose owner was a certain Cesarean Greek; the Jews had endeavored frequently to have purchased the possession of the place, and had offered many times its value for its price; (286) but as the owner overlooked their offers, so did he raise other buildings upon the place, in way of affront to them, and made workingshops of them, and left them but a narrow passage, and such as was very troublesome for them to go along to their synagogue; whereupon the warmer part of the Jewish youth went hastily to the workmen, and forbade them to build there; (287) but as Florus would not permit them to use force, the great men of the Jews, with John the publican, being in the utmost distress what to do, persuaded Florus, with the offer of eight talents, to hinder the work. (288) He then, being intent upon nothing but getting money, promised he would do for them all they desired of him, and then went away from Caesarea to Sebaste, and left the sedition to take its full course, as if he had sold a license to the Jews to fight it out.

"5. (289) Now on the next day, which was the seventh day of the week, when the Jews were crowding apace to their synagogue, a certain man of Caesarea, of a seditious temper, got an earthen vessel, and set it, with the bottom upward, at the entrance of that synagogue, and sacrificed birds. This thing provoked the Jews to an incurable degree, because their laws were affronted, and the place was polluted; (290) whereupon the sober and moderate part of the Jews thought it proper to have recourse to their governors again, while the seditious part, and such as were in the fervor of their youth, were vehemently inflamed to fight. The seditious also among [the Gentiles of] Caesarea stood ready for the same purpose, for they had, by agreement, sent the man to sacrifice beforehand [as ready to support him] so that it soon came to blows. (291) Hereupon Jucundus, the master of the horse, who was ordered to prevent the fight, came thither, and took away the earthen vessel, and endeavored to put a stop to the sedition; but when he was overcome by the violence of the people of Caesarea, the Jews caught up their books of the law, and retired to Narbata, which was a place to them belonging, distant from Caesarea sixty furlongs. (292) But John, and twelve of the principal men with him, went to Florus, to Sebaste, and made a lamentable complaint of their case, and besought him to help them; and with all possible decency, put him in mind of the eight talents they had given him; but he had the men seized upon and put in prison, and accused them for carrying the books of the law out of Caesarea." Flavius Josephus and William Whiston, *The Works of Josephus: Complete and Unabridged* (Peabody: Hendrickson, 1987). *The Wars of the Jews*, 2.284–292

[4] **The Kharabu warriors**: This term is a fictional construct of an elite group of fighters that originated in my novel *Enoch Primordial* and carried on into the rest of the *Chronicles of the Nephilim* series with poetic license. But it was based on the scholarly suggestion of archaeologist David Rohl, who argues that the cherubim may have been a mythological spiritualization of a very human tribe of sentinels called the Kheruba who guarded the Edenic paradise. David Rohl, *From Eden to Exile: The 5000-Year History of the People of the Bible*, (Lebanon, TN: Greenleaf Press, 2002), 31-32.

Did the Biblical writers draw from their ancient Near Eastern neighbors for their concepts of the cherubim or were they distorted pagan memories of the "myth that was true"?

But that's not all. Genesis 3:24 says that the cherubim guard the Tree of Life with "the flame of the whirling sword." Scholar Ronald Hendel has argued that "the 'flame' is an animate divine being, a member of Yahweh's divine host, similar in status to the cherubim; the 'whirling sword' is its appropriate weapon, ever-moving, like the flame itself." Ronald S. Hendel, "'The Flame of the Whirling Sword': A Note on Genesis 3:24," *Journal of Biblical Literature*, Vol. 104, No. 4 (Dec., 1985), pp. 671-674.

Scholar P.D. Miller appeals to passages such as Psalm 104:4 where "fire and flame" are described as "Yahweh's ministers" to conclude a convergence of imagery with ancient Ugaritic texts that describe "fire and flame" as armed deities with flashing swords. He writes that "the cherubim and the flaming sword are probably to be recognized as a reflection of the Canaanite fiery messengers." Thus the Biblically strange, yet strangely Biblical presence in Enoch Primordial of the Cherubim and their divine fiery beings beside them brandishing whirling swords of flashing lightning. Patrick D. Miller, "Fire in the Mythology of Canaan and Israel," *Catholic Biblical Quarterly*, 27 no 3 Jl 1965, p 256-261.

I incorporated all these interpretations with poetic license into my novel *Enoch Primordial*, and the rest of my *Chronicles of the Nephilim* series to fictionalize the theology.

[5] **Paul's word regarding marriage and the impending tribulation**: 1 Corinthians 7:26–31 [26] I think that in view of the impending distress it is good for a person to remain as he is. [27] Are you bound to a wife? Do not seek to be free. Are you free from a wife? Do not seek a wife. [28] But if you do marry, you have not sinned, and if a betrothed woman marries, she has not sinned. Yet those who marry will have worldly troubles, and I would spare you that. [29] This is what I mean, brothers: the appointed time has grown very short. From now on, let those who have wives live as though they had none, [30] and those who mourn as though they were not mourning, and those who rejoice as though they were not rejoicing, and those who buy as though they had no goods, [31] and those who deal with the world as though they had no dealings with it. For the present form of this world is passing away.

CHAPTER 12

[1] **Sleeping arrangements at Qumran**: The members probably did not sleep in the actual settlement, but in the caves of Qumran and in tents outside the walled compound. Gary A. Rendsburg Ph.D., "Lecture 15: Daily Life at Qumran," The Great Courses, The Dead Sea Scrolls, (Rutgers University) Online: https://www.thegreatcoursesplus.com/the-dead-sea-scrolls

[2] **Baptisms for purification at Qumran**: *Cushman's Chronicles* blog, "Baptism Part 4: Common Judaism and Qumran…" Cushman draws from Qumran purity text scholars, Hannah Harrington, Stephen Pfann, Jodi Magness and others. https://cushmanschronicles.com/2011/05/06/baptism-part-four-common-judaism-and-qumran/

[3] **A voice crying in the wilderness and Qumran**: Isaiah 40:3 A voice cries: "In the wilderness prepare the way of the LORD; make straight in the desert a highway for our God.

"Both the Baptizer and the Qumranites shared a preference for prophecy, especially Isaiah (Mark 1:2–3; Matt 3:1–3; Luke 3:4; and esp. John 1:23). The Qumranites clearly and the Baptizer most likely focused upon a stunning and unique interpretation of Isa 40:3: "A Voice is calling: 'In the wilderness prepare the way of YHWH.'"

"The Qumranites clearly understood the verse to mean that the Voice calls the elect ones to come into the wilderness for a purpose (1QS 8.14):17 "In the wilderness prepare the way of the Lord" (or "the way of truth,"); cf. 4QS MS E frag. 1, col. 3:4). For the Qumranites Isa 40:3 has an eschatological purpose: they are to prepare "the way" for the final act of the Lord in the wilderness (1QS 8.13; cf. Luke 3:7–9; Matt 3:7–10). The Qumranites have separated "themselves from the session of the men of deceit in order to depart into the wilderness to prepare the way of the Lord" (1QS 8.13)." James Charlesworth, "John the Baptizer and the Dead Sea Scrolls," *The Bible and the Dead Sea Scrolls Volume Three: The Scrolls and Christian Origins*, Ed. James Charlesworth, (Baylor University Press, 2006), 6-7.

[4] **The number of Essenes in Israel**: "The Essenes were never numerous; Pliny fixed their number at some 4,000 in his day." "Essene" Encyclopaedia Brittanica, Online https://www.britannica.com/topic/Essene

[5] **Hasmoneans as the Congregation of Belial**: "The new apostates corrupted by power, wealth and Hellenism were Hasmonaean kings, Sadducean nobles and even Pharisees, 'seekers of smooth things', who had given up strict observance for an easier life. These formed 'an assembly of worthlessness and a Congregation of Belial', a false leadership that had broken the Holy Covenant, 'interpreters full of guile who led the people astray' and 'prevented the thirsty from drinking the draught of knowledge'." Faulkner, Neil (2012-09-30). *Apocalypse: The Great Jewish Revolt Against Rome AD 66-73* (K-Locations 1544-1547). Amberley Publishing. K-Edition.

See also: Gary A. Rendsburg Ph.D., "Lecture 4: The Historical Backdrop of Ancient Judaism," The Great Courses, The Dead Sea Scrolls, (Rutgers University) Online: https://www.thegreatcoursesplus.com/the-dead-sea-scrolls

"Interestingly, the Qumranians also denounced Jerusalem's priestly system for its murderous conduct: "God will condemn [the wicked priest] to destruction even as he himself planned to destroy the Poor. And as for that which He said, Because of the murders committed in the city and the violence done to the land, the explanation of this is (that) the city is Jerusalem, where the Wicked Priest committed abominable deeds and defiled the Sanctuary of God, and the violence done to the land, these are the towns of Judah where he stole goods of the Poor" (1QpHab 12:5-9).56 They also interpret Habakkuk 2:8 as follows: "Because you have plundered many nations, all the remnant of the people shall plunder you: interpreted this concerns the last Priests of Jerusalem, who shall amass money and wealth by plundering the peoples. But in the last days, their riches and booty shall be delivered into the hands of the army of the Kittim [Romans]" (1QpHab 9:5-7)." Kenneth L. Gentry, Jr., *The Divorce of Israel: A Redemptive-Historical Interpretation of Revelation Vol. 2* (Dallas, GA: Tolle Lege Press, 2016), 430-431.

[6] **War of the Sons of Light Against the Sons of Darkness**: Gary A. Rendsburg Ph.D., "Lecture 10: The War Scroll and Other Apocalyptic Texts," The Great Courses, The Dead Sea Scrolls, (Rutgers University) Online: https://www.thegreatcoursesplus.com/the-dead-sea-scrolls

"The War Scroll (1QM). This scroll consists of nineteen badly deteriorated columns. It was originally somewhat longer, but how much is now impossible to determine. The work is ostensibly a manual to guide the self-styled "Sons of Light" in a final eschatological war, in which they are to face, and eventually vanquish, the "Sons of Darkness." Nevertheless, the text is essentially a theological, not a military, composition.

"Among the topics the War Scroll treats are: preliminary preparations for the war; rules for the sounding and inscription of trumpets used to guide the course of the battle; the dimensions and inscriptions of shields and standards used; the battle array, including who may and may not participate in the conflict; the role of the priests and Levites; and the ebb and flow of the final battle against the Kitti,m (probably the Romans)." M. O. Wise, "Dead Sea Scrolls: General Introduction," ed. Craig A. Evans and Stanley E. Porter, *Dictionary of New Testament Background: A Compendium of Contemporary Biblical Scholarship* (Downers Grove, IL: InterVarsity Press, 2000), 255.

1QM 1.1–7 indicates that the Sons of Light will return from the wilderness (probably Qumran) to encamp in the wilderness of Jerusalem (1.3), after which the armies of the Sons of Light will go forth from Jerusalem (3.11; 7.4).

[7] **Tefillin and phylacteries**: The passage quoted is Deuteronomy 11:18–19. See also, Deuteronomy 6:8, Exodus 13:9, 16.

"A small box containing Scripture verses. One was bound on the forehead and another on the arm during prayer. The word "phylacteries" occurs in the Bible only in Mt. 23:5. The Greek word means "safeguard," "means of protection," "amulet," and as used in Mt. 23:5 is generally identified as the tefillin (lit "prayers"), small boxes containing Scripture verses and worn during prayer, although a less common view identifies the phylacteries of Mt. 23:5 as magical charms or amulets (e.g., Bowman, pp. 523–538; cf. Goodspeed's translation, "They wear wide Scripture texts as charms …"). Tefillin were worn by every adult male at the daily morning prayers in either the home or synagogue except on the Sabbath and high festivals, though originally they were probably worn all day." R. L. Omanson, "Phylactery," ed. Geoffrey W. Bromiley, *The International Standard Bible Encyclopedia, Revised* (Wm. B. Eerdmans, 1979–1988), 864.

[8] **Seekers of smooth things and the Kittim as the Romans**: "The new apostates corrupted by power, wealth and Hellenism were Hasmonaean kings, Sadducean nobles and even Pharisees, 'seekers of smooth things', who had given up strict observance for an easier life. These formed 'an assembly of worthlessness and a Congregation of Belial', a false leadership that had broken the Holy Covenant, 'interpreters full of guile who led the people astray' and 'prevented the thirsty from drinking the draught of knowledge'." Faulkner, Neil (2012-09-30). *Apocalypse: The Great Jewish Revolt Against Rome AD 66-73* (K-Locations 1544-1547). Amberley Publishing. K-Edition.

See also: Gary A. Rendsburg Ph.D., "Lecture 4: The Historical Backdrop of Ancient Judaism," *The Great Courses, The Dead Sea Scrolls*, (Rutgers University) Online: https://www.thegreatcoursesplus.com/the-dead-sea-scrolls

[9] **Morning prayers at Qumran were taken from fragments of the Dead Sea Scrolls, 4Q503-4Q509**: Florentino García Martínez and Eibert J. C. Tigchelaar, *"The Dead Sea Scrolls Study Edition (translations)"* (Leiden; New York: Brill, 1997–1998), 999-1007.

See also: Dennis T. Olson, "Daily and Festival Prayers at Qumran," *The Bible and the Dead Sea Scrolls Volume Two: The Dead Sea Scrolls and the Qumran Community*, Ed. James Charlesworth, (Baylor University Press, 2006), 301-315.

[10] **This description of a day at Qumran was drawn from**: Flavius Josephus, *The Wars of the Jews*, 2.8.5 and the Dead Sea Scrolls 1QS 6:4-6.

See also: Gary A. Rendsburg Ph.D., "Lecture 15: Daily Life at Qumran," *The Great Courses, The Dead Sea Scrolls*, (Rutgers University) Online: https://www.thegreatcoursesplus.com/the-dead-sea-scrolls

[11] **Qumran scriptorium**: Gary A. Rendsburg Ph.D., "Lecture 6: The Dead Sea Site of the Qumran Sect," *The Great Courses, The Dead Sea Scrolls*, (Rutgers University) Online: https://www.thegreatcoursesplus.com/the-dead-sea-scrolls

[12] **Enoch and Melchizedek in the Dead Sea scrolls**: The book of Enoch was extant in the DSS corpus. In 1Enoch we read of Enoch's journey to heaven as well as the war of the giants before the Flood.

11QMelchizedek is a famous scroll from Qumran that spoke of Melchizedek returning as the leader of armies to judge Belial and the fallen Sons of God. In part, it reads:

> 10 about him in the songs of David, who said: Ps 82:1 «Elohim will [st]and in the assem[bly of God,] in the midst of the gods he judges». And about him he sai[d: Ps 7:8–9 «And] above [it,]
> 11 to the heights, return: God will judge the peoples». As for what he sa[id: Ps 82:2 «How long will you] judge unjustly and show partia[lity] to the wicked? [Se]lah.»
> 12 Its interpretation concerns Belial and the spirits of his lot, wh[o …] turn[ing aside] from the commandments of God to [commit evil.]
> 13 But, Melchizedek will carry out the vengeance of Go[d's] judgments, [and on that day he will fr]e[e them from the hand of] Belial and from the hand of all the sp[irits of his lot.]
> 14 To his aid (shall come) all «the gods of [justice»; and h]e is the one w[ho …] all the sons of God, and … […]
> 15 This […] is the day of [peace about whi]ch he said [… through Isa]iah the prophet, who said: [Isa 52:7 «How] beautiful
> 16 upon the mountains are the feet [of] the messen[ger who] announces peace, the mess[enger of good who announces salvati]on, [sa]ying to Zion: your God [reigns.»]

Florentino García Martínez and Eibert J. C. Tigchelaar, *"The Dead Sea Scrolls Study Edition (translations)"* (Leiden; New York: Brill, 1997–1998), 1207–1209.

[13] **Psalms, Isaiah and Deuteronomy most read Scriptures at Qumran**: Gary A. Rendsburg Ph.D., "Lecture 11: Biblical Manuscripts at Qumran" *The Great Courses, The Dead Sea Scrolls*, (Rutgers University) Online: https://www.thegreatcoursesplus.com/the-dead-sea-scrolls

[14] **He is copying** Isaiah 53.

[15] **Two Messiahs and a prophet in the Dead Sea Scrolls**: CD–B Col. xix:10 "These shall escape in the age of the visitation; but those that remain shall be delivered up to the sword when there comes the messiah 11 of Aaron and Israel." Florentino García Martínez and Eibert J. C. Tigchelaar, *"The Dead Sea Scrolls Study Edition (translations)"* (Leiden; New York: Brill, 1997–1998), 577.

1QS Col. ix:11 "until the prophet comes, and the Messiahs of Aaron and Israel." Florentino García Martínez and Eibert J. C. Tigchelaar, *"The Dead Sea Scrolls Study Edition (translations)"* (Leiden; New York: Brill, 1997–1998), 93.

1QS Col. ix:10 "shall be ruled by the first directives which the men of the Community began to be taught 11 until the prophet comes, and the Messiahs of Aaron and Israel." Florentino García Martínez and Eibert J. C. Tigchelaar, *"The Dead Sea Scrolls Study Edition (translations)"* (Leiden; New York: Brill, 1997–1998), 93.

See also: CD–B Col. xx:1; 4Q266 Frag. 10 i:11. CD–A Col. xii:22-xiii:1.

Priestly Messiah and Kingly Messiah: 1Q28a ii:11-21.

Messiah in the Last Days to destroy the wicked:

4Q174 Frags. 1 i, 21, 2:11 I will be a father to him and he will be a son to me.» This (refers to the) «branch of David», who will arise with the Interpreter of the law who 12 [will rise up] in Zi[on in] the [l]ast days, as it is written: Amos 9:11 «I will raise up the hut of David which has fallen», This (refers to) «the hut of 13 David which has fall[en», w]hich he will raise upto save Israel.

4Q174 Frags. 1 i, 21, 2:18 Why ar]e the nations [in turmoil] and hatch the peoples [idle plots? The kings of the earth t]ake up [their posts and the ru]lers conspire together against YHWH and against 19 [his anointed one». Inter]pretation of the saying: [the kings of the na]tions [are in turmoil] and ha[tch idle plots against] the elect ones of Israel in the last days.

Florentino García Martínez and Eibert J. C. Tigchelaar, *"The Dead Sea Scrolls Study Edition (translations)"* (Leiden; New York: Brill, 1997–1998), 353-355.

See also: 4Q458 Frag. 2 ii:3-4.

Messiah as Melchizedek the high priest:

11QMelchizedek is a famous scroll from Qumran that spoke of Melchizedek returning as the leader of armies to judge Belial and the fallen Sons of God. In part, it reads:

> 10 about him in the songs of David, who said: Ps 82:1 «Elohim will [st]and in the assem[bly of God,] in the midst of the gods he judges». And about him he sai[d: Ps 7:8–9 «And] above [it,]
> 11 to the heights, return: God will judge the peoples». As for what he sa[id: Ps 82:2 «How long will you] judge unjustly and show partia[lity] to the wicked? [Se]lah.»
> 12 Its interpretation concerns Belial and the spirits of his lot, wh[o ...] turn[ing aside] from the commandments of God to [commit evil.]
> 13 But, Melchizedek will carry out the vengeance of Go[d's] judgments, [and on that day he will fr]e[e them from the hand of] Belial and from the hand of all the sp[irits of his lot.]
> 14 To his aid (shall come) all «the gods of [justice»; and h]e is the one w[ho ...] all the sons of God, and ... [...]
> 15 This [...] is the day of [peace about whi]ch he said [... through Isa]iah the prophet, who said: [Isa 52:7 «How] beautiful
> 16 upon the mountains are the feet [of] the messen[ger who] announces peace, the mess[enger of good who announces salvati]on, [sa]ying to Zion: your God [reigns.»]

Florentino García Martínez and Eibert J. C. Tigchelaar, *"The Dead Sea Scrolls Study Edition (translations)"* (Leiden; New York: Brill, 1997–1998), 1207–1209

[16] **Aaron here is reading from**: Isaiah 53:1-2, one of the most important messianic prophesies in the Old Testament.

Isaiah 53 [1] Who has believed what he has heard from us? And to whom has the arm of the LORD been revealed? [2] For he grew up before him like a young plant, and like a root out of dry ground; he had no form or majesty that we should look at him, and no beauty that we should desire him. [3] He was despised and rejected by men; a man of sorrows, and acquainted with grief; and as one from whom men hide their faces he was despised, and we esteemed him not. [4] Surely he has borne our griefs and carried our sorrows; yet we esteemed him stricken, smitten by God, and afflicted. [5] But he was pierced for our transgressions; he was crushed for our iniquities; upon him was the chastisement that brought us peace, and with his wounds we are healed. [6] All we like sheep have gone astray; we have turned—every one—to his own way; and the LORD has laid on him the iniquity of us all.

[7] He was oppressed, and he was afflicted, yet he opened not his mouth; like a lamb that is led to the slaughter, and like a sheep that before its shearers is silent, so he opened not his mouth. [8] By oppression and judgment he was taken away; and as for his generation, who considered that he was cut off out of the land of the living, stricken for the transgression of my people? [9] And they made his grave with the wicked and with a rich man in his death, although he had done no violence, and there was no deceit in his mouth.

[10] Yet it was the will of the LORD to crush him; he has put him to grief; when his soul makes an offering for guilt, he shall see his offspring; he shall prolong his days; the will of the LORD shall prosper in his hand. [11] Out of the anguish of his soul he shall see and be satisfied; by his knowledge shall the righteous one, my servant, make many to be accounted righteous, and he shall bear their iniquities. [12] Therefore I will divide him a portion with the many, and he shall divide the spoil with the strong, because he poured out his soul to death and was numbered with the transgressors; yet he bore the sin of many, and makes intercession for the transgressors.

[17] **The oldest example of Jews arguing for a collective interpretation of the servant** can be found in the second century apologetic work of Origen: Origen, Contra Celsum (i.e., Origen Against Celsus), bk. 1, chap. 55 (5:218). Since the Essenes of Qumran considered themselves the true remnant of Israel, it would make sense they might interpret themselves as that righteous collective suffering servant.

[18] **The Gabriel Stone or "Vision of Gabriel":** Israel Knohl, "'By Three Days, Live': Messiahs, Resurrection, and Ascent to Heaven in Hazon Gabriel," *The Journal of Religion*, Vol. 88, No. 2 (April 2008), pp. 147-158.

A recent discovery of an ancient text on stone called "Vision of Gabriel," dated to the first century B.C., has revealed a unique correspondence with the New Testament notion of Messiah rising after three days. This is much more explicit than any Old Testament reference to such a thing. This is not to say that the Vision of Gabriel should be considered Scripture. But it certainly adds outside corroboration to the understanding of the Jewish messianic hope fulfilled in Christ.

[19] **O Death, where is your sting?:** Hosea 13:14.

[20] **This description of a day at Qumran was drawn from:** Flavius Josephus, *The Wars of the Jews*, 2.8.5 and the Dead Sea Scrolls 1QS 6:4-6.

See also: Gary A. Rendsburg Ph.D., "Lecture 15: Daily Life at Qumran," *The Great Courses, The Dead Sea Scrolls,* (Rutgers University) Online: https://www.thegreatcoursesplus.com/the-dead-sea-scrolls.

CHAPTER 13

[1] **For a description of Herod's palace, see:** Flavius Josephus, *The Wars of the Jews*, 5.156-182.

[2] **Agrippa and Bernice incestuous relationship**: "Agrippa II's private life was not exemplary. His sister Bernice came to live with him after their uncle, who was also her second husband, Herod king of Chalcis, died in A.D. 48. Because of the rumors of incest, she resolved to marry Polemo of Cilicia, but shortly after this she returned to her relationship with her brother. This incestuous relationship became the common chatter in Rome (Ant. xx.7.3 [145–47]; Juvenal Satires vi.156–160)." H. W. Hoehner, "Herod," ed. Geoffrey W Bromiley, *The International Standard Bible Encyclopedia, Revised* (Wm. B. Eerdmans, 1979–1988), 697.

[3] For Florus and the riots of Caesarea described here, see: Flavius Josephus, *The Wars of the Jews*, 2.284-292.

[4] **Pilate's atrocities described here, and others**: Flavius Josephus, *The Wars of the Jews*, 2.169-177; *The Antiquities of the Jews*, 18.65-72.

CHAPTER 14

¹ **Ezekiel was called to prophesy judgment against Israel, who would not listen to him**: Ezekiel 3:4–7 ⁴ And he said to me, "Son of man, go to the house of Israel and speak with my words to them… ⁷ But the house of Israel will not be willing to listen to you, for they are not willing to listen to me: because all the house of Israel have a hard forehead and a stubborn heart.

² **These words of the old man, Joshua, are from**: Matthew 23:37-38, Luke 19:43-44 and 1Thes 2:16.

³ **These words of Joshua come from**: Matthew 3:1-3.

⁴ **These words of Joshua come from John the Baptist**: Matthew 3:7-12.

CHAPTER 15

¹ **Temple warning to Gentiles upon pain of death**: "Within a short distance, in the court, a marble screen 4½ feet high, and beautifully ornamented, bore Greek and Latin inscriptions, warning Gentiles not to proceed, on pain of death. One of those very tablets, bearing almost the same words as those given by Josephus, has been discovered in late excavations." Alfred Edersheim, *The Temple, Its Ministry and Services as They Were at the Time of Jesus Christ*. (London: James Clarke & Co., 1959), 46.

² **This description of the Court of Women and the treasury taken from**: Alfred Edersheim, "The Court of Women" and "The Chambers," *The Temple, Its Ministry and Services as They Were at the Time of Jesus Christ*. (London: James Clarke & Co., 1959), 48-50.

³ **This chapter is a creative condensation and simplification of the events described in**: Flavius Josephus, *The Wars of the Jews*, 2.293-308. I integrate Gischala into this scene for creative license purposes, but it still captures the spirit of what happened.

The actual order of the historical events is:
1) Florus goes to the temple treasury and takes 17 talents of gold under the false pretense that Caesar wanted them.
2) Some Jews mocked Florus by handing a basket to collect donations for Florus as if he were poor.
3) Florus is so insulted by the mockery that he sends 50 troops to Jerusalem to demand they hand over the culprits of the prank.
4) The Jews ask for forgiveness on behalf of the pranksters, but protect them from discovery. Most likely one of them was a son of the high priests.
5) Florus sends his men into the Upper Marketplace where they killed 3600 men, women and children. He had some of the men crucified.

¹ **Cassandra quotes from the following passages**: Romans 1:16 For I am not ashamed of the gospel, for it is the power of God for salvation to everyone who believes, to the Jew first and also to the Greek.

Zechariah 12:10–11 ¹⁰ "And I will pour out on the house of David and the inhabitants of Jerusalem a spirit of grace and pleas for mercy, so that, when they look on me, on him whom they have pierced, they shall mourn for him, as one mourns for an only child, and weep bitterly over him, as one weeps over a firstborn. ¹¹ On that day the mourning in Jerusalem will be as great as the mourning for Hadad-rimmon in the plain of Megiddo.

Revelation 1:7 Behold, he is coming with the clouds, and every eye will see him, even those who pierced him, and all tribes of the earth will wail on account of him.

² **Cassandra is quoting from**: Acts 2:23; 1Corinthians 2:8; John 8:4; Matthew 8:11-12; Romans 2:3.

³ **Alexander is quoting from:** Matthew 16:27-28 and 26:64.

⁴ **Know not the day or the hour**: Matthew 24:36.

⁵ **The last hour had arrived**: 1John 2:18.

Jesus was "coming soon" to the first century: Revelation 1:1, 3; 2:26; 3:11; 22:6, 7, 10, 12, 20.

⁶ Demetrius' words of the gospel of "loving one another" come from John's admonitions: 1John 3:11, 23; 4:7, 12; 2John 5.

CHAPTER 17

[1] **These words the lector reads are from**: Revelation 22.

[2] **The Time of the End is distant for Daniel, but near for John**: Revelation 22:10 And he said to me, "Do not seal up the words of the prophecy of this book, for the time is near.

Daniel 12:4 But you, Daniel, shut up the words and seal the book, until the time of the end.

[3] **Skepticism of Johannine authorship of Revelation**: "Differences in writing style (grammar, vocabulary, etc.) from the Johannine Gospel and Epistles cannot be determinative for nonapostolic authorship because such variation would be expected in a writing of a different (apocalyptic-prophetic) genre. Furthermore, differences of occasion and purpose in writing can significantly affect writing style." G. K. Beale, *The Book of Revelation: A Commentary on the Greek Text, New International Greek Testament Commentary* (Grand Rapids, MI; Carlisle, Cumbria: W.B. Eerdmans; Paternoster Press, 1999), 34–35.

The elder Boaz here is wrong. The Revelation does in fact reflect Johanine literary technique: "In fact, the fingerprints of the apostle are all over the apocalypse! One need only open their eyes and ears to apprehend the clues. For example, John, and John alone, identifies Jesus as the Word, or Logos (John 1:1, 14; Revelation 19:13). Likewise, John alone identifies Jesus as the true witness (John 5:31–47; 8:14–18; Revelation 2:13; 3:14), and it is John who most exploits the Mosaic requirement of two witnesses (John 8:12–30; Revelation 11:1–12). Other exclusive parallels between the Gospel of John and Revelation include Jesus's invitation to all who are thirsty to come to him and drink (e.g., John 7:37; Revelation 22:17) and Jesus's reference to his having received authority from his Father (e.g., John 10:18; Revelation 2:27).

"Additional similarities that are not exclusive to John but are clearly parallel in the gospel and the Apocalypse include white garments symbolizing holiness (John 20:12; e.g., Revelation 3:4) and reference to Jesus as the Lamb of God (John 1:29, 36; Revelation 5:6, 8, 12, et al.). More significantly, both the Gospel of John and Revelation present an explicitly high Christology, such that Jesus is God in the flesh and worthy of worship. In fact, it is in these two books that we find perhaps the clearest passages of the divinity of Christ in all of Scripture (see, e.g., John 1:1–3, 14, 18; 20:28; Revelation 4–5).

"Added to all this, there is an undeniable commonality in the symbolic use of the number seven. Says Guthrie: "The Apocalypse is constructed on this pattern and so is the Fourth Gospel (cf. for instance its seven 'signs,' its seven-day opening of the Lord's ministry, its seven-day account of the passion story). This characteristic would not be so significant were it not confined in the New Testament to the Johannine writings."[85] David Chilton likewise points out that "both books are arranged in a series of 'sevens;' both are structured in terms of the Biblical/heavenly liturgy and festive calendar; and both books use numbers in a symbolic sense that transcends their literal significance" Hank Hanegraaff, *The Apocalypse Code: Find Out What the Bible REALLY Says About the End Times... and Why It Matters Today* (Thomas Nelson, 2007), 213.

[4] **All four Gospels (Indeed the whole New Testament) written before A.D. 70**: J.A.T. Robinson's classic, *Redating the New Testament,* remains a legitimate scholarly argument for the early date of all New Testament books written before A.D. 70. Though he was a liberal, he admitted the internal and external evidence warranted the conclusion.

"One of the oddest facts about the New Testament is that what on any showing would appear to be the single most datable and climactic event of the period - the fall of Jerusalem in ad 70, and with it the collapse of institutional Judaism based on the temple - is never once mentioned as a past fact...

"Explanations for this silence have of course been attempted. Yet the simplest explanation of all, that perhaps ... there is extremely little in the New Testament later than ad 70 [Moule, op. cit., 121.] and that its events are not mentioned because they had not yet occurred, seems to me to demand more attention than it has received in critical circles...

"The one conclusion we can draw so far is to agree with Reicke's opening statement that it is indeed 'an amazing example of uncritical dogmatism' that 'the synoptic gospels should be dated after the Jewish War of ad 66-70 because they contain prophecies ex eventu of the destruction of Jerusalem'. Indeed on these grounds alone one might reverse the burden of proof, and reissue Torrey's challenge, which he contended was never taken up:

"It is perhaps conceivable that one evangelist writing after the year 70 might fail to allude to the destruction of the temple by the Roman armies (every reader of the Hebrew Bible knew that the Prophets had definitely predicted that foreign armies would surround the city and destroy it), but that three (or four) should thus fail is quite incredible. [Wink, USQR 26, 48, poses a similar question to Brandon who wishes to put Mark after 70: 'Is it really conceivable that Mark should fail to mention, even by allusion in a single instance, an event so traumatic that it is alleged to be the sole motification for his undertaking to write his gospel?'] On the contrary, what is shown is that all four Gospels were written before the year 70. And indeed, there is no evidence of any sort that will bear examination tending to show that any of the Gospels were written later than about the middle of the century. The challenge to scholars to produce such evidence is hereby presented. [C. C. Torrey, The Apocalypse of John, New Haven, Conn., 1958, 86, quoting his earlier book, The Four Gospels, New York 21947.]"

John A.T. Robinson, *Redating the New Testament*, Online text prepared by Paul Ingram and Todd Dennis, (1976), "II: The Significance of 70."

[5] **For book length treatments on the fulfillment of Matthew 24 during the first century**: Gary DeMar, *Last Days Madness: Obsession of the Modern Church,* Wolgemuth & Hyatt Pub; 4th Revised edition (September 1999); Kenneth L. Gentry, Jr., *The Olivet Discourse Made Easy*, (Apologetics Group. 2010); John L. Bray, *Matthew 24 Fulfilled*, (American Vision; 5th Edition, 2009).

[6] **Jesus prophesied that his coming would occur during the lives of the current generation**: Matthew 16:27–28 [27] For the Son of Man is going to come with his angels in the glory of his Father, and then he will repay each person according to what he has done. [28] Truly, I say to you, there are some standing here who will not taste death until they see the Son of Man coming in his kingdom."

Matthew 26:63–64 [63] But Jesus remained silent. And the high priest said to him, "I adjure you by the living God, tell us if you are the Christ, the Son of God." [64] Jesus said to him, "You have said so. But I tell you, from now on you will see the Son of Man seated at the right hand of Power and coming on the clouds of heaven."

Matthew 10:22–23 [22] and you will be hated by all for my name's sake. But the one who endures to the end will be saved. [23] When they persecute you in one town, flee to the next, for truly, I say to you, you will not have gone through all the towns of Israel before the Son of Man comes.

Matthew 16:27–28 [27] For the Son of Man is going to come with his angels in the glory of his Father, and then he will repay each person according to what he has done. [28] Truly, I say to you, there are some standing here who will not taste death until they see the Son of Man coming in his kingdom."

Matthew 26:63–64 [63] But Jesus remained silent. And the high priest said to him, "I adjure you by the living God, tell us if you are the Christ, the Son of God." [64] Jesus said to him, "You have said so. But I tell you, from now on you will see the Son of Man seated at the right hand of Power and coming on the clouds of heaven."

In Revelation:

• "The things that *must shortly take place*" (1:1).
• "For the time is *near*" (1:3).
• "I am coming to you *quickly*" (2:16).
• "I am coming *quickly*" (3:11).
• "The third woe is coming *quickly*" (11:14).
• "The things which must *shortly take place*" (22:6).
• "Behold, I am coming *quickly*" (22:7).
• "For the time is *near*" (22:10).
• "Behold, I am coming *quickly*" (22:12).
• "Yes, I am coming *quickly*" (22:20)
Gary DeMar, *Left Behind: Separating Fact from Fiction* (Powder Springs, GA: American Vision, 2009), 123–124.

[7] **"The fathers have died" is not a reference to the Patriarchal fathers but the fathers of the New Covenant:** 2 Peter 3:4 They will say, "Where is the promise of his coming? For ever since the fathers fell asleep, all things are continuing as they were from the beginning of creation."

1 Clement 23.3-5 "Let this scripture be far from us where He saith; Wretched are the double-minded, which doubt in their soul and say, These things we did hear in the days of our fathers also, and behold we have grown old, and none of these things hath befallen us. 4Ye fools, compare yourselves unto a tree; take a vine. First it sheddeth its leaves, then a shoot cometh, then a leaf, then a flower, and after these a sour berry, then a full ripe grape. Ye see that in a little time the fruit of the tree attaineth unto mellowness.

5Of a truth quickly and suddenly shall His will be accomplished, the scripture also bearing witness to it, saying; He shall come quickly and shall not tarry; and the Lord shall come suddenly into His temple, even the Holy One, whom ye expect." Joseph Barber Lightfoot and J. R. Harmer, *The Apostolic Fathers* (London: Macmillan and Co., 1891), 67–68. See also: 2 Clem 11:1–7; Herm. Vis. 3:4:3; 3:5:1; 3:8:9.

"The scoffers are saying: "The Parousia was promised before the death of the fathers. Well, the fathers have died and still nothing happens." (2) Second Peter does not answer the objection that a specific time-limit has passed. The reason for this may be that the author does no more than reproduce the answers to the problem of eschatological delay which he found in his Jewish apocalyptic source, and these answers were, of course, designed to meet the general problem of eschatological delay rather than the specifically Christian problem of nonfulfillment within the lifetime of the apostles." Richard J. Bauckham, *2 Peter, Jude, vol. 50, Word Biblical Commentary* (Dallas: Word, Incorporated, 1998), 291–292.

[8] **Did John live past the Tribulation of AD 64-68?:** "about the Apostle John. For when, on the tyrant's death, he returned to Ephesus from the isle of Patmos, he went away, being invited, to the contiguous territories of the nations." *Clement of Rome, Who is the Rich Man That Shall Be Saved?* 42. http://www.earlychristianwritings.com/text/clement-richman.html. Though Eusebius assumes the tyrant here is Trajan, why would it not be Nero, the tyrant on the throne at the time of John?

Jesus prophesied that both James and John would be martyred: Mark 10:35-40 And James and John, the sons of Zebedee, came up to him and said to him, "Teacher, we want you to do for us whatever we ask of you." 36 And he said to them, "What do you want me to do for you?" 37 And they said to him, "Grant us to sit, one at your right hand and one at your left, in your glory." 38 Jesus said to them, "You do not know what you are asking. Are you able to drink the cup that I drink, or to be baptized with the baptism with which I am baptized?" 39 And they said to him, "We are able." And Jesus said to them, "The cup that I drink you will drink, and with the baptism with which I am baptized, you will be baptized, 40 but to sit at my right hand or at my left is not mine to grant, but it is for those for whom it has been prepared."

"Of course, the death of Jesus was uniquely vicarious for sin (Mark 10:45; cf. Ps 49:7). Nevertheless, the cup Jesus spoke of cannot be separated from his death, for that is the manner in which the debt was paid. To say that James and John would drink the cup meant that they would share his fate. Their deaths would have a different effect, but they would be martyred nonetheless." Sean McDowell, *A Historical Evaluation Of The Evidence For The Death Of The Apostles As Martyrs For Their Faith* (Dissertation, The Southern Baptist Theological Seminary, 2014), 249.

"Irenaeus writes: "We will not, however, incur the risk of pronouncing positively as to the name of Antichrist; for if it were necessary that his name should be distinctly revealed in this present time, it would have been announced by him who beheld the apocalyptic vision. For that was seen no very long time since, but almost in our day, towards the end of Domitian's reign…

"Indisputably, the most serious potential objection to the common translation has to do with the understanding of [the Greek words for], "was seen." What is the subject of this verb? Is it "him who saw the Apocalypse" (i.e., John) or "the Apocalypse"? Which of these two antecedents "was seen" "almost" in Irenaeus's time and near "the end of the reign of Domitian"? …Irenaeus twice elsewhere says John lived to Trajan's reign, not just to Domitian's." Kenneth Gentry, *Before Jerusalem Fell* (Institute for Christian Economics, 1989), 47-49, 54.

Gentry argues convincingly that Irenaeus was referring to John being seen around the time of Domitian. But even if Irenaeus meant the Revelation, in either case, John lived past AD 70, so his martyrdom would have been after Domitian and maybe even into Trajan's reign.

[9] **They were in the last hour of the last days:** 1 John 2:18 Children, it is the last hour, and as you have heard that antichrist is coming, so now many antichrists have come. Therefore we know that it is the last hour.

Hebrews 1:1–2 Long ago, at many times and in many ways, God spoke to our fathers by the prophets, [2] but in these last days he has spoken to us by his Son, whom he appointed the heir of all things, through whom also he created the world.

1 Peter 1:20 He was foreknown before the foundation of the world but was made manifest in the last times for the sake of you.

384

The Last Days occurred in the first century during the time of Christ: Hebrews 1:1–2 Long ago, at many times and in many ways, God spoke to our fathers by the prophets, 2 but in these last days he has spoken to us by his Son, whom he appointed the heir of all things, through whom also he created the world.

Hebrews 9:26 But as it is, he has appeared once for all at the end of the ages to put away sin by the sacrifice of himself.

1 Peter 1:20 He was foreknown before the foundation of the world but was made manifest in the last times for the sake of you

Acts 2:16–17 But this is what was uttered through the prophet Joel: 17 " 'And in the last days it shall be, God declares, that I will pour out my Spirit on all flesh…

1 Corinthians 10:11 [11] Now these things happened to them as an example, but they were written down for our instruction, on whom the end of the ages has come.

Hebrews 10:24–25 [24] And let us consider how to stir up one another to love and good works, [25] not neglecting to meet together, as is the habit of some, but encouraging one another, and all the more as you see the Day drawing near.

The Last Days: "One of the first things a Christian must learn in interpreting the Bible is to pay attention to the time texts. Failing to recognize the proximity of a prophetic event will distort its intended meaning. The New Testament clearly states that the "end of all things" was at hand for those who first read 1 Peter 4:7; that is, the Old Covenant with its types and shadows was about to pass away. The Book of Hebrews opens with two verses that put the timing of certain eschatological events into perspective: "God, after He spoke long ago to the fathers in the prophets in many portions and in many ways, in these last days has spoken to us in His Son, whom He appointed heir of all things, through whom also He made the world" (Heb. 1:1–2). Prior to the coming of Jesus, God spoke via dreams, prophets, written revelation, and types. Through the New Covenant God "has made the first obsolete. But whatever is becoming obsolete and growing old is ready [lit., near] to disappear" (8:13).

"The New Covenant is better than the Old Covenant because the blood of Jesus is better than the blood of animals (Heb. 7:22; 8:6). In addition, the way God communicates with His people has changed. For example, under the Old Covenant no man could look upon the face of God and live (Ex. 33:20). At the dawning of the New Covenant, however, God was no longer hidden. He had taken on human flesh in the person of Jesus Christ…

"God spoke in this new way "in these last days." The last days were in operation in the first century when God was manifested in the flesh in the person of Jesus Christ! Those Hebrew Christians who read the letter addressed to them were being told that an important covenantal era was about to end, the era of "the fathers in the prophets." The proof that the last days had come was that God "has spoken in His Son." The last days are not way off in the distant future. The end came to an obsolete covenant in the first century.

"In A.D. 70 the "last days" ended with the dissolution of the temple and the sacrificial system. A similar pronouncement is made in 1 Peter 1:20: "For He was foreknown before the foundation of the world, but has appeared in these last times for the sake of you." Gordon Clark comments on what Peter means by "these last times": " 'The last days,' which so many people think refers to what is still future at the end of this age, clearly means the time of Peter himself. 1 John 2:18 says it is, in his day, the last hour. Acts 2:17 quotes Joel as predicting the last days as the life time of Peter." Gary DeMar, *Last Days Madness: Obsession of the Modern Church, Fourth revised edition* (Powder Springs, GA: American Vision, 1999), 37–38.

[10] **The debate in this chapter reflects the content of 2Peter 2 and 3**: Peter's Day of the Lord was the destruction of Jerusalem and the temple. Those who denied that the judgment was coming could very well be those Judaizers who claimed that the Torah requirements still held. For a detailed explanation of this, see "Appendix: The Day of the Lord in 2Peter" in Brian Godawa, *End Times Bible Prophecy: It's Not What They Told You* (Los Angeles, CA: Embedded Pictures Publishing, 2017) 165-168.

[11] **When Jeremiah prophesied destruction of the temple, false prophets declared he was blaspheming the house of Yahweh**: Jeremiah 6:13–14 "For from the least to the greatest of them, everyone is greedy for unjust gain; and from prophet to priest, everyone deals falsely. 14 They have healed the wound of my people lightly, saying, 'Peace, peace,' when there is no peace.

[12] John the apostle wrote that he and the first century Christians were in the great tribulation and the antichrist persecution they experienced was prophesied:

Revelation 1:9 I, John, your brother and partner in the tribulation and the kingdom and the patient endurance that are in Jesus, was on the island called Patmos on account of the word of God and the testimony of Jesus.

Revelation 3:10 Because you have kept my word about patient endurance, I will keep you from the hour of trial that is coming on the whole world, to try those who dwell on the earth.

1 John 2:18 Children, it is the last hour, and as you have heard that antichrist is coming, so now many antichrists have come. Therefore we know that it is the last hour.

1 John 2:22 Who is the liar but he who denies that Jesus is the Christ? This is the antichrist, he who denies the Father and the Son.

1 John 4:3 and every spirit that does not confess Jesus is not from God. This is the spirit of the antichrist, which you heard was coming and now is in the world already.

2 John 7 For many deceivers have gone out into the world, those who do not confess the coming of Jesus Christ in the flesh. Such a one is the deceiver and the antichrist.

[13] **The blessings and curses of the covenant used as an argument against the Christians**: Jacob is referring to Deuteronomy 28 that lists the blessings and curses in detail that the Jews would experience based on obedience to Torah or not. This is a dominant theme throughout Deuteronomy as well (Deuteronomy 4:1, 10, 40; 5:29-33; 6:1-2, 18, 24; 7:12-13).

Deuteronomy 28:1–2 [1] "And if you faithfully obey the voice of the LORD your God, being careful to do all his commandments that I command you today, the LORD your God will set you high above all the nations of the earth. [2] And all these blessings shall come upon you and overtake you, if you obey the voice of the LORD your God.

Deuteronomy 28:15–16 [15] "But if you will not obey the voice of the LORD your God or be careful to do all his commandments and his statutes that I command you today, then all these curses shall come upon you and overtake you. [16] Cursed shall you be in the city, and cursed shall you be in the field.

Deuteronomy 28:25 "The LORD will cause you to be defeated before your enemies. You shall go out one way against them and flee seven ways before them. And you shall be a horror to all the kingdoms of the earth.

[14] **The false teachers that Peter wrote about were very likely Judaizers**: "There are a number of reasons for believing that Peter's opponents are either Judaizers, Jewish believers within the church who want to stuff the New Covenant into Old Covenant wineskins, or Jewish Christians who have abandoned Christ to return to Judaism outright. Several lines of evidence lead to this conclusion. First, there is the general fact that the main threat to Christianity in the first century came from Judaism. Most of the persecution recorded in the book of Acts comes at the hands of Jews, rather than Romans, and Peter is describing teachers who not only mislead but persecute the faithful. In Paul's ministry, the main threat to the purity of the gospel came from Judaizers and Jews. To be more specific, Peter is dealing with apostates: the false teachers "deny the Master who bought them" (2 Pet. 2:1), and having escaped the "defilements of the world by the knowledge of the Lord and Savior Jesus Christ," they now "are again entangled in them and are overcome" (v. 20). Throughout the New Testament, however, the great apostasy was not reversion to paganism but reversion to Judaism. Especially under threat of persecution, many believers found a safe haven in Judaism, which was recognized as a legal religion in the first century, and this problem is addressed extensively in the letter to the Hebrews. Thus it is prima facie plausible that Peter is dealing with similar opponents.

"There also appears to be a veiled reference to the decision of the council of Jerusalem in the descriptions of the churches' opponents in Revelation. At the council, the elders and apostles decided that they would not impose the ceremonies of the law on Gentile believers beyond the prohibitions required of Gentiles in the Old Covenant: "that you abstain from things sacrificed to idols and from blood and from things strangled and from fornication" (Acts 15:29). When Jesus says in His letters to the churches that Jezebel and Balaam and the false Jews are encouraging Christians to "eat things sacrificed to idols" and to "fornicate," He is saying that they are violating the terms of the Jerusalem Council. In short, this is a provocative way of saying that they are Judaizers.

"Against this background, Peter's charge that the false prophets engaged in sensuality, reveling, and greed takes on a metaphorical coloration. It is likely that Peter was charging false prophets with literal violations of the Ten Commandments, but in the New Testament these sins are related to Judaizing and Judaism.

"Twice Peter charges the false teachers with "fleshliness" and indulgence in the "lusts of the flesh" (2 Pet. 2:10, 18). Modern readers tend to interpret "flesh" as "bodily appetites," especially sexual desires, but "flesh" normally has a very different connotation in the New Testament. On the one hand, it describes the condition of all men in Adam and indeed the entire Old Covenant order, which is a fleshly order in contrast to the New Covenant order of the Spirit. More specifically, Paul frequently connects the "flesh" of circumcision with the "fleshly" interests of the Jews. Judaizers want to be perfected by the flesh (Gal. 3:3) and insist that Gentiles can be perfected only through the fleshly rite of circumcision (Gal. 5:13). Obsession with a ritual that is quite literally "fleshly" is connected with the "fleshly" behavior described in Galatians 5:19–21. When we read the list of the "works of the flesh," we cannot forget that Paul has consistently been describing the Jews and Judaizers as "fleshly." The "works of the flesh," appalling as they might be, are primarily descriptions of the behavior of Judaizers." Peter J. Leithart, *The Promise of His Appearing: An Exposition of Second Peter* (Moscow, ID: Canon Press, 2004), 52–53; 59–61.

"There is plenty of evidence in the Scriptures . . . that there was a group of [false] Christian leaders who claimed to have the anointing (messiah) of apostles, who claimed to be prophets and teachers, and who did indeed mislead many believers. They were a constant danger in the apostolic era, and a great deal of Paul's writings in particular deal with their deceptions. We are thinking, of course, of the Judaizers. The Judaizers were the heirs of the tradition-serving Jewish teachers who were Jesus' worst enemy. The Judaizers are the constant enemy in Acts and the epistles. They are the anti-christs of the Johannine letters, who claimed to have been sent out by the apostles but who were not "of us" (1 John 2:18-19; 4:1). They are the main enemy in the book of Revelation." Gary DeMar, *Identifying the REAL Last Days Scoffers* (Atlanta GA: American Vision, 2012), 150.

[15] **Cassandra is quoting from Galatians regarding the Judaizer doctrines**: Galatians 3:1–3 [1] O foolish Galatians! Who has bewitched you? It was before your eyes that Jesus Christ was publicly portrayed as crucified. [2] Let me ask you only this: Did you receive the Spirit by works of the law or by hearing with faith? [3] Are you so foolish? Having begun by the Spirit, are you now being perfected by the flesh? [fleshly obedience to Torah]

Galatians 4:9 But now that you have come to know God, or rather to be known by God, how can you turn back again to the weak and worthless elementary principles of the world, whose slaves you want to be once more?

"Weak and worthless principles of dead covenant": See note below about *Stoicheia*.

Peter refers to Jewish heresy as "dog returning to its vomit": 2 Peter 2:20–22 [20] For if, after they have escaped the defilements of the world through the knowledge of our Lord and Savior Jesus Christ, they are again entangled in them and overcome, the last state has become worse for them than the first. [21] For it would have been better for them never to have known the way of righteousness than after knowing it to turn back from the holy commandment delivered to them. [22] What the true proverb says has happened to them: "The dog returns to its own vomit, and the sow, after washing herself, returns to wallow in the mire."

The Last Days occurred in the first century during the time of Christ: Hebrews 1:1–2 Long ago, at many times and in many ways, God spoke to our fathers by the prophets, 2 but in **these last days** he has spoken to us by his Son, whom he appointed the heir of all things, through whom also he created the world.

Hebrews 9:26 But as it is, he has appeared once for all at the end of the ages to put away sin by the sacrifice of himself.

1 Peter 1:20 He was foreknown before the foundation of the world but was made manifest in the last times for the sake of you

Acts 2:16–17 But this is what was uttered through the prophet Joel: 17 " 'And in the last days it shall be, God declares, that I will pour out my Spirit on all flesh…

1 Corinthians 10:11 [11] Now these things happened to them as an example, but they were written down for our instruction, on whom the end of the ages has come.

Hebrews 10:24–25 [24] And let us consider how to stir up one another to love and good works, [25] not neglecting to meet together, as is the habit of some, but encouraging one another, and all the more as you see the Day drawing near.

[16] **Cassandra is quoting from**: John 16:2–4 [2] They will put you out of the synagogues. Indeed, the hour is coming when whoever kills you will think he is offering service to God. [3] And they will do these things because they have not known the Father, nor me. [4] But I have said these things to you, that when their hour comes you may remember that I told them to you.

[17] **Scoffers doubting Christ's coming in the first century**: 2 Peter 3:3–4 [3] knowing this first of all, that scoffers will come in the last days with scoffing, following their own sinful desires. [4] They will say, "Where is the promise of his coming? For ever since the fathers fell asleep, all things are continuing as they were from the beginning of creation."

1 Peter 4:7 The end of all things is at hand; therefore be self-controlled and sober-minded for the sake of your prayers.

1 Peter 1:5 who by God's power are being guarded through faith for a salvation ready to be revealed in the last time.

False teachers would plague the Church: 2 Peter 2:1–3 [1] But false prophets also arose among the people, just as there will be false teachers among you, who will secretly bring in destructive heresies, even denying the Master who bought them, bringing upon themselves swift destruction. [2] And many will follow their sensuality, and because of them the way of truth will be blasphemed. [3] And in their greed they will exploit you with false words. Their condemnation from long ago is not idle, and their destruction is not asleep.

Doctrines of demons include a return to dietary restrictions, like that in Torah: 1 Timothy 4:1–3 [1] Now the Spirit expressly says that in later times some will depart from the faith by devoting themselves to deceitful spirits and teachings of demons, [2] through the insincerity of liars whose consciences are seared, [3] who forbid marriage and require abstinence from foods that God created to be received with thanksgiving by those who believe and know the truth.

[18] **Jacob refers to early church reactions to the coming destruction**: Acts 4:32 Now the full number of those who believed were of one heart and soul, and no one said that any of the things that belonged to him was his own, but they had everything in common.

Paul wrote about this same issue of avoiding marriage, though closer to A.D. 70: 1 Corinthians 7:26–29 [26] I think that in view of the present distress it is good for a person to remain as he is. [27] Are you bound to a wife? Do not seek to be free. Are you free from a wife? Do not seek a wife. [28] But if you do marry, you have not sinned, and if a betrothed woman marries, she has not sinned. Yet those who marry will have worldly troubles, and I would spare you that. [29] This is what I mean, brothers: the appointed time has grown very short.

[19] **Women keep silent in the context of a church assembly of worship**: 1 Corinthians 14:33–35 [33] For God is not a God of confusion but of peace. As in all the churches of the saints, [34] the women should keep silent in the churches. For they are not permitted to speak, but should be in submission, as the Law also says. [35] If there is anything they desire to learn, let them ask their husbands at home. For it is shameful for a woman to speak in church.

[20] **Cassandra is quoting from**: 2 Peter 3:8–9 [8] But do not overlook this one fact, beloved, that with the Lord one day is as a thousand years, and a thousand years as one day. [9] The Lord is not slow to fulfill his promise as some count slowness, but is patient toward you, not wishing that any should perish, but that all should reach repentance.

For a detailed explanation of 2Peter Day of the Lord as a reference to the destruction of Jerusalem: see "Appendix: The Day of the Lord in 2Peter" in Brian Godawa, *End Times Bible Prophecy: It's Not What They Told You* (Los Angeles, CA: Embedded Pictures Publishing, 2017) 165-168.

[21] **Stoicheia**: In every place that *stoicheion* shows up in the New Testament it means elementary principle rudiments of a worldview, sometimes a godless worldview (Col. 2:8), but more often the elementary principles of the Old Covenant law described as a "cosmos" (Gal. .4:3; 9; Col. 2:20; Heb. 5:12).

Remember how the cosmic language of creating heavens and earth was used to describe the cosmic significance of God establishing a covenant? And remember how in the Old Testament, the destruction of covenants, nations, and peoples was described in *decreation* terms as the collapsing of the universe?

That is the case in these passages as well, with the term "cosmos" being used metaphorically for the "universe" of God's covenantal order as embodied in the Old Covenant laws of Jewish separation:

Circumcision, dietary restrictions and sabbaths. Paul is telling his readers that the *stoicheion* of the Old Covenant *cosmos* are no longer over them because the people of God are under new *stoicheion*, the elementary principles of faith (Gal. 4:1-11).

"Peter means the same thing. When he says that the heavens will pass away and the *stoicheion* will be burned up, he is claiming that when the Temple in Jerusalem is destroyed, it will be the final passing away of the Old Covenant cosmos, along with all the elementary principles tied to that physical sacramental structure, the laws that once separated Jew and Gentile. The new cosmos is one in which both Jew and Gentile "by God's power are being guarded through faith for a salvation ready to be revealed in the last time" (1 Pet. 1:5)." Leithart, Peter J. *The Promise of His Appearing: An Exposition of Second Peter*. Moscow, ID: Canon Press, 2004, p.101.

Stoichea and the elements: "Kittel's Theological Dictionary of New Testament Words observes that while in pagan literature the word is used in a number of different ways (referring to the "four elements" of the physical world, or to the "notes" on a musical scale, or to the "principles" of geometry or logic), the New Testament writers use the term "in a new way, describing the stoicheia as weak and beggarly. In a transferred sense, the stoicheia are the things on which pre-Christian existence rests, especially in pre-Christian religion. These things are impotent; they bring bondage instead of freedom."20 Throughout the New Testament, the word "elements" (stoicheia) is always used in connection with the Old Covenant order. St. Paul used the term in his stinging rebuke to the Galatian Christians who were tempted to forsake the freedom of the New Covenant for an Old Covenant-style legalism.

"Describing Old Covenant rituals and ceremonies, he says "we were in bondage under the elements (stoicheia) of this world. . . . How is it that you turn again to the weak and beggarly elements (stoicheia), to which you desire again to be in bondage? You observe days and months and seasons and years. . . ." (Gal. 4:3, 9–10). He warns the Colossians: "Beware lest anyone cheat you through philosophy and empty deceit, according to the basic principles (stoicheia) of the world, and not according to Christ. . . . Therefore, if you died with Christ to the basic principles (stoicheia) of the world, why, as though living in the world, do you subject yourselves to regulations — 'Do not touch, do not taste, do not handle'" (Col. 2:8, 20–21).

"The writer to the Hebrews chided them: "For though by this time you ought to be teachers, you have need again for someone to teach you the elements (stoicheia) of the oracles of God, and you have come to need milk and not solid food" (Heb. 5:12). In context, the writer to the Hebrews is clearly speaking of Old Covenant [elements that the book of Hebrews argues have passed away] — particularly since he connects it with the term oracles of God, an expression used elsewhere in the New Testament for the provisional, Old Covenant revelation (see Acts 7:38; Rom. 3:2). These citations from Galatians, Colossians, and Hebrews comprise all the other occurrences in the New Testament of that word "elements" (stoicheia).

"Not one refers to the "elements" of the physical world or universe; all are speaking of the "elements" of the Old Covenant system, which, as the apostles wrote just before the approaching destruction of the Old Covenant Temple in A. D. 70, was "becoming obsolete and growing old" and "ready to vanish away" (Heb. 8:13). And St. Peter uses the same term in exactly the same way. Throughout the Greek New Testament, the word "elements" (stoicheia) always means [covenantal elements], not [physical elements]; the foundational "elements" of a religious system that was doomed to pass away in a fiery judgment [Matt. 22:7]." Gary DeMar, *Identifying the REAL Last Days Scoffers* (Atlanta GA: American Vision, 2012), 122-123.

[22] **Cassandra quotes from**: 2 Peter 3:10 [10] But the day of the Lord will come like a thief, and then the heavens will pass away with a roar, and the heavenly bodies will be burned up and dissolved, and the earth and the works that are done on it will be exposed.

Taken away" of Matthew 24:40 is NOT a "rapture": "Many futurists claim that the phrase "took them all away" (24:39) refers to a rapture that is still in our future. On the contrary. "In the context of 24:37–39, 'taken' presumably means 'taken to judgment' (cf. Jer. 6:11 NASB, NRSV)." The phrase ties the judgment of the world in Noah's day with the judgment of the Jews' world in Israel's day that took place with the destruction of the city of Jerusalem and the temple. Who was taken away in the judgment of the flood? Not Noah and his family. They were left behind to carry on God's work. John Gill writes in his commentary on this passage: "the whole world of the ungodly, every man, woman, and child, except eight persons only; Noah and his wife, and his three sons and their wives...." were taken away in judgment. And what does Gill say about those in the field?: They shall be taken away "by the eagles, the Roman army, and either killed or carried captive by them." The Bible gives its own commentary on the meaning of "took them all away" in Luke 17:27, 29: "Destroyed them all" is equivalent to "took them all away."""Gary DeMar, *Last Days Madness: Obsession of the Modern Church, Fourth revised edition* (Powder Springs, GA: American Vision, 1999), 196–197.

[23] **The Abomination of Desolation in Matthew 24:15 is explained in Luke 21:20 as being Jerusalem surrounded by armies**. It is the same sermon. Matthew was written to Jews who understood the reference, Luke was written to Greeks who would not, so he interpreted it for them.

Matthew 24:15–16 [15] "So when you see the abomination of desolation spoken of by the prophet Daniel, standing in the holy place (let the reader understand), [16] then let those who are in Judea flee to the mountains.

Luke 21:20–21 [20] "But when you see Jerusalem surrounded by armies, then know that its desolation has come near. [21] Then let those who are in Judea flee to the mountains.

[24] **The end of all things is at hand:** Peter was writing to those Christians who were suffering in his time period. The end of all things was not the end of the physical world, but rather the end of all things related to the Old Covenant.

1 Peter 4:7 The end of all things is at hand; therefore be self-controlled and sober-minded for the sake of your prayers.

1 Peter 5:1 So I exhort the elders among you, as a fellow elder and a witness of the sufferings of Christ, as well as a partaker in the glory that is going to be revealed.

The cessation of revelatory gifts upon the arrival of the final consummation of the New Covenant: "Miraculous phenomena are always attached to revelation from God. In Biblical history, eras of new special revelation are punctuated by validating sign-miracles.

• In Exodus God clearly endows Moses with miraculous power in order to underscore the divine origin of his message. When Moses initially balks at his task, he expresses a concern that the people might say: "The Lord hath not appeared to you" (Exod. 4:1). In response to this fear the Lord endued him with miraculous abilities (such as the power to turn his staff into a serpent, Exod. 4:3) "that they may believe that the Lord, the God of their father. . . has appeared to you" (Exod. 4:5; cp. Acts 7:36-38).

"As redemptive history progresses into the post-Pentecost, new covenant era we discover the same purpose in the miracles of the revelation bearing apostles. The Lord confirms their message with many signs and wonders: "Then fear came upon every soul, and many wonders and signs were done through the apostles" (Acts 2:43). "What shall we do to these men? For, indeed, that a notable miracle has been done through them is evident to all who dwell in Jerusalem, and we cannot deny it" (Acts 4:16).

"Consequently, the bestowing of supernatural-miraculous gifts upon believers serves as a confirmation of the apostolic message. This is clearly taught in the locus classicus on the matter: "How shall we escape if we neglect so great a salvation? After it was at the first spoken through the Lord, it was confirmed to us by those who heard, God also bearing witness with them, by signs and wonders and by various miracles and gifts of the Holy Spirit according to His own will" (Heb. 2:3, 4).

"Probably the least understood aspect of the function of tongues is its serving as a sign to Israel of God's covenant curse due to her unbelief. Yet Paul explicitly suggests this in 1 Corinthians 14:21-22: "In the Law it is written: 'By men of strange tongues and by the lips of strangers I will speak to this people, and even so they will not listen to Me,' says the Lord. So then tongues are for a sign, not to those who believe, but to unbelievers."

• Jeremiah 5:15 warns: "'Behold, I am bringing a nation against you from afar, O house of Israel,' declares the Lord, 'It is an enduring nation, it is an ancient nation, a nation whose language, you do not know, nor can you understand what they say.' "

• In rebuke of Israel's sinful dullness of hearing, Isaiah warns: "Indeed, He will speak to this people through stammering lips and a foreign tongue" (Isa. 28:11).

• In speaking of the removal of the curse and the return of covenantal blessing, the sign of curse would be removed, as Isaiah prophesies: "You will no longer see a fierce people, a people of unintelligible speech which no one comprehends, of a stammering tongue which no one understands" (Isa. 33:19).

390

"Clearly, then, the presence of foreign tongues was a sign of curse upon Israel. And all of this is specifically related to the gift of tongues when Paul applies the sign of covenantal curse (Isa. 28:11) to the explanation of tongues:

"In the law it is written: "With men of other tongues and other lips I will speak to this people; and yet, for all that, they will not hear Me," says the Lord. Therefore tongues are for a sign, not to those who believe but to unbelievers. (1 Cor. 14:21-22a).

"Scripture Designates a Terminus Ad Quem: First Corinthians 13:8-10 reads: "Love never fails; but if there are gifts of prophecy, they will be done away; if there are tongues, they will cease; if there is knowledge, it will be done away. For we know in part, and we prophesy in part; but when the perfect comes, the partial will be done away." This passage, properly understood, points to the providential completion of the New Testament canon as that which renders tongues (and other revelatory gifts) inoperative. Tongues, prophecy, and knowledge are specifically designated as having a joint terminus: each will be rendered inoperative at some future date (1 Cor. 13:8). What affects one gift, will affect all three.

"The idea here is simply that during the period between Pentecost and the completion of the canon God gifts a variety of believers in various churches with these revelatory gifts. But these gifts are sporadic in that they give a revelation here and one there, but do not weave a total, complete New Testament revelatory picture. The various prophetic revelations offer at best partial insight into the will of God for the Church.

"But verse 10 speaks of something coming which will contrast the piecemeal, bit-by-bit (Greek: ek merous) revelation of that transitional age. That which supersedes the partial and renders it inoperative is something designated as "perfect" (Gk., to teleion): "But when the perfect comes, the partial will be done away." It is difficult to miss the antithetic parallel between the "partial" thing and the "perfect" (complete, mature, full) thing. Since the "partial" speaks of the sporadic revelatory gifts of tongues, prophecy, and knowledge, then it would seem that the "perfect"—which supplants these—represents the perfect and full New Testament Scripture, in that modes of revelation are being contrasted. The final inscripturated word is not piecemeal—it is perfect (James 1:22-25). Thus, it equips the man of God adequately for all the tasks before him (2 Tim. 3:16-17)." Kenneth L. Gentry, Jr., Th.D., "Tongues Speaking: The Meaning, Purpose and Cessation of Tongues," *Nourished on Sound Words: Studies in Reformed Truth* (Ventura, CA: Nordskog, 2008), 55-78.

[25] **The Judge is standing right at the door**: James 5:7-9 [7] Be patient, therefore, brothers, until the coming of the Lord. See how the farmer waits for the precious fruit of the earth, being patient about it, until it receives the early and the late rains. [8] You also, be patient. Establish your hearts, for the coming of the Lord is at hand. [9] Do not grumble against one another, brothers, so that you may not be judged; behold, the Judge is standing at the door.

CHAPTER 18

[1] **Agrippa was away at Alexandria when Florus had these final showdowns with the Jews**: Flavius Josephus, *Wars of the Jews* 2.309.

[2] **Florus killed 3600 Jews in the upper marketplace and crucified many of them**: "Florus was more provoked at this, and called out aloud to the soldiers to plunder that which was called the Upper Market Place, and to slay such as they met with. So the soldiers, taking this exhortation of their commander in a sense agreeable to their desire of gain, did not only plunder the place they were sent to, but forcing themselves into every house, they slew its inhabitants; (306) so the citizens fled along the narrow lanes, and the soldiers slew those that they caught, and no method of plunder was omitted; they also caught many of the quiet people, and brought them before Florus, whom he first chastised with stripes, and then crucified. (307) Accordingly, the whole number of those that were destroyed that day, with their wives and children (for they did not spare even the infants themselves), was about three thousand and six hundred; (308) and what made this calamity the heavier, was this new method of Roman barbarity; for Florus ventured then to what no one had done before, that is, to have men of the equestrian order whipped, and nailed to the cross before his tribunal; who, although they were by birth Jews, yet were they of Roman dignity notwithstanding." Flavius Josephus and William Whiston, *The Works of Josephus: Complete and Unabridged* (Peabody: Hendrickson, 1987). *Wars of the Jews*, 2.305-308.

[3] **Berenice pleads to Florus**: "Which things Bernice was now performing, and stood barefoot before Florus's tribunal, and besought him [to spare the Jews]. Yet could she neither have reverence paid to her, nor

could she escape without some danger of being slain herself." Flavius Josephus and William Whiston, The Works of Josephus: Complete and Unabridged (Peabody: Hendrickson, 1987). *Wars of the Jews* 2.314.

[4] **Sicarii take Masada and kill Romans there in June AD 66**: "And at this time it was that some of those that principally excited the people to go to war, made an assault upon a certain fortress called Masada. They took it by treachery and slew the Romans that were there, and put others of their own party to keep it." Flavius Josephus and William Whiston, The Works of Josephus: Complete and Unabridged (Peabody: Hendrickson, 1987). *Wars of the Jews* 2.408. Martin Goodman, *Ruling Class of Judaea: The Origins of the Jewish Revolt Against Rome, A. D. 66-70* (Cambridge University Press, 1993), 169.

[5] **Eleazar ben Ananias**: Eleazar ben Ananias was captain of the temple who stopped the sacrifice. But a different Eleazar, son of Simon was a warrior who eventually took over the inner temple. So I combined both of these characters into one in order to simplify the story.

[6] **Eleazer stops the sacrifice, which is considered the final act of war**: Flavius Josephus, *The Wars of the Jews* 2.17.2 §409-410 "Eleazar, the sons of Ananias the high priest, a very bold youth, who was at that time governor of the temple, persuaded those that officiated in the divine service to receive no gift or sacrifice for any foreigner. And this was the true beginning of our war with the Romans; for they rejected the sacrifice of Caesar on this account; (410) and when many of the high priests and principal men besought them not to omit the sacrifice which it was customary for them to offer for their princes, they would not prevailed upon. These relied much upon their multitude, for the most flourishing part of the innovators assisted them, but they had the chief regard to Eleazar, the governor of the temple." Flavius Josephus and William Whiston, *The Works of Josephus: Complete and Unabridged* (Peabody: Hendrickson, 1987), 624.

[7] **There are a few different interpretations of when the 1290 days of Daniel 12:11 occurs**: The ceasing of the daily sacrifice and the abomination being set up in the holy land are two starting points for the 1290 days that ends in the shattering of the power of the holy people. So the ceasing of the sacrifice on behalf of Caesar, which started the war, is the first part in mid-AD 66. But the 1290 days does not start until the second part, the abomination of desolation, is "set up" in the holy land in AD 67. I am basically using the first one, but the second one is just as viable.

"TWO STARTING POINTS FOR THE 1,290 DAYS: Daniel 12:11 gives two starting points to the 1,290 days, seemingly without an end point: "And from the time that the daily sacrifice is taken away, and the abomination of desolation is set up, there shall be one thousand two hundred and ninety days." Because it is unusual to have two beginning points, some view the taking away of the sacrifice as the beginning of the 1,290 days, with the abomination of desolation happening at the end of the 1,290 days. J. E. H. Thomson notes the following on how the grammatical construction of this verse does not support this interpretation:

> And the abomination that maketh desolate set up. At first sight the reader is inclined to… regard this as a statement of the terminus ad quem [end point]. The grammatical difficulties against this view are forcible…Yet it seems strange that two termini a quo [starting points] should be assigned and no terminus ad quem.

That Daniel 12:11 gives two starting points for the 1,290 days (the daily sacrifice taken away and the abomination of desolation) is not as strange as it first seems. The end point has already been supplied in v. 7; it would be the shattering of Daniel's people. Thus, the glorious Man was saying from the time that the daily sacrifice was removed and the one who would make the Jewish nation desolate came (the abomination of desolation) to the shattering of the Jewish nation would be 1,290 days or 43 months.

"I believe the removal of the daily sacrifice that Daniel 12:11 speaks of is not the cessation of sacrifice that happened near the end of the Jewish war (in late July of AD 70) but the removal of the sacrifice the Jews offered twice a day on behalf of the emperor (Josephus, The Jewish War 2, 10, 4); this occurred in the summer of AD 66. This change in the sacrifice marked the beginning of the Jewish war with Rome."

McKenzie PhD, Duncan W.. *The Antichrist and the Second Coming: A Preterist Examination Volume I* (K-Locations 3672-3685). Xulon Press. K-Edition.

"The primary indicator of the Jewish rebellion involved the leaders of the revolt refusing to allow any sacrifices in the Temple from Gentiles. This resulted in the taking away of the daily sacrifice that was being offered for the emperor. According to Josephus, "This action laid the foundation of the war with Rome; for they renounced in consequence the sacrifices offered for Rome and the emperor."

"The outcome of this taking away of the daily sacrifice for the emperor was the coming of the one who would make the Jewish nation desolate; this was the abomination of desolation (Dan. 9:27). Responding to Nero's order to crush the Jewish rebellion, Titus marched the fifteenth legion from Egypt up the length of the Holy Land to rendezvous with his father at Ptolemais on the western border of Galilee. This coming of Titus happened around February of AD 67 as he marched a wing of the Roman army through the sacred land of Israel. This was the abomination of desolation that Jesus warned those in Judea to flee from; all hell literally broke loose at this time (Matt. 24:15-24; cf. Rev. 6).

"Titus' coming was the beginning of the great tribulation; this culminated in the shattering of the Jewish nation 1,290 days later, in August/September of AD 70 (Dan. 12:1-7).

I thus propose that the starting point for the 1,290 days of Daniel 12:11 involved two stages. The first stage was the taking away of the daily sacrifice for the emperor (c. August AD 66); this marked the beginning of the Jewish rebellion. The second stage (which happened about six months later, c. February AD 67) was the abomination of desolation, the coming of the one who would make Israel desolate (Dan. 9:27). It was 1,290 days after Titus' coming to the Holy Land that the Jewish nation was shattered and dispersed into the nations. We thus see the meaning of Daniel 12:11 as follows: From the time that the daily sacrifice is taken away and the abomination of desolation is set up [i.e., the coming of the one who would make Israel desolate, Dan. 9:27], [to the time of the end, the shattering of the Jewish nation, Dan. 12:6-8] there shall be one thousand two hundred and ninety days."

McKenzie PhD, Duncan W.. *The Antichrist and the Second Coming: A Preterist Examination Volume I* (K-Locations 3705-3714). Xulon Press. K-Edition.

A second possibility for the 1290 days:

"It is to be noted that the two measures of time here given, 1290 days and 1335 days, both fall within the period of three years and a part, given in verse 7 as the full measure of the time of the end. This tends still further to confirm the view that by "a time, times, and a part" is meant three full rounds of the annual feasts of the Jews, and part of a fourth.

"It will further be seen from this answer that Daniel's question had reference to the very last epoch of Jewish history; for it was in that very last stage of their national existence that the daily sacrifice was caused to cease, which was by them regarded (when it came to pass in the days of the siege of Jerusalem, as we shall presently show) the harbinger of some dire calamity.

"THE TAKING AWAY OF THE DAILY SACRIFICE

"We take the marginal reading (which is the more literal) as giving the sense, the words of the margin being "and to set up the abomination, " &c. This reading would make the 1290 days the measure of time between the two specified events. But we have lately seen an interpretation, based on the text of the A. V., which makes the taking away of the daily sacrifice, and the setting up of the abomination that maketh desolate, simultaneous events, both governed by the preposition "from." But this obviously leaves the verse without meaning; for it gives a measure of time from two specified events, without stating to what that measure brings us.

"The "daily sacrifice" was the sacrifice of a lamb every morning and evening. This was to be kept up by the children of Israel throughout all their generations, and a special promise was given upon condition that this offering be continued (Ex 29: 38-45). (It should be observed that the causing of the sacrifice and oblation to cease, as foretold in (Da 9: 27), is a very different thing.)

"Now, as a matter of historic fact, the daily sacrifice was taken away during the siege of Jerusalem; and this was counted by the Jews an event of such importance, and such a portent of approaching disaster, that Josephus has recorded the very date on which it occurred, saying: "And now Titus gave orders to his soldiers that were with him to dig up the foundations of the tower of Antonia, and make a ready passage for his army to come up, while he himself had Josephus brought to him; for he had been informed that, on that very day, which was the seventeenth day of Panemus, the sacrifice called 'the daily sacrifice' had failed, and had not been offered to God for want of men to offer it; and that the people were grievously troubled at it" (Wars, VI. 2.1.)."

"The Roman army, which, by comparison of the Lord's words in (Mt 24: 15,16 Lu 21: 20,21,) is clearly seen to be "the abomination which maketh desolate, " encompassed Jerusalem before the failure of the daily sacrifice; whereas it might appear from the wording of the prophecy that those events occurred in the reverse order. But Mr. Farquharson shows that "there is nothing whatever in the verbs of the sentence to indicate which of the events should precede the other; the interval of time between them only is expressed."

"The first approach of the Roman armies under Cestius is described by Josephus in his book of Wars, II 17, 10. This was in the month corresponding to our November, A.D. 66. The taking away of the daily sacrifice was in the month Panemus, corresponding to the Hebrew Tammuz, and our July, A.D. 70 (Hartwell Horne's Chronological Table). Thus the measure of time between the two events was three years, and part of a fourth.

"But more than this: the measure 1290 days is exactly 43 great months (30 days each, according to the Hebrew method of reckoning), and inasmuch as their practice was to reckon by even weeks, months, and years the fulfilment of this part of the prophecy is seen in the fact that it is just 43 even months between the two events, ignoring the parts of the two months in which the events severally occurred."

Mauro, Philip. *The Seventy Weeks and the Great Tribulation* (K-Locations 2288-2319). K-Edition.

A third view is that the Abomination of desolation being set up is the Roman armies surrounding Jerusalem:

"Around the 6th of Av of A.D. 66, Eleazar terminated the daily sacrifice to Caesar fulfilling part of v. 11.12 According to Josephus, this act "was the true beginning of our war with the Romans."13 Hearing about this act of sedition, Agrippa immediately dispatched three thousand horsemen who seized the upper city, Mt. Zion, where they attacked the Jewish rebels who possessed the lower city and Temple.14 The Roman army with their idols to Zeus, Caesar and Rome is the abomination that causes desolation… Thus immediately after Eleazar put an end to the daily sacrifice to Caesar, Roman auxiliaries, the abomination that causes desolation, entered Jerusalem. Thus the starting point of the 1,290 days is the termination of the daily sacrifice to Caesar and the consequent abomination that causes desolation which occurred immediately thereafter.

"Counting 1290 days from these two events ends on Shabat of A.D. 70. This is the month in which the Roman army arrived outside of Jerusalem to begin preparations for what would end up being the final siege of Jerusalem.15 Remember, the Roman army with their idols to Zeus, Caesar and Rome is the abomination that causes desolation. Here one can see that there appears to have been 1,290 days from the cessation of the daily sacrifice to Caesar and the resulting abomination that causes desolation when the Roman auxiliaries fought the rebels inside Jerusalem until the Roman army, the abomination that causes desolation, arrived outside of Jerusalem again in preparation for their final assault on the city."

Daniel Chapter 12: A Preterist Commentary online. http://revelationrevolution.org/daniel-chapter-12-a-preterist-commentary/

[8] **The content of this speech is taken from**: Flavius Josephus, *Wars of the Jews* 2.349-404.

CHAPTER 19

[1] **Hubal and Allah, the Arabic pre-Islamic deities of Nabatea**: "The Qurayshite pantheon was composed principally of idols that were in the haram of Makka, that is, Hubal (the most important and oldest deity), Manaf, Isaf, and Na'ila. The pantheon of the hums and other associations was superimposed on the Qurayshite one; their principal deities were Allah (the god who brought victory to Quraysh against Abraha at the Battle of the Elephant) and three goddesses, Allat, al-'Uzza, and Manat. Allah's shrine was the Ka'ba in Makka, but the three goddesses had neither idols nor a shrine in that city. To find a shrine consecrated to one of them, one must look as far as Buss, about 100 kilometers northeast of Makka, where there was a temple of al-'Uzza. The question has been raised whether Hubal (the main god of Quraysh) and Allah (main god of the entire tribal federation around Quraysh) were not one and the same deity under two successive names: indeed, Allah (which is probably a contracted form of al-Ilah, "the God") could be a designation that consecrated Hubal's superiority over the other gods.

"However, evidence supporting the hypothesis of two distinct gods is not lacking. The temple dedicated to Allah-the Ka'ba-is very different from the rest of the haram. According to some traditions, the Ka'ba contained no statue, but its interior was decorated with images of Mary and Jesus, of prophets, angels, and trees. Another argument is that the two gods clearly had different functions: Hubal was invoked and venerated only by the Qurayshites, while Allah was the supreme God of a large group of individuals belonging to different tribes (Rubin 1986; Robin 2001a). According to this hypothesis, it should be assumed that the temple of Makka was first consecrated to a supreme god named Allah and then hosted the pantheon of Quraysh after the conquest of Makka by that tribe, about a hundred years before Muhammad's time.

"A second question concerns the nature of Allah. Was he the God of the supporters of monotheism or a god of pagan origin? In the oldest revelations of the Qur'an, the name of Allah does not appear. When Muhammad refers to God, he says "the Lord" or, if he want to give him a proper name, it is al-Rahman (the name of the one God of the Jews and Christians of Arabia, but also of the followers of Musaylima) (Peters 1991, 300-301).

"Allah is thus a god originating in polytheism. Inscriptions seem to confirm it. At Qaryat al-Faw, for example, a certain 'Igl entrusts the tomb he has built to "Kahl, Allah, and 'Aththar the Oriental." The text is dated by the writing style to the beginning of the Christian era just before or just after)." Scott Fitzgerald Johnson, *The Oxford Handbook of Late Antiquity* (Oxford University Press, 2012), 304.

"The religion of the Arabs, as well as their political life, was on a thoroughly primitive level...In particular the Semites regarded trees, caves, springs, and large stones as being inhabited by spirits; like the Black Stone of Islam in a corner of the Ka'bah at Mecca, in Petra and other places in Arabia stones were venerated also...Every tribe worshipped its own god, but also recognized the power of other tribal gods in their own sphere...Three goddesses in particular had elevated themselves above the circle of the inferior demons. The goddess of fate, al-Manat, corresponding to the Tyche Soteira of the Greeks, though known in Mecca, was worshipped chiefly among the neighboring Bedouin tribes of the Hudhayl. Allat—"the Goddess," who is Taif was called ar-Rabbah, "the Lady," and whom Herodotus equates with Urania—corresponded to the great mother of the gods, Astarte of the northern Semites; al-'Uzza, "the Mightiest," worshipped in the planet Venus, was merely a variant form... In addition to all these gods and goddesses the Arabs, like many other primitive peoples, believed in a God who was creator of the world, Allah, whom the Arabs did not, as has often been thought, owe to the Jews and Christians...The more the significance of the cult declined, the greater became the value of a general religious temper associated with Allah. Among the Meccans he was already coming to take the place of the old moon-god Hubal as the lord of the Ka'bah...Allah was actually the guardian of contracts, though at first these were still settled at a special ritual locality and so subordinate to the supervision of an idol. In particular he was regarded as the guardian of the alien guest, though consideration for him still lagged behind duty to one's kinsmen." (*History of the Islamic Peoples*, Carl Brockelmann, p 8-10)

"This was especially true of Allah, 'the God, the Divinity', the personification of the divine world in its highest form, creator of the universe and keeper of sworn oaths. In the Hejaz three goddesses had pride of place as the 'daughters of Allah'. The first of these was Allat, mentioned by Herodotus under the name of Alilat. Her name means simply 'the goddess', and she may have stood for one aspect of Venus, the morning star, although hellenized Arabs identified her with Athene. Next came Uzza, 'the all-powerful', whom other sources identify with Venus. The third was Manat, the goddess of fate, who held the shears which cut the thread of life and who was worshipped in a shrine on the sea-shore. The great god of Mecca was Hubal, an idol made of red cornelian." (*Mohammed*, Maxime Rodinson, 1961, translated by Anne Carter, 1971, p 16-17)

"It is not related that the Black Stone was connected with any special god. In the Ka'ba was the statue of the god Hubal who might be called the god of Mecca and of the Ka'ba. Caetani gives great prominence to the connection between the Ka'ba and Hubal. Besides him, however, al-Lat, al-'Uzza, and al-Manat were worshipped and are mentioned in the Kur'an; Hubal is never mentioned there. What position Allah held beside these is not exactly known. The Islamic tradition has certainly elevated him at the expense of other deities. It may be considered certain that the Black Stone was not the only idol in or at the Ka'ba. The Makam Ibrahim was of course a sacred stone from very early times. Its name has not been handed down. Beside it several idols are mentioned, among them the 360 statues. (First Encyclopedia of Islam, E.J. Brill, 1987, Islam, p. 587-591)" http://www.bible.ca/islam/islam-allah-pre-islamic-origin.htm

Hubal and Allah's similarities and connection to the moon: "Clearly "Allah," both as a title and as a proper name, was applied to lunar deities in the ancient Near East. Allah also shares many direct similarities with Ba'al/Hubal. We know that at various times in pre-Islamic Arab regions, Hubal was linked to the same deities with whom Allah was connected. Hoyland informs us that Hubal was worshipped jointly with Manat in the Hijaz portion of the Nabataean kingdom, and that he was served by a priestly office jointly with Dushara and Manat at Hegra, also in the northern Hijaz. Indeed, the earliest inscription to bear Hubal's name shows him to be associated with Manawat, a cognate name of Manat, in the Nabataean kingdom. Also among the Nabataean remains have been found references to Ba'l along with Manat and al-Uzza. All in all, despite the claims of Saifullah and David to the contrary, Hubal does indeed seem to have been "integrated into the divine family" of Allah.

"This is even more enlightening when we consider that the evidence of the much earlier Ras Shamra texts tell us that Ba'al was a god who had three daughters, just like Allah. It is not at all improbable that Ba'al with his three daughters passed, with some modifications and evolution due to the passage of time, to being Hubal with three daughters - Hubal (the lord) known also by the name Allah (the god, al-ilah). It then becomes explicable why the Qur'an would condemn the worship of the daughters of Allah as shirk (association of other deities with Allah), while remaining strangely silent about the worship of Hubal. The worship of Hubal was the worship of Allah - the error of the particular idolatry in question lay solely in associating daughters with Hubal/Allah. Allah, as a title, was applied to Hubal, the god's name, so the writers of the Qur'an did not see a need to raise a row about Hubal. It is likely that only later, when the absolute monotheism of Islam became more crystallized and reference to the names of pre-Islamic deities in conjunction with Allah became discouraged, do we see the traditions arising in which Hubal is opposed to and ultimately defeated by Allah." Timothy W. Dunkin, "Ba'al, Hubal, and Allah: A Rebuttal to the Islamic Awareness Article Entitled "Is Hubal the Same as Allah?" by M.S.M. Saifullah and 'Abdallah David, http://www.studytoanswer.net/islam/hubalallah.html

"Saifullah and David wrote: "Is Hubal the Same as Allah?" dated 24 June 2006. Hubal means "The Baal" just as "Allah" means "The god." The topic of Hubal is pertinent to this paper's focus since some have theorized that Hubal was Allah, Baal, or a rival Mekkan moon-god, and that Hubal was the high-god of Mekka.

"The account of the Battle of Uhud and K 037:125 show that Hubal was not Allah, but rather a rival of Allah. Since the Kaaba was an astral shrine, the natural rival of Allah the moon-god would have been Jupiter. Since the sun in Arabic is feminine, the sun goddess would not be a rival to a male moon-god. Some have said that Hubal could have been the old or the new moon-god, but in syncretistic paganism, the old and new moon-gods would have been easily merged into one moon-god.

"Islamic traditions relate that Hubal came from Syria. Philip Schaff noted that the Greeks and Romans thought of any god called Baal as being Zeus or Jupiter.[24] The International Standard Bible Encyclopedia states that Jupiter was equated with Zeus, and that…

"…in accord with the syncretism of the period, [Jupiter] was identified with countless deities in the local cults of Asia Minor and elsewhere.[25]

"Thus, Hubal was likely thought of as Baal and Jupiter in Syria before the idol was transported to Mekka.

"All the foregoing data correlates well with the idea that Hubal was short for Ha-Baal, which means "the Baal." Torrey wrote about the definite article Ha- (i.e. the): "Ha is so pervasive in all Semitic speech."[26] The difference in spelling between Ha-Baal and Hubal, like that between Syn and Sin mentioned above, is to be expected. The Ha-Baal to Hubal transformation reminds one of how Allah was originally spelled Hallah and Alaha in pre-Islamic inscriptions.[27]

"The Hubal versus Allah clash was an incarnation of the rivalry between the moon-god Sin and the Jupiter-god Marduk that brought down the Babylonian empire. Allah was derived from Sin and Hubal was derived from Marduk. While Allah lost to Hubal at the Battle of Uhud, Allah eventually won the war. Yoel Natan, "Answering Islam and the 'Allah is a pre-islamic moon-god' hypothesis" http://www.answering-islam.org/Responses/Saifullah/moonotheism.htm

[2] **Sodomizing as a means of humiliation**: "The Sufi Martin Lings wrote:
"The Prophet now turned away from the Kaaba toward the idols which surrounded it in a wide circle, three hundred and sixty in all. Between these and the House [the Kaaba] he now rode, repeating the verse of the Revelation: 'The Truth hath come and the false hath vanished. Verily the false is ever a vanisher' [K 017:081], and pointing at the idols one by one with his staff; and each idol as he pointed at it fell forward on its face.

"Of course this was the same stick that Muhammad used to symbolically fecundate the Venus Black Stone in its vulviform casing. This shows that Muhammad symbolically sodomized the 360 idol.

"Sodomizing one's rivals has a long history in the Mideast. Sodomizing was meant to shame and trivialize a would-be competitor and show domination over an opponent. This was a particularly effective technique in the honor-shame obsessive cultures of the Mideast. Gordon Newby wrote:

"In Ibn Ishaq's chronology of [pre-Islamic] Yemen…King Hassan was overthrown by Dhu Shanatir…His [King Hassan's] policy for consolidation of power was either to kill the leaders of the society or to sodomize them, rendering them unfit for rule because of their shame. After Muhammad symbolically charged up his phallic stick with Allah's sexual energy at crescent-shaped Hatim Wall, he used it first to symbolically fecundate the vulviform Black Stone and then to symbolically sodomize the 360 images surrounding the Kaaba."

Yoel Natan, *Moon-o-theism: Religion of a War and Moon God Prophet Volume I of II* (online:2006), 767, http://www.yoel.info/moonotheismv1andv2.pdf

[3] **The details of pre-Islamic Mecca, the Black Stone and the Kaaba as an astral fertility altar for Venus**: "The ancients knew that the Black Stone was Venus since the Black Stone was set into a corner of the cubic Kaaba. The planet Venus was always observed to be near the sun.

"The crescent-shaped Hatim Wall, the cubic Kaaba and the Black Stone were the moon, the sun and Venus. An ancient way of symbolizing the moon, the sun and Venus would be: (crescent-square-star), which looks a lot like the outline of an overhead view of the Hatim Wall, the Kaaba and the Venus Black Stone.

"Malise Ruthven recounts another astral tradition about the Kaaba:
"The earliest Muslim sources suggest that the pre-Islamic cult of the Kaaba had some astronomical significance. The historian Masudi (896-956 [AD]) [in Murudj, iv. 47] stated that certain people had regarded the Kaaba as a temple dedicated to the sun, moon and the five visible planets (making up the mystical figure of seven, the number of circumambulations required for each Tawaf). The story that there were exactly 360 idols placed round the temple also points to an astronomical significance [360 = 12 months of 30 days each…

"Someone might ask what was it about the Black Stone that would make it such an object of worship. The Black Stone was an earthly representation of Venus, which was the goddess Uzza in pre-Islamic times…

"The vulva-look of the silver case around the Black Stone probably extends back to pre-Islamic times when the Kaaba was circumambulated by nude worshippers. The vulva-look would have complemented the Lingam and Yoni worship that was prevalent throughout Arabia and India at the time, and Venus worship, too, since the Black Stone did represent Venus…

"Muhammad sacrificed to the goddess Venus. He also had a custom dating from pre-Islamic times of kissing the Black Stone. These points tend to confirm that the Black Stone represented Venus. The Black Stone is smooth, at least the portion that is visible to the public. How the statue's head was worn down to a smoother state was from a millennium's worth of "extremely passionate….rubbing and kissing," as John of Damascus phrased it…

"A Third Auspicious Stone at the Kaaba Dedicated to Manat There was another auspicious stone in the Kaaba that probably represented Manat. Glassé wrote: In the opposite corner [from the Black Stone], set somewhat lower, is another stone of a reddish color called the 'Stone of Felicity' (Hajar As-Sa'adah). The stone "Felicity," meaning "good fortune," would seem to be connected to Manat, goddess of Fortune…"

Yoel Natan, *Moon-o-theism: Religion of a War and Moon God Prophet Volume I of II* (online:2006), 747-761, http://www.yoel.info/moonotheismv1andv2.pdf

Navel of the earth: "The idea was common in the ancient world that the earth and the deities had body parts located in sacred spots, such as navels and vulvas. The idea behind the earth's navel is that there is an invisible umbilical between the god in the sky and the earth since a goddess had given birth to the earth. The *Encyclopedia Britannica* states:

"Frequently, the altar is regarded as the center or the image of the universe. For the ancient Greeks the grave marker (a mound of earth or a stone) was the earth altar upon which sacrifices to the dead were made and, like other earth altars, it was called the omphalos, 'the navel' of the Earth—i.e. the central point from which terrestrial life originated. In Vedic India the altar was regarded as a microcosm, its parts representing the various parts of the universe and its construction being interpreted as a repetition of the creation of the cosmos.

"The worshippers of Yahveh knew that Yahveh's Faces (2Ch 07:14a) and his eyes, ears and heart were present at the temple (1Ki 09:03; 2Ch 07:15-16). By contrast, fertility cult worshippers were concerned that their gods and goddesses' reproductive organs were at the temple—the Lingam and Yoni."

Yoel Natan, *Moon-o-theism: Religion of a War and Moon God Prophet Volume I of II* (online:2006), 756, http://www.yoel.info/moonotheismv1andv2.pdf

[4] **Hira**: "The Cave of Hira is a talus cave about 3 kilometres (2 mi) from Mecca, on the mountain named Jabal al-Nour in the Hejaz region of present-day Saudi Arabia. It is notable for being the location where Muslims believe Muhammad received his first revelations and where Quran was first revealed…the cave itself is about 3.7 m (12 ft) in length and 1.60 m (5 ft 3 in) in width. The cave is situated at a height of 270 m (890 ft)." "Hira," Wikipedia https://en.wikipedia.org/wiki/Hira

CHAPTER 20

[1] **This translation of the War Scroll comes from**: Michael O. Wise, Martin G. Abegg Jr., and Edward M. Cook, *The Dead Sea Scrolls: A New Translation* (New York: HarperOne, 2005), 148. 1Q33 Col. i:9-i12.

[2] **Qumran, The War Scroll, Daniel's Abomination of Desolation and the End of Days**: In this chapter, the Essenes have the interpretation that the ceasing of the imperial sacrifice, the entrance of the Roman Florus into the temple and the murder of the high priest are the fulfillment of Daniel's prophecy of the time of the end and the coming of the Abomination of Desolation:

Daniel 12:4 But you, Daniel, shut up the words and seal the book, until the time of the end. Many shall run to and fro, and knowledge shall increase."

Daniel 11:31 Forces from him shall appear and profane the temple and fortress, and shall take away the regular burnt offering. And they shall set up the abomination that makes desolate.

But just because they believe this, does not make it true. In fact, the Essenes have a lot in common with the Christian interpretation of the End Times. The difference was that they were only partly right and mostly wrong. I will be showing later in the story when these Danielic prophecies are actually fulfilled. The Essenes were close to the Kingdom, but yet so far. Like the other Jews, they had rejected Jesus as Messiah, so their interpretations and their sectarian manuscripts would ultimately lead them astray.

[3] **Josephus describe the Essenes as deterministic in their philosophy**: Flavius Josephus, *The Antiquities of the Jews*, 18.18.

CHAPTER 22

[1] **The captain quotes Torah's penalty for blasphemy**: Leviticus 24:16 Whoever blasphemes the name of the LORD shall surely be put to death. All the congregation shall stone him. The sojourner as well as the native, when he blasphemes the Name, shall be put to death.

[2] **The Jews laying waste to Pella and other cities in response to Florus' slaughter of Jews in Caesarea**: Flavius Josephus, *Wars of the Jews* 2.457-460 "Now the people of Cesarea had slain the Jews that were among them on the very same day and hour [when the soldiers were slain], which one would think must have come to pass by the direction of Providence; insomuch that in one hour's time above twenty thousand Jews were killed, and all Cesarea was emptied of its Jewish inhabitants; for Florus caught such as ran away, and sent them in bonds to the galleys. (458) Upon which stroke that the Jews received at Cesarea, the whole nation was greatly enraged; so they divided themselves into several parties, and laid waste the villages of the Syrians, and their neighboring cities, Philadelphia, and Sebonitis, and Gerasa, and Pella, and Scythopolis, (459) and after them Gadara, and Hippos; and falling upon Gaulonitis, some cities they destroyed there, and some they set on fire, and then they went to Kedasa, belonging to the Tyrians, and to Ptolemais, and to Gaba, and to Cesarea; (460) nor was either Sabaste (Samaria) or Askelon, able to oppose the violence with which they were attacked; and when they had burned these to the ground, they entirely demolished Anthedon and Gaza; many also of the villages that were about every one of those cities were plundered, and an immense slaughter was made of the men who were caught in them." Flavius Josephus and William Whiston, *The Works of Josephus: Complete and Unabridged* (Peabody: Hendrickson, 1987).

[3] Josephus details the battles between the Jews and Greeks in cities throughout Israel and Syria: Flavius Josephus, *The Wars of the Jews*, 2.18.

[4] **Gurion quotes**: Matthew 26:52 Then Jesus said to him, "Put your sword back into its place. For all who take the sword will perish by the sword.

The three passages about Jesus telling Peter to put away his sword (Matthew 26:51-56; Luke 22:49-53; John 18:10-11), if carefully considered in context are not a universal prohibition against using weapons or righteous violence. Jesus was stopping Peter because of Christ's special calling to be sacrificed. He had the right to call legions of angels to kill those men, but he chose not to for the specific goal of New Covenant atonement. That is not a universal application to all people. However, that does not mean self-defense is always justifiable either. For those called to persecution, the sword would not be appropriate. Neither pacifism nor self-defense is absolute.

[5] **Demetrius quotes**: Luke 22:36 He said to them, "But now let the one who has a moneybag take it, and likewise a knapsack. And let the one who has no sword sell his cloak and buy one.

Psalm 82:4 Rescue the weak and needy; Deliver them out of the hand of the wicked.

Proverbs 24:11 Rescue those who are being taken away to death; hold back those who are stumbling to the slaughter.

Self-Defense in the Law of God: Exodus 22:2–3 [2] If a thief is found breaking in and is struck so that he dies, there shall be no bloodguilt for him, [3] but if the sun has risen on him, there shall be bloodguilt for him. He shall surely pay.

[6] **The whip sword Rahab and its story**: Uriel actually got the sword from Jesus. This weapon has a long fictional history that is told through the entire *Chronicles of the Nephilim* series ending with *Jesus Triumphant*.

[7] **Gathering the elect from the four corners**: Matthew 24:31 And he will send out his angels with a loud trumpet call, and they will gather his elect from the four winds, from one end of heaven to the other.

I see two possible ways of interpreting this verse about the angels gathering the elect. I have both interpretations in this novel. First, it may be a reference to the rescue of the Christians from out of the towns in Israel as they anticipated the Roman armies coming in fulfillment of Luke 21:20. If, as I argue, the 144,000 are the Jewish Christians to be rescued from Jerusalem, and the angels are described in Revelation 7:1 as "holding back the four winds of the land" in order to rescue them, then maybe this going out to the four winds of the land (or four corners of the compass), could be a reference to God gathering the other Christians in Israel away from the judgment coming in Rome. They would have wanted to avoid both the Jewish rebels and the pro-Roman Hellenists in their loyalty. The question arises: Does this gathering not occur AFTER the coming of the Son of Man? Not necessarily. It may simply be an event that is described by Jesus IN RELATION to his coming, namely, that when he talks about his coming in judgement upon Israel, he reminds them that he will first rescue the Christians (the elect). The order of events in Matthew 24 is not intended to be a scientifically precise order of events. They are a complex of events that all occur around the judgment coming. Yes, there is some chronological order ("Immediately after the Tribulation of those days" Matthew 24:29), but surely earthquakes, famines, wars and rumors of wars are sporadic and without the exact order that Jesus said them. Some of Matthew 24 is thematic, NOT chronological. If one compares the order of events in Matthew 24 with Luke 17:22-37 they do not match up in the same exact order, though they are clearly talking about the same complex of events. So the gathering of the elect here in Matthew 24:31 could very well be a thematic reminder that God will save his Christians out of the judgment before his coming is complete. And besides, even the "coming on the clouds" is not a singular one day event (24:30), it consists in the entire complex of events of Jerusalem surrounded by armies, then destroyed, which took 3 and one half years from start to finish.

Another more likely interpretation of the angels gathering the elect: This was a metaphor of God's messengers (Christians) spreading the Gospel on the earth:

After Jesus came in judgment upon Jerusalem and confirmed his authority at the right hand of God by destroying the old covenant symbols for good, he then sent out his angels for a task.

> Matthew 24:31 And he will send out his angels with a loud trumpet call, and they will gather his elect from the four winds, from one end of heaven to the other.

The Greek word for "angel," angelos (or angelous/angelon), does not always mean a divine being from heaven. In fact, its most primary meaning is "messenger." Yes, those messengers are often divine beings from heaven in the Bible. But not always. Sometimes, they are human!

John the Baptist was an angel of God (Matthew 11:10, same Greek word for angel), John the Baptist's disciples were called John's angels (Luke 7:24), The Jewish spies who snuck into Jericho were called angels (James 2:25), and Jesus' own disciples were called angels (Luke 9:52).

Ken Gentry makes a strong biblical argument in his Revelation commentary that the "angels" of the seven churches in Revelation may actually have been the human Christian messengers of the letter to the congregation, lectors who would read the text to the church body, since they didn't have their own Bibles.

Think about it: we Christians are the messengers of the gospel to the world, aren't we? In that sense, we are God's angelous, his angels. We bring the message of the gospel to the four winds of the earth, just as he commanded (Acts 1:8). And God has used the gospel as the means to gather his elect into his kingdom. Whether you believe they are elect first and then believe, or they first believe and are then elect, the end remains the same: they are gathered into God's kingdom through the proclamation of the gospel. The loud trumpet is reminiscent of the shofar trumpet in the temple that would call the Jews to worship, or it could call them to war. Now that the physical temple would be destroyed, this trumpet call is an obvious figurative expression of the call to preach the gospel to the lost.

And historically speaking, this is exactly what happened after Jesus came in judgment upon Jerusalem, destroyed the temple, and led the Jews into captivity; the Christians escaped and were dispersed to spread the gospel to all nations, a gospel that gathered together the children of God from all nations.

> John 11:51 Being high priest that year he prophesied that Jesus would die for the nation, 52 and not for the nation only, but also to gather into one the children of God who are scattered abroad."

As we see in this and other New Testament passages, the growth of the Church is the fulfillment of the promise for God's people to be brought out of exile from the nations (Acts 2; Romans 10, quoting Isaiah 52 and 53 about the return from exile). As New Testament scholar N.T. Wright explains,

> The end of this exile, and the real 'return', are not now future events to be experienced in terms of a cleansed Land, a rebuilt Temple, an intensified Torah. The exile came to its cataclysmic end when Jesus, Israel's representative Messiah, died outside the walls of Jerusalem, bearing the curse, which consisted of exile at the hands of the pagans, to its utmost limit. The return from exile began when Jesus, again as the representative Messiah, emerged from the tomb three days later.

There is one last important piece that can easily be missed in the English translation with our modern Western viewpoint. That Greek word for "gather" that John used for gathering the children of God (11:51) is the word synagogue. That should of course ring bells in the reader's memory. "Synagogue" is the word for the gathering of the Jews in each city. A similar Greek word is used for the angels "gathering" the elect in Matthew 24:31: *episynago* (an expansion of synagogue).

So the "gathering" of the elect by angels is not a miraculous rapture or resurrection, but rather the congregational assembly of God's people. It refers to God building his "church" (ekklesia: "assembly"), the new "assembly" of God's people, by drawing them from every nation into the kingdom through the call of the gospel (Matt 23:37; Acts 2; John 6:44; 10:16; Rom 10:17). And, lo and behold, this is exactly what God prophesied in the Old Testament (LXX).

> Deuteronomy 30:3-4 And the Lord shall heal your sins, and he will show mercy to you, and he will gather (synagogue) you again from all the nations into which the Lord scattered you there. 4 If your dispersion should be from one end of heaven as far as the other end of heaven, from that place the Lord your God will gather (synagogue) you and from that place the Lord your God will take you.

CHAPTER 23

[1] **Alexander is quoting from the following passages to make the argument that the earthly temple is no longer a part of God's spiritual economy under the New Covenant**: Hebrews 9:11–12 [11] But when Christ appeared as a high priest of the good things that have come, then through the greater and more perfect tent (not made with hands, that is, not of this creation) [12] he entered once for all into the holy places, not by means of the blood of goats and calves but by means of his own blood, thus securing an eternal redemption.

Hebrews 9:24 For Christ has entered, not into holy places made with hands, which are copies of the true things, but into heaven itself, now to appear in the presence of God on our behalf.

Hebrews 10:1 For since the law has but a shadow of the good things to come instead of the true form of these realities, it can never, by the same sacrifices that are continually offered every year, make perfect those who draw near.

Hebrews 10:9–10 [9] then he added, "Behold, I have come to do your will." He does away with the first in order to establish the second. [10] And by that will we have been sanctified through the offering of the body of Jesus Christ once for all.

Hebrews 10:12–14 [12] But when Christ had offered for all time a single sacrifice for sins, he sat down at the right hand of God, [13] waiting from that time until his enemies should be made a footstool for his feet. [14] For by a single offering he has perfected for all time those who are being sanctified.

[2] **Because the temple is no longer God's temple, to worship at it is to worship at the temple of the Beast**: "So then, in 13:13 it appears that the Land beast's fire under the authority of the sea beast represents the Jewish high priesthood's conducting temple sacrifices at God's heaven-fired altar. In this context involving his submission to the sea beast, John has specifically in view the priestly sacrifices in behalf of the Roman emperor. We know from history that the priestly hierarchy offers "sacrifices twice every day for Caesar, and the Roman people" (J.W. 2:10:4 §197; Philo, Embassy 32 §157, 232; 40 §317; 45 §355)…

"In fact, elsewhere Josephus writes: "we also offer perpetual sacrifices for them; nor do we only offer them every day at the common expenses of all the Jews, but although we offer no other such sacrifices out of our common expenses, no, not for our own children, yet do we this as a peculiar honor to the emperors, and to them alone, while we do the same to no other person whomsoever" (Ap. 2:6 §77-78; cp. J.W. 2:10:4 §197). Thus, "just as Caesar was linked with traditional gods and heroes elsewhere in the East, so in the Jerusalem Temple, the priests 'offered sacrifice twice daily for Caesar and the Roman people" (Horsley 1995: 122)…

"The temple worship of that day is all for men, and not for God, because God turns from it to establish a new temple (see Exc 11 at 13:12). We see this clearly in Rev's conclusion: "I saw no temple in it, for the Lord God, the Almighty, and the Lamb, are its temple" (Rev 21:22). The temple system is "obsolete" (pepalaiōken) in John's day and "ready to disappear" (Heb 8:1380). The physical temple and its ritual service have become Israel's idol. Their religious authorities themselves sell out their temple to Rome when they reject the true temple, Christ (cf. Mk 14:58//; 15:29//). Their declaration in favor of Caesar over Christ in Jn 19:15 "was a clear renunciation of their Messianic hope, a virtual abolition of the Theocracy — a deliberate abandonment of their place and purpose as a nation" (Whitelaw 1993: 397). The temple service and religious rituals are deceptive, no longer functioning as God's blessing (13:14; cp. Gal 4:10; 5:6, 12; Php 3:2-3; Heb 9-10). The Land beast's deceiving activity entails his operating within Israel, for his "imagery and background suggest deception within the covenant community itself" (Beale 708).

"Revelation is dramatically presenting the temple itself as the image of the beast. Its rulers align themselves with the Emperor over against Christ and his followers, encouraged sacrifices for Caesar (Exc 11 at 13:12), and violently resist the Christian witness against the temple and ceremonial features of the law. The charge against Stephen, the first martyr, is that "this man incessantly speaks against this holy place, and the Law; for we have heard him say that this Nazarene, Jesus, will destroy this place and alter the customs which Moses handed down to us"86 (Ac 6:13). But ironically, despite the temple authorities' formal and external resistance to images, they spiritually commit idolatry by denying God and his Messiah by trusting in the old temple and its ritual instead of trusting in the true Temple and his redemption. Thus it befalls them as their fathers before them that "he who burns incense is like the one who blesses an idol" (Isa 66:3d). It is probably significant that John employs the word "image" (eikōn) rather than "idol" (eidōla), for just as men are the "image [eikona] of God" (Ge 1:26; 1Co 11:7), the Jewish hierarchy so control the temple system that it becomes an image of their god, Caesar — and ultimately of his god, Satan (13:2; cp. 2:9; 3:9; Jn 8:44)." Kenneth L. Gentry, Jr., *The Divorce of Israel: A Redemptive-Historical Interpretation of Revelation Vol. 2* (Dallas, GA: Tolle Lege Press, 2016), 273.

[3] **Alexander quotes from these passages to argue that Jesus is the new temple of God**: Hebrews 10:19–20 [19] Therefore, brothers, since we have confidence to enter the holy places by the blood of Jesus, [20] by the new and living way that he opened for us through the curtain, that is, through his flesh,

John 1:14 And the Word became flesh and dwelt among us, and we have seen his glory, glory as of the only Son from the Father, full of grace and truth.

Revelation 21:22 And I saw no temple in the city, for its temple is the Lord God the Almighty and the Lamb.

1 Peter 2:4–6 [4] As you come to him, a living stone rejected by men but in the sight of God chosen and precious, [5] you yourselves like living stones are being built up as a spiritual house, to be a holy priesthood, to offer spiritual sacrifices acceptable to God through Jesus Christ.

Ephesians 2:19–22 [19] So then you are no longer strangers and aliens, but you are fellow citizens with the saints and members of the household of God, [20] built on the foundation of the apostles and prophets, Christ Jesus himself being the cornerstone, [21] in whom the whole structure, being joined together, grows into a holy temple in the Lord. [22] In him you also are being built together into a dwelling place for God by the Spirit.

Matthew 21:42 [42] Jesus said to them, "Have you never read in the Scriptures: " 'The stone that the builders rejected has become the cornerstone; this was the Lord's doing, and it is marvelous in our eyes'?

[4] **Boaz quotes from these passages to argue that the temple is still in effect because the apostles used the temple**: Paul prayed in the temple at Jerusalem: Acts 22:17.
Paul engaged in a Nazarite vow and ritual purification in the temple: Acts 21:17-26.
Paul had Timothy circumcised: Acts 16:3.

[5] **Alexander quotes from these passages to argue that the temple is obsolete in the New Covenant**: Galatians 4:3–5 [3] In the same way we also, when we were children, were enslaved to the elementary principles of the world. [4] But when the fullness of time had come, God sent forth his Son, born of woman, born under the law, [5] to redeem those who were under the law, so that we might receive adoption as sons.

Galatians 4:9–11 [9] But now that you have come to know God, or rather to be known by God, how can you turn back again to the weak and worthless elementary principles of the world, whose slaves you want to be once more? [10] You observe days and months and seasons and years! [11] I am afraid I may have labored over you in vain.

1 Corinthians 9:19–22 [19] For though I am free from all, I have made myself a servant to all, that I might win more of them. [20] To the Jews I became as a Jew, in order to win Jews. To those under the law I became as one under the law (though not being myself under the law) that I might win those under the law. [21] To those outside the law I became as one outside the law (not being outside the law of God but under the law of Christ) that I might win those outside the law. [22] To the weak I became weak, that I might win the weak. I have become all things to all people, that by all means I might save some.

Hebrews 8:13 [13] In speaking of a new covenant, he makes the first one obsolete. And what is becoming obsolete and growing old is ready to vanish away.

[6] **Alexander quotes from Galatians to argue that the promise to Abraham's seed was to Jesus as Messiah, NOT to physical descendants of Abraham**: Galatians 3:16 [16] Now the promises were made to Abraham and to his offspring. It does not say, "And to offsprings," referring to many, but referring to one, "And to your offspring," who is Christ.

Galatians 3:29 And if you are Christ's, then you are Abraham's offspring, heirs according to promise.

Romans 2:17–18 But if you call yourself a Jew and rely on the law and boast in God [18] and know his will

Romans 2:25 For circumcision indeed is of value if you obey the law, but if you break the law, your circumcision becomes uncircumcision.

Romans 2:28–29 [28] For no one is a Jew who is merely one outwardly, nor is circumcision outward and physical. [29] But a Jew is one inwardly, and circumcision is a matter of the heart, by the Spirit, not by the letter. His praise is not from man but from God.

[7] **Paul called the Judaizers, "the Mutilators"**: Philippians 3:2–3 [2] Look out for the dogs, look out for the evildoers, look out for those who mutilate the flesh. [3] For we are the circumcision, who worship by the Spirit of God and glory in Christ Jesus and put no confidence in the flesh.

"The force of Paul's rhetoric in this statement is nearly impossible to communicate in English translation. In Greek, the statement consists of three clauses all beginning with the same verb ("watch out"!) and each verb's direct object begins with a "k" sound. We can almost catch the rhetorical effectiveness of the phrase with the translation, "Beware the curs! Beware the criminals! Beware the cutters!" Paul is referring to Jewish Christians who teach that circumcision, dietary observance, and Sabbath-keeping are all necessary requirements, in addition to faith in Christ, for salvation. By calling them "dogs" Paul is turning their own advocacy of ritual purity back upon them. Because ancient streets were often home to dogs (Ps. 59:6, 14), who ate whatever they found, they may have been considered a symbol of nonobservance in matters of diet. The term "mutilators" (katatomē) is a play on the term "circumcision" (peritomē), which Paul uses in the next verse. Since circumcision was not necessary for salvation, those who promoted it were only mutilating the flesh, something that Leviticus 21:5 forbids as a pagan ritual." Clinton E. Arnold, *Zondervan Illustrated Bible Backgrounds Commentary: Romans to Philemon., vol. 3* (Grand Rapids, MI: Zondervan, 2002), 359–360.

You have severed yourselves from Christ: Galatians 5:1–5 [1] For freedom Christ has set us free; stand firm therefore, and do not submit again to a yoke of slavery. [2] Look: I, Paul, say to you that if you accept circumcision, Christ will be of no advantage to you. [3] I testify again to every man who accepts circumcision that he is obligated to keep the whole law. [4] You are severed from Christ, you who would be justified by the law; you have fallen away from grace. [5] For through the Spirit, by faith, we ourselves eagerly wait for the hope of righteousness.

[8] **Alexander quotes from these Bible passages to argue that true Jews are believers in Messiah, not physical descendants**: Romans 9:6–8 6 But it is not as though the word of God has failed. For not all who are descended from Israel belong to Israel, 7 and not all are children of Abraham because they are his offspring, but "Through Isaac shall your offspring be named." 8 This means that it is not the children of the flesh who are the children of God, but the children of the promise are counted as offspring.

Romans 4:13–16 [13] For the promise to Abraham and his offspring that he would be heir of the world did not come through the law but through the righteousness of faith. [14] For if it is the adherents of the law who are to be the heirs, faith is null and the promise is void. [15] For the law brings wrath, but where there is no law there is no transgression. [16] That is why it depends on faith, in order that the promise may rest on grace and be guaranteed to all his offspring—not only to the adherent of the law but also to the one who shares the faith of Abraham, who is the father of us all,

Remnant theology is that only the true believers WITHIN Israel are the true Israel: Romans 11:1–6 [1] I ask, then, has God rejected his people? By no means! For I myself am an Israelite, a descendant of Abraham, a member of the tribe of Benjamin. [2] God has not rejected his people whom he foreknew. Do you not know what the Scripture says of Elijah, how he appeals to God against Israel? [3] "Lord, they have killed your prophets, they have demolished your altars, and I alone am left, and they seek my life." [4] But what is God's reply to him? "I have kept for myself seven thousand men who have not bowed the knee to Baal." [5] So too at the present time there is a remnant, chosen by grace. [6] But if it is by grace, it is no longer on the basis of works; otherwise grace would no longer be grace.

Jesus is coming to judge the Jews of the first century because they killed him. He will then give the kingdom to another "people" a new congregation of the Lord: Matthew 21:33-44

Also: Luke 19:11, 27 As they heard these things, he proceeded to tell a parable, because he was near to Jerusalem, and because they supposed that the kingdom of God was to appear immediately…But as for these enemies of mine, who did not want me to reign over them, bring them here and slaughter them before me.' " (parable about Israel not prepared for God's arrival in Messiah)

Also: Matthew 22:2–7 "The kingdom of heaven may be compared to a king who gave a wedding feast for his son, [3] and sent his servants to call those who were invited to the wedding feast, but they would not come…[5] But they paid no attention and went off, one to his farm, another to his business, [6] while the rest seized his servants, treated them shamefully, and killed them. [7] The king was angry, and he sent his troops and destroyed those murderers and burned their city.

Gentiles who were not God's people are now God's people: Romans 9:23–26 [23] in order to make known the riches of his glory for vessels of mercy, which he has prepared beforehand for glory— [24] even us whom he has called, not from the Jews only but also from the Gentiles? [25] As indeed he says in Hosea, "Those who were not my people I will call 'my people,' and her who was not beloved I will call 'beloved.' " [26] "And in the very place where it was said to them, 'You are not my people,' there they will be called 'sons of the living God.' "

[9] **This part of the debate is a creative anachronism**. The ideas of two peoples of God, the Church and Israel, versus the church "replacing" Israel is only a recent dichotomy of Dispensational theology of the 19th century. However it greatly affects modern prophecy interpretation, and since there was much debate in the first century over theology, it was not too unreasonable to suppose that there may have been those who suggested such a thing, though it would surely have been considered heresy.

[10] **The root of Israel and the branches of Jew and Gentile can be found in**: Romans 11:11-24.

[11] **Boaz appeals here to**: Romans 11:28-32.

The gathering of remnant Israel back to the land prophesied in the Old Testament: "Ezekiel 36:24 I will take you from the nations and gather you from all the countries and bring you into your own land.

> Amos 9:9–15 [9] "For behold, I will command, and shake the house of Israel among all the nations as one shakes with a sieve…[14] I will restore the fortunes of my people Israel, and they shall rebuild the ruined cities and inhabit them;…[15] I will plant them on their land, and they shall never again be uprooted.

> Micah 2:12 I will surely assemble all of you, O Jacob; I will gather the remnant of Israel; I will set them together like sheep in a fold.

> "Isaiah 11:10–12 In that day the Lord will extend his hand yet a second time to recover the remnant that remains of his people, from Assyria, from Egypt, from Pathros, from Cush, from Elam, from Shinar, from Hamath, and from the coastlands of the sea. [12] He will raise a signal for the nations and will assemble the banished of Israel, and gather the dispersed of Judah from the four corners of the earth.

[12] **The Gospel of the New Covenant is the first century fulfillment of the gathering of Israel promised in the Old Testament**: Ezekiel 37:7-14 describes a vision that Ezekiel was given about the regathering and restoration of Israel depicted as a massive resurrection. Then in his further explanation of everything that restoration entailed, he writes this from the mouth of God:

> Ezekiel 37:21–28 [21] then say to them, Thus says the Lord GOD: Behold, I will take the people of Israel from the nations among which they have gone, and will gather them from all around, and bring them to their own land. [22] And I will make them one nation in the land, on the mountains of Israel. And one king shall be king over them all, and they shall be no longer two nations, and no longer divided into two kingdoms… [24] "My servant David shall be king over them, and they shall all have one shepherd. They shall walk in my rules and be careful to obey my statutes. [25] They shall dwell in the land that I gave to my servant Jacob, where your fathers lived. They and their children and their children's children shall dwell there forever, and David my servant shall be their prince forever. [26] I will make a covenant of peace with them. It shall be an everlasting covenant with them. And I will set them in their land and multiply them, and will set my sanctuary in their midst forevermore. [27] My dwelling place shall be with them, and I will be their God, and they shall be my people. [28] Then the nations will know that I am the LORD who sanctifies Israel, when my sanctuary is in their midst forevermore."

"In an expansion of that prophecy earlier in the text, God adds another promise that he will place his spirit within them and give them a heart of flesh to replace their heart of stone.

> Ezekiel 36:24–28 [24] I will take you from the nations and gather you from all the countries and bring you into your own land. [25] I will sprinkle clean water on you, and you shall be clean from all your uncleannesses, and from all your idols I will cleanse you. [26] And I will give you a new heart, and a new spirit I will put within you. And I will remove the heart of stone from your flesh and give you a heart of flesh. [27] And I will put my Spirit within you, and cause you to walk in my statutes and be careful to obey my rules. [28] You shall dwell in the land that I gave to your fathers, and you shall be my people, and I will be your God.

"On every level, this entire prophecy is about the arrival of the New Covenant, not some distant future reinstitution of the Old Covenant shadows of physical temple and land. Each of the prophecy's constituent elements are fulfilled in the New Testament Scriptures *at the time of the first century*. Let's take a look at those elements:

1. The gathering of Israel from all the nations (v. 21): This was already explained above as starting to occur in AD 30 at Pentecost (Acts 2). The New Covenant beginning in the first century.

2. One nation with one king, David (v. 24-25): It was already detailed above that this messianic reference was Jesus seated on David's throne at his resurrection and ascension (Acts 2:30-33) and uniting his sheepfolds (Jn 10:16). That's the New Covenant beginning in the first century.

3. The everlasting covenant of peace with Israel (v. 26): The New Testament says that this everlasting covenant of peace is the New Covenant brought through Christ beginning in the first century.

> Hebrews 13:20 [20] Now may the God of peace who brought again from the dead our Lord Jesus, the great shepherd of the sheep, by the blood of the eternal covenant,

> Colossians 1:20 [20] and through him to reconcile to himself all things, whether on earth or in heaven, making peace by the blood of his cross.

4. God's dwelling place shall be with them (v. 27-28): In multiple places in the New Testament the Church of believers in Jesus are described as God's temple (1Cor 3:16-17; Eph 2:19-22), but Paul explicitly quotes the Ezekiel prophecy of the regathering and God's dwelling as fulfilled in the New Covenant Church beginning in the first century.

> 2 Corinthians 6:16 [16] What agreement has the temple of God with idols? For we are the temple of the living God; as God said, "I will make my dwelling among them and walk among them, and I will be their God, and they shall be my people.

5. Remove the heart of stone, replace with a heart of flesh (36:26): Paul wrote that this promise of heart replacement was fulfilled in the arrival of the New Covenant of Christ beginning in the first century.

> 2 Corinthians 3:3 [3] And you show that you are a letter from Christ delivered by us, written not with ink but with the Spirit of the living God, not on tablets of stone but on tablets of human hearts.

6. God will put his Spirit in them and causing them to obey (36:27)

7. He will be their God and they will be His people (36:27): Not only does the Old Testament link these phrases to the New Covenant (Jer 31:31-34), but the New Testament also claims this promise was fulfilled beginning in the first century with the arrival of the New Covenant.

> Ephesians 1:13 [13] In him you also, when you heard the word of truth, the gospel of your salvation, and believed in him, were sealed with the promised Holy Spirit. (see also Jn 7:37-39, 1Cor 6:19)

> Hebrews 8:6–13 [6] "Behold, the days are coming, declares the Lord, when I will establish a new covenant with the house of Israel and with the house of Judah... I will put my laws into their minds, and write them on their hearts, and I will be their God, and they shall be my people... [13] In speaking of a new covenant, he makes the first one obsolete. And what is becoming obsolete and growing old is ready to vanish away.

"Notice how the Holy Spirit-authorized writer of Hebrews says right up front that the promise to the house of Israel and Judah is fulfilled in the arrival of the New Covenant in the first century, *not* in a future time yet to come. God places his Spirit in all believers in Jesus, they are his people of the New Covenant.

"Dispensationalists claim that the gathering of the Gentiles occurred with the coming of Jesus but not the promised gathering of Judah and Israel, which has yet to take place. But the New Testament over and over again claims that the New Covenant fulfills that promise to Judah and Israel of their gathering. If the New Testament claims a prophecy has been fulfilled, then it is literally anti-biblical to deny that fulfillment.

"Ezekiel 36-37 is pregnant with motifs and promises of the New Covenant arrival of Messiah, not a second coming and reinstitution of Old Covenant shadows. It is important to remember that the Old Testament contains no theology of the second coming of Messiah. It's all about the first coming for them. The second coming is a New Testament doctrine, not an Old Testament one. The whole point to the prophets was that when Messiah came, he would fulfill the promises and usher in the messianic age to come. The New Covenant is that messianic age, complete with Jesus seated on the throne of David (Eph 1:20-23). So when Christians read these prophecies as if they are intended to be split into pieces of fulfillment, the last of which will occur at a second coming of Christ, they are quite simply imposing their preconceived theology onto the text that has already been fulfilled instead of reading it within its original Old Covenant context." This was excerpted from Brian Godawa, *Israel in Bible Prophecy: The New Testament Fulfillment of the Promise to Abraham* (Embedded Pictures Publishing, 2017), 60-64.

The Kingdom of God is the "inheritance" of eternal life in the New Covenant that replaces the "inheritance" of physical land in the Old Covenant:

Galatians 4:30 30 But what does the Scripture say? "Cast out the slave woman and her son, for the son of the slave woman shall not inherit with the son of the free woman."

Galatians 3:18 For if the inheritance comes by the law, it no longer comes by promise; but God gave it to Abraham by a promise.

Ephesians 1:14 who is the guarantee of our inheritance until we acquire possession of it, to the praise of his glory.

Ephesians 1:18 having the eyes of your hearts enlightened, that you may know what is the hope to which he has called you, what are the riches of his glorious inheritance in the saints,

Hebrews 9:15 Therefore he is the mediator of a new covenant, so that those who are called may receive the promised eternal inheritance, since a death has occurred that redeems them from the transgressions committed under the first covenant.

Hebrews 11:8 By faith Abraham obeyed when he was called to go out to a place that he was to receive as an inheritance. And he went out, not knowing where he was going.

1 Peter 1:4 to an inheritance that is imperishable, undefiled, and unfading, kept in heaven for you,

For Jesus as the fulfillment of all the eternal promises to Abraham see: Brian Godawa, Israel in Bible Prophecy: The New Testament Fulfillment of the Promise to Abraham. books2read.com/u/m0zAAP

[14] Alexander quotes from this Bible passage to prove that earthly Jews and Jerusalem are rejected by God but Jew and Gentile who believe in Jesus are his true sons: Galatians 4:22-31.

[15] **Alexander quotes from Jesus' parables about God judging Israel by destroying the city and excluding the Jews from the kingdom**: Matthew 23:37–24:2 37 "O Jerusalem, Jerusalem, the city that kills the prophets and stones those who are sent to it! How often would I have gathered your children together as a hen gathers her brood under her wings, and you were not willing! 38 See, your house is left to you desolate. 39 For I tell you, you will not see me again, until you say, 'Blessed is he who comes in the name of the Lord.' " 1 Jesus left the temple and was going away, when his disciples came to point out to him the buildings of the temple. 2 But he answered them, "You see all these, do you not? Truly, I say to you, there will not be left here one stone upon another that will not be thrown down."

Matthew 22:4–9 [4] Again he sent other servants, saying, 'Come to the wedding feast.' ' [5] But they paid no attention and went off, one to his farm, another to his business, [6] while the rest seized his servants, treated them shamefully, and killed them. [7] The king was angry, and he sent his troops and destroyed those murderers and burned their city. [8] Then he said to his servants, 'The wedding feast is ready, but those invited were not worthy. [9] Go therefore to the main roads and invite to the wedding feast as many as you find.'

Matthew 21:37–43[37] Finally he sent his son to them, saying, 'They will respect my son.' [38] But when the tenants saw the son, they said to themselves, 'This is the heir. Come, let us kill him and have his inheritance.' [39] And they took him and threw him out of the vineyard and killed him. [40] When therefore the owner of the vineyard comes, what will he do to those tenants?" [41] They said to him, "He will put those wretches to a miserable death and let out the vineyard to other tenants who will give him the fruits in their seasons." [42] Jesus said to them, "Have you never read in the Scriptures: " 'The stone that the builders rejected has become the cornerstone; this was the Lord's doing, and it is marvelous in our eyes'? [43] Therefore I tell you, the kingdom of God will be taken away from you and given to a people producing its fruits."

Matthew 8:11–12 [11] I tell you, many will come from east and west and recline at table with Abraham, Isaac, and Jacob in the kingdom of heaven, [12] while the sons of the kingdom will be thrown into the outer darkness. In that place there will be weeping and gnashing of teeth."

Wrath has come upon the Jews to the utmost: 1 Thessalonians 2:14–15 [14] For you, brothers, became imitators of the churches of God in Christ Jesus that are in Judea. For you suffered the same things from your own countrymen as they did from the Jews, [15] who killed both the Lord Jesus and the prophets, and drove us out, and displease God and oppose all mankind

CHAPTER 24

[1] **Cassandra remembers this Bible passage**: Revelation 13:11–14.

[2] **Fire from heaven on the altar**: "Here in [Revelation] 13:13 John is presenting an important and relevant element of the first-century high priest's work which involves the manipulation of fire—though it is not a literal miracle. In that his "signs" (sēmeia) are exhibited in the presence of men (v. 13) and are designed to deceive men regarding matters of worship (vv. 14–15), John may be portraying them as miraculous for dramatic purposes. The Jews were especially influenced by signs (1Co 1:22; cp. Mt 12:38–39), even responding to good signs for the wrong reasons (Jn 2:23–25). But these "signs" may not have been miracles at all. The primary meaning of sēmeion is: "sign, token, indication or portent" (cf. BAGD 920). It is used in non-miraculous contexts regarding the baby Jesus in a manger (Lk 2:12), Judas' kiss (Mt 26:48), covenantal circumcision (Ro 4:11), Paul's signature (2Th 3:17), and so forth—none of which were miraculous…

"Since the altar is God-fired, Leviticus warns that "the fire on the altar shall be kept burning on it. It shall not go out, but the priest shall burn wood on it every morning; and he shall lay out the burnt offering on it, and offer up in smoke the fat portions of the peace offerings on it. Fire shall be kept burning continually on the altar; it is not to go out" (Lev 6:12-13)…

"So then, in 13:13 it appears that the Land beast's fire under the authority of the sea beast represents the Jewish high priesthood's conducting temple sacrifices at God's heaven-fired altar. In this context involving his submission to the sea beast, John has specifically in view the priestly sacrifices on behalf of the Roman emperor. We know from history that the priestly hierarchy offered "sacrifices twice every day for Caesar, and the Roman people" (J.W. 2:10:4 §197; Philo, Embassy 32 §157, 232; 40 §317; 45 §355). In fact, elsewhere Josephus writes: "We also offer perpetual sacrifices for them; nor do we only offer them every day at the common expenses of all the Jews, but although we offer no other such sacrifices out of our common expenses, no, not for our own children, yet do we this as a peculiar honor to the emperors, and to them alone, while we do the same to no other person whomsoever" (Ap. 2:6 §77-78; cp. J.W. 2:10:4 §197). Thus, "just as Caesar was linked with traditional gods and heroes elsewhere in the East, so in the Jerusalem Temple, the priests 'offered sacrifice twice daily for Caesar and the Roman people'" (Horsley 1995: 122).

"By his symbolically linking the Land beast (the high priest) to the sea beast (Rome), John appears to be taking a jab at the Jewish sacrifice in honor of the emperor. Sacrifices on the altar speak of atonement and forgiveness of sin, peace with God, and other such spiritual realities. How then can they offer sacrifices in honor of the idolatrous emperor? Sacrifices on behalf of the emperor involve a selling-out of the priestly system so that they might preserve their own power." Kenneth L. Gentry, Jr., *The Divorce of Israel: A Redemptive-Historical Interpretation of Revelation Vol. 2* (Dallas, GA: Tolle Lege Press, 2016), 265, 269.

[3] **Because the temple is no longer God's temple, to worship at it is to worship at the temple of the Beast**: "So then, in 13:13 it appears that the Land beast's fire under the authority of the sea beast represents the Jewish high priesthood's conducting temple sacrifices at God's heaven-fired altar. In this context involving his submission to the sea beast, John has specifically in view the priestly sacrifices in behalf of the Roman emperor. We know from history that the priestly hierarchy offers "sacrifices twice every day for Caesar, and the Roman people" (J.W. 2:10:4 §197; Philo, Embassy 32 §157, 232; 40 §317; 45 §355)…

"In fact, elsewhere Josephus writes: "we also offer perpetual sacrifices for them; nor do we only offer them every day at the common expenses of all the Jews, but although we offer no other such sacrifices out of our common expenses, no, not for our own children, yet do we this as a peculiar honor to the emperors, and to them alone, while we do the same to no other person whomsoever" (Ap. 2:6 §77-78; cp. J.W. 2:10:4 §197). Thus, "just as Caesar was linked with traditional gods and heroes elsewhere in the East, so in the Jerusalem Temple, the priests 'offered sacrifice twice daily for Caesar and the Roman people" (Horsley 1995: 122)…

"The temple worship of that day is all for men, and not for God, because God turns from it to establish a new temple (see Exc 11 at 13:12). We see this clearly in Rev's conclusion: "I saw no temple in it, for the Lord God, the Almighty, and the Lamb, are its temple" (Rev 21:22). The temple system is "obsolete" (pepalaiōken) in John's day and "ready to disappear" (Heb 8:1380). The physical temple and its ritual service have become Israel's idol. Their religious authorities themselves sell out their temple to Rome when they reject the true temple, Christ (cf. Mk 14:58//; 15:29//). Their declaration in favor of Caesar over Christ in Jn

19:15 "was a clear renunciation of their Messianic hope, a virtual abolition of the Theocracy — a deliberate abandonment of their place and purpose as a nation" (Whitelaw 1993: 397). The temple service and religious rituals are deceptive, no longer functioning as God's blessing (13:14; cp. Gal 4:10; 5:6, 12; Php 3:2-3; Heb 9-10). The Land beast's deceiving activity entails his operating within Israel, for his "imagery and background suggest deception within the covenant community itself" (Beale 708).

"Revelation is dramatically presenting the temple itself as the image of the beast. Its rulers align themselves with the Emperor over against Christ and his followers, encouraged sacrifices for Caesar (Exc 11 at 13:12), and violently resist the Christian witness against the temple and ceremonial features of the law. The charge against Stephen, the first martyr, is that "this man incessantly speaks against this holy place, and the Law; for we have heard him say that this Nazarene, Jesus, will destroy this place and alter the customs which Moses handed down to us"86 (Ac 6:13). But ironically, despite the temple authorities' formal and external resistance to images, they spiritually commit idolatry by denying God and his Messiah by trusting in the old temple and its ritual instead of trusting in the true Temple and his redemption. Thus it befalls them as their fathers before them that "he who burns incense is like the one who blesses an idol" (Isa 66:3d). It is probably significant that John employs the word "image" (eikōn) rather than "idol" (eidōla), for just as men are the "image [eikona] of God" (Ge 1:26; 1Co 11:7), the Jewish hierarchy so control the temple system that it becomes an image of their god, Caesar — and ultimately of his god, Satan (13:2; cp. 2:9; 3:9; Jn 8:44)…

"We must recall that the Land beast "spoke as a dragon," that is, deceptively. And since John is casting their beloved (but doomed, Mt 24:2//) temple and its services as an idolatrous image, the speaking of the image may refer to either (1) the deceptively alluring temple liturgy as speaking delusory words of peace and acceptance to all who submit; or (2) the satanically inspired orders (Jn 8:44; 13:2) from Jewish temple authorities against Christ and his followers." Kenneth L. Gentry, Jr., *The Divorce of Israel: A Redemptive-Historical Interpretation of Revelation Vol. 2* (Dallas, GA: Tolle Lege Press, 2016), 273, 274.

⁴ **The harlot that rides the beast**: Revelation 17:3-6; 13:11.

Israel as adulterous harlot with idols: Ezekiel 16:15-59; Ezekiel 23; 2Kings 17:7-17; Jeremiah 3:1-11; Hosea 1-2.

The harlot that rides the beast represents the corrupt Jewish leaders: "Since the harlot is dressed in the distinctive robe of the high priest which is worn only on holy occasions (Ex 28:2-4, 41, 43), and since she possesses a "gold cup" as used in libations (Ex 25:29; 1Ki 7:50; cp. m. Yoma 3:10), Rev is presenting the holy city (cp. 11:1) under the guise of the high-priest engaged in his sacerdotal duties…

"That the gold cup is "full of abominations and of the unclean things of her immorality further identifies the harlot as Jerusalem. The kai here is probably epexegetical, signifying that she is "full of abominations, which are, the uncleanness of her immorality." In the OT, the word *abominations* is often a religious term signifying that which the God of Israel detests and "uncleanness" is a cultic term related to Israel's separation to God. This religio-cultic concern is strongly Jewish, well fitting first-century Jerusalem…

"So in John's drama the priestly libations God ordains for holy worship are replaced in Jerusalem's high-priestly system: their golden libation bowls now are filled with uncleanness because of their spilling the innocent blood of Christ and Christians. Rather than offering humble sacrifices to God in true worship, the temple system destroys the followers of the Lamb…

"John portrays Jerusalem's situation as a sexual liaison (she is a "harlot" committing "immorality," 17:2, 4-5) with Rome. In the background of ch 17 is the "league of friendship and mutual alliance" with Rome, beginning with Julius Caesar (1 Macc 8:17–30; 14:24, 40; Jos. Ant. 12:10:6 §414–19; 13:5:8 §163–65; 14:10:1–8 §185–216; 16:6:2–3 §162–66; 19:9:2 §360–65).36 In 1 Macc 14:40 the Jews call themselves "friends, allies, and brothers of Rome," and were, according to Smallwood (2001: 7) "immensely proud of the alliance." Josephus (Ant. 14:10:1 §186) writes: "it seems to me to be necessary here to give an account of all the honors that the Romans and their emperors paid to our nation, and of the leagues of mutual assistance they have made with it." Philo also mentions that the Jews are "friends to Caesar"… John is painting Jerusalem in the same way Isaiah and Jeremiah did as they spoke of the first temple's destruction: "How the faithful city has become a harlot, / She who was full of justice! / Righteousness once lodged in her, / But now murderers" (Isa 1:21). "You have lain down as a harlot . . . . Also on your skirts is found / The lifeblood of the innocent poor" (Jer 2:20d; 34a; cp. 7:6; 19:3-4; 22:11, 17)." Kenneth L. Gentry, Jr., *The Divorce of Israel: A Redemptive-Historical Interpretation of Revelation Vol. 2* (Dallas, GA: Tolle Lege Press, 2016), 435, 429, 430, 416-417.

[5] **This passage on the False Prophet comes from**: Revelation 19:20.

[6] **The false prophet as the high priest of first century Israel**: Alexander is remembering Revelation 16:13-16 about the false prophet and the battle of Armageddon.

"Corsini (333) perceptively observes that "the beast-prostitute pair... constitute a repetition of the two beasts of ch. 13, described here not only in their complementary aspect, but also in the complexity involved in the symbol." On the same page he continues: "The symbol of the prostitute, like the beast from the land / false prophet, also points to Judaism. The symbol signifies Judaism's perversion, through the metaphor of prostitution. Prostitution means idolatry and Judaism has become idolatrous because it adores the beast and its statue, political authority. This is the case not because it accepts the political domination of the Romans.... Judaism adopts their mentality, their means and their goals."

"The angelomorphic Christ now declares that Babylon-Jerusalem has become a dwelling place of demons (18:2b). Here we see Babylon-Jerusalem associated with "demons" — and "every unclean spirit" (18:2c). This is not surprising in that the "false prophet" (the high-priestly aristocracy) issues death decrees against Christ and Christians (Ac 9:1-2, 21) when prompted by "unclean spirits," the "spirits of demons" (cf. 16:13-14). Kenneth L. Gentry, Jr., *The Divorce of Israel: A Redemptive-Historical Interpretation of Revelation Vol. 2* (Dallas, GA: Tolle Lege Press, 2016), 492.

[7] **Two horns on the Land Beast**: "The second beast symbolizes apostate Judaism as concentrated in its religious leadership embodied in its high priestly aristocracy. That being the case, his two horns could possibly represent the high priest and the "captain of the temple guard [stratēgos tou hierou]" (Ac 4:1; 5:24, 26).

"Footnote: 5 According to Jeremias (1969: 161), "the highest ranking priest after the high priest was the captain of the Temple.... His privileged position is illustrated by the fact that the assisted the high priest in the solemn performance of his ceremonial duties, and therefore had a special place at his right hand (M. Yom. iii.9; iv.1; M. Tam. vii.3; j. Yom. iii.8, 41a.4; cf. M. Yom. vii.i; M. Sot. vii.7-8). When the high priest gave or received condolences the captain of the Temple stood on his right (T. Sanh. iv.1, 420; b. Sanh. 19a)." His significance is also seen in that the high priest had to first serve as Captain of the Temple before becoming high priest (j. Yoma 3:8, 41a.5)." Kenneth L. Gentry, Jr., *The Divorce of Israel: A Redemptive-Historical Interpretation of Revelation Vol. 2* (Dallas, GA: Tolle Lege Press, 2016), 236.

[8] **Israel/Jerusalem described in Revelation as Sodom, Egypt and Babylon**: Revelation 11:8 ...the great city that symbolically is called Sodom and Egypt, where their Lord was crucified.

Revelation 16:19 The great city was split into three parts, and the cities of the nations fell, and God remembered Babylon the great, to make her drain the cup of the wine of the fury of his wrath.

"We may discern that this storm-theophany is particularly aimed at Jerusalem from the statement that the great city was split into three parts (16:19a) and Babylon the great was remembered before God (16:19c). This evidently refers to Jerusalem under the appellation of "Babylon" in that: (1) Revelation's theme strongly suggest that Israel's capital, the home of the old covenant temple, should be the key target of judgment (1:7). And Babylon certainly has a strong presence in the next two, climactic chapters of Revelation. (2) We learned earlier in 11:8 that "the great city" is where the "Lord was crucified." John also informs us there that the once holy city can be "mystically [pneumatikōs]" called by pagan names (such as "Babylon"). Like the great city Jerusalem in 11:8, the great city in 16:19 is also subjected to a "great earthquake... (3) In a separate statement from his comment regarding "the great city," John states that the cities of the nations fell (16:19b). This indicates that "Babylon the great" is not one of the "cities of the Gentiles" but of the Jews. As Oecumenius put it in the sixth century: "By the great city he means Jerusalem, and he clearly contrasts with the cities of the nations." Ruiz agrees: "Contrary to the opinion of the majority of commentators, the data presented above indicate that hē polis hē megalē in 16:19c refers to Jerusalem." Kenneth L. Gentry, Jr., *The Divorce of Israel: A Redemptive-Historical Interpretation of Revelation Vol. 2* (Dallas, GA: Tolle Lege Press, 2016), 375.

[9] **The first century generation of Jews were wicked and spiritually adulterous for rejecting Jesus as Messiah**: Matt. 11:16 "But to what shall I compare this generation? 18 "For John came neither eating nor drinking, and they say, 'He has a demon!' 19 "The Son of Man came eating and drinking, and they say, 'Behold, a gluttonous man and a drunkard, a friend of tax collectors and sinners!' Yet wisdom is vindicated by her deeds."

Luke 11:29 As the crowds were increasing, He began to say, "This generation is a wicked generation; it seeks for a sign, and yet no sign will be given to it but the sign of Jonah,"

Matt 12:41 "The men of Nineveh will stand up with <u>this generation</u> at the judgment, and will condemn it because they repented at the preaching of Jonah; and behold, something greater than Jonah is here. 42 "The Queen of the South will rise up with <u>this generation</u> at the judgment and will condemn it, because she came from the ends of the earth to hear the wisdom of Solomon; and behold, something greater than Solomon is here.

Matt. 12:45 "Then it goes and takes along with it seven other spirits more wicked than itself, and they go in and live there; and the last state of that man becomes worse than the first. That is the way it will also be with <u>this evil generation</u>."

Matt. 17:17 And Jesus answered and said, "You <u>unbelieving and perverted generation</u>, how long shall I be with you? How long shall I put up with you?

Mark 8:38 "For whoever is ashamed of Me and My words in <u>this adulterous and sinful generation</u>, the Son of Man will also be ashamed of him <u>when He comes in the glory of His Father with the holy angels</u>."

CHAPTER 25

[1] **The vindication of the martyrs beneath heaven's altar**: Revelation 6:9–11 When he opened the fifth seal, I saw under the altar the souls of those who had been slain for the word of God and for the witness they had borne. [10] They cried out with a loud voice, "O Sovereign Lord, holy and true, how long before you will judge and avenge our blood on those who dwell on the earth?" [11] Then they were each given a white robe and told to rest a little longer, until the number of their fellow servants and their brothers should be complete, who were to be killed as they themselves had been.

The martyrs of Christ in the first century is a dominant theme and purpose of Revelation: Revelation 1:9; 2:9-10; 3:9-10; 6:9-11; 11:7-8, 11-13, 18; 12:10; 13:10; 14:11-13; 16:5-6; 17:6; 18:20, 24; 19:2; 20:4, 6.

The Jews were the first persecutors of the church: Ac 4:3; 5:18-33; 6:12; 7:58-60; 8:1; 9:1-3, 13, 23; 11:19; 12:1-4; 13:45-50; 14:2-5, 19; 16:23; 17:5-13; 18:6, 12; 20:3, 19; 21:11, 27; 22:4, 30; 23:12-15, 20, 27, 30; 24:5-9, 27; 25:2-15; 25:24; 26:10, 21. See also: Ro 15:31; 2Co 11:24; 2Th 2:14-15; Heb 10:32-34.

The Neronic persecution marks the entry of Rome into the Great Tribulation. Until then, they had considered Christians to be a sect of Judaism. With the Neronic persecution, Christianity became singled out for attack. And even then, it was the Jews who instigated it by persuading Nero most likely through Poppea, Aliturius the mime and possibly Josephus who was there when the Great Fire occurred. To God, both Rome and Israel were guilty of crucifying Christ (Acts 2:22-24, see below), but because Israel was in covenant with God, her sin was greater and was the focus of God's wrath in the destruction of the city and temple (Matthew 23:31-38, see below).

Acts 2:22–24 [22] "Men of Israel, hear these words: Jesus of Nazareth, a man attested to you by God with mighty works and wonders and signs that God did through him in your midst, as you yourselves know— [23] this Jesus, delivered up according to the definite plan and foreknowledge of God, <u>you crucified and killed by the hands of lawless men.</u> [24] God raised him up, loosing the pangs of death, because it was not possible for him to be held by it.

Matthew 23:31–38 [31] Thus you witness against yourselves that you are sons of those who murdered the prophets. [32] Fill up, then, the measure of your fathers. [33] You serpents, you brood of vipers, how are you to escape being sentenced to hell? [34] Therefore I send you prophets and wise men and scribes, some of whom you will kill and crucify, and some you will flog in your synagogues and persecute from town to town, [35] so that on you may come all the righteous blood shed on earth, from the blood of righteous Abel to the blood of Zechariah the son of Barachiah, whom you murdered between the sanctuary and the altar. [36] Truly, I say to you, all these things will come upon this generation. [37] "O Jerusalem, Jerusalem, the city that kills the prophets and stones those who are sent to it! How often would I have gathered your children together as a hen gathers her brood under her wings, and you were not willing! [38] See, your house is left to you desolate.

[2] **Eleazer ben Ananias**: Josephus, *Wars of the Jews* 2.409-410 "Eleazar, son of the murdered high priest Ananias. This Eleazar first proposed the cessation of the sacrifices, and was a staunch supporter of the ordinary priests against the high priests. He was responsible for leading the war party in its early attacks on the peace party in the upper city, for the assassination of the rebel leader Menahem, and for the perfidious murder of the Roman garrison under Metilius." Tessa Rajak, *Josephus* (Bristol Classical Press; 2nd edition, 2002) 129.

On taking over the inner temple: Actually, it was Manahem, leader of the Sicarii, who first took over the inner temple and killed Ananias the high priest. Shortly afterward, Eleazar took it from Manahem and killed the latter. So I combined that sequence of events and telescoped them for the sake of simplicity.

Manahem, leader of the Sicarii: Flavius Josephus, *Wars of the Jews* 2.433-40, 44-48 "An even better known son [of Judas, the originator of the Zealot's "Fourth Philosophy"] was Menahem, leader of the sicarii until his murder in autumn 66. He is described interestingly as a sophistes (teacher of the law?), and was arrogant enough to appear at the Temple for ritual purposes in regal array, accompanied by an armed bodyguard of devoted followers." See also, Tessa Rajak, *Josephus* (Bristol Classical Press; 2nd edition, 2002), 116.

[3] **The Jewish response to Caesarea**: Flavius Josephus, *The Wars of the Jews*, 2.18.1 §458-460 "Upon which stroke that the Jews received at Caesarea, the whole nation was greatly enraged; so they divided themselves into several parties, and laid waste the villages of the Syrians, and their neighboring cities, Philadelphia, and Sebonitis, and Gerasa, and Pella, and Scythopolis, (459) and after them Gadara, and Hippos; and falling upon Gaulonitis, some cities they destroyed there, and some they set on fire, and then they went to Kedasa, belonging to the Tyrians, and to Ptolemais, and to Gaba, and to Cesarea; (460) nor was either Sabaste (Samaria) or Askelon, able to oppose the violence with which they were attacked; and when they had burned these to the ground, they entirely demolished Anthedon and Gaza; many also of the villages that were about every one of those cities were plundered, and an immense slaughter was made of the men who were caught in them." Flavius Josephus and William Whiston, *The Works of Josephus: Complete and Unabridged* (Peabody: Hendrickson, 1987), 627.

[4] **The prophecies of Israel's destruction that Cassandra quotes here**: 1 Thessalonians 2:14–16 For you, brothers, became imitators of the churches of God in Christ Jesus that are in Judea. For you suffered the same things from your own countrymen as they did from the Jews, [15] who killed both the Lord Jesus and the prophets, and drove us out, and displease God and oppose all mankind [16] by hindering us from speaking to the Gentiles that they might be saved—so as always to fill up the measure of their sins. But wrath has come upon them at last!

Revelation 1:7 Behold, he is coming with the clouds, and every eye will see him, even those who pierced him, and all tribes of the earth will wail on account of him.

CHAPTER 26

[1] **Christ's triumphal procession, with victory over the spiritual powers**: Colossians 2:15 [15] He disarmed the rulers and authorities and put them to open shame, by triumphing over them in him.

Ephesians 4:8–10 [8] Therefore it says, "When he ascended on high he led a host of captives, and he gave gifts to men." [9] (In saying, "He ascended," what does it mean but that he had also descended into the lower regions, the earth? [10] He who descended is the one who also ascended far above all the heavens, that he might fill all things.)

1 Peter 3:21–22 [21] Jesus Christ, [22] who has gone into heaven and is at the right hand of God, with angels, authorities, and powers having been subjected to him.

Ephesians 1:20–22 [20] that he worked in Christ when he raised him from the dead and seated him at his right hand in the heavenly places, [21] far above all rule and authority and power and dominion, and above every name that is named, not only in this age but also in the one to come. [22] And he put all things under his feet.

[2] **The Gates of Hades**: "In Matthew 16:13-20 is the famous story of Peter's confession of Jesus as the Christ, who then responds, "I tell you, you are Peter, and on this rock I will build my church, and the gates of hell [Hades] shall not prevail against it" (v. 18). Shortly after, Jesus leads them up to a high mountain where he is transfigured.

"In order to understand the spiritual reality of what is going on in this polemical sequence and its relevance to the cosmic War of the Seed, we must first understand where it is going on.

"Verse 13 says that Peter's confession takes place in the district of Caesarea Philippi. This city was in the heart of Bashan on a rocky terrace in the foothills of Mount Hermon. This was the celebrated location of the grotto of Banias or Panias, where the satyr goat god Pan was worshipped and from where the mouth

411

of the Jordan river flowed. This very location was what was known as the "gates of Hades," the underworld abode of dead souls.

"As scholar Judd Burton points out, this is a kind of ground zero for the gods against whom Jesus was fighting his cosmic spiritual war. Mount Hermon was the location where the Watchers came to earth, led their rebellion and miscegenation, which birthed the Nephilim (1 Enoch 13:7-10). It was their headquarters, in Bashan, the place of the Serpent, where Azazel may have been worshipped before Pan as a desert goat idol.

"When Jesus speaks of building his church upon a rock, it is as much a polemical contrast with the pagan city upon the rock, as it may have been a word play off of Peter's name, meaning "stone." In the ancient world, mountains were not only a gateway between heaven, earth, and the underworld, but also the habitations of the gods that represented their heavenly power and authority. The mountain before them, Hermon, was considered the heavenly habitation of Canaanite gods as well as the very Watchers before whose gates of Hades Jesus now stood. The polemics become clearer when one realizes that gates are not offensive weapons, but defensive means. Christ's kingship is storming the very gates of Hades/Sheol in the heart of darkness and he will build his cosmic holy mountain upon its ruins." Brian Godawa, *When Giants Were Upon the Earth: The Watchers, the Nephilim, and the Biblical Cosmic War of the Seed* (Embedded Pictures, 2014), 295-296.

[3] **Sons of God as shining beings**: "In Job 38, the sons of God are referred to as "morning stars." That same description is found outside the Bible in ancient texts from the biblical world. Ancient people thought the stars were living entities. Their reasoning was simple: Many stars moved. That was a sign of life to the ancient mind. Stars were the shining glory of living beings.

"The stars also inhabited the divine realm—literally, in the sense that they existed off the earth. The ancients believed that divine beings lived far away from humans, in remote places where human habitation wasn't possible. The most remote place of all was the sky, the heavens."

Michael S. Heiser, The Unseen Realm: Recovering the Supernatural Worldview of the Bible, First Edition (Bellingham, WA: Lexham Press, 2015), 24.

"Let's reconsider the gemstones that describe the appearance of the "the sealer" in Ezekiel 28:13. As I mentioned earlier, proponents of the view that Ezekiel is drawing on Adam's rebellion for his analogous portrayal of the prince of Tyre want to argue that the gemstones point to a human priest-king. But the "adornment" can quite easily be telegraphing something else—divinity. All of the gems have one thing in common—they shine or sparkle. Luminescence is a characteristic of divine beings or divine presence across the ancient Near Eastern world and the Old Testament (e.g., Ezek 1:4–7, 27–28 [cf. Ezek 10:19–20]; Dan 10:6; Rev 1:15). This description of the divine cherub in Eden is designed to convey divinity—a shining presence.

"There are more details. The anointed cherub ultimately gets cast out of Eden, out from "the midst of the stones of fire." We already know from other data that Eden is the place of the council. The "stones of fire" is another clue in that direction. This phrase is associated in other Jewish texts (1 Enoch 18:6–11; 1 Enoch 24–25) with the supernatural, mountainous dwelling of God and the divine council.

"It may be objected here that Eden was the dwelling place of God and so the "stones of fire" do not only point to the divine beings of Yahweh's council. That much is true, but there's more to the phrase than a dwelling place. Other scholars have also drawn attention to the ancient Near Eastern propensity to describe divine beings as stars. Job 38:7 refers to the sons of God as "stars," and Isaiah 14:12–13 refers to a being fallen from heaven as the "Day Star, son of Dawn" (ESV) who wanted to ascend above the "stars of God" in the divine realm. The "stones of fire" therefore do not only describe an abode, but also divine entities in that abode." Michael S. Heiser, *The Unseen Realm: Recovering the Supernatural Worldview of the Bible, First Edition* (Bellingham, WA: Lexham Press, 2015), 79–80.

Jesus as the unique Son of God: "Readers of Psalm 82 often raise a specific question about Jesus. If there are other divine sons of God, what do we make of the description of Jesus as the "only begotten" son of God (John 1:14, 18; 3:16, 18; 1 John 4:9)? How could Jesus be the only divine son when there were others?

"Only begotten" is an unfortunately confusing translation, especially to modern ears. Not only does the translation "only begotten" seem to contradict the obvious statements in the Old Testament about other sons of God, it implies that there was a time when the Son did not exist—that he had a beginning.

"The Greek word translated by this phrase is monogenes. It doesn't mean "only begotten" in some sort of "birthing" sense. The confusion extends from an old misunderstanding of the root of the Greek word. For years monogenes was thought to have derived from two Greek terms, monos ("only") and gennao ("to beget, bear"). Greek scholars later discovered that the second part of the word monogenes does not come from the Greek verb gennao, but rather from the noun genos ("class, kind"). The term literally means "one of a kind" or "unique" without connotation of created origin. Consequently, since Jesus is indeed identified with Yahweh and is therefore, with Yahweh, unique among the elohim that serve God, the term monogenes does not contradict the Old Testament language.

"The validity of this understanding is borne out by the New Testament itself. In Hebrews 11:17, Isaac is called Abraham's monogenes. If you know your Old Testament you know that Isaac was not the "only begotten" son of Abraham. Abraham had earlier fathered Ishmael (cf. Gen 16:15; 21:3). The term must mean that Isaac was Abraham's unique son, for he was the son of the covenant promises. Isaac's genealogical line would be the one through which Messiah would come. Just as Yahweh is an elohim, and no other elohim are Yahweh, so Jesus is the unique Son, and no other sons of God are like him." Michael S. Heiser, *The Unseen Realm: Recovering the Supernatural Worldview of the Bible, First Edition* (Bellingham, WA: Lexham Press, 2015), 36–37.

The Transfiguration and the Mountain of Bashan (Hermon) replaced by Mount Zion: But the battle is only beginning. Because the very next incident that occurs is the transfiguration (Matt. 17:1-13). The text says that Jesus led three disciples up a high mountain. But it doesn't say which mountain. Though tradition has often concluded it was Mount Tabor, a more likely candidate is Mount Hermon itself. The reasons are because Tabor is not a high mountain at only 1800 feet compared to Hermon's 9000 feet height, and Tabor was a well traveled location which would not allow Jesus to be alone with his disciples (17:1).

"Then the text says, that Jesus "was transfigured before them, and his face shone like the sun, and his clothes became white as light. And behold, there appeared to them Moses and Elijah, talking with him" (Matthew 17:2–3). When Peter offers to put up three tabernacles for each of his heroes, he hears a voice from the cloud say, "This is my beloved Son with whom I am well pleased, listen to him" (vs. 4-5). The theological point of this being that Moses and Elijah are the representatives of the Old Covenant, summed up as the Law (Moses) and the Prophets (Elijah), but Jesus is the anointed King (Messiah) that both Law and Prophets pointed toward.

"So God is anointing Jesus and transferring all covenantal authority to him as God's own Son. And for what purpose? To become king upon the new cosmic mountain that God was establishing: Mount Zion in the city of God. In the Mosaic Covenant, Mount Sinai was considered the cosmic mountain of God where God had his assembly of divine holy ones (Deut. 33:2-3). But now, as pronounced by the prophets, that mountain was being transferred out of the wilderness wandering into a new home in the Promised Land as Mount Zion (ultimately in Jerusalem). And that new mountain was the displacement and replacement of the previous divine occupants of Mount Hermon. Of course, just like David the messianic type, Jesus was anointed as king, but there would be a delay of time before he would take that rightful throne because he had some Goliaths yet to conquer (1 Sam. 16:13; 2 Sam. 5:3).

"Take a look at this Psalm and see how the language of cosmic war against the anointed Messiah is portrayed as a victory of God establishing his new cosmic mountain. We see a repeat of the language of Jesus' transfiguration at Hermon.

> Psalm 2:1–8 (NASB95) 1 Why are the nations in an uproar And the peoples devising a vain thing? 2 The kings of the earth take their stand And the rulers [heavenly as well?] take counsel together Against the LORD and against His Anointed [Messiah], saying, 3 "Let us tear their fetters apart And cast away their cords from us!" 4 He who sits in the heavens laughs, The Lord scoffs at them. 5 Then He will speak to them in His anger And terrify them in His fury, saying, 6 "But as for Me, I have installed My King Upon Zion, My holy mountain." 7 "I will surely tell of the decree of the LORD: He said to Me, 'You are My Son, Today I have begotten You. 8 'Ask of Me, and I will surely give the nations as Your inheritance, And the very ends of the earth as Your possession.

"Like Moses' transfiguration in Exodus 34:29, Jesus' body was transformed by his anointing to shine with the glory of those who surround God's throne (Dan. 10:6; Ezek 1:14-16, 21ff.; 10:9). But that description is no where near the ending of this spiritual parade of triumph being previewed in God's Word. One last passage illustrates the conquering change of ownership of the cosmic mountain in Bashan. Notice the ironic language used of Bashan as God's mountain, and the spiritual warfare imagery of its replacement.

413

Psalm 68:15–22 O mountain of God, mountain of Bashan; O many-peaked mountain, mountain of Bashan! 16 Why do you look with hatred, O many-peaked mountain, at the mount that God desired for his abode, yes, where the LORD will dwell forever? 17 The chariots of God are twice ten thousand, thousands upon thousands; the Lord is among them; Sinai is now in the sanctuary. 18 You ascended on high, leading a host of captives in your train and receiving gifts among men, even among the rebellious, that the LORD God may dwell there… 21 But God will strike the heads of his enemies, the hairy crown of him who walks in his guilty ways. 22 The Lord said, "I will bring them back from Bashan, I will bring them back from the depths of the sea.

"In this Psalm, God takes ownership of Bashan with his heavenly host of warriors, but then replaces it and refers to Sinai (soon to be Zion). It is not that God is making Bashan his mountain literally, but conquering its divinities and theologically replacing it with his new cosmic mountain elsewhere. In verse 18 we see a foreshadowing of Christ's own victorious heavenly ascension, where he leads captives in triumphal procession and receives tribute from them as spoils of war (v. 18). He will own and live where once the rebellious ruled (v. 18). He strikes the "hairy crown" (seir) of the people of that area (v. 21), the descendants of the cursed hairy Esau/Seir, who worshipped the goat demons (as depicted in Joshua Valiant and Caleb Vigilant). He will bring them all out from the sea of chaos, that wilderness where Leviathan symbolically reigns.

"But first, the Messiah must descend into that sea to claim his victory." Brian Godawa, *When Giants Were Upon the Earth: The Watchers, the Nephilim, and the Biblical Cosmic War of the Seed* (Los Angeles, CA: Embedded Pictures Publishing, 2014), 296-298.

[4] **Psalm of the gates of Hades being opened and Yahweh, king of glory**: Psalm 24:7-10.

[5] **Christ's Descent Into Hades/Sheol**: "One of the most difficult and strange passages in the New Testament is 1 Peter 3:18-22. It's oddity approaches that of Genesis 6:1-4 that speaks of the Sons of God mating with the daughters of men in the days of Noah and breeding Nephilim giants that lead to the judgment of the Flood. Perhaps its oddity is tied to the fact that it is most likely connected directly to Genesis 6 and therefore of particular importance for the Cosmic War of the Seed.

"This 1 Peter 3 passage is notorious for its difficult obscurity and lack of consensus among scholarly interpretation. Views are divided over it with a variety of speculative interpretations to pick from. So, let's take a look at it more closely with an attempt to clarify its meaning.

1 Peter 3:18–22 For Christ also suffered once for sins, the righteous for the unrighteous, that he might bring us to God, being put to death in the flesh but made alive in the spirit, 19in which he went and proclaimed to the spirits in prison, 20because they formerly did not obey, when God's patience waited in the days of Noah, while the ark was being prepared, in which a few, that is, eight persons, were brought safely through water. 21Baptism, which corresponds to this, now saves you, not as a removal of dirt from the body but as an appeal to God for a good conscience, through the resurrection of Jesus Christ, 22who has gone into heaven and is at the right hand of God, with angels, authorities, and powers having been subjected to him.

"The context of this letter is the suffering of believers for their faith under the persecution of the Roman empire (3:13-17). Peter is encouraging them to persevere in doing good despite the evil done against them because they will be a witness to the watching world just as Christ was in his suffering. He then launches into this section as an analogy of what Christ did for us in his journey of suffering, death, resurrection, and ascension.

The questions begin to pile up:
When did Christ go on this journey? (v. 18)
Where did he go to proclaim to the spirits? (v. 19)
What did he proclaim? (v. 19)
Who are the spirits? (v. 19)
Where is this prison that they are in? (v. 19)

I believe the answers to these questions are very much in line with the storyline of the War of the Seed.

"When Did Christ Go on His Journey? When Christ "went" to proclaim to the spirits in prison, it says he was "put to death in the flesh but made alive in the spirit, in which he went…" In the original Greek, "he went" does not contain a notion of direction as in ascent to heaven or descent to hell. It can only be determined by the context. So let's look at that context.

414

Some scholars interpret this being "made alive in the spirit" as a reference to the physical resurrection of Christ from the dead, repeated later in v. 21. As Bible commentator Ramsey Michaels says, "the distinction here indicated by "flesh" and "Spirit" is not between the material and immaterial parts of Christ's person (i.e., his "body" and "soul"), but rather between his earthly existence and his risen state." Scholar William Dalton argues that the idea of being made alive in the spirit was a New Testament reference to the resurrection of Christ's physical body by the power of the Holy Spirit, not a reference to Christ's disembodied soul. He writes, "General New Testament anthropology insists on the unity of the human person. Terms such as "flesh" and "spirit" are aspects of human existence, not parts of a human compound. Bodily resurrection is stressed, not the immortality of the soul." This venerable interpretation sees Christ proclaiming to the spirits in Hades, as a resurrected body, sometime before he ascended.

Another scholarly interpretation is that Christ's journey of proclamation occurred in a disembodied state between his death and resurrection. While his body was dead for three days, his spirit was alive and in Sheol. This understands the flesh/spirit distinction as a conjunction of opposites. "Put to death in the flesh but made alive in the spirit" is not talking about the fleshly death and fleshly resurrection, but a fleshly death and a spiritual life. The "spirit" in which he was made alive in this view is not the Holy Spirit, but rather his disembodied soul in the spiritual realm. That "spirit" then corresponds to the "spirits" to whom he proclaimed in the very next verse (v. 19).

This view that Christ's soul or spirit went down into the underworld of Sheol between his death and resurrection is the most ancient and most traditional view, as attested in the Apostle's Creed. The Greek for "made alive" is never used of Christ's physical resurrection in the New Testament, but it is used of the spiritual reality of the believer "being made alive" in Christ (Eph. 2:5-6). Christ suffered the spiritual death of separation from the Father when he died on the cross (Isa. 53:4-6; 1 Pet. 2:24; Matt. 27:46). How the second person of the Trinity can experience separation from the Father remains a Biblical mystery. But in this interpretation, it is Christ's disembodied spirit that makes the journey to proclaim to the spirits, not his resurrected body.

"Where is the "Prison"? One interpretation of the prison is that it is a metaphor for human beings on earth who are "imprisoned" in their sin. But the context of the passage mitigates against this view. When the New Testament refers to preaching the Gospel to people on earth, the Greek term for "soul," is used (psyche). But this is not a term about a ghost in a machine, but rather an expression of the life of an individual human, their inner being, their "person," or their "self." Thus, Peter writes in 3:20 that "eight persons (psyche) were brought safely through the waters" in the ark during the Flood. When Peter preaches the Gospel in Acts 2, it says that "those who received his word were baptized, and there were added that day about three thousand souls [psyche]… and awe came upon every soul [psyche]" (Acts 2:42-43). "Soul" could be used synonymously with "individuals" or "persons."

But in 1 Peter 3, the distinct Greek term for "spirit" (pneuma), not "soul" (psyche), is used in contrast to the physical flesh. And these "spirits" are those who were disobedient in the days of Noah (v. 20), so they could not be people on earth at the time of Christ. Christ was proclaiming to spirits. During the time of Christ, those who were around in the days of Noah could only be in one place according to the Old Testament: The underworld of Hades or Sheol.

"Hades was well known in the Greco-Roman world as the holding cell of the spirits of the dead until the judgment. Sheol was the Hebrew equivalent for Hades so the two could be used interchangeably. Prisons in that time period were exactly that, holding cells for punishment. So when Peter refers to a prison for spirits, this view concludes that he is referring to Hades, just as he did in 2 Peter 2:4 when he said that the disobedient angels were cast into Tartarus, the lowest point in Hades.

There are orthodox traditions of Christian scholars who have supported this passage as referring to Christ's proclamation as occurring at his physical ascension into heaven and others as referring to Christ's spiritual descent into Hades. I take the position in Jesus Triumphant that Christ spiritually descended into Hades. So did early church fathers like Tertullian, Augustine, Jerome, Clement of Alexandria, Irenaeus, Cyril, and Origen, as well as Medieval scholastics like Robert Bellarmine, John Calvin, Thomas Aquinas, and modern scholars like Charles B. Cranfield, and Bo Reicke. But I also incorporate the post-resurrection interpretation when it comes to the angelic Sons of God (Watchers) reigning on earth.

"William Dalton agrees with Reicke that Jesus is cast as a typological Enoch, but then argues that in 2 Enoch, Enoch visits the bound angels in the lower regions of heaven, not Hades. This is true of 2 Enoch, but unfortunately, the text is of such late origin (2nd century after Christ) that it cannot have been part of the original Enochian corpus used as a source in the Bible.

415

"In contrast, 1 Enoch, which seems to be the source of the Biblical text, does in fact depict Enoch as visiting the place of the condemned Watchers who were "formerly in heaven" (1 Enoch 16:2), and that place is described as a "deep pit," in the bottom of a mountain, just like Tartarus of Hades (Sheol), "an empty place with neither heaven above nor an earth below" (1 Enoch 21:1-2).

"The descent of Christ in 1 Pet. 3:19 is poetically structured to counterbalance the ascent of Christ into heaven in verse 22. In the same way that Christ went down into Sheol, he later ascended up into heaven. But more importantly, if Christ makes a proclamation to the spirits in prison, those dead and bound prisoners are certainly not in heaven. They are most likely in Sheol.

"Another passage, Ephesians 4:8 quotes Psalms 68:18 about Christ "ascending on high and leading a host of captives." Paul then adds a parenthetical,

> Ephesians 4:9-10 "In saying, 'He ascended,' what does it mean but that he had also descended into the lower regions, the earth? He who descended is the one who also ascended far above all the heavens, that he might fill all things."

"Christ "descending into the lower regions, the earth" can legitimately be interpreted as referring to Christ's incarnation or even his descent in the Spirit on Pentecost. But other scholarship argues that the phrase is better translated as "descending into the lowest parts of the earth," in other words into Sheol.

"This underworld (Sheol) interpretation would seem to coincide with the memes presented in 1 Peter 3. The contrast of the heights of heaven with the depths of Sheol, and the tying of Christ's death, descent into Sheol, resurrection, and ascension into the totality of his victory over the angelic principalities and powers.

"Psalm 68 says that after leading the host of captives, God "received gifts from men," a reference to the notion of ancient victors receiving tribute from their conquered foes. Paul changes that "receiving of gifts" into "giving of gifts" as a expansion of that victory over foes into a sharing of victory with his army, the people of God. Perhaps this is the meaning of the Old Testament saints resurrected at the time of Christ's resurrection (Matt. 27:52-53). They too were sharing in the long awaited victory train of Messiah to free them from Hades and ascend into heaven.

"The context of conquest over the angelic powers is also apparent in Eph. 1:20-21, "when he raised [Jesus] from the dead and seated him at his right hand in the heavenly places, far above all rule and authority and power and dominion, and above every name that is named."

"Christ's death on the Cross becomes the apparent defeat by God's enemies, led by angelic principalities and powers. But it turns around and becomes a disarming of those spiritual powers and the beginning of his triumph over them (Col. 2:15). In this view, Christ goes down into Sheol (in his spirit or later, in his resurrected body) to make a proclamation to the original minions of evil, now held captive. After he raises from the dead, he ascends into heaven to be coronated as king over all authority and powers of heaven and earth (Eph. 1:20-21). And that victory over spiritual powers brings us to the next element of 1 Peter 3:18-22. For the rest of this exegesis on Christ's descent, and for a fictionalized account of that supernatural event, see Brian Godawa, *Jesus Triumphant*, (Embedded Pictures Publishing, 2015).

The saints resurrected by Christ at his resurrection: Matthew 27:51–53 [51] And behold, the curtain of the temple was torn in two, from top to bottom. And the earth shook, and the rocks were split. [52] The tombs also were opened. And many bodies of the saints who had fallen asleep were raised, [53] and coming out of the tombs after his resurrection they went into the holy city and appeared to many.

The fall of Satan to earth like lighting during the ministry of Christ, as his binding: "Through the entire *Chronicles* series, I have used a concept called "binding" of angels, demons, and Watchers. This binding is accomplished through imprisonment in the earth or Tartarus.

"This binding notion originates theologically from the binding of Satan in the ministry of Christ as noted above in Matthew 12. The binding of angels in "chains of gloomy darkness" in Tartarus in Jude 6 and 2 Peter 2:4 is a different kind of binding than what was done to the satan during Christ's ministry.

"The idea of binding spirits is a common one in ancient religion and magic. Michael Fishbane notes that in the ancient Near East, incantations and spells were used by sorcerers and enchanters to bind people and spirits in spiritual "traps, pits, snares, and nets," using venomous curses from their lips like serpents. In response to some of these verbal sorceries, the Psalmist himself calls upon Yahweh in similar utterances to reverse the spells upon his enemies that they would be trapped, ensnared and bound by their own magical devices (Psalm 140; 64; 57:4-6).[5] Exorcists of the first century used incantations to cast out demons in Jesus' name (Acts 16:18), the same incantation used by Demons *against* Jesus before being cast out (Mk 1:27).

"Scholars have pointed out that the binding of Satan that occurs in Matthew 12 is evidently not an exhaustive or absolute binding, since he is still active after the ministry of Christ and even into the New Testament era (Acts 5:3; Rom. 16:20; 2Cor. 12:7; 1Thes. 2:18; Rev. 2:13). But then how does this continuing satanic activity fit with the notion that Satan "was thrown down to the earth" (Rev. 12:9), "fell like lightning from heaven" (Luke 10:18), was disarmed and overthrown in triumph (Col. 2:15), destroyed along with his power of death (Heb. 2:14), and all of this accomplished through the death, resurrection and ascension of Christ (Matt. 12:28-29; Heb. 2:14)?

> Matt. 12:26–29 And if the satan casts out the satan, he is divided against himself. How then will his kingdom stand?...But if it is by the Spirit of God that I cast out demons, then the kingdom of God has come upon you. Or how can someone enter a strong man's house and plunder his goods, unless he first binds the strong man? Then indeed he may plunder his house.

"Jesus said that his ministry on earth of casting out demons from the Promised Land was a binding of the satan. The satan could not stop the kingdom of God (ie: the Gospel) from inaugurating on earth. The binding of the satan that occurs in Revelation 20 is a different kind of binding. It involves casting the satan into the Abyss. That comes later in our *Chronicles of the Apocalypse*.

"This current binding is like a legal restraining order on the satan. In the Old Testament, the satan is a divinely ordained legal role as a kind of prosecutor within God's heavenly court. He would test God's law and righteousness through accusation against God's people (1Kgs. 22; Job 1, 2; Zech 3). In Rev. 12:10, it describes the satan's fall from heaven as "the Accuser of our brethren being thrown down," also at the inauguration of God's kingdom. With the advent of Christ, the satan/Accuser has effectively been exiled from the divine council of Yahweh and no longer has any legal power of accusation against God's people (Rom. 8:1-4). Brian Godawa, *When Giants Were Upon the Earth: The Watchers, the Nephilim, and the Biblical Cosmic War of the Seed* (Embedded Pictures, 2014), 293-294.

[6] **Apollyon has the key to the Abyss**: Revelation 9:1 And I saw a star fallen from heaven to earth, and he was given the key to the shaft of the bottomless pit.

The Abyss: "The Abyss was believed to be the underworld prison of evil spirits. When the demons were cast out of the demoniac by Jesus, they pleaded with him not to send them to the Abyss (Luke 8:30–31). The Abyss was also considered the realm of the dead. Jesus, after his death, descended into the Abyss ("deep" NIV; Rom. 10:7 quoting Deut. 30:13 LXX). However, in Revelation the name Hades is used for the realm of the dead (cf. Rev. 1:18; 6:8; 20:13, 14), reflecting the Septuagint in which the Hebrew Sheol is translated by "Hades" rather than "Abyss."Clinton E. Arnold, *Zondervan Illustrated Bible Backgrounds Commentary: Hebrews to Revelation., vol. 4* (Grand Rapids, MI: Zondervan, 2002), 304.

"While the key to the abyss is mentioned again in 20:1, the notion of a shaft that could be locked and unlocked is implied rather than explicitly stated. In the other two references, in Rev 11:7 and 17:8, the abyss is the place from which the beast is said to ascend. PGM XIII.169–70, 481–83 indicates a belief in a supernatural being who rules over the abyss: "a god appeared, he was put in charge of the abyss." David E. Aune, *Revelation 6–16, vol. 52B, Word Biblical Commentary* (Dallas: Word, Incorporated, 1998), 526.

"In Job the "abyss" (41:23[22]–24[23]) is the abode of the cosmic sea dragon (40:17[12]; 40:25[20]; 41:10[9]); cf. also Isa. 27:1 and Ps. 73(74):12–13, with Amos 9:3), who has "the appearance of the morning star" (41:10[9]), is "king of all" in his realm (41:26[25]), and is antagonistic to God (e.g., 40:32[27]). This abode became symbolic for the forces of evil (Ps. 76(77):16). The "abyss" is synonymous with the concept of Hades (Job 38:16; Ezek. 31:15; Jonah 2:6) and is the realm of suffering (Ps. 70[71]:20) and death (Exod. 15:5 [AΣΘ]; Isa. 51:10; 63:13; Wis. 10:19). Isa. 24:21–22 says that God will punish angels and evil kings, and "they will be gathered together as prisoners in the pit [bôr], and will be confined in prison, and after many days will be punished. Fallen angels were said to be imprisoned in the pit to await final judgment (1 En. 10:4–14; 18:11–16; 19:1; 21:7; 54:1–6; 88:1–3; 90:23–26; Jub. 5:6–14; 2 Pet. 2:4; cf. 4 Ezra 7:36; Prayer of Manasseh 3)." G. K. Beale, The Book of Revelation: A Commentary on the Greek Text, New International Greek Testament Commentary (Grand Rapids, MI; Carlisle, Cumbria: W.B. Eerdmans; Paternoster Press, 1999), 493.

"The "bottomless pit" translates the phrase *tou phreatos tēs abussou* which literally means: "the shaft of the abyss." The word *phreatos* means "a relatively deep pit or shaft in the ground" (L-N 12). It is apparently the narrow entryway to the *abussos*, which literally means "without bottom": the a is a negative and is attached to buthos ("depths"), i.e., the unfathomable deep… Wright (2011: 86) puts the matter picturesquely: "John's conception of the present creation includes a bottomless pit which, like a black-hole in modern astrophysics, is a place of anticreation, anti-matter, or destruction and chaos." Kenneth L. Gentry, Jr., *The Divorce of Israel: A Redemptive-Historical Interpretation of Revelation Vol. 1* (Dallas, GA: Tolle Lege Press, 2016), 729.

The Abyss and the Gates of Hades: "In Matthew 16:13-20 is the famous story of Peter's confession of Jesus as the Christ, who then responds, "I tell you, you are Peter, and on this rock I will build my church, and the gates of hell [Hades] shall not prevail against it" (v. 18). Shortly after, Jesus leads them up to a high mountain where he is transfigured.

"In order to understand the spiritual reality of what is going on in this polemical sequence and its relevance to the cosmic War of the Seed, we must first understand where it is going on.

"Verse 13 says that Peter's confession takes place in the district of Caesarea Philippi. This city was in the heart of Bashan on a rocky terrace in the foothills of Mount Hermon. This was the celebrated location of the grotto of Banias or Panias, where the satyr goat god Pan was worshipped and from where the mouth of the Jordan river flowed. This very location was what was known as the "gates of Hades," the underworld abode of dead souls.

"The Jewish historian Josephus wrote of this sacred grotto during his time,

> "a dark cave opens itself; within which there is a horrible precipice, that descends abruptly to a vast depth; it contains a mighty quantity of water, which is immovable; and when anybody lets down anything to measure the depth of the earth beneath the water, no length of cord is sufficient to reach it (Wars of the Jews 1:405)."

"As scholar Judd Burton points out, this is a kind of ground zero for the gods against whom Jesus was fighting his cosmic spiritual war. Mount Hermon was the location where the Watchers came to earth, led their rebellion and miscegenation, which birthed the Nephilim (1 Enoch 13:7-10). It was their headquarters, in Bashan, the place of the Serpent, where Azazel may have been worshipped before Pan as a desert goat idol." Brian Godawa, *When Giants Were Upon the Earth: The Watchers, The Nephilim and the Biblical Cosmic War of the Seed* (Embedded Pictures Publishing 2014), 295-296.

Satan as Angel of the Abyss with key to the Abyss:

> Revelation 9:1–3 1 And the fifth angel blew his trumpet, and I saw a star fallen from heaven to earth, and he was given the key to the shaft of the bottomless pit [Abyss]. 2 He opened the shaft of the bottomless pit [Abyss], and from the shaft rose smoke like the smoke of a great furnace, and the sun and the air were darkened with the smoke from the shaft. 3 Then from the smoke came locusts on the earth, and they were given power like the power of scorpions of the earth… 9:10–11 They have tails and stings like scorpions, and their power to hurt people for five months is in their tails. 11 They have as king over them the angel of the bottomless pit [Abyss]. His name in Hebrew is Abaddon, and in Greek he is called Apollyon.

The Beast also comes out of the Abyss:

> Revelation 11:7–8 And when they have finished their testimony, the beast that rises from the bottomless pit [Abyss] will make war on them and conquer them and kill them, 8 and their dead bodies will lie in the street of the great city that symbolically is called Sodom and Egypt, where their Lord was crucified.

> Revelation 17:8 The beast that you saw was, and is not, and is about to rise from the bottomless pit and go to destruction. And the dwellers on earth whose names have not been written in the book of life from the foundation of the world will marvel to see the beast, because it was and is not and is to come.

"Down through history he repeatedly "comes up out of the Abyss" to harass and, if it were possible, to destroy the people of God. He is the little horn of Daniel 7 (Antiochus Epiphanes) who rises out of the fourth kingdom (the "most terrifying" fourth beast, Dan 7:19) to make war against the saints (Dan 7:21). He is Nero, who instigates a persecution of the Christians to avert suspicion that he is responsible for the burning of Rome." Robert H. Mounce, *The Book of Revelation, The New International Commentary on the New Testament* (Grand Rapids, MI: Wm. B. Eerdmans Publishing Co., 1997), 314.

Primeval Wars: The reference to the War on Eden and the War of Gods and Men are fictional wars depicted in the first two books of Chronicles of the Nephilim, *Noah Primeval* and *Enoch Primordial*. But they are fictional expressions of the theological reality.

Azazel: One of the lead Watchers that led the rebellion on Mount Hermon found in detail in 1 Enoch (1 Enoch 8:1; 9:6; 10:4–8; 13:1–2; 54:5; 55:4; 69:2). The reference to Azazel revealing occultic secrets is also in that book. The notion of him using Leviathan is a fictional component of a storyline that threads through the entire Chronicles of the Nephilim series. But Azazel is not some fictional creation of 1Enoch. He also appears in the Bible.

"In Leviticus 16, we read of the sacrificial offering on the Day of Atonement. Among other sacrifices, the high priest would take two goats for atonement of the people. One, he would kill as blood sacrifice on the altar, and the other, he would transfer the sins of the people onto the goat by confession and the laying on of his hands. This action of transferring the bloodguilt onto the "other" is where we got the concept of "scapegoat."

"But that is not the most fascinating piece of this puzzle. For in verses 8–10 and 26, the priest is told to send the goat "away into the wilderness to Azazel" (v. 10)! You read that right: Azazel.

> Leviticus 16:7-10 Then he shall take the two goats and set them before the Lord at the entrance of the Tent of Meeting. And Aaron shall cast lots over the two goats, one lot for the Lord and the other lot for Azazel.And Aaron shall present the goat on which the lot fell for the Lord and use it as a sin offering, but the goat on which the lot fell for Azazel shall be presented alive before the Lord to make atonement over it, that it may be sent away into the wilderness to Azazel.

"The name Azazel is not explained anywhere in the Old Testament, but we've heard that name before in the book of 1Enoch. Azazel was one of the lead Watchers who led the rebellion of 200 Watchers to mate with the daughters of men. And that Watcher was considered bound in the desert of Dudael.

"The natural question arises whether this is the same sacrifice to goat demons that Yahweh condemns in the very Leviticus and Isaiah passages we already looked at. But a closer look dispels such concerns.

"The first goat was "for Yahweh" and the second "for Azazel" (v. 8). But whereas the first goat was a sacrifice, the second was not. As commentator Jacob Milgrom claims, "In pre-Israelite practice [Azazel] was surely a true demon, perhaps a satyr, who ruled in the wilderness—in the Priestly ritual he is no longer a personality but just a name, designating the place to which impurities and sins are banished."

"Milgrom then explains that in the ancient world, purgation and elimination rites went together. The sending out of the scapegoat to Azazel in the wilderness was a way of banishing evil to its place of origin which was described as the netherworld of chaos, where its malevolent powers could no longer do harm to the sender. This wilderness of "tohu and wabohu" or emptiness and wasteland was precisely the chaos that Yahweh pushed back to establish his covenantal order of the heavens and earth, so it was where all demonic entities were considered to reside." Brian Godawa, *When Giants Were Upon the Earth: The Watchers, the Nephilim, and the Biblical Cosmic War of the Seed* (Embedded Pictures, 2014), 216-217.

Leviathan as a many-headed sea dragon of chaos: "As Job 41 describes Leviathan, this is no known species on earth. From the smoke and fire out of its mouth to the armor plating on back and belly, this monster of the abyss was more than a mere example of showcasing God's omnipotent power over the mightiest of creatures, it was symbolic of something much more. And that much more can be found by understanding Leviathan in its ancient Near Eastern (ANE) and Biblical covenantal background.

"In ANE religious mythologies, the sea and the sea dragon were symbols of chaos that had to be overcome to bring order to the universe, or more exactly, the political world order of the myth's originating culture. Some scholars call this battle Chaoskampf—the divine struggle to create order out of chaos...

"Creation accounts were often veiled polemics for the establishment of a king or kingdom's claim to sovereignty. Richard Clifford quotes, "In Mesopotamia, Ugarit, and Israel the Chaoskampf appears not only in cosmological contexts but just as frequently—and this was fundamentally true right from the first—in political contexts. The repulsion and the destruction of the enemy, and thereby the maintenance of political order, always constitute one of the major dimensions of the battle against chaos."

"Perhaps the closest comparison with the Biblical Leviathan comes from Canaanite texts at Ugarit as John Day argued. In 1929, an archeological excavation at a mound in northern Syria called Ras Shamra unearthed the remains of a significant port city called Ugarit whose developed culture reaches back as far as 3000 B.C. Among the important finds were literary tablets written in multiple ancient languages, which opened the door to a deeper understanding of ancient Near Eastern culture and the Bible. Ugaritic language and culture shares much in common with Hebrew that sheds light on the meaning of things such as Leviathan.

"A side-by-side comparison of some Ugaritic religious texts about the Canaanite god Baal with Old Testament passages reveals a common narrative: Yahweh, the charioteer of the clouds, metaphorically battles with Sea (Hebrew: yam) and River (Hebrew: nahar), just as Baal, the charioteer of the clouds, struggled with Yam (sea) and Nahar (river), which is also linked to victory over a sea dragon/serpent.

"Baal fights Sea and River to establish his sovereignty. He wins by drinking up Sea and River, draining them dry, which results in Baal's supremacy over the pantheon and the Canaanite world order. In the second passage, Baal's battle with Sea and River is retold in other words as a battle with a "dragon," the "writhing serpent" with seven heads. Another Baal text calls this same dragon, "Lotan, the wriggling serpent." The Hebrew equivalents of the Ugaritic words tannin (dragon) and lotan are tannin (dragon) and liwyatan (Leviathan) respectively. The words are etymologically equivalent. Not only that, but so are the Ugaritic words describing the serpent as "wriggling" and "writhing" in the Ugaritic text (brh and 'qltn) with the words Isaiah 27 uses of Leviathan as "fleeing" and "twisting" (bariah and 'aqalaton). Notice the last Scripture in the chart that refers to Leviathan as having multiple heads just like the Canaanite Leviathan. Bible scholar Mitchell Dahood argued that in that passage of Psalm 74:12-17 the author implied the seven heads by using seven "you" references to God's powerful activities surrounding this mythopoeic defeat of Leviathan.

"The Apostle John adapted this seven-headed dragon into his Revelation as a symbol of Satan as well as a chaotic demonic empire (Rev 12:3; 13:1; 17:3). Jewish Christians in the first century carried on this motif in texts such as the Odes of Solomon that explain Christ as overthrowing "the dragon with seven heads… that I might destroy his seed."

"The story of deity battling the river, the sea, and the sea dragon Leviathan/Rahab is clearly a common covenant motif in the Old Testament and its surrounding ancient Near Eastern cultures. The fact that Hebrew Scripture shares common words, concepts, and stories with Ugaritic scripture does not mean that Israel is affirming the same mythology or pantheon of deities, but rather that Israel lives within a common cultural environment, and God uses that cultural connection to subvert those words, concepts and stories with his own poetic meaning and purpose.

"Chaoskampf and creation language are used as word pictures for God's covenant activity in the Bible. For God, describing the creation of the heavens and earth was a way of saying he has established his covenant with his people through exodus into the Promised Land, reaffirming that covenant with the kingly line of David, and finalizing the covenant by bringing them out of exile. The reader should understand that the Scriptures listed above, exemplary of Chaoskampf, were deliberately abbreviated to make a further point below. I will now add the missing text in those passages in underline to reveal a deeper motif at play in the text—a motif of creation language as covenantal formation.

Psa. 74:12-17
Psa. 89:9-12; 19-29
Isa 51:9-16
Isa. 27:1; 6-13

"In these texts, and others, God does not merely appeal to his power of creation as justification for the authority of his covenant. More importantly, God uses the creation of the heavens and earth, involving subjugation of rivers, seas, and dragon (Leviathan), as poetic descriptions of his covenant with his people, rooted in the Exodus story, and reiterated in the Davidic covenant. The creation of the covenant is the creation of the heavens and the earth which includes a subjugation of chaos by the new order. The covenant is a cosmos—not a material one centered in astronomical location and abstract impersonal forces as modern worldview demands, but a theological one, centered in the sacred space of land, temple, and cult as the ancient Near Eastern worldview demands." Brian Godawa, *When Giants Were Upon the Earth: The Watchers, the Nephilim, and the Biblical Cosmic War of the Seed* (Embedded Pictures, 2014), 82-92.

[8] **Titanomachy of primordial days**: "Titanomachy" is a term about the Greek mythological rebellion of the Titans. The premise of Chronicles of the Nephilim is that this myth may be rooted in the historical fact of the Genesis 6 Nephilim outbreak that is explained with more detail in 1Enoch. I fictionalize this story of the Titanomachy as it might have been in consistency with the Biblical story in my novel *Enoch Primordial*, book 2 of Chronicles of the Nephilim.

The Nephilim as rebellious giants: "It has been long known by scholars that the letter of Jude not only quotes a verse from the non-canonical book of 1 Enoch (v. 14 with 1 Enoch 1:9), but that Jude 6-7 and 2 Peter 2:4-10 both paraphrase content from 1 Enoch, thus supporting the notion that the inspired authors intended an Enochian interpretation of "angels" called the Watchers (sons of God) having sexual intercourse with humans. 1 Enoch extrapolates the Nephilim pre-flood story from the Bible as speaking of angels violating their supernatural separation and having sex with humans who bear them giants.

"Any question regarding the authenticity of this interpretation in Jude and Peter is quickly answered by another commonality that the New Testament authors share with the Enochian interpretation. Their combination of the angelic sexual sin with the sexual sin of Sodom is a poetic doublet that does not occur in the Old Testament, but does appear in multiple Second Temple Jewish manuscripts circulating in the New Testament time period. Jude and Peter are alluding to a common understanding of their culture that the angelic sin (and its hybrid fruit of giants) was an unnatural sexual violation of the divine and human separation. Here are some of those texts:

> Sirach 16:7-8 He forgave not the giants of old, [the fruit of angelic sin]
> Who revolted in their might.
> He spared not the place where Lot sojourned,
> Who were arrogant in their pride.

> Testament of Naphtali 3:4-5 [D]iscern the Lord who made all things, so that you do not become like Sodom, which departed from the order of nature. Likewise the Watchers departed from nature's order; the Lord pronounced a curse on them at the Flood.

> 3 Maccabees 2:4-5 Thou didst destroy those who aforetime did iniquity, among whom were giants trusting in their strength and boldness, bringing upon them a boundless flood of water. Thou didst burn up with fire and brimstone the men of Sodom, workers of arrogance, who had become known of all for their crimes, and didst make them an example to those who should come after. [notice "making an example for those after" that is also in Jude 7]

> Jubilees 20:4-5 [L]et them not take to themselves wives from the daughters of Canaan; for the seed of Canaan will be rooted out of the land. And he told them of the judgment of the giants, and the judgment of the Sodomites, how they had been judged on account of their wickedness, and had died on account of their fornication, and uncleanness, and mutual corruption through fornication.

"This is critical for understanding the Nephilim as unholy giant progeny because the Nephilim are the result of this sexual union between angel and human." Brian Godawa, *When Giants Were Upon the Earth: The Watchers, the Nephilim, and the Biblical Cosmic War of the Seed* (Embedded Pictures, 2014), 68-70.

[9] **The Rephaim**: The events described here are fictionalized in the novel *Enoch Primordial*, Book 2 of *Chronicles of the Nephilim* by Brian Godawa.

"The Rephaim have an interesting Biblical history that connects them literarily to the Nephilim in the Bible. First, the Nephilim are described as gibborim, or "mighty men," "men of renown" in Genesis 6:4. This word gibborim is used extensively throughout the Old Testament of warriors such as David's "mighty men" (2 Sam. 16:6) and even of the giant Goliath (1Sam. 17:51) and many others. The Nephilim were mighty warriors. The Rephaim were mighty warrior kings.

"In the Bible, Rephaim were Anakim giants, descendants of the Nephilim (Deut. 2:11; Num. 13:33), who were so significant they even had a valley named after them ("Valley of the Rephaim," Josh. 15:8). But there is more to the Rephaim than that. Og, king of Bashan, was a Rephaim giant, and all his portion of the land of Bashan was called "the land of the Rephaim" (Deut. 3:13), an ambiguous wording that could equally be translated as "the 'hell' of the Rephaim." Bashan was a deeply significant spiritual location to the Canaanites and the Hebrews. And as the *Dictionary of Deities and Demons in the Bible* puts it, Biblical geographical tradition agrees with the mythological and cultic data of the Canaanites of Ugarit that "the Bashan region, or a part of it, clearly represented 'Hell', the celestial and infernal abode of their deified dead kings," the Rephaim.

"Mount Hermon was in Bashan, and Mount Hermon was a location in the Bible that was linked to the Rephaim (Josh. 12:1-5), but was also the legendary location where the sons of God were considered to have come to earth and have sexual union with the daughters of men to produce the giant Nephilim.

"There are two places in the Bible that hint at the Rephaim being warrior kings brought down to Sheol in similar language to the Ugaritic notion of the Rephaim warrior kings in the underworld:

Is. 14:9 Sheol beneath is stirred up to meet you when you come;
it rouses the [Rephaim] to greet you,
all who were leaders of the earth;
it raises from their thrones
all who were kings of the nations.

Ezek. 32:21 They shall fall amid those who are slain by the sword… The mighty [Rephaim] shall speak of them, with their helpers, out of the midst of Sheol: "They have come down, they lie still, the uncircumcised, slain by the sword."

"Scholar Michael S. Heiser concludes about this connection of Rephaim with dead warrior kings in Sheol and Bashan:

"That the Israelites and the biblical writers considered the spirits of the dead giant warrior kings to be demonic is evident from the fearful aura attached to the geographical location of Bashan. As noted above, Bashan is the region of the cities Ashtaroth and Edrei, which both the Bible and the Ugaritic texts mention as abodes of the Rephaim. What's even more fascinating is that in the Ugaritic language, this region was known not as Bashan, but Bathan—the Semitic people of Ugarit pronounced the Hebrew "sh" as "th" in their dialect. Why is that of interest? Because "Bathan" is a common word across all the Semitic languages, biblical Hebrew included, for "serpent." The region of Bashan was known as "the place of the serpent." It was ground zero for the Rephaim giant clan and, spiritually speaking, the gateway to the abode of the infernal deified Rephaim spirits." Brian Godawa, *When Giants Were Upon the Earth: The Watchers, the Nephilim, and the Biblical Cosmic War of the Seed* (Embedded Pictures, 2014), 74-76.

[10] **Josephus writes about the slaughter of the Alexandrian Jews**: Flavius Josephus, *The Wars of the Jews*, 2.18.7-9.

CHAPTER 28

[1] **Josephus on Jerusalem as the navel**: "The city Jerusalem is situated in the very middle; on which account some have, with sagacity enough, called that city the Navel of the country." Flavius Josephus, The Wars of the Jews, 3.3.2 §52 Flavius Josephus and William Whiston, *The Works of Josephus: Complete and Unabridged* (Peabody: Hendrickson, 1987), 641.

Mount Zion as primordial hill of creation: "These two passages from the Talmudic tractate Yoma present Mount Zion as the point from which creation proceeded, in other words, the one place of a genuinely primordial character in our world. The following midrash shows that the notion of increasing orders of centrality can be found even on the mountain itself:

"Just as the navel is positioned in the center of a man, thus is the Land of Israel positioned in the center of the world, as the Bible says, "dwelling at the very navel of the earth" (Ezek. 38:12), and from it the foundation of the world proceeds.... And the Temple is in the center of Jerusalem, and the Great Hall is in the center of the Temple, and the Ark is in the center of the Great Hall, and the Foundation Stone is in front of the Ark, and beginning with it the world was put on its foundation."

"In short, the Temple is a visible, tangible token of the act of creation, the point of origin of the world, the "focus" of the universe." Jon Levenson, "The Temple and the World," *The Journal of Religion*, Vol. 64, No. 3 (Jul., 1984), pp. 283.

"Perhaps chief among the symbols expressing the sacred centrality of the Temple is the idea that Zion, and the Temple built there, is the cosmic mountain (Clifford 1972; 1984; Levenson 1985: 111–75). The temple building, on a mountain and a platform, replicates the heavenly mountain of Yahweh (cf. Ps 48:1–4) and also its earlier manifestation at Sinai. It also reaches back to the beginning of time, to the creation of the world (cf. the seven years of Solomonic temple-building activity in relation to the seven days of creation). The foundation of the Temple thus becomes a protological event, going back to the beginnings of time and established by God, not by either David or Solomon (see Ps 78:69–70)." Carol Meyers, "Temple, Jerusalem," ed. David Noel Freedman, *The Anchor Yale Bible Dictionary* (New York: Doubleday, 1992), 359–360.

The temple as cosmic mountain: "The Temple of Yahweh in Israel was naturally associated with a cosmic mountain dwelling like Sinai because it was situated in Jerusalem on Mount Zion, the new Sinai. Psalm 48 makes this quite clear:

1 Great is the LORD and greatly to be praised
in the city of our God!
His holy mountain, 2 beautiful in elevation,
is the joy of all the earth,
Mount Zion, in the far north [Lit.: heights of the north],
the city of the great King (Psa 48:1–2 ESV).

"Zechariah 8:3 (ESV) echoes the same notion: "Thus says the LORD: I have returned to Zion and will dwell [literally, "will tabernacle"; shakan] in the midst of Jerusalem, and Jerusalem shall be called the faithful city, and the mountain of the LORD of hosts, the holy mountain."

"As anyone who has been to Jerusalem knows, Mount Zion isn't much of a mountain. It certainly isn't located in the geographical north—it's actually in the southern part of the country. So what's meant by "the heights of the north"?

"This description would be a familiar one to Israel's pagan neighbors, particularly at Ugarit. It's actually taken out of their literature. The "heights of the north" (Ugaritic: "the heights of tsaphon") is the place where Baal lived and, supposedly, ran the cosmos at the behest of the high god El and the divine council. The psalmist is stealing glory from Baal, restoring it to the One to whom it rightfully belongs—Yahweh. It's a theological and literary slap in the face, another polemic.

"This explains why the description sounds odd in terms of Jerusalem's actual geography. This is why Isaiah and Micah used phrases like "the mountain of the house of Yahweh" (Isa 2:2; Mic 4:1). The description is designed to make a theological point, not a geographical one. Zion is the center of the cosmos, and Yahweh and his council are its king and administrators, not Baal." Michael S. Heiser, *The Unseen Realm: Recovering the Supernatural Worldview of the Bible*, First Edition (Bellingham, WA: Lexham Press, 2015), 226–227.

[2] **The cosmic link between earthly and heavenly temples**: "Temples had names in the ancient world (since naming was an expression of function and existence), and a name such as "Bond between Heaven and Earth" certainly captures the ideology beautifully.

"From the standpoint of deity, the temple is his/her estate and residence. The earthly temple was a symbol, an echo, a shadow of the heavenly residence. As such it served as a link, a bond, or even a portal to the heavenly residence. The heavenly archetypal temple can sometimes be identified as the cosmos itself. In Mesopotamia the ziggurat stood beside the temple as the place where the deity descended from the heavens to reside among the people and to receive their worship." John H. Walton, *Ancient Near Eastern Thought and the Old Testament: Introducing the Conceptual World of the Hebrew Bible* (Grand Rapids, MI: Baker Academic, 2006), 113–114.

God's throne in the waters above the firmament: Psa. 104:2-3 Stretching out the heavens like a tent. He lays the beams of his chambers on the waters;

Psa. 148:4 Praise him, you highest heavens, and you waters above the heavens!

Paul Seely shows how the modern scientific bias has guided the translators to render the word for "firmament" (raqia) as "expanse." Raqia in the Bible consistently means a solid material such as a metal that is hammered out by a craftsman (Ex. 39:3; Isa. 40:19). And when raqia is used elsewhere in the Bible for the heavens, it clearly refers to a solid material, sometimes even metal! (Paul H. Seely, *The Westminster Theological Journal* 53 (1991) 227-40).

Job 37:18 Can you, like him, spread out [raqia] the skies, hard as a cast metal mirror?

Ex. 24:10 And they saw the God of Israel. There was under his feet as it were a pavement [raqia] of sapphire stone, like the very heaven for clearness.

Ezek. 1:22-23 Over the heads of the living creatures there was the likeness of an expanse [raqia], shining like awe-inspiring crystal, spread out above their heads. And under the expanse [raqia] their wings were stretched out straight.

Prov. 8:27-28 When he established the heavens... when he made firm the skies above.

Job 22:14 He walks on the vault of heaven.

Amos 9:6 [God] builds his upper chambers in the heavens and founds his vault upon the earth.

[3] **Temple as microcosm of heavens and earth**: "YHWH is building a new Temple, therefore creating a new world, and vice versa. In light of Gosta Ahlstrom's astute argument that Syro-Palestinian temples were meant to be "heaven and earth," I am led to wonder whether "heaven and earth" in Isa. 65:17 and elsewhere is not functioning as a name for the Jerusalem Temple. The Sumerian parallels are strong. The Temple at Nippur (and elsewhere) was called Duranki, "bond of heaven and earth," and in Babylon we find Etemenanki, "the house where the foundation of heaven and earth is."64 Perhaps it is not coincidence that the Hebrew Bible begins with an account of the creation of heaven and earth by the command of God (Gen. 1:1) and ends with the command of the God of heaven "to build him a Temple in Jerusalem" (2 Chron. 35:23). It goes from creation (Temple) to Temple (creation) in twenty four books." Jon Levenson, The Temple and the World, The Journal of Religion, Vol. 64, No. 3 (Jul., 1984), pp. 295.

Flavius Josephus, The Wars of the Jews, 5.5.5
"Now, the seven lamps signified the seven planets; for so many there were springing out of the candlestick. Now, the twelve loaves that were upon the table signified the circle of the zodiac and the year; (218) but the altar of incense, by its thirteen kinds of sweet-smelling spices with which the sea replenished it, signified that God is the possessor of all things that are both in the uninhabitable and habitable parts of the earth, and that they are all to be dedicated to his use." Flavius Josephus and William Whiston, The Works of Josephus: Complete and Unabridged (Peabody: Hendrickson, 1987), 707.

Flavius Josephus, The Antiquities of the Jews, 3.7.7
"Moses distinguished the tabernacle into three parts, and allowed two of them to the priests, as a place accessible and common, he denoted the land and the sea, these being of general access to all; but he set apart the third division for God, because heaven is inaccessible to men. (182) And when he ordered twelve loaves to be set on the table, he denoted the year, as distinguished into so many months. By branching out the candlestick into seventy parts, he secretly intimated the Decani, or seventy divisions of the planets; and as to the seven lamps upon the candlesticks, they referred to the course of the planets, of which that is the number. (183) The veils, too, which were composed of four things, they declared the four elements; for the fine linen was proper to signify the earth, because the flax grows out of the earth; the purple signified the sea, because that color is dyed by the blood of a sea shell fish; the blue is fit to signify the air; and the scarlet will naturally be an indication of fire. (184) Now the vestment of the high priest being made of linen, signified the earth; the blue denoted the sky, being like lightning in its pomegranates, and in the noise of the bells resembling thunder. And for the ephod, it showed that God had made the universe of four [elements]; and as for the gold interwoven, I suppose it related to the splendor by which all things are enlightened. (185) He also appointed the breastplate to be placed in the middle of the ephod, to resemble the earth, for that has the very middle place of the world. And the girdle which encompassed the high priest round, signified the ocean, for that goes round about and includes the universe. Each of the sardonyxes declare to us the sun and the moon; those, I mean, that were in the nature of buttons on the high priest's shoulders. (186) And for the twelve stones, whether we understand by them the months, or whether we understand the like number of the signs of that circle which the Greeks call the Zodiac, we shall not be mistaken in their meaning." Flavius Josephus and William Whiston, The Works of Josephus: Complete and Unabridged (Peabody: Hendrickson, 1987), 90–91.

"Ancient Near Eastern archaeology and texts portray ancient temples as microcosms of heavenly temples or of the universe. One of the best examples of this is the connection of the arboreal lampstand of Israel's Temple with 'cosmic trees' in ancient temples.15 That the bronze 'sea' basin in the courtyard represented the cosmic seas is borne out by ancient New Eastern temples that also have artificial replicas of seas symbolizing either the chaotic forces stilled by the god or the waters of life at the cosmic centre.

"In other respects ancient temples reflected cosmic symbolism. For instance, temples were symbolically the 'embodiment of the cosmic mountain' representing the original hillock first emerging from the primordial waters at the beginning of creation; such waters themselves were symbolized in temples together with fertile trees receiving life from the waters…

"In this respect there are hints that the Garden of Eden was the archetypal Temple in which the first man worshipped God.

"First, Israel's Temple was the place where the priest experienced God's unique presence, and Eden was the place where Adam walked and talked with God. The same Hebrew verbal form (hithpael), hithallek, used for God's 'walking back and forth' in the Garden (Gen. 3:8), describes God's presence in the Tabernacle (Lev. 26:12; Deut. 23:14 [15]; 2 Sam. 7:6–7).

"Secondly, Genesis 2:15 says God placed Adam in the Garden 'to cultivate [work] it and to keep it'. The two Hebrew words for 'cultivate and keep' are usually translated 'serve and guard' elsewhere in the Old Testament. When these two words (verbal ['abad and shamar] and nominal forms) occur together in the Old Testament (within an approximately fifteen-word range), they sometimes have this meaning and refer either to Israelites 'serving' God and 'guarding [keeping]' God's word (approximately ten times) or to priests who 'keep' the 'service' (or 'charge') of the Tabernacle (see Num. 3:7–8; 8:25–26; 18:5–6; 1 Chr. 23:32; Ezek. 44:14).

"Thirdly, when Adam failed to guard the Temple by sinning and letting in an unclean serpent to defile the sanctuary, Adam lost his priestly role, and the two cherubim took over the responsibility of 'guarding' the Garden Temple: God 'stationed the cherubim … to guard the way to the tree of life' (so Gen. 3:24). Likely, their role became memorialized in Israel's later Temple when God commanded Moses to make two statues of cherubim and stationed them on either side of the 'ark of the covenant' in the 'holy of holies'.

"Fourthly, the 'tree of life' itself was probably the model for the lampstand placed directly outside the 'holy of holies'. The lampstand looked like a small, flowering tree with seven protruding branches from a central trunk, three on one side and three on the other, and one branch going straight up from the trunk in the middle. Exodus 25:31–36 pictures the lampstand having a flowering and fructifying appearance of a tree with 'bulbs and flowers', 'branches' and 'almond blossoms' (see Exod. 25:31–36; likewise, see Josephus, Ant. III:145).

"Fifthly, that the Garden of Eden was the first Temple is also suggested by observing that Israel's later Temple had wood carvings which gave it a garden-like atmosphere: 1 Kings 6:18, 29 says there was 'cedar … carved in the shape of gourds and open flowers' (v. 18); 'on the walls of the temple round about' and on the wood doors of the inner sanctuary were 'carvings of cherubim, palm trees, and open flowers' (vv. 29, 32, 35); beneath the heads of the two pillars placed at the entrance of the holy place were 'carved pomegranates' (1 Kgs. 7:18–20).

"Sixthly, Eden was on a mountain (Ezek. 28:14, 16); Israel's Temple was on Mount Zion (e.g. Exod. 15:17); and the eschatological Temple was to be located on a mountain (Ezek. 40:2; 43:12; Rev. 21:10).

"Seventhly, just as a river flowed out from Eden (Gen. 2:10), so the eschatological Temple in both Ezekiel 47:1–12 and Revelation 21:1–2 has a river flowing out from its centre (and likewise Rev. 7:15–17 and probably Zech. 14:8–9). Later Judaism understood that from 'the tree of life' streams flowed (Midr. Rab. Gen. 15:6; 2 Enoch [J] 8:3, 5). Indeed, Ezekiel generally depicts eschatological Mount Zion (and its Temple) in the colours of Eden in an attempt to show that the promises originally inherent in Eden would be realized in the fulfilment of his vision.

"Eighthly, Genesis 2:12 says that 'good gold' and 'bdellium and onyx stone' were in 'the land of Havilah', apparently where Eden was. Of course, various items of Tabernacle furniture were made of gold, as were the walls, ceiling, and floor of the holy of holies in Solomon's Temple (1 Kgs. 6:20–22). Furthermore, the onyx stones decorated both the Tabernacle and Temple, as well as the high priestly garments (Exod. 25:7; 28:9–12, 20; 1 Chr. 29:2). Gold and onyx are also found together in the priest's clothing (Exod. 28:6–27) and are mentioned together as composing parts of the Temple (1 Chr. 29:2).

"Ninethly, the ark in the holy of holies, which contained the Law (that led to wisdom), echoes the tree of the knowledge of good and evil (that also led to wisdom). The touching of both the ark and this tree resulted in death.

"Tenthly, the entrance to Eden was from the east (Gen. 3:24), which was also the direction from which one entered the Tabernacle and later Temples of Israel and would be the same direction from which the latter-day Temple would be entered (Ezek. 40:6)." Gregory Beale, "The Final Vision of the Apocalypse and Its Implications for a Biblical Theology of the Temple," in *Heaven on Earth*, ed. T. Desmond Alexander and Simon Gathercole (Carlisle [England: Paternoster Press, 2004), 195, 197–199.

Creation of the world linked to creation and dedication of the temple: "I should like to draw attention to two texts that connect the creation of the world and the construction of the Temple which have not been remarked before. 1 Kings 6:38b tells us that it took Solomon seven years to build his Temple. According to 1 Kings 8, he dedicated it during the Feast of Booths (Sukkot), which occurs in the seventh month (verse 2) and which, in Deuteronomic tradition, is a festival of seven days' duration (Deut. 16:13-

15). Moreover, the speech in which Solomon dedicates his shrine, just completed, is structured around seven petitions (1 Kings 8:31-55).47 Can the significance of the number seven in this Temple dedication be coincidence? In light of the argument on other grounds that Temple building and creation were thought to be congeneric, this is improbable. It is more likely that the construction of the Temple is presented here as a parallel to the construction of the world in seven days (Gen. 1:1-2:4)." Jon Levenson, "The Temple and the World," *The Journal of Religion*, Vol. 64, No. 3 (Jul., 1984), pp. 289.

[4] **Altar hearth as "mountain of El":** Bible scholar Michael Heiser talks of this phrase altar hearth (*ha ari-el*)in Ezekiel 43 as meaning "mountain of El" and "bosom of the earth," in The Naked Bible Podcast #157 Ezekiel 40-48 Part 2 https://www.nakedbiblepodcast.com/naked-bible-157-ezekiel-40-48-part-2/

[5] **Carvings of garden imagery in architecture of the temple**: "Other symbols constitutive of the cosmic order made visual and vital in the Temple can be identified in the exuberant presence of floral and faunal motifs in the interior decoration of the building and in the construction and decoration of its appurtenances. The trees carved on the walls, the groves on the Temple Mount, and perhaps even the sacred lampstands, are part of the symbolic expression of the mythic Tree of Life that stood on the Cosmic Mountain, and in the paradisial garden at creation. Similarly, the waters of the Molten Sea and the great fountains of the deep present in God's habitation on Zion (Ps 46:4) contribute to the notion of the Temple as cosmic center." Carol Meyers, "Temple, Jerusalem," ed. David Noel Freedman, *The Anchor Yale Bible Dictionary* (New York: Doubleday, 1992), 360.

Menorah lampstand as symbol of the tree of life: "Fourthly, the 'tree of life' itself was probably the model for the lampstand placed directly outside the 'holy of holies'. The lampstand looked like a small, flowering tree with seven protruding branches from a central trunk, three on one side and three on the other, and one branch going straight up from the trunk in the middle. Exodus 25:31–36 pictures the lampstand having a flowering and fructifying appearance of a tree with 'bulbs and flowers', 'branches' and 'almond blossoms' (see Exod. 25:31–36; likewise, see Josephus, Ant. III:145)." Gregory Beale, "The Final Vision of the Apocalypse and Its Implications for a Biblical Theology of the Temple," in *Heaven on Earth*, ed. T. Desmond Alexander and Simon Gathercole (Carlisle [England: Paternoster Press, 2004), 195, 197–199.

[6] **The veil of the temple as a picture of the universe**: Flavius Josephus, The Wars of the Jews, 5.5.4 §212-214 "It was a Babylonian curtain, embroidered with blue, and fine linen, and scarlet, and purple, and of a contexture that was truly wonderful. Nor was this mixture of colors without its mystical interpretation, but was a kind of image of the universe; (213) for by the scarlet there seemed to be enigmatically signified fire, by the fine flax the earth, by the blue the air, and by the purple the sea; two of them having their colors the foundation of this resemblance; but the fine flax and the purple have their own origin for that foundation, the earth producing the one, and the sea the other. (214) This curtain had also embroidered upon it all that was mystical in the heavens, excepting that of the [twelve] signs, representing living creatures." Flavius Josephus and William Whiston, *The Works of Josephus: Complete and Unabridged* (Peabody: Hendrickson, 1987), 707.

[7] **Ichabod as a term to describe the glory of God departing from Israel when the ark was taken**: 1 Samuel 4:21–22 And she named the child Ichabod, saying, "The glory has departed from Israel!" because the ark of God had been captured and because of her father-in-law and her husband. 22 And she said, "The glory has departed from Israel, for the ark of God has been captured."

The missing ark of the covenant: Michael Heiser examines 9 theories of where the ark is and concludes that the most likely biblical evidence is that the ark of the covenant was destroyed when Babylon destroyed the temple and took its vessels. The Naked Bible podcast #158 The Fate of the Ark of the Covenant. https://www.nakedbiblepodcast.com/naked-bible-158-the-fate-of-the-ark-of-the-covenant/

Though not explicit, this is implied in several Scriptures. First…

Ezekiel prophesies the jealousy of God (and therefore, the ark of God's presence) departing when Babylon destroys the ark:
Ezekiel 16:41–42 And they shall burn your houses and execute judgments upon you in the sight of many women. I will make you stop playing the whore, and you shall also give payment no more. 42 So will I satisfy my wrath on you, and my jealousy shall depart from you. I will be calm and will no more be angry.

Jeremiah implies that the ark is gone (Yahweh's footstool and glory), but will not be missed with the coming of Messiah and the new covenant:
Jeremiah 3:16 And when you have multiplied and been fruitful in the land, in those days, declares the

LORD, they shall no more say, "The ark of the covenant of the LORD." It shall not come to mind or be remembered or missed; it shall not be made again.

The ark is Yahweh's footstool Jeremiah implies again that it is gone and will not be remembered: Lamentations 2:1 How the Lord in his anger has set the daughter of Zion under a cloud! He has cast down from heaven to earth the splendor of Israel; he has not remembered his footstool in the day of his anger.

When Babylon came and destroyed the temple: 2 Esdras 10:22 Our psaltery is laid on the ground, our song is put to silence, our rejoicing is at an end, the light of our candlestick is put out, the ark of our covenant is spoiled, our holy things are defiled. The Apocrypha: King James Version (Bellingham, WA: Logos Research Systems, Inc., 1995), 2 Esd 10:22.

Revelation says that the ark of the covenant was in heaven in the first century: Revelation 11:19 Then God's temple in heaven was opened, and the ark of his covenant was seen within his temple. There were flashes of lightning, rumblings, peals of thunder, an earthquake, and heavy hail.

The power of the people of God was about to be shattered by the Roman abomination of desolation: Daniel 12:7–11 "when the shattering of the power of the holy people comes to an end all these things would be finished. [8] I heard, but I did not understand. Then I said, "O my lord, what shall be the outcome of these things?" [9] He said, "Go your way, Daniel, for the words are shut up and sealed until the time of the end... [11] And from the time that the regular burnt offering is taken away and the abomination that makes desolate is set up, there shall be 1,290 days.

[8] **Simon bar Giora's presence at Masada and his intentions**: "Simon became successful conquering the countryside and taking booty from the wealthy. When Ananus sent out an army to capture him and end his banditry, Simon fled to Masada and sought temporary refuge with the Sicarii there. After Ananus's death and the fall of the provisional government, Simon left Masada and continued his conquests. He soon gained control of other areas, including Idumea...

"Simon presented himself as a champion of the lower classes, attacking the rich and proclaiming "liberty for slaves and rewards for the free." In his actions, some have seen messianic overtones. As he gained territory and popularity, Simon attracted an ever-growing army of loyal followers, which now included freed slaves, the remnants of other bandit groups, and also "many respectable citizens who obeyed him like a king." Kent P. Jackson, "Revolutionaries in the First Century," Brigham Young University Studies, Vol. 36, No. 3, *Masada and the World of the New Testament* (1996-97), pp. 129-140.

CHAPTER 29

[1] **The Slaughter of Scythopolis Jews**: Flavius Josephus, *The Wars of the Jews*, 2.18.3 (§466-468) "3. (466) And thus far the conflict had been between Jews and foreigners; but when they made excursions to Scythopolis they found Jews that acted as enemies; for as they stood in battle array with those of Scythopolis, and preferred their own safety before their relation to us; they fought against their own countrymen; (467) nay, their alacrity was so very great that those of Scythopolis suspected them. These were afraid therefore, lest they should make an assault upon the city in the nighttime, and to their great misfortune, should thereby make an apology for themselves to their own people for their revolt on them. So they commanded them, that in case they would confirm their agreement and demonstrate their fidelity to them, who were of a different nation, they should go out of the city, with their families, to a neighboring grove: (468) and when they had done as they were commanded, without suspecting anything, the people of Scythopolis lay still for the interval of two days, to tempt them to be secure, but on the third night they watched their opportunity, and cut all their throats, some of them as they lay unguarded, and some as they were asleep. The number that was slain was above thirteen thousand, and then they plundered them of all that they had." Flavius Josephus and William Whiston, *The Works of Josephus: Complete and Unabridged* (Peabody: Hendrickson, 1987), 627.

[2] **The horrible atrocities written of here**: Flavius Josephus, *The Wars of the Jews*, 2.18.2 (§465) "It was then common to see cities filled with dead bodies, still lying unburied, and those of old men, mixed with infants, all dead, and scattered about together; women also lay amongst them, without any covering for their nakedness: you might then see the whole province full of inexpressible calamities, while the dread of still more barbarous practices which were threatened, was everywhere greater than what had been already perpetrated." Flavius Josephus and William Whiston, *The Works of Josephus: Complete and Unabridged* (Peabody: Hendrickson, 1987), 627.

[3] **Safe cities in Israel and Syria**: Flavius Josephus, *The Wars of the Jews*, 2.18.5 (§479-480)"479) only the Antiochians, the Sidonians, and Apamians, spared those that dwelt with them, and they would not endure either to kill any of the Jews, or to put them in bonds. And perhaps they spared them, because their own number was so great that they despised their attempts. But I think that the greatest part of this favor was owing to their commiseration of those whom they saw to make no innovations. (480) As for the Gerasens, they did no harm to those that abode with them; and for those who had a mind to go away, they conducted them as far as their borders reached." Flavius Josephus and William Whiston, *The Works of Josephus: Complete and Unabridged* (Peabody: Hendrickson, 1987), 628.

[4] **Sarcasm in the Bible**: "Some Christians feel that sarcasm or satire is harsh and unloving—not befitting a Christ-like treatment of people. And a cursory look at American culture confirms that concern. We are drenched in sarcastic humor that often approaches cynical cruelty. Comedians ruthlessly mock everything from the sanctity of sex to the holiness of God. Chic nihilism reigns in music, movies and television. But does all this sophistry preclude a proper use of sarcasm? What is the Christian's responsibility regarding this dark angle on humor? It turns out that an examination of the Bible yields a rather startling revelation: God uses sarcasm and mockery as an important tool of truth-telling.

"God is often sarcastic in his humor. And particularly in relation to sin. In response to the foolishness of sinners gathering together, plotting against God and his anointed Son, King David writes, "He who sits in the heavens laughs, The Lord scoffs at them" (Ps 2:4-5). God scoffs. He mocks the folly of wicked men (Ps 37:12-13), He mocks nations of sinners who "howl like dogs," and "belch forth with their mouths" (Ps 59:6-8). Arrogant rebels deserve to be mocked when comparing them to the glory of God.

"But God does not reserve his acerbic wit for the reprobate alone. He also employs it against his own regenerate children when they get out of line. When Job's sincere desire to accept the deep ways of God turns into a questioning demand to account for alleged injustice, God responds with eighty-plus sarcastic questions meant to humiliate Job in his hubris. And God prefaces those questions by mockingly saying, "I will ask you, and you instruct Me!" (Job 38:3). As if God has anything to learn from the brightest star of human intelligence. As if God is obligated to give an account of his ways to man (Job 33:13). Questioning God deserves to be scorned, especially when it is engaged in by a believer who ought to know better.

"Sarcasm is not below God's character, and neither is it below his people's character. The same laughing derision that God himself employs toward the wicked is also played out dramatically through God's appointed mockers—I mean messengers, the prophets…

"ISAIAH: In Isaiah 44 the prophet mocks those who worship idols made of the same wood used for common household tasks. One can hear the sarcasm bellowing in the words put into the idolater's mouth by Isaiah:

> "Aha! I am warm, I have seen the fire." But the rest of it he makes into a god, his graven image. He falls down before it and worships; he also prays to it and says, "Deliver me, for you are my god." (Is 44:16-17)

"And atheists think they have a corner on mocking religion. God has the longest-running gag about religion yet—false religion, that is.

"JESUS: But what about Jesus? The man of love and kindness—surely he never used sarcasm or mockery to get a point across.

"As the prophet Micaiah would say, go ahead and believe what you want. But here's the truth: Jesus mocked.

"In Luke 13:32, for example, Jesus called King Herod a "fox." In ancient Jewish literature, the image of a fox was not only used as a derogatory metaphor for lowly cunning, but more particularly was a reference to people who were of little importance. The fox was a political nuisance who, like the jackal, would scavenge off the kill of a lion (imagery for truly powerful people) and try to dodge the consequences. By using the image of a fox for Herod, Jesus is insulting him in the same way we might today insultingly refer to politicians as "publicity hounds," "weasels," or "sleazebags."

But that's not all. By using the feminine form of the word Jesus is actually calling Herod a "vixen," a female fox, insinuating he was dominated by his unlawful wife Herodias." Brian Godawa, *The Imagination of God: Art, Creativity and Truth in the Bible* (Los Angeles, CA: Embedded Pictures Publishing, 2016) 155-160.

[5] **The source stories for this chapter's battle**: Josephus' Life 1-73 tells the story of the civil war in Galilee and Josephus' battles with John of Gischala and others to stabilize the region. Also, Wars of the Jews 2.18.1-11 (§457-510) describes the civil war. This chapter draws from several of those incidents and combines characters in order to keep the narrative flowing. Josephus had several battles of Tiberias, some with Gischala and one with Justus. In this story, I combined Justus' story with Gischala into one character. I have also compressed and accelerated the chronology for the sake of my story.

Flavius Josephus, *The Life of Flavius Josephus*, 66 (§368-372) "66. (368) Now, when I had settled the affairs of Tiberias, and had assembled my friends as a sanhedrin, I consulted what I should do as to John: whereupon it appeared to be the opinion of all the Galileans that I should arm them all, and march against John, and punish him as the author of all the disorders that had happened. (369) Yet was not I pleased with their determination; as purposing to compose these troubles without bloodshed. Upon this I exhorted them to use the utmost care to learn the names of all that were under John; (370) which when they had done, and I thereby was apprised who the men were, I published an edict, wherein I offered security and my right hand to such of John's party as had a mind to repent; and I allowed twenty days' time to such as would take this most advantageous course for themselves. I also threatened, that unless they threw down their arms, I would burn their houses, and expose their goods to public sale. (371) When the men heard of this, they were in no small disorder, and deserted John; and to the number of four thousand threw down their arms, and came to me. (372) So that no others staid with John but his own citizens, and about fifteen hundred strangers that came from the metropolis of Tyre; and when John saw that he had been outwitted by my stratagem, he continued afterward in his own country, and was in great fear of me." Flavius Josephus and William Whiston, The Works of Josephus: Complete and Unabridged (Peabody: Hendrickson, 1987), 22–23.

The story of Tiberias and Sylla, the commander helping Justus, that I changed to John of Gischala: Flavius Josephus, The Life of Flavius Josephus, 70-72 (§390-401) "70. (390) About this time it was that Justus, the son of Pistus, without my knowledge, ran away to the king; the occasion of which I will here relate. (391) Upon the beginning of the war between the Jews and the Romans, the people of Tiberias resolved to submit to the king, and not to revolt from the Romans; while Justus tried to persuade them to betake themselves to their arms, as being himself desirous of innovations, and having hopes of obtaining the government of Galilee, as well as of his own country [Tiberias] also…

"69. (385) When I heard this, I was in doubt what to do, and hesitated by what means I might deliver Tiberias from the rage of the Galileans; for I could not deny that those of Tiberias had written to the king, and invited him to come to them; for his letters to them, in answer thereto, would fully prove the truth of that…

"401) At the same time also there came forces, both horsemen and footmen, from the king, and Sylla their commander, who was the captain of his guard; this Sylla pitched his camp at five furlongs distance from Julias, and set a guard upon the the roads, both that which led to Cana, and that which led to the fortress Gamala, that he might hinder their inhabitants from getting provisions out of Galilee. 72. (399) As soon as I had got intelligence of this, I sent two thousand armed men, and a captain over them, whose name was Jeremiah, who raised a bank a furlong off Julias, near to the river Jordan, and did no more than skirmish with the enemy; till I took three thousand soldiers myself, and came to them. (400) But on the next day, when I had laid an ambush in a certain valley, not far from the banks, I provoked those that belonged to the king to come to a battle, and gave orders to my own soldiers to turn their backs upon them, until they should have drawn the enemy away from their camp, and brought them out into the field, which was done accordingly; (401)" Flavius Josephus and William Whiston, *The Works of Josephus: Complete and Unabridged* (Peabody: Hendrickson, 1987), 23.

[6] **Josephus' injury**: Flavius Josephus, *The Life of Flavius Josephus*, 72 (§401-404) "for Sylla, supposing that our party did really run away, was ready to pursue them, when our soldiers that lay in ambush took them on their backs, and put them all into great disorder. (402) I also immediately made a sudden turn with my own forces, and met those of the king's party, and put them to flight. And I had performed great things that day, if a certain fate had not been my hindrance; (403) for the horse on which I rode, and upon whose back I fought, fell into a quagmire, and threw me on the ground; and I was bruised on my wrist, and carried into a village named Cepharnome, or Capernaum. (404) When my soldiers heard of this, they were afraid I had been worse hurt than I was; and so they did not go on with their pursuit any further, but returned in very great concern for me. I therefore sent for the physicians, and while I was under their hands, I continued feverish that day; and as the physicians directed." Flavius Josephus and William Whiston, *The Works of Josephus: Complete and Unabridged* (Peabody: Hendrickson, 1987), 24.

[7] **Uriel carrying Noah out of Tartarus**: This story is fictionalized in Brian Godawa, *Noah Primeval* (Los Angeles, Embedded Pictures 2011).

CHAPTER 30

[1] **The riotous living of young Titus**: "Besides cruelty, he was also suspected of riotous living, since he protracted his revels until the middle of the night with the most prodigal of his friends; likewise of unchastity because of his troops of catamites and eunuchs, and his notorious passion for queen Berenice, to whom it was even said that he promised marriage. He was suspected of greed as well; for it was well known that in cases which came before his father he put a price on his influence and accepted bribes. In short, people not only thought, but openly declared, that he would be a second Nero. But this reputation turned out to his advantage and gave place to the highest praise, when no fault was discovered in him, but on the contrary the highest virtues." Suetonius, *Lives of the Twelve Caesars, Titus* 7.

[2] **Titus divorced Marcia Furnilla because her family was linked to the Pisonian Conspiracy**: Gavin Townend, "Some Flavian Connections," *The Journal of Roman Studies* (1961), p 57; Suetonius, *Lives of the Twelve Caesars, Titus* 4.

[3] **On Nero's poisoning of Britannicus, Titus' beloved friend**: Suetonius, *Lives of the Twelve Caesars, Nero* 33; *Lives of the Twelve Caesars, Titus* 2.

Britannicus, his relationship to Nero and his poisoning: Tacitus, *The Annals* 13.14-16; Cassius Dio, *Roman History*, 60.32, 34, 61.1, 7.4.

[4] **Cassius Dio on Sporus and Pythagoras**: "Nero missed her so that [after her death, at first, on learning that there was a woman resembling her he sent for and kept this female: later] because a boy of the liberti class, named Sporus, resembled Sabina, he had him castrated and used him in every way like a woman; and in due time he formally married him though he [Nero] was already married to a freedman Pythagoras. He assigned the boy a regular dowry according to contract, and Romans as well as others held a public celebration of their wedding." Cassius Dio, *Roman History*, 62.28.2-3.

"Now Nero called Sporus Sabina… Nero took to himself two bedfellows, Pythagoras to treat as a man and Sporus as a woman. The latter, in addition to other forms of address, was termed lady, queen, and mistress. Cassius Dio, *Roman History*, 63.13.1-2.

Dio Chrysostom, a young contemporary of Nero, on Sporus: "Take Nero for instance: we all know how in our own time that he not only castrated the youth whom he loved, but also changed his name for a woman's, that of the girl whom he loved and his subsequent wife, for whom he conceived a passion and wedded after openly incarcerating his former wife, to whom he was already married when he became Emperor.

"But that youth of Nero's actually wore his hair parted, young women attended him whenever he went for a walk, he wore women's clothes, and was forced to do everything else a woman does in the same way. And, to cap the climax, great honours and boundless sums of money were actually offered to anyone who should make him his wife. Dio Chrysostom, *Discourses* 21.6-7.

Suetonius on Sporus: "He castrated the boy Sporus and actually tried to make a woman of him; and he married him with all the usual ceremonies, including a dowry and a bridal veil, took him to his house attended by a great throng, and treated him as his wife… This Sporus, decked out with the finery of the empresses and riding in a litter, he took with him to the assizes and marts of Greece, and later at Rome through the Street of the Images, fondly kissing him from time to time." Suetonius, *Lives of the Twelve Caesars, Nero* 28.1-2.

[5] **Vespasian's rule defined as "notorious and hated" by Tacitus, but "with great justice and high honor" by Suetonius**: Tacitus, *The Histories* 2.97; Suetonius, *Lives of the Twelve Caesars, Vespasian* 4.3

[6] **Vespasian's insult toward Nero of falling asleep on his performance**: "On the tour through Greece, among the companions of Nero, he bitterly offended the emperor by either going out often while Nero was singing, or falling asleep, if he remained. Being in consequence banished, not only from intimacy with the emperor but even with his public receptions, he withdrew to a little out-of-the-way town, until a province and an army were offered him while he was in hiding and in fear of his life." Suetonius, *Lives of the Twelve Caesars, Vespasian* 4.4

[7] **Vespasian the Muleteer**: Suetonius, *Lives of the Twelve Caesars, Vespasian* 4.2.

[8] **Vespasian was probably given control over the Judean campaign after Cestius failed to bring order there**: "And as he was deliberating to whom he should commit the care of the east, now it was in so great a commotion, and who might be best able to punish the Jews for their rebellion, and might prevent the same distemper from seizing upon the neighboring nations also,—(4) he found no one but Vespasian equal to the task, and able to undergo the great burden of so mighty a war, seeing he was growing an old man already in the camp, and from his youth had been exercised in warlike exploits: he was also a man that had long ago pacified the west, and made it subject to the Romans, when it had been put into disorder by the Germans: he had also recovered to them Britain by his arms, (5) which had been little known before; whereby he procured to his father Claudius to have a triumph bestowed on him without any sweat or labor of his own.

"So Nero esteemed these circumstances as favorable omens, and saw that Vespasian's age gave him sure experience, and great skill, and that he had his sons as hostages for his fidelity to himself, and that the flourishing age they were in would make them fit instruments under their father's prudence. Perhaps also there was some interposition of Providence, which was paving the way for Vespasian's being himself emperor afterwards." Flavius Josephus and William Whiston, *The Works of Josephus: Complete and Unabridged* (Peabody: Hendrickson, 1987). Flavius Josephus, *The Wars of the Jews*, 3.3-6.

[9] **Cestius Gallus**: Though the Jews did try to send a company of ambassadors to appeal to Caesar, Cestius was actually called upon directly by Agrippa and Berenice to help quell the uprising (Flavius Josephus, *The Wars of the Jews*, 2.333-343). Berenice actually came to Rome after the revolt, where she lived for a time as Titus' mistress (Cassius Dio, *Roman History*, 16.15). I used this creative license in order to show Berenice's connection to Rome and set up her love affair with Titus that did in fact occur during the revolt (Tacitus, *The Histories* 2.1-2).

[10] **On Nero's ravaging of victims' genitals**: "Yet why should one wonder at this, seeing that this monarch would fasten naked boys and girls to poles, and then putting on the hide of a wild beast would approach them and satisfy his brutal lust under the appearance of devouring parts of their bodies? Such were the indecencies of Nero." Cassius Dio, *Roman History*, 63.13.2.

"He so prostituted his own chastity that after defiling almost every part of his body, he at last devised a kind of game, in which, covered with the skin of some wild animal, he was let loose from a cage and attacked the private parts of men and women, who were bound to stakes, and when he had sated his mad lust, was dispatched by his freedman Doryphorus; for he was even married to this man in the same way that he himself had married Sporus, going so far as to imitate the cries and lamentations of a maiden being deflowered." Suetonius, *Lives of the Twelve Caesars, Nero* 29.1.

[11] **It was common in the first century for both Christians and pagans to call Nero a "beast", even a many-headed beast:** "I have seen hosts of Arabian and Indian wild beasts; but as to this wild beast, which many call a tyrant, I know not either how many heads he has, nor whether he has crooked talons and jagged teeth…this one is only roused to greater cruelty than before by those who stroke him, so that he rends and devours all alike. And again there is no animal anyhow of which you can say that it ever devours its own mother, but Nero is gorged with such quarry. Philostratus, Life of Apollonius 4.36-40 (translation by F.C. Conybeare, published in 1912 in the Loeb Classical Library) http://www.livius.org/sources/content/philostratus-life-of-apollonius/philostratus-life-of-apollonius-4.36-40/

[12] **Azazel taught the implements of war and seduction to the primeval humans**: 1Enoch 8:1-2 "And Azaz'el taught the people (the art of) making swords and knives, and shields, and breastplates; and he showed to their chosen ones bracelets, decorations, (shadowing of the eye) with antimony, ornamentation, the beautifying of the eyelids, all kinds of precious stones, and all coloring tinctures and alchemy. And there were many wicked ones and they committed adultery and erred, and all their conduct became corrupt." James H. Charlesworth, *The Old Testament Pseudepigrapha, vol. 1* (New York; London: Yale University Press, 1983), 16.

CHAPTER 31

[1] **The Sibylline prophecy about Nero:** "Thrice three hundred years having run their course of fulfillment, Rome by the strife of her people shall perish. Last of the sons of Aeneas, a mother-slayer shall govern." Cassius Dio, *Roman History*, 62.17.4.

[2] **Prophecy of a "ruler from the east" or "from Judea":** "But now, what did most elevate them [the Jews] in undertaking this war was an ambiguous oracle that was found in their sacred writings, how,

"about that time, one from their country should become governor of the habitable earth." The Jews took this prediction to belong to themselves in particular; and many of their wise men were thereby deceived in their determination. Now, this oracle certainly denoted the government of Vespasian, who was appointed emperor in Judea." Flavius Josephus, *The Wars of the Jews*, 6.5.4.

[Some understand that this meant Herod, others the crucified wonder-worker Jesus, others again Vespasian.] *Slavonic addition, Loeb*, vol. 2, p. 658.

"The majority were convinced that the ancient scriptures of their priests alluded to the present as the very time when the Orient would triumph and from Judaea would go forth men destined to rule the world. This mysterious prophecy really referred to Vespasian and Titus, but the common people, true to the selfish ambitions of mankind, thought that this exalted destiny was reserved for them, and not even their calamities opened their eyes to the truth." Tacitus, *The Histories*, 5.13.

"It may be that mysterious prophecies were already circulating, and that portents and oracles promised Vespasian and his sons the purple; but it was only after the rise of the Flavians that we Romans believed in such stories." Tacitus, *The Histories*, 1. 10.

"An ancient superstition was current in the East, that out of Judea would come the rulers of the world. This prediction, as it later proved, referred to the two Roman Emperors, Vespasian and his son Titus; but the rebellious Jews, who read it as referring to themselves, murdered their Procurator, routed the Governor-general of Syria when he came down to restore order, and captured an Eagle." Suetonius, *Lives of the Twelve Caesars, Vespasian*, 4.

These passages were drawn from a chart by C.N. Carrington on his article, "The Flavian Testament" that details the oracles surrounding Vespasian as "the ruler" and their interpretations at the time. http://carrington-arts.com/cliff/FlavSyn.htm

[3] A Son of David as ruler of the nations: read Isaiah 11; Psalm 2;

[4] **Berenice is referencing**: Psalm 82:1–8 [1] God has taken his place in the divine council; in the midst of the gods he holds judgment: [2] "How long will you judge unjustly and show partiality to the wicked? *Selah* [3] Give justice to the weak and the fatherless; maintain the right of the afflicted and the destitute. [4] Rescue the weak and the needy; deliver them from the hand of the wicked." [5] They have neither knowledge nor understanding, they walk about in darkness; all the foundations of the earth are shaken. [6] I said, "You are gods, sons of the Most High, all of you; [7] nevertheless, like men you shall die, and fall like any prince." [8] Arise, O God, judge the earth; for you shall inherit all the nations!

[5] **Titus' affair with Berenice:**
Suetonius, Lives of the Twelve Caesars, Titus 1.1
"because of his troops of catamites and eunuchs, and his notorious passion for queen Berenice, to whom it was even said that he promised marriage."
http://penelope.uchicago.edu/Thayer/E/Roman/Texts/Suetonius/12Caesars/Titus*.html

Cassius Dio, *Roman History*, 66.15.3-5
[after AD 70]"Berenice was at the very height of her power and consequently came to Rome along with her brother Agrippa. 4 The latter was given the rank of praetor, while she dwelt in the palace, cohabiting with Titus. She expected to marry him and was already behaving in every respect as if she were his wife; but when he perceived that the Romans were displeased with the situation, he sent her away."
http://penelope.uchicago.edu/Thayer/E/Roman/Texts/Cassius_Dio/65*.html

CHAPTER 31

[1] **20,000 Jews murdered in Caesarea Maritima**: Flavius Josephus, The Wars of the Jews 2.18.1 §457
"1. (457) Now the people of Cesarea had slain the Jews that were among them on the very same day and hour [when the soldiers were slain], which one would think must have come to pass by the direction of Providence; insomuch that in one hour's time above twenty thousand Jews were killed, and all Cesarea was emptied of its Jewish inhabitants; for Florus caught such as ran away, and sent them in bonds to the galleys." Flavius Josephus and William Whiston, The Works of Josephus: Complete and Unabridged (Peabody: Hendrickson, 1987), 627.

[2] **Cestius' age**: "Cestius was old. Apparently he had been a member of the Senate since A.D. 21...To have met the qualifying age of 25 for the quaestorship in A.D. 21, Cestius must have been born not later

432

than 4/3 B.C. Assuming that latest possible birthdate, he must have been 69 or 70 when he led the expedition to Judaea…When we think of this, his activities on horseback for weeks at a time and his escape from Beit-Horon seem quite impressive." Steve Mason, *A History of the Jewish War, AD 66-74* (Cambridge University Press, 2016) 321.

[3] **Cestius Gallus campaign from Caesarea Maritima**: Flavius Josephus, *The Wars of the Jews*, 2.18.10-11 §507-510 "10. (507) And now Cestius himself marched from Ptolemais, and came to Cesarea; but he sent part of his army before him to Joppa, and gave orders that if they could take that city [by surprise] they should keep it; but that in case the citizens should perceive they were coming to attack them they then should stay for him and for the rest of the army. (508) So some of them made a brisk march by the seaside, and some by land, and so coming upon them on both sides, they took the city with ease; and as the inhabitants had made no provision aforehand for a flight, nor had gotten anything ready for fighting, the soldiers fell upon them, and slew them all, with their families, and then plundered and burnt the city. (509) The number of the slain was eight thousand four hundred. In like manner Cestius sent also a considerable body of horsemen to the toparchy of Narbatene, that adjoined to Cesarea, who destroyed the country and slew a great multitude of its people; they also plundered what they had and burnt their villages.

"11. (510) But Cestius sent Gallus, the commander of the twelfth legion, into Galilee, and delivered to him as many of his forces as he supposed sufficient to subdue that nation. (511) He was received by the strongest city of Galilee, which was Sepphoris, with acclamations of joy; which wise conduct of that city occasioned the rest of the cities to be in quiet; while the seditious part and the robbers ran away to that mountain which lies in the very middle of Galilee, and is situated over against Sepphoris; it is called Asamon." Flavius Josephus and William Whiston, *The Works of Josephus: Complete and Unabridged* (Peabody: Hendrickson, 1987), 629–630.

[4] **Florus' execution**: Florus was replaced by Marcus Antonius Julianus, but there is no evidence he was executed. This scene is creative license for the story.

CHAPTER 33

[1] The 144,000 as Jewish Christians in Revelation 7 and 14:

Revelation 7:1–8 After this I saw four angels standing at the four corners of the earth, holding back the four winds of the earth, that no wind might blow on earth or sea or against any tree. [2] Then I saw another angel ascending from the rising of the sun, with the seal of the living God, and he called with a loud voice to the four angels who had been given power to harm earth and sea, [3] saying, "Do not harm the earth or the sea or the trees, until we have sealed the servants of our God on their foreheads." [4] And I heard the number of the sealed, 144,000, sealed from every tribe of the sons of Israel: [5] 12,000 from the tribe of Judah were sealed, 12,000 from the tribe of Reuben, 12,000 from the tribe of Gad, [6] 12,000 from the tribe of Asher, 12,000 from the tribe of Naphtali, 12,000 from the tribe of Manasseh, [7] 12,000 from the tribe of Simeon, 12,000 from the tribe of Levi, 12,000 from the tribe of Issachar, [8] 12,000 from the tribe of Zebulun, 12,000 from the tribe of Joseph, 12,000 from the tribe of Benjamin were sealed.

Revelation 14:1–5 Then I looked, and behold, on Mount Zion stood the Lamb, and with him 144,000 who had his name and his Father's name written on their foreheads. [2] And I heard a voice from heaven like the roar of many waters and like the sound of loud thunder. The voice I heard was like the sound of harpists playing on their harps, [3] and they were singing a new song before the throne and before the four living creatures and before the elders. No one could learn that song except the 144,000 who had been redeemed from the earth. [4] It is these who have not defiled themselves with women, for they are virgins. It is these who follow the Lamb wherever he goes. These have been redeemed from mankind as firstfruits for God and the Lamb, [5] and in their mouth no lie was found, for they are blameless.

In his Revelation commentary, Kenneth Gentry argues for these 144,000 being Jewish Christians in Israel, and in Jerusalem:

"First, this view fits the overriding character of Revelation… As I am arguing in this commentary, Revelation is dealing with God's judgment of Israel and her temple in AD 70 (1:7; cp. 11:1–2). Consequently, in this light (along with John's specific statements in 7:4–8, see below) the burden of proof rests on any view that denies the Jewish identity of this group…

"Second, this view fits the remnant expectations of Scripture. In the Old Testament we frequently hear of the remnant reserved out of Israel (e.g., Isa 6:31, 10:20–21, 11:11, 16, 28:5, Jer 23:3, 50:20, Eze 6:8, Mic 2:12, Zec 8:11–12). For instance, a prophecy similar to the 144,000 on Mount Zion in Revelation 14:1 appears in Isaiah 37:31–32: "For out of Jerusalem will go forth a remnant and out of Mount Zion survivors. The zeal of the LORD of hosts will perform this." In his day Paul sees that despite the wide-scale rebellion of Israel as a body, "There has also come to be at the present time a remnant according to God's gracious choice...

"This is the "remnant" of Israel, the few in Israel who were chosen from the many Christ called in the first century (Mt 22:14).12 They are the "true" Jews contrary to the ethnic Jews who remain within Judaism and who thereby "lie" (2:9, 3:9).

"Third, this view fits John's specific Old Testament backdrop. As I note above at 7:3, John clearly draws from Ezekiel 9. In that vision the angel with the writing case is to go through Jerusalem "and put a mark on the foreheads of the men who sigh and groan over all the abominations which are being committed in its midst" (9:4). But the other angels are to "go through the city after him and strike, do not let your eye have pity and do not spare" (9:5). This backdrop in the context of the first temple's destruction well matches that which will occur in the second temple's destruction, which is the result of the very theme of Revelation (1:7). I see in Revelation the protection of the Christian Jews during the Jewish War.

"Fourth, this view picks up on the prophecy of Christ in his Olivet Discourse—which prophecy exercises a great influence on the seals (see discussion in Rev 6). We must also recall that John's theme in 1:7 not only speaks of Israel's approaching judgment, but is itself also influenced by the Olivet Discourse. In both Matthew 24:30 and Revelation 1:7 we see a unique merging of Zechariah 12:10 and Daniel 7:13 (see Exc. 3 at 1:7). Thus, we should not be surprised to discover that Jesus warns Jewish Christians within Jerusalem to flee when they see certain events coming to pass (Mt 24:16). Their flight in that context will allow the Jerusalem Christians to survive the holocaust.

"Fifth, this view fits well with the redemptive-historical facts regarding the church's Jewish origins. In Revelation 14 the 144,000 (14:1a) are deemed the "first fruits to God and to the Lamb" (14:4c). The New Testament everywhere witnesses to the Jewish origins of Christianity. In fact, even Christ himself declares: "salvation is of the Jews" (Jn 4:22).

"Sixth, this view fits well with the New Testament recognition of differences between Jew and Gentile believers in the early development of Christianity. We seethis distinction in many New Testament passages...

"Though some scholars argue that Revelation makes no distinction between Jewish and Gentile Christians, this seems to be the very case here in 7:4–8 where God protects the Jewish Christians in Israel (those "from every tribe of the sons of Israel"), whereas in 7:9–17 the whole church from "every nation and all tribes and peoples and tongues" are mentioned separately...

"Seventh, this view fits well with the association of the 144,000 with a Jewish geographical referent. In 14:1 John writes: "I looked, and behold, the Lamb was standing on Mount Zion, and with Him one hundred and forty-four thousand, having His name and the name of His Father written on their foreheads." The sealing action in Revelation 7 is marking the Jews in Jerusalem (where Mount Zion is located) for protection. We also see the reference to "the Land" in the immediate context (7:1) as well as in 14:3 where we hear of "the one hundred and forty-four thousand who had been purchased from the Land" (see Exc. 7 at 6:10). I would also point out that archaeologists argue from evidence found in Jerusalem that we have found remains of a pre-AD 70 Jewish-Christian synagogue on Mount Zion (Scott 1998).

"Eighth, this view fits well with the specific designation in our text. Here we read that John hears the number of the 144,000 who are "sealed from every tribe of the sons of Israel" (7:4b). The word "Israel" appears only twice in Revelation, here and in 21:12. In 21:12 it indisputably refers to the tribes of ethnic Israel as it mentions their names on the gates of the new Jerusalem...

"Eleventh, this view works well with the sorting of Israel into its various tribes. It does not, however, seem reasonable to present the church in terms of the particular tribes. The New Testament references to the church as the new Israel use basic, corporate designations ("the seed of Abraham," "the true circumcision," "the Israel of God," and so forth). It never presents the church in terms of Israel's distinct tribal divisions...

434

"Twelfth, this view comports with the idea of mentioning the specific number of 12,000 from each tribe. We can discern a need for showing that all the Jewish Christians from whatever tribe will escape Jerusalem's destruction. Though the number is undoubtedly symbolic, there appears no reason to number them separately in a symbolic portrayal of the church. A symbolic sum does not demand a symbolic people, whereas a symbolic sum can apply to a literal people.

"Thirteenth, this view fits well with the drawing out of some from among the wider body of Jews. In his lead statement John notes that the sealed are "from every tribe of the sons of Israel": ek pasēs phulēs huiōn Israēl. This employs ek with the partitive genitive (phulēs) to note their being separated out from among the others. He continues this in presenting each of the tribes, for after 7:4 he repeatedly states: "from the tribe of x," ek phulēs..." (7:5–8). This uses the same ek + partitive genitive structure. If Israel represents the church (the new Israel), why are only some drawn out of it? Whereas if the tribes of Israel are the literal Jewish tribes, then we see why the Christian prophet John would distinguish some Jews from the larger ethnic body: these have become followers of the Lamb (cp. Ro 11:7). Note that elsewhere in Revelation John dismisses unconverted Jews as those "who say they are Jews and are not" (2:9, 3:9)." Kenneth L. Gentry, Jr., *The Divorce of Israel: A Redemptive-Historical Interpretation of Revelation Vol. 1* (Dallas, GA: Tolle Lege Press, 2016), 661-664.

The gathering of Israel or "return from exile" is fulfilled in the New Covenant: This is a complex theological issue. The single best source for understanding this principle is probably N. T. Wright, *The New Testament and the People of God, Christian Origins and the Question of God* (London: Society for Promoting Christian Knowledge, 1992).

But one example can show how the language of the gathering into the land is a reference not to a modern geopolitical nation-state and physical land, but rather a metaphorical image of God drawing both Jew and Gentile from all over the earth.

> Eze 36:24–28 I will take you from the nations and gather you from all the countries and bring you into your own land. [25] I will sprinkle clean water on you, and you shall be clean from all your uncleannesses, and from all your idols I will cleanse you. [26] And I will give you a new heart, and a new spirit I will put within you. And I will remove the heart of stone from your flesh and give you a heart of flesh. [27] And I will put my Spirit within you, and cause you to walk in my statutes and be careful to obey my rules. [28] You shall dwell in the land that I gave to your fathers, and you shall be my people, and I will be your God.

The language in this passage is all related to the new covenant. Notice the elements of the promise in Ezekiel 36: 1) sprinkle clean water on you (the sprinkled water of our clean conscience in the new covenant Hebrews 10:22); 2) I will give you a new heart of flesh and new spirit (the new heart and spirit of the new covenant Romans 2:28-29; Hebrews 10:22); 3) I will put my Spirit within you (The new covenant Holy Spirit is in us 2Corinthians 1:22; Ephesisan 1:13); 4) Cause you to walk in my statutes (This Scripture is fulfilled in the new covenant Hebrews 8:10; 10:15-18) 5) Take you from the nations and bring you into your own land (Acts 2). This last promise has transformed from the literal land of Israel into all the earth because when Messiah came, the whole earth became his inheritance, not merely the single plot of land on the coast of the Mediterranean Sea. Jesus is our "inheritance," he is the Promised Land. For a more in depth examination of this notion, see Brian Godawa, *Israel in Bible Prophecy: The New Testament Fulfillment of the Promise to Abraham* (Embedded Pictures Publishing, 2017).

[2] **Comparison of the worshippers of the Beast with the worshippers of the Lamb**: These comparisons are drawn from Revelation 13 about the Beast and Revelation 14 that is placed right after it:

> Revelation 14:1–5 Then I looked, and behold, on Mount Zion stood the Lamb, and with him 144,000 who had his name and his Father's name written on their foreheads. [2] And I heard a voice from heaven like the roar of many waters and like the sound of loud thunder. The voice I heard was like the sound of harpists playing on their harps, [3] and they were singing a new song before the throne and before the four living creatures and before the elders. No one could learn that song except the 144,000 who had been redeemed from the earth. [4] It is these who have not defiled themselves with women, for they are virgins. It is these who follow the Lamb wherever he goes. These have been redeemed from mankind as firstfruits for God and the Lamb, [5] and in their mouth no lie was found, for they are blameless.

Chart from Kenneth L. Gentry, Jr., The Divorce of Israel: A Redemptive-Historical Interpretation of Revelation Vol. 2 (Dallas, GA: Tolle Lege Press, 2016), 296.

Land Beast Vision	Zion Lamb Vision
Appears as a "lamb" (*arniō*) (13:11)	Appears as the "Lamb" (*arnion*) (14:1)
Beast arises from the "Land" (13:11)	Lamb stands on Mount Zion (14:1)
Speaking as a dragon (13:11)	Singing godly praise (14:3)
Land dwellers align with first beast (13:12, 14)	Remnant (144,000) align with Lamb (14:1)
In presence (*enōpion*) of first beast (13:12)	In presence (*enōpion*) of God's throne (14:3)
Fatal wound healed (13:12)	Lamb standing though slain (14:1; cp. 5:6)
Land (*tēn gēn*) worships (13:12, 14)	Redeemed from the Land (*tēs gēs*) (14:3)
Worship first beast (13:12)	Worship God (14:3, cp. v. 7)
Makes (*poiei*) men worship first Beast (13:12)	Men freely follow Lamb (14:4)
Fire from heaven (*ek tou ouranou*) (13:13)	Voice from heaven (*ek tou ouranou*) 14:13
Sings before (*enōpion*) men (13:13)	Sings before (*enōpion*) the throne (14:3)
Deception (13:14)	No lie (14:5)
Image speaks (13:15)	Heaven sings (14:3)
Men forbidden to buy (*agorasai*) (13:17)	Men bought by Lamb (*ēgorasthēsan*) (14:4)
All marked on forehead (*metōpon*) (13:16)	144,000 named on forehead (*metōpōn*) (14:1)
Mark requires wisdom to figure (13:18)	Song known only to 144,000 (14:3)
Forehead has beast's name (*onoma*) (13:18)	Forehead has name (*onoma*) of Father (14:1)

[3] **Remnant as "virgins"**: These are the ones who have not been defiled with women, for they have kept themselves chaste (14:4a). This portion of the verse has generated enormous debates over the centuries, especially regarding monasticism. If taken literally it urges celibacy—at least among the 144,000. This literalistic interpretation has been ably rebutted by many scholars. John's drama, however, employs these words metaphorically of the remnant redeemed from out of debased Israel. When they commit to Christ's kingdom they do not look back (Lk 9:62); they do not wither under the heat of persecution (Mt 13:3, 5-6; cp. Mt 10:17-18). They are not like the Jewish converts to Christ who eventually turn from him to tread under foot the blood of the covenant (Heb 10:26-29; cp. Heb 6:1-6; Jn 6:66; 1Jn 2:19). As faithful converts to the Lamb, who will soon marry him (19:9; 21:2, 9; cp. Mt 22:1–14), once his divorce of old covenant Israel is complete, they keep themselves "chaste" (lit.: they are "virgins," parthenoi) in their redeemed estate. This representation of the remnant contrasts with Israel's Old Testament practice of "fornication" (Isa 57:3; Jer 13:37) and harlotry (Isa 1:21; Jer 2:20; 3:1, 6, 8; Eze 16:5-17; 23:5, 19; Hos 2:5)—as well as her then current situation in which she acted as a harlot with Rome (17:1–4, 15; 18:3; 19:2)… This is "a picture of those (who) have not had (figurative) illegitimate intercourse with 'the great harlot.'" Kenneth L. Gentry, Jr., *The Divorce of Israel: A Redemptive-Historical Interpretation of Revelation Vol. 2* (Dallas, GA: Tolle Lege Press, 2016), 301.

[4] **The Remnant 144,000 as "firstfruits"**: "These have been purchased from among men as first fruits to God and to the Lamb (Revelation 14:4c)…

"In that these are "first fruits," this reference alone undermines any notion that Revelation is referring to the distant future beyond our own day: how could these be first fruits? This is underscored in that Revelation's events must shortly take place (1:1, 3; 22:6, 12). We must remember that the gospel was to the Jew first (Ac 3:26; Ro 1:16; 2:9; cp. Mt 10:6; 15:24). As noted above, John is reflecting on Jeremiah 2:2–3 where virgin Israel follows God into the wilderness to marry him. There she is declared "the first [archē] of His harvest" (Jer 2:3a; cp. Hos 9:10). Under the Old Testament ritual calendar, the first of the harvest required an offering as evidence of God's ownership and blessing (Chilton 357). Leviticus 23:9 introduces the first fruits legislation: "When you enter the land which I am going to give to you" (cp. Ex 22:29; 23:16; Lev 23:9-21; Dt 18:4-5; Ne 10:35-37). The first-fruits harvest promised a wider, fuller harvest to follow: through the worldwide progress of the gospel that flowed from the faithfulness of the Jewish remnant who weathered the storm of Jewish and Roman persecution in the 60s (cp. 7:9ff; 12:17)." Kenneth L. Gentry, Jr., *The Divorce of Israel: A Redemptive-Historical Interpretation of Revelation Vol. 2* (Dallas, GA: Tolle Lege Press, 2016), 302-303.

[5] **The great multitude of Revelation 7**: John said that he was partaking in "the Tribulation" at that very time in the first century: Revelation 1:9 I, John, your brother and partner in the tribulation and the kingdom and the patient endurance that are in Jesus, was on the island called Patmos.

Kenneth Gentry explains: "John is speaking of those who are presently coming out of the great tribulation and who are entering into heaven because of their relationship to the Lamb: they have washed their robes and made them white in his blood (see below). As I note at 7:9c these are not martyrs, or at least not all of them are. They are the ones who are faithfully enduring through that great tribulation era and who die by whatever means and enter into heaven. In fact, that they are currently continuing to come out of the great tribulation implies that the church of Jesus Christ will continue on into the future despite the first-century tribulation she encountered…

"Rather, we must remember that John is writing to particular people (1:4, 11) at a particular time (1:1, 3): the first-century church in the time of Christianity's infancy. The infant church is not only enduring persecution from Jerusalem and Rome, but will also witness God's wrath on Jerusalem where Christianity was born. To interpret "the great tribulation" as involving general circumstances encountered by Christians at all times— including you as you read this commentary in the comfort of your air conditioned office—surely reduces the significance not only of John's phrase, and of the suffering of many severely persecuted Christians, but also of Revelation itself. Revelation's drama is too dramatic for that. John is speaking of a particular episode: tēs thlipseōs tēs megalēs, "the tribulation, the great one." It is a "superlatively great crisis" (Swete 102). This articular phrase is anaphoric, indicating that John's audience is well aware of this period as the particular, unique event." Kenneth L. Gentry, Jr., *The Divorce of Israel: A Redemptive-Historical Interpretation of Revelation Vol. 1* (Dallas, GA: Tolle Lege Press, 2016), 682-683.

[6] **No lie was found in their mouth**: "And no lie was found in their mouth; they are blameless (Revelation 14:5). Filling out the picture of the faithful Jewish remnant in the Land, John extols their virtue as true Jews. "Unlike those who deny Christ, and yet claim to be the true people of God (2.9; 3.9), and in stark contrast to the beast from the earth who deceives the earth's inhabitants (13.13-15), the members of the new Israel are evidently truthful". Interestingly, the Old Testament backdrop to this statement is Zephaniah 3:13 regarding the remnant of Israel: "The remnant of Israel will do no wrong / And tell no lies, / Nor will a deceitful tongue / Be found in their mouths." Kenneth L. Gentry, Jr., *The Divorce of Israel: A Redemptive-Historical Interpretation of Revelation Vol. 2* (Dallas, GA: Tolle Lege Press, 2016), 303.

[7] The two harvests spoken of here come from:

> Revelation 14:14–20 [14] Then I looked, and behold, a white cloud, and seated on the cloud one like a son of man, with a golden crown on his head, and a sharp sickle in his hand. [15] And another angel came out of the temple, calling with a loud voice to him who sat on the cloud, "Put in your sickle, and reap, for the hour to reap has come, for the harvest of the earth is fully ripe." [16] So he who sat on the cloud swung his sickle across the earth, and the earth was reaped. [17] Then another angel came out of the temple in heaven, and he too had a sharp sickle. [18] And another angel came out from the altar, the angel who has authority over the fire, and he called with a loud voice to the one who had the sharp sickle, "Put in your sickle and gather the clusters from the vine of the earth, for its grapes are ripe." [19] So the angel swung his sickle across the earth and gathered the grape harvest of the earth and threw it into the great winepress of the wrath of God. [20] And the winepress was trodden outside the city, and blood flowed from the winepress, as high as a horse's bridle, for 1,600 stadia.

[8] **The harvest of judgment**: Kenneth Gentry writes: "Put in your sharp sickle, and gather the clusters from the vine of the earth because her grapes are ripe (Revelation 14:18b). Though the grain harvest (14:14) reflects the "first fruits" (14:4), this vintage picks up on the earlier mention of "Babylon" making the nations "drink of the wine of the passion of her immorality" (14:8b). Consequently, John will soon refer to the judgment as one that occurs "outside the city" (14:20), that is, outside of Babylon-Jerusalem.

437

"This envisions a judgment against Israel in that it notes that this vine is "of the Land [tēs gēs]." And the vine is a familiar image of Israel in the Old Testament (Ps 80:1, 8-9,14-15; Isa 5:1-7; Eze 15:6). That "her grapes are ripe" indicates the ripeness of Israel for judgment. We should remember the words of Christ and of Paul about Israel's ripening process: "Fill up then the measure of the guilt of your fathers.... that upon you may fall the guilt of all the righteous blood shed on earth, from the blood of righteous Abel to the blood of Zechariah, the son of Berechiah, whom you murdered between the temple and the altar" (Mt 23:32, 35). Paul writes that the Jews are "hindering us from speaking to the Gentiles that they might be saved; with the result that they always fill up the measure of their sins. But wrath has come upon them to the utmost" (1Th 2:16).

"Israel is now ripe for judgment, which is clearly portrayed in the angel's action: Though John proleptically refers to Babylon's fall (14:8), he will actually "reach the destruction of the city in chs. 17, 18, but now he is concerned only about those 'outside the city'" (Ford 250). This is an image of the devastation wreaked by the Roman forces marching through the Land as they furiously approach their goal, Jerusalem. "It corresponds in history to the overrunning of Palestine and approach on Jerusalem of the armies of Vespasian" (Carrington 247). The distance of the bloodshed is "two hundred miles" (stadiōn chiliōn exakosiōn, "1600 stadia"). According to the Itinerarum (ca. AD 200) of Antonius of Piacenza, Palestine's length is 1664 stadia. Thus, "the distance [is]... approximately the length of Palestine from north to south". This prophecy refers to the enormous blood flow in Israel during the Jewish War so that "the streams of running blood become a great Red Sea, reaching 'up to the horses' bridles' in a recapitulation of the overthrow of Pharaoh's horses and chariots (Ex. 14:23, 28; 15:19)". This is the Land that should have been "flowing with milk and honey" (Ex 13:5), but instead it will flow with blood.

"Such blood flow is a common hyperbolic image of enormous loss of life during war. Isaiah likens massive bloodshed to "the waters . . . full of blood" (Isa 15:9). We see this language in other ancient writings. "And the horse will walk up to its chest in the blood of sinners" (1 En. 100:3). "And there shall be blood from the sword as high as a horse's belly and a man's thigh and a camel's hock" (4 Ezra 15:35-36). "Blood will flow up to the bank of deep eddying rivers" (Sib. Or. 5:372). "The bloody ocean will be filled with flesh and blood of the senseless, from evil war" (Sib. Or. 5:472-73). "They killed among them until the horse sank up to the nostrils in blood. And the blood rolled along rocks of 40 se'ah in weight, until it reached four miles into the sea" (y. Ta'an. 4:8; Rabbah Lam. 2:2:4). "They slew in it men, women and children, until their blood flowed and poured into the great sea"...

"Josephus's Jewish War records various particularly bloody battles: "the whole space of ground whereon they fought ran with blood, and the wall might have been ascended over by the bodies of the dead carcasses" (J. W. 3:7:23 §249); "the sea was bloody a long way" (3:9:3 §426); "one might then see the lake all bloody, and full of dead bodies" (3:10:9 §529); "the whole of the country through which they had fled was filled with slaughter, and Jordan could not be passed over, by reason of the dead bodies that were in it" (4:7:6; §437). Even in Jerusalem itself we learn that eventually "blood ran down over all the lower parts of the city, from the upper city" (4:1:10 §72); "the outer temple was all of it overflowed with blood" (4:5:1 §313); "the blood of all sorts of dead carcases stood in lakes in the holy courts" (5:1:3 §18); and "the whole city ran down with blood, to such a degree indeed that the fire of many of the houses was quenched with these men's blood" (6:8:5 §406)." Kenneth L. Gentry, Jr., *The Divorce of Israel: A Redemptive-Historical Interpretation of Revelation Vol. 2* (Dallas, GA: Tolle Lege Press, 2016), 321-323.

[9] **The harvest of rescue**: Kenneth Gentry writes: "(I see the harvest referring to the remnant in first-century Israel rather than the elect at the consummation—though as a "first fruits" action it certainly anticipates that final harvest). That it portrays a positive ingathering of his people appears from the following:

"(1) This vision occurs immediately after positive statements of the perseverance of the faithful (14:12), the benediction upon them (14:13a), and the promise of rest from their labors (14:13b). Since they are so blessed, this fits well with this vision speaking of the Son of Man protectively gathering his own.

"(2) The "white" color of the cloud upon which the Son of Man sits is not an appropriate image for the storm of God's judgment. In Revelation judgment phenomena involve thunder, lightning, hail and so forth (4:5; 8:5; 10:3; 11:19; 16:18; 19:6) which are more naturally associated with dark clouds (see the storm clouds rolling ominously across the sky in 6:14). Darkness characterizes judgment in Revelation (8:12; 9:2; 16:10; 18:23). Besides, John's Gospel speaks of the evangelistic opportunity as fields being "white for harvest" (Jn 4:35) which may impact the whole picture as a positive thought.

"(3) This harvesting of grain picks up on the earlier positive statement in 4c which declares the "blameless" 144,000 to be the "first fruits." First fruits are harvested as a token of the favor of God (cp. Lev 23:9-14) so that it becomes a time of celebration (Dt 16:9ff).

"(5) The vision of the 144,000 in the protective presence of the Lamb on Mount Zion (14:1–5) fits the notion of protective ingathering in this vision. The positive image of this grain harvest is presented before the negative portrayal of the vintage. This follows the pattern of the original number of the 144,000 (7:4–8) preceding the trumpet judgments (8:1ff) and of the measuring of the inner temple preceding the outer temple's destruction (11:1-2). John repeatedly emphasizes God's protective presence during times of great judgment. In fact, God's care for his own in the midst of judgment is a strong theme in Revelation.

"(6) Some New Testament references elsewhere speak of a protective ingathering of the harvest. At least one of these involves a (first fruits!) harvest at the end of the old covenant era as God's judgment befalls Israel in AD 70: "His winnowing fork is in His hand, and He will thoroughly clear His threshing floor; and He will gather His wheat into the barn, but He will burn up the chaff with unquenchable fire" (Mt 3:12; cp. 3:11 with Acts 1:5; 2:16-21). This does not require a physical resurrection but most likely represents a spiritual gathering into the church (which involves a spiritual resurrection, cp. Jn 5:24-26)." Kenneth L. Gentry, Jr., *The Divorce of Israel: A Redemptive-Historical Interpretation of Revelation Vol. 2* (Dallas, GA: Tolle Lege Press, 2016), 318-320.

[10] **The winnowing of the wheat from the chaff**: This reference about John the Baptizer's prophecy is often assumed to refer to the end of the world. But as described elsewhere, it is not, it is the "end of the age" which is the end of the old covenant age or era. But this is the case with most of Jesus' parables as well. They refer to the coming judgment on Israel and Jerusalem as the end of the old covenant age. Those who rejected Jesus as Messiah in that first century would be judged.

> Matthew 3:11–12 [11] "I baptize you with water for repentance, but he who is coming after me is mightier than I, whose sandals I am not worthy to carry. He will baptize you with the Holy Spirit and fire. [12] His winnowing fork is in his hand, and he will clear his threshing floor and gather his wheat into the barn, but the chaff he will burn with unquenchable fire."

Jesus parable of the Tenants reinforces this judgment upon the first generation and Jerusalem for rejecting Messiah:

> Matthew 21:38–43 [38] But when the tenants saw the son, they said to themselves, 'This is the heir. Come, let us kill him and have his inheritance.' [39] And they took him and threw him out of the vineyard and killed him. [40] When therefore the owner of the vineyard comes, what will he do to those tenants?" [41] They said to him, "He will put those wretches to a miserable death and let out the vineyard to other tenants who will give him the fruits in their seasons." [42] Jesus said to them, "Have you never read in the Scriptures: " 'The stone that the builders rejected has become the cornerstone; this was the Lord's doing, and it is marvelous in our eyes'? [43] Therefore I tell you, the kingdom of God will be taken away from you and given to a people producing its fruits.

Jesus' parable right after the Tenants is the parable of the Wedding Feast, another affirmation of the destruction of Jerusalem and the first century Jews who rejected him, which then resulted in the spread of the Gospel to the Gentiles.

> Matthew 22:7–9 [7] The king was angry, and he sent his troops and destroyed those murderers and burned their city. [8] Then he said to his servants, 'The wedding feast is ready, but those invited were not worthy. [9] Go therefore to the main roads and invite to the wedding feast as many as you find.'

The parables of the "end of the age" are not the end of the world, but the end of the old covenant age, so the pulling out of the weeds and their burning in the parable of the weeds is not the final judgment at the end of the world, but the judgment of the Jews and the destruction of their temple in the fires of God's judgment in AD 70. But first, God's servants are spared.

> Matthew 13:39–43 [39] and the enemy who sowed them is the devil. The harvest is the end of the age, and the reapers are angels. [40] Just as the weeds are gathered and burned with fire, so will it be at the end of the age. [41] The Son of Man will send his angels, and they will gather out of his kingdom all causes of sin and all law-breakers, [42] and throw them into the fiery furnace. In that place there will be weeping and gnashing of teeth. [43] Then the righteous will shine like the sun in the kingdom of their Father. He who has ears, let him hear.

439

The parable of the net is the same thing. The end of the age is the end of the old covenant age, not the end of the world.

> Matthew 13:47–50 [47] "Again, the kingdom of heaven is like a net that was thrown into the sea and gathered fish of every kind. [48] When it was full, men drew it ashore and sat down and sorted the good into containers but threw away the bad. [49] So it will be at the end of the age. The angels will come out and separate the evil from the righteous [50] and throw them into the fiery furnace. In that place there will be weeping and gnashing of teeth.

The End of the Age is NOT the end of the world, but the end of the old covenant age: "My first hint was that the Greek word for "age" that Jesus used was aion, which Louw-Nida defines as "a unit of time as a particular stage or period of history—age, era."

"This notion of the end of the age shows up in other teachings from Jesus. At the end of Matthew, Jesus said to his disciples, "Behold, I am with you always, to the end of the age" (28:20). In another place he said that those who followed him would receive both persecutions and spiritual family in this age, "and in the age to come eternal life" (Mark 10:30).

"The notion of the present age and the messianic age to come was prevalent in Jewish understanding and in the New Testament as well. Paul wrote of the Christians living in "this age" (1 Cor 3:18), "this present evil age" (Gal 1:4) that had evil spiritual rulers of this age (1 Cor 2:8; 2 Cor 4:4); but there was the messianic "age to come" (Eph 1:21, Heb 6:4). When Messiah came, he would usher in a new covenant, a new age of spiritual transformation in the world.

"Well, of course, Messiah had come. That "age to come" was not a reference to a second coming of Jesus, but his first coming, bringing the kingdom of God (the kingdom age to come), a kingdom that was both now and not yet. It was inaugurated but not consummated.

"This "age to come" was the new covenant age. Paul wrote elsewhere that the gospel (the new covenant) was "hidden for ages, but now revealed to his saints (Col 1:26). In 1 Corinthians 10:11, he wrote that the old covenant events occurred as an example "for our instruction upon whom the end of the ages has come." Did you catch that? The temple had not yet been destroyed, and Paul was saying that his generation was at the end of the ages! He said that it had come upon that first century of believers. The end of the age is not a future event that hasn't happened yet; it occurred in the first century with the coming of the new covenant, confirmed in the destruction of the temple. But Paul isn't the only one who wrote that in the New Testament.

"Hebrews 9:26 says that Jesus suffered on the cross, "once for all at the end of the ages to put away sin by the sacrifice of himself." The end of the ages is not the end of history or the end of the world as we understand it. The end of the ages had already occurred at the time of the crucifixion of Christ. The end of the ages was the end of the old covenant era and the beginning of the new covenant in Christ's blood!

"But get this: that same writer of Hebrews talked about the new covenant in Christ being superior to the old covenant in Hebrews 8. He quoted Jeremiah confirming that the prophets predicted the arrival of the new covenant age. And then he said, "In speaking of a new covenant, he makes the first one obsolete. And what is becoming obsolete and growing old is ready to vanish away" (8:13).

"What was growing old and ready to vanish at that time?

"It blew my theology when I realized that he was talking about the destruction of the temple as the final culmination of the new covenant replacement of the old covenant! He was writing in the time period after Christ's death and resurrection and right before the temple had been destroyed. So the new covenant had been established in Christ's blood, but it was not consummated with historical finality. Like Paul, the writer believed they were at the end of the ages. The new covenant would make the old covenant obsolete. But take a closer look at the language he used. He said that the old is "becoming obsolete and is ready to vanish away," as if the old covenant had not vanished yet. It was only in the process of becoming obsolete. "Becoming," not "had become," and not "would become" thousands of years in the future. What could that mean?

"Well, the writer was writing within the generation that Jesus said would see the destruction of the temple. The temple had not yet been destroyed. Hebrews 8 says that they were in a time period of change between covenants and that change had not yet been fully or historically consummated. That first century generation was in the transition period between ages or covenants. So, what would be the event that would embody the theological claim that the old covenant was obsolete and the new covenant had replaced it? The destruction of the symbol of the old covenant, the temple! The old covenant would not be obsolete until its symbolic incarnation, the temple, was made desolate." Brian Godawa, *End Times Bible Prophecy: It's Not What They Told You* (Los Angeles, CA: Embedded Pictures Publishing, 2017), 72-74.

[11] **Stoicheia:** In every place that *stoicheion* shows up in the New Testament it means elementary principle rudiments of a worldview, sometimes a godless worldview (Col. 2:8), but more often the elementary principles of the Old Covenant law described as a "cosmos" (Gal. .4:3; 9; Col. 2:20; Heb. 5:12).[11]

Remember how the cosmic language of creating heavens and earth was used to describe the cosmic significance of God establishing a covenant? And remember how in the Old Testament, the destruction of covenants, nations, and peoples was described in *decreation* terms as the collapsing of the universe?

That is the case in these passages as well, with the term "cosmos" being used metaphorically for the "universe" of God's covenantal order as embodied in the Old Covenant laws of Jewish separation: Circumcision, dietary restrictions and Sabbaths. Paul is telling his readers that the *stoicheion* of the Old Covenant *cosmos* are no longer over them because the people of God are under new *stoicheion*, the elementary principles of faith (Gal. 4:1-11).

Peter means the same thing. When he says that the heavens will pass away and the *stoicheion* will be burned up, he is claiming that when the Temple in Jerusalem is destroyed, it will be the final passing away of the Old Covenant cosmos, along with all the elementary principles tied to that physical sacramental structure, the laws that once separated Jew and Gentile. The new cosmos is one in which both Jew and Gentile "by God's power are being guarded through faith for a salvation ready to be revealed in the last time" (1 Pet. 1:5).

Leithart, Peter J. *The Promise of His Appearing: An Exposition of Second Peter*. Moscow, ID: Canon Press, 2004, p.101. Bauckham argues that "The heavenly bodies (sun, moon and stars) is the interpretation favored by most commentators," for *stoicheion*. But then we are right back to the sun, moon, and stars as figurative language of covenantal elements. Bauckham, *2 Peter, Jude*, 316. But I doubt this interpretation because the clear words for "heavenly bodies" are not stoicheion, but epouranios soma (1 Cor. 15:40-41).

CHAPTER 34

[1] **Paul wrote about this same issue of avoiding marriage, though closer to A.D. 70**: 1 Corinthians 7:26–29 [26] I think that in view of the present distress it is good for a person to remain as he is. [27] Are you bound to a wife? Do not seek to be free. Are you free from a wife? Do not seek a wife. [28] But if you do marry, you have not sinned, and if a betrothed woman marries, she has not sinned. Yet those who marry will have worldly troubles, and I would spare you that. [29] This is what I mean, brothers: the appointed time has grown very short.

CHAPTER 35

[1] **The Anakim in Gaza in the days of Joshua**: Joshua 11:21–22 And Joshua came at that time and cut off the Anakim from the hill country, from Hebron, from Debir, from Anab, and from all the hill country of Judah, and from all the hill country of Israel. Joshua devoted them to destruction with their cities. [22] There was none of the Anakim left in the land of the people of Israel. Only in Gaza, in Gath, and in Ashdod did some remain.

Numbers 13:32–33 So they brought to the people of Israel a bad report of the land that they had spied out, saying, "The land, through which we have gone to spy it out, is a land that devours its inhabitants, and all the people that we saw in it are of great height. [33] And there we saw the Nephilim (the sons of Anak, who come from the Nephilim), and we seemed to ourselves like grasshoppers, and so we seemed to them."

[2] **Gaza as described here**: "Gaza was one of the most important cities of Palestine in ancient times for two main reasons: its role as a major emporium for the lucrative luxury-goods trade from Arabia Felix and the Far East, and its location on the Via Maris leading from Asia Minor and Syria to Egypt. Strategically, it served as a bridgehead for Egyptian rulers who launched campaigns to conquer Palestine and Syria, just as it served as a springboard for conquering Egypt from the N. The city already became an international commercial center under the reign of the Achaemenid Persians."

"It is no surprise that in the reign of Jehoram of Judah, when Judah and its former ally Israel were weakened by Aram, the Philistine city-states, together with the Arabs, sought revenge on Judah (2 Chr 21:16–17). From this point, the trade route from Arabia to Gaza was in the hands of Gaza's friends (2 Kgs 8:20)."

"After Herod's death Gaza enjoyed the status of partially autonomous polis under the aegis of the Roman governor in Syria (Ant 17.320; JW 2.97; Rosenberger 1975: 54). In Emperor Claudius' days Gaza was flourishing once again and was even described as an important city (Schürer HJP² 2: 102, n. 79). In 66 C.E. Gaza and Anthedon were attacked by Jewish zealotic rebels. Josephus (JW 2.460) states that the two cities were totally destroyed, but numismatic evidence indicates that this report was greatly exaggerated." Katzenstein H. J., "Gaza (Place): PreHellenistic Gaza," ed. David Noel Freedman, The Anchor Yale Bible Dictionary (New York: Doubleday, 1992), 913.Aryeh Kasher, "Gaza (Place): Gaza in the Greco-Roman Period," ed. David Noel Freedman, *The Anchor Yale Bible Dictionary* (New York: Doubleday, 1992), 913-916.

[3] **Dagon**: "In the Bible, Dagon is described as the chief god of the Philistines. The story of Samson's death in Judges 16 takes place in the temple of Dagon, god of the Philistines. In 1 Chron. 10:10 the Philistines are said to have hung the decapitated head of King Saul in a temple of Dagon at Beth-shan. 1 Sam. 5 tells the story of Philistines capturing the ark of the covenant and placing it in the temple of Dagon in Ashdod. Two mornings in a row, the statue of Dagon was found flat on its face before the ark, the second time, with its head and hands "cut off." Severing hands and heads was a common tactic of ancient Near Eastern powers, both Mesopotamian and Canaanite. This supernatural "power encounter" between Yahweh and Dagon becomes then a spiritual polemic of warfare and conquest between gods. But beyond these mentions, nothing more is revealed in the Old Testament.

"The meaning of the name Dagon is uncertain. Early scholarly interpreters argued that it came from the Hebrew word for "fish," thus one tradition depicts him as a hybrid deity with the upper torso of a man and the lower bottom of a fish. The 1 Samuel passage describing the lower part of the Dagon statue has been interpreted by some as "his fishy part." Later scholars argued the name Dagon came from the Hebrew word for "grain," thus another tradition understands him as a god of fertility or grain. Still others have argued Dagon was a storm god, whose name came from the Arabic word for cloudy rain. No scholarly consensus has been reached on these interpretations, though the earlier ones have fallen out of favor.

"Dagon had a strong presence in Mesopotamia and Syria primarily as a storm god, spelled Dagan, and likened to the Babylonian weather god Enlil. The Syrians included Dagon in their pantheon at Ugarit, which was in Syria, but nowhere in Canaan. The Canaanite champion deity Ba'al is described throughout the Ugaritic texts as the "Son of Dagon" which made him an outsider to the family of gods ruled over by the high god El and his wife, Athirat (Asherah), the Mother of the Gods.

"But since the Philistines were known for adapting customs and gods from their newly conquered lands it is entirely possible that Dagon was imported from Philistine contact with Syria and adapted to the interests of the coastal Sea People.

[4] **Uriel's special sword move**: If you don't know what this is from the series *Chronicles of the Nephilim*, you will eventually find out before *Chronicles of the Apocalypse* is through.

[5] **Angels are not pure spirits. They have flesh**: "the ontological nature or "material being" of the angels as revealed in the Bible would seem to preclude these fallen angels from being the Old Testament or New Testament demons. While angels are multidimensional in their ability to traverse between the heavenlies and the earth, they are described as having flesh that eats food (Gen. 18; 19:1), and can have sexual congress with human beings (Gen. 6:1-4). This is a heavenly flesh that is different from human flesh (1 Cor. 15:39-40), but is flesh nonetheless. This would make angels or divine beings such as the Watchers unlikely candidates for incorporeal spirits." Brian Godawa, *When Giants Were Upon the Earth: The Watchers, the Nephilim, and the Biblical Cosmic War of the Seed* (Los Angeles, CA: Embedded Pictures Publishing, 2014), 277.

Angels have a heavenly flesh that is unlike earthly flesh: Jude 6–7 (NASB95) [6] And angels who did not keep their own domain, but abandoned their proper abode, He has kept in eternal bonds under darkness for the judgment of the great day, [7] just as Sodom and Gomorrah and the cities around them, since they in the same way as these indulged in gross immorality and went after strange flesh.

[6] **This incident of Michael's dismemberment by Asherah and Dagon is fictionalized in my previous novel**: Brian Godawa, *David Ascendant* (Embedded Pictures Publishing, 2014).

[7] **The kings of the east whose angels are bound at the Euphrates**: Zeus is the god of Commagene, Hubal of Arabia and Ba'al of Syria. All these gods were over the nation's forces that made up the Roman army that marched down upon Jerusalem. At this point, they are being bound by the angels until their appointed time. "Contrary to dispensationalists, these kings do not represent modern-day, "Oriental rulers" (Walvoord 236). Rather, they are "kings from the east," who are mentioned in a book which declares its events are near (1:3; 22:10). We should recall that the Roman forces set against Israel were comprised not only of Roman legionary troops but others from various auxiliary kings. Josephus notes that in the initial imperial engagement of the war, Vespasian added to his legions, "a considerable number of auxiliaries... from the kings Antiochus, and Agrippa, and Sohemus, each of them contributing one thousand footmen that were archers, and a thousand horsemen. Malchus also, the king of Arabia, sent a thousand horsemen, besides five thousand footmen, the greatest part of whom were archers" (J.W. 3:4:2 §68). The same held true for the final stages of the war under Titus, beside "whom marched those auxiliaries that came from the kings, being now more in number than before, together with a considerable number that came to his assistance from Syria" (J.W.5:1:6 §42–44). So then, not only did Titus draw troops from the Euphrates in the east (J.W. 5:1:6 §44), but Antiochus IV is the king of Commagene, and "Samoseta, the capital of Commagene, lies upon Euphrates" (J.W. 7:7:1 §224). In addition, Titus called the tenth legion through Jericho (J.W. 5:1:6 §42; 5:2:3 §69), which is east of Jerusalem (cf. Jos 13:32; 16:1; 20:8)—though not near the Euphrates. These important troop movements from east of Jerusalem involved the tenth legion, one of "the most eminent legions of all" (J.W. 3:4:2 §65)." Kenneth L. Gentry, Jr., *The Divorce of Israel: A Redemptive-Historical Interpretation of Revelation Vol. 2* (Dallas, GA: Tolle Lege Press, 2016), 360.

Commagene's gods: "The restored freedom of Commagene, now allied to Rome, allowed Antiochus leisure for his great religious expression still visible atop Nemrud Dagh. His remarkable fusions of Greek and Iranian gods satisfied the composite population, which could now worship Zeus-Oromasdes (Ahuramazda), Heracles-Artagnes, and the grandly titled Apollo-Mithras-Helios-Hermes!" Richard D. Sullivan, "Commagene (Place)," ed. David Noel Freedman, *The Anchor Yale Bible Dictionary* (New York: Doubleday, 1992), 1096.

Baal Haddad was the chief storm god of Syria: "The tablets from Ebla contain a pantheon of Canaanite gods, but some of the names and relationships are different from those at Ugarit. Concerning the deity Baal, there were either two storm gods or one storm god with two names, Baal and Hadad. By the time of Ugarit, Hadad had definitely become another name for Baal, and some cultures (e.g., the Arameans) worshiped Baal by the name Hadad. The greater prominence of the god Dagon as head of the pantheon at Ebla may explain the Ugaritic reference to Baal as "Son of Dagon." Winfried Corduan, "Baal," ed. John D. Barry et al., *The Lexham Bible Dictionary* (Bellingham, WA: Lexham Press, 2016).

""Hadad" appears only once in the biblical text. Among the Canaanites, Hadad was known by his title Baal ("Lord"), by which he more commonly appears in the Bible. The biblical text also attests to the cult of Hadad via several theophoric names belonging to the rulers of Aram-Damascus and to the early rulers of the tribes of Edom." Justin L. Kelley, "Hadad," ed. John D. Barry et al., *The Lexham Bible Dictionary* (Bellingham, WA: Lexham Press, 2016).

Serapis was a god in Alexandria from where Titus brought the 15th Legion into Judea. Tacitus and Suetonius both claim Vespasian had an encounter with Serapis in Alexandria right before he was declared emperor after the death of Nero. Tacitus *Histories* 4.81-82; Suetonius, *Vespasian* 7.1.

CHAPTER 36

[1] **Revelation 11 and the measuring of the temple**: Revelation 11:1 Then I was given a measuring rod like a staff, and I was told, "Rise and measure the temple of God and the altar and those who worship there

[2] **Measuring as a metaphor for God's protection**: Ezekiel 40:3; 47:3; Zechariah 1:16; 2:1-8.

[3] **Revelation 11 and the measuring and destruction of the temple**: Revelation 11:1–2 Then I was given a measuring rod like a staff, and I was told, "Rise and measure the temple of God and the altar and those who worship there, [2] but do not measure the court outside the temple; leave that out, for it is given over to the nations, and they will trample the holy city for forty-two months.

The 42 months: "Providentially then, this forty-two month period actually does conform very closely to the length of the Jewish War that ended with the destruction of "the holy city" and the temple. And this is not merely a "curious coincidence"...

"John would likely count the beginning of the war from the time that the white horseman actually "went out [exēlthon]" to conquer (6:2), that is, when Vespasian initially entered Israel to engage military operations. Shortly thereafter, "the war began in earnest only in March or April of 67, when Vespasian and his son Titus gathered their legions in Ptolemais...

"This figure [42 months] represents "the duration of the final struggle with Rome [for] Vespasian entered Galilee with his armies in the Spring of 67 CE (War 3:29-34) and Jerusalem fell forty-two months later, in September 70 CE." From Spring of AD 67 to August/September of AD 70, the time of formal imperial engagement against Jerusalem, is a period right at forty-two months." Kenneth L. Gentry, Jr., *The Divorce of Israel: A Redemptive-Historical Interpretation of Revelation Vol. 2* (Dallas, GA: Tolle Lege Press, 2016), 52-54.

[4] **He quotes from**: Luke 21:5–6 [5] And while some were speaking of the temple, how it was adorned with noble stones and offerings, he said, [6] "As for these things that you see, the days will come when there will not be left here one stone upon another that will not be thrown down."

Luke 21:20–24 "But when you see Jerusalem surrounded by armies, then know that its desolation has come near. [21] Then let those who are in Judea flee to the mountains, and let those who are inside the city depart, and let not those who are out in the country enter it, [22] for these are days of vengeance, to fulfill all that is written. [23] Alas for women who are pregnant and for those who are nursing infants in those days! For there will be great distress upon the earth and wrath against this people. [24] They will fall by the edge of the sword and be led captive among all nations, and Jerusalem will be trampled underfoot by the Gentiles, until the times of the Gentiles are fulfilled.

[5] **The meaning of the inner temple about outer temple**: "The correspondence between Revelation 11:2 and Luke 21:24 virtually demands first-century Jerusalem be in view (Lk 21:5–6, 20; cp. Zec 12:3). The lexical similarity between Luke and Revelation is hard to dismiss. Compare the italicized words:

Luke 21:24b
Jerusalem will be trampled [patēsousin]
under foot by the Gentiles [ethnesin]
until the times of the Gentiles be fulfilled.

Revelation 11:2b
It has been given to the nations [enthnōn];
and they will tread [patoumenē] under
foot the holy city for forty-two months

"John is not to measure the entire temple complex, but only the inner "temple" (naos), "the altar," and "those who worship in it." Josephus calls this naos "that most sacred part of the temple" (J.W. 5:5:4 §207). Aune (605) notes that the word "measure" (metrein) can also mean "count," which would fit well with John's counting of persons, that is, "those who worship [proskunountas] in it,"27 as well as with the counting of the 144,000 in 7:3–8. The people he is to "measure" are following the example of the elders in the heavenly temple above who "worshiped" [prosekunēson] God (11:16; cp. 4:10; 5:14; 19:4). The "altar" in the inner temple is the place where redemptive contact with God occurs on earth; its heavenly counterpart is where "the prayers of the saints" are heard (8:3; cp. 16:7) and from whence God's judgment—against rebellious Israel flows (8:5; 14:18)...

"So then, this protective measuring of the inner temple, altar, and worshipers (11:1b), along with the omission of the unmeasured outer court to the Gentiles (11:2), pictures the judgmental removal of the old covenant's external temple (and the redemptive economy for which it stands) and the protection of Christian Jews within Jerusalem (and the Christian church of which they are the seed and the representatives). This image does not picture a future rebuilt temple (as per some commentators), rather here the purpose is "to note that certain righteous persons will be protected from the oncoming woe" (Vogelgesasng 118). The unbelieving Jews (represented by their temple which defined their religious faith)31 have become like Gentiles: they are a "Sodom and Egypt" (11:8), worthy of judgment. As in Hebrews, the earthly tabernacle/temple elements are but transient copies of the heavenly (Heb 8:5; 9:24; cp. Ex 25:9, 40; 26:30; 27:8; Ac 7:44). As the old covenant expired, its central feature (the physical temple) was finally and forever removed in AD 70, thereby fulfilling Christ's wrath against those who pierced him (1:7; cp. Mt 24:30).(the Kenneth L. Gentry, Jr., *The Divorce of Israel: A Redemptive-Historical Interpretation of Revelation Vol. 2* (Dallas, GA: Tolle Lege Press, 2016), 36, 44, 50.

[6] **Jesus is the new temple of God, and so is his body, the church**: Ephesians 2:19–22 [19] So then you are no longer strangers and aliens, but you are fellow citizens with the saints and members of the household of God, [20] built on the foundation of the apostles and prophets, Christ Jesus himself being the cornerstone, [21] in whom the whole structure, being joined together, grows into a holy temple in the Lord. [22] In him you also are being built together into a dwelling place for God by the Spirit.

[7] **Christians are the priesthood and the temple**: 1 Peter 2:4–5 [4] As you come to him, a living stone rejected by men but in the sight of God chosen and precious, [5] you yourselves like living stones are being built up as a spiritual house, to be a holy priesthood, to offer spiritual sacrifices acceptable to God through Jesus Christ.

[8] **Jesus is the Shekinah Glory of the temple**: The glory left the temple in the days of Ezekiel: Ezekiel 10:18,19 "...the glory of the LORD departed from the threshold of the temple and stood over the cherubim. And the cherubim lifted their wings and mounted up from the earth in my sight. When they went out, the wheels were beside them; and they stood at the door of the east gate of the LORD'S house, and the glory of the God of Israel was above them."

Ezekiel 11:22-25 ...the cherubim lifted up their wings, with the wheels beside them, and the glory of the God of Israel was high above them. And the glory of the LORD went up from the midst of the city and stood on the mountain, which is on the east side of the city [the Mount of Olives]. Then the Spirit took me up and brought me in a vision by the Spirit of God into Chaldea, to those in captivity. And the vision that I had seen went up from me. So I spoke to those in captivity of all the things the LORD had shown me."

Messiah prophesied to be the return of God's glory (The very words of John the Baptist about Jesus):

Isaiah 40:3–5 [3] A voice cries: "In the wilderness prepare the way of the LORD; make straight in the desert a highway for our God. [4] Every valley shall be lifted up, and every mountain and hill be made low; the uneven ground shall become level, and the rough places a plain. [5] And the glory of the LORD shall be revealed, and all flesh shall see it together, for the mouth of the LORD has spoken."

John 1:14–18 And the Word became flesh and dwelt among us, and we have seen his glory, glory as of the only Son from the Father, full of grace and truth... [16] For from his fullness we have all received, grace upon grace. [17] For the law was given through Moses; grace and truth came through Jesus Christ. [18] No one has ever seen God; the only God, who is at the Father's side, he has made him known.

[9] **The great harlot of Revelation is apostate Jerusalem**:

Israel as adulterous harlot with idols: Ezekiel 16:15-59; Ezekiel 23; 2Kings 17:7-17; Jeremiah 3:1-11; Hosea 1-2.

The harlot that rides the beast represents the corrupt Jewish leaders: "Since the harlot is dressed in the distinctive robe of the high priest which is worn only on holy occasions (Ex 28:2-4, 41, 43), and since she possesses a "gold cup" as used in libations (Ex 25:29; 1Ki 7:50; cp. m. Yoma 3:10), Rev is presenting the holy city (cp. 11:1) under the guise of the high-priest engaged in his sacerdotal duties...

"That the gold cup is "full of abominations and of the unclean things of her immorality further identifies the harlot as Jerusalem. The kai here is probably epexegetical, signifying that she is "full of abominations, which are, the uncleanness of her immorality." In the OT, the word *abominations* is often a religious term signifying that which the God of Israel detests and "uncleanness" is a cultic term related to Israel's separation to God. This religio-cultic concern is strongly Jewish, well fitting first-century Jerusalem...

"So in John's drama the priestly libations God ordains for holy worship are replaced in Jerusalem's high-priestly system: their golden libation bowls now are filled with uncleanness because of their spilling the innocent blood of Christ and Christians. Rather than offering humble sacrifices to God in true worship, the temple system destroys the followers of the Lamb...

"John portrays Jerusalem's situation as a sexual liaison (she is a "harlot" committing "immorality," 17:2, 4-5) with Rome. In the background of ch 17 is the "league of friendship and mutual alliance" with Rome, beginning with Julius Caesar (1 Macc 8:17–30; 14:24, 40; Jos. Ant. 12:10:6 §414–19; 13:5:8 §163–65; 14:10:1–8 §185–216; 16:6:2–3 §162–66; 19:9:2 §360–65).36 In 1 Macc 14:40 the Jews call themselves "friends, allies, and brothers of Rome," and were, according to Smallwood (2001: 7) "immensely proud of the alliance." Josephus (Ant. 14:10:1 §186) writes: "it seems to me to be necessary here to give an account of all the honors that the Romans and their emperors paid to our nation, and of the leagues of mutual assistance they have made with it." Philo also mentions that the Jews are "friends to Caesar"...

445

John is painting Jerusalem in the same way Isaiah and Jeremiah did as they spoke of the first temple's destruction: "How the faithful city has become a harlot, / She who was full of justice! / Righteousness once lodged in her, / But now murderers" (Isa 1:21). "You have lain down as a harlot . . . . Also on your skirts is found / The lifeblood of the innocent poor" (Jer 2:20d; 34a; cp. 7:6; 19:3-4; 22:11, 17)." Kenneth L. Gentry, Jr., *The Divorce of Israel: A Redemptive-Historical Interpretation of Revelation Vol. 2* (Dallas, GA: Tolle Lege Press, 2016), 435, 429, 430, 416-417.

The scroll of Revelation 5 as a divorce certificate: "Rev comes late in the period of canonical revelation as the great redemptive-historical juncture is reached in the first century. Soon God will finally and permanently remove his central temple, which forever opens the door to the Gentiles. The AD 70 catastrophe is a major issue in redemptive history that an intensely Jewish-flavored book such as Rev would not overlook. This strongly suggests that the scroll in Rev 5 represents God's legal judgment against Israel, especially given the large role that AD 70 plays elsewhere in the NT record (note for instance Luke's four Jerusalem oracles, 13:32–35; 19:41–44; 21:20–24; 23:38–31; cf. Walker 1996: 69–80). The seven seal judgments "are best understood in the light of the 'sevenfold chastisement' that is evolved within Jewish legal theology as a scheme of punishment for disobedience to God". This is affirmed by a mass of contextual evidence in Rev as well, which I will develop as I work through the material.

"More specifically the evidence even suggests that this judgment scroll is a divorce decree against God's unfaithful wife, Israel. According to Christ's own teaching, a man may not divorce his wife to take another apart from proper moral justification and his securing a divorce certificate (Mt 5:31-32; 19:9). God certainly did this in the OT when Israel committed harlotry (Jer 3:8). The moral justification Christ demands for such a radical breach of covenant is porneia (fornication"), which happens to be related to the word used for Rev's "harlot": pornēs. In fact, the harlot is guilty of porneia (14:8; 17:1–2; 18:2–3). Rev shows God issuing a divorce decree against his harlot-wife in a dramatic court-room setting before presenting the new bride, the "new Jerusalem," the Church of Jesus Christ. The local movement in Rev is from God's throne (ch 4), the presentation of the divorce decree and Christ's receiving it in order to open it (ch 5), God's judgments flowing from it (ch 6) to a pause to consider the faithful remnant of Jews (the 144,000 from the 12 tribes) and the resulting universal growth of the Christian church (ch 7). This movement parallels in important respects the revisiting of the scroll (ch 10), the destruction of the temple in the holy city (11:1–2) in the presence of witnesses (11:3–8), with a reiteration of its universal consequences (11:15) and its viewing of the heavenly temple (11:16–18) which is now forever opened (11:19). The divorce of Israel leads to enormous redemptive-historical changes as the true faith is permanently universalized.

"Clearly "in Israel some kind of written document appears to have been necessary" to effect divorce, and this required formal court proceedings and proper witnesses (as the Mishnah. Consequently, I believe Ford's (original) approach is generally correct: "the bride and adulteress motifs in Revelation . . point to such a scroll. It might easily be a bill of divorce; the Lamb divorces unfaithful Jerusalem and marries the new Jerusalem" (Ford 93). This identification of the scroll and the consequent dramatic movement of Rev will become more evident as I continue in ch 5 and through the remainder of the book." Kenneth L. Gentry, Jr., *The Divorce of Israel: A Redemptive-Historical Interpretation of Revelation Vol. 1* (Dallas, GA: Tolle Lege Press, 2016), 545-546.

Yahweh's marriage to a new bride, the body of Christ: Matthew 22:1-14; 25:1-13; Luke 5:33-35; John 3:28-29; Revelation 19:6–9; 21:2, 9; 22:17

[10] **The new covenant church is the New Jerusalem, the new Mount Zion**: Hebrews 12:22–24 [22] But <u>you have come to Mount Zion and to the city of the living God, the heavenly Jerusalem</u>, and to innumerable angels in festal gathering, [23] <u>and to the assembly of the firstborn</u> who are enrolled in heaven, and to God, the judge of all, and to the spirits of the righteous made perfect, [24] and to <u>Jesus, the mediator of a new covenant.</u>

John explains clearly that the new Jerusalem in Revelation 21 is a symbolic picture of the new covenant bride of Christ: Revelation 21:2–3 And I saw the holy city, new Jerusalem, coming down out of heaven from God, prepared as a bride adorned for her husband. [3] And I heard a loud voice from the throne saying, "Behold, the dwelling place of God is with man. He will dwell with them, and they will be his people, and God himself will be with them as their God.

Revelation 21:9–10 [9] "Come, I will show you the Bride, the wife of the Lamb." [10] And he carried me away in the Spirit to a great, high mountain, and showed me the holy city Jerusalem coming down out of heaven from God.

446

[1] **The secrets of the Watchers**: 1 Enoch 8:1-3 "And Azaz'el taught the people (the art of) making swords and knives, and shields, and breastplates; and he showed to their chosen ones bracelets, decorations, (shadowing of the eye) with antimony, ornamentation, the beautifying of the eyelids, all kinds of precious stones, and all coloring tinctures and alchemy. 2 And there were many wicked ones and they committed adultery and erred, and all their conduct became corrupt. 3* Amasras taught incantation and the cutting of roots; and Armaros the resolving of incantations; and Baraqiyal astrology, and Kokarer'el (the knowledge of) the signs, and Tam'el taught the seeing of the stars, and Asder'el taught the course of the moon as well as the deception of man." James H. Charlesworth, *The Old Testament Pseudepigrapha, vol. 1* (New York; London: Yale University Press, 1983), 16.

The ancient spell mentioned here: Has a storied history in the War on Eden and the War of Gods and Men. These are fictional wars depicted in the first two books of Chronicles of the Nephilim, Noah Primeval and Enoch Primordial. But they are fictional expressions of the theological reality.

[2] **This description of Leviathan is taken from**: Job 41:1–34 "Can you draw out Leviathan with a fishhook or press down his tongue with a cord? 2 Can you put a rope in his nose or pierce his jaw with a hook? 3 Will he make many pleas to you? Will he speak to you soft words? 4 Will he make a covenant with you to take him for your servant forever? 5 Will you play with him as with a bird, or will you put him on a leash for your girls? 6 Will traders bargain over him? Will they divide him up among the merchants? 7 Can you fill his skin with harpoons or his head with fishing spears? 8 Lay your hands on him; remember the battle—you will not do it again! 9 Behold, the hope of a man is false; he is laid low even at the sight of him. 10 No one is so fierce that he dares to stir him up. Who then is he who can stand before me? 11 Who has first given to me, that I should repay him? Whatever is under the whole heaven is mine. 12 "I will not keep silence concerning his limbs, or his mighty strength, or his goodly frame. 13 Who can strip off his outer garment? Who would come near him with a bridle? 14 Who can open the doors of his face? Around his teeth is terror. 15 His back is made of rows of shields, shut up closely as with a seal. 16 One is so near to another that no air can come between them. 17 They are joined one to another; they clasp each other and cannot be separated. 18 His sneezings flash forth light, and his eyes are like the eyelids of the dawn. 19 Out of his mouth go flaming torches; sparks of fire leap forth. 20 Out of his nostrils comes forth smoke, as from a boiling pot and burning rushes. 21 His breath kindles coals, and a flame comes forth from his mouth. 22 In his neck abides strength, and terror dances before him. 23 The folds of his flesh stick together, firmly cast on him and immovable. 24 His heart is hard as a stone, hard as the lower millstone. 25 When he raises himself up, the mighty are afraid; at the crashing they are beside themselves. 26 Though the sword reaches him, it does not avail, nor the spear, the dart, or the javelin. 27 He counts iron as straw, and bronze as rotten wood. 28 The arrow cannot make him flee; for him, sling stones are turned to stubble. 29 Clubs are counted as stubble; he laughs at the rattle of javelins. 30 His underparts are like sharp potsherds; he spreads himself like a threshing sledge on the mire. 31 He makes the deep boil like a pot; he makes the sea like a pot of ointment. 32 Behind him he leaves a shining wake; one would think the deep to be white-haired. 33 On earth there is not his like, a creature without fear. 34 He sees everything that is high; he is king over all the sons of pride."

As this chapter describes, this is no known species on earth. From the smoke and fire out of its mouth to the armor plating on back and belly, this monster of the abyss was more than a mere example of showcasing God's omnipotent power over the mightiest of creatures, it was symbolic of something much more. And that much more can be found by understanding Leviathan in its ancient Near Eastern (ANE) and Biblical covenantal background.

For more details on Leviathan see note 8 in chapter 26 here.

[3] **Severus is referring to this Scripture:** 1 Timothy 1:12–16 I thank him who has given me strength, Christ Jesus our Lord, because he judged me faithful, appointing me to his service, 13 though formerly I was a blasphemer, persecutor, and insolent opponent. But I received mercy because I had acted ignorantly in unbelief, 14 and the grace of our Lord overflowed for me with the faith and love that are in Christ Jesus. 15 The saying is trustworthy and deserving of full acceptance, that Christ Jesus came into the world to save sinners, of whom I am the foremost. 16 But I received mercy for this reason, that in me, as the foremost, Jesus Christ might display his perfect patience as an example to those who were to believe in him for eternal life.

¹ **Cestius' forces go to Joppa and Galilee**: Flavius Josephus, *The Wars of the Jews* 2.18.10-11 § 507-512. "And now Cestius himself marched from Ptolemais, and came to Cesarea; but he sent part of his army before him to Joppa, and gave orders that if they could take that city [by surprise] they should keep it; ...the soldiers fell upon them, and slew them all, with their families, and then plundered and burnt the city. (509) The number of the slain was eight thousand four hundred. In like manner Cestius sent also a considerable body of horsemen to the toparchy of Narbatene, that adjoined to Cesarea, who destroyed the country and slew a great multitude of its people; they also plundered what they had and burnt their villages.

11. (510) But Cestius sent Gallus, the commander of the twelfth legion, into Galilee, and delivered to him as many of his forces as he supposed sufficient to subdue that nation. (511) He was received by the strongest city of Galilee, which was Sepphoris, with acclamations of joy; which wise conduct of that city occasioned the rest of the cities to be in quiet; while the seditious part and the robbers ran away to that mountain which lies in the very middle of Galilee, and is situated over against Sepphoris; it is called Asamon. So Gallus brought his forces against them; ... only some few concealed themselves in certain places hard to come at, among the mountains, while the rest, above two thousand in number, were slain."Flavius Josephus and William Whiston, *The Works of Josephus: Complete and Unabridged* (Peabody: Hendrickson, 1987), 629–630.

² **The campaign mentioned here is described in detail**: Flavius Josephus, *The Wars of the Jews*, 2.19.1-4 §513-527.

³ **Jerusalem aristocracy meets with Cestius to help him into the city**: Flavius Josephus, *The Wars of the Jews*, 2.19.4 §533 "5. (533) In the meantime, many of the principal men of the city were persuaded by Ananus, the son of Jonathan, and invited Cestius into the city, and were about to open the gates for him; (534) but he overlooked this offer, partly out of his anger at the Jews, and partly because he did not thoroughly believe they were in earnest." Flavius Josephus and William Whiston, *The Works of Josephus: Complete and Unabridged* (Peabody: Hendrickson, 1987), 631.

I chose not to name Ananus in the story to avoid confusing him with the major character of the high priest Ananus ben Ananus.

CHAPTER 39

¹ **The nobles who sought to negotiate with Cestius were thrown from the walls**: Flavius Josephus, *The Wars of the Jews*, 2.19.4 §533 "5. (533) In the meantime, many of the principal men of the city were persuaded by Ananus, the son of Jonathan, and invited Cestius into the city, and were about to open the gates for him; (534) but he overlooked this offer, partly out of his anger at the Jews, and partly because he did not thoroughly believe they were in earnest; whence it was that he delayed in the matter so long, that the seditious perceived the treachery, and threw Ananus and those of his party down from the wall." Flavius Josephus and William Whiston, *The Works of Josephus: Complete and Unabridged* (Peabody: Hendrickson, 1987), 631

CHAPTER 40

¹ **The angel of the Lord protects his people**: Psalm 34:7 The angel of the LORD encamps around those who fear Him, And rescues them.

Psalm 91:11–13 ¹¹ For he will command his angels concerning you to guard you in all your ways. ¹² On their hands they will bear you up, lest you strike your foot against a stone. ¹³ You will tread on the lion and the adder; the young lion and the serpent you will trample underfoot.

² **Michael the archangel rises up to protect God's people in the last days of Jerusalem and the temple**: Daniel 12:1 "At that time shall arise Michael, the great prince who has charge of your people. And there shall be a time of trouble, such as never has been since there was a nation till that time. But at that time your people shall be delivered, everyone whose name shall be found written in the book."

Matthew 24:21 "For then there will be great tribulation, such as has not been from the beginning of the world until now, no, and never will be."

"Jude speaks of "Michael the archangel" as contending with the devil about the body of Moses (Jude 9); and in (Re 12: 7), Michael is again seen in conflict with the devil. Paul mentions the archangel (without naming him) as having to do with the resurrection of the saints (1Th 4: 16). In Daniel there are three references to Michael, all in this prophecy given by the angel who appeared to Daniel on the banks of the Tigris. The first reference is in (Da 10: 13,) where the angel says that the prince of the kingdom of Persia had withstood him, but Michael, one of the chief princes, came to his aid. Again in the same chapter (Da 10: 20,21) are the words: "And now I will return to fight with the prince of Persia; and when I am gone forth, lo, the prince of Grecia shall come.... And there is none that holdeth with me in these things, but Michael your prince." From these words it appears that the political destinies of the great heathen nations of earth are presided over by mighty beings, who are rebels against the authority of God, high potentates in the Kingdom of Satan. None of those angelic beings stands for God "in these things"— i.e., the affairs of the world— except Michael, the archangel. This is in accord with the words of the Lord Jesus who speaks of the devil as "the prince of this world" (Joh 14: 30, etc.)." Mauro, Philip. *The Seventy Weeks And The Great Tribulation* (K-Locations 2083-2097), K-Edition.

Michael the archangel and the temple: In the Pseudepigrapha: "'lofty abode:' is where the heavenly Jerusalem, the Temple, and the altar are built, and Michael, principal prince, stands and offers an offering on it." (b. Hag. 12B) Jacob Neusner, *The Babylonian Talmud: A Translation and Commentary, vol. 7d* (Peabody, MA: Hendrickson Publishers, 2011), 49

"there was a noise from the highest heaven like triple thunder. And I Baruch said, "Lord, what is this noise?" And he said to me, "Michael is descending to accept the prayers of men." (3 Baruch 11:3-4) James H. Charlesworth, *The Old Testament Pseudepigrapha, vol. 1* (New York; London: Yale University Press, 1983), 674.

CHAPTER 41

[1] **Cestius burns the New City and prepares to burn the north gate of the temple**: Flavius Josephus, The Wars of the Jews 2.19.4, §527-530 "4. (527) But now Cestius, observing that the disturbances that were begun among the Jews afforded him a proper opportunity to attack them, took his whole army along with him, and put the Jews to flight, and pursued them to Jerusalem. (528) He then pitched his camp upon the elevation called Scopus [or watchtower], which was distance seven furlongs from the city; yet did he not assault them in three days' time, out of expectation that those within might perhaps yield a little; and in the meantime he sent out a great many of his soldiers into neighboring villages, to seize upon their corn; and on the fourth day, which was the thirtieth of the month Hyperbereteus [Tisri], when he put his army in array, he brought it into the city. (529) Now for the people, they were kept under by the seditious; but the seditious themselves were greatly affrighted at the good order of the Romans, and retired from the suburbs, and retreated into the inner part of the city, and into the temple. (530) But when Cestius was come into the city, he set the part called Bezetha, which is also called Cenopolis, [or the new city], on fire; as he did also to the timber market; after which he came into the upper city, and pitched his camp over against the royal palace." Flavius Josephus and William Whiston, *The Works of Josephus: Complete and Unabridged* (Peabody: Hendrickson, 1987), 631.

Flavius Josephus, The Wars of the Jews 2.19.5, §35-537 "(535) Thus did the Romans make their attack against the wall for five days, but to no purpose. But on the next day, Cestius took a great many of his choicest men, and with them the archers, and attempted to break into the temple at the northern quarter of it; (536) but the Jews beat them off from the cloisters, and repulsed them several times when they were gotten near to the wall, till at length the multitude of the darts cut them off, and made them retire; (537) but the first rank of the Romans rested their shields upon the wall, and so did those that were behind them, and the like did those that were still more backward, and guarded themselves with what they call Testudo, [the back of] a tortoise, upon which the darts that were thrown fell, and slided off without doing them any harm; so the soldiers undermined the wall, without being themselves hurt, and got all things ready for setting fire to the gate of the temple." Flavius Josephus and William Whiston, *The Works of Josephus: Complete and Unabridged* (Peabody: Hendrickson, 1987), 631.

[2] **Mithraeum temples and tauroctony**: "The typical mithraeum was a small rectangular subterranean chamber, on the order of 75 feet by 30 feet with a vaulted ceiling. An aisle usually ran lengthwise down the center of the temple, with a stone bench on either side two or three feet high on which the cult's members would recline during their meetings. On average a mithraeum could hold perhaps twenty to thirty people at a time. At the back of the mithraeum at the end of the aisle was always found a representation-- usually a carved relief but sometimes a statue or painting-- of the central icon of Mithraism: the so-called tauroctony or "bull-slaying scene" in which the god of the cult, Mithras, accompanied by a dog, a snake, a raven, and a scorpion, is shown in the act of killing a bull. Other parts

of the temple were decorated with various scenes and figures." Online: "Mithraism: The Cosmic Mysteries of Mithras" adapted from David Ulansey, *The Origins of the Mithraic Mysteries* (Oxford University Press, 1991). http://www.mysterium.com/mithras.html

"The event takes place in a cavern, into which Mithras has carried the bull, after having hunted it, ridden it and overwhelmed its strength.30 Sometimes the cavern is surrounded by a circle, on which the twelve signs of the zodiac appear. Outside the cavern, top left, is Sol the sun, with his flaming crown." http://www.tertullian.org/rpearse/mithras/display.php?page=main

Banquet of the Sun: "The second most important scene after the tauroctony in Mithraic art is the so-called banquet scene. The two scenes are sometimes sculpted on the opposite sides of the same relief. The banquet scene features Mithras and the Sun god banqueting on the hide of the slaughtered bull." http://www.tertullian.org/rpearse/mithras/display.php?page=main

[3] **Mithraeum outside the walls of the Antonia**: "In the nineteenth century, a French explorer named Charles Clermont-Ganneau conducted excavations in caverns beneath the basements of houses on the north side of the Via Dolorosa, to the west of the Sheep's Pools… The discovery of vases decorated with Mithraic imagery in underground caverns by the Via Dolorosa suggests that this was the site of a Mithraeum (a shrine of Mithras), a possibility supported by the cult's popularity among Roman soldiers." Jodi Magness, *The Archaeology of the Holy Land : From the Destruction of Solomon's Temple to the Muslim Conquest* (NY: Cambridge, 2012) 278-279.

Cestius visits the mithraeum: Though the existence of the mithraeum and its location are historical, Cestius' visit and encounter is not. Mithras was however the god of the legions, so Cestius no doubt participated in the cultus.

[4] **Mithraeum temple as microcosm of the universe**: "the ancient author Porphyry records the tradition that the Mithraic cave was intended to be "an image of the cosmos." Of course, the hollow cave would have to be an image of the cosmos as seen from the inside, looking out at the enclosing, cave-like sphere of the stars." Online: "Mithraism: The Cosmic Mysteries of Mithras" adapted from David Ulansey, *The Origins of the Mithraic Mysteries* (Oxford University Press, 1991). http://www.mysterium.com/mithras.html

[5] **Officers sympathetic to Florus impeded Cestius' strategy**: Flavius Josephus, *The Wars of the Jews* 2.19.4, §531-532 "had [Cestius] but at this very time attempted to get within the walls by force, he had won the city presently, and the war had been put an end to at once; but Tyrannius Priscus, the muster-master of the army, and a great number of the officers of the horse, and been corrupted by Florus, and diverted him from that attempt; (532) and that was the occasion that this war lasted so very long, and thereby the Jews were involved in such incurable calamities." Flavius Josephus and William Whiston, *The Works of Josephus: Complete and Unabridged* (Peabody: Hendrickson, 1987), 631.

[6] **The Northern Sheep Gate (Tadi Gate)**: "Josephus gives a hint of the decoration on these gates, recording that when Titus set fire to the outer gates during his siege of the Temple Mount, that the silver plating covering them melted and revealed a wooden interior before it too burned (War 6.4.2; 232-35)… On the north, there was an old gate, the Tadi Gate, which had been closed since Hasmonean times (Middot 2:1)." *Rose Guide to the Temple* (Rose Publishing, 2013) 500, 502.

[7] **The flight of the seditious inside the temple**: Flavius Josephus, *The Wars of the Jews* 2.19.6 §538-539 "(538) And now it was that a horrible fear seized upon the seditious, insomuch that many of them ran out of the city, as though it were to be taken immediately; but the people upon this took courage, and where the wicked part of the city gave ground, thither did they come, in order to set open the gates, and to admit Cestius as their benefactor, (539) who, had he but continued the siege a little longer, had certainly taken the city; but it was, I suppose, owing to the aversion God had already at the city and the sanctuary, that he was hindered from putting an end to the war that very day." Flavius Josephus and William Whiston, *The Works of Josephus: Complete and Unabridged* (Peabody: Hendrickson, 1987), 631.

All rights lost upon first hit of battering ram: "Under Roman law, any defenders who failed to surrender before the first ram touched their wall were denied any rights. The moment they heard the ram hit the wall, those inside the city knew that the siege proper had begun and there was no turning back." "Roman Siege Engines," Wikipedia https://en.wikipedia.org/wiki/Roman_siege_engines

[8] **Cestius stops his siege of Jerusalem unexpectedly**: Flavius Josephus, *The Wars of the Jews* 2.19.7, §540-541. "7. (540) It then happened that Cestius was not conscious either how the besieged despaired of success, nor how courageous the people were for him; and so he recalled his soldiers from the place, and

by despairing of any expectation of taking it, without having received any disgrace, he retired from the city, without any reason in the world. (541) That when the robbers perceived this unexpected retreat of his, they resumed their courage, and ran after the hinder parts of his army, and destroyed a considerable number of both their horsemen and footmen." Josephus, Wars, 2:18:9–19:9 §499–555. Flavius Josephus and William Whiston, *The Works of Josephus: Complete and Unabridged* (Peabody: Hendrickson, 1987). See also Tacitus, *Histories* 5:10

[9] **Eleazar quotes from**: Isaiah 61:1-2.

CHAPTER 42

[1] **The religious significance of the Beth-Horon pass**: "The choice of Beth-Horon as the place to confront Cestius was surely guided by the knowledge of that earlier Heaven-sent victory. Cestius would have been seen as Seron, and doubtless many different Judaean commanders saw themselves as the next Judah Maccabee.

"Joshua himself pursued the five kings of the Amorites through the pass at Beth-Horon, where the Israelites received Heavenly assistance:

> As they fled before Israel, while they were going down the slope of Beth-Horon, the Lord threw down huge stones from heaven on them as far as Azekah, and they died...
> On the day when the Lord gave the Amorites over to the Israelites, Joshua spoke to the Lord; and he said in the sight of Israel, "Sun, stand still at Gibeon, and Moon, in the valley of Aijalon." And the sun stood still, and the moon stopped, until the nation took vengeance on their enemies. (Joshua 10:10-13)

"Thus Beth-Horon was the sight of some of the most famous and miraculous victories in Jewish history. So it is not surprising when Josephus tells us how elated the rebels were at this, proof that Heaven was indeed with them -- proof so compelling that the pro-Roman faction was completely silenced: "Distinguished Jews abandoned the city like swimmers from a sinking ship", says Josephus (*Wars* 2.20.1 556). And moderates throughout Judaea were swayed to the cause -- including, it appears, Josephus himself." G.J. Goldberg, "A War Chronology - Part 2: The Campaign of Cestius Gallus and the Defeat of the Twelfth Legion" http://www.josephus.org/warChronology2.htm

[2] **Cestius killing pack animals to increase speed**: Flavius Josephus, *The Wars of the Jews* 2.19.8 §546 "8. (546) That therefore he might fly the faster, he gave orders to cast away what might hinder his army's march; so they killed the mules and the other creatures, excepting those that carried their darts and machines, which they retained for their own use, and this principally because they were afraid lest the Jews should seize upon them." Flavius Josephus and William Whiston, *The Works of Josephus: Complete and Unabridged* (Peabody: Hendrickson, 1987), 632.

[3] **Simon's attack on Cestius**: Simon bar Giora attacked Cestius at Beth-Horon while Cestius was on his way to besiege Jerusalem. I left that out of the story for the sake of simplifying. Simon is not mentioned by Josephus in the attack on Cestius on his return to Caesarea, but it is certainly reasonable that he was part of that force again.

Flavius Josephus, *The Wars of the Jews* 2.19.2 §521 "Simon the son of Giora, fell upon the back of the Romans as they were ascending up Bethoron, and put the hindmost of the army into disorder, and carried off many of the beasts that carried the weapons of war, and led them into the city." Flavius Josephus and William Whiston, *The Works of Josephus: Complete and Unabridged* (Peabody: Hendrickson, 1987), 630.

[4] **The grave disadvantage of the Romans on their retreat**: Flavius Josephus, *The Wars of the Jews* 2.19.7 §542-544. "[Cestius] invited the enemy to follow him, who still fell upon the hindmost, and destroyed them; they also fell upon the flank on each side of the army, and threw darts upon them obliquely, (543) nor durst those that were hindmost turn back upon those who wounded them behind, as imagining that the multitude of those that pursued them was immense; nor did they venture to drive away those that pressed upon them on each side, because they were heavy with their arms, and were afraid of breaking their ranks to pieces, and because they saw the Jews were light and ready for making incursions upon them. And this was the reason why the Romans suffered greatly, without being able to revenge themselves upon their enemies; (544) so they were galled all the way, and their ranks were put into disorder; and those that were thus put out of their ranks were slain." Flavius Josephus and William Whiston, *The Works of Josephus: Complete and Unabridged* (Peabody: Hendrickson, 1987), 632.

[5] **The Roman disadvantage in the Beth-Horon pass**: Flavius Josephus, *The Wars of the Jews* 2.19.8 §546-548 "[Cestius] then made his army march on as far as Bethoron. (547) Now the Jews did not so much press upon them when they were in large open places; but when they were penned up in their descent through narrow passages, then did some of them get before, and hindered them from getting out of them; and others of them thrust the hindermost down into the lower places; and the whole multitude extended themselves over against the neck of the passage, and covered the Roman army with their darts. (548) In which circumstances, as the footmen knew not how to defend themselves, so the danger pressed the horsemen still more, for they were so pelted, that they could not march along the road in their ranks, and the ascents were so high that the cavalry were not able to march against the enemy." Flavius Josephus and William Whiston, *The Works of Josephus: Complete and Unabridged* (Peabody: Hendrickson, 1987), 632.

[6] **Roman losses at Beth-Horon**: Flavius Josephus, *The Wars of the Jews* 2.19.9 §555 "while they had themselves lost a few only, but had slain of the Romans five thousand and three hundred footmen, and three hundred and eighty horsemen." Flavius Josephus and William Whiston, *The Works of Josephus: Complete and Unabridged* (Peabody: Hendrickson, 1987), 633.

[7] **Cestius' age**: "Cestius was old. Apparently he had been a member of the Senate since A.D. 21…To have met the qualifying age of 25 for the quaestorship in A.D. 21, Cestius must have been born not later than 4/3 B.C. Assuming that latest possible birthdate, he must have been 69 or 70 when he led the expedition to Judaea…When we think of this, his activities on horseback for weeks at a time and his escape from Beit-Horon seem quite impressive." Steve Mason, *A History of the Jewish War, AD 66-74* (Cambridge University Press, 2016) 321.

[8] **On Cestius' death**: Though Simon bar Giora did attack the Romans at Beth-Horon, he did not kill Cestius. Tacitus implies that Cestius died in dishonor from his failure after he returned to Syria. (Tacitus, *Histories*, 5:10).

"Tacitus is unsure, though, whether [Cestius] died because of men's ordinary fate (i.e., natural causes) or through taedium – a word that could mean simple weariness or rather "loathsomeness" – to Nero (Hist. 5.10). The latter possibility recalls Tacitus' remark about Caesennius Paetus, when Nero returned the Armenian portfolio to Corbulo because "Paetus had inspired disgust (Paeti piguerat)."…Given Cestius' disgrace and Roman aristocratic tradition, we might conjecture that he took his own life. Tacitus apparently did not know how he died, however, and if Josephus knew he did not say. We do not know either." Steve, Mason, *A History of the Jewish War, AD 66-74* (Cambridge University Press, 2016) 325-326.

[9] **Nightfall saved Cestius from complete defeat**: Flavius Josephus, *The Wars of the Jews* 2.19.8 §550 "Indeed these things were come to such a pass, that the Jews had almost taken Cestius's entire army prisoners, had not the night come on, when the Romans fled to Bethoron." Flavius Josephus and William Whiston, *The Works of Josephus: Complete and Unabridged* (Peabody: Hendrickson, 1987), 632.

[10] **Cestius lost the standard of the legion to the Jewish rebels**: "Over the course of the retreat the Romans lost… the greatest disgrace of all, the eagle standard of the legio XII Fulminata." Si Sheppard, *The Jewish Revolt AD 66-74* (Oxford, Osprey Publishing, 2013) 16.

Roman standards: "The Roman Standard (Latin: Signum or Signa Romanum) was a pennant, flag, or banner, suspended or attached to a staff or pole, which identified a Roman legion (infantry) or Equites (cavalry). The Standard of a cavalry unit was emblazoned with the symbol of the serpent (Draconarius) while a legion of infantry was represented by a totemic animal. The most famous of these is the eagle (Aquila)…

"Besides the Serpent and Eagle symbols, there were also the Imago (a Standard displaying the image of the emperor), the Manus (an open hand at the top of the banner), the Vexillum (a rectangular cut cloth of a certain color, sometimes with a number, attached to a pole), and Banners which designated military hierarchy (a red banner, for example, would designate a general). The Vexillum designated the type of unit (legion or cohort) and which legion it was. The Manus of the open hand symbolized the loyalty of the soldiers and the trust they had in their leaders. The Imago reminded the troops of the emperor they fought for and symbolically stood for the will of Rome among them. A Standard would have more than one banner on it except for the Vexillum which was used to direct the troops' movements." "Roman Standard," *Ancient History Encyclopedia* Online http://www.ancient.eu/Roman_Standard/

Roman standards ("ensigns") were considered idolatrous by the Jews: Flavius Josephus, *The Wars of the Jews* 2.9.2 §169-170 "Now Pilate, who was sent as procurator into Judea by Tiberius, sent by night those images of Caesar that are called Ensigns, into Jerusalem. (170) This excited a very great tumult among the Jews when it was day; for those that were near them were astonished at the sight of them, as indications that their laws were trodden underfoot: for those laws do not permit any sort of image to be brought into the city." Flavius Josephus and William Whiston, *The Works of Josephus: Complete and Unabridged* (Peabody: Hendrickson, 1987), 608.

[11] **War engines left behind**: Flavius Josephus, *The Wars of the Jews* 2.19.9 §553 "Insomuch, that the soldiers, through the astonishment and fear they were in, left behind them their engines for sieges, and for throwing of stones, and a great part of the instruments of war." Flavius Josephus and William Whiston, *The Works of Josephus: Complete and Unabridged* (Peabody: Hendrickson, 1987), 632.

Eleazar ben Simon captured the Roman pay chest:

Flavius Josephus, *The Wars of the Jews* 2.20.3 §564 "[Eleazar] had gotten into his possession the prey they had taken from the Romans, and the money they had taken from Cestius." Flavius Josephus and William Whiston, *The Works of Josephus: Complete and Unabridged* (Peabody: Hendrickson, 1987), 633.

[12] Cestius' attack provoked the full scale war to begin: "By late October / early November, C. Cestius Gallus (the Roman legate of the Syrian province which included Judaea) led a Roman military force to Jerusalem in an attempt to put down the uprising. He assembled "an army of over thirty thousand men in Antioch—the whole of one of the Syrian legions, XII Fulminata, and vexillations from the others, ten auxiliary units, and large contingents supplied by Agrippa, who led his force in person, and two other client kings, Antiochus IV of Commagene and Sohaemus of Emesa" (Smallwood 2001: 296). But after surrounding Jerusalem, he unexpectedly withdrew for reasons that are unclear (J.W. 2:18:9–19:9 §499–555; Tacitus, Hist. 5:10). His withdrawal was disastrous, encouraging the Jews in their revolt by giving them hope of success against Rome (J.W. 6:6:2 §341). This transformed the regional revolt against the procurator Gessius Florus into a full-scale war against the emperor Nero Caesar." Kenneth L. Gentry, Jr., *The Divorce of Israel: A Redemptive-Historical Interpretation of Revelation Vol. 2* (Dallas, GA: Tolle Lege Press, 2016), 53.

CHAPTER 43

[1] **Ananus ben Ananus was a Sadducee** (Josephus, *Antiquities* 20.199).

[2] **The casualties of the battle of Beth-Horon**: Flavius Josephus, *The Wars of the Jews* 2.19.9 §555 "while they had themselves lost a few only, but had slain of the Romans five thousand and three hundred footmen, and three hundred and eighty horsemen." Flavius Josephus and William Whiston, *The Works of Josephus: Complete and Unabridged* (Peabody: Hendrickson, 1987), 633.

[3] **Ananus appointed governor of Jerusalem forces, and Eleazar in the temple**: Flavius Josephus, *The Wars of the Jews* 2.20.3 §563-564 "Joseph also, the son of Gorion, and Ananus the high priest, were chosen as governors of all affairs within the city, and with a particular charge to repair the walls of the city; (564) for they did not ordain Eleazar the son of Simon to that office, although he had gotten into his possession the prey they had taken from the Romans, and the money they had taken from Cestius, together with a great part of the public treasures." Flavius Josephus and William Whiston, *The Works of Josephus: Complete and Unabridged* (Peabody: Hendrickson, 1987), 633.

[4] **The generals appointed for the regions and cities in Israel**: Flavius Josephus, *The Wars of the Jews* 2.20.4 §566-568 "4. (566) They also chose other generals for Idumea; Jesus the son of Sapphias, one of the high priests; and Eleazar the son of Ananias, the high priest; they also enjoined Niger, the then governor of Idumea, who was of a family that belonged to Perea, beyond Jordan, and was thence called the Peraite, that he should be obedient to those forenamed commanders. (567) Nor did they neglect the care of other parts of the country; but Joseph the son of Simon was sent as general to Jericho, as was Manasseh to Perea, and John, the Essene, to the toparchy of Thamma; Lydda was also added to his portion, and Joppa and Emmaus. (568) But John, the son of Matthias, was made the governor of the toparchies of Gophritica and Acrabastene; as was Josephus, the son of Matthias, of both the Galilees. Gamala also, which was the strongest city in those parts, was put under his command." Flavius Josephus and William Whiston, *The Works of Josephus: Complete and Unabridged* (Peabody: Hendrickson, 1987), 633.

[5] **When did the Christians leave Jerusalem for the mountains?**: Yamauchi cites R. A. Pritz who shows Josephus' record of several flight opportunities leading up to Jerusalem's final destruction in August and September of AD 70: November of AD 66 (J.W. 2:19:6 §538, 2:20:1 §556), Winter of AD 67/68 (J.W. 4:6:1, 3 §353, 377, 4:7:1, 3 § 397, 410), and June of AD 70 (J.W. 4:7:4 §420, 4:8:1 §446–50). The two most likely pauses are: (1) After the initial attack by Cestius Gallus, Roman governor of Syria, in

November, AD 66. This is before the Jewish War is formally declared by Nero. After surrounding the city Cestius surprisingly withdraws for reasons that we do not know (J.W. 2:17--22, Tac., Hist. 5:10).7 This delays the full outbreak of war from November, AD 66 to Spring, AD 67 at which time Nero formally commissions Vespasian to put down the Jewish revolt. But the most famous and most likely opportunity for escape occurs in June, AD 68. After Vespasian and Titus "encompass the city [Jerusalem] round about on all sides" (J.W. 4:9:1 §490), Vespasian is "informed that Nero was dead" (4:9:2 §491). Consequently, he and Titus do "not go on with their expedition against the Jews" (4:9:2 §502, cp. Pref. 9 §23, 4:10:2 §590)." Kenneth L. Gentry, Jr., *The Divorce of Israel: A Redemptive-Historical Interpretation of Revelation Vol. 1* (Dallas, GA: Tolle Lege Press, 2016), 655.

[6] **The population of Christians in Jerusalem**: See <u>footnote 47 in Chapter 7</u>.

[7] **Abraham and Sarah's name change**: Genesis 17:4–5 [4] "Behold, my covenant is with you, and you shall be the father of a multitude of nations. [5] No longer shall your name be called Abram, but your name shall be Abraham, for I have made you the father of a multitude of nations.

Genesis 17:15–16 [15] And God said to Abraham, "As for Sarai your wife, you shall not call her name Sarai, but Sarah shall be her name. [16] I will bless her, and moreover, I will give you a son by her. I will bless her, and she shall become nations; kings of peoples shall come from her."

Jacob's name change: Genesis 32:28 [28] Then he said, "Your name shall no longer be called Jacob, but Israel, for you have striven with God and with men, and have prevailed."

Peter's name change: John 1:42 [42] He brought him to Jesus. Jesus looked at him and said, "You are Simon the son of John. You shall be called Cephas" (which means Peter).

God's "name change": Exodus 6:2–3 [2] God spoke to Moses and said to him, "I am the LORD. [3] I appeared to Abraham, to Isaac, and to Jacob, as God Almighty [El Shaddai], but by my name the LORD [Yahweh] I did not make myself known to them.

[8] **Prophets and the covenant lawsuit in Revelation**: Another kind of Biblical lawsuit saw Old Testament prophets as Yahweh's prosecuting attorneys indicting Israel for breaking her covenant with God. The prophet would stand before God's divine council and make the summons and charges against Israel before calling her to respond to the charges. Then Yahweh as judge would pronounce his verdict. One of the qualifications of a prophet's authority to speak for God was that he had stood in this divine council (Jer. 23:18, 22).

"The structure of the Biblical Covenant bears striking similarities to the established form for peace treaties in the ancient Near East. s2 This is how it worked: After a war, the victorious king would make a covenant with his defeated foe, making certain promises and guaranteeing protection on condition that the vassal-king and all under his authority would obey their new lord. Both lord and vassal would swear an oath, and they would thenceforth be united in covenant…

"As Kline explains, the standard treaty-form in the ancient world was structured in five parts, all of which appear in the Biblical covenants:

1. Preamble (identifying the lordship of the Great King, stressing both his transcendence [greatness and power] and his immanence [nearness and presence]);
2. Historical Prologue (surveying the lord's previous relationship to the vassal, especially emphasizing the blessings bestowed);
3. Ethical Stipulations (expounding the vassal's obligations, his "guide to citizenship" in the covenant);
4. Sanctions (outlining the blessings for obedience and curses for disobedience);
5. Succession Arrangements (dealing with the continuity of the covenant relationship over future generations).

Deuteronomy
1. Preamble (1:1-5)
2. Historical Prologue (1:6-4:49)
3. Ethical Stipulations (5:1-26:19)
4. Sanctions (27:1-30:20)
5. Succession Arrangements (31:1-34:12)

"If a vassal kingdom violated the terms of the covenant, the lord would send messengers to the vassal, warning the offenders of coming judgment, in which the curse-sanctions of the covenant would be enforced. This turns out to be the function of the Biblical prophets, as I mentioned above: They were prosecuting attorneys, bringing God's message of Covenant Lawsuit to the offending nations of Israel and Judah. And the structure of the lawsuit was always patterned after the original structure of the covenant. In other words, just as the Biblical covenants themselves follow the standard five-part treaty structure, the Biblical prophecies follow the treaty form as well.

"Like many other Biblical prophecies, the Book of Revelation is a prophecy of Covenant wrath against apostate Israel, which irrevocably turned away from the Covenant in her rejection of Christ. And, like many other Biblical prophecies, the Book of Revelation is written in the form of the Covenant Lawsuit, with five parts, conforming to the treaty structure of the Covenant." David Chilton, *The Days of Vengeance: An Exposition of the Book of Revelation* (Texas: Dominion Press, 1987, 1990) 14-15.

"[Revelation 11] portrays a first-century, Jerusalem-focused episode. Furthermore, we should observe that the events in the prophetic oracle in 11:3ff involve a "witness" (11:3, 7) against Jerusalem/Israel (11:8, 10), that is resisted by the Jews (11:5, 10), though approved by heaven above (11:4, 11–12). Like the Old Testament prophets upon whom John models these two prophets, these are legal "witnesses" against Jerusalem-Israel for its covenantal rebellion against God (Isa 30:8–11; 59:12; Jer 14:7; Hos 5:5; Am 3:13–14; Mic 1:2–5). These prophets effectively serve as prosecuting covenant-lawsuit prophets rather than promising covenant-mediator prophets...

"The two witnesses clearly bear a judicial significance in that: (1) John specifically and deliberately designates them as "witnesses" (martusin) immediately upon their appearing (11:3). (2) He presents us with two witnesses. According to biblical law, legal testimony in capital cases (such as in the case of the murderous, Jerusalem-harlot, 17:5–6; 18:24; 19:2; see Exc. 13 at 17:1) requires two witnesses (Nu 35:30; Dt 17:6; 19:15; 1Ki 21:10)." Kenneth L. Gentry, Jr., *The Divorce of Israel: A Redemptive-Historical Interpretation of Revelation Vol. 2* (Dallas, GA: Tolle Lege Press, 2016), 75-76.

The seven-fold judgment of Revelation a fulfillment of Leviticus/Deuteronomy seven-fold judgment on Israel: "In order to grasp the five-part structure of Revelation, we must first consider how St. John's prophecy is related to the message of Leviticus 26. Like Deuteronomy 28, Leviticus 26 sets forth the sanctions of the Covenant: If Israel obeys God, she will be blessed in every area of life (Lev. 26:1-13; Deut. 28:1-14); if she disobeys, however, she will be visited with the Curse, spelled out in horrifying detail (Lev. 26:14-39; Deut. 28:15-68). (These curses were most fully poured out in the progressive desolation of Israel during the Last Days, culminating in the Great Tribulation of A.D. 67-70, as punishment for her apostasy and rejection of her True Husband, the Lord Jesus Christ). One of the striking features of the Leviticus passage is that the curses are arranged in a special pattern: Four times in this chapter God says, "I will punish you seven times for your sins" (Lev. 26:18,21,24, 28). The number seven, as we will see abundantly throughout Revelation, is a Biblical number for completeness or fullness (taken from the seven-day pattern laid down at the creation in Genesis 1). The number four is used in Scripture in connection with the earth, especially the Land of Israel; thus four rivers flowed out of Eden to water the whole earth (Gen. 2:10); the Land, like the Altar, is pictured as having four corners (Isa. 11:12; cf. Ex. 27:1-2), from which the four winds blow (Jer. 49:36); the camp of Israel was arranged in four groups around the sides of the Tabernacle (Num. 2); and so on (see your concordance and Bible dictionary). So by speaking of four sevenfold judgments in Leviticus 26, God is saying that a full, complete judgment will come upon the Land of Israel for its sins...

"The imagery of a sevenfold judgment coming four times is most fully developed in the Book of Revelation, which is explicitly divided into four sets of seven: the Letters to the Seven Churches, the opening of the Seven Seals, the sounding of the Seven Trumpets, and the outpouring of the Seven Chalices. In thus following the formal structure of the covenantal curse in Leviticus, St. John underscores the nature of his prophecy as a declaration of covenant wrath against Jerusalem." David Chilton, *The Days of Vengeance: An Exposition of the Book of Revelation* (Texas: Dominion Press, 1987, 1990) 16-17.

[9] **Two witnesses, 1260 days, 42 months, trampling Jerusalem underfoot in the times of the Gentiles**: Revelation 11:2–3 [2] but do not measure the court outside the temple; leave that out, for it is given over to the nations, and they will trample the holy city for forty-two months. [3] And I will grant authority to my two witnesses, and they will prophesy for 1,260 days, clothed in sackcloth."

Luke 21:20–24 [20] "But when you see Jerusalem surrounded by armies, then know that its desolation has come near...For there will be great distress upon the earth and wrath against this people. [24] They will fall by the edge of the sword and be led captive among all nations, and Jerusalem will be trampled underfoot by the Gentiles, until the times of the Gentiles are fulfilled.

455

The 42 months of holy city being trampled underfoot by the Gentiles: "From Spring of AD 67 to August/September of AD 70, the time of formal imperial engagement against Jerusalem, is a period right at forty-two months. Court (87) speaks of "the period of the Flavian war, from the spring of AD 67 to 29 August 70, during which time Jerusalem was 'profaned.'" Even in Rabbinic tradition we read: "for three and a half years Vespasian surrounded Jerusalem" (Lam. R. 1:31)."

"That John's reference to the two witnesses' prophesying "for twelve hundred and sixty days" (11:3) apparently covers the same period of "forty-two months" during which the Gentiles trample the holy city...

The two witnesses' period of service seems ultimately to pick up on Daniel's "time, times, and half a time" (i.e., three-and-one-half years) that appears in Daniel 7:25; 9:27; 12:7. As such it symbolizes a "halved" period, that is, a period of a "broken seven". The 1,260 days and forty-two months are also three and one-half years, which is half of a seven year period. Seven represents perfection, having a "qualitative significance" so that "seven became the symbol of the fulfilled and perfectly completed." Kenneth L. Gentry, Jr., *The Divorce of Israel: A Redemptive-Historical Interpretation of Revelation Vol. 2* (Dallas, GA: Tolle Lege Press, 2016), 54, 88-89.

[10] **Alexander quotes from**: Luke 6:27–29 [27] "But I say to you who hear, Love your enemies, do good to those who hate you, [28] bless those who curse you, pray for those who abuse you. [29] To one who strikes you on the cheek, offer the other also, and from one who takes away your cloak do not withhold your tunic either.

[11] **Agrippa quotes common apocalyptic metaphors for the fall of earthly powers**: Hosea 10:8 The sin of Israel, shall be destroyed. Thorn and thistle shall grow up on their altars, and they shall say to the mountains, "Cover us," and to the hills, "Fall on us."

Agrippa also unwittingly quotes Revelation text without realizing it: Revelation 6:12–16 [12] When he opened the sixth seal, I looked, and behold, there was a great earthquake, and the sun became black as sackcloth, the full moon became like blood, [13] and the stars of the sky fell to the earth as the fig tree sheds its winter fruit when shaken by a gale. [14] The sky vanished like a scroll that is being rolled up, and every mountain and island was removed from its place. [15] Then the kings of the earth and the great ones and the generals and the rich and the powerful, and everyone, slave and free, hid themselves in the caves and among the rocks of the mountains, [16] calling to the mountains and rocks, "Fall on us and hide us from the face of him who is seated on the throne, and from the wrath of the Lamb."

Revelation 9:6 And in those days people will seek death and will not find it. They will long to die, but death will flee from them.

The destruction and captivity of Israel by Nebuchadnezzar and his invasion that occurred in 606-586 BC was described as the universe collapsing: Isaiah 24:1-9 Behold, the LORD lays the earth waste, devastates it, distorts its surface, and scatters its inhabitants...3 The earth will be completely laid waste and completely despoiled, for the LORD has spoken this word. 4 The earth mourns {and} withers, the world fades {and} withers, the exalted of the people of the earth fade away. 5 The earth is also polluted by its inhabitants, for they transgressed laws, violated statutes, broke the everlasting covenant. 6 Therefore, a curse devours the earth, and those who live in it are held guilty. Therefore, the inhabitants of the earth are burned, and few men are left....19 The earth is broken asunder, The earth is split through, The earth is shaken violently. 20 The earth reels to and fro like a drunkard, And it totters like a shack, For its transgression is heavy upon it, And it will fall, never to rise again. 21 So it will happen in that day, That the LORD will punish the host of heaven, on high, And the kings of the earth, on earth....23 Then the moon will be abashed and the sun ashamed, ...26:9 For when the earth experiences Thy judgments The inhabitants of the world learn righteousness....

The destruction of Edom fulfilled in the Babylonian Invasion of Judah 587-586 BC: Isaiah 34:4–5 [4] All the host of heaven shall rot away, and the skies roll up like a scroll. All their host shall fall, as leaves fall from the vine, like leaves falling from the fig tree. [5] For my sword has drunk its fill in the heavens; behold, it descends for judgment upon Edom, upon the people I have devoted to destruction.

[12] **Ten Thousand Jews murdered in Damascus in response to the victory over Cestius**: Flavius Josephus, *The Wars of the Jews* 2.20.2 §559-561. "2. (559) In the meantime, the people of Damascus, when they were informed of the destruction of the Romans, set about the slaughter of those Jews that were among them; (560) and as they had them already cooped up together in the place of public exercises,...so they came upon the Jews, and cut their throats, as being in a narrow place, in number ten thousand, and all of them unarmed, and this in one hour's time, without any body to disturb them."Flavius

Josephus and William Whiston, *The Works of Josephus: Complete and Unabridged* (Peabody: Hendrickson, 1987), 633.

[13] **The kings of the east whose angels are bound at the Euphrates**: Zeus is the god of Commagene, Hubal of Arabia and Ba'al of Syria. All these gods were over the nation's forces that made up the Roman army that marched down upon Jerusalem. At this point, they are being bound by the angels until their appointed time. "Contrary to dispensationalists, these kings do not represent modern-day, "Oriental rulers" (Walvoord 236). Rather, they are "kings from the east," who are mentioned in a book which declares its events are near (1:3; 22:10). We should recall that the Roman forces set against Israel were comprised not only of Roman legionary troops but others from various auxiliary kings. Josephus notes that in the initial imperial engagement of the war, Vespasian added to his legions, "a considerable number of auxiliaries… from the kings Antiochus, and Agrippa, and Sohemus, each of them contributing one thousand footmen that were archers, and a thousand horsemen. Malchus also, the king of Arabia, sent a thousand horsemen, besides five thousand footmen, the greatest part of whom were archers" (J.W. 3:4:2 §68). The same held true for the final stages of the war under Titus, beside "whom marched those auxiliaries that came from the kings, being now more in number than before, together with a considerable number that came to his assistance from Syria" (J.W.5:1:6 §42–44). So then, not only did Titus draw troops from the Euphrates in the east (J.W. 5:1:6 §44), but Antiochus IV is the king of Commagene, and "Samoseta, the capital of Commagene, lies upon Euphrates" (J.W. 7:7:1 §224). In addition, Titus called the tenth legion through Jericho (J.W. 5:1:6 §42; 5:2:3 §69), which is east of Jerusalem (cf. Jos 13:32; 16:1; 20:8)—though not near the Euphrates. These important troop movements from east of Jerusalem involved the tenth legion, one of "the most eminent legions of all" (J.W. 3:4:2 §65)." Kenneth L. Gentry, Jr., *The Divorce of Israel: A Redemptive-Historical Interpretation of Revelation Vol. 2* (Dallas, GA: Tolle Lege Press, 2016), 360.

Commagene's gods: "The restored freedom of Commagene, now allied to Rome, allowed Antiochus leisure for his great religious expression still visible atop Nemrud Dagh. His remarkable fusions of Greek and Iranian gods satisfied the composite population, which could now worship Zeus-Oromasdes (Ahuramazda), Heracles-Artagnes, and the grandly titled Apollo-Mithras-Helios-Hermes!" Richard D. Sullivan, "Commagene (Place)," ed. David Noel Freedman, *The Anchor Yale Bible Dictionary* (New York: Doubleday, 1992), 1096.

Baal Haddad was the chief storm god of Syria: "The tablets from Ebla contain a pantheon of Canaanite gods, but some of the names and relationships are different from those at Ugarit. Concerning the deity Baal, there were either two storm gods or one storm god with two names, Baal and Hadad. By the time of Ugarit, Hadad had definitely become another name for Baal, and some cultures (e.g., the Arameans) worshiped Baal by the name Hadad. The greater prominence of the god Dagon as head of the pantheon at Ebla may explain the Ugaritic reference to Baal as "Son of Dagon." Winfried Corduan, "Baal," ed. John D. Barry et al., *The Lexham Bible Dictionary* (Bellingham, WA: Lexham Press, 2016).

""Hadad" appears only once in the biblical text. Among the Canaanites, Hadad was known by his title Baal ("Lord"), by which he more commonly appears in the Bible. The biblical text also attests to the cult of Hadad via several theophoric names belonging to the rulers of Aram-Damascus and to the early rulers of the tribes of Edom." Justin L. Kelley, "Hadad," ed. John D. Barry et al., *The Lexham Bible Dictionary* (Bellingham, WA: Lexham Press, 2016).

Serapis was a god in Alexandria from where Titus brought the 15th Legion into Judea. Tacitus and Suetonius both claim Vespasian had an encounter with Serapis in Alexandria right before he was declared emperor after the death of Nero. Tacitus *Histories* 4.81-82; Suetonius, *Vespasian* 7.1.

CHAPTER 44

[1] **The Christian flight to Pella**: "Two important fourth-century sources relate the tradition that the disciples heeded the warnings of Jesus and fled to the Transjordanian town of Pella from Jerusalem before it fell.

Eusebius (H.E. 3.5.3) relates:

> On the other hand, the people of the church in Jerusalem were commanded by an oracle given by revelation before the war to those in the city who were worthy of it to depart and dwell in one of the cities of Perea which they called Pella.

According to Epiphanius (De mens, et pond. [*Treatise on Weights and Measures*] 15):

When the city (Jerusalem) was about to be taken by the Romans, it was revealed to all the disciples by an angel of God that they should remove from the city, as it was going to be completely destroyed. They sojourned as emigrants in Pella…in TransJordania. And this city is said to be of the Decapolis.38

According to Epiphanius (Haer. 29.7.7f. and 30.2.7):

"This heresy of the Nazoraeans exists in Beroea in the neighbourhood of Coele Syria and the Decapolis in the region of Pella and in Basanitis in the so-called Kokaba, Chochabe in Hebrew. For from there it took its beginnings after the exodus from Jerusalem when all the disciples went to live in Pella because Christ had told them to leave Jerusalem and to go away since it would undergo a siege After all those who believed in Christ had generally come to live in Perea, in a city called Pella of the Decapolis of which it is written in the Gospel and which is situated in the neighbourhood of the region of Batanaea and Basanitis.

"Some scholars believe that Epiphanius and Eusebius derived their accounts from Hegesippus, a second-century source. But an even more probable source was Aristo, an apologist from Pella, who wrote in the mid-second century."

"Pella was a Gentile city of the Decapolis. The choice of Pella as a place of refuge may have been influenced by a Gentile church in the city. Sowers suggests, "The antipathy of that city toward political revolt against Rome made the city a logical choice for the Jerusalem Church, seeking a haven from rebellious territory, to settle in." Brandon has exaggerated the damage which might have been done to Pella by the Jewish and Roman attacks on it. Gray notes, "Careful examination of the evidence shows that Pella was not the complete ruin that has been suggested; in fact, compared with other Palestinian towns, it fared quite well during the war/'48 She states, "We may say, in conclusion, that there is nothing incredible in a settlement of members of the Jerusalem Church in Pella, at least in part, between the years A.D. 66-8."

"Indeed, it became a commonplace motif among the church fathers to allege that the destruction of Jerusalem and its temple was God's punishment upon the Jews for the death of Christ. This judgment was first expressed by Justin Martyr (1 Apol. 47). Eusebius (H.E. 3.5.3), after reporting the flight of the Christians to Pella, expresses his opinion as follows:

"To it those who believed on Christ migrated from Jerusalem, that when holy men had altogether deserted the royal capital of the Jews and the whole land of Judaea the judgment of God might at last overtake them for all their crimes against the Christ and his Apostles, and all that generation of the wicked be utterly blotted out from among men.

"This same motif was to be repeated by Hilary, Jerome, Sulpicius Severus, and Augustine. To be sure, this is a theological reflection, but it is surely more probable that it was founded on the historical reality of the Pella tradition." Edwin M. Yamauchi, "Christians and the Jewish revolts against Rome," *Fides et historia,* 23 no 2 Sum 1991, p 18, 20, 22.

This passage from the Pseudo-Clementines affirms the belief that Christians fled to Pella because they believed the destruction of Jerusalem was the proof that Jesus was Messiah:

Pseudo-Clement of Rome, *Recognitions of Clement,* 1.37 (2nd or 4th century AD)
"In addition to these things, he also appointed a place [Pella] in which alone it should be lawful to them to sacrifice to God…
"This place [Jerusalem], which seemed chosen for a time, often harassed as it had been by hostile invasions and plunderings, was at last to be wholly destroyed. And in order to impress this upon them, even before the coming of the true Prophet [Jesus], who was to reject at once the sacrifices and the place, it was often plundered by enemies and burnt with fire, and the people carried into captivity among foreign nations, and then brought back when they betook themselves to the mercy of God; that by these things they might be taught that a people who offer sacrifices are driven away and delivered up into the hands of the enemy, but they who do mercy and righteousness are without sacrifices freed from captivity, and restored to their native land."

Pseudo-Clement of Rome, "Recognitions of Clement," in *Fathers of the Third and Fourth Centuries: The Twelve Patriarchs, Excerpts and Epistles, the Clementina, Apocrypha, Decretals, Memoirs of Edessa and Syriac Documents, Remains of the First Ages*, ed. Alexander Roberts, James Donaldson, and A. Cleveland Coxe, trans. M. B. Riddle, vol. 8, The Ante-Nicene Fathers (Buffalo, NY: Christian Literature Company, 1886), 87.

Exactly when did the Christians flee Jerusalem?: "We might surmise that once Jerusalem had been surrounded, it was already too late to flee. But the city was surrounded on several occasions before Titus' final circumvallation. For instance, before the Jewish revolt became a full-scale war, Cestius Gallus surrounded the city, only to suddenly cease operations and leave. Josephus notes that he surrounded the city "on all sides" (Gk.: pantothen), allowing him to besiege her walls for five days (J.W. 2:19:5 §535). At that time "many of the most eminent of the Jews swam away from the city, as from a ship when it was going to sink" (J.W. 2:20:1 §556). Perhaps the Christians escaped at this time also. Later in AD 68, generals Vespasian and Titus "had fortified all the places round about Jerusalem. . . encompassing the city round about on all sides" (Josephus, J.W. 4:9:1§486). But when Vespasian and Titus were "informed that Nero was dead" (4:9:2 §491), they "did not go on with their expedition against the Jews" (4:9:2 §497; cp. 4:10:2 §590) until after Vespasian became emperor in AD 69 (4:11:5 §567). This would have been the last reasonable opportunity for escape from Jerusalem because eventually Titus built "a wall round about the whole city" (J.W. 5:12:1 §499). With this action he largely sealed off Jerusalem, for he had "encompassed the city with this wall, and put garrisons into proper places" (J.W. 5:12:2 §510).Though even then Jews could escape, as Titus recognized (J.W. 5:12:1 §496)." Kenneth L. Gentry, Jr., *The Divorce of Israel: A Redemptive-Historical Interpretation of Revelation Vol. 2* (Dallas, GA: Tolle Lege Press, 2016), 515-516.

Josephus on the flight of Jews after Cestius left: "After this calamity had befallen Cestius, many of the most eminent of the Jews swam away from the city, as from a ship when it was going to sink." (*Wars* 2.20.1 556).

Josephus on Pella being devastated before Christians fled to it: "Upon which stroke that the Jews received at Caesarea, the whole nation was greatly enraged; so they divided themselves into several parties, and laid waste the villages of the Syrians, and their neighboring cities, Philadelphia, and Sebonitis, and Gerasa, and Pella, and Scythopolis." (*Wars* 2.458)

CHAPTER 45

[1] **Cassandra quotes from several verses in Song of Solomon**: Song 4:9; 2:1, 4, 8, 16.

[2] **Demetrius quotes from**: 1 Thessalonians 3:12-13; Revelation 22:20-21.

[3] **Alexander quotes from**: Song of Solomon 6:4,

[4] **Jesus is coming quickly**: The time texts in Revelation and Jesus' prophecies of his judgment coming are perhaps the death knell to futurist interpretations that want to postpone their fulfillment into the far distant future. The very urgency of Revelation speaks to its encouragement of persecuted believers in the first century. Revelation would be a mockery of their suffering if the repetitive comfort of Christ's coming was not for them. Look at how often the text affirms the nearness of his coming:

- "The things that *must shortly take place*" (1:1).
- "For the time is *near*" (1:3).
- "I am coming to you *quickly*" (2:16).
- "I am coming *quickly*" (3:11).
- "The third woe is coming *quickly*" (11:14).
- "A *little while longer*" (6:11).
- "*no more delay*" (10:6).
- "his *time is short*" (12:12).
- "The things which must *shortly take place*" (22:6).
- "Behold, I am coming *quickly*" (22:7).
- "For the time is *near*" (22:10).
- "Behold, I am coming *quickly*" (22:12).
- "Yes, I am coming *quickly*" (22:20).

This list was drawn from Gary DeMar, *Left Behind: Separating Fact from Fiction* (Powder Springs, GA: American Vision, 2009), 123–124.

Notice how the futurist must force an alien symbolism onto the historical referent that completely altars the first century context in which the letter was written. In a usually literalistic scheme, the seven churches must now become allegories or symbols or the comfort of Revelation becomes a fraud. And their usually literalistic bias now switches to symbolism and turns meanings into their opposites. "Shortly take place" becomes "distantly takes place," "near" becomes "far," "quickly" becomes "slowly," "a little

459

while longer" becomes "long long while," "not more delay," becomes "massive delay," and "short" becomes "long."

But it is not merely Revelation that uses the language of these fulfillments occurring within their lifetime. Jesus himself stressed over and over that he was coming soon.

Jesus taught that his judgment coming was to happen within *his own* generation, the generation of his hearers:

Matthew 16:27–28 27 For the Son of Man is going to come with his angels in the glory of his Father, and then he will repay each person according to what he has done. 28 Truly, I say to you, there are some standing here who will not taste death until they see the Son of Man coming in his kingdom."

Matthew 26:63–64 63 But Jesus remained silent. And the high priest said to him, "I adjure you by the living God, tell us if you are the Christ, the Son of God." 64 Jesus said to him, "You have said so. But I tell you, from now on you will see the Son of Man seated at the right hand of Power and coming on the clouds of heaven."

Matthew 10:22–23 22 and you will be hated by all for my name's sake. But the one who endures to the end will be saved. 23 When they persecute you in one town, flee to the next, for truly, I say to you, you will not have gone through all the towns of Israel before the Son of Man comes.

Matthew 23:36 36 Truly, I say to you, all these things will come upon this generation.

Matthew 24:30 30 Then will appear in heaven the sign of the Son of Man, and then all the tribes of the earth will mourn, and they will see the Son of Man coming on the clouds of heaven with power and great glory.

Matthew 24:33–34 33 So also, when you see all these things, you know that he is near, at the very gates. 34 Truly, I say to you, this generation will not pass away until all these things take place.

John 21:20–23 20 Peter turned and saw the disciple whom Jesus loved following them, the one who also had leaned back against him during the supper and had said, "Lord, who is it that is going to betray you?" 21 When Peter saw him, he said to Jesus, "Lord, what about this man?" 22 Jesus said to him, "If it is my will that he remain until I come, what is that to you? You follow me!"

The New Testament writers indicated that the coming of the Lord was to happen within their own time period:

James 5:7-9 Be patient, therefore, brethren, until the coming of the Lord. Behold, the farmer waits for the precious produce of the soil, being patient about it, until it gets the early and late rains. 8 You too be patient; strengthen your hearts, for the coming of the Lord is at hand. 9 Do not complain, brethren, against one another, that you yourselves may not be judged; behold, the Judge is standing right at the door.

2 Thessalonians 2:1–9 1 Now concerning the coming of our Lord Jesus Christ and our being gathered together to him, … For that day will not come, unless the rebellion comes first, and the man of lawlessness is revealed, the son of destruction… 6 And you know what is restraining him now so that he may be revealed in his time. 7 For the mystery of lawlessness is already at work. Only he who now restrains it will do so until he is out of the way. 8 And then the lawless one will be revealed, whom the Lord Jesus will kill with the breath of his mouth and bring to nothing by the appearance of his coming.

Philippians 4:4–5 4 Rejoice in the Lord always; again I will say, rejoice. 5 Let your reasonableness be known to everyone. The Lord is at hand;

Hebrews 10:25 25 not neglecting to meet together, as is the habit of some, but encouraging one another, and all the more as you see the Day drawing near.

The New Testament writers all said that their own generation was the generation of the last days:

Hebr. 1:1 God, after He spoke long ago to the fathers in the prophets in many portions and in many ways, 2 in these last days has spoken to us in His Son,...

Hebrews 9:26 but now once at the consummation of the ages He has been manifested to put away sin by the sacrifice of Himself.

1Peter 1:20 For [Jesus] was foreknown before the foundation of the world, but has appeared in these last times for the sake of you

460

1Pet. 4:7 <u>The end of all things is at hand</u>; therefore, be of sound judgment and sober spirit for the purpose of prayer.

1John 2:18 Children, <u>it is the last hour</u>; and just as you heard that antichrist is coming, even now many antichrists have arisen; from this we know that <u>it is the last hour</u>.

1John 4:3 and every spirit that does not confess Jesus is not from God; and this is the spirit of the <u>antichrist, of which you have heard that it is coming, and now it is already in the world</u>.

Jude 17–19 [17] But you must remember, beloved, the predictions of the apostles of our Lord Jesus Christ. [18] They said to you, "<u>In the last time there will be scoffers</u>, following their own ungodly passions." [19] <u>It is these who cause divisions</u>, worldly people, devoid of the Spirit.

2Tim. 3:1 But realize this, that <u>in the last days</u> difficult times will come.... 5 holding to a form of godliness, although they have denied its power; and avoid such men as these. [**these men were around at THAT time**] 6 For among them are those who enter into households and captivate weak women weighed down with sins, led on by various impulses, 7 always learning and never able to come to the knowledge of the truth. 8 And just as Jannes and Jambres opposed Moses, so these {men} also oppose the truth, men of depraved mind, rejected as regards the faith.

Acts 2:15–20 [15] For these people are not drunk, as you suppose, since it is only the third hour of the day. [16] But <u>this is what was uttered through the prophet Joel</u>: [17] " 'And in the last days it shall be, God declares, that I will pour out my Spirit on all flesh, and your sons and your daughters shall prophesy, and your young men shall see visions, and your old men shall dream dreams; [18] even on my male servants and female servants in those days I will pour out my Spirit, and they shall prophesy. [19] And I will show wonders in the heavens above and signs on the earth below, blood, and fire, and vapor of smoke; [20] the sun shall be turned to darkness and the moon to blood, <u>before the day of the Lord comes, the great and magnificent day</u>.

1Cor 10:11 Now these things happened to them as an example, and they were written <u>for our instruction, upon whom the ends of the ages have come</u>.

Jude 17 But, beloved, ought to remember the words that were spoken beforehand by the apostles of our Lord Jesus Christ, 18 that they were saying to you, "<u>In the last time</u> there shall be mockers, following after their own ungodly lusts." 19 <u>These are the ones who cause divisions, worldly-minded, devoid of the Spirit</u>.

1 Cor 7:26 I think then that this is good <u>in view of the present distress</u>, that it is good for a man to remain as he is...But this I say, brethren, <u>the time has been shortened</u>, so that from now on those who have wives should be as though they had none; ... for <u>the form of this world (*kosmos*) is passing away</u>.

"Modern prophecy pundits have tried to spin these texts by saying that Christ's coming was imminent; that is, it could have come at any moment. Even though he would come thousands of years from then, when he did come he would surprise everyone. This is how futurists try to explain away the contradiction of Paul expecting the Lord's coming in his lifetime, while concluding that he never came. But that is not taking the text literally. The text does not say he could come at any moment for millennia to come, but that he was "at hand" for those first century believers. This phrase "at hand" is used throughout the Gospels to mean within their lifetime (Matt 26:18; 26:45-46; Luke 21:20; John 2:13; 6:4; 7:2; 7:6; 11:55), not thousands of years later, which would make the phrase "at hand" meaningless. In fact, Jesus used this same "at hand" in Matthew 24:32 of the Olivet Discourse when he said that his coming could be compared to a fig tree with leaves that predicts the summer is "near" (same Greek word). A summer for a fig tree is not thousands of weeks away; it is a few weeks away. Near means near; at hand means within the lifetime of the hearers. It is never used to mean far or many years beyond the lifetime of the hearers.

"The book of Revelation repeatedly explains that its end times events would "shortly take place" (1:1, 22:6), that "the time is near" (1:3), that Jesus and those events were "coming quickly" (2:16; 3:11; 11:14; 22:7; 22:12; 22:20). "Near," "quickly," and "at hand" cannot mean thousands of years from now. That would make the words nonsense.

"Although futurists try to redefine "near" to mean thousands of years from New Testament times, they will admit that when they use the words "near" and "soon," they mean within their own lifetimes. They will say "The end is near," "the Day of the Lord is at hand," and "Jesus is coming soon." And what do they mean? They mean that they believe Jesus is coming within their own generation.

"And that is exactly what the Bible authors meant as well when they wrote "near," "at hand," and "soon." They meant what Jesus meant when he said "this generation." They meant within their lifetime."

Brian Godawa, *End Times Bible Prophecy: It's Not What They Told You* (Los Angeles, CA: Embedded Pictures Publishing, 2017) 126-127.

[5] **The new song of the 144,000**: Notice it comes right before the seven angels with seven plagues begins. They are sealed and kept from the wrath to come:

Revelation 15:1–7 1 Then I saw another sign in heaven, great and amazing, seven angels with seven plagues, which are the last, for with them the wrath of God is finished. 2 And I saw what appeared to be a sea of glass mingled with fire—and also those who had conquered the beast and its image and the number of its name, standing beside the sea of glass with harps of God in their hands. 3 And they sing the song of Moses, the servant of God, and the song of the Lamb, saying, "Great and amazing are your deeds, O Lord God the Almighty! Just and true are your ways, O King of the nations! 4 Who will not fear, O Lord, and glorify your name? For you alone are holy. All nations will come and worship you, for your righteous acts have been revealed."

[5] After this I looked, and the sanctuary of the tent of witness in heaven was opened, [6] and out of the sanctuary came the seven angels with the seven plagues, clothed in pure, bright linen, with golden sashes around their chests. [7] And one of the four living creatures gave to the seven angels seven golden bowls full of the wrath of God...

Revelation 14:1–3 [1] Then I looked, and behold, on Mount Zion stood the Lamb, and with him 144,000 who had his name and his Father's name written on their foreheads. [2] And I heard a voice from heaven like the roar of many waters and like the sound of loud thunder. The voice I heard was like the sound of harpists playing on their harps, [3] and they were singing a new song before the throne and before the four living creatures and before the elders. No one could learn that song except the 144,000 who had been redeemed from the earth.

"In the light of this it is not surprising that the author of Revelation himself reintroduces the Exodus theme through the "sea" and the "song." The crystal sea stands in contrast to the one from which the sea monster emerged, and the singing conquerors stand in a position comparable to the Israelites after their escape through the Reed Sea from idolatrous Egypt; one recalls that the city in Rev 11:8 was allegorically called "Sodom" and "Egypt." The righteous will be saved but the "Egyptian plagues" will visit the faithless (Rev 16).

"In Rev 15:2 the author sees those who win a three-fold victory, over the beast, his image, and the number of his name. The tense of "prevail" is present, not perfect; these people are triumphing at the present over the beast, etc. They appear to be the same people as the redeemed remnant portrayed in 14:1–5. They are standing either on or by a sea, which is probably the counterpart of the heavenly one in 4:6, and they hold harps of God, probably harps used in the worship of God.

"Although their song is called the song of Moses, it is not one of triumph such as is found in Exod 15; it is more like Deut 32, also called Song of Moses...

"The song seems to be more influenced by Deut 32 than Exod 15, but this is understandable in the light of the stress on wrath and justice in the Deuteronomic writings; cf. Hanson, pp. 5, 37. Rev 15:4a is akin to Deut 32:3, Rev 15:3b to Deut 32:4, and Rev 15:4b to Deut 32:4b. Further, the theme of the fire of God's anger is found in Deut 32:22. Some of the plagues—hunger, burning heat, pestilence, wild beasts, vermin, the sword—are reflected in Deut 32:23–27. Moreover, Deut 32:32 refers to the vine of Sodom and the fields of Gomorrah and describes their wine as the poison of serpents; cf. Rev 14:8, 10; 17:1–6." J. Massyngberde Ford, *Revelation: Introduction, Translation, and Commentary, vol. 38, Anchor Yale Bible* (New Haven; London: Yale University Press, 2008), 257.

[6] **This song of the Lamb comes from**: Revelation 15:1-4.

[7] **This song of Moses is shortened from**: Deuteronomy 32.

EPILOGUE

[1] **On the conspiracy of the Scribonii and Corbulo's suicides, I have taken some creative license. The basic story is true**: "In June A.D. 66, just before Nero sailed for Greece, there had been discovered a second smaller plot with its headquarters at Beneventum. The details of this "Vinician Conspiracy" are

the most meagre possible and little else is known save the names of the victims. That it accounted in any way for Nero's attacks upon the Stoics we do not hold, inasmuch as Tacitus never mentions it at all As it seems to have been centered at Beneventum it is possible that its purpose was to intercept and slay Nero as he passed through the town on his way to the coast to take ship for Greece. On a former such journey he had halted at, and turned back from, the city. It is also more possible (and herein lies the chief interest of the plot), that the conspirators had meant to replace Nero by Corbulo. If the greater conspiracy had shipwrecked upon the unworthiness of its protagonist Piso, the lesser would not run this risk. We grope our way in a mist hesitatingly through all this story, for little but darkness appears on all sides. Annius Vinicianus was son of a former unlucky conspirator against Claudius' life, and himself had married Corbulo's daughter. He had served with the general through the Armenian war, and had been sent by him to escort Tiridates to Rome in A.D. 66. For this he was rewarded by Nero with the consulship, though he was not yet thirty years old. He gives his name to the plot, for the discovery of which the Arval Brotherhood pay thanks to the Gods on June 19 of this year. Then he vanishes, not even expressly numbered among its victims. Nero proceeded three months later to Greece. While there he had to appoint a general to the now very serious Jewish war. He passed over Corbulo in silence and chose Vespasian. Corbulo was not even reappointed to the legateship of Syria. Then, while in Greece, the Emperor suddenly sent friendly messages, not only to Corbulo in the East, but also to two brothers, who then were governors of the two German provinces, Sulpicius Scribonius Rufus and Scribonius Proculus, bidding all three come to him at once in Greece. They hastened to obey. The Scribonii were not admitted to his presence. Paccius Africanus an informer denounced them with accusations suitable to the occasion," says the. chronicler enigmatically, and they committed suicide. Corbulo on landing at Cenchreae, the port of Corinth on the Saronic gulf, received Nero's command to die. He obeyed instantly." Bernard W. Henderson, *The Life and Principate of the Emperor Nero* (London, Methuen and Co. 1903) 387-388.

Cassius Dio, *Roman History*, 68.17.2-5 "I shall, however, mention Corbulo and the two Sulpicii Scribonii, Rufus and Proculus. 3 The latter two were brothers of about the same age, and had never done anything separately but had remained united in purpose and in property as they were in family; they had for a long time administered the two Germanies together, and now came to Greece at the summons of Nero, who pretended to want them for something. 4 Complaints of the kind in which that period abounded were lodged against them, but they could neither obtain a hearing nor get within sight of Nero; and as this caused them to be slighted by everybody alike, they began to long for death and so met their end by opening their veins. 5 I mention Corbulo, because the emperor, after sending him also a most courteous summons and invariably calling him, among other names, "father" and "benefactor," then, when this general landed at Cenchreae, commanded that he should be slain before he had even entered his presence." http://penelope.uchicago.edu/Thayer/E/Roman/Texts/Cassius_Dio/62*.html.

[2] **References used for description of Roman sacrifice as depicted here**: The Illustrated History of the Roman Empire online http://www.roman-empire.net/religion/sacrifice.html & "Sacrifices in Roman Religion," The Roman Military Research Society online http://www.romanarmy.net/sacrifices.shtml

[3] **Nero appoints Vespasian as legate to prosecute the war against the Jews**: "Thus, "such was the situation when Nero, in February 67, appointed Titus Flavius Vespasianus with the rank of legatus to carry on the war" (CAH 10:858). Bunson (1991: 443) states that Vespasian "was given command of the legions in Palestine in February 67, the rank of governor of Judaea, and the task of suppressing the revolt of the Jews." John would likely count the beginning of the war from the time that the white horseman actually "went out [exēlthon]" to conquer (6:2), that is, when Vespasian initially entered Israel to engage military operations. Shortly thereafter, "the war began in earnest only in March or April of 67, when Vespasian and his son Titus gathered their legions in Ptolemais." Kenneth L. Gentry, Jr., *The Divorce of Israel: A Redemptive-Historical Interpretation of Revelation Vol. 2* (Dallas, GA: Tolle Lege Press, 2016), 53.

Legatus: "The legion's commanding officer, who may or may not have had much military experience, carried mainly political weight. Selected by the emperor as his personal representative (legatus)." Steve Mason, *A History of the Jewish War, AD 66-74* (Cambridge University Press, 2016) 148.

[4] **The rider on the white horse**: "Many ancient writers, as well as some modern scholars, see this as a picture of Christ. Some such as Ladd see it as a personification of the spread of Christ's gospel. They argue that this white horse appears again in 19:11 where we see Christ seated on him. The following reasons, however, weigh against this interpretation:

"(1) The "white horse" is the only similarity with the vision of Christ in chapter 19. In fact, in 19:15, 21 Christ does not even possess the bow mentioned here, but a sword. And the sword is often associated with him in Revelation (1:16; 2:12, 16; 19:15, 21) while the bow never is. Also the horseman is given a victor's wreath (stephanos translated "crown"), whereas Christ wears many "diadems [diadēmata]" in 19:12. The stephanos sometimes appears on evil beings (9:7) and conquering often applies to them (nikaō) (11:7; 13:7).

"(2) Christ's appearance here would be awkward, even for non-logical apocalyptic imagery. Per Ladd (131), Mounce (142), and Beasley-Murray (131) it would be strange for Jesus both to open the scroll and to be in its contents (6:1–2).

"(3) It also would seem inappropriate for an angel ("living creature") to command the Son of Man to "come" (6:2).3 (4) Furthermore, the rider is "given" a crown. This involves a providential granting that John associates with divine permission for evil powers to perform their tasks (Caird 81; Mulholland 1990:168). These passiva Divina statements usually apply to divine authorization for non-Christian entities to operate under God's sovereign administration (6:2, 4, 8; 9:1, 3; 11:2; 13:5, 14, 15).

"We must keep in mind Revelation's Hebraic character, near-term time constraints (1:1, 3), and its Israel-judgment theme (1:7). This image symbolizes either a generic representation of the Roman army in its victorious march toward Jerusalem, or (most probably) a specific symbol of the Roman general Vespasian who begins subduing Israel in the Spring of 67. Vespasian is Nero's "most experienced general," whom Nero commissions to put down the Jewish revolt. This commissioning elevates the uprising (the Jewish Revolt) to an official war (the Jewish War) engaging a full-scale Roman military response (see comments at 11:2; J.W. 3:1 §1–8). It is no longer a local police action under the oversight of the provincial governor, Cesitus Gallus (J.W. 2:17–22 §405–652); it is now an imperial problem. Josephus considers Nero's choice of Vespasian as inspired by God (J.W. 3:1:3 §6). As John puts it: he is sent to Israel "conquering and to conquer" (6:2), that is, conquering in order to gain conquest. In a speech by Titus to his troops he refers to his father Vespasian, noting that "it is usual for my father to conquer [ta nikan ethos" (J.W. 3:10:2 §482).

"In a parable prophesying Jerusalem's destruction, Jesus calls the Romans "his [God's] armies" (Mt 22:7). This is like God calling Assyria the "rod of my anger" (Isa 10:5; cp. Hab 1:6), though he will eventually punish Assyria for its arrogance (Isa 10:12). Or like God calling Nebuchadnezzar "My Servant" (Jer 25:9; 27:6; cp. 2Ki 24:2; Jer 4:11–13), though he will soon destroy this evil ruler (Jer 25:12).

"But more probably this white color represents victory. I hold this for four reasons: (1) White commonly represents victory in antiquity.5 (2) The text states that this rider goes forth "to conquer" (6:2b), which involves victory. (3) The "bow" is a symbol of victory (Zec 9:13–14), just as breaking bows is a symbol of peace resulting from victory (Ps 46:9; cp. 1Sa 2:4). (4) The color white then relates its effect—"conquering"—like the other horse's colors reflect their results (e.g., red = bloodshed [6:4]; black =starvation by famine [6:5]; pale = death [6:8]). The Romans will certainly prevail, just as Josephus warns his fellow Jews that "they must know the Roman power was invincible" (J.W. 5:9:3 364; cp. 5:9:1 §353), for "the power of the Romans is invincible in all parts of the habitable earth" (J.W. 2:16:4 §388; cp. 2:20:7 §577; 5:9:3 §364)." Kenneth L. Gentry, Jr., *The Divorce of Israel: A Redemptive-Historical Interpretation of Revelation Vol. 1* (Dallas, GA: Tolle Lege Press, 2016), 577-580.

AFTERWORD

[1] For documentation of the repeated failures of millennarians to predict Bible prophecy events see, Francis Gummerlock, *The Day and the Hour: Christianity's Perennial Fascination with Predicting the End of the World* (American Vision, 2000); Richard Kyle, *Apocalyptic Fever: End-Time Prophecies in Modern America* (Cascade Books, 2012). See also Gary DeMar, *Left Behind: Separating Fact from Fiction* (American Vision, 2010); Jerry Bower, Jay Ryan, Charles Bower, Joel McDurmon, *Shemitah Years And Blood Moons As Market Timing Tools* (AmericanVision.org, 2015); Richard Abanes, *End-Time Visions: The Road to Armageddon* (Four Walls Eight Windows, 1998).

Made in the USA
Las Vegas, NV
03 December 2023

81992730R00262